Jilly Cooper is a well-known journalist, writer and media superstar. The author of many number one bestselling novels, including *Riders, Rivals, Polo, The Man Who Made Husbands Jealous, Appassionata* and *Score!*, she and her husband live in Gloucestershire with several dogs and cats.

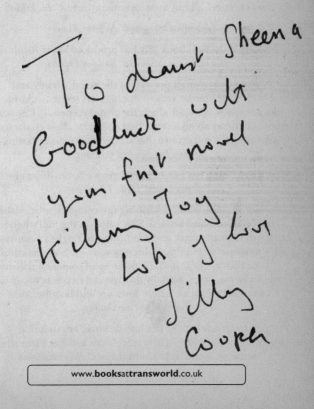

To dearest Sheena
Goodluck with
your first novel
Killing Joy
with I love
Jilly
Cooper

'Open the covers of Jilly Cooper's latest novel and you lift the lid of a Pandora's box. From the pages flies a host of delicious and deadly vices . . . Cooper's sheer exuberance and energy are contagious . . . Cooper fans will be waiting eagerly for the next novel' *The Times*

'There is enough plot for several novels here (enough sex for dozens), all vividly conveyed in the author's excitable style . . . Her many fans will not be disappointed' *Literary Review*

'Cooper plays out a deliciously entertaining drama of promiscuous artists, unfaithful spouses and inevitably, illegitimate children whose true parentage is only revealed in the closing chapters . . . Compelling comedy'
Independent on Sunday

'This is Jilly in top form with her most sparkling novel to date'
Yorkshire Post

'Her priapic fictions – of which *Pandora* is among the best – are a definite force for good. They vibrate with glee and gusto: qualities of which we all need an infusion every now and then'
Observer

'Cooper possesses story-telling skills that bypass many an aspiring Booker Prize winner . . . Under the playful rollicking and nonsensical high jinks, she deals in serious archetypes . . . Cooper outshines all others' *Glasgow Herald*

'Great fun' *Good Housekeeping*

'You relish the sheer breathless gusto of her writing, the way she adores her own characters . . . Constantly diverting: funny, inventive and graphic' *Daily Mail*

'Well constructed and totally gripping . . . A wonderful, romantic spectacular of a novel' *Spectator*

'A new Jilly Cooper is always a treat. *Pandora* is all that you expect from one of her novels; a rollick with some exquisitely naughty people, some of whom we have met before in previous novels . . . Oh the swaggering lives! It's wonderful . . . It's a book readers will sneak peeks at, eager to find out if lovers are reunited and villains get their comeuppance. It's lively. It's frothy and funny. You have as much fun reading it as you feel Jilly had writing it' *Waterstone's Book Quarterly*

PANDORA

Jilly Cooper

CORGI BOOKS

PANDORA
A CORGI BOOK : 0 552 14850 4

Originally published in Great Britain by Bantam Press,
a division of Transworld Publishers

PRINTING HISTORY
Bantam Press edition published 2002
Corgi edition published 2003

1 3 5 7 9 10 8 6 4 2

Set in 10/11 pt New Baskerville by
Phoenix Typesetting, Burley-in-Wharfedale, West Yorkshire.

Corgi Books are published by Transworld Publishers,
61–63 Uxbridge Road, London W5 5SA,
a division of The Random House Group Ltd,
in Australia by Random House Australia (Pty) Ltd,
20 Alfred Street, Milsons Point, Sydney, NSW 2061, Australia,
in New Zealand by Random House New Zealand Ltd,
18 Poland Road, Glenfield, Auckland 10, New Zealand
and in South Africa by Random House (Pty) Ltd,
Endulini, 5a Jubilee Road, Parktown 2193, South Africa.

Printed and bound in Germany by
Elsnerdruck, Berlin

To Mark Barty-King, a hero in every way,
with huge love and gratitude

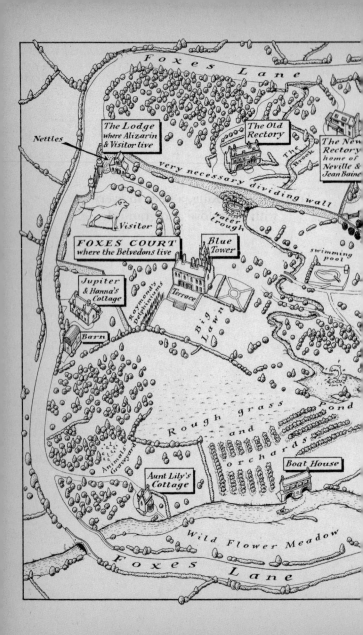

Foxes Lane

Nettles

The Lodge
where the Alizarin
& Visitor live

The Old Rectory

The New Rectory
home of Neville & Jean Baines

The Brook

very necessary dividing wall

water trough

Visitor

FOXES COURT
where the Belvedons live

Blue Tower

swimming pool

Jupiter & Hanna's Cottage

Raymond's delphiniums

Terrace

Big Lawn

Barn

Rough grass and orchards

Pond

Animals Graveyard

Aunt Lily's Cottage

Boat House

Wild Flower Meadow

Foxes Lane

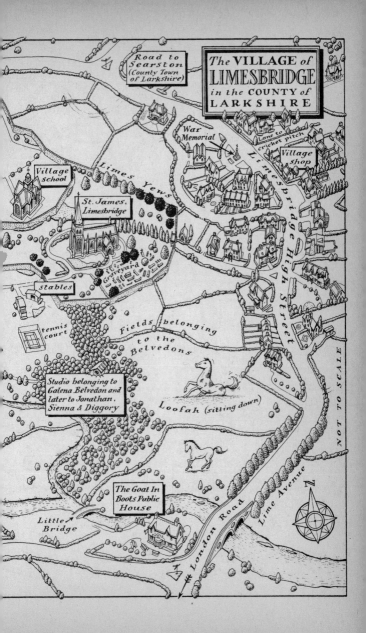

THE LEGEND OF PANDORA'S BOX

There are many variations on the legend of Pandora but I have used the one that begins with a heroic mortal called Prometheus boldly storming Mount Olympus, the home of the Gods. As if on an SAS mission, he stole fire, which had hitherto been the preserve of the Gods. This audacity outraged Jupiter, their King, not least because he feared that mortals might now have a means of overthrowing him.

As retribution, he therefore instructed his Gods and Goddesses to create the most beautiful mortal ever seen: a woman called Pandora, which means 'all-gifted'. Jupiter then ordered his messenger, Mercury, to deliver this exquisite creature to the door of Prometheus's brother, Epimetheus. A susceptible young man, Epimetheus ignored his brother's warning not to accept any presents from the Gods and promptly asked the lovely Pandora to marry him. His only condition was that she should never open the oak chest in the corner of the room.

The newly married Pandora, however, was overwhelmed with curiosity, and one day when Epimetheus was out hunting she yielded to temptation and opened the chest. Immediately all the evils and diseases of the world, which had been trapped inside, flew out. After viciously stinging Pandora and a returning Epimetheus, they flew off, contaminating the earth with a biological storm and bringing dreadful pain and misfortune to the human race.

Pandora and Epimetheus were still weeping and writhing in agony when they heard tapping on the inside of the oak chest and out stepped a radiant, angelically smiling fairy.

'My name is Hope,' she told them, 'and I have come to bring comfort and to relieve the suffering of you and all mankind.'

CAST OF CHARACTERS

GENERAL ALDRIDGE	Lord-Lieutenant of Larkshire – so boring he's known locally as 'General Anaesthetic'.
COLIN CASEY ANDREWS	England's greatest painter, according to Casey Andrews. A Belvedon Gallery artist with exalted ideas of his own genius and sexual prowess. Long-term lover of Galena Borochova.
ZACHARY ANSTEIG	Zac the Wanderer. An American journalist of Austro-Jewish extraction, whose tigerish beauty and air of suppressed violence in no way conjure up cheery images of *The Sound of Music*.
NEVILLE BAINES	Vicar of St James, Limesbridge, predictably known as 'Neville-on-Sundays'.
JEAN BAINES	His very tiresome, ecologically correct wife, known as 'Green Jean'.

RAYMOND BELVEDON	An extremely successful art-dealer, owner of the Belvedon Gallery in Cork Street.
JUPITER BELVEDON	Raymond's machiavellian eldest son, who, after Cambridge, joins him in the gallery.
HANNA BELVEDON	Jupiter's blonde Junoesque wife, a very gifted painter of flowers.
ALIZARIN BELVEDON	Raymond's second son, a genius tormented by a social conscience. Produces vast tortured canvasses no-one wants to buy.
JONATHAN BELVEDON	Raymond's colossally glamorous younger son. A genius as yet unhampered by any conscience at all.
SIENNA BELVEDON	Raymond's elder daughter. A truculent, talented wild child.
DICKY BELVEDON	Raymond's youngest son – an artful dodger.
DORA BELVEDON	Raymond's younger daughter and Dicky's horse-mad twin sister.
JOAN BIDEFORD	A Belvedon Gallery artist and splendid bruiser with a fondness for her own sex. Unenthusiastically married to Colin Casey Andrews.

SOPHY CARTWRIGHT	Patience and Ian's younger adopted daughter, a teacher of splendid proportions and great charm.
NAOMI COHEN	Zachary Ansteig's lawyer, as ambitious as she is bright and beautiful.
KEVIN COLEY	A perfectly awful petfood billionaire, Chairman of Doggie Dins. A collector of art as an investment and sponsor of the British Portrait Awards.
ENID COLEY	His overweight, overbearing wife.
EDDIE	Raymond Belvedon's packer.
MR JUSTICE CARADOC WILLOUGHBY EVANS	A high court judge.
FIONA	Raymond Belvedon's gallery assistant, a glamorous well-bred half-wit.
DETECTIVE INSPECTOR GABLECROSS	A super sleuth.
SI GREENBRIDGE	A mega-rich American arms-dealer and a serious collector of pictures.
GINNY GREENBRIDGE	Si's trophy wife, a former Miss New Jersey.
LILY HAMILTON	Raymond Belvedon's older sister.
DAME HERMIONE HAREFIELD	World-famous diva, seriously tiresome, brings out the Crippen in all.

HARRIET	A radiant henna-haired reporter from *Oo-ah!* magazine.
ABDUL KARAMAGI	An amorous Saudi with a penchant for saucy pictures.
KEITHIE	Somerford Keynes's boyfriend, an exquisite piece of rough trade and sometime burglar.
SOMERFORD KEYNES	A malevolent gay art critic, known as the 'Poisoned Pansy'.
ESTHER KNIGHT	Raymond Belvedon's comely cleaner.
MINSKY KRASKOV	An unnerving Russian Mafia hood, who uses art as collateral to raise money for dodgy deals.
JEAN-JACQUES LE BRUN	A very great French painter.
NATACHA	A glamorous member of Sotheby's Client Advisory Department.
SIR MERVYN NEWTON	A rather self-regarding dry-cleaning millionaire.
LADY NEWTON	His grander wife, given to gardening and Pekineses.
ROSEMARY NEWTON	Their daughter – an absolute brick.
PASCAL	An American interior designer.
PATTI	Another glamorous member of Sotheby's Client Advisory Department.

GERALDINE PAXTON	A networking nympho, a mover and shaker in the art world.
PEREGRINE	Sampson Brunning's junior.
GORDON PRITCHARD	A very exalted specialist.
CHRIS PROUDLOVE	The genial, indefatigable press officer at Sotheby's.
DAVID PULBOROUGH	A Cambridge undergraduate employed to coach the Belvedon children in the vac. Later a highly successful art-dealer with his own gallery, the Pulborough.
BARNEY PULBOROUGH	David's son – a seriously dodgy slug in a Savile Row suit.
ROBENS	Raymond Belvedon's gardener/chauffeur whose wandering eye is overlooked because of his green fingers.
MRS ROBENS	His long-suffering wife. Raymond Belvedon's cook and housekeeper – a treasure.
ANTHEA ROOKHOPE	A very tempting temp, who becomes permanent at the Belvedon Gallery in all senses of the word.
TAMZIN	Raymond's gallery assistant in 1999 – the 'Dimbo'.
TRAFFORD	Jonathan Belvedon's unspeakably scrofulous best friend and painter-in-crime. A Young British Artist.

SLANEY WATTS	A glamorous New Yorker and PRO of the Greychurch Museum.
HENRY WYNDHAM	The charismatic Chairman of Sotheby's.
ZELDA	An American art student.
ZOE	David Pulborough's subtly understated assistant.

THE ANIMALS

Badger	Rupert Campbell-Black's black Labrador.
The Brigadier	Lily Hamilton's white cat.
Choirboy	Trafford's Newfoundland puppy, as intent on destruction as his master.
Diggory	Jonathan Belvedon's sharp-toothed Jack Russell.
Grenville	Raymond Belvedon's brindle greyhound.
Loofah	Dora Belvedon's delinquent skewbald pony.
Maud	Raymond Belvedon's blue greyhound.
Shadrach, Meshach and Abednego	Rosemary Pulborough's marmalade cats.
Shrimpy	Galena Borochova's Jack Russell.
Visitor	Alizarin Belvedon's yellow Labrador, great-great-grandson of Rupert Campbell-Black's Badger. Socialite and ballroom dancer.

PROLOGUE

In the early hours of 24 August 1944, Raymond Belvedon, a recently commissioned young subaltern in the Larkshire Light Infantry, waited in a poplar copse for first light, when he was to lead an attack on the village of Bonfleuve, which lay below. His platoon, who had been fiercely fighting their way through Normandy since D-Day and who had had little sleep for three days, dozed fitfully around him.

Raymond was too tense to sleep and, with a torch, was reading Tennyson in a lichen-green leather-bound volume given him by his older brother, Viridian, for his twentieth birthday back in May. The volume, which he kept in the breast pocket of his battledress, had saved his life a few days before, when it had deflected a sniper's bullet headed for his heart.

In the flyleaf, Raymond had stuck a photograph of his family. His mother, father and elder sister, Lily, a beautiful, much-sought-after Wren, were grouped round Viridian, always the centre of attention, and here laughing on a garden bench with Hereward, the wire-haired terrier, bristling on his knee.

In the background rose Foxes Court, the glorious golden-stoned family home in Larkshire, reminding Raymond of the pat of tennis balls, chocolate cake under the walnut tree, Beethoven drifting out of the study window, his father grumbling to visitors that the garden had gone over, his mother sending him inside to fetch her a cardigan because the evenings were drawing in – all those clichés of country-house life, which seem so precious in wartime.

And the starry nights were so quiet in Larkshire. By contrast, here, as though time had stopped on 5 November, a monstrous everlasting firework party crashed, banged, thundered, roared and exploded all around him, with flashing and flickerings constantly lighting the sky until his brain seemed to crumple like a kicked-in compo tin.

It was already hot and close, but Raymond couldn't stop shivering. It wasn't just from butterflies over the task ahead. The day before yesterday, during a lull in the fighting, he had been scribbling a letter to Viridian, who was serving with the regiment in Italy, about the deflection of the sniper's bullet.

'Your birthday present stood me in further stead', he had written, when he became aware of the wireless operator receiving a signal, which he had immediately taken to the adjutant.

Raymond had noticed them talking gravely, then wondered if he had failed the company in some way, as the adjutant approached him with a solemn face.

But instead he had said, 'Awfully sorry, Raymond. Got some bad news.'

Viridian had been killed near Cassino. As yet there were no details.

The worst part was imagining the village postmistress pedalling up the drive with the fatal telegram and not being able to ring home to comfort his parents.

For how would they ever recover from the loss of such a golden boy? Viridian, as the elder son, would have inherited Foxes Court and its fifty acres and the family business, the art gallery in Cork Street, both of which he would have run effortlessly and with such panache.

Now the task would fall to Raymond, who had long

dreamt of a gentle academic career, writing books on art, and who felt less equipped to run a business than Hereward the dog. Raymond had been so sorry for poor shy, stammering George VI, having to step into the polished brogues of the glamorous, adored Edward VIII. Now he was in the same position.

And how would he himself survive without Viridian, whom he had loved so dearly, and who had been so fearless and certain of life, always shielding Raymond from bigger boys, never embarrassed to have a much younger brother hanging around?

Raymond glanced back at his volume of Tennyson, and at Viridian's strong, sunburnt, laughing face in the photograph, and quoted despairingly: '"Death has made his darkness beautiful with thee."'

Oh lucky, lucky death. Raymond had thought he was bearing up awfully well until last night, when he had stumbled on a poor lone cow on the verge of a road. Refusing to abandon her dead calf, whose back legs had been blown off, unmilked for several days, she was bellowing in pain and desperation. Having been brought up with animals, Raymond settled down to milk her. Only as he finished did he realize her reddy-brown flank, where his dark head had rested, was soaked with tears.

His platoon, most of whom had been recruited from Larkshire or next-door Gloucestershire and who knew Viridian and his parents, had been so kind. They hadn't said much, but Private Treays, who was the son of the local blacksmith, had given him a four-leaf clover, Private Turner had handed over the remains of a bottle of Calvados, and Lance-Corporal Formby, who had the charm of the devil, had wheedled three brown eggs out of a nearby French farmer, which had been scrambled for Raymond's supper last night.

On the other hand, the anguish of losing Viridian had made Raymond even more aware of his responsibility to bring his men safely through the coming action.

Beside him Private Treays had fallen asleep, head on his knapsack. From the faint pink glow in the east, rose doré mixed with a touch of raw sienna, Raymond could see the boy's thin face darkened with stubble, long lashes drooping over purple shadows, a half-eaten apple browning in his hand. Raymond wished he had pastels and paper.

'You must draw for at least a quarter of an hour a day,' his father was always telling him. 'Then you'll realize how bloody difficult it is for the artists.'

Once again Raymond wondered how he would ever live up to Viridian, who had so charmed both artists and collectors. He had never felt more lonely nor more inadequate.

Unknown to Raymond, however, his platoon sergeant, John 'Spider' Webster, whose face was so round and red it could have risen instead of the sun, was keeping an eye on him. Raymond's fortitude worried Sergeant Webster. The lad pushed himself too hard, constantly living in Viridian's shadow, worrying he wouldn't be up to the job. In fact he was first rate, brave as a lion and loved by officers and men alike. Some of those young subalterns were such berks, but Raymond was so kind, so modest, so unaware of his good looks, so outwardly unflappable. Spider had only once seen the boy lose his temper – when Private Turner, mistaking a big black hound silhouetted in a doorway for a ferocious guard dog, had shot it dead.

Raymond glanced at his watch, and shoved Tennyson back into his breast pocket. Nearly time to attack; he had better wake the others. The fields, heavy with dew, gleamed like sheets of silver in the half light; a slight breeze bent the corn. Beyond the village on the far side of a little river, rising out of the mist, he could see the grey pointed turrets of the château, which was rumoured to be occupied by a Nazi gauleiter, one of Goering's favourites.

Just before five a.m., his platoon moved off. Raymond's task was to attack on the right, advancing stealthily through orchards and back gardens. The distant chatter of Spandaus suggested that the other platoons had already made contact. There was no time to lose.

'"Into the jaws of Death, Into the mouth of Hell,"' muttered Raymond. He had always worried he wouldn't be able to kill the enemy, but with Viridian gone, he had no compunction and was soon shooting everything in his path in a blind fury.

Hearing shells exploding and the chilling swish of rockets, which indicated both the Artillery and the RAF were pitching in, Raymond battled his way choking through a smoke-filled café out into the high street, which had been reduced to rubble. Passing a little girl sobbing over a dead kitten, he gathered her up, shoving her into the arms of an old woman, also weeping in a doorway, and ran on.

By midday, after ferocious fighting, the village was in British hands. Germans had been winkled out of every other building. In a barn near the river, the other platoons had cornered forty prisoners. As they approached with their hands above their heads, Raymond was struck by how young they were and how old they looked; their hair prematurely grey with dust from the rubble, their faces seamed with despair and exhaustion like a defeated boat-race crew.

A delighted Lance-Corporal Formby, for whom needles leapt out of haystacks, had discovered a bottle of schnapps in an abandoned German staff car and gave Raymond a swig. A highly satisfied Company Commander was conferring with Spider Webster, his red face now blackened with smoke. Spider put a hand on Raymond's shoulder: 'You did very well there, sir.'

Delighted but embarrassed by such praise, Raymond quickly asked if everyone had been accounted for.

'I'm afraid Private Treays bought it, sir. Corporal

Turner was hurt, but only a flesh wound, thank God. The rest of us got through.'

Noticing Raymond's face working and his sudden pallor beneath the grime, Spider pointed to the château across the river, parts of which were now ablaze after a direct hit.

Disappointingly, however, no Nazi gauleiter had emerged.

'The bird seems to have flown,' observed the Company Commander. 'Just check if there's anyone inside, could you, Raymond?'

Numbly remembering how often Private Treays's father had shod his pony when he was a little boy, Raymond pushed open the rusty gates of the château and ran across a shaggy yellowing lawn. Kicking in a door, he wandered into a deserted drawing room where he found a cigar stubbed out in a Sèvres plate, with a three-quarters-drunk bottle of Calvados beside it, and some exquisite Louis-Quatorze furniture.

He was about to empty several bullets into Hitler's portrait over the fireplace, when his heart stopped at the beauty of a painting hanging on the right-hand wall. Drawing closer, he realized the subject was Pandora's Box. Pretty Pandora, in her sky-blue dress, and her rather insipid husband were writhing from the stings of the world's evils, newly released from a highly polished oak chest. To their left, the clearly defined Seven Deadly Sins were lumbering out of a side door, grumbling like drunks evicted from the pub. To the right, through a window, shone the full moon, bathing in light the iridescent rainbow-clad figure of Hope. She was so lovely, so serene, so radiant with promise of another world, compared with the bloody carnage and loss around Raymond.

The painting, particularly of the oak chest, was so wonderful, the colours so glowing, the faces so vivid, that Raymond, having been brought up with pictures, suspected it could be a Raphael. Drawing closer, he noticed a Latin tag, 'Malum infra latet', painted in gold letters along the bottom of the picture, meaning 'Trouble lies below'.

Trouble was also breaking out above as crashing beams and the warning shouts of his comrades brought him back to earth. He couldn't leave Pandora to burn, or fall back into the hands of the Nazis, who had after all just murdered Viridian and Private Treays, and only a philistine would hang a Raphael over a radiator.

Draining the Calvados, Raymond whipped out his knife and cut the picture out of its frame as his father had taught him. It was small, only twenty-two inches by eighteen, and easy to roll up, picture-side outwards, so as not to crack the paint. Glancing round for something in which to hide it, Raymond found a German First World War shell case holding fire-irons – the ideal solution and souvenir.

As the building collapsed, Raymond escaped into the sunlight.

1

1

1961

Raymond succeeded beyond everyone's wildest dreams. After the excitement of liberating Europe and a brief stint at Cambridge, he found equal thrills in transforming the respectable but slightly sleepy family gallery, the Belvedon in Cork Street, into one of the most successful in London.

To begin with, he worked all hours to blot out the horror of Viridian's death, but gradually he began to enjoy himself, developing a distinctly buccaneering attitude to art. Draconian export laws he felt deserved to be broken. Nor should one question too closely where a beautiful picture came from. Many a masterpiece was soon being smuggled abroad in the false bottom of his briefcase or brought home in the hold of the boat in which he took holidays each summer. Winter saw him with a permanent ski tan acquired while depositing illegal currency in the gallery's Swiss bank account.

Back in London, collectors fainted when given the occasional peep at the Old Masters stored in the Belvedon vaults. Raymond knew where to find a treasure and where to place it. Each time he was invited to stay in some great house, he left a less faded square on the damask wallpaper, having gently convinced his hostess that this was the optimum time to part with the Velásquez.

As the gallery's success increased, so did Raymond's eligibility. Invitations poured in for dances, but as Raymond circled the ballrooms of the Hyde Park Hotel and Claridge's, fluttering the hearts of the debs and their mothers, he made sure he got his name in the address book of the fathers: aristocrats who might want to flog a Gainsborough to pay for the season, *nouveau riche* businessmen who needed guidance on adorning the walls of their big new houses.

Raymond was such a charming chap, so unsnooty, he could be relied on to act as an advisor and to sell you something really good when it came along – even if sadly he showed no signs of marrying your daughter.

Only in the same area had Raymond disappointed his parents. At nearly thirty-seven, he had still failed to marry and produce an heir. Raymond's mother had a weak chest and his father, who was champing to retire permanently to the house in Provence, was threatening to hand Foxes Court, the main family home, over to Raymond's elder sister and her husband, who was thinking of leaving the diplomatic service, if Raymond didn't get a move on. But Raymond was a romantic. He could no more marry a woman he didn't love than exhibit an artist whose work he didn't admire.

Raymond, who had a flair for anticipating changes in taste, had specialized not only in Old Masters and Pre-Raphaelites, which were beginning to rise in value, but also living artists. Two of the latter were a married couple in their thirties: Colin Casey Andrews and Joan Bideford. Casey Andrews's huge part-abstract land-scapes of the Cornish coast were already selling well and in early May 1961, Joan had just completed such a successful debut show at the Belvedon that she had felt justified in throwing a party to celebrate.

She chose a beautiful Saturday evening – Viridian's

birthday, in fact – Viridian the virile, who would have produced half a dozen heirs by now, had he not been blown to bits leading his men at Monte Cassino without even a grave on which to put flowers.

Having taken down Joan Bideford's exhibition on the Friday before her party, Raymond and Eddie, his packer, had spent hours hanging the paintings of Raymond's latest discovery, a Frenchman called Etienne de Montigny, for the private view on Monday. Was it deliberately to eradicate the memory of Viridian's death that, at two o'clock in the morning, a sleepless Raymond had wandered down from the flat above the gallery and, deciding the pictures looked irredeemably garish and vulgar, had summoned Eddie the packer from the warmth of his girlfriend's bed in Battersea to repaint the stark white walls behind them?

Against a background of two coats of Prussian blue emulsion, the pictures looked sensational, like lit-up liners in a night-dark sea. Nor had Eddie minded labouring all night and through Saturday. At seven shillings an hour, he could take his girlfriend out on the toot this evening, and sleep it off tomorrow.

And Raymond was such a lovely bloke to work for, even if he did have mad notions and was picky about pictures being hung a millimetre too far to the left. He was so appreciative. He never talked down, and the tales he'd told Eddie about the Gods and Goddesses as they rehung the paintings would make your hair curl.

'That nymph being poked by that bull, Eddie, is actually the wife of the French Minister of Agriculture.'

Having showered upstairs and emerged beautiful as the evening star in his dinner jacket, Raymond had been distracted by a small oil of a languid youth admiring his white naked reflection in a pond.

'Exquisite,' he murmured.

'He'll get sunburn if he don't put on his shirt, and you're going to be late for that party,' chided Eddie, taking a pale pink rose from the vase on the reception desk and slotting it into Raymond's buttonhole. 'I'll lock up. Don't let Joan and Casey Andrews bully you. Invitation said bring a bottle.'

'Oh hell.'

'Here, take the Jack Daniel's that Yank brought you.'

'Thanks, Eddie.' Raymond gazed round happily. 'That blue's made all the difference. I can't thank you enough. See you Monday.'

As he emerged from the white-fronted eighteenth-century terrace house, with the dark blue Belvedon Gallery sign swaying in the warm breeze, the prostitutes who plied their trade along Cork Street wolf-whistled.

'Who's the lovely toff?' shouted a handsome blonde.

A pretty brunette started singing a pop song called 'Wooden Heart', imploring Raymond not to break hers.

Raymond laughed and danced a few steps with her before coiling his long length into his bottle-green E-Type. The girls were his friends, whom he often sketched and invited into the gallery on cold nights for a glass of brandy. Last Christmas they had clubbed together and given him a bottle of Armagnac.

As he drove towards Hampstead, he found the sudden heatwave had brought out good-looking couples, laughing outside pubs or wandering hand in hand along pavements strewn with pink and white blossom. Knowing she'd be desolate remembering Viridian, he'd rung his mother earlier.

'You're such a dear, Raymond,' her voice had trembled, 'you'd make such a wonderful husband.'

In the spring, the not-so-young man's fancy, reflected Raymond heavily, turns to thoughts of love.

He felt as though he'd been imprisoned in the gallery for so long he'd missed the spring. The creamy-white hawthorns were turning brown in the parks, the chestnut candles already over. But as he passed houses garlanded in cobalt-violet wisteria and breathed in a heady scent of rainsoaked lilac, it was impossible not to feel optimistic. He had sold a Reynolds to the National Gallery and a fine Zoffany to a Canadian collector, and Joan Bideford's nudes had gone so well that the big bumpy freckled nose of her far more famous husband was thoroughly out of joint.

Casey, as he was usually known, and Joan were such a repulsive couple: greedy, egotistical, sexually predatory, insanely jealous of one another and other artists, that, as an escape route, Raymond had arranged to dine at nine o'clock back in Mayfair with a rich collector and some of his friends – hence the dinner jacket. Later he would take them in wine-jolly strip-club mood back to the gallery for large drinks and a preview of Etienne de Montigny's erotic pictures.

2

Arriving at Joan and Casey's red-brick Victorian house, Raymond tripped over bicycles and a CND placard in the hall. At a recent demo, Joan had been arrested for socking a policeman. It was rumoured that during a subsequent stint in Holloway, she had developed a taste for her own sex.

Judging by the uproar, the party had been going on for several hours. People were crammed into a double-roomed studio with big sash windows opening onto the Heath. Lights like striped snowballs had just been turned on. Even on their walls Joan and Casey slugged it out. The only paintings on view were Joan's nudes and Casey's lowering seascapes, bright yellow cliffs over Antwerp-blue seas.

Raymond had forgotten the party was fancy dress. He could hardly see the paint-stained floorboards for Whistler's Mothers, florid Rembrandt self-portraits, Bardots, John F. Kennedys and Macmillans with drooping moustaches and winged grey hair. A famously drunken sculptor was causing howls of mirth because he'd arrived as Margot Fonteyn complete with white tulle tutu and ballet shoes but had refused to shave off his beard or wear tights over his hairy legs.

Raymond was desperate for a decent drink before he tackled the crowd, but the common denominator of the bottles lined up on the sideboard beside sweating

cheese and greying pâté was their cheapness and nasti-
ness. Some still had raffle tickets attached. Clinging to
his bottle of Jack Daniel's, Raymond searched for a
glass, but his hostess saw him first.

'Raymond Belvedon!' she bellowed. 'Have you come
as a waiter, or are you pushing off somewhere else as per
usual?'

Everyone swung round because they associated
Raymond's name with the gallery's success. Then they
stayed looking because of his height and beauty and the
warmth of his smile, which was belied by the wistfulness
in his big turned-down manganese-blue eyes.

As a jury had recently decided *Lady Chatterley's Lover*
was not obscene, Joan Bideford had dressed as Mellors
the gamekeeper in breeches, lace-up boots and a tweed
checked cut-away jacket with a fox fur slung over her
shoulders. The fox's eyes were marginally more glassy
than hers.

On a plate, like some instrument of torture, she was
brandishing a half-grapefruit bristling with cocktail
sticks threaded with cubes of cheese and pineapple.
Raymond could never look at her without thinking of
Tennyson's poem 'The Revenge', and Sir Richard
Grenville's wounded sailors: 'Men of Bideford in
Devon, And we laid them on the ballast down below.'

Raymond had no desire to lay Joan anywhere. Her big
handsome face was carmine with drink. He decided
against kissing her jutting oblong jaw.

'Just dropped in to congratulate you,' he said.
'Exhibition went awfully well.'

'Sold any more since yesterday?' demanded Joan.
'No? Well, my monthly cheque didn't arrive this
morning either.'

And I've just bust a gut flogging fourteen of your
pictures, you avaricious bitch, thought Raymond, who
had kindly paid her a retainer to live on while she
produced enough canvasses for an exhibition. But it was
no time to argue, Joan weighed more than he did and

her beady bloodshot eyes had lighted on the Jack Daniel's.

'Casey and I like bourbon, don't waste it on these gannets.' Grabbing the bottle, she shoved it behind an African mask.

Fortunately she was diverted by the arrival of Somerford Keynes, the *Daily Post* art critic, who'd come as Oscar Wilde and who was nicknamed the Poisoned Pansy because of his lethal reviews.

'Somerford,' howled Joan, 'did you bring a carbon of your piece?'

Raymond had managed to find a teacup and was just raiding the Jack Daniel's bottle when he was accosted by two pretty girls who thought it hilarious that they'd both rolled up as Lady Chatterley. Recognizing them as the entwined nudes in Joan's paintings, Raymond thought how much more attractive artists' models looked with their clothes on.

'Hello, handsome,' giggled the first. 'We're not going to find any decent John Thomas here, and none of us are safe from Joan or Casey. Want to come to another party?'

'You'd have much more fun with us,' added the second.

'What a pity, I've got to go out to dinner,' sighed Raymond.

'We know who you are,' they chorused. 'Will you tell your other artists we're very good models? Casey and Joan are so tight.'

Then they went scarlet, because towering over them, resplendent as Neptune in a slipping loincloth, with sea horses and seaweed painted all over his mighty torso and massive thighs, was Casey Andrews.

'Dance with you young women later,' he boomed, whacking them on the bottom with his trident. 'Now push off.'

With his jutting red-bearded jaw almost meeting his

huge bumpy nose, his angry little eyes and vigorous russet curls, Casey looked more like Raphael's drawing of Hercules wrestling with the Nemean lion than Neptune. But he was just as capable of causing storms.

It was strange, reflected Raymond, how the picture of Pandora, which had turned out to be by Raphael and which now hung at the top of the house at Foxes Court, influenced his judgement of people. Casey Andrews was guilty of at least six of the Deadly Sins: pride, wrath, envy, avarice, lust and certainly greed, as he devoured a huge Stilton sandwich washed down with red wine from a pint mug. Casey also felt it was his right to seduce every woman, and their privilege to capitulate. Raymond had nightmare visions of having to represent thousands of odious Casey Andrews offspring when he was a doddering old dealer.

Like Joan, Casey immediately got on to money. Had Raymond sold any pictures, had he heard from Rome and if not why not, and what about an American exhibition?

'An American car company's interested in that oil of St Mawes,' countered Raymond and, when Casey looked bootfaced: 'They'd like two more for the boardroom.'

But, as usual, Casey wasn't happy with the price. Commercial concerns should pay twice as much.

'Andras Kalman's invited me to lunch,' he said bullyingly.

'You'll enjoy it.' Raymond just managed to control his anger. 'Andras is a charmer, and runs a great gallery.'

Casey stormed off.

Nearby two art critics dressed as Roman senators were admiring Joan's grapefruit hedgehog, which she'd abandoned on a sofa.

'I didn't know Bideford was tackling sculpture,' said one. 'That piece is very fine.'

Raymond suppressed a smile. He was so kind and courteous that the moment Casey abandoned him, the crowd moved in: artists who wanted to show him their work; collectors who wanted free advice or jobs in the gallery for their daughters; critics who wanted praise for a review. Casey returned for another row and, finding Raymond surrounded, shoved off again.

'I can't think how you endure those two,' said a soft lisping voice.

It was the Poisoned Pansy, Somerford Keynes. Everything about Somerford seemed to flop downwards: his straight sandy locks from an Oscar Wilde middle parting, his droopy blond moustache concealing a large flapping upper lip, even his bow tie wilted in the heat. But he had knowing eyes, as if he were aware of secrets Raymond didn't want divulged. Somerford's taste for working-class louts was equalled only by his desire to be the darling of society hostesses, among whom he did not list Joan Bideford.

'Thank you for giving Joan such a good review,' murmured Raymond.

'If I hadn't been devoted to you, dear boy, I'd have annihilated her; so crude those lardlike bodies, I've perjured myself invoking the name of Gauguin.'

'Stop, you're driving me crazy,' sang the record player.

A large tabby cat was thoughtfully licking the sardine pâté.

'Can you chaps shove through to the next room?' ordered Joan.

'Got to go,' said Raymond, meekly shuffling a few feet forward.

'I'm meeting Francis Bacon at Muriel's later,' murmured Somerford, 'why not join us after dinner?'

Raymond felt overwhelmed with tiredness, nor did he want to be sucked into Somerford's underworld.

'I don't seem to have been to bed for days,' he apologized. 'Going to crash out the moment dinner's over.'

But as he glanced briefly into the second room his exhaustion fell away, for lounging against the piano, dressed as a pirate, was the sexiest boy he had ever seen. He was about five foot nine, with straight dark hair hanging in a thick fringe and tied back by a black ribbon. His shoulders were broadened by the horizontal stripes of a matelot T-shirt, his hips narrowed by dark blue trousers tucked into shiny black boots. His face was dominated by long slanting sloe-dark eyes above very high cheekbones, with a black moustache and line of beard emphasizing a big sulky red mouth.

But it was the provocative thrust of his body and the disdainful lift of his head that made him so attractive, as if he were going to leap onto the deck of Sir Richard Grenville's *Revenge*, cutlass hissing, and slay every man alive.

Oh dear, dear God, marvelled Raymond.

Then, as the pirate reached back for his glass on the window, the striped T-shirt tightened against a high breast and jutting nipple and Raymond realized that he was a girl, that her moustache and beard were of smudged cork and that several men who normally showed no interest in women were circling her as though she were covered in sexual aniseed.

'"A queen, with swarthy cheeks and bold black eyes",' muttered Raymond, but this time there was no Viridian's Tennyson in his breast pocket to shield his heart from Cupid's arrow.

'More like one of the waiters at La Popote,' mocked Somerford. 'Even I wouldn't mind giving her a jolly roger.'

'Who is she?' asked Raymond.

'Galena Borochova, playgirl of the Mid-European world, defected last year from Czechoslovakia, rumoured to have slept with half the secret police in the process, drinks too much to forget, been causing havoc in Paris. Casey and Joan are equally besotted and fighting over her. Rumoured to be a good painter. Needs a dealer' – Somerford looked slyly at a spell-bound Raymond – 'to take her under his wing.'

The pirate was now emptying a bottle of Riesling out of the window, shouting, 'Nothing good ever came out of Yugoslavia,' and helping herself to more red.

'That's wasteful, Galena, sweetie.' Appearing from behind, Joan Bideford lifted up the girl's T-shirt and grabbed her breasts with huge red paint-stained hands.

'Go avay, Joan.' Galena's voice was deep and husky like a cello played all its life in smoky nightclubs. 'Just bugger off.'

Then, when Joan didn't, Galena calmly stubbed out her cigarette on a groping finger.

'You bitch,' howled Joan. Tugging down Galena's T-shirt, she kissed her bare shoulder. 'But I love you for it.'

Galena shrugged then went berserk as a man dressed as Picasso tried to take her photograph. Screaming in Slovak, she snatched his camera, hurling it against the wall with a sickening crunch.

By the time Raymond had fought his way over, Casey Andrews had seen off the opposition and, armed with a refilled pint of red and another Stilton sandwich, his red beard smeared with butter and crumbs, was trying to persuade Galena to dance.

Closer up, Raymond discovered she looked older, perhaps thirty. He was also reassured to see a few grey hairs in her black fringe, and lines round the arrogant mouth.

'Who is this?' she demanded, then, examining Raymond's face, 'Ve have met before.'

'We certainly haven't.'

'I am never wrong.'

'Where are you from?'

'Bohemia.'

Raymond smiled. 'That figures.'

'Who are you?' she asked impatiently.

'Raymond Belvedon,' snapped Casey, 'Joan and I show at his gallery.'

'You make a stunning pirate,' stammered Raymond. God, how wet could one get?

'I come from country viz no coast line,' said Galena. 'In England ven you feel trapped, you can run and run until you reach the sea. In Czechoslovakia you end up in Austria, East Germany or Poland. Now I am here, I can be pirate.'

Noticing a bacon-and-egg pie being carried past, she speared a big triangle with her cutlass.

Raymond couldn't take his eyes off her huge sulky mouth. He longed to stand up the rich collectors and whisk her off to Annabel's, but she probably wouldn't get in without a tie.

'Somerford likened my work to Gauguin,' Joan was telling everyone. She and most of the men in the room were preparing to launch another attack on Galena, who was now arguing with Casey, wolfing bacon-and-egg pie, waving her cigarette around, coughing, taking gulps of red wine and all the time keeping her narrowed, appraising eyes on Raymond.

Finally the drunken sculptor dressed as Margot Fonteyn could bear it no longer and pirouetted up to Galena, arms, hairy legs and mug of Spanish Burgundy going everywhere. An outraged Casey shoved him away. Margot Fonteyn swayed and fell backwards on Joan's grapefruit hedgehog with a bellow of pain.

'Lucky thing,' grumbled Somerford, 'to have so many pricks in one go.'

'Poor chap.' Raymond struggled not to laugh.

Galena had no such reserve. Unrestrained guffaws seemed to bubble up from inside her like lava.

'You said you were going ages ago, Raymond,' said Casey pointedly.

'I am.'

'You must see my vork.' Grabbing Casey's sketch-book, left on the piano to be looked at, Galena tore off half a page.

'I've drawn on that,' bellowed Casey.

'My signature will be more vorth than all your drawing one day,' taunted Galena.

Scribbling down her name, a street which Raymond had never heard of and a Battersea telephone number, she shoved the piece of paper into his breast pocket, then removed the pink rose from his buttonhole.

'In Czechoslovakia, it is unlucky to give people even number of flowers. One rose is OK.'

As Casey was about to run him through with his trident, Raymond fled.

3

Raymond remembered nothing about dinner. Having downed two large dry Martinis and left all his Dover sole, he took no-one to see Etienne de Montigny's erotic pictures. Making a lame excuse about having to get home to the West Country, he turned south at Hyde Park and drove over the river.

It was still terribly hot. He had removed his dinner jacket and his tie and rolled up his sleeves, but his shirt was dripping. Galena lived in a rough area. No-one was enjoying noisy after-dinner drinks in their back gardens. He located her room before the number of the house by the sound of *Don Giovanni* pouring out of an open second-floor window.

Raymond ran upstairs, hardly needing to hammer on the door, his heart was banging so loudly. Galena welcomed him, a glass in one hand, paintbrush in the other, her fringe drenched with sweat, paint all over her matelot jersey. She had kicked off her new boots and put them beside Casey's sketchbook and the remains of Raymond's bottle of Jack Daniel's on the only chair.

'Casey, vile peeg, vas swigging it from the bottle, then he give me great cheesy kiss, I slap his face and run away.' She filled a tooth mug with whiskey for Raymond.

'Perhaps you should give back his sketchbook? Those drawings are probably worth something.'

'Good, I need money for paints.'

Galena's room was dreadful, only large enough to contain a single bed, stacked up canvasses, an easel, a small rickety table for her tubes of paint, brushes and palettes, and an ancient gramophone. The LPs, apart from *Don Giovanni*, were by Slav composers: Suk, Bartók, Dvořák and Smetana. On top of the books piled up by the bed was a collapsing copy of Kafka's *Castle*. In between big damp patches on the wall were rough sketches and far too many scribbled telephone numbers. Did they all belong to men? Donna Giovanna? Raymond was appalled by his jealousy.

Galena had gone back to her easel, thickly applying paint. Raymond edged towards the canvasses.

'May I?'

'Of course, that is vy you are here.'

And Raymond was overwhelmed by the same churning excitement he had felt when he first saw the Raphael Pandora in the flaming château. Galena's subject matter was hideous. Farms and entire villages being sliced in half by the Iron Curtain. Humans and animals being blown to pieces or burnt to death on high-voltage electric fences.

'As children,' Galena said flatly, 'we were tormented by the screams and bangs as foxes, hares, dogs and cats tread on mines.'

The pictures were made more sinister by homely touches: storks nesting in watchtower chimneys, window boxes filled with orange nasturtiums. As if in defiance against the horrors and the greyness of Communist life, Galena revelled like Matisse in the brightest, most exuberant of palettes.

One large canvas took Raymond's breath away. On the Slovak side, from a watchtower above the electric fence, border guards were mowing down defectors in case the mines didn't get them. Everywhere were screaming mouths, waving hands, terrified eyes, severed limbs. On the Austrian side, a bunch of grandees were blasting away at partridge against brilliant autumn colours. A horse and cart followed, weighed down by picnic hampers and crates of wine. The contrast made the behaviour of both sides more reprehensible. It had the power of a *Guernica*. Galena could capture sadistic arrogance in a brush stroke.

'These are amazing, has anyone seen them?'

'No. In Prague, I vas banned from college for protesting against Communists. The Volpos, secret police, vatch me and my friends. They close down my first two exhibitions.' Galena had put on *The Bartered Bride*, side one, which was even more scratchy.

'Things get too hot, my father vas arrested for political activity, he didn't come home much, my mother die earlier.'

'How did you escape?'

'I get to know Volpos, who arrange for me and my sister to escape over border. She vas four years younger.'

Tears were trickling down Galena's face as she went to the window.

'As we get to other side, my sister tread on mine, it blow off her leg, and knock me unconscious. I came round to hear her last screams, border guards leave her to die.

'I crawl to safety. A shooting party nearly shoot me instead of birds. Then they take me to people I know in Vienna. My last memory of Czechoslovakia is my sister screaming. That is the picture.' She pointed to the huge canvas.

Raymond longed to comfort her. Her face was a wreckage of smudged mascara and burnt cork.

'I betray artist friends by leaving Prague, but how can I show protest if no-one sees it? We live all our lives in Czechoslovakia under tyranny.'

'The artist has a different loyalty,' said Raymond gently. 'To the future as well as the present. You were right to come here. I am so sorry about your sister.'

The music grew louder. Someone banged angrily on the wall. Galena promptly turned up the volume.

If she were happy, thought Raymond, she might paint happier pictures. Casey and Joan were like some foul witch and wizard. He was just dreaming of rescuing Galena from their clutches like an Arthurian knight when the telephone rang. Galena pounced on it, tears turning in a trice to fury. Even across the room, Raymond could hear the caller at the other end roaring as if dinner had been delayed in the lion house.

A grinning Galena held out the receiver.

'I bought you those boots only yesterday,' Casey was yelling.

Finally Galena caved in and hung up.

'He's coming over,' she told a despairing Raymond, then she laughed: 'So we must go. Take me to the sea.'

'I'll take you home to Limesbridge, there's a river and a boat.'

Normally the great motorway being built to the west caused endless hold-ups, but tonight, as if conspiring to catapult him into committing himself more quickly, there were no roadworks nor traffic jams.

As they sped through deserted Farringdon and Lechlade, deeper into the country, it was like a film being played backwards. Candles once more lit the horse chestnuts, cow parsley frothed white along the roadside, hawthorn exploded in creamy fountains in the fields, and wild garlic rioted over the woodland floor mirroring the Milky Way streaming across the sky above.

Escaping from their velvet ribbon, tendrils of hair striped Galena's face. As she took swigs of Jack Daniel's, and sang drunken snatches of the Czech national anthem, her long muscular thighs spread at right angles, taunting Raymond to stroke them.

Never had the hundred-mile journey home passed more quickly. As they dropped into the Silver Valley, a full moon, ringed with pale flame, was shining down on the sleeping village of Limesbridge – so named because of the splendid avenue of limes on either side of the bridge over the River Fleet. There were also limes round the village green and the churchyard where all the Belvedon ancestors were buried except Viridian. Foxes Court, built in Queen Anne's day, lay to the west of the village with two acres of walled garden, several cottages and barns and fields stretching down to the river.

Cherry trees forming a white guard of honour scattered their last petals like confetti on the E-Type as Raymond and Galena roared up the drive. Stone nymphs and cherubs peeped round yew corridors for a first glimpse. The stench of wild garlic from the church-yard next door overwhelmed the sweet delicate smell of the pink clematis which swarmed over pergolas and up the north side of the house.

Swaying like a pirate ship, a bare-footed Galena picked her way over the gravel. Inside the hall, the yellow Cotswold stone was covered in faded blue and crimson rugs, the walls with shiny dark panelling. Half-way up the stairs hung a Matisse of equally swaying green dancers.

Galena examined it closely, frantically trying not to be too impressed, nor as she reeled from room to ravishing room to get too excited over the Courbet flower girl, nor the Pissarro snow scene, nor the Leonardo drawing of a lion, nor Rossetti's sly sketch of Tennyson, nor Rodin's maquette of a female nude: enchantments even a dealer couldn't bear to part with.

There was a patter of feet, and a yawning blue grey-hound, claws sliding, spiny tail banging against the panelling, came bounding down the stairs.

'This is Maud,' said Raymond as the bitch circled him ecstatically. 'She likes lazing on beds all day, so we spend our time yelling: "Come into the garden, Maud."'

'How beautiful she is.' Galena fell to her knees, hug-ging Maud, smoothing her velvet ears. 'Like Wenceslas's dog on the Charles Bridge.'

She recognized the Matisse; she loves my dog. It was

like Bassanio passing the tests set him by Portia with flying colours, thought Raymond.

The kitchen, painted cold air-force blue with fluorescent lighting, was less seductive than the other rooms. Galena, however, discovered rare delights in the refrigerator, and was soon wolfing vegetable pâté, made for tomorrow's luncheon party, and sharing slices of chicken *estragon* with a delighted Maud.

'How did you get this house?'

'My parents live here, they're coming back tomorrow.'

'And the gallery?'

'Some have greatness thrust upon them, my elder brother was killed in the war, so I inherited it.'

With her sloe-dark eyes beneath drooping eyelids and that luminous gold skin, Galena looked very like a Raphael, he thought. She was now attacking tomorrow's pudding: pale yellow syllabub in six blue glasses, only awaiting a sprinkling of bitter chocolate.

Pondering on his next move, Raymond said, 'Teach me some Czech.'

'You should ask: *mate znamost.*'

'What does it mean?'

'Do you have a boyfriend?'

'Well, do you?'

'Not until now.'

As Raymond felt dizzy with happiness, Galena grabbed another blue glass. Out of the window, she could see a moonlit lawn as smooth as a pale grey fitted carpet disappearing into dark shrubberies.

'This is big house with much land. Are you a lord?'

'No, not at all.'

'In 1949, when the Communists took over' – another black mood swept over Galena – 'the Czech aristocrats who lived in the big houses fetched coaches that hadn't been used in years out of the stables, piling them up with their belongings – leaving in fine style – smiling bravely. I will never forget the silhouette of those coaches and horses going along the horizon to Austria.'

'Why didn't you go too?'

'My mother vas housekeeper to one of these houses. She wouldn't leave without my father who was away. The Communists stormed the house. They took chandeliers and central heating before starting on the wine in the cellar. Then the most drunken hurled our puppy down into the courtyard.'

Shaking violently, Galena huddled over Maud, convulsively stroking her sleek blue coat.

'They play football with puppy, kicking him to death, laughing. Sylvie, my sister, vas such a pretty little girl that my mother hid her in our part of the house, but when she hear puppy's howls, she rushed into the courtyard, kicking the soldiers.

'The Cossack Colonel vas pervert, who didn't bother with my mother. Even I vas too old at sixteen, but Sylvie vas only ten, so he raped her. My mother tried to knife him. The soldiers killed her.'

Embarrassed by such tragic outpourings, soaked with tears, Maud slid out of the room.

'Christ, I'm so sorry.' Removing the syllabub from Galena's clutches, Raymond pulled her to her feet. Wailing helplessly, she collapsed against him.

'I try to make it up to Sylvie. I sleep with Volpos, so we can escape. I thought if we reach Vest, I could paint and make a home for her. Why did she tread on mine not me?'

No wonder she had gone berserk over the photographer at the party, thought Raymond. Spying Volpos must have been behind every bush.

'It wasn't a millionth as bad for me.' Raymond stroked her damp hair, trying to still her shuddering. 'But my brother was blown up in North Italy. You feel so guilty you're the one who survived.'

Gradually Galena's sobs subsided enough for her to grab her glass and light a cigarette.

'What did he look like, your brother?'

Raymond took her into the study. To the right of the fireplace was a portrait of Viridian by Rex Whistler, who had also been killed in the last war.

The Fates must have been jealous of anyone so clear-eyed and confident, thought Galena.

'He is very handsome, like Sylvie,' she observed, 'but his face is not as kind, nor as clever as yours.'

Glancing up through lowered black lashes, she suddenly pressed a hand against Raymond's cock and, pulling his head down, flickered a wine-darkened tongue along his lips.

'Show me your bedroom, now!'

4

Raymond led her up two flights of stairs and along dark winding passages, but when they reached the steep uncarpeted steps up to his turret bedroom, known as the Blue Tower, she bounded ahead, flaunting her delectably high bottom like a cabin boy climbing the rigging.

Moonlight silvered the bare floorboards. Above the crimson-curtained four-poster, the dark blue vaulted ceiling had been painted with stars. As Raymond turned on a bedside light, Galena noticed the walls covered in exquisite erotic paintings.

'It was my parents' love nest,' explained Raymond, unbuttoning his cork-smudged dress shirt. 'They believed if you had beautiful things to look at, you would produce beautiful children.'

But Galena was racing round the room, gazing out of the four windows, at the gold weathercock topping the church spire, at black yew rides and ivy-clad ruins, and over a cloud of apple blossom, down to a boathouse and a gleaming silver river.

'It is good escape tower. Ve can hide ven Casey comes. Oh my God!' The smile froze on her face as she caught sight of the Raphael. 'Is it yours?'

Raymond nodded, gazing in wonder at her gazing in such wonder as she fingered the folds of Pandora's sky-blue dress, examining each deadly sinner, stopping longest at Hope, shaking her head in bewilderment.

'It is breath-tooking. Has it belong to your family for years?'

'Well, quite a long time.'

Raymond had never identified so much with Lust in his vermilion coat, leering at Pandora. Unable to hold back any longer, he crossed the room; he tugged off Galena's ribbon, so her dark hair fell like a weeping ash to her shoulders. As he took her lithe sinewy body in his arms, he could smell sweat, and feel muscles heavily developed by painting and lugging around huge canvasses. Her mouth tasted of cigarette smoke and Jack Daniel's.

He could have picked her up in a dockland bar in Marseilles. It was illegal to prefer men to girls, and in those agonizing encounters with his own sex in the dark, when he was abroad, any ecstasy had been followed by a descent into a hell of guilt. But now there was only ecstasy.

There were no underclothes to rip off once he'd removed her hipsters and striped T-shirt. Terrified his erection might collapse, he delayed and delayed, laying her on the patchwork counterpane, kissing her big lascivious mouth, absurdly turned on by the faintest stubble where the cork moustache had been, kissing each breast and sticking-out rib. At the end of a sweep of white belly, her pubic hair rose spiky as a blackthorn copse in the snow. If there were no sea around Czechoslovakia, there was a river bubbling between Galena's legs.

Once inside her, her muscles gripped him like an octopus, and her normally narrowed eyes stayed wide open.

'My beautiful Raymond.'

The bed's creaking grew faster, her gold cross bounced on her breasts, the smoky whispered endearments grew more incomprehensible. He felt she was gouging out his heart with her cutlass, as if he were a little sailing boat on the roughest sea as she bucked beneath him. Then, spitting on a nail-bitten finger, she reached round and plunged it deep inside him. Raymond gave a groan of pleasure and came. Very, very slowly, he returned to earth.

'God, I'm so sorry. I meant you to come.'

'I drink too much,' mumbled Galena, 'I'm too numb to come,' and, laughing softly as she kissed him on the shoulder, she passed out.

Raymond was woken by the church bell ringing for early service, and the sun shining through the thickly cob-webbed eastern window. Galena, wearing only his dress shirt, was standing on the bed, gazing at the Raphael. On the bedside table was a large cup of black coffee and a half-eaten croissant smothered in butter and black cherry jam.

Grabbing her strong tawny ankle, sliding his hand upwards, Raymond apologized for sleeping so long. But Galena was preoccupied with the painting:

'Hesiod describe Pandora as meddlesome Nosy Parker, who bring all evils of world on mankind, because she open box she vas told not to. So vot? Every-one open box. We got few presents at Christmas, but whenever my mother go out, Sylvie and I went through her drawer, to find out what we were getting. Without curiosity there is no art.

'If Epimetheus' – disdainfully Galena waved a hand at Pandora's writhing, insect-covered husband – 'had had the self-control not to marry Pandora – Prometheus, his brother had already warned him not to – none of these evils would have escaped and plagued the world.'

If Epimetheus had been overwhelmed with a quarter of my lust . . . thought Raymond, as his hand caressed the soft underside of her bottom.

'Raphael also give La Fornarina's face to Pandora,' added Galena.

And Raymond was lost. No debutante he'd trundled dutifully round Claridge's ballroom had ever heard of Hesiod or had known that La Fornarina was Raphael's last beloved mistress.

'"Let me not to the marriage of true minds . . ."' he murmured.

Galena jumped triumphantly off the bed.

'I know where I see you before,' she cried. 'It vas in Venice. On the left-hand side of Bellini's *Coronation of Christ*, there is a portrait of Jesus, thin faced but strong jawed' – she ran a finger down Raymond's cheek – 'and with thick hair that springs up if it is not kept down with water, a beautiful mouth' – she stroked his lower lip – 'and the saddest eyes in the world. As you look at his face, you see the pain setting in. You know he's going to suffer. It's the only sexy Christ I ever see.'

Galena took a gulp of coffee, then, kneeling down, put her warm mouth round Raymond's cock, sucking gently. Instantly Raymond sprang to life.

'My God, where d'you learn these tricks?'

'I need them to convince Volpos.'

The shadows were creeping over her face again.

'It's all right, darling, don't think about them any more.'

Once again came the lightning mood switch. Running her finger along the top of her half-eaten croissant, Galena smiled wickedly: 'I do even more exciting things with butter.'

The coffee went cold. Maud, unnoticed, pinched the rest of the croissant.

'Will you marry me?' asked Raymond.

Galena looked at him appraisingly.

'I should like to live in this house, and for you to put on big exhibition of my vork and buy me my own dog.

56

But I must be free spirit. If I paint all night, I cannot stop to cook your dinner. Don't expect me to be housevife. Never trap me.'

Raymond pushed back her lank black hair.

'"God gives us love",' he quoted slowly, '"Something to love he lends us". You will always be free. No more electric fences, no watchtowers, no secret police nor mines. There's the river.' He pointed out of the window. 'You can sail away whenever you want, as long as you come back.'

Raymond's parents didn't mind in the slightest about their ransacked lunch, and swept all their guests, including Galena, wearing another of Raymond's shirts, out to lunch at the Lark Ascending on the Cheltenham Road.

They soon decided, particularly Raymond's father, that Galena was adorable, and immensely talented, with just the right degree of vitality and realism to offset Raymond's excessive kindness and dreamy romantic chivalry. Their critical faculties were slightly blurred by their relief that Raymond had finally taken the plunge.

Or as Somerford Keynes pointed out to a fulminating Casey Andrews: 'Those desirous of grandchildren do not look a gift whore in the mouth.'

Casey was so angry he would have left the Belvedon and moved to another gallery, if it hadn't meant less access to Galena.

'There's no way one man's enough for her,' he roared at Raymond. 'You'll be forced to share her.'

Joan Bideford, relieved that Galena hadn't run off with Casey, was more philosophical.

'Of course we can go on seeing each other, darling,' she told Galena as she smothered poached salmon with Hollandaise sauce during lunch at the Ritz. 'But try not to hurt Raymond, he's a nice man, and we don't want anything to distract him from selling our pictures. The only thing that worries me is the money. You've coped so brilliantly with being destitute, sweetie. I'm not sure how you'll handle being rich.'

'I must be free spirit,' insisted Galena, waving for another bottle of champagne.

5

Maybe it was the result of gazing at erotic paintings in the Blue Tower, but within a year, Galena had delighted Raymond and (almost more) her new in-laws by producing a beautiful heir, called Jupiter. A second son, Alizarin, named after Galena's favourite colour, alizarin crimson, arrived two years later.

Raymond returned the compliment by ensuring Galena's first exhibitions were both critical and commercial successes. After the monotony of the Czech countryside, Limesbridge and the surrounding Silver Valley haunted her like a passion. Wandering in a trance, she had captured the wooded ravines, mist from the river merging into white orchards, the locals in the Goat in Boots, Foxes Court serene and golden behind its armoury of ancient trees, in joyful light-filled paintings that Raymond sold as soon as she produced them.

The gallery profits soared throughout the Sixties. But as Joan Bideford had predicted, Galena coped with riches far less well than poverty. Professing a scorn for commercialism, she claimed no great painting had ever sold in its lifetime. Denied the need to work, she started drinking heavily, ranting at Raymond that he had taken away the hunger necessary to a great artist.

Even worse, during the crushing of the Prague Spring by the Communists in 1968, a young friend of hers had died setting fire to himself in protest against Russian brutality. Galena suffered appalling guilt, and her paintings became violent and tortured again.

Why, she stormed, had Raymond forced her to abandon her fellow artists? Why had Chamberlain sold the Czechs down the river in the first place? Why was she trapped in a gilded cage? Over and over she portrayed as prison bars the trunks of the trees round Foxes Court with herself screaming and anguished at every window. This gave her the excuse to escape to London, lounging around with Casey and Joan on big silk cushions smoking dope and – since she was now an extremely expensive spirit as well as a free one – gorging on caviare, foie gras and crates of priceless wine.

These days of lethargy and excess would eventually be followed by more guilt and frenzied work sessions when she would yell at anyone, particularly the little boys and Raymond, if they disturbed her.

The Belvedon Gallery in fact did spectacularly well in the Sixties because Raymond was working night and day to forget the horror of his marriage. For in addition to the drunken ranting, the ingratitude and the over-spending, Galena was sadistically unfaithful.

From the first, she had deliberately picked Raymond's gallery artists. These included not just Casey and Joan but also Etienne de Montigny, the handsome Frenchman whose semi-pornographic paintings Raymond had been hanging the night he met Galena. All of their revenue Raymond would have lost if he had refused to represent them any more. Plenty of other lovers soon joined the circus.

'I need new men,' shouted Galena, 'I get tired of drawing the same one.'

Raymond might have retaliated in kind, if she hadn't so demoralized him sexually.

'Am I big enough for you?' he had begged her on their honeymoon, to which she had mockingly replied:

'If you have small villy, you must become genius at sucking off.'

A mortified Raymond had tried so hard, but, putting his mouth to Galena's gaping red, not very well-washed gash, he found himself gagging, which Galena in turn construed as rejection, and their sex life deteriorated. Sometimes, to help him get it up, she would describe what another wonderful lover looked like or had done to her, which made Raymond come immediately and Galena in turn more scornful.

Most men would have cuffed her, or walked out, but it was the Sixties when everyone was far too cool to admit rage or heartbreak. And, like his hero, King Arthur, whose world collapsed because of his wife's infidelity, Raymond still loved her.

For when she smiled, the flowers came out. She could be enchanting, funny, playful, affectionate. She was a glorious, imaginative cook. She painted wonderful murals in strong Slav colours all over the house, and she told marvellous stories to little Jupiter and Alizarin, who absolutely adored her. Raymond in turn doted on his boys. There was no way they were going to be subjected to a divorce. Finally he felt it his duty, like Theo Van Gogh, who had so heroically bolstered and bankrolled his mad tragic brother, to keep Galena on an even keel to create the masterpieces of which he knew she was capable.

One of the lowest points in his marriage was in early July 1970. At four o'clock in the morning, still trembling from a row the night before, he lay on the edge of the crimson-curtained four-poster listening to the piping of Tennyson's 'half-awakened birds', and imagining the icicles of white light between the carelessly drawn dark blue curtains were being plunged into his heart.

For a start, he was convinced Galena had a new lover. He had left a bottle of champagne in the fridge, which was gone when he returned yesterday from a couple of days in Venice. The orchids in the drawing room had certainly not come from the garden. There was also a pretty new Lalique bowl on her dressing table.

As clinching evidence, she had been grumbling non-stop about Alizarin and Jupiter being home from school for an eight-week summer holiday, getting under her feet. After the over-excited little boys had been sent to bed, Raymond and Galena had had a drink outside in the twilight. A fresh soapy smell of meadowsweet drifted up from the river. White and pale pink roses cascaded frivolously over the dark green shoulders of the yews.

As he wandered round the terrace, deadheading geraniums and stepping over Maud, who was stretched out soothing her stiff old bones on the still warm flag-stones, Raymond broke the good news, that he had employed an undergraduate for the summer to amuse the boys and teach them to draw, leaving Galena free to paint.

'Vere did you meet him?' asked Galena silkily as she topped up her third drink.

'At Cambridge when I gave that lecture on the Pre-Raphaelites. This boy, David Pulborough, ex-grammar school, reading history of art at King's, was assigned to look after me. Later, at dinner' – Raymond swatted a midge on his forearm – 'we talked about Arthurian legend, painting and the awful factory jobs he's been forced to take in the vac to make ends meet. Parents live near Leeds. Sound a bit repressive.' Fingering the dry earth in a tub of white agapanthus, Raymond reached for the watering can. 'Father's in local govern-ment, regards art as sissy, wanted David to read law or medicine.'

Raymond didn't add that David Pulborough had wavy tawny hair to his shoulders, big navy blue eyes and a fair skin that flushed easily. Nor did he say how touched he'd been that David, obviously short of money, had tried to pay for dinner.

'He's a sweet boy. You'll like him,' Raymond went on, then, appealing to Galena's fondness for comparing people in real life with those in paintings, he added,

'Looks exactly like St John Evangelista in Raphael's painting of St Cecilia.'

'Ven does he arrive?'

'Tomorrow in time for supper.'

At first he thought Galena's silence was delighted assent. Then she went berserk. How could Raymond spring this surprise on her, then push off to London, probably abroad, leaving her to entertain some boorish youth in the evenings?

'How dare you employ pop squeak to spy on me and to teach the boys to draw? Do you want their paintings to hang on Green Park fences?'

Maud, who loathed rows, beat a limping retreat into the house.

The intensity of Galena's rage indicated that she had other mischief planned for the first weeks of the holidays, particularly when she yelled at Raymond that she was off to France first thing. No doubt to stay with Etienne de Montigny, thought Raymond despairingly.

'And you can bloody vell stay down in country, to velcome your little queer when he arrives tomorrow,' was her final shot. 'Are you sure you're safe leaving the boys viz him?'

As she slammed the french windows behind her, she had broken two panes.

It was now growing light in the Blue Tower. Raymond, listening to the rusty key-jangling cries of the jackdaws in the tall chimneys, was still shaking. Alizarin and Jupiter were almost more obsessed with the Raphael than with their mother, and, oblivious of grubby sheets that had harboured God knew who, took every opportunity to creep into their parents' bed in the early mornings and wait for Hope, Pandora and the rest of the gang to creep out of the shadows. Raymond, who longed to make love to his wife, tried not to resent the boys.

He was amazed Galena could sleep so deeply after such a shattering row. Possessed of earthy charms that in early life don't need much upkeep, she was a couple of stone heavier than the boyish pirate he had first married. But she still attracted him unbearably and he couldn't resist putting a hand on her breast. Galena stirred, smiling sleepily, not yet identifying the hand. If only he could psych himself into getting it up . . . but the next moment there was a crash on the door and the boys charged in. Sighing, Raymond threw a towel over their mother.

Jupiter at eight had just finished his first term away from home at prep school, and was consequently tougher, steelier, more withdrawn. With his cool turned-down sage-green eyes, dark brown hair and thin freckled face, he was like Raymond, but without Raymond's openness and generosity. As conniving but colder than his mother, Jupiter wished he had inherited her talent.

Alizarin, on the other hand, had Galena's looks: black brows, slitty dark eyes, high cheekbones and straight dark flopping hair. Gangling and unco-ordinated, as tall as Jupiter, he had inherited his father's sweet nature and anxiously commuted between his parents trying to keep the peace.

Knowing their mother would soon be off to paint, or, worse, to London, the boys always tried to waylay her and weave stories round the Raphael. This morning Jupiter collapsed on the bed snoring loudly.

'Which deadly sin am I?'

'Sloth,' smiled Raymond.

'Who am I?' Alizarin put a finger under his long grey-hound nose, pushing it into the air. 'I'm Pride.'

He looked so absurd, Raymond and Galena burst out laughing.

'I'm Envy,' snapped Jupiter, pinching his younger brother savagely on the arm. 'Don't be a drip,' he hissed as Alizarin started to cry.

Jupiter was extremely jealous of his brother, whom he surpassed in everything except art, which he knew

64

meant more to their mother than anything else. He detested the way Galena doted on Alizarin, calling him her little Slav. Jupiter intended to make Alizarin his little slave all summer.

Alizarin admired and feared his brother, who after a term of prep school cricket and swimming seemed ten times more powerful.

'Tell us about Pandora,' he begged as he crept under the sheet.

'She was a beautiful woman, cruelly treated by the Gods, who married a feeble husband' – Galena shot a malevolent look at Raymond – 'who couldn't control her.'

'Tell us about the lion of Prague with two tails,' asked Jupiter, but, seeing the clock, Galena had leapt out of bed, not even bothering to keep the towel round her.

'Haven't got time, got a plane to catch.'

Alizarin's tears, despite Jupiter's thumping, lasted for over an hour. Galena was always cruellest to those who loved her the most.

6

David Pulborough's summer with the Belvedons began disastrously. Bidden to arrive around six in the evening of the Thursday morning Galena had fled, he had left home near Leeds too late and run into holiday traffic. The second-hand Ford he'd paid too much for in order to escape from Foxes Court in the evenings proceeded to overheat all down the recently opened M1. To stop his fashionable new flared trousers flapping on the ground, he had invested in some high-heeled boots, in which he soon discovered he couldn't drive, so he had resorted to bare feet. These swelled up so much in the heat that he couldn't get into his boots again when, having forgotten Raymond's map, he had to keep diving into pubs and garages to ask the way.

Worst of all, he had agreed under parental pressure to have a haircut before Auntie Dot's funeral last Saturday. No doubt tipped off by David's father, who thought his son looked sissy with long flowing locks, the local barber had waited until David was immersed in 'Jennifer's Diary', dreaming of being part of that gilded set, to give him a hideous short back and sides.

David also had grave doubts about committing himself like Jane Eyre to eight weeks at Foxes Court. Would he be expected to eat in the kitchen or in his room or alone with his two charges? Would tall, dark and extremely handsome Raymond turn into Mr

Rochester, and jump on him all summer? Probably not, now – like Samson – he had lost his dark gold locks.

The charm of Limesbridge with its higgledy-piggledy houses clustered at all levels round the High Street was totally lost on David. Grunting and belching, the Ford only just made it up the drive as the church clock struck eight-fifteen.

'Some awful drip's rolled up,' announced Jupiter, who was as outraged as his mother at the prospect of a stranger monitoring his every move this summer.

Having been allowed to stay up for an early dinner at seven, both boys were starving and irritable. But not so cross as Mrs Robens, the cook, who not only felt her dinner had been ruined but that her position, looking after the boys, had been usurped.

Distracted by the beauty of John Newcombe cruising, mahogany-limbed, through the Wimbledon semi-finals, Raymond had not minded the delay. But glancing out of the study window, his heart sank. Had he allowed the Third World War to break out within his marriage for this? St John Evangelista appeared to have turned into a sweaty, red-faced Shropshire Lad with a frightful haircut, emphasizing a goose neck and sticking-out ears. David was also wearing a club tie, a dreadful cheap blazer with a badge and a battery of pens on the breast pocket and acrylic fawn flares. Raymond the dandy shuddered.

'Go and welcome him,' he told the boys faintly.

'Traffic was terrible,' apologized David as he limped through the front door, clutching a pile of parcels and some moulting mauve roses. 'I hope I haven't made you late for your tea.'

'You have. Dinner's been ready since seven,' said Jupiter coldly.

'We were able to stay up later,' added Alizarin kindly.

Confronted by two pudding-basin haircuts with posh voices, David put up his first black by assuming the taller was the older.

'You're obviously Jupiter,' he said, shaking Alizarin heartily by the hand, 'the great athlete, and you're the arty one, Alizarin,' as he turned to Jupiter.

'Wrong again,' drawled Jupiter.

Oh dear, thought Raymond coming out of the study, the boys are going to pick up the most frightful Yorkshire accent by the end of the holidays. Granny Belvedon, a fearful snob, would be demented.

Then, feeling thoroughly ashamed of himself, Raymond smiled, and shook David's sweaty hand.

'My poor boy, what a ghastly hot day to drive down on. You must be exhausted. Would you like a bath or a large drink?'

'I'd love a gin, please. I've brought these from Dad's herbaceous border for Mrs Belvedon.' David brandished the roses, which he'd purchased in a motorway garage, and which promptly shed more petals.

'My wife's away.' Raymond relieved him of the flowers. 'She'll be thrilled when she gets back.'

'When *is* she coming home?' asked Alizarin for the thousandth time.

'Oh shut up,' snapped Jupiter.

There were tears in Raymond's eyes after he opened David's present of a little red leather-bound first edition of Tennyson's *Maud*.

'My dear boy, nothing could give me greater pleasure. "Maud with her exquisite face, And wild voice peeling up to the sunny sky." I have a passion for Tennyson, but also my ancient greyhound' – Maud, lying languidly on the olive-green study sofa, lifted her tail a centimetre – 'is called Maud. It's so appropriate. Thank you, thank you.'

David had brought Alizarin a Polaroid camera. 'Very useful when you're painting and the light changes or someone moves their position. I'll show you how it works tomorrow.'

Alizarin was speechless with pleasure. Jupiter was less thrilled with his metal detector.

'Only trogs use them.'

'Jupiter!' growled Raymond.

'As this is such an old property,' said David coolly, 'there are bound to be ancient coins in the garden and around the church.'

'I'll be able to find my collection money. They're wonderful presents,' said Raymond, sweeping David through the drawing room, where pictures covered virtually every square inch of the priceless, hand-painted, primrose-yellow Japanese wallpaper, through the french windows out onto the terrace.

'Oh my God,' gasped David, 'what a stunning garden.'

Herbaceous borders on each side of the lawn were dominated by huge proud delphiniums in every shade of blue, and banks of regale lilies opening their carmine beaks and pouring forth scent. Each dark tree and yew hedge had tossed a pale frivolous boa of roses round its shoulders. In the orchard beyond, apples were reddening. Across the valley, houses were turning a soft rose and the Cambridge-blue sky was covered in fluffy salmon-pink clouds, indicating the sun was setting behind the trees, which sheltered Foxes Court from the north-west winds.

'If only Cézanne were alive to paint it,' sighed David, 'you could reach out and touch those houses. Thanks.' He accepted a huge drink from Raymond. 'Newcombe won presumably?'

Then remembering Raymond's passion for Tennyson, he added, 'If they ever filmed Tennyson's "Revenge", John Newcombe, with those lean, hawklike features, that glossy black moustache, should play Sir Richard Grenville.'

'You're right,' said a delighted Raymond. 'That is such a good poem: My Lord Howard and his five ships of war, melting like a cloud in the silent summer heaven.'

'Bor-ing.' Jupiter rolled his eyes.

'I love tennis.' David, who had been in the team at Sorley Grammar School, saw a chance to shine. 'I'll have to teach you to play, Jupe and Aly.'

'My name's Jupiter, I can play,' snapped Jupiter, 'and I'm starving.'

'Let David get his breath back,' said Raymond sharply.

A great deal of ice and tonic had not disguised the brute strength of the gin in David's glass. He was perking up.

'Can I use your toilet before dinner?'

The downstairs lavatory was a shrine to the sporting achievements of generations of Belvedons. There was Raymond's father playing hockey for Cambridge, Viridian hitting a six in the Rugby–Marlborough match at Lord's, and a framed telegram from the Forties, its pencil message fading: 'Raymond 120 not out against Uppingham today.' On the left of the mirror was a newly framed photograph of Jupiter already in a cricket team at Bagley Hall. David decided he must try and win the little sod over.

As they sat down to dinner, he smiled at Jupiter: 'See you made the under-nines.'

'I'm captaining them,' said Jupiter haughtily.

'That's great, what are you going to do when you grow up?'

'Run the country.'

'Ted's already doing a grand job,' said David, who'd been euphoric last month when Edward Heath had been the first grammar-school boy to become prime minister.

'Too keen to push us into Europe,' said Jupiter dismissively. 'As an island, it's better for England to remain autonomous.'

Wow! thought David, who was just about to tuck his napkin into his collar to protect his new blazer, when he noticed Raymond and the boys had laid theirs over their knees. All round the walls, portraits of Belvedons

70

gazed snootily down checking his table manners.

The large lugubrious Mrs Robens, struggling in with a shiny dark gold chicken dripping in butter and tarragon, might sigh like a force eight gale, but she was a brilliant cook. Her roast potatoes were crisp and brown as crème brûlée on the outside, her new peas and tiny carrots had a minty sweetness that never came out of a packet. The feathery light bread sauce bore no resemblance to the stodgy porridge run up by his mother. Apple pie and thickest cream followed. David, who'd survived on a diet of baked beans and sliced bread all term, had seconds of everything.

Dinner was interrupted by several telephone calls. Each time Alizarin leapt up, longing to learn his mother had arrived safely, then drooped when it was some man wanting to speak to her or no-one there. What a waste of divine wine, thought David, as Raymond mopped up spilt Pouilly-Fumé with a desperately shaking hand.

'Did you come through Cheltenham?' he said to David.

'That's the third time you've asked him that,' taunted Jupiter.

I must pull myself together, thought Raymond. Were David's parents interested in pictures? he enquired.

'Not very,' sighed David.

His mother, he explained, was kept so busy running her boutique in a fashionable part of town. His father was in charge of traffic in Leeds, which had become dreadfully congested with so many more cars on the road.

Alizarin was yawning his head off.

'Bed,' said Raymond firmly.

'We were going to show him round,' protested Jupiter.

'Come down and say goodnight in your pyjamas.'

'I'd love,' said David, 'to see some of the pictures.'

To Raymond's amazement, David identified ninety per cent of them: Raymond's grandfather by Orpen, his father by Augustus John, Viridian, carelessly romantic and death defying, by Rex Whistler.

'That's an Etienne de Montigny, isn't it?' David paused in front of a drawing of Galena. 'What a striking woman.'

'That's my wife.'

'Painted before you were married,' observed David archly. 'No wedding ring.'

'Etienne was reluctant to paint it in.' Raymond tried to make a joke of it.

'Montigny divorces sex from the soul,' said David dismissively. 'I admire him as a painter, but he never touches my heart.'

David would have seen passionate gratitude on his new boss's face if he hadn't turned to a portrait of Raymond himself in a dark blue open-necked shirt, sleeves rolled up to reveal suntanned arms, a happy, confident, amused smile playing round the greeny-blue eyes.

'John Minton clearly adored you,' observed David. 'Was that painted while you were at King's?'

'No, shortly before I was married.'

Christ, he's aged, thought David, that was only nine years ago. Things are not right in this marriage.

In the next oil, the artist had transformed great hanging clumps of violet aubretia into portly bishops in Lenten purple. Slumped against a Cotswold stone wall, they were swigging beer out of bottles, having a fag, and eyeing up some young nuns. The picture was bitchy, blasphemous and strangely beautiful.

'This is distinctly disturbing' – David shook his head – 'but that picture reminds me very much of a marvellous Czech artist called Galena Borochova.'

As the boys returned, wearing only striped pyjama bottoms, because of the heat, Jupiter said, 'That's our mother.'

'When's she coming back?' asked Alizarin.

'Your mother's Galena Borochova?' said an

astounded David, then he took in the wild doodles beside the telephone, the rich sapphire-blue sofas, the exotic Eastern European preponderance of gilt and clapped his hand to his forehead.

'Of course, she showed at the Belvedon last year. I never put two and two together.' Then, turning back to the aubretia bishops: 'This is a masterpiece.'

'It is,' said Alizarin proudly, taking David's hand. 'Come and see our rooms. Mummy painted Noah's Ark in mine. Jupiter's is Orpheus with all the animals.'

'I can tell him,' snarled Jupiter.

Raymond shook his head as David was led off. He must have been seriously drunk that evening at King's. He was sure he'd told David he was married to Galena. Still, it was good the boys had taken to him.

Then another icicle was plunged into his heart as he noticed yet another bottle of champagne flung casually in the waste-paper basket. In summer, Mrs Robens did the big downstairs rooms every Monday. Some admirer of Galena's must have looked at the pictures since then.

Once the boys were in bed, Raymond took David and a bottle of Armagnac out on the terrace. He knew he shouldn't tank the boy up on his first night, but he needed company and the comfort.

The Good Friday Music from *Parsifal* was now drifting out of the study window. Rose petals floated down in the windless air like freefall butterflies. Ravishing scents wafting in from all over the garden reminded David of how his mother used to drag him as a little boy through Marshall and Snelgrove's perfume department, claiming she had no time or money to waste on such dangerous frippery.

'So lucky to be able to play music loudly,' said David enviously.

'We've got a very deaf old parson in the rectory next door.'

'Marvellous pictures inside. What's the secret of being a good dealer?'

'Tremendous energy,' sighed Raymond, remembering his sleepless night, 'no stone unturned, even though one uncovers a lot of woodlice. A good eye. Proof of that is how much more you sell the picture for in twenty years' time. We're lucky we've got lots of storage space here. My father bought Turners before the war, kept them until the early Sixties and made a killing. I'm hoping to do the same with the Pre-Raphaelites. Basically it's the same as shares, hold on to the good ones, sell at the top of the market.'

In the dusk David looked beautiful again, his face no longer red from the heat, his eyes huge and trusting.

'How did you enjoy the summer term?' asked Raymond. 'I was at King's just after the war. One was so glad to be alive, we talked all night, forging such strong friendships.'

'I found it a let-down,' grumbled David, 'no-one talks about their feelings any more,' then paused, hoping Raymond might confide in him about his marriage.

'I imagined you whooping it up.'

'You can't swing if you haven't any money,' said David bitterly. 'I've never been to a nightclub, nor got stoned. I was so green when I arrived, a girl handed me a joint, I thought it was a fag and stubbed it out.'

'You shouldn't have bought us so many presents,' protested Raymond.

The Good Friday Music had just given way to the March of the Knights.

'So beautiful,' sighed David. 'I'd love to have heard Melchior in the title role.'

Overhead the clouds had rolled away, leaving the stage to the stars.

'"Now glowed the firmament With living sapphires",' quoted David. Throwing back his head, delectable brandy trickling down his throat, he idly identified the various constellations.

'There's the Swan flying past, the Eagle, the Lyre, the Herdsman, Hercules striding in the wrong direction and there' – David tilted his chair back even further – 'is the tail of the Great Bear disappearing into the wood.'

Admiring the lovely curve of David's neck, Raymond decided he did look good with short hair. What an incredibly accomplished young man, he thought hazily, such a knowledge of stars, music, pictures, poetry, particularly Tennyson.

'I can't imagine a more w-w-w-wonderful place.' David often emphasized a slight stammer to sound more vulnerable and appealing. 'That evening in Cambridge changed my life and the boys are great,' he added, only fifty per cent truthfully.

'I'd be glad if you kept an eye on Jupiter,' murmured Raymond, 'he's going to be form prefect next term, and poor Alizarin's the only person he can practise on.'

'I can handle Jupiter.' David suppressed a yawn.

'Go to bed,' said Raymond.

David's bedroom was perfect. The dark green silk curtains of the four-poster were repeated on either side of a window situated above the front door. Intensely nosy, David would thus be able to monitor all comings and goings. Across a sweep of gravel, a waterfall tumbled into a water trough.

Inside the room, Galena had covered the Nile-green walls with dryads, satyrs and nymphs in various states of undress peering out from the trees. Hares and deer frolicked in the ferns. To avoid the attentions of Apollo, Daphne was turning herself into a laurel.

Also on the walls were a John Bratby of Galena surrounded by birds, a Samuel Palmer of flowering cherries under an orange moon, and a bluey-mauve Sickert of Battersea Power Station. On the dressing table paced a proud little Degas horse. A wardrobe large enough to accommodate an army of lovers contained only Raymond's morning coat with a cornflower shrivelling in the buttonhole.

In the chest of drawers lined with yellowing art magazines David found lavender bags, and bloody hell! his clothes all neatly folded. Mrs Robens must have nipped upstairs between courses and unpacked for him. Racing across the room, David unzipped the pocket in the top of his suitcase and gasped with relief. The pile of cuttings and Xeroxes were undisturbed.

Heart still thumping, David flipped through them. The big piece, from a 1965 *Sunday Times* colour magazine, had told him everything about Galena and Raymond. There was also an excellent *Ideal Home* feature on Foxes Court detailing its wonderful pictures, particularly those by Galena and other Belvedon artists, an *Observer* review of Galena's last exhibition, and a huge profile of Raymond in the *Telegraph*.

Other goodies included details of the night sky in July from *The Times*, which David had memorized last night, and a photostat of Tennyson's ten-page entry in the *Oxford Dictionary of Quotations* from which David had been learning thirty lines a day. Listening to Raymond on *Desert Island Discs* had familiarized him with his new boss's taste in music. Lives of the Pre-Raphaelites would stand him in good stead when Raymond showed him the rest of the pictures tomorrow.

'Hey diddly dee, a dealer's life for me,' sang David.

What dividends had been reaped from a couple of days in Leeds Library – and he must learn to rhyme 'one' with 'fun' rather than 'gone' in future.

He was so proud of the delighted surprise in his voice: 'Galena Borochova's your mother!' That little sod, Jupiter, was going to need watching, he was much too sharp. Lifting up a rug, David found a loose floorboard and shoved the cuttings underneath it.

David Pulborough was heterosexual but extremely self-seeking, and so anxious to escape from the stultifying world of lower-middle-class Sorley (where his mother actually worked in a draper's shop and his father as a clerk in the traffic department at the Town Hall) that he was prepared to use his looks to achieve his own ends with either sex.

Women were drawn to his rather spiritual beauty, particularly as he had perfected a technique of standing very close, gazing into their eyes, and flattering them outrageously. He had also realized that an almost effortless way up the social scale was to become the plaything of some rich, grand old queen, and with luck be remembered in his will.

In his first two years at Cambridge, unbeknownst to each other, he had been enjoying the favours of his homosexual tutor and that tutor's good-looking unsatisfied wife. He had only needed to let a slender arm rub against the shoulders of the former during tutorials to gain excellent marks, along with invitations to smart parties and the task of looking after the famous Raymond Belvedon when he visited the college.

The tutor's wife, Petra, was very demanding in bed. In fact young David had improved so dramatically under her tuition that she was threatening to leave her husband. David had countered this move, which would have caused an awful scandal and jeopardized his degree next summer, by persuading Petra to lend him her running away money of £500 to pay off his pressing end-of-term debts. Instead he had blued the money on the second-hand Ford, which appeared to be a write-off, new clothes and presents for the Belvedons.

David knew that Raymond was attracted to him, but Raymond was not an old queen, he was hugely glamorous, and could introduce David to everyone in the art world.

For two months, I am going to live on the fat of the land, thought David as he soaked in a green-scented bath. The waterfall outside sounded like a running tap. What bliss not to be shouted at for leaving it on. As he dried himself on a soft emerald-green towel, admiring his slender body, which would look even better when he had a tan, he could hear Raymond talking loving nonsense to Maud as he took her out for a last walk.

Happily David slid between cool white linen sheets. On his bedside table was a Collected Tennyson, a wireless switched to Radio Three and a harebell-blue enamel box filled with pink iced biscuits.

'Not after you've cleaned your teeth.' He could hear his mother's reproof, as he defiantly bit into one.

Poetry recited last thing at night could often be retained perfectly in the memory the following morning.

'Till last by Philips farm I flow
To join the brimming river,' mumbled David,
'For men may come and men may go,
But I go on for ever.'

As the waterfall outside converged with Tennyson's 'Brook', he fell into a deep sleep.

7

For the next few days David absorbed the wonder of Foxes Court: the glorious pictures, the vast library of books and records, the romantic garden, the barns and cottages, the prettiest of which he had earmarked for himself in the future, and Galena's studio off to the left through ancient woodland.

He helped Alizarin dam the stream which ran through the water trough under the house, down the garden to the river, which gave him ample opportunity to quote Tennyson's 'Brook'. He taught Alizarin to crawl in the swimming pool, the bottom of which was all looking-glass. In addition, he bowled endlessly to Jupiter, and let the little beast beat him at tennis, croquet and chess – not difficult with the hangovers he had most mornings after drinking and talking long into the night with Raymond.

As he suspected, his new boss was under colossal strain and, despite his sweetness, had a short temper. He would shout if anyone forgot to fill up Maud's water bowl, or opened his beloved *Times* in the morning before he did. When he wasn't working in his study, Raymond spent a lot of the day masterminding the garden like Leonardo, yelling from top-floor bedrooms, 'We need more vermilion over there, Robbie, and a splash of purple lake to the right next to those crimson phlox.'

Robbie the gardener, Mrs Robens's husband, a lech with a good body and wandering eyes, was very jealous of Raymond's partiality for David. Nor was he pleased when his plump, gloomy wife couldn't praise the lad enough.

'Room's neat as a new pin, makes his bed, brings in plates from the garden, gave me a box of chocolates for unpacking his clothes and he really keeps those boys amused.'

Having been employed to teach Jupiter and Alizarin to draw, David put this into practice one morning before lunch, escaping from the heatwave into the shade of a vast oriental plane on the edge of the lawn.

Bumblebees hung upside down in the catmint. Maud inspected her master's delphiniums, trying to remember where she'd buried a pork chop. The Good Friday Music floated once more out of the study, where Raymond had retreated with a pile of transparencies to write catalogue blurbs.

'What shall we draw?' asked Alizarin.

'You can draw me,' said David.

'Boring, boring, drawing's boring,' intoned Jupiter.

'Not if you find something new in my face, there's always a different way of looking at things.'

Jupiter smirked and drew a Hitler moustache. Alizarin chewed his pencil, dark eyes intent, tongue slightly out.

'Tell us about Pandora,' he asked.

'Pandora's troubles all began because the Gods invented fire,' explained David. 'They didn't want to share this fire with humans who they thought would burn themselves like children or, worse still, set fire to Heaven where the Gods lived.'

'This isn't Pandora,' scoffed Jupiter, training David's hair to the right over one eye and giving him sticking-out ears.

'It is. Prometheus, who was very brave, raided Heaven and stole fire like an Olympic torch. Your namesake,

Jupiter' – David raised an eyebrow – 'the King of the Gods, was so angry that in revenge he created the most beautiful woman ever seen.'

'Like Mummy,' piped up Alizarin.

'Only when she dresses up,' sneered Jupiter.

'And he called her Pandora,' went on David, 'and ordered Mercury, his messenger, to deliver her to the house of Prometheus's younger brother, Epimetheus.'

'Ah, your story begins differently.' Jupiter put down his pencil to listen. Alizarin, frowning, looking constantly up and down from his pad to David's face, carried on drawing.

'And Prometheus pleaded with his younger brother, who he protected, just as you protect Alizarin,' said David so sarcastically that Jupiter blushed. 'He pleaded: Don't accept anything from Mercury. But when Mercury rolled up with such a stunning girl, Epimetheus couldn't resist marrying her – on one condition that she never opened the casket on the shelf.'

'It was a chest in *our* story,' crowed Jupiter, adding a Mick Jagger pout beneath the Hitler moustache.

'Having opened the box and been stung all over far worse than snakes or scorpions by the evils of the world that flew out,' David was saying five minutes later, 'Pandora wept and said she wished she'd listened to her husband Epimetheus – like I'm sure your mum listens to your dad.'

'She don't,' said Alizarin. 'When's she coming back? Ouch!' he howled as Jupiter kicked him on an ankle already purple from a croquet ball.

'Stop it,' exploded David.

Thank God, there was Mrs Robens coming out to lay lunch.

'How d'you know so much about Pandora?' asked David, getting up to inspect the sketchpads: 'Jesus Christ!' for Alizarin's drawing was brilliant.

How, at only six, could he have captured the

demurely lowered lashes, the calculated innocence, the nose twitching in curiosity, the deeply sensual lower lip? It was like looking in a discerning mirror.

'Look at that!' David seized the tray from Mrs Robens. Mrs Robens glanced from the drawing to David in wonder.

'It's more like you than you are yourself,' she cried. 'You'll be as famous as your mum one day, Alizarin.' Then, catching sight of the murderous expression on Jupiter's face, 'And yours is very good too, Jupey.'

'A more abstract concept,' said David, noting the Hitler moustache and the squint. Don't rise, he told himself.

Parsifal finished, Raymond wandered out into the garden.

'What a lovely day. If only I didn't have to go to London.'

'Alizarin's going to keep you in your old age,' said David, who was fed up with Jupiter.

Alizarin had certainly captured David's beauty, thought Raymond wistfully, but praising him at the expense of Jupiter only encouraged more bullying.

'Excellent, both of you,' he said heartily, then, as Mrs Robens staggered out bearing tomatoes green with chopped basil, new potatoes, and cold chicken blanketed with mayonnaise: 'It all looks wonderful, Mrs R., could you possibly bring out a bottle of wine?'

'That was great,' David told Mrs Robens, opening the washing-up machine later, as he brought back the plates.

'Put them on the side,' hissed Mrs Robens. 'Mr Belvedon's given me that wretched dishwasher. Can't get to grips with it at all. I'm not risking coffee cups worth five hundred pounds. After he's gone, I'll wash everything by hand.'

'I'll show you how to work it later,' hissed back David.

After Raymond had finally dragged himself away and

Robens had gone to skittles, David despatched the furious boys to bed and dined on macaroni cheese and summer pudding in the kitchen with Mrs Robens. Immediately he steered the conversation onto Jupiter.

'The little bastard deliberately serves balls into Alizarin's back, and yesterday hit him on the ankle with a croquet ball.'

'Jupiter, being the first son, was the apple of everyone's eye,' said Mrs Robens as she filled up their glasses with cider. 'Then Al comes along, sickly, not nearly so bonny, but his mother loved him to death. And he's such a dear little fellow – like his dad. Raymond gave me that dishwasher because he says I work too hard.'

'You do, it's a brilliantly run house. Such wonderful sugar biscuits, such a shine on the furniture, I've never stayed in such a well-appointed spare room.' No need to point out he'd never stayed in a spare room at all.

Mrs Robens turned pink.

'Robbie and I came here when we first married. Old Mrs Belvedon trained me. Like Raymond she was only interested in seeing her guests were comfortable and happy. "Look after my Raymond," she pleaded, when she and Raymond's dad moved to France. Galena's not a cherisher.'

After a third glass of cider, Mrs Robens confessed she only stayed because of Raymond and the boys.

Here we go, thought David happily.

'Isn't Galena a good wife?'

'Not for me to say,' said Mrs Robens and did. 'All those letters marked *Private* piling up for her?'

'Let's get out the kettle and steam them open.'

'Get on with you.'

They both jumped guiltily as the telephone rang.

David took it in the hall.

'May I speak to Mrs Belvedon?' It was a toff's voice, clipped, light, yet curiously arrogant.

'I'm afraid she's away.'

'When's she back?'

'We don't know.'

'Tell her Rupert rang.'

'That must be Rupert Campbell-Black.' Mrs Robens puffed out her cheeks, going even redder in the face. 'He was at the Bath and West Show earlier this summer, phoned once or twice – trouble if you ask me.'

Not yet twenty-one, Rupert Campbell-Black was the *enfant terrible* of British showjumping, as beautiful as he was bloody minded.

'Mrs Belvedon's old enough to be his grandmother,' said David, appalled.

'Never stopped her in the past. He's Jupiter's hero.'

'That figures, monsters attract little monsters.'

'Would you like some coffee?' said Mrs Robens.

Both felt they had gone too far.

'I wish I could help,' sighed David.

'You have already. The boys are much happier, and Raymond's more relaxed and staying home more. He's such a good kind man.'

Raymond might be the 'parfit gentil knight', thought David disapprovingly, but, like the knight in chess, he slid to one side to avoid confrontation. He should have beaten the hell out of Jupiter for terrorizing Alizarin, and out of Galena for neglecting both the boys and himself.

Gradually, David set about making himself indispensable to his new boss, opening bottles, collecting newspapers, helping him with research for an Old Masters exhibition, boosting Raymond's shattered self-esteem by asking his advice.

'How does one get rid of girls without hurting them?'

He also took charge of the telephone, fending off collectors, artists and hostesses who, avid for a handsome spare man now Galena was away, were equally demanding.

'Mr Belvedon's been overworking, he needs peace,' David told all of them.

He also saved Raymond hurt, fielding calls from Galena's admirers, trying to distinguish the different accents: French, German, Cornish and clipped upper-class: 'Where the fuck is she?' which he assumed was Rupert Campbell-Black again.

Filled out with Mrs Robens's good food, David drifted round in shorts, his smooth skin warming to the colour of butterscotch.

'Let me run you a bath, Raymond,' he would suggest, or, having persuaded Raymond to take off his shirt, 'Let me oil you,' and feel Raymond quivering with longing beneath his languid tender caresses.

How could he ever have thought David's Yorkshire accent boorish? wondered Raymond. It was such a long time since he'd been stroked by anyone. Did he imagine it, or during tennis games, did David bend over a fraction too long retrieving a ball, to show off white jutting buttocks above tanned thighs? Aesthetically offended by David's cheap wardrobe, Raymond threw out a lot of old Harvie & Hudson shirts, which had gone in the collar.

Flush with his new salary David bought Raymond the latest recording of Debussy's *Prélude à l'après-midi d'un faune*, with its haunting theme of emerging sexuality on a hot summer afternoon.

Unfaithful to *Parsifal*, Raymond played the LP repeatedly, dreaming of David joining the gallery when he came down from Cambridge in a year's time. What a joy and asset he'd be.

At the beginning of the third week, deciding he couldn't justify any more time at home, Raymond flew to Aberdeenshire, where some bachelor laird had died, leaving a large collection of pictures. The boys were spending the day with friends. The Robenses had the day off. David decided to snoop. He was irked to find the door to the Blue Tower was locked.

Thwarted, he explored Galena's dressing room below, removing the stopper of a big bottle of Mitsouko, breathing in its sweet, musky, disturbing smell. He opened Galena's wardrobe, billowing with brilliantly coloured silks and taffetas, then jumped out of his sweating skin, as the telephone rang.

'Dear boy' – it was Raymond calling from Scotland – 'if only you were here, such marvellous watercolours, I'll be home around seven, but in case I forget, can you put a date in the diary? Sir Mervyn Newton and his daughter Rosemary are driving up from Cornwall on Thursday week to buy a picture for his wife's sixtieth birthday. He's bought Casey Andrews and Etienne de Montigny before, so we must remember to hang a few on the walls. But he might go for an Old Master this time. I've invited them to supper.'

Just as David was writing 'Supper Sir Mervyn Newton' on the wall calendar in the study, Raymond telephoned again in complete panic.

'Galena's just rung, she's landing at Heathrow at four o'clock. It's an Air France flight from Paris. I don't get into Birmingham until six. Can you meet her? Is Mrs Robbie there?'

'It's her day off, but she's left a cold supper,' said David soothingly. 'The boys won't be back till after seven.'

'Take the Rover.'

Wanting something more flash, David took the E-Type.

8

The country had reached the stage when it needed a good haircut. Blond grasses rusted with docks collapsed in the fields, awaiting the tractors which were in other fields sailing across bleached stubble, piling up bales like tower blocks. As the temperature soared into the nineties, the smell of new-mown hay drifted through the window each time David slowed down, which was not often. The E-Type was superb once he got the hang of it.

He was excited, yet nervous of meeting Galena. At least on the drive home he intended to give her a piece of his muddled mind – he felt she treated Raymond so appallingly. Having parked the car at Heathrow, he dived into the Gents to wash off the sweat and comb his hair. Thank God it had grown a bit and he had a great tan. Perhaps he should have worn trousers instead of frayed denim shorts, but Raymond had begged him to hurry. Out in the arrivals lounge, all the women eyed him up.

'"In the summertime, you can reach up and touch the sky,"' sang David happily.

Next moment he was spitting. Why hadn't anyone told him Galena was at least eight months pregnant? She came striding through the barrier, trailing men, who were buckling under easels, canvasses, suitcases, and pushing trolleys groaning with duty free. A French army officer was even carrying her handbag.

David would have recognized her instantly, such was the force of her personality, and the wafts of the same sweet heavy Mitsouko that had hung around her dressing room this afternoon. Instead of a wedding ring on her left hand, a huge ruby glowed. A scarlet cheesecloth smock clung to her breasts and swollen belly. She looked about to pop. But unlike most heavily pregnant women, she didn't waddle, she prowled like a huntress.

'Mrs Belvedon?' David approached her cautiously.

Galena looked him up and down, taking in the streaked blond hair flopping over the freckled forehead and Raymond's blue-striped shirt, with the collar cut off, unbuttoned to reveal a smooth gold chest, and promptly bid farewell to her fleet of porters.

'It is good being pregnant,' she told David, 'I was given first-class seat, champagne, and all those men carry my things.'

Despite living in England for nearly nine years, her Slav accent was still very strong, her voice deep and husky. David was worried there wouldn't be room for all her luggage; as it was he had to make three journeys to the car park.

Only when they were safely on the motorway did he steal a second glance. Close up, she wasn't beautiful. Her make-up was old fashioned, too much eyeliner on the heavy lids, too much blood-red lipstick. Her broad nose was too low in her face, her dark hair streaked with grey and needing washing. As well as Mitsouko, he could smell BO and brandy fumes. She'd clearly had more than champagne on the flight.

His mother would have been appalled. She didn't approve of pregnant women drinking or wearing such short dresses. Galena had wonderful ankles although a few black hairs were sprouting on them. His cousin Denise had had hippopotamus's ankles when she was pregnant.

Galena was now slotting a fag into her drooping red mouth, not offering him one, demanding a light, sending him fumbling round the unfamiliar dashboard.

'Good trip?' he asked.

'I was vorking.'

'When's your baby due?'

'In one hour.'

David went green. What happened if her waters broke all over Raymond's beloved car? Would they be flooded out? Might he have to deliver the baby in a lay-by? He speeded up, then slowed down as the car bumped over a dead rabbit. He didn't want to jolt her into giving birth any quicker. Raymond and Mrs Robens should have bloody well told him.

Deciding to soothe her with flattery, he told her her pictures, all over the house, were wonderful.

'Too accessible.'

'But so beautiful.'

'Great art should never seem beautiful on first acquaintance. I hate my first dry Martini, and my first blow job.' Seeing the shock on David's face, she burst out laughing.

'How are my boys?'

'Fine – sweet.'

'Sveet! Jupiter!' Galena's unplucked ebony eyebrows vanished under her fringe.

'He's highly intelligent,' said David firmly. 'Yesterday he nearly strangled a boy in the village for bullying Alizarin.'

'Hates anyone taking over his job.' Galena shrugged. 'Perhaps he learn. And Alizarin?' Her voice softened.

'A genius, I can't teach him anything,' said David, reaching into the dashboard. 'This is a drawing he did of me.'

'Alizarin has third eye, sees vot other people don't.'

Galena was pleased with the sketch, but soon distracted.

'I met Picasso in Paris.'

'My God.' David nearly rammed the car in front. 'What was he like?'

'Very old, but still attractive; he give me the hot eye.'

Coals to Newcastle, thought David, Galena's eyes could scorch the blond hairs off his chest.

'Raymond tell me you were spitting image of Raphael's St John Evangelista.'

'He did?'

'Patron saint of virgins.'

David wished she wouldn't make such risqué remarks.

'When's your next exhibition?' he asked.

'Too soon. How's my husband?'

'Wonderful, the nicest person I've ever met.'

'And I'm the nastiest.' Laughing uproariously, Galena lit one cigarette from another, dropping the first on the floor.

If the car catches fire, perhaps her waters will break and put it out, thought David sourly.

As they came off the motorway, nature seemed to be putting on a huge banquet to welcome Galena. Every elderbush was covered in lacy tablemats. Hogweed, like plates borne aloft by waiters, crowded every verge.

'Raymond and I have huge row when he announce you are coming,' said Galena. 'I vas furious that he provide dull youth to bore me in evenings, but' – she glanced at David under her eyelashes – 'maybe you vill do.'

Here's to you, Mrs Robinson, thought David smugly.

'But perhaps' – Galena gave her deep throaty laugh again – 'Raymond provide himself with little catamite?'

'Certainly not,' exploded David, going crimson, 'that's the last thing.'

Desperate to change the subject, he asked her what presents she had bought for the boys.

'Nothing, I forget. Raymond can have brandy, I only drink little from bottle.' Then, seeing David's look of disapproval: 'Children are given too much in England.

As a child I was lucky to get present at Christmas.'

David's disapproval cost him. Galena borrowed his last fiver to buy a box of Quality Street for the boys in Cirencester and kept the change, which meant he couldn't escape to the Goat in Boots this evening if she and Raymond had a row.

Arriving at Foxes Court, she bounded into the house.

'Where would you like these put?' he asked sulkily, having humped all her loot into the hall.

'I'd like you to open a bottle of red.'

She was flipping through her skyscraper of post. Opening two blue envelopes marked *Private*, skimming the contents, she smirked, and shoved the letters into her bag. She then insisted he had a drink with her.

'Bit early, the boys might want to play tennis.'

'Don't be a little prude.'

When he had filled two glasses, she drained hers in one gulp, then groaned and clutched her belly.

'My baby is due. Help! I am in labour.'

'Oh my God, I'll phone the hospital.'

But next minute, Galena had whipped up her scarlet dress to reveal strong white thighs, a pair of knickers as red as the wine she'd just drunk, edged with curls of black pubic hair. Tied round her waist, resting on her flat belly, was a huge leather money bag. Next moment, she had unzipped it, and, roaring with laughter, was scooping out hundreds of notes and throwing them in the air so they fluttered all over the room.

'This is my beautiful baby. I sell eight pictures. This vay I pay no tax.'

As she chucked the empty money bag on the sofa, a car door slammed and the boys came racing in. Alizarin couldn't speak, he just mouthed in ecstasy, then threw himself into Galena's arms. Jupiter paused, casting an eye over the green carpet of money.

'Mummy go a-hunting,' crowed Galena, then scooping up a handful of notes divided them between the boys. 'The banks will change it. David will find chocolate I buy you. He tell me you paint very well, darling.' She smiled at Alizarin. 'And you do everything else brilliant,' she added vaguely to Jupiter.

You cow, thought David. And for a woman who was alleged to have such contempt for commercialism, she'd got a very shrewd business head.

For a moment, she bombarded the boys with questions, then the telephone rang. Galena took it in the study.

'That vas Etienne,' she announced when she emerged ten minutes later, slap into Raymond who was accompanied by Maud, who, forgetting her rheumatism, was leaping joyfully around him.

'Don't let her tear the money,' cried Jupiter in horror and, helped by David, he started shovelling it back into the money bag.

Over their bowed heads and scrabbling hands, Raymond and Galena gazed at each other. Like so many high-complexioned Englishmen, Raymond quadrupled his good looks with a tan. His brushed back hair was striped black and grey like corduroy, his upper lip stiff as papier mâché, long dark lashes tipped with grey fringed the hurt, bewildered turquoise-blue eyes. As he kissed his wife, his hands were clenched to stop them trembling.

'You're very brown,' she mocked him. 'While I vork, you enjoy yourself. See, you are not the only person in this house who sell picture. I sell five to a friend of Etienne's, three to a collector from Munich who wants four more.'

'That's awfully good,' said Raymond slowly.

'And you bring me St John Evangelista, who was horrified when I fooled him I vas about to give birth.' Her eyes slid towards David. 'Is that a hint for me to become more virginal?'

'Can we stay up for supper?' begged Alizarin.

'That mean ve dine too early.' Galena glanced at her

watch. 'I vant to paint for a couple of hours. Ve'll have dinner at nine. You can stay up tomorrow. For now you can help David take my stuff upstairs.'

Grabbing the bottle of red, she wandered out through the french windows.

What a bitch, thought David, what an absolutely horrible, bloody gorgeous bitch.

Galena didn't return from her studio until eleven o'clock, by which time David was drunk and Raymond deathly pale and beyond eating.

'Painting is like a drug to my wife,' he told David apologetically, 'she probably hasn't done much while abroad, and was desperate for a fix.'

9

Life changed completely after Galena came home. Meal-times were awry. Everyone fought for her attention. The household trembled when her work was going badly. Life was a series of deep glooms followed by irresistible high spirits. David was in turmoil: the more he disapproved, the more he was captivated.

Working late, Galena slept under the stars on the flat roof of her studio, then wandered out naked into the garden to paint, dipping her brushes in the stream. As the heatwave increased its stranglehold and the earth cracked, David and Robens fought over the watering, so they could surreptitiously watch her. Her body had thickened, no longer as good as she thought it was, but David was mesmerized by the sight of her swimming naked, the mirror on the bottom of the pool reflecting her bush whisking up and down like some furry water rat.

David soon made himself as useful to Galena as everyone else, picking up paints from Bristol, helping her cook Sunday lunch before she got too drunk, carrying her easels and canvasses through the countryside, coming back later with a picnic basket, breathing in the smell of wild mint as he cooled the white wine in the stream.

One morning he was sketching the river with the boys.

'Most buses have "Searston" or "Cheltenham" on the front,' he told them, 'but one magic psychedelic bus had "Further" as its destination, and that's where you want to go. As an artist you must always try to go further, and see things in a new way. That acacia tree, for example, has got yellow in it, which makes it seem warmer and nearer, but if you want to create distance, like those hills, add blue.'

A shadow fell across his pad.

'You are better teacher than artist,' mocked Galena, 'you better join Raymond in the gallery.'

The following day, when she opened her paintbox, Galena found four lines in David's handwriting:

> She was a phantom of delight
> When first she gleamed upon my sight;
> A lovely apparition, sent
> To be a moment's ornament.

Galena smirked. Like an all-over suntan, one could never have too many men in love with one. David was a silly little lapdog, but a useful one.

Raymond meanwhile was aware that he had spent too much of the summer hanging round David, neglecting the gallery. As July drew to a close, he set off abroad to sell and replenish stock. David rose at sunrise to see him off. The brilliant hard light anticipated autumn as it gilded the trees.

'I'm going to miss you.' David emphasized his stammer. 'I think I'm turning into Sir Galahad: "Live pure, speak true, right wrong, follow the King – Else, wherefore born?" You're my King Arthur.'

'Look after my Guinevere.' Raymond tried not to betray how moved he felt.

'I'll ward off any Lancelot.' Hugging Raymond, David kissed him briefly on the cheek. 'Please come home soon.'

David's ardour was somewhat cooled by having to watch
Jupiter's hero, Rupert Campbell-Black, triumphing at
Wembley all week. 'The handsomest man in England',
according to the *Daily Mail,* he was greeted by screaming
teenagers each time he entered the show ring. It had
become a sudden bond between Jupiter and Galena,
who out-screamed any teenagers whenever he won.

The first night Raymond was away David was resolutely
reading Tennyson in the dusk on the terrace:

'To love one maiden only . . .' ('maiden' was pushing
it – Galena must be nearly forty) '. . . and worship her
by years of noble deeds . . . for indeed I knew of no more
subtle master under heaven . . . to keep down the base
in man.'

He mustn't make a pass at Galena, Raymond was his
friend.

The base in David however rocketed sharply a
moment later, as Galena came onto the terrace utterly
transformed. A flamingo-pink dress, short and sleeveless, caressed her hot, newly bathed body from which
Mitsouko rose like incense. Her hair was clean and
glossy, her make-up for once applied with all the skills
of a great artist. She also smelled of toothpaste rather
than fags and booze.

Well away from herself, she was carrying a still-wet
canvas, which she propped up on a chair. A developer
had bought the big field on the other side of the river,
which was rumoured to contain over a hundred
different wild flowers, and was planning to slap houses
all over it.

In Galena's painting of the same field, pink grasses,
merging into olive-green woods and a sky the bright
blue of Rupert Campbell-Black's eyes, were dominated
by a full moon, as gold as the plates Mrs Robens refused
to put in the dishwasher.

'It's stunning,' sighed David, 'show it to the Council

and they'll never grant the developers permission to ruin such a lovely spot.'

But all he could think of was that Galena had made herself beautiful for him on Raymond's first night away.

'Vy did you put that verse in my paintbox?' she asked.

Collapsing onto a nearby chair, she spread her legs. There was still enough light to see she was wearing no knickers. David hastily looked away.

Galena laughed: 'I'm vaiting.'

And David was lost.

'I've fought it and fought it,' he mumbled, 'but from the moment you walked out at Heathrow, I realized I'd met my Waterloo. You're going to break my heart, I know you will' – he seized her hand and covered it with kisses – 'because I'm so vulnerable and you're so far out of my league.'

'Hearts mend very quickly at your age,' observed Galena.

'Never! I want to be your cavaliere servente and serve you in every way.'

'You can start off by opening a bottle,' mocked Galena. 'And I'm out of sketchbooks, so you can pop into Searston tomorrow, and first thing you can run up to the village shop and get me some Tampax.'

'Oh, I couldn't.' David blushed furiously, not least imagining where the Tampax was destined. He was about to kiss his way up her arm, to hell with the boys or Robens looking out of the window, when everything was spoilt by the telephone ringing. Galena bolted inside.

'Come at once,' he could hear her saying. 'I'll vait in the studio, and hurry, my darling.'

Smiling cruelly, she drifted out again.

'If you vant to serve me,' she purred, 'get me a bottle of Dom Pérignon and tell Raymond, or anyone else who rings, that I'm painting.'

'The town red,' fumed David.

Dying of humiliation, he retired upstairs, checking the boys on the way. Tired after another long hot day, they were too fast asleep to witness their mother's feck-lessness.

A prom of Beethoven's Ninth on Radio Three couldn't comfort David as he lay on his bed smoking. In despair, he took Maud out for a last walk. The mocking moon overhead was a voyeur like himself. Next moment, a Rolls-Royce with blacked-out windows blaring 'In the Summertime' stormed up the drive.

Lurking behind a huge chestnut, putting a hand round Maud's jaws to stop her barking, David saw the car take the bumpy wooded path to Galena's studio. There he caught a glimpse of sleek fair hair, and a cold statue's face, as a man jumped out and bolted up the steps, to be greeted by screams of joy from Galena. If Rupert Campbell-Bloody-Black jumped for England, he'd have no difficulty leaping on Galena.

Ten minutes later, she had the gall to return to the house for a bottle of whisky.

'Don't look so sulky,' she taunted David. 'Keep your pretty mouth shut, and don't forget those sketchbooks in the morning.'

Tearing the July page off the calendar to draw on, she was gone. As a final straw, the stream that ran through the garden had dried up, so there was no waterfall to soothe him to sleep.

In the morning, Rupert had gone but his presence was everywhere. David had only just returned from the village shop where he'd been subjected to hideous embarrassment when the short-sighted owner, unable to find a price on David's purchase, bellowed, 'How much is Tampax, Mother?' in front of a long queue of giggling women.

David had nearly died, particularly when Galena, walking bow-legged if not wounded after a night's rogering, sent him straight back for the *Daily Telegraph*, which had a piece on Rupert, describing him in terms of gross hyperbole as 'charismatic as the newly launched

Concorde'. As well as being a deb's delight and showjumping's golden boy, Rupert was evidently a hell-raiser, given to letting off thunder flashes in church and lopping the tails of yew peacocks.

And he's the same fucking age as me, brooded David.

10

Galena retired to her studio to paint. Tormented by doubts about the direction her painting was going, influenced by the Abstract Expressionists who laid canvasses on the floor and dripped paint on them in manic squiggles, she had decided to drench her pubic hair in cobalt violet. She was just face down writhing on a piece of white paper when her husband's least favourite artist, Colin Casey Andrews, marched in. Having dropped into the gallery in Cork Street and found Raymond abroad, Casey had decided to enjoy a few days at Foxes Court. Picking Galena up, he threw her dripping paint on the bed. After the ensuing session, the sheets themselves should have been framed.

David had never met anyone so arrogant, so unpleasant, so grotesque as this spoilt roaring giant. Casey Andrews treated all the staff like navvies, and kept dispatching David to Searston to buy foie gras, caviare and champagne on Raymond's account. David, having forgotten his own modest pass at Galena, was violently disapproving. He spent his time protecting the boys, taking them out on jaunts, while Galena and Casey painted each other, binged and made drunken love on the roof of the studio. Robens spent a lot of time up a ladder pruning an oak, so he could watch them.

Mrs Robens's mouth disappeared totally, as she ceased to find solace even in indignation meetings with

David. She was such a 'treasure', however, that people were always offering her jobs. Earlier in the week, the newly married and utterly undomesticated Lady Waterlane from Rutminster Park had telephoned. Mrs Robens was consequently going for an interview on Thursday, disguising the fact by asking Galena if she and Robens could have the afternoon off to go and see her mother.

'Take the whole day,' shouted Galena, who was fed up with being spied on.

On Thursday afternoon, Casey finally passed out on the studio floor, and Galena, overwhelmed with guilt about not working, told David she was not to be disturbed. Her first interruption was Jean Baines, the curate's prim wife, who'd rolled up to snoop and bum a buckshee picture for the village fête. Galena was so incensed by the intrusion she picked up the remains of a still life of fruit she'd started ten days ago, and bombarded her visitor with rotten kumquats and pomegranates.

Storming over to the house, Galena shouted at David for letting Jean in.

'How can I paint in this madhouse?'

'Van Gogh did his most brilliant work in an asylum, so cool it, Mum,' said Jupiter, not looking up from *Swallows and Amazons*.

'Don't speak to me like that,' howled Galena, then, turning on David, 'I'm going to paint in the Blue Tower. Take the boys out somevere to play. Then come back and don't you dare allow anyone up there.'

David had hardly been back five minutes from farming out the boys when a Rolls-Royce with blacked-out windows roared up and a young man jumped out. He had white-blond hair, a brown face, long blue eyes, a Greek nose and a brutally determined mouth. He wore only a white shirt and breeches. His feet were bare, his beauty, despite its familiarity from the papers all summer, astonishing. In the back of the car, through a lowered window, could be seen a red coat, several silver cups and a genial black Labrador.

David rushed out feeling hot, sweaty and very unbrave.

'Mrs Belvedon gave orders she wasn't to be disturbed.'

'Not by me, she didn't.'

Rupert was a good five inches taller than David, much broader in the shoulder and fighting fit.

'Get out of my way, you little twerp.'

Picking David up, disdainfully shoving him to one side like a bollard, he bounded up the stairs.

Next moment, Galena had thundered down to meet him, crying, 'Oh Rupert!' and throwing herself into his arms.

From below David could see Rupert's long fingers going straight under her skirt:

'I've got some amyl nitrate, it'll blow your mind.'

'I'm not going to bed, it's only seven o'clock,' hissed a returning Jupiter.

'Nor am I,' said Alizarin, 'I'm going to see Mummy in her studio.'

Christ, they'd stumble on a drunken Casey.

'She's in the Blue Tower,' said David hastily.

'Fine, we'll go and see her.' Jupiter turned towards the stairs.

David had a brainwave. Robens had painted a shed such a revolting shade of hen's diarrhoea green that Raymond had asked David to get a Dulux colour chart, which he now brandished before the boys.

'I'll give you a pound each,' he said in desperation, 'if you can match as many colours as possible with flowers from the garden. Now buzz off.'

David was extremely upset. He might have a monstrous crush on Galena, but he adored Raymond a great deal more, and hated such things occurring in what should have been a happy family. Out of the window, he noticed Rupert's car, which he'd better move under the trees, before the boys saw it. Thank God, the key was still in the ignition.

I want to be six foot two, upper class, self-confident, as charismatic as Concorde, he thought longingly, and have a black-windowed Roller that I park across the drives of hostesses I screw.

Back in the house, his brooding was interrupted by Maud barking at the doorbell. Outside a large, self-important, balding man in a very well-pressed suit was standing beside a rather plain girl.

'I'm afraid we're a bit early,' said the man. 'We heard dire stories of hold-ups and holiday traffic, but it wasn't too bad.'

Twigging they must be Sir Mervyn Newton, the dry-cleaning king, and his daughter Rosemary come to buy a picture for Lady Newton's sixtieth birthday, David's heart sank.

'I'm afraid Mr Belvedon isn't back from abroad.'

'He will be soon,' said Sir Mervyn, clearly a man of importance, unused to being forgotten.

'We can just sit in his lovely garden,' said the plain daughter. 'We're so looking forward to meeting Mrs Belvedon.'

'Ah!' As they entered the dark hall, Sir Mervyn put on his bi-focals to admire a yellow and dark blue oil. 'That's one of Casey Andrews', one of my favourite artists, I'd love to shake him by the hand.'

Not if you knew where it had been recently, thought David. Like a gorilla in a safari park, Raymond kept Casey away from collectors.

'Go through into the garden,' he said, 'I'll get you both a long cool drink.'

Meanwhile, in the Blue Tower, post-coital for a second time, Galena found exquisite pleasure in watching a long-limbed, golden, naked Rupert examining the pictures, and reached for her sketchbook.

She wished she were a sculptor. He was so beautiful, and what a body to sculpt; Borochova's Rupert would stand alongside the Davids of Donatello and Michelangelo. It was the utter stillness of the face, followed by the amazing smile, that made him so irresistible. He also had the same Greek nose as Pride in the Raphael.

'Nice arse,' Rupert admired a plump Boucher bottom.

Galena explained Raymond's father's theory about beautiful pictures inspiring beautiful children.

'My parents were probably gazing at a Stubbs foxhound when I was conceived,' said Rupert. 'Still, it worked with Raymond. Good-looking bloke, what's he like in bed?'

Galena pointed contemptuously to a working drawing of Raphael's *The Battle of Nude Men*, hanging by the door, which showed a lot of warriors with minute penises hurling spears and arrows at one another.

'Like that,' she sneered, 'like a little shrimp villy, help-lessly thrashing around.'

'Some have smallness thrust upon them. Not my problem,' said Rupert, gazing in satisfaction at his suntanned belly and magnificent already rising cock.

'Nor Colin Casey Andrews's,' said Galena, to puncture his self-esteem.

'Column Casey Andrews,' said Rupert, emptying the last of the champagne into their glasses. 'Are you going to get another bottle? Is he bigger than me?'

'Much, but not as beautiful.'

As Rupert slid his hand between her legs, Galena carried on drawing, squinting up at his face.

Was that why he was so attracted to her, wondered Rupert, because she didn't give a damn? She was fantastic in bed, licking one everywhere, fingers in every pie, sucking one in like a whirlpool, but even when she gave you a blow job, you felt she was still watching your face to see how your hair fell.

'They should bring back National Service for people

like you,' he grumbled. 'Shrimp Villy's a sweet man, gives you everything, sells your pictures, allows you the run of this ravishing house. All you do is moan.'

'Not viz desire for him. He's impotent.'

'Probably queer like my brother Adrian, who works in an art gallery. Maybe all dealers are queer.'

'Freud cured Mahler's impotence,' observed Galena.

'He'd better cure Raymond then.'

'Freud's dead, stupid. Ven I marry Raymond I told him I must have freedom to do vot I like.'

'To have and to cuckhold.' Rupert shook his golden head. 'I couldn't cope with an unfaithful wife.'

He picked up Galena's sketch.

'That's good, can I have it?'

'Ven I've signed it.' Galena scrawled G.B. on the bottom.

'Thank you.' Rupert laughed. 'We should all have G.B. tattooed on our bumpers to show we've been to bed with you. Now that *is* nice.' Rupert had just noticed the Raphael Pandora, on the right of the bed. 'Where did Shrimp Villy find that?'

'In some flea market in France.'

'Did he buy that little flea who tried to stop me coming up here? Who is he?'

'David someone, Raymond hired him for the summer to coach the boys. Are you jealous?'

'Of that?' asked Rupert incredulously.

I love his arrogance almost more than his beauty, thought Galena, holding out her arms. 'Come back to bed.'

Her breath reeked of drink and fags. Fucking Galena, reflected Rupert, was like going to the pub. They were interrupted by thunderous banging.

'Bugger off!' Rupert hurled the empty champagne bottle at the door.

'Mrs Belvedon! Galena!'

'Go away.'

'I'm sorry to bother you, the boys are back, and Sir Mervyn Newton and his daughter, Rosemary, have been downstairs for half an hour.'

'Tell them I'm vorking.'

'They've come all the way from Cornwall to see you.'

'Well, tell Mrs Robens to give them a drink and get rid of them.'

'You gave the Robenses the day off. She's gone to see her sister. Sir Mervyn's expecting supper.'

'Oh, you sort something out.'

11

Having left Sir Mervyn and Rosemary on the terrace with more huge drinks, David belted back to the kitchen. Perhaps supper had been left, but as he opened the fridge, only a large raw fish, as balefully uncooperative as Mrs Robens, glared out at him.

He telephoned Raymond's favourite local restaurant, the Lark Ascending, only to be told they were fully booked.

'It's for Raymond Belvedon,' protested David.

There was a pause, followed by a different voice.

'We've got a wedding party, but we could fit Mr Belvedon into our private room any time after nine.'

It was only seven now. By nine, Sir Mervyn would be horizontal in the delphiniums.

'Leave it,' snapped David.

When he was rich and famous, he vowed, people would empty restaurants to accommodate him and his guests. He was roused by an excited squeak as Maud heaved herself out of her basket and limped out of the kitchen. For the second time, Galena and Rupert were interrupted by thundering on the door.

'Mrs Belvedon, Mr Belvedon's home.'

'Holy shit.' Rupert ran to the window. 'Holy even shittier.'

Seeing Maud joyfully dancing on her rheumaticky legs to greet her master, Badger, Rupert's Labrador, bored of being confined to the Rolls, had wriggled through the lowered black glass window, and was now cavorting on the lawn with her.

Examining the label on Badger's collar, Raymond read: 'Campbell-Black, Penscombe 204'. So that was why Galena had been so manic recently.

Having yelled to David that she'd be down in a minute, Galena ordered Rupert to stay put.

'Raymond'll change in his dressing room, then go back downstairs to sell pictures. The deal is all. I'll smuggle you out later.'

Drenching herself in Mitsouko to disguise the reek of sex, Galena slipped into her flamingo-pink dress and, not bothering to wash or comb her hair, ran downstairs out onto the terrace.

'Forgeeve me, Sir Mervyn, I have been painting since early this morning.' She clasped Mervyn's hand, then, turning to Rosemary: 'This must be your charming daughter. Vy have you got empty glasses, vy didn't anyone tell me you vere coming? I sack my housekeeper. You should have known!' She turned furiously on David.

Fortunately at that moment Raymond came through the french windows. His suit was crumpled and much in need of Sir Mervyn's pressing services, his eyes bloodshot, his face grey, but his smile as warm as ever.

'My dear fellow, how lovely to see you, and dear Rosemary.' He bent to kiss her.

'No-one told me they vere coming,' snapped Galena.

'Never mind, we're all in one piece,' said Raymond evenly. 'I'm late, Mervyn, because I've been looking for something really nice for darling Margaret. Why don't you go along to the warehouse and browse around while I get out of this suit? David, dear boy, could you unload the car?'

By the time Raymond rejoined Mervyn, the dealer had reasserted itself. The barn which he used as a warehouse was high and cheerless. Normally Raymond would have turned off the overhead lights, and orchestrated the viewing, placing one carefully lit picture on an easel, its colours enhanced by some specially chosen flowers on a side table. Now he had to plunge straight in. He found Sir Mervyn rootling through stacked-up canvasses, frustrated they didn't have any prices. One didn't like to admit that one's choice was determined less by a picture's beauty than by its likelihood of rocketing in value.

'Good trip?' he asked.

'I think so,' said Raymond lightly. 'Grubbing around a sale room in Paris, I found a picture listed as a copy of a Gainsborough. I've got a gut feeling it's the real thing. Can't wait to get it back to my restorer in London. Now, about Margaret's picture.'

But Sir Mervyn's purple-veined nose was twitching.

'What sort of price were you thinking about?'

'If it were the real thing, about twenty thousand. Probably isn't. Now, this is something Margaret might like.' Raymond picked up his feckless wife's painting of the wild-flower meadow. 'I'm not going to tell you who this is by, a contemporary artist, very talented.'

'Beautiful,' Sir Mervyn murmured, 'very serene.'

He mostly bought contemporary work, but also considered himself an authority on early English paintings. After all, a wife wasn't sixty every day, and Margaret had been a tower of strength.

'Could I have a look at the Gainsborough, even if it is dirty?'

The subject was a handsome couple, their children and a supercilious King Charles spaniel grouped in lush parkland. Age had turned the husband's breeches yellow. The spaniel looked as though it had been rolling.

'Stunning,' gasped David, who'd popped in with bottles to check drinks.

Raising a hand to hush him, Raymond moved next to

Mervyn, seeing who could maintain a silence longest. The ice melted in Raymond's whisky.

'Interesting,' said Mervyn non-committally.

Raymond shook himself out of a trance, and smiled gently. 'Indeed it is.'

Another silence ensued.

'Can I see it without its frame?'

'Certainly.'

Sir Mervyn put on his bi-focals, examining the picture on both sides. What's he looking for? A sticker saying Woolworths, 5s 6d? wondered David. Turning, Raymond gave him a wink.

'It's not signed.' Mervyn puffed out his cheeks importantly.

'No, but the husband looks rather like Gainsborough in the early portraits. These artists love including themselves. And a very happy charming couple like you and Margaret.'

'If it was Gainsborough, it would go up in value?'

'Oh certainly. But I'm hoping whoever buys it appreciates it as great art.'

Like myself, thought Sir Mervyn smugly. People would certainly sit up to learn he'd bought Margaret a Gainsborough.

Raymond changed tack.

'Probably isn't a Gainsborough, but I know how Margaret loves dogs. Maybe a pupil did it. I'll be able to tell you more next week.'

Mervyn took a gulp of his freshened gin and tonic, and pursed his lips.

'I'd like to chance it.'

Once again Raymond raised his hand.

'No, no, I can't let you, we've got till the end of August. Now, what else have we got that Margaret might like?'

'Promise not to sell it to someone else?'

'I promise.'

There was lots of hearty laughter as Sir Mervyn accused Raymond of being too honest.

'I'd never give you a job in my company,' then, picking up Galena's *Wild-Flower Meadow*, he said, 'I'd like to buy this picture as well. And while we're here, have you got any early Casey Andrews?'

David was enraptured – never had he seen such an example of grace under pressure. A thunderous rumble from Sir Mervyn's large tummy brought him back to earth. Rosemary's drink must be empty by now. He raced back to the terrace to find her alone. Galena must have buggered off upstairs.

'Like a Pimm's?'

'Oh, how delicious. Shall I come and help you make it?'

For a moment David's panic about dinner subsided. The Belvedons were always comparing people to characters in paintings. Now he had the fleeting pleasure of recognizing Rosemary Newton as the bouncy grey horse in Raphael's *St George and the Dragon*.

In the picture, the horse looked very secure, almost smug, as if he knew his master was a dab hand with a sword, and wouldn't let the fierce dragon bite even a fetlock. Like Rosemary, he had merry, knowing, round, rather small eyes, a curly forelock, and a long white face capable of jauntiness but never beauty. From what he could see, Rosemary also had St George's horse's strong white cobby body. David guessed she was about twenty-nine.

'So kind of them to invite us to kitchen sups,' she was saying as she followed him into the kitchen. 'Daddy so adores his sessions with Raymond.' Then, seeing David's face: 'They forgot we were coming?'

David deliberated.

'Well, Mrs Belvedon's been away too and someone's torn off July from the calendar.'

'I'll help,' said Rosemary, in her brisk Roedean voice.

'I've been a chalet girl for the last three years. Let's see what we can rustle up.

'There's a lovely sea trout in here,' she said, opening the fridge. 'I'll gut it and take its head off.' For a second she cradled the fish in her capable white hands. 'It'll take about forty minutes. Let's see if we can find a fish kettle. We'll need half a bottle of cheap white and lots of herbs from the garden. I know a quick mayonnaise which we can turn into *sauce verte* while the fish is cooking.'

'I'll dig up some potatoes,' said David gratefully.

'And get some mint too.'

Rosemary was absolutely wonderful and when Jupiter and Alizarin staggered up to the kitchen door, bearing half Raymond's herbaceous border to match David's colour chart, she praised them to the skies. Then she averted Raymond and Robens's wrath by putting the flowers in vases and decorating the dining-room table with the broken flower heads.

'You're both staying up for supper,' she told the delighted boys.

Judging by the laughter on the terrace, Galena was down again.

'Raymond speak of you often, he tell me you are great collector and connoisseur,' she was lying to Sir Mervyn.

'I collect for the sheer pleasure of possessing beauty,' Sir Mervyn lied back. 'I've just bought your flower meadow. You stand in front of a picture like that, as Paul Mellon, a good friend of mine, is always saying, and you think: "And what is money?"'

'Vot indeed?' purred Galena. 'I would love to meet Paul Mellon.'

'I'm sure it can be arranged,' said Mervyn warmly.

Leaving them, Raymond found Rosemary and David in the kitchen.

'Let it cool,' Rosemary was saying as she lifted the sea

112

trout out of the fish kettle, 'and I'll skin it. If you could chop up some cucumber, David.'

'I'm so sorry about the cock-up,' said Raymond. 'You two children are such bricks.'

'It's our secret,' whispered Rosemary, 'we mustn't tell Daddy, he doesn't understand about being forgotten. Dinner'll be ready in ten minutes.'

Outside two magpies were having a domestic and big black clouds were moving in like gangsters. It was growing even hotter. As Rosemary laid the sea trout on a big green plate shaped like a lettuce leaf, and decorated it with chopped cucumber and slices of fennel, David told her about Prometheus carrying fire from Heaven in a fennel stalk.

'How clever to know Greek things,' said Rosemary.

She's really nice, decided David, watching her tossing new potatoes in chopped-up mint and melted butter. Rosemary for remembrance. She'd certainly remember dentist appointments, and the names of collectors' wives and children, and whether they were coming to dinner. And all that dry-cleaning dosh would make an ascent up the social scale so much easier.

12

'Supper,' announced David triumphantly, then groaned, for, staggering up the lawn, a leaning tower of pissed artist, his eyes red as traffic lights, his face creased by sheets, his body not remotely covered by Galena's crocus-yellow dressing gown, came Casey Andrews.

Not a trace of anguish that Casey must have been down here screwing Galena and was about to screw up any deal showed on Raymond's face.

'My dear Casey,' he murmured, 'what an extraordinary coincidence. I've been showing your pictures to Sir Mervyn, who you know is a great fan. Perhaps you'd like to explain them to him yourself?'

'My work defies explanation,' said Casey pompously, helping himself to a huge Scotch.

'We'd better lay another place,' whispered Rosemary.

'And put arsenic in his sea trout,' whispered back David, letting his lips touch her very clean ear.

'Thrilling for Daddy to meet such a famous artist,' giggled Rosemary, 'but isn't he awful?'

'We're about to dine, Casey,' said Raymond firmly, 'but I suppose we can wait another five minutes.'

'I'll have another gin then,' said Sir Mervyn.

Wearily Raymond led them off to the warehouse. Such were their monumental egos, he daren't leave them alone.

*　　*　　*

By the time they returned, Galena had vanished, but dinner couldn't be held up any longer. The boys were drooping; Casey and Mervyn both drunk. Searching for his wife, Raymond discovered her back in the Blue Tower sketching a naked Rupert, who was asleep like the young Endymion, his legs longer than Maud's. Raymond didn't know which was more beautiful, Rupert or Galena's drawing of him.

On the chair near the door was a far more explicit drawing of Rupert, entitled: *Orgasm – July 26th.* Raymond flipped it over. So that was where the July page of the calendar had gone.

'What the fuck are you playing at?' he hissed. 'This place is like a whorehouse. First Casey, then Rupert – don't you give a stuff the effect it has on the boys, David and the servants?'

'I tell you, I need new models. This one' – she waved her pencil at Rupert – 'sits like a rock, he's got the stillest face I've ever seen.'

Somehow Raymond gained control of himself.

'Dinner's ready, I don't imagine he's staying.'

He glanced up at the Raphael, particularly at Hope, with her sweet soothing smile.

'You lying jade,' he told her bitterly.

After dinner, they had more drinks outside. Casey, who'd eaten most of the sea trout, was getting stuck into the kümmel. Having been impressed by other artists' portraits on the dining-room walls, Sir Mervyn asked Casey if he'd be interested in painting Margaret. Having decided that Margaret would probably be as plain as her daughter Rosemary, Casey said he didn't do portraits.

'Don't be silly, Casey,' chided Galena.

'I like the work of that Froggy who also exhibits at the Belvedon,' said Mervyn, who didn't understand professional jealousy.

'Etienne de Montigny?' Galena glanced mockingly at Casey.

115

'That's the fellow, got some of his racy stuff.' Then, checking across the terrace that Rosemary was still totally preoccupied with David: 'Mind you, I keep it away from the wife.'

Casey, who couldn't bear any competition, rose to his feet, blotting out a rising moon more effectively than any gathering black cloud.

'Wait one minute, I want to show you something.'

Unable to sleep because of the din, Alizarin crept into the spare room overlooking the terrace. Lurking undetected on the balcony, he breathed in the sweet tobacco smell of buddleia which that afternoon had been covered in butterflies. The moon looked like a slice of lemon waiting to be dropped into one of Sir Mervyn's gins and tonic. Why were grown-ups so thirsty? They didn't run about much.

Alizarin detested Casey Andrews. He was so loud, bossy and rude to his father. He was also disgusting, with food in his beard and bogeys in his hairy nose, which this evening he had buried in a stinking piece of cheese before deciding to cut himself a piece. Alizarin shuddered. But worst of all was the way Casey monopolized his mother. He'd seen the horrible giant slide his hand over Galena's bottom once too often. Alizarin was a stoical little boy, but, aware he was his mother's favourite, he felt neglected.

To the left he could hear the sound of blinds rattling up, as sleeping pigeons were roused by Casey's noisy return from Galena's studio.

'Come and give me a hand,' he yelled to David. 'Careful, the paint isn't dry. Who says I can't do portraits?' he asked boastfully as the canvas was leant against a bench, and one of the terrace lights retrained onto a huge nude of Galena.

There were gasps followed by stunned silence. Half-woman, half-goat, Galena's lips were drawn back from her long yellow teeth in a hideous grimace, vine leaves entwined her horned head, a Gauloise glowed between a cloven hoof, bouncing pink udders hung below her belly button, with a bleeding slit below.

The stunned silence continued.

'I've called it: *In Season*,' said Casey sententiously.

'Interesting,' volunteered Sir Mervyn.

Raymond was quivering with rage. But Alizarin lurking on the balcony was quicker.

'It's a horrible painting,' he shouted. Then, as everyone jumped and looked up: 'My mother's the most beautiful woman in the world, and she hasn't got long teef and her bosoms don't hang down.'

And before anyone could stop him, he tipped an entire tin of hen's-diarrhoea-green emulsion all over the canvas and the furious upturned face of Casey Andrews.

'You bastard,' spluttered Casey.

'You horrible little bourgeois,' screamed Galena. 'How dare you destroy great vork of art?'

'Bollocks,' drawled a voice.

It was a barefoot Rupert, back in his white shirt and breeches, with a great grin on his face.

'Evening, Raymond. Evening, Mervyn, sorry I didn't get back to you over that sponsorship deal, I've been abroad. And well done, you,' he shouted up to a trembling Alizarin, 'fucking marvellous.'

Then he walked towards the dripping canvas.

'That painting is perfectly frightful. Any self-respecting goat would take you to court, Casey.' Peering at the few bits not drenched in green emulsion: 'And I don't think your brush strokes are very smooth either. I certainly won't employ you to paint my stable doors.'

'How dare you!' roared Casey.

'Very easily.' Turning to bolt, Rupert looked frantically round for his moved car. Having located it under the plane tree, however, he had to wait for Badger, who was bidding a lingering farewell to a smug-looking Maud. This enabled Casey to catch up with him and grab him by his shirt.

'You little weasel.'

'And you're about to go pop.' Swinging round, Rupert smashed his fist into Casey's furious face.

For the second time that day, England's self-confessed greatest painter passed out cold. A second later, his wife Joan Bideford came storming up the drive on a Harley Davidson.

'I thought I'd find you here, Casey,' she bellowed.

'Can I have your autograph, Mr Campbell-Black?' said Jupiter admiringly.

'What a brave little chap that Alizarin is,' sighed Rosemary as she and David loaded Mrs Robens's dish-washer.

'Would you like a walk round the garden?'

'Yes please.' Then, as soon as they drew out of earshot: 'That painting's Mrs Belvedon, isn't it, and she had two chaps here, Casey and Rupert?'

David nodded.

'What a tart! Raymond's such a dear. He always remembers one's name and gives one a kiss at parties.'

'He's wonderful,' said David.

Rosemary had a nice voice, he decided, slightly raucous, but definitely patrician. It turned him on.

Having waved Rupert off, Raymond went upstairs to see the boys and found Rosemary saying goodnight to Alizarin.

'You were very brave to pour paint on that revolting man.'

'Shall I show you a picture I've done of him?'

'Yes, please.'

Rosemary didn't realize Alizarin had put Casey's red roaring face on the body of Gluttony, portrayed in the Raphael.

'It's awfully good!' She couldn't stop laughing. 'I'd love to buy it, would you accept two pounds?'

'Rupert Campbell-Black's already given me a tenner,' said Alizarin. 'You can have it for ten shillings.'

'I think you're going to need a really good dealer to handle the business side,' said Rosemary smiling up at Raymond.

Rosemary drove home to her parents' house near Oxford. Mervyn, very drunk, couldn't stop laughing. Not for nothing did his colleagues call him 'Pissed-as-a-Newton'.

'Bohemians always behave like that. We've been seeing life, Rosie. Damned attractive woman, that Galena, good painter, going to buy more of her stuff.'

Rosemary was about to say she thought Galena was a slut, when her father switched to Rupert.

'His father Eddie's got a marvellous shoot. Rupert's going to do some adverts for us. Bloody good-looking chap.'

David's much nicer-looking, thought Rosemary, and he'd taken her telephone number.

At Foxes Court at four in the morning, they were woken by thunder and deluge. Checking his garden when he got up, Raymond was distraught to find all his delphiniums snapped in two, their proud blue heads hanging. Galena, helped by David, cooked lunch: beef goulash, dumplings with sour cream and lemon and cranberry sauce.

'You did well yesterday, Evangelista,' she said mockingly, and kissed him briefly on the mouth.

David was in turmoil. Perhaps he should get out now, escape back to Yorkshire, out of charm's way.

Despite a black eye and green hair Casey as well as Joan stayed on for lunch as if nothing had happened. For pudding there was cherry pie. Alizarin was dreamily counting his cherry stones: 'Rich man, poor man, bugger man, thief.'

Galena burst out laughing. 'It's your father who's the bugger man.'

Raymond threw down his napkin and walked off into the garden. David tracked him down in the boathouse by the river, crying helplessly.

'My delphiniums, my delphiniums.' Raymond groped for a green silk handkerchief. 'So sorry, whole thing's been a bit of a strain.'

David patted Raymond awkwardly on the shoulder. 'It's my fault. You asked me to look after Mrs Belvedon. I'm utterly on your side, we all are. She's such a bitch.'

Raymond looked up, eyes streaming.

'Will you come and work in the gallery when you come down from Cambridge?'

David's face lit up the gloom of the boathouse like a Leonardo.

'I can't think of anything more wonderful. Despite the dramas, this has been the happiest summer of my life.'

13

On 6 April 1971, on the alleged anniversary both of Raphael's birth and his death, Galena gave birth not to wads of francs and Deutschmarks, but to a third son, Jonathan. Five weeks premature, early for the last time in his life, Jonathan was a charming, indolent Aries, who smiled, ate and, unlike his elder brothers, slept through the night.

When he didn't look like Etienne, nor Rupert, nor Casey Andrews, nor even Joan Bideford, as Somerford Keynes, the *Daily Post* critic, bitchily observed, the art world charitably assumed he must be Raymond's – particularly when Raymond seemed even more besotted with this little chap than either of the others.

The art world was even more excited that autumn when David came down from Cambridge and joined the Belvedon, enviously assuming David was Raymond's boyfriend, and the old dear had finally come out.

Envy quadrupled when they realized the Boy David, as he was known, was not just a pretty face. He had a cool head, and didn't get carried away at auctions. He also had huge energy. At weekends, when he wasn't at Foxes Court, bouncing baby Jonathan on his knee, or dispatching Jupiter and Alizarin to match autumn leaves to colour charts, he toured the provincial galleries and art schools ever searching for new talent.

Raymond was exhausted by hard work and ten years

not sleeping over Galena. David on the other hand could whoop it up all night, discussing ideas with these new artists or with collectors, and still be bright and alert at his desk the following morning.

A delighted Raymond fed off the boy's daring and youthful enthusiasm, took advantage of his fresh eye and occasionally boxed David's ears when he got too big for his new hand-made ankle boots.

Early on David discovered Raymond wasn't perfect. He might spend hours mopping up the tears of an old duchess worried about selling a family painting, but, having acquired the painting, he had no scruples about disposing of it profitably.

'Always remember,' he told David, 'that a thing of beauty is infinitely more of a joy for ever if you can sell it for four times as much.'

David approved of the gallery making money and enjoyed spending it even more. From the moment he arrived, there was never any petty cash in the till. Fiona, Raymond's assistant, a glamorous well-bred half-wit, spent her time cashing cheques at the pub round the corner.

David had a hill sheep's ability to climb socially, aping Raymond's every mannerism, his pronunciation, his wonderful Trumper's aftershave: West Indian Extract of Lime, his style of dressing. The man-made fibres were chucked in the bin. A snob with expensive tastes, David was unable to resist the siren call of tailors in Savile Row, shirts in Jermyn Street, restaurants in Soho, Fortnum's, Hatchards and Burlington Arcade, teeming with expensive little presents for the impossibly chic and beautiful girls gliding up and down nearby Bond Street. It was soon clear David was not going to be able to live on his salary. Petra, his still unpaid-back tutor's wife, was threatening to sue him. The bank manager's letters grew nastier.

One April afternoon at Foxes Court, when Raymond was proudly wheeling a year-old Jonathan in his push-chair round the village, David discussed the problem with Galena. He was immensely flattered because she had asked him to sit for her. He was now perched on the window seat in the drawing room, with Shrimpy, the Jack Russell which Rupert had given Galena for her birthday, perched on his knee.

'You need a vife,' said Galena.

'If I married someone as sexy as you,' grumbled David, 'I'd be too worried to concentrate on work.'

'You vant someone plain, rich, capable and kind,' said Galena, 'then you have safety net to come home to.

'Jealousy is stupid. Shrimpy,' she went on, blowing a kiss at her little dog, 'screw everything. Every bitch he meet, table leg, ankle of vicar, but he love me best and always come back to me. What do I care what he gets up to?'

Although David had made himself useful putting Galena's ill-gotten gains into Swiss bank accounts when he went abroad, she was getting tired of picking up bills for him, suspecting Raymond did the same.

'Why don't you marry Rosemary Newton?'

'The thought had crossed my mind.'

David had been very impressed the summer before last by her calm resourcefulness, and her father's dry-cleaning fortune. He had taken her to a couple of concerts, but had ducked out when she asked him to a ball. You didn't dance the last waltz with St George's horse.

'She's a nice girl,' said Galena with rare enthusiasm. 'She sent me large bottle of scent and a Tiffany christening mug when Jonathan was born. She often drop in. Alizarin and Jupiter adore her. You must not appear gold-digger.' Mixing terra rosa with burnt sienna, she began painting Shrimpy's red patches.

'The rich detest freeloaders. Take her to nice restaurants, buy her pretty undervear, write her charming notes, flatter her, cherish her. It vork with my husband,' Galena added slyly. 'He vas eating out of your hand in a few days that first summer.'

'Oh come on,' David flushed, 'I love the bloke.'

'But you don't vant to be roped to his apron for ever.'

Shrimpy was getting bored, bristling after the vicar's tabby who was padding through the daffodils, trying to wriggle out of David's clutches.

'Can't we have a break?'

'Two more minutes.'

David supposed it was worth it. Galena was beginning to stockpile pictures for her exhibition in October. A handsome portrait of himself would do his reputation no harm. He could see Somerford Keynes's definitive biography: 'The greatest influence on Borochova's painting was undoubtedly David Pulborough, seen here with her beloved Jack Russell, Shrimpy.'

If he were going to woo Rosemary seriously, he needed an advance.

'Can you lend me fifteen hundred? Ouch, you little bugger.' Seeing Raymond, Maud and baby Jonathan returning from their walk, Shrimpy had plunged his claws into David's thighs and shot out of the room.

'It's OK. I've finished.'

Preparing a charming compliment, that only god-desses could confer immortality on mere mortals, David crossed the room to admire his portrait. Bloody hell! The bitch had only painted Shrimpy and left him out altogether. He'd have shouted at her, if he hadn't needed the money.

Galena gave it to him in cash: 'Be careful, it needs laundering.'

'Perhaps Sir Mervyn will dry clean it,' said David sourly.

The IRA were incredibly active in London that summer. Most of the restaurants were boarded up with sandbags. On their third date, for a more relaxed atmosphere, David drove Rosemary out to a very smart expensive restaurant overlooking the Thames.

He had written her wonderful letters, liberally spiced

with Lamartine and Catullus. He had also given her Ma Griffe, pretty underwear, a pale blue Hermès scarf covered in butterflies, and a navy blue cashmere jumper from Burlington Arcade, all of which Rosemary was wearing that evening.

Attempting to be fashionable, she had bought a pair of flared trousers, which unfortunately emphasized her cobby thighs. Catching sight of them in a nearby mirror, she had hastily covered her lap with her table napkin.

Rosemary had been at a very low ebb when David had called her. On the eve of her thirty-first birthday, she had discovered the impoverished young charmer who'd been wooing her had been simultaneously sleeping with two of her girlfriends. David had picked up the pieces, making her laugh by writing 'Ban Fortune-Hunting' on a sticker in large letters to put in her rear window.

David's jokes made Rosemary laugh anyway, because she was already curly head over flat heels in love with him. Used to attracting women easily, David recognized the terror of betraying this longing in her round, normally merry little eyes, and was touched.

The menu was colossally expensive; he'd have to wrap this courtship up soon. He hadn't made a pass yet, because he had no desire to, and because he wanted her to think his intentions were honourable. He ordered a bottle of Moët et Chandon. Rosemary, so churned up with nerves she could hardly eat, asked for Dover sole off the bone. David chose duck à l'orange. Restaurants had ceased to frighten him: he had mastered gulls' eggs, artichokes, asparagus, avocado pears. He no longer asked for vichyssoise and steak tartare to be heated up.

He had just taken delivery of his first bespoke suit, pinstripe and single breasted; it made him look taller, and older, as did the spectacles he put on to read the menu.

Perhaps a nine-year gap wasn't too impossible, thought Rosemary. David was so good looking, she tried not to stare; such a sweet sensitive face, and his big dark eyes so full of sincerity.

They had lots to talk about: the Belvedons, ghastly Casey Andrews, Rupert Campbell-Black's latest atrocity, and Fiona, Raymond's ravishing assistant, who had been in the Upper Fourth at boarding school when Rosemary had been head girl.

'Every Friday, Fiona leaves at lunchtime,' grumbled David, 'having phoned home and said: "Mummy, can you arrange to have the train stopped?" Evidently the Carlisle Express runs across her parents' estate, so she just jumps down from her first-class carriage and scampers across the fields to some mansion.' David tried to keep the envy and antagonism out of his voice. Fiona had recently repelled his advances.

'She is so thick,' he went on, 'but Raymond likes her contacts.'

'She's a duck,' said Rosemary, very relieved that David wasn't smitten.

'And talking of duck, here's mine,' said David.

God, it looked divine, pity he was supposed to be off his food with love, he must remember not to eat too much.

'This is fun,' said Rosemary as the waiter placed her sole in front of her.

The word 'macho' was beginning to be bandied around in London. David took one look at Rosemary's Dover sole, and summoning the head waiter loudly ticked him off for not taking it off the bone.

'It doesn't matter,' mumbled Rosemary.

'Yes it does, I do not expect restaurants of your calibre to make mistakes.'

The head waiter, who didn't like upstarts, let David run, by which time the entire restaurant was listening; then, as David drew breath, said: 'Sir, you have paid me the greatest compliment.'

'Don't be bloody rude.'

In answer the head waiter lifted the top half of the sole. 'My chef removed the bone, without you noticing it.'

David was hugely and furiously embarrassed, a little boy being laughed at in the playground again. It took all Rosemary's tact and sweetness to calm him down.

'I just want everything to be perfect for you,' he mumbled.

It was a warm evening, and the cashmere jersey had turned her face scarlet. They were both relieved to retreat for coffee outside. As a peace-offering, the head waiter offered them a liqueur on the house with their After Eights. The river reminded David of Foxes Court: lights on the opposite side sending gold snakes writhing across the river, the water birds calling to each other sleepily, the dip of the oars of a late-night rower, the smell of wet vegetation.

'Shall we have lunch tomorrow?'

'I can't,' wailed Rosemary, 'I've got to collect for the Cats Protection League outside Gloucester Road Station.' She could have wept with disappointment, particularly when he didn't suggest another date.

'It's been such a lovely evening.' Rosemary pointed to the new moon disentangling itself from the black branches of the alders on the opposite bank. 'Did you book her to appear too?'

'I'm learning a huge amount from Raymond,' said David idly, 'but one day I'd like my own gallery.'

David was so thoughtful, he made the waiter pack up all the duck he hadn't been able to eat in foil for Elspeth, Rosemary's mother's Pekinese.

In the car going home, he sang along to a tape of Schubert songs. In one about a beautiful wild rose in the hedgerow, he changed 'Röslein' to 'Rosemary'. Rosemary's little house in Chelsea had lift gates on the window to keep out burglars. Embarrassed he might think she expected him to kiss her, Rosemary opened the door quickly, but David grabbed her right hand.

'Don't g-g-go,' he stepped up his stammer. 'I can't bear it, I know I've had a lot of girls in the past but you are so lovely.'

'Don't be silly,' squeaked Rosemary.

'Beauty is in the eye of the b-b-beholder, and I've got a good eye, Raymond tells me. You're the most beautiful girl I have ever seen. I've met my Waterloo, Rosemary, I know you're going to break my heart.'

'Don't be a clot.'

'Yes, you will.' David put his head in his hands. 'Because I've fallen in love with you. It's utterly presumptuous, the desire of the moth for the star. Your family are wealthy, so far above me.'

'We're not grand.' Rosemary cast around desperately: 'I like boneless soles much better than chinless wonders.'

'Don't mock me,' said David in anguish. 'I love you. The first moment at Foxes Court, I thought: "She was a phantom of delight When first she gleamed upon my sight."'

'That's so lovely,' sobbed Rosemary. 'I've loved you too, ever since we cooked that sea trout together.'

'You love me?' said David incredulously. 'I don't believe it. Oh darling.'

She tasted of brandy and After Eights. He was touched by her clumsy enthusiasm and lack of experience. Under the cashmere, he discovered firm, delightfully full breasts, and was just getting her really worked up, when he pushed her away.

'I still can't ask you to marry me. I'm only twenty-two. My salary all goes on supporting Mum and Dad.'

'Oh, poor you.' Rosemary was mortified. 'You shouldn't have bought me that lovely dinner and all those presents.'

'I couldn't help myself. Raymond gives me a small commission. I sold a drawing by Ingres last week.'

'That's why you've lost weight, you can't afford to eat. I'm not poor,' she went on tearfully. 'I've got enough for both of us and your parents, I'm an only child, so one day all Daddy's money . . .'

'I'll make a fortune one day.'

'Of course you will.'

David rather wanted another feel of those wonderful breasts, but thought now was the right cut-off moment.

'I can't expect you to wait for me. You must have lots of kids and a big house.'

'I don't want—'

But David had leapt out of the car and, belting round, opened the door; then, as she stumbled out, cried dramatically: 'Goodbye, Rosemary darling, I love you too much to pull you down to my level.'

As he roared off, instantly switching to Radio One, in his driving mirror, he could see she was crying. She'd also forgotten her duck doggie bag, which he could eat when he got home.

David sang 'Who wants to be a millionaire?' at the top of his voice all the way back to his bedsitter in Bayswater.

Rosemary dolefully clanked her tin in Gloucester Road. She'd been too dispirited to accost anyone and after half an hour had only collected half a crown and an Irish penny for the Cats Protection League. How would the poor strays survive? Catching sight of her, shoppers scuttled past, not wanting to be nabbed, clutching their fares as they plunged into the womb of the tube station. It gave her a dreadful feeling of déjà vu: young men at deb parties had long ago shot into darkened discos with the same averted eyes.

She jumped at a screech of brakes.

'"Oh Rosemar-ee, I love you,"' sang a wonderfully familiar tenor.

Rosemary started to cry. Slowly, through her tears, she became aware of a heavenly vision, a young Apollo framed in the window of Raymond's dark blue E-Type. The boot was full of canvasses.

'Jump in,' yelled David.

Rosemary blushed furiously, aware of astonished passers-by.

'I'm on duty till two o'clock.'

'Fuck duty. Get in.'

Rosemary did, straight into David's arms, to be kissed on and on, until every outraged motorist in London seemed to be hooting to the drumming accompaniment of her heart.

'I must go back,' she gasped as a grinning David finally drove off, making V signs to left and to right.

'You must *not*.' Fumbling in the dashboard, David handed her a wad of Galena's unlaundered greenbacks. 'That should protect a few pussies.'

'You can't give me all that money.'

'I've booked us into the Royal Garden for a quicky, but only if you promise to marry me to make it respectable.'

'Yes, please,' gasped Rosemary, as he pulled up in front of the hotel and, throwing his car keys to the door man, seized Rosemary's hand and belted inside.

'I've only been to bed with one and a half men,' mumbled Rosemary as he wrestled with the endless buttons of her flowered Laura Ashley.

'What didn't the half one do?'

'Couldn't get it up.' Rosemary hung her curly head. 'Probably didn't find me exciting enough.'

'Unlike me,' sighed David, as white breasts flew like doves out of an even whiter bra, 'I find you wildly exciting.' Then, dropping to his knees: 'This is definitely one pussy I want to protect.'

St George's horse, he reflected afterwards, gave him one of the nicest rides he'd ever had.

'But you mustn't tell anyone,' he begged, 'until I've asked your father's permission.'

He was simply dreading breaking the news to Raymond.

14

Having made his pile and married very far up, Sir Mervyn Newton approved of young men on the make. He had adored sponsoring Rupert Campbell-Black and seeing the 'Good as Newton' slogan emblazoned across Rupert's showjumping lorry, but he had sadly recognized that Rupert was not going to offer for Rosemary. It looked likely the poor lass might never get a husband. Sir Mervyn was so disappointed there would be no grandson to carry on the line that he had, as a means of acquiring immortality, become obsessed with his art collection.

The morning after David and Rosemary's lunchtime romp in the Royal Garden, Mervyn dropped into the Belvedon. Having just acquired a Romney from a somewhat dodgy gallery, he wanted Raymond's opinion that it was 'right'. As Raymond was out at Trumper's having his hair cut, David hastily shoved another foul letter from his bank manager into his top drawer and, after one look, told Mervyn he must take the picture straight back.

'You can still smell the turpentine, sir, probably painted in 1972 rather than 1772,' then, subtly applauding Mervyn's taste, 'but it's an extraordinarily good copy.'

'How can you tell it's a copy?'

'It's like asking a farmer the difference between Guernseys and Friesians.'

Mervyn was most impressed. Why didn't he buy David lunch, while his chauffeur took the Romney plus a flea in the ear back to the rogue gallery?

'Only if you'll let me pay, sir.'

'We'll argue about that later.'

Raymond in fact had double dated, and David had been just about to ring the Ritz and cancel his boss's favourite table overlooking Green Park, but decided to hang on to it for himself and Mervyn.

Not only did David remember he drank gin and tonic but never had Mervyn met anyone who found the dry-cleaning business quite so fascinating. Gazing at Mervyn's gleaming, pinky-brown pate and face, David decided he had never met anyone so like a baked bean. And I won't have to eat you on toast any more if I marry your daughter, he thought resolutely. His landlady in Bayswater was hectoring him for last month's rent.

Staring into a cup of coffee, black as Galena's eyes, David took a gulp of Pouilly-Fumé.

'I must pay for lunch, sir, because I'm about to ask you a huge favour.'

An interview for his cousin, thought Mervyn in disappointment. A biro mark his mother can't get off her new coat. For a second, he didn't take in the words: 'daughter's hand in marriage'.

'I know I'm nine years younger than R-r-r-r-rosemary' – there were tears in the boy's eyes – 'I know she's had a rough time with other chaps. But I truly love, admire and long to cherish her and I'm certain, with her by my side, I could do really well in the art world.' Impatiently he shook his head at a hovering waiter: 'Unless you'd like a brandy, sir?'

'I would indeed,' cried Sir Mervyn joyfully.

Margaret, his wife, had been seven years older and much better bred than he. He had never been faithful to her, but she had her garden (which was opened more often than her legs these days), and her Pekes, and last year the title (which his hard work had bestowed on her), and they rubbed along very well. David seemed so genuine when he outlined his plans for the future.

'I like Yorkshire folk,' said Mervyn. 'They call a spade a spade.'

All the better to gold-dig with. David fought a hysterical desire to laugh.

He insisted on paying the bill with the last of Galena's money.

Cash, noted Mervyn.

'Sometimes we do deals on paintings,' murmured David. 'People are happy to accept considerably less for cash. If you were interested . . . I know you're in a hurry, sir, but if you really feel it's OK for me to marry Rosemary, I did go ahead and buy her a ring, just as a present.'

'What does Rosebud feel?' asked Mervyn fondly. 'Old girl keeps her feelings reined in.'

Horses should, thought David.

'She admits she cares for me, enough to marry me. I know I can make her happy, but I wouldn't dream of putting this on her finger until I knew you and Lady Newton had agreed.'

On a bed of dark blue velvet lay a huge heart-shaped diamond also paid for by Galena.

'Lovely setting.' Mervyn examined it. 'Couldn't have chosen anything nicer myself. I'm sure Lady N. will be just as pleased. Where are you planning to live?'

'Well, Rosie's got her little house, and I've got plans to rent one of the cottages down at Foxes Court. I imagine Rosie'll want kids very soon, and I'd like to get her out of the way of the IRA.'

And I could visit them, reflected Sir Mervyn, and take that sexy Galena out to lunch.

Having tipped the waiter exactly ten per cent, David said he ought to get back to the gallery.

Good conscientious lad, thought Mervyn approvingly.

'I'll come with you,' he said. 'Chauffeur can drive us. What are you showing?'

'Marvellous Pre-Raphaelites downstairs, Casey Andrews drawings upstairs.'

'Loved it when Rupert hit him across the lawn,' admitted Mervyn. 'Presumptuous oaf, thinking a lovely woman like Galena could fancy him.'

'I'm the luckiest, happiest man in the world,' said David, realizing as they glided up Old Bond Street that he could now afford all the ravishing girls they were passing.

Hey diddly dee, a fat cat's life for me, sang David under his breath.

Raymond, who was examining a Rossetti of a redhead in a green silk dress, turned pale and dropped his eyeglass when David broke the news. But true to form, he immediately pulled himself together, congratulated David warmly, and, having sent him off to open a bottle of champagne, told Mervyn what a charming, kind, trustworthy, clever husband he would make.

'Galena, I and the boys are devoted to him.'

Fiona, Raymond's fair assistant, got the giggles.

'Just like winning the pools, David.'

Later, more bottles were opened, Rosemary came over and was given her ring, and Mervyn bought the Rossetti.

'We must tell Mummy,' sighed a starry-eyed Rosemary, 'she hates being left out.

'We're to go over to drinks later,' she said, putting down the telephone. 'Mummy sounds pleased. Are you the Tadcaster Pulboroughs?' she asked.

'No, he's the Pull-everything-in-sightborough,' muttered Eddie the packer, who'd just returned from a delivery.

'Hush,' giggled Fiona, 'and have some fizz.'

Passers-by, seeing the merry-making and assuming it was a private view, came in from the street, and Raymond ended up selling a Millais and two of Casey's drawings.

'Do you really love her?' he asked David.

'Not as you love Galena, but I think I can make her happy. She looks happy.' David glanced across the gallery at a flushed Rosemary, who was shrieking with laughter with Fiona as she whispered about the wad of greenbacks for the Cats Protection League.

'Quite frankly,' he went on, putting a hand on Raymond's arm, 'I gave my heart away two years ago. Being with you, working with you, is the most important thing in my life, and there's no way R-R-R-Rosebud's going to change that. Anyway, she adores you. First day I met her at Foxes Court, she said you were the most smashing chap she'd ever met.'

'I hope she thinks you've taken over that role,' said Raymond drily, but he felt happier.

'Fallen on his fucking feet, hasn't he, Guv,' grumbled Eddie as a half-cut David was led off to meet Lady Newton.

'I hope so,' mused Raymond. 'He's spurned Aphrodite in favour of Mammon. Reject the Goddess at your peril.'

'There you go, rabbiting on like Fiona about people I've never 'eard of,' grumbled Eddie. 'Let's open another bottle.'

Margaret Newton, who, with her lack of chin and bulging eyes, resembled a well-upholstered turbot, was less of a pushover than her husband. Dom Pérignon was opened, toasts drunk, futures discussed, the exciting art collection admired, by which time David was plastered and terrified of letting his accent slip. Instead

135

his glass slipped out of his hand, splashing the polished floor with champagne, which David proceeded absent-mindedly to wipe up with Elspeth, his future mother-in-law's Pekinese. Thank God, Mervyn, not a fan of his wife's dog, thought this extremely funny.

15

For both social and financial reasons, David was anxious to get married as quickly and quietly as possible. To his relief, his grandmother, with unusual tact, died in June, which gave an excuse for a tiny wedding, to which none of his common relations were invited. To encourage wedding presents, Sir Mervyn threw a drinks party at his club, the RAC, to which David invited his more glamorous Cambridge and art world friends.

As the Boy David's fortunes prospered, Raymond entered a time of hell. In July, his busiest month, the newly wed Mr and Mrs Pulborough took off on an extended honeymoon to Geneva, Florence, Venice and Kenya. A far worse hammerblow fell a week later. Alizarin, never strong, contracted rheumatoid arthritis. The doctors were hopeful he would grow out of it, but it meant he couldn't join Jupiter at prep school in September. This in turn meant that when he wasn't staggering around on crutches, Alizarin spent his time in his parents' bed, reading, painting or gazing at the Raphael. This made Galena very bad tempered. Worried stiff about her favourite child, she was drinking heavily, not amassing enough paintings for her long-awaited October exhibition and unable to see her lovers.

Fed up with her moods, nannies employed to look after Alizarin and baby Jonathan came and went. As a result, Galena took it out on Raymond. Devastated by David's marriage, still tormented by jealousy of Casey, Rupert, Etienne and the rest of Galena's fan club, Raymond was dealt a further blow when thick decorative Fiona announced she wanted a six-month sabbatical from the gallery. She was needed to provide moral support while her sister had her first baby in Hong Kong.

Raymond was appalled. He loathed change. He desperately needed Fiona to organize Galena's exhibition. She knew all the people that mattered and how to address them on invitations. She had enough taste to send the right flowers, and who would buy all his Christmas presents? She understood all his ways.

'You can't abandon me. I need you.'

'So does my sister. I asked the agency to send you an upmarket older woman.'

'Sounds like Margaret Newton,' said Raymond gloomily.

On the Monday the temporary was due to arrive, he felt even gloomier. Jonathan, however adorable, had formed a wrecking party with Shrimpy the Jack Russell. Jonathan had smashed some priceless porcelain and glass. Shrimpy had chewed up the first edition of *Maud* given him by David and, almost more disastrously, Raymond's address book. Another nanny had given in her notice. Galena had given Raymond hell for abandoning her to drive up to Cork Street.

'Gallery can't run itself without David and Fiona,' he had finally shouted at her. 'We've got to get your fucking invitations out.'

Arriving still shaking at the gallery, failing to find the invitation list, complete with addresses, which Fiona had promised to type, he was dispiritedly opening the post, when out fell David and Rosemary's wedding photographs.

Rosemary, who'd been incredibly relieved not to have

to wear her mother's tiara, looked happy and jaunty, like a seaside donkey in one of those straw hats that keep off the flies. Beside her David looked heartbreakingly young. Raymond groaned. He hadn't believed it was possible to miss anyone so much. Even when David finally came back from his honeymoon, it wouldn't be the same. David would confide in Rosemary now.

There was a knock on the door, or was it on the inside of Pandora's Box? Hope seemed to have jumped down from the Raphael and flown up to London, as in came one of the prettiest girls he had ever seen. Her short fair curls were swept off an angelic heart-shaped face, which was enhanced by big eyes the colour of love-in-a-mist, a wild-rose complexion, a soft pink smiling mouth, and a little turned-up nose. She was also tiny, with the sweet unformed figure of a twelve-year-old, and gave an impression of being swathed in rainbows. Perhaps he had died of a broken heart and gone to heaven.

Having an Irish mother, Raymond believed in fairies. Then he realized the rainbow effect came from a violet cardigan, a pink floating scarf and a short skirt made out of a patchwork of pastel colours.

'Mr Belvedon' – she even had a tiny squeaky fairy's voice – 'I'm Anthea Rookhope, your new temp.'

My God, any moment he'd be making jokes about hoping she'd become permanent.

She seemed to dance over to him, a peacock butterfly fluttering across the gallery.

'I am *so* excited. I know you wanted someone older and more public schooly' – her smiling pink lips parted to show beautiful little white teeth – 'but I adored art school and I've always wanted to work in a gallery. What lovely pictures.' She gazed round in wonder. 'Who painted them?'

'Rory Balniel, one of our younger artists,' stammered Raymond, 'lives in France, used to paint angry tormented stuff; now he's happily married, he paints his wife and children.'

'Oh, I love happy marriages,' sighed Anthea. 'Look at those lovely kiddies. You look tired, Mr Belvedon, let me make you a coffee.'

The telephone rang.

'Oh God, I don't know how to work the bloody thing,' moaned Raymond.

'I'll answer it,' said Anthea, going rather pink after a minute, and putting her hand over the receiver. 'It's a Mr Casey Andrews saying he hasn't been paid, shall I tell him you're not here?'

Raymond seized the telephone. 'We have paid you, Casey, and if you can't keep a civil tongue in your swollen head, then I suggest you push off to another gallery.'

The sound of clapping made them both jump.

It was Eddie.

'Well done, Mr B. Stand up to the old bugger,' then, wolf-whistling at Anthea: 'Things is definitely looking up.'

Things certainly were. Raymond came back from lunching at the Connaught with a client to find Anthea had worked through her lunch hour.

'I've tracked down the list for Mrs Belvedon's exhibition, such exciting people, are you really asking Paul McCartney and Rupert Campbell-Black? I also discovered a lot of filing.'

'Where did you find it?'

'Well, quite by chance, it was in the dustbin, a lot of yogurt spilled on the top pages, but I sponged it off, I'm sure Fiona didn't mean to chuck it all away, just had other things on her mind before going away.'

Raymond wasn't so sure. Anthea was clearly one of those sweethearts who saw the best in everyone.

'And I found Mr Casey Andrews's cheque.'

'Oh God.'

'No, it was OK. He popped in half an hour ago, I explained about being a new girl and it probably being my fault. He couldn't have been kinder. I gave him a coffee and he went off with his cheque like a lamb.'

All the letters Raymond had dictated that morning came back immaculately typed.

'These are fine,' said Raymond, signing them, then smiling at her, 'but in future could you possibly put Esq. rather than Mr on the envelope, and I prefer to write in the Dear Somerford or Dear Lady X at the top, more intimate somehow. I've got a boring dinner this evening, so I'm going to have a shower. See you in the morning.'

'Give me your jacket,' said Anthea. 'I can't have my handsome boss going out with a button hanging loose.'

Wiping a hole in the misted-up mirror, Raymond wondered if he was still handsome. When he came out, Anthea had retyped all the letters.

'You should have gone,' said a shocked Raymond, accustomed to Fiona's insistence that anything after six o'clock was well past her party time. 'Particularly with all the tube strikes.'

'I only like leaving an empty in-tray.' Anthea stood on tiptoe to adjust his collar as she helped him on with his jacket. 'You do look smart. Have a lovely evening. Thank you for such a wonderful day.'

The next day she brought him home-made cake and a jar of pear jelly.

'I live in Purley, which means "Pear tree lee".'

She really was the most conscientious child. She never took lunch hours except to shop for the gallery. She revolutionized Fiona's sloppy filing, despatched Galena's invitations, had a mug printed with Raymond's name. She also brought in a small wireless.

'So we could have a dance when we're not too busy. I so wanted to be a dancer, but I was too little,' she told Raymond, 'but working in a gallery's so much more exciting.'

Soon she was adding womanly touches: making

cushions and chair-covers to enhance the pictures being shown; arranging wonderful flowers, which she'd bought early in Covent Garden; finding pretty frames for the photographs of Galena and the three boys, pointing out Mr Belvedon's beautiful family to everyone.

Raymond found himself missing David less and less. Anthea was so slender, smelled so sweet and, scorning the flares and long skirts that were fashionable, stuck to short, tightly belted frocks and pleated skirts which showed off her pretty legs and tiny waist.

'I'm into femininity, not feminism,' she was always saying.

At the end of the week, the agency rang. They had found an older more experienced woman to replace Anthea.

'Oh no,' said Raymond in horror, 'we all love her, we want Miss Er, Miss Er . . .'

'Rookhope,' whispered Anthea.

'Miss Rookhope to stay as long as possible.'

When he came off the telephone, Anthea gave him a little kiss.

'It's pronounced Rookh'p,' she giggled, 'after a little village in Durham.'

'I shall call you "Hopey",' said Raymond happily, 'after a character in a picture at home, which one day I'll show you. I must remember: Rookhope pronounced Rookh'p.'

'To rhyme with suck'p and shack'p,' muttered Eddie, who was much less taken.

It was clear Raymond had developed a sodding great crush on Anthea. Eddie had hoped with David and Fiona out of the way, it would be him and the Governor together again. Anthea, he noticed, turned on the charm like an electric kettle. She never remembered he didn't take sugar and only gave him a slice of home-made cake if Raymond were about.

'I'm a good listener,' she was always saying in her silly

142

squeaky voice, but, like the Boy David, she was more interested in storing information that could be used later.

She praised everything Raymond did, noticing dark rings under his eyes, a different tie, laughing at his most insane quips. Important collectors and artists got the same treatment.

She might charm the birds off the trees, reflected Eddie, but he didn't think she'd take them to the RSPCA if they broke a wing in the fall.

The person she creepily reminded Eddie of was David. Like him, she was frantic to escape from her dull, relatively impoverished, suburban background. There would be a battle royal for Raymond's affections when David returned.

Eddie retired to the basement to smoke dope and photocopy his cock in the smart new machine ordered by Anthea. Hearing how pretty she was from other artists, Somerford Keynes, the demon critic and a great fan of Eddie's, waddled down to the Belvedon to have a butcher's.

'She's very small,' he murmured.

'So was Napoleon,' snapped Eddie, 'and about as defenceless.'

In early September, Galena came up to London for a party at the Tate, and spent the afternoon at Vidal Sassoon, emerging with gleaming collar-length hair falling over one eye from a side parting. Dramatic make-up, and a beautiful vermilion dress, floating to avoid the spreading waist, but slightly see-through to show off the still exciting breasts, completed the picture. Raymond felt all the old tugging of his heart strings. Galena's latest tipple was a pinch of cocaine in a glass of champagne, repeated throughout the night.

All the art world were at the party, all smiling brightly to conceal their envy and animosity. Galena received a lot of attention. She'd been stuck in the country for months, and news had filtered out that an important new exhibition was imminent.

Everyone stopped talking as an extraordinarily handsome Pakistani – a young artist called Khalid – walked in.

'You'd like him, wouldn't you?' Galena murmured mockingly to Raymond.

It took her precisely half an hour. She and Khalid left the party together. Raymond returned to the flat in Duke Street, St James's, which he'd acquired after the top floor of the gallery in Cork Street had been given over to pictures. Here he waited up, churning with rage, humiliation and misery, until a dull dawn broke over the dirty city.

'What is life to me without her?'

Arriving at the gallery, he thought he'd been burgled. A little Watteau was missing from the wall, then he realized Anthea was dusting its frame. Coffee bubbled in the percolator. The peel of the oranges she had squeezed for him lay in the waste-paper basket, a croissant was keeping warm in a drying-up cloth. He also recognized the opening bars of the Sanctus from the *Missa Solemnis*, on the score of which Beethoven had written, 'From the heart, may it again go to the heart.'

'We're singing it in the choir at home,' explained Anthea. 'I bought you a tape. Whatever's the matter, didn't you have a lovely party?'

A desolate contrast to her new, bright-coloured cushions, Raymond had slumped on the sofa, his head in his hands, his shoulders shaking.

'Galena never came home.'

'Oh, you poor dear.' Anthea ran over and put her arms round him. She was so tiny, it was like being comforted by Alizarin.

'Don't be upset, Daddy, please don't.'

It was Eddie's day off, so they stayed quietly in the gallery. As Anthea cosseted him with chicken soup and

144

tomato sandwiches made with fresh basil, further details emerged.

'I want to drop her horrible party list in the dustbin,' raged Anthea.

There was also a train strike. Anthea rang home.

'Mr Belvedon's very kindly lent me his flat, Mum. He's going to work late and sleep in the gallery, we're so busy.'

She and Raymond were planning to go out to dinner, but over a bottle of Chablis still more details emerged.

'I can't satisfy Galena. Her contempt makes me impotent. She complains I'm too small.'

'How beastly of her. I'm so tiny, you'd be quite big enough for me.' Anthea was edging up to him on the sofa.

'I'm far too old for you.'

'You're not, you're so distinguished looking and you've got a figure most young fellows would die for.'

Much encouraged, Raymond put an arm round her shoulders, expecting to encounter angel's wings. He felt like a collector, taking an exquisite figurine out of a glass case, fondling, examining, making a miraculous discovery: that he could give her pleasure. She was so perfect, so responsive, wriggling on his knee like a little girl, letting him play with her for hours.

'I've got a real daddy at last.'

Anthea's fortnight ran into months.

16

It was a bright crisp morning at the beginning of October; dry plane leaves rattled along the gutters. The sun was no longer hot or high enough to necessitate the green-and-white-striped awning outside the gallery. Anthea on the telephone could see cobalt-blue sky between the houses.

'We're showing Kit Eskine this week, Lord Partridge. We're open till six. We don't close for din— sorry, lunch. Lovely, see you later.'

The switchboard meant power and knowledge. Anthea had also received increasing abuse from Galena, whose pictures were due in today. The Boy David was due back tomorrow. Anthea had pinned his postcards on Raymond's cork board.

'I'm like a coffee machine,' she joked to a passing Raymond, 'that's twenty cups I've made this morning.'

'You shouldn't attract so many collectors,' said Raymond fondly as he retired into the inner office with one of the madder and richer. 'We don't want to be disturbed.'

David was thrilled to be back in London. His honey-moon had been pleasant enough. Rosemary had proved a surprisingly easy companion. He had made good contacts in Florence and Venice, put more of Galena's money into a Swiss bank while admiring wild flowers around Geneva, and enjoyed the game reserves. Although after a bit one giraffe looks very like another.

Leaving his bride to wake up slowly, anxious to show off his wedding present, he thundered up Piccadilly, only to be distracted by a beige windmill. It was a frantically waving Somerford Keynes.

'Dear boy, dear boy, how are you enjoying the lap of luxury? Lovely party at the RAC. Liked your new wife, but aren't people bitchy? "There goes David and his pension fund," said some wag. I can't remember who. "Don't knock it," I reproved them, "a young lad has to get on," particularly now it looks as if you've got competition at the gallery. Raymond is positively besotted by his new popsy.'

David was shocked. In private he might fawn over Raymond, but he hated outsiders thinking there might be something sexual between them.

'Don't be ridiculous,' he said sharply.

Somerford's sleepy crocodile eyes were suddenly alight with malice.

'We all know you're Raymond's boy.'

Somehow David managed not to betray his fury. He had expected widespread envy when he married money. He'd bloody well show them.

Parking meters had replaced the prostitutes of the Sixties in Cork Street. Fortunately David found a space right outside the Belvedon.

What a lovely brown man, and what a posh car, thought Anthea, checking her curls in the little gilt mirror she'd bought to hang by her reception desk. Since David's absence, there had always been plenty of petty cash.

'Where's Raymond?' David asked her curtly.

'With a client.' Then, as David strode towards Raymond's door: 'You can't go in. He shouldn't be long.'

David's lips tightened. Fiona had often let in the wrong people. Not wanting his searchlight charm diffused, Raymond preferred dealing with one person at a time.

'Would you like a catalogue?' asked Anthea. 'It explains about the pictures.'

And I wrote the fucking blurb, thought David.

Anthea went back to her press cuttings. David mooched around, noticing the number of red spots, pausing in front of an exquisite watercolour of a black girl cuddling an off-white baby.

Anthea decided to charm this unfriendly stranger. He was so good looking in that white suit and lovely shiny shoes.

'D'you like that picture?'

'Very much.'

She was wearing Penhaligon's Bluebell, noticed David, which Raymond often gave to clients' wives.

'Well, I'll let you into a little secret,' she whispered, 'that's Mr Belvedon's favourite. I know he'd like to keep it himself, but they've got so many pictures already in their beautiful Limesbridge home. I expect you've visited it.'

'Frequently,' snapped David.

'Perhaps you'd like to be invited to Mrs Belvedon's private view next week? If I ask Mr Belvedon nicely, I'm sure we can smuggle you in.'

'How very kind,' murmured David. Let me let you into a little secret, he wanted to shout, I'm Mr Belvedon's favourite.

Next moment Raymond came out of the back room with the rich mad old collector, who was clutching a china Alsatian wrapped in the *Daily Mirror*.

'This clearly has huge sentimental value,' he was saying to her. 'Unfortunately public taste has yet to catch up with it. But hang on to it. Who knows what may happen. Thank you so much, I'll get my assistant to find you a bag.'

Looking round, he caught sight of David, and his face lit up.

'My dear boy, you look so well.'

'So do you.' Spontaneously David crossed the gallery, embracing Raymond, kissing him on both cheeks.

'How were the game reserves?'

'Rather tame after Casey and Joan. It was all fine, but it's great to be back. Come and see my new car.'

Outside was an olive-green Aston Martin.

'Won't show up when it's parked under trees on summer evenings.' David grinned wickedly. 'It's Rosemary's wedding present.'

'What did you give her?' said Raymond, laughing yet disapproving.

'My undying respect.'

'You must come and meet Anthea.'

Anthea was scarlet – ready to explode like a hurled tomato. How dare David make a fool of her?

'I'd no idea. You must think me *so* stupid.'

'I think you're a great operator. She nearly sold me a picture, Raymond. Your favourite evidently.'

'Anthea's wonderful,' said Raymond, detecting tension.

'How about some fresh coffee and home-made chocolate cake?' asked Anthea, frantic to regain the ascendancy.

'I'd like something stronger,' said David, who for the past month at half past ten in the burning sunshine had been enjoying Bloody Marys that scorched the roof off one's mouth.

'Bit early,' said Anthea primly.

David raised an eyebrow: 'I'm still on Kenya time. Come on, Raymond. Where's Fiona?'

'Gone to Hong Kong for six months.'

'You must miss her terribly.'

'Not now I've got Hopey.' Raymond smiled at Anthea.

'Hopey?'

'Mr Belvedon's nickname for me, my name's Rookhope after a village in Durham.'

'Well, you've certainly made some changes, gallery

looks like Laura Ashley. Are we selling cushions as well?'

Wandering into Raymond's office, he picked up the photographs of Galena and the children. Asking after each one to emphasize his intimacy, he was appalled to learn of Alizarin's rheumatoid arthritis.

'That's terrible. Rosemary and I'll drive down and see him. I don't suppose all this has helped Galena.'

'No, she's had a terrible time. We're expecting her pictures any minute. Eddie's gone down with the van.'

David noticed Anthea hovering in the doorway. To get rid of her, he asked her to bring in the party list.

'When I've finished updating it,' said Anthea coolly.

'How is Rosemary?' asked Raymond hastily.

'About to start househunting, for somewhere near you.' With every sentence, David tried to exclude Anthea, emphasizing his and Raymond's closeness. Why the hell didn't she fuck off and leave them?

'Where shall we have lunch?' he asked Raymond. 'I'll take you to the Capital in Basil Street – it's wonderful.'

Oh, the joy of a joint bank account!

'I expected you tomorrow,' sighed Raymond, 'I'm committed to taking Somerford to Wilton's, softening him up for Galena's private view.'

'Pity,' said David lightly, then, turning to Anthea, 'Come and have lunch and tell me' – he smiled slyly at Raymond – 'what the old fox has been up to.'

Anthea thawed like butter in a microwave.

'I've got to chase up the press who haven't replied, and I told Lord Partridge we stayed open through the dinner hour. Perhaps Eddie could hold the fort when he gets back.'

Raymond felt distinctly deflated to see his new little friend going off with his old little friend, but after all, he was ashamed to find himself thinking, they were the same age and class.

David took Anthea to Jules Bar in Jermyn Street. Outside on the wall was a giant royal-blue cocktail glass.

Inside was filled with sleek young bloods in pinstripe suits, noisily discussing the afternoon's racing as they downed large gins and tonic. They all eyed up Anthea, who confessed to David she was not much of a drinker. David suggested Pimm's and surreptitiously persuaded the waiter to add a double measure of gin.

'I'm going to have a steak, very rare,' he announced. He didn't like bloody meat any more than he liked black coffee, but asked for them because Raymond did.

'I fancy a prawn cocktail and perhaps a dessert. That gâteau looks tasty,' observed Anthea. 'We mustn't be longer than an hour, Fiona took such frightful liberties.'

She was clearly beady about her predecessor, justifying her anger by cataloguing Fiona's misdemeanours: 'She left everything in such a mess.'

'One mustn't speak ill of the deb,' confided David, 'but Fiona's tiny mind was on other things: Wimbledon, Henley, Ascot, Goodwood, skiing. Raymond loved her because she was *very* glamorous and knew all the right people. She's a particularly good friend of my wife, Rosemary.'

Then, seeing Anthea was feeling upstaged, softened his approach.

'Raymond's very pleased with you. He adores small pictures, so easy to smuggle, and they don't take up too much room on the gallery walls. Similarly he likes small, very feminine ladies; you've stepped out of a Fragonard.'

'He's such a gentleman,' sighed Anthea, taking a delicate sip of Pimm's. 'We have so much in common, despite the age gap: classical music, fine wine, lovely restaurants.'

She and Raymond had clearly been spending a lot of time in the latter recently. She was also able to give David a detailed update of Raymond's family life and the dark horror of Galena's moods and Alizarin's illness.

'Little Jonathan seems the only ray of sunshine.

151

Sometimes I feel Mr Belvedon can't wait to get back to town. He was so distressed when Shrimpy chewed up his address book. I've been making him a new one.'

'With Rookhope at the top of the Rs,' teased David.

Anthea's soft pink lips lifted, but her big blue eyes were serious.

'Mr Belvedon seems so lost.'

'That's because I haven't been around,' said David brutally. 'If I'd known Fiona wasn't going to be here, I'd have come back early from Kenya.'

'We've managed,' said Anthea shirtily.

'You've done a wonderful job filling in while I've been away.'

Anthea rootled around in the shredded lettuce and pink sauce for more prawns. David, she decided, was very glamorous, but on the make, and not to be trusted. Yet she was so anxious to emphasize her value as a help-mate that, after the second Pimm's, which was really a meal in itself if you spooned out all the fruit, she told him about Galena's leaving the Tate party with Khalid the handsome Pakistani.

'Poor Ray, I mean Mr B., staggered into the gallery like a sleep-walker the following morning.'

'I thought she'd given up that sort of caper.' David plunged his knife into his steak with such viciousness that the blood spurted out.

'She sounds a bit of a b.,' admitted Anthea. 'She always calls me Fiona on the phone, and never says please or thank you.'

Back at the gallery, Anthea swayed off to the bog. David rang Rosemary saying he was going to have a drink with Raymond after work.

'I'll be home around eight.' Lowering his voice, he added: 'Galena trouble.'

'How lucky he's got you. Have you had lunch?'

Checking Anthea was still out of earshot, probably throwing up, David said he'd grabbed a sandwich.

'I'll cook you something nice. Love you, darling.'

'Love you too, Rosie.'

As Raymond had confided in David in the past, it was natural after a few drinks for him to confess that he'd fallen for Anthea.

'She's such a poppet. Don't know what the collective noun for collectors is, but it should be an Anthea. They all flock to see her. The artists all want to paint her, Casey and Joan are positively moony. Never makes me feel my age. She's so sweet and unaffected.'

'Unaffected?' said David incredulously.

But Raymond wasn't listening. 'She's just like King Cophetua's beggar maid,' he quoted happily.

> 'In robe and crown the king stept down
> To meet and greet her on her way;
> "It is no wonder," said the lords,
> "She is more beautiful than day" . . .
> One praised her ankle, one her eyes.'

'The Beggar Maid was dark,' protested David, who much preferred Raymond as cuckolded King Arthur than randy King Cophetua.

Aware that David might be a little jealous, Raymond said hastily, 'So glad you're back, particularly to help me hang Galena's pictures.'

'Rosemary and I,' said David grandly, 'would like to lend *The Wild-Flower Meadow*,' which Mervyn had given them to commemorate the evening they first met, 'with a red spot on to start the ball rolling, although I'm sure it won't be necessary.'

Later, brooding on Galena's lapse at the Tate party, David decided she needed taking down several pegs. Searching for houses around Limesbridge at the weekend, hoping Raymond might rent them the lovely cottage overlooking the river, David and Rosemary dropped in, as promised, on Foxes Court, bringing presents for little Alizarin. Both were appalled by how ill he looked. Refereeing rows between his parents, thought David grimly.

While Rosemary read Alizarin *Just William*, David and Galena wandered round the garden. Deliberately misreading her very real worries about Alizarin and her forthcoming exhibition, David reassured her she mustn't feel remotely guilty about getting off with the ravishing Khalid, because Raymond was utterly besotted with his new assistant at the gallery.

At the time Galena made absolutely no comment.

Two days before the private view, most of Galena's pictures had been hung. Having no idea that Khalid was actually Somerford's latest boyfriend, Raymond had been persuaded over lunch at Wilton's to let a simmering Somerford have an even earlier view.

Alas, this coincided with a further and totally new picture being carried in by a grinning Eddie.

'Paint's not the only fing wot isn't dry. Mornin', Somerford.'

David, who'd been glaring at Galena's charming portrait of Shrimpy, still furious he'd been left out, looked round at the picture and gave a gasp of laughter.

One of the most famous cartoons attributed to Raphael at Windsor Castle is entitled *The Battle of Nude Men*. It shows a crowd of naked warriors, one side with spears, the other with bows and arrows, a few armed with just shields, having a free-for-all.

All the warriors have the same short curls and even shorter penises; Raymond had a version of the drawing up in the Blue Tower. Galena, clearly outraged by news of Raymond's crush on Anthea, had copied the picture, including instead her lovers.

There were Rupert Campbell-Black, Casey Andrews, Etienne de Montigny, Robens (that must have been a joke) and Somerford's Khalid, et alia, all splendidly endowed. And, oh God, there was Raymond with the minutest cock, and next to him – David gave a shout of laughter – clutching a large shield with 'Newton Dry Cleaners' blazoned across the front, was a very pot-bellied Sir Mervyn. The old goat!

Raymond and Somerford were up the other end of the gallery, examining a moonlit view of the River Fleet, when David aroused their attention.

'Sorry to interrupt, but I don't think we can show this.'

Raymond, who went dreadfully pale, agreed they couldn't – without evoking the wrath of the Director of Public Prosecutions.

'I'd be terribly grateful if you could pretend you haven't seen it,' he begged Somerford, who'd whipped out his magnifying glass.

'Must go and get some cigarettes,' muttered David.

In the telephone box round the corner, he rang his father-in-law.

'Are you alone?'

'What is it? Nothing's happened to Rosie?'

David explained about the painting. 'We're withdrawing it.'

Mervyn was almost incoherent with rage.

'Woman's made the whole thing up.'

'There's an appendix scar and a cornplaster.' David had great difficulty containing his laughter. 'And a tattoo of Cupid above your belly button,' which was admittedly almost hidden by rolls of fat. 'I'd just deny it.'

Mervyn decided to throw himself on David's mercy, rather than his sword.

'Bloody hell, what a bitch, just a bit of fun.'

'Sure, sure, it's all in hand,' said David soothingly, which sounded even worse. 'Raymond will lock the picture away, mortifying for him, of course.'

'Is he? Am I?' spluttered Mervyn.

'Much bigger. In fact you come out of it' – there he went again – 'very well indeed. But I thought you'd like to know in advance.'

'Forewarned is forearmed,' said Mervyn heartily. 'How's the househunting?'

'Raymond is not going to let us have River Cottage, wants to give it to his sister Lily.'

There was a pause.

'The Old Rectory next door to Raymond,' said David idly, 'has just come onto the market. Lovely property, needs a lot of work, but it'd be a terrific investment. Plenty of rooms for a large family.'

'Sounds ideal.' Mervyn suddenly realized he was wringing with sweat. 'You won't mention anything to Rosie? Awfully loyal to her mother.'

'Of course not.'

'How much do they want for that house?'

'About twenty thousand, and quite a bit more spent on it.'

'Let's drive down and see it at the weekend,' said Mervyn.

17

Somerford, who was not so complaisant as Raymond and who had loved his handsome Khalid, put the boot in. On the morning before Galena's exhibition opened, his review appeared claiming the only reason Galena had a show in Cork Street was because her incredibly tolerant and usually aesthetically foolproof husband owned a gallery. She might have produced good if self-indulgent work in the past, but this new collection was derivative tosh.

'Galena Borrowoff-absolutely-everyone', announced the headline.

Unfortunately Somerford had been to a private view at the Fine Arts Society the night before and had lost no time in telling every other influential critic what junk was about to be shown at the Belvedon. He had even produced a proof of what he had written, which pointed out that *The Battle of Nude Men* had been withdrawn.

Like lemmings, the rest of the critics, even those who found they admired the pictures, followed suit. Even worse, their reviews were all accompanied by sexy six-year-old photographs of Galena, which ensured everyone read the copy.

Galena was so devastated by Somerford's piece she refused to attend the private view. Raymond had just coaxed her round, when Casey rang to report even worse reviews in the London evening papers, which both mentioned *The Battle of Nude Men*. This meant Galena's legion of admirers, who'd accepted invitations and might have bought paintings, alarmed they might be in the picture, had failed to show up.

Rupert Campbell-Black, who didn't read reviews and who was in London cleaning up at the Horse of the Year Show, sauntered in, laughed at the nude of himself asleep in the Blue Tower, and bought it for his mother for Christmas. He also bought the watercolour of Shrimpy and, against his better judgement, even chatted up Anthea, delicate as a harebell in mauve frills.

The private view was a total disaster, with only Rupert's nude, Shrimpy and *The Wild-Flower Meadow* displaying red spots. Galena was suicidal. Utterly unused to rejection, she knew she hadn't worked hard enough, hadn't bothered to go sufficiently deeply into her landscapes, or the characters of her sitters, relying on technique rather than the heart. After the private view, Raymond drove straight down to comfort her, but she had merely been offensive.

'Why didn't you varn me Khalid was Somerford's boyfriend?'

'I had no idea.'

'If you were *au courant* with art vorld, you would know. I cannot go on here. That vaterfall drive me crazy, those church bells send me crackers.'

Poor Alizarin, who couldn't bear to hear his mother crying, stumbled between his parents trying to patch things up.

If only Raymond would stand up to me, thought Galena despairingly.

Next morning, Raymond drove back to London without a word. When Galena tried to call him, Anthea refused to put her through. By mid-morning, an already drunk Galena decided to go to London. Desperate for reassurance, she needed to see if her pictures were as awful as Somerford said they were and to check out

Raymond's new assistant, who sounded like Violet Elizabeth Bott on the telephone.

Up in London, Raymond and David had taken Anthea out to a very long lunch at Overton's to celebrate her nineteenth birthday and thank her for working so hard. Staging an exhibition was a big emotional experience. Galena's might have started disastrously, but there were still twelve days to go, and in November they might recoup any losses when they showed Joan Bideford.

'We'll have to supply Anthea with a chastity belt,' teased David.

Around four o'clock, Anthea had been dropped tight and giggling back at the gallery while Raymond and David took a Reynolds they'd picked up cheaply at an auction over to the National Portrait Gallery.

Having arranged some pink chrysanthemums which had arrived for her from Casey Andrews, Anthea settled down to stick the latest reviews in the cuttings book.

She didn't recognize her boss's wife when she walked in. Galena's lank hair was more grey than black, her face puffy, her once white skin criss-crossed with red veins. Her famously sexy eyes were hidden by dark glasses.

When her fur coat fell open, Anthea could see her black dress had split under the armpit and was wrinkled over the thick waist. But there was something about the lift of the head, a queenliness about the walk.

'Vere is Raymond?' Galena whipped off her dark glasses, revealing protruding bloodshot eyes, which were crudely ringed with black. Anthea nearly dropped the cuttings book.

'He's just popped out, Mrs Belvedon. Pleased to meet you, I'm Anthea.'

She was nearly asphyxiated by fumes of wine and bad digestion. Cannoning off the reception desk, Galena looked round disbelievingly at her canvasses.

'And this is vot Somerford Keynes dismiss as self-indulgent tosh.'

'I'm so furious with him,' stormed Anthea, 'and all the other reviewers.'

'There are more?'

'I'm not going to let you see them.'

If she hadn't been a bit tiddly, reflected Anthea, she would have been quite scared of Galena.

'I'm sticking them in for the record,' she added, 'so we don't invite the same horrid pigs to our next party for Joan Bideford. Joan always does well. Can I get you a coffee?'

'I vant a drink, give me those reviews.' Galena glared at Anthea and then round the gallery.

'And vot are all those flowers doing? It looks like funeral shop!'

'They've been sent to me. It's my birthday,' simpered Anthea, opening the drinks cupboard. 'We've only got sherry or Armagnac, that's Mr Belvedon's tipple.' The old cow might say happy birthday.

'Mr Belvedon and David have just taken me out for a nice meal,' she went on. 'It was a scream because he and David gave me the same gift, a lovely Hermès scarf with famous painters on. David's was navy, Raymond's baby blue. And Casey sent me those lovely chrysanths. Isn't he a sweetheart?'

Galena, who had endured Casey's lack of sympathy last night, went on reading her cuttings.

'Even Somerford sent me a PC,' sighed Anthea. 'I think one just has to know how to handle him, Galena, and look at this lovely lacy little card from Raymond.'

'"Dearest Hopey, Thank you for bringing sunshine into my life",' read Galena. '"Hopey"?' she asked ominously.

'After a fairy called "Hope" in an Old Master in your house.' Anthea poured Galena a tiny Armagnac.

'I felt really choked this morning, reaching nineteen. It seems *so* old. My last year in my teens.' Then, looking at Galena solicitously: 'Would you like to sit down? Come and rest on the sofa. Do you like the new covers?

I chose ones that would be nice and feminine for your exhibition. Let me carry your glass.'

Anthea was like a small and very skilled picador plunging darts into a lumbering old bull. Finally, having no idea that David was a long-term admirer of Galena, she added: 'David is *such* a naughty boy, he keeps trying to get me into bed. He said the moment he saw me, he'd met his Waterloo. He knew I was going to break his heart, because I was out of his league. And he's only just back from honeymoon. I know Rosemary's very old, at least thirty, and no oil paintin', but he rang her from here the other night, saying, "I'm in Suffolk with an artist. Can't you hear the birds singing and all the little squirrels crunching their nuts?" I was shocked, Galena. The moment he put the phone down, he rubbed his hands and asked me out for a drink. He's so suave and charming. I said I'd got to get back to Purley; he said, "I'll drive you. It's a warm night, we'll have the roof down." He sent me this lovely card of a Constable, with such lovely words inside.'

'She was a phantom of delight When first she gleamed upon my sight', read Galena. Quivering with rage, she filled up her glass with Armagnac until it spilled over.

'Pity you missed your do,' sighed Anthea. 'It was such a good party. Rupert Campbell-Black bought a painting and was very attentive. He's only twenty-two you know, same age as David, who got quite cross when Rupert asked me out for a noggin.' Then, as Galena drained her glass and refilled it, 'I think you've had enough, Galena.'

'And you are the face of hell,' said Galena, and picking up a little bronze Degas dancer, she hurled it with a sickening crash through the gallery's front window.

18

Like most wildly promiscuous people, Galena couldn't tolerate infidelity in others. Maddened with jealousy, she insisted Raymond sack Anthea, not least for her gross impertinence.

'She couldn't have meant it nastily,' pleaded Raymond, 'she's only a child.'

'So once was Adolf Eichmann.'

In an agonizing, tearful renunciation scene, Raymond told a devastated Anthea she must leave the gallery at once:

'Galena wants to try again. I can't desert her after a flop like this and I can't abandon the boys, particularly when she's so unstable. I'm so dreadfully sorry.'

'Just like Tristan and Sharon,' sighed David, highly delighted by the turn of events, as he watched Anthea sobbing all the way down Cork Street.

As if trying to disguise the death of an apple tree by growing a rambler rose over it, Raymond and Galena's attempt at reconciliation was fleeting. Galena was of the pre-pill generation and invariably forgot to put her Dutch cap back in its box. As a result of the rubber being punctured by Shrimpy's sharp teeth, she was enraged in February to find herself pregnant again. But abortions were not on the cards for healthy married women, unless you could prove mental instability – which admittedly would not have been difficult.

As the nine months passed, Galena sank deeper into depression. Her doctor had banned alcohol; but finding his desperately needed glass of whisky having no effect in the evenings, Raymond discovered the Bell's bottle had been three-quarters filled with water. The following day, he found Galena swigging green mouth-wash from the bottle. This turned out to be crème de menthe. During previous pregnancies, Galena had decorated a bedroom for each child, but this time no Orpheus and his bewitched entourage sprang to life on the walls of the new baby's room.

Lovers also fell away. Casey and Joan were painting in Australia, Etienne de Montigny had a new mistress, Rupert had married an American beauty appropriately called Helen, a great fan of Galena's, who even wanted a picture as a wedding present.

'Fuck off,' had screamed Galena.

Her inability to forgive him for trying to bed Anthea had also soured her relationship with her little lap-dog David. This was highly embarrassing, as he and Rosemary had been bought the Old Rectory next door by Sir Mervyn. David avoided Foxes Court by spending most of his time working in London. Rosemary, busy supervising builders, however, saw a lot of Galena. Rosemary was about to give birth herself, but found time to play with Jonathan and read to Alizarin who, still ill, was bearing the brunt of his mother's histrionics.

Jupiter, when he came home from Bagley Hall, worried Rosemary the most. Withdrawn, cold eyed, he was still desperately jealous of his younger brother. Winning the history prize and scoring endless tries for the second fifteen were no substitute for being the centre of his mother's constant if neurotic attention.

Galena spent a lot of time scribbling dark thoughts in her diary. Right up to the birth, which she insisted on having at home so she could continue to drink, she also carried on painting: producing doomladen landscapes dominated by thunderclouds and birds of prey, eerily reminiscent of the black crows in Van Gogh's last corn-fields.

On 7 October 1973, she gave birth to a beautiful six-pound daughter, Sienna Sylvie, who did not emerge, as Rupert Campbell-Black predicted, with a glass of red in one hand and a fag in the other.

Two days later, whilst Mr and Mrs Robens were having an afternoon off, Galena unaccountably despatched the maternity nurse to the cinema. Alone at Foxes Court with Alizarin and the baby, she haemorrhaged and was found dead in a sea of blood at the bottom of the stairs.

People were alerted to the tragedy by the hysterical yapping of a blood-stained Shrimpy and the screams of Alizarin who, having been unaccountably locked in his room, despite his arthritis, had somehow clambered onto the roof. Utterly traumatized, he was unable to tell the police what had happened.

Poor Raymond was arrested for twenty-four hours and then released. There was no proof of misconduct. No-one had picked up on the fact that Galena had clean hair and was wearing scent and make-up for the first time in months. Her diary, which might have provided clues, and which on her instructions was not to be read before October 2000, had been seized and hidden by Raymond's elder sister Lily, who had recently moved into the cottage overlooking the river. Suicide was suspected but could not be proved. The coroner recorded a verdict of death by misadventure.

At midnight a week later, Anthea Rookhope was returning from a very spartan package holiday in Spain, where none of the men were as gentlemanly as Raymond. It was over a year since she'd joined the Belvedon Gallery and enjoyed the happiest weeks of her life. Poor darling Raymond, she prayed every day that he would have the courage to leave that awful bitch. But he was so vague, he'd probably lost her address, particularly now that dopey Fiona was back working for him.

Barcelona Airport had been on strike and at mid-night was still unbearably hot, with the flights all up the creek. Anthea had already waited three hours.

'Go away,' she hissed at a leering porter, 'I don't want anything carried.'

Tomorrow, she'd have to start looking for a job, though it'd be simpler to go into a convent. She was desperately hungry and thirsty, but only had enough money for her fare back to Purley. If she reached England before the trains started she couldn't afford a taxi.

Flipping through a discarded *Sunday Express*, she gave a shriek and collapsed onto a luggage trolley. Galena, it appeared, had killed herself falling down the stair-well. Drunk again, thought Anthea. Her heartbroken husband had evidently been left with three little boys and a new-born baby.

'My sister-in-law had been depressed,' Raymond's sister, Lily, was quoted as saying, 'but she was thrilled to have a daughter. We are all convinced it was an accident.'

There was a photograph of Raymond looking devastated and devastating outside Foxes Court, and another earlier one of him, with the three boys and Galena, who had turned into a monster with several heads in Anthea's imagination, but who here appeared both happy and beautiful.

Even venomous Somerford Keynes was quoted as saying: 'Galena was one of the most exciting painters since the war, tragically cut off in her prime.'

'Not what you wrote this time last year,' muttered Anthea.

Then, abandoning her suitcase, she rushed round begging for change.

'A friend has passed away, I must phone home.'

The Foxes Court number was engraved on her thumping heart. Perhaps she shouldn't ring so late, people always thought there'd been an accident. But no

165

worse accident could have befallen those poor little children.

'Hello, who's that?' The deep musical voice was hoarse with tears and telling the press to bugger off.

'Raymond, it's Anthea, I'm so sorry.'

'Oh Hopey, I need you, please come at once.'

Anthea left all her luggage and her old life in Barcelona. Robens met her at the airport. The sun was just creeping over the horizon, warming the great golden limes as she arrived at Foxes Court.

Running out of the front door, feeling as if he'd been stung by every misfortune in the world, Raymond saw his own Hope emerging from the dark depths of the Bentley. Anthea looked so thin, pale and ill, that he realized in wonder, despite his anguish, that she had missed him quite as much as he had missed her.

'Oh my darling, never leave me again.'

No-one was remotely surprised when they were quietly married at Searston Register Office on Raymond's fiftieth birthday in May 1974. Anthea was twenty.

In a very happy marriage, one of the only setbacks was in 1987, when the Boy David, who was nearing forty, came to the realization that Raymond, who believed in primogeniture, would eventually hand over the entire business to his eldest son, Jupiter, who had joined the gallery after coming down from Cambridge.

David couldn't face working for steely, arrogant Jupiter. He was also fed up with being patronized and told to go off and open a bottle if he suggested a painting was 'wrong'. He also felt Raymond had taken too much credit for an Etienne de Montigny retrospective at the Tate for which David had done all the leg work.

In turn, Raymond and Jupiter felt too many people, when they rang the gallery, were asking for the Pulborough. David was getting far too much post and too many critics were putting 'the Belvedon and the Pulborough' in reviews, three extra words which would be better employed saying, 'staggeringly beautiful pictures', observed Jupiter.

In 1987, therefore, David had walked out of the Belvedon with all Raymond's contacts and mailing lists, taking with him several of the gallery's biggest artists.

As Sir Mervyn had died in 1986, Rosemary's inheritance had been plundered to start up David's own gallery, which was named the Pulborough and which was defiantly situated right opposite the Belvedon in Cork Street. Both galleries did well in the art boom of the Eighties, survived the disastrous slump of the early Nineties, but by 1998, the Pulborough, to Jupiter's fury, was edging ahead of the Belvedon.

In 1995, David had been joined in the business by his son Barney, a fat pinstripe-suited slug, who also had shares in a Mayfair gambling club, which came in useful laundering any of the Pulborough's shadily gotten gains. Barney was very dodgy indeed.

Raymond's six children, who now included the twins, Dicky and Dora, born to him and Anthea in 1990, referred to Barney and David as 'Punch and Judas'. Raymond, who'd been devastated by David's defection, still loved him, but there was spiky and bitter competition between the two galleries and the two adjoining households in Limesbridge.

2

19

1998

As Sir Raymond Belvedon prepared to leave Foxes
Court on a chilly October morning in 1998, gold leaves
were tumbling thickly out of the lime trees, symbolizing
the money his gallery had made and the spiritual riches
his programmes had brought to so many viewers.
Having consolingly patted his brindle greyhound,
Grenville, who was sulking on the bed, Raymond briefly
admired his reflection in his dressing-room mirror. Still
spare and splendid looking at seventy-four, with bright
blue eyes and a shock of silvery white hair, Raymond
had, as a result of his second wife's constant flattery and
expert laundering, become even more of a dandy, with
a penchant for pastel ties, mauve silk handkerchiefs
wafting Extract of Lime and slightly waisted pearl-grey
suits.

This flamboyance, together with a belief that you
must entertain any audience in front of you, and an
ability to listen and gently draw out the most difficult
artist or critic, had made him in the last ten years a great
hit on television.

On the doorstep, Raymond said goodbye to his
eight-year-old twins, Dicky and Dora, who were on half-
term, and to his wife. Soft and fragile in pearls and
cornflower-blue cashmere, Anthea at forty-five was still

enchantingly pretty without a wrinkle or a grey hair. Raymond gave her a special hug, knowing she was dying to accompany him. Wild horses, however, couldn't have dragged Anthea away from a meeting that afternoon of the Limesbridge Improvement Society in which a Galena Borochova Memorial would be discussed yet again.

As Galena had immortalized Limesbridge and stopped developers slapping houses all over the Silver Valley (which was now designated an Area of Outstanding Natural Beauty), there was a desire in the village to honour her memory with a statue in the High Street. There was also pressure on Raymond to transform one of his nicer cottages into a museum of Galena memorabilia.

Anthea, who had a hang-up about Raymond's first wife, had managed to quash any public recognition of the twenty-fifth anniversary of Galena's death last week. She was also opposing any statue on the false grounds that it would evoke painful memories for Raymond and Galena's four children. There was no way she was going to let the pro-Galena faction gain ground behind her back, and so she reluctantly waved her husband and his chauffeur-cum-head gardener Robens off in the Bentley.

'Cheerio, cheerio.' Anthea's once squeaky little voice had become very grand over the years, particularly since she had become Lady Belvedon when Raymond was knighted last April.

Great mirth had been caused earlier in the month when Anthea had gone into the crowded village shop, asked for *The Times*, then, opening it on the social page, had shrieked, 'Oh heavens, *how* embarrassing, they've remembered my birthday.'

Nor was she amused now when Rosemary Pulborough, in awful gardening clothes, reared up over the wall of the Old Rectory next door and sarcastically asked the departing Raymond to give her love to David, if he saw him later.

'David definitely told me he was going to Penscombe,' Anthea called out to Rosemary. It gave her pleasure to remind Rosemary that she and David confided on a regular basis. Serve Rosemary right for supporting the idea of a memorial to Galena.

Raymond sighed and closed the window. At the bottom of the drive Robens turned right past the Lodge where Alizarin lived, with its garden full of nettles, past the approaching scarlet post van buckling under Raymond's fan mail, past Visitor, Alizarin's rotund, grinning yellow Labrador, rustling purposefully through the leaves. Thursdays were dustbin days: all sorts of goodies would be forthcoming inside punctured black bags.

Raymond sighed again. The Limesbridge Improvement Society this afternoon would no doubt complain yet again about Alizarin's nettles and Visitor's binning habits.

The whole day was bound to stir up painful memories. There had been much fuss in the press recently about owners of national treasures reneging on pledges to make them accessible to the public in return for huge tax benefits.

Rupert Campbell-Black, for example, had stalled and stalled, but today had finally agreed to put his stunning collection of pictures on show in his beautiful house in nearby Gloucestershire. Raymond was covering the event for the BBC and as an old friend of Rupert, who had sold the odd picture to pay for a horse or a Campbell-Black wedding, was being allowed a preview before the crowds poured in. He smiled slightly when he heard, on the car wireless, that there was a ten-mile tailback on the M4, caused by busloads of eager women and gays storming down from London to gaze at the divinely handsome Rupert rather than his paintings.

Raymond turned to his morning ritual, checking the

three Ds: Divorce, Deaths and Debtors in his beloved *Times*, sussing out who might suddenly be flush or needing money, or getting rid of an important picture.

Ever since he had comforted Rupert's ex-wife Helen after the murder of Roberto Rannaldini, her famous conductor husband, in 1996, and been rewarded with the task of selling the Murillo Madonna which he had achieved at a record price, Raymond had been nick-named 'the widow's mate'. Beside him on the back seat was a delicious cake in a beribboned striped box, which, after visiting Rupert, Raymond would take on to the recently widowed Clemency Waterlane at Rutminster Hall, urging her to eat to keep up her strength, and gently persuading her that parting with the Waterlane Titian would be the easiest way out of estate duty.

A great favourite with the Queen Mother and Lady Thatcher, Raymond had long advised both the royal family and the Tories, and was currently looking for an artist to paint Prince William.

And there was Rupert's house, lounging like a vol-uptuous blonde against its orange pillow of beech woods. In the early Eighties Rupert had switched from showjumping to national hunt racing, branching out into flat racing as well in the early Nineties. His extremely successful yard lay to the west of the house.

Rupert, not wanting to be ogled by the masses, had clearly done a bunk. Raymond was relieved to be able to walk through the rooms admiring the often dirty and badly lit pictures on his own, overwhelmed by a sick, churning, very painful excitement as so much of Galena's past returned.

At the top of Rupert's stairs hung a huge oil by her long-term lover, Etienne de Montigny. This showed Galena as Circe turning men into swine. There had been a row at the time, because Rupert had complained the pigs were saddlebacks, a breed not invented in 2000 BC, and demanded his money back.

Next door was *A Storm on Exmoor* by Casey Andrews, who with brutal insensitivity was, even twenty-five years after Galena's death, giving interviews claiming to be her greatest love. Raymond was ashamed he hadn't sacked Casey as a gallery artist, but as poetic justice he had at least made a killing out of the disgusting old goat.

And there in the dark of the landing – Raymond caught his breath, heart pounding – was Galena's ravishing drawing of a naked Rupert asleep in the crimson-curtained four-poster in the Blue Tower. Raymond so clearly remembered that warm summer evening when Sir Mervyn and Rosemary had arrived unexpectedly and Galena had ordered Rupert to remain upstairs.

Galena had later described how Rupert had made love to her and on occasions even allowed Raymond, through the two-way mirror she had had installed in the Blue Tower door, to watch her with Rupert or other lovers. This had been the greatest turn-on of Raymond's life. He had been so happy with Anthea, she had put him first, built up his career and confidence. He owed her everything, but she had never turned his loins to liquid as Galena had done.

To discourage the crowds, Rupert had turned off the central heating. Raymond shivered, then jumped as his mobile rang. He was due to join his television crew in a minute, but it was Anthea checking he was all right.

'*Newsnight* wondered if you'd be in town this evening, Melvyn wants you on the *South Bank Show* next month, and you'll never guess: *Good Housekeeping* want to interview me,' Anthea giggled, 'for a feature on wonderful wives. I can't think why.'

'I can, my darling, you *are* wonderful.'

'Well, don't forget to give my special love to Rupert.'

'I won't, and, Hopey, don't forget to turn on the alarm when you go out.'

Alizarin, glowering like Cerberus at the bottom of the drive, was not a sufficient deterrent to burglars. Now

Raymond had become a cult figure, they couldn't be too careful.

Raymond was glad Anthea had not accompanied him. She had a totally unreciprocated crush on Rupert, who could be embarrassingly curt with those he didn't like. And she would certainly have acted up at the number of Galena's pictures on the walls. This caused Raymond pain of a different kind. Galena's work had rocketed in value since her death. What a tragedy that on Anthea's insistence he'd sold so many of them back in 1974. They'd be worth a fortune today. He'd also tragically let Anthea paint over Galena's murals. The fiercely protected children's rooms were about the only ones left intact.

As he moved towards the film crew at the end of the long gallery, admiring on the way the Lucian Freud of a muscular nude lying beside a whippet striped like a humbug, Raymond found himself still trembling. Galena's end had been so terrible, what with the ghastly haemorrhaging, and baby Sienna screaming herself blue, and Alizarin never mentioning his mother's name again, and Raymond himself discovering blood-baths in the Blue Tower as well as the bottom of the stairs, and all with the Raphael smiling serenely down.

'Oh Christ.' Raymond sucked in his breath.

For there on the wall was Galena's adorable drawing of Shrimpy, her little Jack Russell, who'd been found bloodstained and whimpering under her skirts.

After her death, Raymond couldn't face the thought of sleeping in the Blue Tower so Anthea, with the help of Mary Fox Linton, had knocked through walls to make a beautiful bedroom on the floor below. The Raphael, on the other hand, had remained locked away in the Blue Tower, so no-one saw it except the children when they asked permission, or he and Anthea when less and less frequently they made love up there.

'We're ready, Sir Raymond.' It was his director. 'Are you OK? You look dreadfully pale. Make-up's in the bootroom, I'll get you a coffee. Stunning collection, isn't it? We thought we'd kick off with the Turner.'

'And end up with the Rubens,' said Raymond, which he knew Rupert was keen to sell.

As Raymond finished filming, the crowds started pouring in, mobbing him, because he was a star and exuded such kindness on television that everyone thought they knew him.

As he quickly signed autographs, he was suddenly aware of a beautiful girl thrusting out her catalogue. She was ravishingly but rather unsuitably dressed for sight-seeing in a waisted royal blue and green striped velvet suit, sheer dark tights and very high heels. She had long black shiny Pre-Raphaelite hair, luminous white skin, with the peach flush of an August sunset, the tiniest nose, smudged pink lips as though she'd eaten too many raspberries, and she smelt deliciously of violets.

Her demurely cast-down eyelids with their thick dark brown fringe of lash seemed almost too heavy to lift as she watched him scrawl his name. Then slowly she looked up, her eyes like huge green traffic lights. Go, they seemed to entice him. Go deep into my soul. Go fall in love with me. Raymond was jolted.

'Dear God, but someone must paint you, my child. Your destiny is to see your face endlessly immortalized in pictures.'

'On the contrary,' replied the girl in a surprisingly clipped Sloaney voice. 'It's me who wants to immortalize you.'

Her name, she told him, was Emerald Cartwright. She was a sculptor who'd just left Chelsea College of Art and never missed his programmes.

'I want to do your head, it's such a noble one. Will you look at my portfolio?'

'Where's Rupert, where's Rupert?' demanded the crowd behind, which was getting larger and more impatient by the second and which included, as well as gays, Knightsbridge beauties and wrinklies, a tidal wave of schoolgirls on half-term and secretaries on spurious sick leave.

'Ring the gallery and make an appointment,' a blushing Raymond shouted over the din as he handed Emerald his card.

'What's your next programme about?' she shouted back.

'I'm working on a documentary about Raphael.'

Next moment, a tall man in a gorilla mask pushed his way through the screaming masses and disappeared through a door marked 'Private'. It was Rupert avoiding the crush.

20

Raymond, who was feeling exhausted, was so grateful he'd been invited to lunch. On his way to Rupert's private quarters, he laughed to see Somerford Keynes mincing along, almost concave from trying to tuck in his fat bottom and tummy, getting out a huge spy-glass to examine Galena's drawing of Rupert's very public hindquarters.

Raymond met Rupert on the way in. Nimrod the lurcher and assorted dogs were noisily and joyfully weaving round their master, who was immediately called away to answer the telephone, which gave Raymond a chance to look round.

The house, surprisingly shabby, was packed with beautiful, chipped and often threadbare pieces, gathered at random over the last 250 years by a family who'd always been more interested in horses, dogs and each other. Anthea's exquisite needlework would have worked wonders.

Raymond admired a huge oil of a rotund black Labrador, the great-great-grandfather of Alizarin's yellow Labrador, Visitor. He was also gratified to see charming pastels of Rupert's children and grandchildren by one of the Belvedon's most successful gallery artists, Daisy France-Lynch.

Daisy was so pretty, but so had been that ravishing Emerald Cartwright. And now Raymond found himself embraced by another beauty almost as tall as himself . . . for a second he was pressed against the soft breasts, tickled by the cloudy dark hair, bewitched by the silver-grey eyes and sweet anxious smile of Rupert's wife, Taggie.

'Oh, how lovely to see you, Raymond, you look frozen, you poor thing, would you like one of Rupert's jerseys? There's a nice fire in the drawing room. I've got to race, too rude but I promised to take Bianca to *Cats*. I've left you a sort of picnic.' Then, lowering her voice: 'I'm so pleased you're here to cheer up Rupert. He's absolutely fed up with all these people.'

Rupert had gone into the drawing room.

'There he is,' mouthed eager voices at the window; a second later it was filled with screaming excited faces.

'Fuck off,' snarled Rupert, nearly bringing down the curtains as he dragged them together.

The sight of Rupert's wife and daughter disappearing in the familiar dark blue helicopter stepped up the fever.

Seated at the kitchen table with his back to the Aga, Raymond felt much more cheerful after a large glass of claret, a bowl of leek soup and home-made brown bread. He had been a friend of Rupert's profligate father Eddie, often selling pictures for him to pay off various wives and gambling debts. He had also just after the war sold Eddie a Rubens of a nude Diana bathing with her naked nymphs for £5,000. Rupert, who wanted more capital to buy horses, was interested in selling it.

'Beautiful picture,' enthused Raymond.

'My father loved it for obvious reasons, I can't stand great lardy lesbians. What's it worth?'

'Five or six million.'

Rupert whistled.

'Wouldn't go through the auction houses. The Louvre, the Met and the National Gallery would certainly be interested. I could have a word.' Raymond tried to keep the excitement out of his voice.

Rupert picked up this excitement as he placed a Stilton, a glistening apricot flan and a jug of thick cream on the table.

He approved of Raymond's venal streak. Old Shrimp Villy had also been amazingly forgiving over Galena. Rupert felt he owed him.

'OK,' he said, 'you handle it.'

While they argued idly over commission and what horses Rupert had running at Cheltenham next month, Rupert spooned up apricot flan with great speed. It was so delicious, Raymond took his time.

'Marvellous cook, your Taggie.'

Rupert, like Raymond, had profited from an extremely happy second marriage. He was still arrogant, short fused, irrational and spoilt, but, tamed by the sweet, gentle Taggie, he was no longer relentlessly promiscuous nor insanely possessive. He was also a wonderful father and a fiercely loyal friend. Age had given character and strength and a few lines to the flawless face, but no extra flesh. In his presence, Raymond could look nowhere else.

'Did you see that incredibly beautiful dark girl?' he asked. 'Thought she might be one of yours.'

'Christ, I hope not – one can't be too careful with DNA.'

Briefly they discussed Rupert's adopted children, who were both black. Xavier, the boy, who was at Bagley Hall with Raymond's son, Dicky, had gone hunting.

'He won't get many more chances,' grumbled Rupert, 'with Blair fucking up the country, or "rural areas" as it's now known. Can you imagine fighting for King and rural area? I wonder how the saboteurs will play it. Xav could sue them for racism if they pull him off his pony. How's that very stylish child who tipped green paint over Casey Andrews?'

'Alizarin? Hardly a child. He's thirty-four and six foot two and insists on haunting war zones portraying human suffering on huge canvasses – probably still trying to blot out the horror of Galena's death. I really shouldn't,' he added, as Rupert filled up his glass.

'Do you good, you're not driving,' said Rupert, who thought Raymond was looking very fragile. 'Alizarin got over his rheumatoid arthritis then?'

'Mostly. He gets stiff and he limps in damp weather. But he never complains about it.' Raymond shook his head sadly. 'I can't get close to Alizarin. And he'll never forgive Jupiter, who always had it in for him, for stealing and marrying the only girl Al ever really loved. Alizarin used to be incredibly close to Jonathan. Now they're separated by Alizarin's failure to sell anything and Jonathan's huge success.

'Jonathan reminds me of you when you were a boy,' went on Raymond with a smile, 'far too successful and good looking for his own good. He just had to bat his long lashes at the masters at school.'

'Thanks,' said Rupert acidly. 'From what I've read Jonathan spends his time shagging and punching critics. What about the girl?'

'Sienna? Most screwed up of the lot,' said Raymond wearily. 'Gives poor darling Anthea a frightful time. I had to stop vilifying the Turner Prize when she was shortlisted last year, but it was frightfully embarrassing.'

Sienna's entry, he explained, following the trend for celebrating bodily fluids, had been called *Tampax Tower*, and was built of used tampons sent her by women of substance. Women beyond menopausal age had been allowed to cheat and dip theirs in red ink.

'It wasn't funny,' protested Raymond as Rupert started to laugh. 'What boundaries are there left for young artists to push through?'

Sienna had been much photographed riding round Limesbridge on a motorbike in the nude.

'I know they had a rackety start,' said Raymond dolefully, 'but Anthea and I have tried so hard to make up for it.'

It was such a relief to be able to discuss his and Galena's children. He always found it difficult in front of Anthea.

'How are your lot?' he asked. 'I heard Marcus's prom. He gets better and better.'

'Perdita's playing polo for the American team,' said Rupert, shoving the Stilton in Raymond's direction, 'Tab's expecting a baby any minute, then she's going to train for the Sydney Olympics – got a great horse. She and Wolfie (he's a dream) are in France. He's producing Tristan de Montigny's latest film.'

'They've done terribly well,' said Raymond enviously.

'They were hellish on the way up,' conceded Rupert. 'It's all due to Taggie, she's been a wonderfully unwicked stepmother.'

'Anthea's been wonderful too,' said Raymond with slightly less conviction, then his eyes filled with tears. 'And I can never fail to be amazed that such a lovely young girl, thirty years younger than me, has given me nearly twenty-five years of undivided love.'

Rupert, who passionately regretted a one-minute stand with Anthea in the back of his Rolls on the night of Galena's last disastrous exhibition, said nothing.

Watching his host ripping off black grapes with still sun-tanned fingers which must have once given Galena such pleasure, Raymond was overwhelmed with a sick craving to bring her back by asking Rupert the extent of their affaire. But Rupert was getting restless, longing to get back to the yard. Jumping up, he peered through the curtains.

'Oh Christ, here comes Augustus John Thomas.'

Casey Andrews, in a big velour hat and Norfolk jacket, could be seen striding towards the house, bellowing like an MFH on Boxing Day, so the crowd would recognize England's greatest painter.

'His prices are bigger than his canvasses,' said Rupert

sourly, 'and his last exhibition looked as though you'd unleashed an orang-utan with a space gun. The old bugger's only here to see his picture's hung where everyone can see it and to try and persuade me to let him paint Taggie. Christ!'

'Casey's a trustee of the Tate,' Raymond shook his head sadly, 'so one has to be nice to him. Means he can block any artist he chooses from being hung there. Alizarin hasn't a hope after drenching him with paint.'

As Rupert, back in his gorilla mask, saw Raymond off, they laughed to see David Pulborough scuttling in from the car park, smoothing his thinning tawny hair and adjusting his clothes over a spreading waistline.

'He's got so grand now he won't travel in the same car as his chauffeur,' observed Rupert, 'but you should hear him dropping his haitches when he's called in to tell New Labour what to put on their walls.'

'He's covered his drive with gravel that looks like chopped chicken breast,' said Raymond. 'Oh God, I mustn't be bitchy.'

'Probably late because he's been screwing some slag,' pronounced Rupert with all the disapproval of the reformed rake.

'Expect it's Geraldine Paxton. Yes, it is,' said Raymond, as a gaunt beauty, pretending to arrive from another part of the car park, holding up a hand mirror as she frantically applied scarlet lipstick, rushed towards them.

'Ghastly whore,' added Raymond with unusual venom. 'But we have to suck up to her, like Casey, because she's on the Arts Council and has such a pull with Saatchi and the Tate. Geraldine, my *dear*, how lovely to see you,' he called out. 'Rupert's pictures are to die for. You have a treat in store. Afternoon, David,' he added acidly. 'Saw your wife earlier, she sent lots of love.'

Geraldine and David's mouths became even tighter than Rupert's security, as Robens, who'd been enjoying the crumpet still queueing up to enter the house, noticed his master and drove up in the Bentley.

'Hope today hasn't been too much of a bugger,' said Rupert, lowering his voice as he opened the door for Raymond, 'Galena would have loathed growing old. Couldn't survive without male adulation. Her looks were beginning to go.'

'So are yours in that ridiculous mask,' chided Raymond to hide how touched he was by Rupert's solicitude. Then, unable to resist asking: 'Do you miss her?'

'Oh, of course,' lied Rupert.

'Thank you,' mumbled Raymond, then rallying: 'Lady Belvedon sent her love.'

Meanwhile, over in Larkshire in the village hall, Anthea was addressing a not entirely compliant Limesbridge Improvement Society.

'My husband's late wife had many unsuitable men friends with whom she indulged in – well, orgies at Foxes Court. Do we really want our village associated with that sort of thing? The press so love muck-raking and Ay cannot have Sir Raymond upset. After all, he is no longer young.'

If Galena had lived, Anthea thought fretfully, she'd now be sixty-six, a bloated old wino living in Cardboard City, who'd never have coped with her frightful children. But because she was dead everyone idolized her. And there was ghastly Rosemary Pulborough, still in her gardening clothes, with an Alice band rammed into her electrocuted haystack hair, fanning the flames.

Whatever jokes Anthea and David made about Rosemary, nicknaming her the 'Wardress' because she was always watching them, it irritated the hell out of Anthea that her stepchildren were all unaccountably devoted to Rosemary.

Not wanting to snore or dribble in front of Robens, Raymond fought sleep. He should never have accepted that third glass of claret. As the Bentley rolled down Rupert's drive, he observed the Stubbs-like serenity of sleek, beautiful horses grazing beneath amber trees, and thought wryly of the worry Galena's children caused him: Sienna, drinking too much, sleeping around, rowing with Anthea; Alizarin, tormented and unapproachable; Jonathan always in trouble. He'd started conducting with his cock during a boring television programme last week. Worst of all was Jupiter, constantly questioning his father's every decision, implying it was high time Raymond retired.

'"A doubtful throne is ice on summer seas,"' sighed Raymond.

Jupiter's eye, alas, was not as good as David's, nor was he as adept at buttering up clients and wooing young artists – which was one of the reasons the Belvedon was in danger of dropping behind the Pulborough. Odd how it still upset him to see David.

Lying back, Raymond shut his eyes. Tomorrow he would ring the National Gallery about Rupert's Rubens, and perhaps that ravishing child with green eyes would turn up to sculpt his head.

Quoting his favourite Tennyson:

'Death closes all: but something e'er the end,
Some work of noble note, may yet be done,
Not unbecoming men that strove with gods.'

Raymond fell asleep.

21

Emerald Cartwright, the girl with green eyes, had been adopted as a very small baby by parents who had adored and hopelessly indulged her for the past twenty-five years. Despite being brought up in a beautiful Georgian house in Yorkshire with stables, tennis courts, a long drive and fields, despite being sent to a smart boarding school in the south, and later to art college in London, where she had been bought a sweet little house in Fulham to share with her sister Sophy, Emerald felt fate had dealt her a cruel hand.

A great fantasist, who regarded herself as a cross between Carmen and Scarlett O'Hara, Emerald imagined she was a princess's daughter who'd been kidnapped at birth. She hadn't fallen in love with any of the hordes of men who ran after her because in her dreams she was saving herself for the prince or great artist she knew to be her real father.

Rupert Campbell-Black had had legions of women before falling for his second wife, Taggie. Maybe while he'd been married to his first wife, thought Emerald longingly, he'd had a fling with some dark beauty too proud to tell him she was pregnant, who had given her baby girl up for adoption.

Always the winner of any head-turner prize, Emerald was unfazed by everyone staring at her as she wandered round the house. She was only interested in catching sight of Rupert and looking at his pictures.

Emerald was small, only five feet. As the crowds in front of her suddenly became a screaming mob, desperate for a glimpse of their idol, she wailed that she couldn't see. Next moment a pair of hands closed round her tiny waist, lifting her up, and she saw the back of Rupert's sleek blond head as he vanished like the White Rabbit through another door.

'Hell, I've missed him again.'

Breathing in expensive aftershave which she recognized as CK One, Emerald glanced down and noticed the hands were suntanned and ringless. Returned to earth, she swung round and gasped because the man towering over her was twenty years younger than Rupert but almost as handsome. Her eyes were level with his breast bone. Between the second and third button of his black shirt, she could see a silver Star of David. A charcoal-grey bomber jacket emphasized wide shoulders, black jeans showed off lean gym-honed hips and long legs. Glancing up she saw black stubble on a square jaw, a jutting pudgy lower lip, hawklike Mephistophelean features, a smooth olive complexion, thick dark lashes fringing unblinking yellow eyes. Although his black glossy close-cropped hair was flecked with grey, he didn't look a day over thirty.

Wow, thought Emerald, he's like Bagheera in *The Jungle Book*.

He then introduced himself in Bagheera's deep purring voice as Zachary Ansteig, an American journalist doing a piece on Rupert's open day for a New York art magazine called *Mercury*.

'This guy's like the Pied Piper,' he drawled. 'If he walked into that lake over there, there wouldn't be a faggot or a woman left in England. What's his interest in art?'

'Mostly dynastic,' said Emerald. 'He chiefly commissions contemporary portraits of his family and his animals. The rest are Old Masters handed down by previous generations.'

'Lot of Borochovas,' observed Zac, turning to Galena's drawing of Shrimpy. 'She's getting really big in the States. I guess she and Rupert were an item.'

Emerald, who didn't want to think of Rupert being an item with anyone but herself, was thrilled nevertheless that Zac was following her round.

But although she showed off her knowledge of art, making risqué remarks about the pictures and regaling him with gossip about Casey Andrews and Somerford Keynes, who nearly put his neck out gazing at Zac as he passed them, Zac didn't react. There was a sinister stillness about him. He seemed only interested in examining each picture, and kept diving into cordoned-off rooms for recces, until Rupert's minions chucked him out. He made no notes for his piece.

'Are you a burglar?' asked Emerald.

'Maybe,' said Zac.

She found it disconcerting that the crowds, perhaps as compensation for not seeing Rupert, gazed at Zac, rather than herself, and was gratified when a passing David Pulborough gave her an undressing glance behind Geraldine Paxton's immaculately tailored back.

'I should have done a number on that guy,' she taunted Zac, 'he's rumoured to be even better hung than his pictures and the Pulborough's hotter for young artists than the Belvedon these days. That's his mistress with him – one of the great movers and shakers of the art world.'

They had reached the last room on the tour. As anxious to see Rupert as Emerald, the sinking sun was peering in through the jasmine-covered window, casting lace patterns on a lovely Constable of Cotchester Cathedral. Outside the crowds could be seen trailing disconsolately towards the car park.

'Let's try and get to see him,' Emerald begged Zac,

'I'm sure he'd give you a quick interview if you plugged his racehorses and the yard.'

Glancing at his watch, Zac shook his head.

'I've got to catch a train to Paddington. Great meeting you.'

Irked by his indifference, Emerald was amazed to find herself offering Zac a lift back to London, when she was in fact headed for a dance in Dorset.

As they walked towards her car, a young boy on a muddy grey pony came hurtling across the fields, flying over stone wall and fence, haughtily scattering the crowds on his way into the yard.

'That must be Xavier, Rupert's adopted son,' said Emerald in excitement.

This is the world I belong to, she told herself firmly.

Reaching her car, a Golf convertible which smelled like she did of violets, she plugged in a CD of Abigail Rosen playing Tchaikovsky's violin concerto and kicked off her shoes. She was so small, her car seat had to be pushed so far forward that the long-legged Zac found himself addressing the back of her head.

He also clocked the emerald earrings, the Tiffany cross, the Cartier watch with diamond numbers, the black leather Dunhill case in the back. She was a fast but excellent driver. Her mobile rang the whole time, all men with trembling voices asking for dates.

'I guess that's the reason there's a man shortage in London,' mocked Zac, 'all the guys are calling you.'

Away from Rupert's pictures he became more chatty. Without eye contact, Emerald also found herself expanding under his questioning, explaining that like Rupert's younger children, she was adopted, but had never felt she fitted in.

'Plato believed in adoption,' observed Zac. 'He said kids were much better raised by other people, whose expectations weren't so high.'

'I just feel I'm with the wrong family,' sighed Emerald. 'My adoptive parents are so straight and horsey, and I *hate* horses, and they're so buttoned up about their feelings. They've been good to me, so it seems ungrateful to ask about my natural parents.'

'Who were they anyway?'

'My natural father didn't have the guts to sign the birth certificate,' said Emerald bitterly.

'Perhaps he was a God who turned into a swan or a shower of gold to impregnate your mom,' teased Zac. 'You look kinda goddess-like. He could hardly put Shower of Gold on a birth certificate.'

Emerald was not in the mood for jokes.

'I often think he could have been high profile, and not wanted a scandal. My mother worked in an art gallery.

'If you want to know what it's like to be blind, walk around with your eyes shut,' she added bitterly. 'But if you want to find out what it's like to be adopted, go on the tube and look at any couple sitting next to you, smart, ugly, arguing, holding hands – they could be your parents. Any guy I go out with could be my brother or my father. I feel like an unstarted symphony.' Emerald's voice was rattling now. 'I have no past.'

'It's your future that matters.'

As Abigail Rosen launched into the last stampeding movement of the Tchaikovsky, Emerald reached the motorway, and symbolically rammed her foot down.

'I always feel as though I'm hurtling into a future without knowing where I've come from. You've no idea how hard that is.' She glanced round at Zac: so fit, tanned and elitist. 'I bet you come from a glamorous family.'

'They were mostly wiped out in concentration camps,' said Zac flatly, 'I've got no past either, that makes two of us.'

'Oh God, I'm sorry.' Jolted out of her self-absorption, Emerald felt ashamed. 'They always tell you adopted children are chosen, so I'm a member of the Chosen Race too.'

Then she nearly drove off the road as Zac lifted her cascade of hair and laid a warm, caressing hand on the back of her neck.

'I was teased at school for being adopted,' she gabbled. 'They told me the reason I was small was because I hadn't come out of my mother's tummy.'

'I was beaten up for being a "Yid",' countered Zac, 'and, because I had a slight Austrian accent (which they assumed was German), for being a Nazi as well. Then the rabbi arranged for me to have judo lessons. No-one beat me up again,' he added grimly.

'You're Austrian?' said Emerald in surprise. 'I must say you don't conjure up cheery images of the Blue Danube, Glühwein and *The Sound of Music*.'

Turning to him as they reached the outskirts of London, she noticed Zac's strange gleaming cat's eyes, his face orange from the glare of the street lights, and felt unsettled and wildly attracted to him.

'When are you going back to America?' she asked and was shocked at her desolation when he said, 'Tomorrow.'

He was yawning now and talking about getting an early night. Emerald couldn't bear it. She must keep him interested.

'Did you see Raymond Belvedon? He's such a duck, he gave me his card, he wants me to sculpt his head.'

'We get his programmes on PBS,' said Zac. 'They just adore him in the States. He used to be married to Borochova, that explains why he was there.'

'His next programme's on Raphael.'

As they reached Hammersmith, Emerald was again astounded to hear herself, who never made the running, asking Zac if he'd like to come back to Fulham for a drink.

'Sure,' he said, 'I've woken up now. Has Raymond Belvedon started shooting the programme on Raphael?'

22

Emerald lived in a charming part of Fulham, just off Parsons Green. The street of pastel houses was lined with cherry trees, whose tawny pink leaves carpeted the pavements to welcome them. Number eighteen was painted pale blue. The tiny front garden was crowded out by two dreadful-smelling dustbins and a large bicycle leaning like a dinosaur against a window box of browning plants. All the lights were blazing.

'I've been away so I don't know if my sister Sophy's here,' said Emerald, opening the bottle-green front door, then she flipped.

Sophy must have been giving a riotous lunch party for some of her obnoxious teacher friends, and they'd all pushed off to the cinema. There were flowing ashtrays, half-empty glasses everywhere, pudding plates still on the table. The sink in the kitchen was full of dirty pans. Emerald was gibbering with rage, misdialling Sophy on her mobile, which refused to answer.

'Sophy sure is a terrific cook,' said a grinning Zac who was calmly finishing up the shepherd's pie.

'Surrounding herself with lame ducks, I'm amazed she didn't feed them crusts,' raged Emerald. 'Look at her clothes hung like drunks over the radiators. Look at my plants she hasn't watered.'

The pictures were crooked, there was no milk, no loo paper downstairs, no light bulbs, drink all over the drawing-room carpets, the washing machine was full and queuing up, and there was fluff left on top of the tumble dryer.

'Bugger bugger Sophy,' screeched Emerald.

As Zac progressed to Sophy's rhubarb crumble, he wandered round the room admiring Emerald's smart invitations, interspersed with coloured cards to Sophy: all on a hangover theme.

'Darling Sophy, thanks for a wild party.'

Sophy was obviously quite a raver. Examining the photographs of a big plain raw-boned woman in hunting kit on a large horse and a straight-backed man with a moustache in a colonel's uniform, Zac could see why Emerald didn't fit in with her adopted parents. A chihuahua among mastiffs, she looked as though she came from a different planet. There was also a rather bad watercolour of a big, dark grey Georgian house at the end of a drive, over the fireplace.

'That's where we live and the bloody cow's drunk my last bottle of champagne. Thank Christ she can't fit into my clothes. Come on, let's go upstairs.

'Don't look in there!' She slammed the door on a mountain of discarded clothes on the first landing. 'That's Sophy's bedroom.'

The next flight of stairs led to a door on which hung a tapestry cushion embroidered with the words: 'Go Away'. Inside they entered a different world: serene and beautiful.

Black and white tiles covered the entire floor. In one half were emerald green curtains, a huge bed with a green and white striped counterpane, and white armchairs with bright green and cobalt-blue cushions. On the dressing table were bottles of Penhaligon's Violetta, which explained the enticing smell of violets. In the other half, equally tidy, the room was lined with white pillars topped with terracotta and bronze heads sculpted by Emerald and of astonishing brilliance. Zac was amazed that someone quite so self-absorbed should create people so distinctive and so alive. Dotted round the room were works in progress, shrouded like hooded monks in black or green plastic bags to keep the clay damp.

In the shelves were books on Epstein, Michelangelo, Rodin and Picasso. On the walls were photographs of people nose to nose with their own sculptured heads and drawings of great beauty. Zac looked at Emerald with new respect.

'This stuff is awesome.'

He was particularly drawn to a curiously romanticized painting of a darling old lady, white hair drawn back in a bun. On her lap lay knitting: a blue jumper with the word 'Charlene' in pink on the front. She was holding out her arms and smiling. Along the bottom of the painting, Emerald had written in green ink: 'My real grandmother'.

Zac whistled.

'Omigod, what did your adopted grandmom say?'

'She went ballistic,' said Emerald happily. 'It won a prize at school. They printed it in the local paper. Forget Whistler's *Mother*. Emerald's Real Granny got much better reviews. She's such a bitch, Granny Cartwright. One day, she said: "Isn't it a pity none of my grandchildren have green eyes." Mummy protested: "Emerald does." And Granny Cartwright said, "No, I mean my real grandchildren."'

Emerald had taken a bottle of Chablis from the fridge, but even with one of those foolproof silver fish corkscrews, her hands were shaking so much, she buggered the cork. Zac took it from her.

'It's OK, baby.' Putting the bottle down, he ran a soothing hand down her hair.

'It isn't,' snapped Emerald. 'Look at my mother and father.' She pointed to another photograph of the plain, straight, middle-aged couple, this time in evening dress. 'We're light years apart.'

Glancing into the other half of the room, Zac noticed

above the bed a ravishingly executed painting of a beautiful prince and princess, who bore a strong resemblance to Rupert and Taggie Campbell-Black, and again in green writing underneath: 'My real parents'.

Below hung a beautiful drawing of a cat, which Zac recognized as by Galena Borochova. On a table was a little glass case containing a musical box, a fluffy green hippo and a yellowing once-white cardigan.

'Those were presents given me by my real mother,' explained Emerald in a trembling voice, 'before she handed me over. I was only three days old. What kind of a woman gives up a baby?'

'A very brave one,' said Zac gently. Christ, she was screwed up.

As he gouged out the cork and poured the Chablis into two glasses, he asked her why, as someone so slender and fragile, she'd taken up such a back-breaking profession as sculpture.

'If you're adopted *and* small, you have to prove yourself.'

'When did you start?'

'When I was eight, I brought a rock from the moors into the kitchen and picked up a knife. My parents were terrified until they saw I was carving an angel.'

'A self-portrait,' murmured Zac, the irony lost on Emerald.

They were interrupted by her mobile ringing, some young man in Dorset whose family were expecting her to arrive for dinner before the dance.

'I'm not coming. Last time I stayed, your mother called me Emeline all weekend,' snapped Emerald.

Having furiously cut him off, she proceeded to play back her messages.

'Emo, can you come to this?' 'Are you doing anything on Thursday night?' 'It's the Bramham Moor Hunt Ball on Saturday.' 'My Uncle Jimmy wondered if you'd like to sculpt my cousin's head for Aunt Molly's birthday.'

Some of them sounded like tentative Hugh Grants; others, probably fellow art students, had flat London accents. No girls rang Emerald, reflected Zac.

Emerald let the tape run to the end to wind him up. Zac didn't react, picking up a book on Degas. He'd hardly touched his drink. Out of nerves Emerald had knocked back one glass and nearly finished a second. She couldn't help herself to a third yet without appearing an old soak.

'What happened to your family?' she blurted out.

Despite his suntan, Zac's face turned as grey as the flecks in his dark hair.

'My mom was deported to a detention camp called Theresienstadt when she was two. My grandmother remained there with her briefly before being dragged off to Auschwitz. Somehow Mom survived. After the war she joined my Great-aunt Leah in New York. They were the only family left.'

Zac's voice was so matter-of-fact he might have been describing a baseball match.

'Your poor mother,' moaned Emerald. 'Did she ever get over it?'

'She died of cancer last year,' said Zac flatly. 'Just beforehand, we travelled to Auschwitz, and found my grandmother's name and convoy number in a memorial book. I guess it helped Mom to grieve. I figure the chemo zapped her; she wasn't strong enough to resist it.'

'What about your father?'

'He was a survivor – just – of Belsen. He was much older than Mom and died a couple of years after I was born.'

'Did your mother marry again?'

Zac shrugged. 'She married out. My stepfather was a car mechanic with fists.'

Emerald burst into tears. 'I'm so sorry I banged on. But at least you know who your parents were. The awful part is not knowing.'

197

'Only if someone tells you it's awful.'

Crossing the room, Zac took her in his arms; his heart was level with her ears and she could hear its steady beat. Unlike her other fumbling boyfriends, the hands that removed her velvet suit and dark blue jersey were completely steady. Pushing her gently away, he sat down on the bed.

'Let me look at you.'

Emerald tossed her head haughtily, Carmen again, so her shiny hair cascaded over her breasts. Very slowly, never taking her huge green eyes off his, she removed a pink lace bra.

What the hell was she playing at? She never went to bed with men until the fifth or sixth date, usually never, but Zac had robbed her of all willpower.

'Put your arms above your head,' he ordered.

Emerald turned around proudly and slowly. Her breasts and bottom were high, curved and full, compared with her tiny frame. The throbbing and bubbling between her legs was getting more insistent.

'Beautiful,' said Zac softly. 'My little Munch Madonna. Come here.'

Slowly he kissed her nipples until they were as hard and red as rosehips, gently rubbing her pink silk knickers over her clitoris until it stiffened in the same way.

'I mustn't,' gasped Emerald. 'Too soon. These things ought to be taken slowly,' yet found herself pulling off his shirt.

Only a long scar above his heart marred the smooth gold rippling perfection of his chest.

'Oh Zac, you're beautiful.'

Zac laughed, the stretch of perfect white teeth, the enigmatic eyes, the flying black brows reminding her unnervingly again of Mephistopheles. But his shoulders were as smooth, hard and warm as a bronze in the afternoon sun. As her sculptor's fingers moved downwards, moulding, kneading, Zac also gasped with pleasure. His black jeans fell to the floor, followed by Calvin Klein underpants.

Emerald had never been very keen on penises. Having seen too many hanging like purple wistaria on male models, she felt they were better hidden by figleaves. But Zac's sprang out so joyfully, so big, smooth and strong below his taut belly, as if it couldn't wait to give her pleasure.

Gathering her up like a doll, kissing first one lip, then another, his tongue lazily exploring her mouth, murmuring endearments, he laid her on the white counterpane. Then ripping off her knickers, he kissed her thighs above her black hold-ups, burying his face in the soft white flesh, teasing her, letting his tongue stray into every crevice. Then, just as she was quivering on the edge of orgasm, drawing away, mocking her as she begged him to go on. Now he was lying beside her, his fingers probing deeply, testing and stroking, strafing her with his thumb knuckle, until she was rigid and moaning on the brink.

'Go on, my darling,' then once more he withdrew his hand.

'*Please*, don't stop, go on,' begged Emerald.

Moving down the bed, Zac put his tongue between her legs again, mumbling that, like clay, he mustn't let her dry up.

'Don't make bloody jokes!' she sobbed.

Satisfied she was wet enough, he was on top of her, driving his wonderful cock inside her, deeper and deeper, balancing on one elbow, as his left hand cupped her tiny right hip, his stroking thumb never losing touch with her clitoris.

'Go for it, baby, go on.'

At last I know what all the fuss is about, marvelled Emerald.

Her pleasure was so intense that it was some time before she realized Zac was in the shower next door.

'That was a-mazing,' she called out to him.

'A-mazing.' A returning Zac kissed her, then, pulling his clothes onto his still wet body: 'I've got to go.'

'Can't you stay?'

'I've got a guy to meet and a very early flight.'

Emerald was in a panic: 'When are you coming back?'

'Sometime. I'll call you.' He took one of her cards from the pile on the desk.

'Where did you get that scar?'

'My stepfather threw a knife at me. What d'you expect from a goy?' and he was gone.

Bastard, thought Emerald, transporting me up to heaven, then down to hell. She was also furious when she staggered out of bed to find she'd lost Raymond Belvedon's card.

23

Emerald was so angry, she picked up the telephone and vented her rage on Sophy.

'For someone who works in a sink school, it would be nice if you could occasionally leave your own sink tidy.'

She was so busy listing Sophy's misdemeanours that it was several minutes before Sophy could get a word in edgeways.

'For God's sake, Emo, shut up, I had to come home in the middle of lunch. Daddy's been fired and it appears we've lost all our money.'

Emerald then had the temerity to go into a rant because she hadn't been told first.

'I'm the elder sister. Why are you always the one people tell things to?'

Emerald drove up to Yorkshire the following morning and found things were much worse. Colonel Ian Cartwright, her father, had for the last ten years been managing director of a small, very profitable engineering business in Pikely-in-Wharfedale. As the former commanding officer of a tank regiment, Ian Cartwright had made a successful transition to the business world because he was intelligent, hard working and very straight, which appealed to his customers. This straightness, however, combined with a military brusqueness, expecting others to jump, and an inability to flatter and drink with the boys, had not endeared him to his fellow directors.

These directors had taken him aside the previous month and persuaded him that if the business were to prosper, he must tell the chairman, who owned the company, that he ought to retire, and let Ian make the major decisions.

After nights without sleep, Ian was more brusque in his ultimatum than he intended. The chairman, a vain old tosser who liked reading Chaucer out loud to Ian's wife Patience in the evenings, was understandably outraged, and, turning furiously to the other directors, announced that Ian Cartwright wanted him out. Whereupon they denied all knowledge. Ian was sacked the following morning.

Without the back-up of his salary, Ian Cartwright admitted to his wife that he had been gambling heavily on the stock market to keep up the mortgage payments on the Fulham house which he had bought for his beloved Emerald and Sophy. Worst of all, the two sisters had not appreciated that their grand house, Pikely Hall, with its rose gardens, tennis court, swimming pool, fields and stables for their mother's two hunters, had only ever been rented. Ian had used a wing of the house as company offices, for which the gardens were a splendid showpiece.

So overnight everything was wiped out. Pikely Hall had to be vacated, the Fulham house sold. The horses, to Emerald's mother's anguish, had to go and a three-bedroom flat, in a rather seedy part of Shepherd's Bush, rented in London.

Ironically what most worried the family, the day Emerald arrived from London, was how she would cope with this change. The answer was with utter hysterics. She had always denigrated the solidarity and durability of Pikely Hall, a charcoal-grey pile with castellated turrets, only softened by Virginia creeper and shielded from the gales by great banks of rhododendrons, spiky monkey puzzles and towering Wellingtonias. But how impressed the other girls at boarding school had been when she'd scrawled Pikely Hall, Yorkshire on her infrequent letters home. Emerald wept and returned to London the next day.

She didn't return to Pikely until early January, the weekend her parents moved out. Furious to be travelling by train because her beloved Golf had had to be sold, she had nipped into the Ladies at Leeds while waiting for a connecting train.

'Baby-changing facilities', said a large sign.

Pity I can't change my parents, thought Emerald savagely.

Arriving at the Hall, finding Pickfords vans outside, she suddenly realized, despite the leafless trees and the moors stretching bleakly above, what a beautiful place it was. If only she'd been able to bring Zac here. He'd have been knocked out by such a splendid old place. Now he'd think she was worth nothing. Or he would if he'd bothered to ring her.

Overwhelmed by self-pity, Emerald sat on the balustrade gazing across the valley at the stubble of pines and the hairnet of stone walls keeping the exuberant khaki hills in check. Why the hell hadn't she painted the view while she had the chance? She sobbed so violently she developed a migraine and the local GP had to be summoned to give her some Valium.

'Does your mother get migraines?' he asked solicitously.

'I don't know,' wept Emerald, 'being adopted I have no medical history!'

Retiring to lie down, Emerald left everyone else to pack up.

The removal vans had been deliberately booked on a Saturday so Ian Cartwright's employees wouldn't be there to gloat or be embarrassed. The secretaries and lower management had loved Ian, appreciating the kind heart beneath the fierce exterior.

While her parents' rather smeary furniture disappeared into the vans, Emerald rallied and wasted her best scarlet Dior lipstick writing 'May you rot' on each Monday in the new 1999 diary of the treacherous incoming managing director.

While her mother's beloved hunters, Jake and Toby, were loaded up to be driven to a new home, Emerald glued the naked body of Marilyn Monroe, cut from a poster, onto the portrait of the chairman hanging in the boardroom, so his wrinkled petulant face peered over the top. When Emerald showed this to her mother, Patience laughed for the first time in days, then found she couldn't stop.

Having in the past spurned Sohrab, the smelly old family golden retriever, Emerald sobbed and sobbed when he was given away to a friend, because with Patience and Ian being forced out to work, it wouldn't be fair to leave a big dog all day in a London flat.

Hordes of locals with bottles turned up to say goodbye to sweet plump Sophy and her parents. Again Emerald wept.

'Why isn't anyone coming to say goodbye to me? It must be because you opted to go to the grammar school, Sophy, and have more local friends. And why haven't they mentioned my name in all the good-luck cards?'

Why the hell should they, when you played Little Lady Muck on the rare times you came up here? thought Sophy furiously.

She looked at her grey-faced, red-eyed parents as they clumsily tried to comfort a hysterical Emerald, who had not helped matters by adding her student loan and her large overdraft to her father's other debts. Why did Emerald always have to be the centre of attention?

*   *   *

Arriving in Shepherd's Bush, Patience Cartwright tried to make the best of things. Just think if they'd been kicked out of Bosnia. At least they were all together, and as Sophy'd been sweet enough to accept the tiny bedroom next to the kitchen, this meant that Emerald would be able to sleep and sculpt in the biggest bedroom overlooking the communal gardens.

Patience Cartwright was a good old girl, big boned, loud voiced, badly dressed, a dire cook, and terrible at houses, having not had to bother too hard when she was an army wife. She had tried valiantly to get on with Ian's business colleagues and their wives, but had much preferred her horsey friends. Every night and every Sunday in Pikely church, she had prayed that Tony Blair wouldn't abolish hunting.

Devastated not to be able to have her own children, she felt humbly privileged to have been able to adopt Emerald and Sophy, but when Emerald turned out so difficult, she had blamed herself for being a bad mother. Patience was not, however, deficient in guts. Having only worked hitherto on charity committees, she found a job in a local pub. The landlord had felt so sorry for her. At the age of fifty-eight, she seemed unlikely to raid the till and her ringing voice would come in useful at closing time.

Ian, who had kept going during the move, running it like a military operation – even the removal vans were his tanks – went to pieces when he reached London. Sitting for hours, he gazed into space, twisting his signet ring round and round. Demoralized by endless interviews which came to nothing, he finally took a job as a minicab driver, and had started getting fearful headaches, ostensibly from familiarizing himself with London streets, but actually because he was drinking heavily.

Sophy was wonderful and helped out with her teacher's wages. Emerald was hell, bemoaning her lot more than ever. It was OK for Sophy escaping into the excitement and bustle of the classroom, but she (Emerald) had nothing to distract her from this nightmare.

She knew she ought to be pushing for commissions, hawking her portfolio round galleries. She still hadn't been to see Raymond Belvedon. But how could she sculpt without her beautiful studio, and what would Zac, who had dominated her dreams since October, say when he saw her living in such a grotty flat?

24

Matters reached a head on a cold Saturday evening in March, just before Mothering Sunday. Ian Cartwright was gazing unseeingly at a half-finished *Daily Telegraph* crossword. His wife Patience was cooking supper, using a cheap-cut recipe for middle neck with swedes and parsnips which she had found in the *Big Issue* and which was filling the flat with a disgusting smell of stewed sheep.

Sophy, hoping to spoil her dinner by eating her way through a bar of Toblerone, was writing reports in the sitting room. Her papers littered the only part of the threadbare Persian carpet which wasn't covered with dark ugly furniture her parents couldn't afford to store.

Unashamedly plump, cheerfully referring to herself as Cellulite City, Sophy had a sweet face, lovely skin, soft blond ringlets and a merry heart beating beneath a splendid bosom. She was also a colossal trimmer. To avoid being duffed up, she always told the fearsome parents at her rough school that even the most delinquent of their children were 'real sweethearts doing brilliantly'.

'Jason has made a real contribution to the class', she was now writing in her clear round hand about the school dunce.

Jason's bricklayer dad was not the only father who after school had sidled up and asked Sophy for a date.

Sophy cheerfully slagged off Emerald behind her back, but always gave in to her face to avoid the screaming fits which so distressed their parents. Now it seemed she was too late, as a quivering Emerald flung open the sitting-room door, scattering papers.

'How dare you shrink my black drawstring flares! I was about to handwash them and you've put them on a hot wash. Now they're two inches above my ankles. They're the first pair of trousers I've bought in years, so I could save on tights, and you've gone and wrecked them.'

'That's enough, darling,' reproved her father, 'Sophy was only trying to help.'

'You always stick up for her,' Emerald turned on her father, shouting so loudly she didn't hear the clanking of the ancient lift.

It was Patience, her grey hair on end, her big face red and shiny, who, hoping to escape the storm by putting the rubbish outside, discovered a man on the doorstep. He was wearing a leather jacket, a dark grey cashmere polo neck to match his sleek flecked hair, and those black army trousers which needed such long arms to reach the pockets. He had a mahogany ski tan, strange unblinking catlike yellow eyes and smelled of the most delicious aftershave. He was so good looking, Patience was about to direct him one floor up to the charming gay actors, who to her delight had asked her if she'd mind catsitting occasionally. Then the man said in a wonderfully deep husky voice, 'I guess I've come to the wrong apartment. I'm looking for Emerald Cartwright.'

'Oh no, you haven't,' cried Patience joyfully, thinking this ravishing stranger, if anything, would lift Emerald's spirits. 'Come in, I'm her mother.'

To economize at weekends, Patience tried to wear out really old clothes. Underneath a holey brown tank top, she was sporting an orange flower-patterned shirt with a long pointed collar, a tweed knee-length gardening skirt, purple legwarmers and bedroom slippers.

Apologizing for dropping by, he'd lost Emerald's

phone number, Zac said he'd found a skip outside the house in Fulham and bags of cement in the front garden.

'A guy knocking through rooms gave me this address and sent you his best.'

'How kind,' brayed Patience. 'Such a sweet couple, one always minds less if people are nice . . . Emo's in the drawing room. Emo!'

A door slammed, rattling even Zac's strong, excellent white teeth, and a fury in a navy-blue camisole top and French knickers erupted into the hall.

'*You* must have shrunk my flares, Mum.'

Then as if a dimmer switch had been turned up and the sound turned down, light flooded Emerald's face and the screaming faded to a stammering whisper.

'Zac – how lovely to see you, what are you doing here? This is my mother.'

God, why did Patience have to look quite so grotesque?

Emerald had been turning out her room. Underwear littered the unmade bed, so she pulled on a red silk dressing gown and reluctantly led Zac into the over-crowded sitting room.

Sophy, who was lying on the carpet, gathering up her scattered reports, looked up.

'Jesus!' she gasped in wonder.

Zac grinned. 'Not quite.'

As Emerald introduced them, Zac half-mockingly clicked his heels together.

'Colonel Cartwright. Sophy.'

For the first time, Emerald noticed the trace of a German accent. Her father, whose own father had died in a POW camp, clocked it too, and rose unsteadily to his feet.

'How d'you do,' he said stiffly.

'Zac's a journalist from New York, Daddy, we met at Rupert Campbell-Black's open day,' said Emerald, rushing round, plumping cushions, gathering up

Toblerone paper, and emptying ashtrays. Oh Christ, there was an empty glass hidden under her father's chair.

'What would you like to drink? Red, white or whisky?' she asked.

Removing Emerald's tapestry, Zac sat down on the sofa, saying he'd like a Scotch and soda.

'I'll get it,' said Patience, fleeing.

Emerald had forgotten Zac's ability not to fill silences, letting others stumble into inanities.

'Did *Mercury* ever do your piece on Rupert?' she mumbled.

'It's scheduled for May.'

He was beautiful, but not awfully cosy, decided Sophy.

'What are you working on?' he asked her.

'Reports. I'm a teacher. Where did you go?'

'The Hebrew School in New York, then the University of New Hampshire.'

Emerald's father, Zac decided, was a basket case, gazing into space, food stains all over his green cardigan, his hand shaking as he checked his flies. He was also plastered.

'I'll go and help Mummy with the drinks,' said Emerald, running out of the room in despair.

She found Patience gazing at an empty cupboard. There had been a bottle of red and half-full bottle of whisky that morning.

'Bloody Daddy must have drunk it,' hissed Emerald.

'Don't say anything,' pleaded Patience, 'he'll only deny it.'

'There isn't a drop in the house. Have you got any money?'

'Not enough,' sighed Patience.

Back in the drawing room, Ian and Zac were spikily discussing England's collapse in the Melbourne Test.

'Stewart's only bat who showed any gumption,' Ian was complaining. 'Fairbrother was a waste of space. Hick made a duck.'

'Hussain might make a good captain,' said Zac idly.

'Hussain?' exploded the colonel. 'Can't have a black captaining England!' Then, seeing Zac's raised eyebrow: 'Man was out first ball.'

Zac looked at Ian in amusement.

'I think you'll find it was the second.'

'Didn't know you people knew so much about cricket.'

'Jews, you mean?' said Zac politely.

'No, no.' Ian's face flushed an even darker red. 'Americans.'

Sophy, sorry for her father but trying not to laugh, was relieved when her mother and Emerald returned.

Scenting trouble, Patience said, 'I do hope you'll stay and take pot luck, Zac.'

Behind her mother, Emerald was frantically shaking her head.

'I was hoping Emerald might be free for dinner,' said Zac.

'What fun, I'm sure she'd love to,' cried Patience, trying to hide her relief.

'I can answer for myself,' snapped Emerald.

It was so uncool not to be going out on a Saturday night.

'I was actually just changing to go out to a party,' she went on untruthfully. 'But it wasn't very exciting. Thanks, I'd love to.'

'Chap's a bounder,' said Ian as Emerald, in a silver sequinned suit and a spring-like cloud of Violetta, left with Zac.

'I'm afraid he'll break Emo's heart,' sighed Patience.

'Only if he smashes it with a pickaxe,' said Sophy crossly.

25

Outside, the sky was the dull pink of a pigeon's breast; the air reeked of curry and hamburgers. As Zac flagged down a rare taxi, a tramp lurched up to Emerald.

'Give us a fiver, darlin'.'

'It's me who ought to be asking you,' Emerald told him acidly, and shot across the road into the taxi.

Zac took her to an extremely cool restaurant in Savile Row called Sartoria, where diners relaxed in squashy dark brown leather sofas, and Emerald's first course of mozzarella, zucchini, mint and basil was so beautifully laid out it should have been hung on the wall.

Zac ordered a very expensive bottle of red, a light Barolo, a '95 vintage.

'And drink it slowly,' he chided, as Emerald took a great gulp to steady her nerves. 'I figure I get more turned on by wine menus than pornography these days.'

'Is that why you haven't been in touch?'

'I've been busy. Since I saw you I've been to Tokyo, Moscow, Paris, B.A. and the Hermitage.'

'And a few ski slopes.'

'That too.'

'Zac the wanderer,' said Emerald sulkily. 'I haven't been anywhere.'

'What happened to the mansion in Yorkshire?'

Emerald was still telling him when their next course

arrived. Zac forked up her mozzarella and pushed the zucchini to one side, to make room for her scallops.

'And don't expect me to finish up those. Jews don't eat shellfish. Why didn't your father go to the Industrial Tribunal?'

'Says he's not the grumbling generation.'

Unlike his daughter, thought Zac.

'He used to be so macho,' sighed Emerald. 'I can't bear seeing him reduced to a shivering jelly, driving minicabs.'

'Not tonight, I hope,' grinned Zac.

'It's not funny. I don't really blame Daddy for drinking' – Emerald drained her glass of red – 'we've lost everything.'

'Except your talent.'

'That's gone. I gaze into space like Daddy.'

'Don't be a wimp, talent doesn't go away, only the guts to apply it.'

Emerald was as exotically beautiful, reflected Zac, as the scarlet anemones in the glass vase on the table, which had sucked up most of their water. Like her, they needed constantly topping up, but in her case with endless approval and attention. And then you thought of the parents with whom she'd been lumbered: that raucous technicolour scarecrow, and that bigoted drunk. Zac had disliked Ian Cartwright intensely, he was the kind of goy who'd think it terribly cool to have a 'clever little Jew, as sharp as ten monkeys', as his accountant. The whiff of Ian's anti-Semitism had been even more unattractive than the smell of his wife's casserole. Zac shuddered. Picking up Emerald's delicate white hand with the wild-rose-pink fingernails, he examined the fragile wrists.

'Must be some good blood somewhere, you ever thought of tracing your birth mother?'

Emerald, who'd been thrown into turmoil by his touching her, couldn't think straight.

'It'd be like opening Pandora's Box,' she stammered. 'She might be a junky, or in gaol or even a prostitute. She might get fixated on me and want to see me all the time. She might live in a ghastly house, although it couldn't be worse than the dump we've got in Shepherd's Bush.'

'She might want to borrow money off you,' said Zac with a grin.

'She gave me a dreadfully common name: "Charlene".' Emerald was shocked at her own snobbishness.

'Charlene is my darling.' Zac suppressed a yawn.

'Am I?' asked Emerald. She wasn't sure. She must try and talk about him for a change. 'How long are you here for?'

'Tomorrow, maybe Monday.'

'Oh no,' Emerald was appalled, 'I'm so sorry, I've banged on.'

'Good Jewish proverb, "It's better to light a candle than grumble in the dark".'

Later, when Zac got his Amex card out of his wallet, Emerald noticed a photograph of a very dark handsome man. Perhaps Zac was bi-sexual, but it looked like an old snapshot. Zac read her thoughts.

'My Great-uncle Jacob,' adding so bleakly that Emerald shivered: 'He was murdered by the Gestapo.'

'God, how awful.' Then, because she was frantic for Zac to make love to her again: 'Where are you staying?'

'Lancaster Gate. An apartment.'

'It's on the way home,' hinted Emerald. Then when he didn't react, she took a deep breath. 'If I look for my birth mother, will you help me?' Anything to keep him in the country. 'She worked in an art gallery, she was only nineteen, I was born on 7 July 1973. We've got a file at home. I know the name of the adoption society in Yorkshire.'

'In America,' Zac was clearly bored with the subject,

'with the necessary information and a credit card, it's easy. You can order your birth certificate over the phone.'

'My mother's bound to be married now and called something different,' said Emerald fretfully.

She had chewed off all her pink lipstick, leaving her mouth pale and trembling; her big eyes were shadowed and pleading.

'I can't ask Mummy and Daddy to help me, they've had enough grief recently.'

'What was your mother's name?'

'She was called Anthea Rookhope.'

There was a pause, only interrupted by the hiss of the coffee machine, as Zac put the bill and his Amex card back in his wallet. She couldn't read the expression on his face: triumph, pity, calculation.

'OK. I'll help you.'

People were coming out of the theatres. As Zac and Emerald wandered down Piccadilly, they passed Hatchards with a window filled with flowers, ribbons and books by Maeve Binchy, Penny Vincenzi and Rosamund Pilcher, chosen to give pleasure on Mothering Sunday.

'Oh hell, I forgot,' said Emerald crossly. 'Bloody Sophy should have reminded me. I bet she did it on purpose to be one up. I'll have to rush out first thing and get Mummy a card.' Emerald turned to Zac. 'Did you remember?'

'My mother's dead,' said Zac, so icily he could have directed a blizzard into her face.

'Oh Christ, I'm sorry, I'm so off the wall at the moment, I forget everything, what did she die of?'

'Cancer,' snapped Zac, who had flagged down a taxi.

The moment Emerald was inside, he slammed the door.

'Aren't you coming with me?' She was suddenly distraught.

'I'll call you Monday, when I've figured out the best way to trace your mom.' He handed her a £20 note, then told the driver, 'Five Cowfield Court.'

'But where are you going?' sobbed Emerald.

'I'm gonna walk.'

Almost running towards Hyde Park Corner, Zac noticed hanging above the bare plane trees a three-quarters-full moon, with the same sweet, wistful face as his mother, after she'd lost all her lustrous hair.

'Oh Mom,' groaned Zac, 'why did you have to leave me?'

Zac's family had been almost entirely wiped out by the death camps. His hero, Great-uncle Jacob, had had a gallery in Vienna, which had been closed down by the Nazis. Jacob had later been murdered by the Gestapo for smuggling Jews out of occupied Europe. Art therefore was in Zac's blood and the impact of Hitler's mass murder burnt deep in his soul.

When his widowed mother had married a second time, the three-year-old Zac had taken his goy stepfather's name of Anderson. But on leaving home in his late teens, he had changed his name from Anderson to Ansteig, which means 'ascent' in Austrian. This was to symbolize his escape from the poverty of his childhood and the brutality of his stepfather, who drank and beat up both him and his mother.

Now aged twenty-nine, Zac prowled the world, scouting for rich American collectors and writing pieces for art magazines. Eternally questioning like a psychiatrist, he seldom volunteered information about himself. His tigerish-yellow eyes, wonderful gym- and judo-honed body and deceptive cool made him wildly exciting to women. Zac, however, was more interested in unravelling his past and avenging himself on those who'd destroyed it. Hard on the outside, he refused to admit how much he missed the warmth and sympathetic closeness of the Jewish community he'd left behind in New York. When he allowed himself, he could be kind and wryly funny, but at heart he was angry and desolate, identifying with Schubert's Wanderer. 'Wherever I am, happiness is not.'

26

Next day, as promised, Zac applied for a form from the Adoption Contact Register in Southport. This was where parents who'd given children up for adoption left their names and addresses, in the hope that if these children came searching for them, they would know they'd receive a warm welcome.

'If both sides register,' explained Zac, 'a reunion after counselling can be arranged.'

'Can I give your Lancaster Gate address?' asked Emerald as she filled in the form. 'I don't want Mummy and Daddy to know what I'm up to.'

'I'm going away,' said Zac.

'You can't leave me! At least let me stay in the flat and keep it nice for you, or give me a key in case a letter arrives.'

'No,' said Zac firmly. 'The form'll take time to process, you won't hear from them for a few weeks, I'll be back by then.'

Although she was livid with Zac for abandoning her, Emerald couldn't resist working herself up into a fever of excitement.

'Imagine my real mother thinking of me every birthday and Christmas and at the beginning of every term. Every day she must wonder if I've met Mr Right.' Emerald looked up under her lashes at Zac. 'A woman on LBC yesterday said not a day passed, since her daughter was eighteen and officially allowed to search for her, that she didn't expect a knock on the door, or the telephone to ring and a voice to say, "Hi, Mum".'

Instead, three weeks later at the beginning of April, a kind letter arrived from Southport, saying they regretted that no Anthea Rookhope had registered but if, and when, she did she would find Emerald's, or rather Charlene's, name waiting for her.

Emerald, with predictable mood swings, had right up to the last moment been wondering whether she really wanted to meet her birth mother. Denied the opportunity, she was shattered. Zac, back from America, was wonderfully reassuring and patient. The Adoption Contact Register wasn't widely publicized, he kept telling her. Emerald's birth mother probably didn't know it existed.

'You must remember, times were very different when you were born. Young moms gave up their babies expecting never to see or hear from them again. They were forced to make a fresh start. Often they moved abroad to start a new life.'

'I ought to have counselling,' wailed Emerald, 'I need a support group.'

'You've got me,' said Zac.

The next step in the search was to go to the Public Record Office near the Angel, Islington.

'All marriages and births are listed there in year and alphabetical order,' Zac told Emerald. 'You've seen your original birth certificate, which told you your mom worked in a gallery. So this time, try looking for her marriage certificate. Start from July 1973, when she gave you up for adoption, and troll through the relevant volumes till you come to Rookhope, Anthea. If she was a quarter as pretty as you, she'll have been snapped up quickly, and it shouldn't take long.

'This entry,' he continued, 'will give you the date and place where she married and the name of her husband.

Then you can apply for the marriage certificate, which will give an address you can follow up, and the husband's profession. If he's a lawyer or a doctor, it'll be easy to trace him. Once you know your birth mom's married name you can also check through the births while you're there and find out if you've got any siblings.'

'It all sounds fearfully complicated,' grumbled Emerald, 'I'll never understand it, unless you come with me.'

'I'm busy, Moaner Lisa,' said Zac firmly, 'you can do it yourself.'

Sulkily, Emerald took a bus to the Angel. How dare Zac accuse her of moaning? She wouldn't if he made love to her more often and allowed her to stay over in his flat which he kept so private.

It was a very warm spring afternoon, daffodils nodded approval in the parks, blossom danced in all the squares, but Emerald's teeth were chattering frantically as she arrived at the Public Record Office. She allowed the men on the door to search her handbag, but ignored the sign telling her to switch off her mobile. In a big light room, below huge signs saying 'Deaths', 'Births', 'Marriages', with 'Adoptions', typically, sidelined round the corner, were shelves and shelves filled with huge leather-bound books. Everything – walls, carpets, a mass of potted plants, big armchairs – was green; that traditionally restful colour to soothe those making earth-shattering discoveries.

Green linoleum even covered the reading table on which Emerald laid the big sap-green book which said: 'Marriages registered in England and Wales in the months August, September, October 1973' in gold lettering on the spine. Inside the names had been listed on an old-fashioned typewriter, with the occasional correction in ink.

'Rainsworth, Ralph, Ramm,' read Emerald, 'Reed, Rees, Roberts, Rookes,' but no Rookhope. Her hands were clammy and trembling, as she moved to the next volume, and then the next – still with no luck.

Perhaps art students of the future would one day come here to look up her marriage to Zac: Sculptor and Wanderer, thought Emerald dreamily as she took down February to May 1974. She adored Zac so much, she'd happily convert to Judaism. Next door a man with a beard was purposefully working his way through a volume of recent births. Perhaps his wife had been up to no good.

'Ramsey, Ralton, Reading, Rollinson,' read Emerald, then jumped as the hallowed silence was broken by desperate weeping.

'My mother confessed on her deathbed that in 1949 she gave up a daughter for adoption,' a distraught grey-haired woman was telling two kindly officials over at the reception desk. 'Her dying wish was that this child should know how loved she'd been,' she sobbed. 'The social workers in Wales know where she is, but they won't tell me.'

'That's a bloody disgrace.' Dropping February to May with a crash, Emerald rushed across the room. 'You get a lawyer onto it at once,' she said, putting her arm round the woman's heaving shoulders.

'She's my sister,' cried the woman. 'Now that Mother's passed away, she's the only family I've got.'

It was a few seconds before Emerald realized the disapproval on the faces of the kindly officials was not entirely directed at Welsh social workers, and that her mobile was ringing.

'So sorry,' she mumbled, then seeing *call* on the blank screen of her mobile, which must be the unlisted Zac ringing, she scuttled off past a sign saying 'Marine and Consular Births' to answer it.

'You can stop hunting, baby,' said a deep jubilant voice, 'I've found your mom.'

'Omigod, where is she?'

'Get in a taxi, I'll tell you.'

'I haven't any money.'

'I'll pay the other end.'

'Where are you?'

It was the first time he'd given her his Lancaster Gate address.

'Don't forget to get yourself a lawyer,' Emerald yelled to the distraught grey-haired woman as she ran out into the sunshine.

Emerald felt she'd ascended to heaven as she stepped out of the lift into such a beautiful penthouse flat. Zac was waiting with a bottle of Pouilly-Fumé.

'Who is she? Tell me, *tell me.*'

For a minute Zac teased her like the Nurse in *Romeo and Juliet.* First he couldn't find the corkscrew, then there were smears on the glasses. Then he laughed.

'You are not going to believe this. Adrian Campbell-Black called me at lunchtime wanting info on Galena Borochova.'

'What's she got to do with it? She's not my mother. For Christ's sake, Zac.'

'I know, but I knew she was married to Raymond Belvedon, so I picked up *Who's Who* to find out the year she died, and guess who was his second wife?'

'Who, who?'

'Anthea Rookhope.'

Emerald sat down very suddenly on a black leather sofa.

'I am certain,' Zac told her, 'that your mom is living in Limesbridge, one of the prettiest villages in the Cotswolds, and she is now Anthea Belvedon, the wife of Sir Raymond Belvedon.'

'I don't believe it!' screamed Emerald. 'It must be fate. And I even spoke to Raymond, my real father, at Rupert Campbell-Black's. He's such a darling. And, my God, that means Jonathan and Sienna Belvedon are my brother and sister. Christ! I mean they are the two great monster superbrats of the art world. Jonathan is so gorgeous, students stretch his canvasses for nothing, he's got a loft off Hoxton Square and a barn in the country. Hardly starving in a garret and Sienna was shortlisted for the Turner, no wonder I'm so arty. What a lovely man to have as my father, if he's a Sir does that make me an Hon.?'

Emerald was hysterical with excitement, flying round the room like a fairy, knocking back gulps of wine, facts spilling out of her like a fax machine. Zac brought her down to earth.

'Anthea's your mother, but I don't figure Raymond's your pop. I've been digging around. It seems Anthea went to work at the Belvedon in the early Seventies. Raymond was married to Borochova then, who died in October 1973. Anthea didn't marry Raymond until May 1974, a quiet register office wedding, ten months after you were born.'

Zac chucked a pile of photostats down on the table.

'So the four elder Belvedon kids,' he continued, 'probably aren't your blood relatives, but you've got a young half-brother and -sister, Dicky and Dora. It's a bit blurred on that stat, but they must be about eight and awfully cute. Also I bought this round the corner.'

It was a feature on Anthea in April's *Good Housekeeping*. 'Little woman, good wife', said the headline.

'Omigod, I recognize her.' Emerald's tears spattered the pages as she pored over the pictures, frantic for likenesses. 'Of course, Lady Belvedon! She's always in *Hello* and *Tatler*. God, she's pretty, and tiny like me, look how much smaller she is than Raymond. I wonder who my father was. If Raymond had been my dad, they'd surely have gone to court and got me back. Shall we drive down and give her the thrill of her life?'

Then, catching a glimpse of her reflection in a huge mirror, Emerald decided she first needed a haircut. Far down below, she could see the crimson blur on the trees in Hyde Park turning to buff and green. As an omen, the clouds suddenly stopped going east, and surged westwards towards Limesbridge.

'I guess we ought to take things slowly,' said Zac, topping up Emerald's glass. 'I know it's hard, but let Anthea get used to the idea.'

'But she'll be over the moon.'

Zac shook his head.

'It was only in 1976 that adopted kids were given the right to have access to their records. You were born in 1973, that puts Anthea in the frame of women who would never expect to be contacted. She may not have told Raymond about you.'

'In a happy marriage, that's lasted nearly twenty-five years?' scoffed Emerald, who was back studying the *Good Housekeeping* photographs. 'Of course he must know about me.'

In the end Zac agreed to write Anthea a private and confidential letter.

'I'll make it kind of neutral. Just saying "I know of a young woman called Charlene Rookhope, who was born on 7 July 1973, who thinks she might be related to you. It may not be your branch of the family, but if it is, she'd love to get in touch." I'll give your mobile as a contact number. If she calls at an awkward moment, you can always say you'll call her back.'

Emerald insisted they post the letter straight away, kissing the envelope before she popped it in the pillar box, then flinging herself into Zac's arms.

'You are so brilliant. Let's go back and go to bed to celebrate.'

Fucking Emerald, reflected Zac, as Emerald drifted off to sleep beside him, was rather like cycling in the Rockies: wonderful views, but you had to do all the work yourself.

Emerald was still in raging high spirits when she later floated back to Shepherd's Bush. Sophy, who was eating baked beans and reading *Bridget Jones's Diary*, was amazed to see her sister so cheerful. After their parents had gone to bed, Patience exhausted, Ian plastered, Emerald told Sophy about tracking down Anthea. Sophy was appalled and begged Emerald to come clean.

'Daddy and particularly Mummy will want to support you through this, they'll be gutted if they're left in the dark.'

'Zac's helping me, that's all I need,' said Emerald defensively. 'Let me find my mother in my own way, then I'll tell them. They'll be happy if I'm happy. I need to discover my roots.'

'Whenever I discover mine, I take them straight to the colourist.'

'Why d'you always make stupid jokes, just like Zac?' replied Emerald through gritted teeth. 'I need to find my real mother.'

'Bollocks!' Sophy lost her temper. 'Your real mother was Mummy who fed, clothed, and looked after you when you were ill, and put up with your tantrums.'

'Don't you have any desire to find your family?' demanded Emerald.

'I don't need another family,' snapped Sophy, 'I've got a perfectly good one already.'

Emerald, who expected Anthea to be on the telephone next morning, or at least on the doorstep by midday, rushed out first thing to have her hair done, then spent the afternoon trying on different clothes to wear to meet her new mother.

But as the days passed with no reaction, she became increasingly uptight. Zac's big hands had to do a lot of soothing, massaging oil into her tense tiny body, lighting candles round the scented double bath, bringing her to orgasm to make sure – just in case Anthea got in touch the following day – that she got her nine hours' beauty sleep. Meanwhile, he paced the floorboards next door.

Despite this solicitude, Emerald's mood swings became increasingly extreme.

'It was your idea to get in touch with her in the first place,' she would storm, then, two minutes later: 'Of course I can handle any response. All I want from Anthea is information, who my father is, what medical problems she had. Naturally, I'll respect her desire for privacy.'

But alas, the course of maternal love never runs smooth.

Anthea neither replied to Zac's letter nor telephoned. By the end of a fortnight, Emerald was in a frenzy of disappointment, snatching at her mobile.

'It's worse than waiting for you to ring,' she raged at Zac, who sat down and wrote a second letter: 'Your daughter, Charlene, would like to meet with you. You will be very proud of her.' He signed himself Daniel Abelman.

When there was no answer to this and April moved into May, he winkled Raymond's ex-directory number out of a fellow art correspondent, and called Foxes Court. A furious Anthea hung up on him. Next day, a recorded delivery arrived with a Limesbridge postmark. Inside was a brief letter.

Dear Mr Abelman,

I gave Charlene up for adoption more than twenty-five years ago, and have now closed the book. Your getting in touch has unleashed memories of an extremely traumatic time in my life that were buried long since. I wish Charlene well but have no desire to see her. If she gets in touch with me again, I shall have no option but to seek the advice of my solicitors.

Anthea's handwriting, Zac decided, was very shaky.

'She clearly hasn't told Sir Raymond or the rest of the family.'

'I cannot believe it,' whispered a devastated Emerald. 'This isn't a can of worms, it's a can of adders, all hissing out of Pandora's Box. Anthea rejected me, giving me up as a baby, now she's kicking me in the teeth a second time.

'We should have approached her through social workers,' she turned on Zac furiously, 'then she wouldn't be worried about blackmail or fraud. She probably thinks we're a couple of con artists, particularly with you signing yourself "Abelman".'

Her hysteria was rising so rapidly that Zac was tempted to hit her, or throw her out, but being a journalist he wanted to know the end of the story.

'We are *not* giving up so easily.'

Zac had also noticed a paragraph in *Oo-ah!* magazine, whose circulation was creeping up on that of *Hello* and *OK*, announcing that Sir Raymond and Lady Belvedon were giving a big party in late May, to celebrate Raymond's seventy-fifth birthday. They were also intending to reaffirm their marriage vows in a silver wedding ceremony in St James, Limesbridge, beforehand. No wonder Anthea didn't want her little pre-marital lapse popping out of the woodwork at a time like this.

'You and I are getting into Foxes Court another way,' Zac told Emerald.

'I'm not sure I want to after that horrible letter.'

'Sure you do. Have you still got that card Raymond gave you?'

'I lost it.'

'Doesn't matter.'

Zac, to Emerald's horror, proceeded to ring up the Belvedon and made an appointment for her to show Raymond her portfolio at twelve-thirty the following Tuesday.

'But I haven't done any proper work for months.'

'Time you did,' said Zac. 'Get your ass into gear.'

'Can I draw you over the weekend?' Which would at least give her more time with him.

'Only if I have the test match on.'

One beautiful drawing brought Emerald's confidence back. At college, her party trick had been to take a piece of clay and sculpt someone's head in two hours.

'I'm going to try this on Raymond.'

'Your idol will have a head of clay,' said Zac.

27

Jupiter Belvedon had abandoned a career as a sculptor and joined his father in the gallery because he realized his brothers and sister had much more talent. Nor did Jupiter have Raymond or David's eye, but he had excellent business sense and was a genius at hanging and lighting pictures. He was also driven crackers by his father's kind heart and the time he wasted giving free advice.

Tall, fine featured, too thin both in face and body, Jupiter looked effete, but a passer-by who'd tried to steal a Caravaggio from the gallery had been hit halfway down Cork Street. A control-freak, Jupiter loved bashing things into shape. He utterly dominated Hanna, his stunning blonde wife. He had plans to open a satellite gallery in the East End, concentrating on contemporary artists, but his real ambition was to oust William Hague and totally resculpt the Tory Party and later the country.

On the morning of Emerald's appointment, Jupiter was not in carnival mood. Nor for that matter was Emerald. As the taxi bowled down Bond Street, then turned left and left again into Cork Street, she reflected how often, nearly twenty-seven years ago, her real mother must have walked the same way. There was the pretty Regency terraced house with the green-and-white-striped awning and a Casey Andrews in the window. Here Anthea must have come with love in her heart, thought Emerald as, quaking with nerves, she lugged her folding table, her tools, her lump of clay and her portfolio through a glass-fronted door flanked by two bay trees.

She found the gallery in disarray. Casey Andrews's huge oils were coming down, Daisy France-Lynch's delicate portraits were going up, canvasses were stacked against every wall.

I'm going to faint, thought Emerald in panic, but I can't do a runner with all this stuff.

'Yes?' A tall haughty-looking man, probably in his late thirties, and very like the Duke of Wellington painted by Thomas Lawrence, shot out of the inside office.

'I've come to see Sir Raymond Belvedon.'

'Well you can't,' snapped Jupiter.

Raymond had just buggered off to do a television programme he'd forgotten clean about. Tamzin, their dozy assistant, was having a sickie, probably a hangover, and Jupiter had been left manning the gallery. In five minutes he was expecting a major client, an American arms-dealer called Si Greenbridge. Jupiter was about to lock up and take him to lunch.

He was therefore extremely unfriendly, telling Emerald to buzz off and come back and see his doddering old father another day. Enraged, Emerald tried to talk her way in. This austere, handsome crosspatch might after all be her first blood relation.

'Just let me show you my portfolio,' she pleaded, opening a huge shiny black book, almost as big as herself.

Jupiter noted glowing testimonials from Chelsea College of Art and Brighton College, both admittedly from men, and that her heads were astonishingly good. There was however no market for heads, unless they were of someone important.

She was also astonishingly pretty, and with her short upper lip, crazed eyes and rippling dark hair, a dead ringer for Rossetti's Pandora.

'I can't give you any more time,' he said curtly. 'The client coming here any second has walls which need pictures. If I can get inside his head for ten minutes, I can sell them to him, but he's got so much else to occupy his mind, it's taken me three months to pin him down today.'

Jupiter would never have bothered with these explanations if the girl hadn't been so attractive. Just for a second Emerald's eyes hardened: a tantrum hovering.

My first bloody relation, she thought.

'Go on, beat it,' said Jupiter.

But as he opened the glass door, about to dump her stuff outside, the telephone rang. Keeping his eyes on her, in case she swiped a picture, he retreated to the reception desk.

'Belvedon Gallery. It's Jupiter here.' Not by a flicker as he flipped through some Polaroids did he show how furious he was.

'Sure. I understand. Traffic's been awful all day. Shall we make another appointment? OK, you call me when you've got a moment. Fuck, fuck, fuck, fuck,' said Jupiter, wondering if the fucks had started before he'd hung up. He didn't care.

'He cancelled?' asked Emerald.

Jupiter nodded. 'He got away.'

'You were right to show him you didn't give a stuff, he'll ring again.'

'With half the dealers in the world trailing their wares?' sighed Jupiter. 'Si Greenbridge is so newly crazy about art, he's slinging out all his racehorses so he can hang pictures in their boxes.'

'I'm very sorry.'

Emerald was now ensconced on the pale grey velvet sofa, showing off her pretty legs beneath a tight leather mini. Jupiter had only had black coffee for breakfast. An enticing smell of Irish stew drifted over from Mulligan's oyster bar, where he'd booked a table for himself and Si.

'Would you like some lunch?' he was amazed to hear himself saying.

'Have you got time?'

'I have now.'

'I'd rather sculpt your head.'

'What?'

'It'll only take a couple of hours, I promise you. I was going to do your father anyway.'

In no time at all, Emerald had tied back her hair with a violet silk scarf, set up her folding table in the back office, and on a revolving podium placed a lump of clay, already formed into a head with rough features. On a side table was more clay in a white pie dish and her tools: knives, pointed sticks and sticks with wire loops on the end like fairy dog-catchers. Jupiter meanwhile had opened a bottle of red, locked the outside door and put on the answering machine.

'Could you possibly keep your face still and not talk too much,' begged Emerald, 'just to begin with, so I can see what's coming out?'

This man is perhaps my brother, she thought as she gazed into his cool fern-green eyes as if into a mirror. He had the complex, ascetic, ruthless face of a Robespierre or a young Italian cardinal on the make in fifteenth-century Rome. Unable to stop herself, she reached out like a blind man and ran a trembling hand over his features. Jupiter flinched. Perhaps she was a stalker or a nutter. She was deathly pale now.

'I'm sorry.' Emerald blushed. 'It helps me to feel the faces I'm sculpting.' She ran a finger down the long, gritted curve of his jaw. 'I want my work to be touched as well as looked at.'

They both jumped as the telephone rang. It was Casey Andrews fulminating away on the machine like one of the giants in *The Ring*. Casey's latest reviews and sales had not been as good as hoped.

'All art correspondents write about these days is the

stratospheric price of Impressionists and my brother Jonathan's sex life,' grumbled Jupiter.

Sitting opposite him, Emerald applied wooden callipers to Jupiter's temples, to the sides of his aquiline nose, to the distance from brushed eyebrow to smooth hairline, from nose to ears, ears to mouth, then transferred each measurement to the lump of clay. The *Guardian* had described him as 'thin lipped' last week. Jupiter tried to make his mouth fuller.

'Wonderful eyes, wonderful strong face,' murmured Emerald. 'So nice to sculpt someone older,' then, with a smile: 'I'm so used to doing boring students.'

Jupiter was amazed by her total concentration. For the first time in years, he looked at someone else's face for more than two minutes. Emerald's green eyes, practically hidden by narrowed feathery dark lashes, looked through him and at him, flickering constantly back to the head as she modelled and gouged, adding then removing little sausages of clay.

Her slightly parted black knees were an inch away from his. The E set with emeralds, practically the only piece of Cartwright jewellery unpawned, rose and fell on her cashmere bosom. As she worked she told him about the disaster that had befallen her family and how her father had been cruelly ousted by a boardroom coup.

Jupiter wryly wished he could get shot of Raymond as easily. As Emerald crawled round on the carpet to catch different views of him, he was amazed to find himself offering to introduce her to other dealers and clients. Pouring himself another glass of wine, he tried to persuade her to join him, but she still would only accept water.

'Do you mind coming a bit nearer?'

Jupiter edged his chair forward, their knees almost touching. He could smell violets and the sweetness of her breath. The milky green of her jersey was the colour of the dewy lawn at Limesbridge.

To start with he had kept glancing impatiently at his watch, but now he wanted time to go slower and slower, fascinated to see the head emerging more human than himself. That man had mortgage problems, and shouldn't have bought a big house in Chester Terrace to impress the Tory Party. That man needed to nail Si Greenbridge, curb his father's excesses and sell more than David Pulborough.

Jupiter loved his wife Hanna, but he was suddenly filled with lust for this girl with her black legs apart, the soft curve of her breast and her darting eyes.

'You're very good at keeping still.' She smiled at him adorably, head on one side. 'Apparently the person with the stillest face is the Duke of Edinburgh. I haven't made your eyes deep set enough.'

Telephone messages for Raymond from Greyhound Rescue, from television producers and newspapers, from the NSPCC wanting him to open a fête, from artists wanting money, piled up on the machine.

Emerald was now doing Jupiter's thick dark locks – his one vanity – applying clay in a frenzy. The sculpture took on even more reality with his hair. Emerald's eyes were darting quicker and quicker, her little hands and nails burnt umber like his Aunt Lily's after gardening.

I've met this girl before, he thought. Next moment she leant back, stretching and flexing her aching fingers and shoulders.

'OK. Thanks awfully.'

It was a few moments before they realized the bell was ringing insistently accompanied with banging. Outside was Kevin Coley, a petfood billionaire, whom the Belvedons nicknamed Mr Ditherer, because of his infuriating habit of buying paintings after a good lunch and changing his mind next day.

Kevin caught sight of Jupiter's head. 'Bloody hell, who did that? Bloody fantastic.'

'I did,' said Emerald.

To Jupiter's outrage, David Pulborough from his gallery opposite sidled in in Kevin's wake. Knowing Jupiter couldn't chuck him out in front of a client, he instantly started chatting up Emerald.

'You've really caught the old devil, captured all the arrogance and ice of the grand master. Flattered him, of course, Jupey's more lined and his eyes are closer together.'

Emerald looked at the head, constantly smoothing the texture.

'It needs more work.'

'Give us a drink, Jupey,' said Kevin, 'I've dropped in to have a butcher's at Daisy France-Lynch's new stuff. Thinking of commissioning her to paint our Cuddles and the wife in the orangery.'

'Daisy France-Lynch is so passé,' drawled David, who never said anything nice about other dealers' pictures, 'her work's far too pretty for today's look.'

'Probably one of the reasons she sells out before every exhibition opens,' snapped Jupiter.

'I sold a Sickert to the National Gallery this morning,' boasted David as he flipped through Emerald's portfolio. 'These are very good. You should get some postcards printed or a poster of that one. You must give me your card.'

'Me too,' added Kevin, who was admiring one of Daisy France-Lynch's grinning English setters. 'Wonder how that would work on a petfood can?'

'We've met before. That's a nice big girl . . .' David paused to admire a nude of Sophy. 'At Rupert Campbell-Black's open day. I never forget a face.' Then, gazing deep into Emerald's eyes, 'When you walked past me I thought:

'She was a phantom of delight
When first she gleamed upon my sight;
A lovely apparition, sent
To be a moment's ornament.'

'That is so beautiful,' sighed a blushing Emerald.

Having taken Polaroid photographs of Jupiter from all angles, she was now, because she was poor, gathering up all the discarded pieces of clay to use again. It was so nice to be chatted up and praised by such an attractive man. Emerald liked David's warm dark eyes and, not being tall, he didn't dwarf her.

'Lovely name, Emerald Cartwright.' He examined the green card she handed him. 'You are so promotable, darling.'

Stepping out of the back office, David noticed his assistant waving frantically from across the road. One of his best clients, also flushed from a good lunch, had just rolled up.

'I'll call you,' David told Emerald, and shot back to the Pulborough, shortly to be followed by Kevin Coley, saying he'd almost certainly buy the drawing of the English setter.

'Put a red spot on it, Jupey, Daisy could make a fortune if we used it commercially. Can I have one of your cards too?' he asked Emerald.

Shaking with rage, Jupiter poured himself and Emerald glasses of wine, and asked her if she were hungry. Emerald looked at him from under her lashes: 'Could I have another half an hour on the head?'

Sitting in position again, Jupiter failed to control his anger.

'How dare fucking David Pulborough swan in here when he's just poached my brother Jonathan and signed him up for an exhibition in the autumn?'

'Has he?' asked Emerald in amazement. 'That's atrocious.'

'Broke my father's heart. Jonathan's always been his favourite child,' said Jupiter bitterly. 'David'll make a fortune if he can get any work out of him. Dad never managed to. Jonathan won't like it. I concede work suffers if you're too generous on the advance front, but at least he got paid when we represented him. David's not only tight, he isn't straight.'

Even more upsetting, without his brother as an incentive, all Jonathan's wild Young British Artist friends would no longer be so keen to show their work at Jupiter's proposed East End gallery.

'That's terribly disloyal of Jonathan,' said Emerald crossly and hypocritically, 'family should *always* come first.'

She was on the floor again, her hair escaping from its violet scarf. As she looked up at his chin and jawline, a smudge of clay enhanced her flawless face like a beauty spot. Jupiter was appalled how much he wanted to rip off her clothes.

'Have you got a boyfriend?'

'Sort of.' Emerald waved a pointed stick at the last drawing in her still-open portfolio.

'What nationality is he?' asked Jupiter.

'American Jewish, originally from Vienna.'

'Great face.'

Emerald shrugged: 'I suppose so. He disappears for weeks on end, never says he loves me, I'm not sure of him.'

Jupiter sighed and said he wasn't at all sure of his wild sister Sienna and his curmudgeonly brother Alizarin, who had once painted so brilliantly but now exhausted himself producing grotesque unsellable rubbish.

'Alizarin's pictures should be stuck on the ceiling at the dentist's, to show people how much fun it is having one's teeth drilled.'

Emerald giggled. Such had been her excitement at sculpting Jupiter, she was astounded that she had clean forgotten her original mission.

'How does your mother cope with such a large family?' she asked innocently.

Jupiter, whose last memory of Galena was of her being so drunk, she had had to be locked in Raymond's

Bentley during a Bagley Hall Speech Day, said that his mother was dead.

'We've got a stepmother.'

'Is she nice?' Emerald nearly sliced off Jupiter's clay eyebrow, her hand was suddenly shaking so much.

'Wonderful,' said Jupiter with unusual warmth. 'She's held our family together despite Alizarin and Sienna giving her so much aggro. She and I have always got on and she's great with Dad, who's an old drama queen who needs keeping in check, but she always does it nicely.'

Jupiter's flat tummy gave a great rumble, as he added, 'Anthea came to this gallery at eighteen, as a temp, and was so pretty the clients flocked. Dad was her first lover. She picked up the pieces after our mother died.'

Maybe Raymond *was* her father. Emerald was enchanted. She felt so grateful to Jupiter for being sweet about Anthea.

By three-thirty, more punters were trickling in, Jupiter had to get down to hanging Daisy's pictures and Emerald had nearly finished his head. Jupiter was inwardly ecstatic, in a situation of which every dealer dreams: finding a brilliant young artist whom no-one is yet on to, who can still be bought cheap – and who also he wants to fuck insensible. But all he said was: 'It's coming on nicely. Needs another sitting.'

In the past Jupiter had been accused of giving unimaginative presents. Emerald's head, he decided, would be the perfect silver wedding present for his father and Anthea.

As Emerald sprayed the head with water and wrapped it in plastic, Jupiter told her about the party. There would be lots of important dealers and clients there. He would see Emerald and her boyfriend got an invite.

Quite forgetting he needed a squeaky-clean image if he were to oust William Hague and take over the Tory Party, Jupiter suggested Emerald left the head behind and finished it off tomorrow evening.

'I'll buy you dinner and we can discuss your career.'

It was crucial, he told himself in justification, that he signed her up before David Pulborough got his grubby hands on her.

'Limesbridge here I come,' murmured Emerald in ecstasy as he put her into a taxi. 'One gorgeous older brother down and two to go.'

But as they passed the Ritz, she had to jump out and dive into the Ladies, where she threw up and up and up; then she cried her heart out all the way home from shock and nervous tension.

28

Two nights later, Emerald finished Jupiter's head. Afterwards she dined with him at Langan's and was so anxious to learn more about Anthea and the Belvedons that for once she didn't talk obsessively about herself, except to thank Jupiter when he promised to help her with her career. Jupiter misconstrued her frantic dive into a taxi afterwards as an attempt to prevent him jumping on her, when it was only to stop him coming home with her and discovering in what a squalid area she lived. This in no way diminished his lust. Next day Emerald fired the head, leaving it in the kiln for a day, filling in the cracks with car body filler and painting them over, before sending it round to the Belvedon in a taxi.

As the day of the silver wedding party approached, she became more and more histrionic, picking fights, tidying frenziedly, driving Zac further into himself.

'Jupiter'll loathe me for tricking him,' she shouted over the Dyson as she yet again cleaned Zac's flat, 'and I really like him. Anthea may look like a fairy princess, but underneath she's probably more like the wicked stepmother in *Snow White*. She'll reject me even more when she realizes we've wormed our way in. I don't know if I'm Charlene or Emerald, or Belvedon or Cartwright or Rookhope. Will I get swallowed up in a big

240

family who are "careless with other people's lives"? Will I lose Mum, Dad and Sophy, who've been good to me in their bumbling way?'

Zac yawned, turned the page of *The Art Newspaper* and reached for his bourbon and soda.

'For Christ's sake, turn that fucking thing off, you'll wear out the carpet,' he yelled over the din. 'You and Anthea are like push you, pull me. The person doing the searching agonizes about rejection, the person sought out feels invaded and unable to control events. Anthea'll be fine once she sees you.'

'How d'you know?' Furiously Emerald banged the hoover against the skirting board. 'What's in it for you anyway? You just want to get inside the Belvedon house, to do a number on all those artists and clients.'

'What the fuck are you talking about?'

'There must be some reason you're forcing me to do this.'

For a second, Zac's face was as blank as the Rothko on the wall behind him, then he drained his drink and got to his feet.

'Where are you going?'

'Out – I've had you up to here.'

'You can't leave me, I need to work this through, you're the only person I can talk to. Sophy's so disapproving. I haven't dared tell her we're crashing Anthea's party. Fucking hoover. Fuse must have blown.'

But Zac had pulled out the plug and walked out of the flat slamming the door.

What was he really up to? wondered Emerald. He'd retreat for hours into his office, endlessly surfing the net, sifting through catalogues and auction lists, gabbling away on the telephone in French, German, Italian and even Russian. He went out a lot; he disappeared to the gym, working out his rage on those huge machines. He wore wonderful designer clothes, but always in blacks, greys or muted umbers as befitting a creature of the night. He devoured German novels and watched cricket on television, but he never seemed to do any writing. The flat was filled with beautiful abstract sculpture and pictures, but it bore no stamp of Zac's personality – she didn't even know if he owned it.

When he came back three hours later, Zac caught her going through his briefcase and really yelled at her.

'Don't ever do that again.'

'Who's that woman?'

'My mother, for God's sake.'

'She's very beautiful, but at least you were brought up by your own mother. Hearing how lovely Anthea is from Jupiter makes me realize what I've missed.'

As she became more uncertain of Zac, the more demands she made on him. She was still fretting two days before the party over what she was going to give Raymond and Anthea as a present.

'Thirty pieces of silver,' said Zac.

'Don't be stupid and I must have something new to wear. I can't face Anthea unless I feel really good. That's the trouble with being tiny, you can't buy things off the peg, skirts flap on the ground, shirts are like shift dresses. I'll never find anything to fit unless I go to a top designer.'

As she grabbed Zac's empty glass, Zac grabbed it back again.

'I might want another bourbon.'

'Jupiter's promised to give me a thousand pounds for that head,' pleaded Emerald. 'Will you lend it to me?'

In the end Zac gave her £300 for a present and a dress.

'It won't be enough, you come with me and see.'

'I'm going to Lord's,' snapped Zac.

Sulkily Emerald set off, and after wandering up and down Bond Street, she settled for a silver candle-snuffer from Tiffany's and a beautiful card. Pouring rain, which kinked her hair, made her even more bad tempered. Moving on to Knightsbridge, she found nothing that fitted or suited her at Harvey Nichols or Harrods, so she drifted towards Joseph – and there it was, on the rail, a dress in clinging chiffon, flower-patterned in green, crimson and Venetian red, with a frilly neckline and a knee-length skirt. It looked infinitely more ravishing on, demure yet seductive, and picking up the green of Emerald's eyes, with the crimsons and reds showing off her white skin. What would Charlene Rookhope have done if she needed a beautiful dress?

Emerald had never shoplifted before, but she was in such a turmoil and perhaps wanted to jolt Zac, who'd become increasingly withdrawn, into a reaction.

Sliding the chiffon dress into the Tiffany bag alongside the silver candle-snuffer, she still had enough cash to buy one of Joseph's sleeveless orange T-shirts and leave change over. It was so easy. In seconds she was out into the pouring rain and into the womblike safety of a taxi. That was the sort of wild prank Sienna Belvedon would have pulled off, she thought excitedly, as she transferred the chiffon dress to the Joseph bag. Back at the flat, she was unnerved to find cricket rained off, and Zac already home watching a video of one of Raymond's programmes.

'How d'you get on?' he asked, switching down the sound.

'Really well,' said Emerald, brandishing the candle-snuffer. 'Such a romantic idea – dousing the flickering lights before a night of passion. Oh look, there's my darling stepfather. Do turn it up.'

Raymond, in a pale yellow tie and a miraculously cut pinstripe suit, was drifting round the National Gallery followed by a languid-looking greyhound.

'Raphael wasn't just a miraculous artist,' he was telling the camera confidingly, 'he also had such a sweet and generous nature that, according to Vasari, the great Renaissance art historian, not only was he honoured by men, but even by the very animals, who would constantly follow his steps and always love him.' Raymond paused to put a fond hand on the greyhound's striped head. 'Now that, in a not particularly animal-loving country, is a huge recommendation.'

'Raphael would have got on with my mother,' said Emerald, edging towards the bedroom as the camera panned in on the proud bay horse leading Raphael's *Procession to Calvary*.

But Zac had caught sight of the Joseph bag.

'What else did you buy?'

Flustered, Emerald muttered that she'd got a dress and T-shirt cheap in a Joseph sale, and fled next door. Alas, Zac the journalist rang Joseph. Discovering there was no sale on, he stalked into the bedroom and slapped Emerald really hard across the face.

'Thou shalt not steal, for Chrissake! Don't ever do that again, you stupid bitch. You could so easily have been caught. What would have happened if you'd been photographed by *Oo-ah!* wearing it at the silver wedding party?'

Grabbing the dress and his wallet, he was off once again, slamming the door behind him. Emerald was still sobbing on the sofa when he returned long after midnight. The rain had turned the grey flecks as black as the rest of his hair; his face was wet and shiny. He chucked a Joseph bag at her. Inside was the dress.

'How did you fiddle it?' stammered Emerald.

'Said you picked it up by mistake,' said Zac acidly, 'and eyed up the assistant. She was so touched by my honesty, she let me have it at a discount.'

'Oh God, I'm so sorry.' Emerald hung her head. 'I've never stolen anything before.'

'Except hearts.' Zac's face softened. 'C'mon, honey, come here.' Emerald shot across the room into the warmth and security of his arms. This was really the only home she wanted.

'I'm sorry I hit you,' muttered Zac. 'We're both uptight, but we're so nearly there. Let's go to bed.'

Emerald came almost immediately.

'I love you, Zac,' she whispered and within seconds was asleep.

Zac wandered into the bathroom, not bothering to switch on the light. The marble basin, magnifying mirror, silver-backed brushes, CK One bottles, all gleamed in the moonlight. Moving towards the window, Zac caught sight of the moon: wistful, huge eyed, desperately not wanting to die. Overwhelmed with sadness, Zac banged his forehead against the window pane.

'We're getting there, Mom, I promise.'

29

Anthea woke early on her silver wedding day, delighted to see blue sky outside, and feel an already warm breeze ruffling her beautiful new white linen curtains, trimmed with crimson glass beads, which made a lovely clatter when drawn. Although she had just had most of the house redecorated, this room was her favourite. The walls had been repapered in crimson toile de Jouy: a glorious extravaganza of fishing Chinamen, pagodas, parrots, monkeys and joyful dolphins designed by Nina Campbell herself.

Nina, who'd become 'such a friend', had also suggested blinds of the same crimson pattern behind the white linen curtains, cream Tibetan rugs on the polished floor and, on Anthea's four-poster, luxurious self-lined cream linen curtains edged with more crimson.

An enchantingly pretty room for an enchantingly pretty lady, thought Anthea smugly. Crimson, of course, had been Galena's favourite colour, but she'd matched it with such strident royal blues and emerald greens. It required taste – like Nina's, and of course Anthea's – to bring out the true potential of the colour with creams and whites.

Anthea sighed. What a tragedy the women this evening wouldn't be able to admire the new décor when they left their coats on the bed, but there were too many precious things in the house to let guests rove unsupervised.

Anthea had pandered to her husband's every whim over the last twenty-five years, as she was fond of saying. But last night, to ensure nine hours' sleep before their special day, she had banished Raymond, who snored, to the dressing room. Raymond had been rather relieved. It had enabled him to read Tennyson into the small hours and have Grenville the greyhound on his bed.

In an hour or so, after she'd done her exercises, Anthea would creep downstairs and load up a tray with presents, a posy of lilies of the valley, freshly squeezed orange juice, and a half-bottle of champagne, and sing 'Happy Birthday, Sir Raymond' outside his door.

Anthea stretched. One of Raymond's sex games, early on in the marriage, had been to take her out of a specially built glass case, and examine and caress her as if she were a Sèvres milkmaid. The case, which stood by the window, was now filled with pieces of Anthea's favourite porcelain. On the rare times that she and Raymond made love, they would climb the stairs to the Blue Tower, which still seemed to arouse Raymond. As Anthea dutifully slid up and down his cock, she would gaze up at the Raphael and at her nicknamesake emerging from Pandora's Box.

Anthea gave a shiver as reality reasserted itself. Never more had she needed the help of the Radiant Fairy.

'Oh please, Hope and God too' – Anthea fell to her knees – 'please make Charlene go away.'

As most art galleries are undercapitalized, and Raymond and Anthea were not as flush as they appeared, Anthea had brokered a wizard £100,000 deal – a Silver Wedding in a Silver Valley – with *Oo-ah!* magazine. *Oo-ah!* were not only picking up the bill for her £6,000 wedding suit, £3,000 hat and £10,000 ball dress for the dinner dance afterwards, but also paying for bridesmaid and page clothes in fashionable lilac for Dicky and Dora.

In addition, Anthea had dropped a line to guests saying untruthfully that she and Raymond had been so bombarded with requests as to what they wanted as silver wedding presents that they had arranged a list at Asprey's. They would particularly like pieces of their beloved 'Violets' dinner service, on which Anthea's favourite flower, the violet, had been hand-painted. Everyone had belted off there and bought 'Violets' mugs which at £48 were the cheapest thing on the list.

Anthea had hired a lilac-and-white-striped marquee, with an Old Masters theme inside, which practically covered the big lawn which Robens had spent so many weeks perfecting. Robens was also hopping, as was Raymond, at Anthea's last-minute decision to disrupt the exquisite pastel harmony of the herbaceous border by planting a bloody great battalion of red geraniums to add a splash of colour.

Anthea had made more enemies by her decision to use the tent again the following day for a drinks party for the village and friends considered too second eleven to be asked to the silver wedding. These included the local doctor, who had not been forgiven for suggesting Anthea's panic attacks could be the onset of the menopause.

As the day grew hotter and more muggy with a forecast of thunder, tempers were further inflamed by an interview Anthea had defiantly given to Lynda Lee Potter, which had appeared in the *Mail* that morning.

After slagging off Galena: 'If your hubby's first wife hurt him by taking lovers, you make sure you are quadruply faithful and loving,' which enraged her stepchildren, Anthea had then been quoted as saying her life was made complete eight years ago by the arrival of the twins: 'our little autumn crocuses. Oh, the wonder of holding one's first born in one's arms.'

This enraged not only Emerald, working herself into

248

a frenzy back at Lancaster Gate, and the twins, already mutinying about their frightful lilac wedding clothes, but also *Oo-ah!*, who felt they'd been scooped.

Determined to get their kilo of flesh, *Oo-ah!* had photographed Anthea flapping around her newly decorated bedroom; shoving vast flower arrangements in front of Galena's few remaining pictures; seated at the 'pe-arno' playing Chopin ('I am one of nature's accompanists'); and posing by a terrifyingly good new portrait of herself in a silver tunic by Emma Sergeant. This she had given to Raymond as a joint birthday and silver wedding present. The portrait was now hanging in the hall upstaging the Matisse, and ready to be admired by arriving guests, before they were shepherded out through a side door into the garden and the marquee.

The seating plan was also driving Anthea crackers. Somerford Keynes had attacked Colin Casey Andrews in *The Times* that morning, so those two could no longer sit at the same table, and Somerford's burglar boyfriend, Keithie, a heavily tattooed bit of rough trade, had to be kept away from Anthea's porcelain collection. Keithie carried such huge handbags.

Anthea was livid that her very good friend and next-door neighbour, David Pulborough, was bringing his ugly wife, Rosemary, as well as Geraldine Paxton from the Arts Council. They had far too many spare women as it was. Thank God there were tons of gays in the art world, which would at least give an illusion of even numbers in the photographs.

'What a tragedy Rupert Campbell-Black has influenza,' she was now telling Harriet, the svelte henna-haired reporter from *Oo-ah!*, 'such a very old friend. And who on earth are Emerald Cartwright and Zachary Ansteig?' she shrieked.

'Friends of Jupiter's, Lady B.,' said Jean Baines, the vicar's wife and Anthea's best friend, who helped out at Foxes Court when things got too hectic.

'Oh, that's all right then.'

Jupiter's friends, reflected Anthea fondly, could be relied on to be charming and not cause trouble, which was more than could be said for Alizarin, Jonathan and Sienna's.

Anthea might have tried hard at first with her step-children, but she had tended to make beds rather than allowances. She had doted on Jonathan as a little boy, but gone off him as he grew wilder and less respectful. Alizarin was a left-wing bum, living rent free in the Lodge, which Anthea longed to renovate for holiday lets, and Sienna, with her wide drooping mouth, long heavy-lidded eyes and thick dark hair the colour of Marmite, was the image of Galena and quite beyond the pale, calling Anthea 'Hyacanthea Bucket' to her face.

Even on their father and Anthea's special day, none of the three had lifted a paint-stained finger to help. Alizarin was no doubt labouring away at some hideous canvas you wouldn't hang in a slaughterhouse – how he had the nerve to be so arrogant when his last exhibition had been a complete flop . . . And because she had banned his best friend Trafford (who was always sick and broke the place up) from the party, wretched Jonathan had deliberately poached Anthea's extremely comely cleaner, Esther Knight, to pose naked for him in her lunch hour. Mrs Knight and Jonathan were no doubt now getting stoned.

Even worse, Sienna had just stormed by on her motor-bike to get some cigarettes. And all the workmen putting the finishing touches to the marquee had dropped their hammers, because apart from her tattoos and studs in her belly button, ears, nose and tongue, Sienna had been completely in the nuddy. Only wrapping herself in the *Limesbridge Echo* before going into the village shop, she had on the way back pinched a bottle of champagne from the caterer's ice bath.

The twins Dicky and Dora were also acting up. Dicky had been teased at school about being an autumn crocus, and Dora wanted to take her delinquent pony Loofah to a gymkhana. Anthea was fed up with the lot of them. She must keep calm.

'"How do I love thee? Let me count the ways,"' she murmured, rehearsing the poem she was reciting in church.

How could she get herself into the mood for an exchange of vows and a celebration of true love when she was even fed up with Raymond? Annoyed that Anthea had badmouthed Galena in the *Mail*, dismissing the party as women's business, he had disappeared to the tennis court to play his traditional birthday match with his three eldest sons. He was then furious because he and Alizarin had been well beaten for the first time by Jupiter and an already drunk Jonathan. Alizarin kept missing the ball, until Raymond had been captured by *Oo-ah!* yelling at his middle son.

'This is the loveliest time of the year,' Raymond announced every month, but looking out of his dressing-room window as he changed after tennis, he decided that late May had the edge and nature was really putting on her glad rags for Anthea's party. Roads, fields and the churchyard frothed with cow parsley. Wild garlic, hawthorn and cherry blossom all added bridal whiteness. Beyond the pink foam of the orchard, proud trees admired their pale green reflections in the lazily winding river, and beyond that Galena's wild-flower meadow was streaked with cowslips and buttercups. In the muggy heat, the scent of lilac was overpowering.

Raymond was painfully reminded that it was at this time of year he had first brought Galena to Foxes Court. The candles lighting the great horse chestnuts were so askew, Galena could have clipped them on when she was plastered.

Gazing down, he was pleased with his flower beds, except for Anthea's clashing geraniums. He should have banned them as he should have curbed her spending in every direction. She was so competitive. David, living next door, was even worse. If ever a film crew came down to Foxes Court, the sound would instantly be blotted out by the Old Rectory mowing machines at full throttle. Below, Raymond could see David's gardener lobbing snails over their dividing wall as he also rerouted the best rambler roses and clematis over to the Pulborough side. And David has stolen my beloved Jonathan, thought Raymond dolefully.

A shriek from Anthea brought him back to earth. She was clean out of vases to contain the flowers that kept arriving to wish her and Raymond a happy day. Next moment henna-haired Harriet from *Oo-ah!* had butted in:

'We're taking a lunch break, Lady Belvedon. Can we photograph you getting dressed for the church service immediately afterwards?'

'Why don't you like take them upstairs to admire the Raphael?' mocked Sienna, who'd rolled up to steal another bottle.

'Shut up,' hissed Anthea. 'And who's put cow parsley on that table? I will not have it shedding in the house. Where on earth's Knightie? She should be back by now.'

'Knight and Day you are the one,' sang Jonathan as he foxtrotted a naked Mrs Knight round his studio.

Armed with her bottle, Sienna noticed Dicky's football on what was left of the big lawn.

'Ball-ee,' she cried, kicking it deep into Anthea's geraniums, sending Visitor the Labrador flatfooting after it.

252

30

'Why, you look younger than the day I married you, Sir Raymond,' cried Anthea, straightening her husband's dove-grey tie.

'And you look even more beautiful,' said Raymond truthfully.

The church, through an ancient gate and a hundred yards across the grass from Foxes Court, also looked beautiful, decorated with forget-me-nots and cow parsley, which here Anthea didn't mind shedding at all.

Waiting to welcome her and Raymond was dear Neville Baines, the vicar of St James, Limesbridge, a beaming happy clappy in his early fifties, known predictably as 'Neville-on-Sundays'. His beady wife, Jean, who found working occasionally for Lady Belvedon infinitely more exciting than being married to a clergyman, was acting as matron-of-honour. Appropriately dressed in droopy olive green, she was locally nicknamed 'Green Jean' because of her extreme ecological correctness. Jonathan and Sienna's inability to recycle their bottles drove her to a frenzy. In fact, thought Jean furiously, out of Raymond's six children, only Jupiter, who walked his stepmother up the aisle before taking his place beside his wife Hanna in the family pew and later reading: 'Sweet is the breath of morn', from *Paradise Lost*, behaved with any respect.

Galena's other three, spurning the family pew, sat in

a truculent row at the back. Sienna, menacing in a leather catsuit, was reading out Anthea's interview with Lynda Lee Potter:

'"Ay always bowled to may stepsons in the hols." Did she?'

'A wicket stepmother,' said Jonathan, taking a slug out of his bottle of champagne, and falling about at his own joke.

Alizarin, tieless as always, had put his old Rugbeian tie on Visitor, the Labrador who sat grinning in the pew beside him.

The moment Neville-on-Sundays started his pep talk on the sanctity of marriage, the incensed bridesmaid and page belted back to sit with their half-brothers and -sister. Dora, livid she had been banned from bringing Loofah into church, dropped her bouquet and said, 'Bugger.'

Dicky was still seething over his lilac suit. If his mother had worn a veil, he'd have broken her neck treading on it. As it was, Alizarin only just stopped him letting off a stink bomb.

'We could always have said Visitor had farted,' said Jonathan.

The entire pew rocked with giggles.

Poor, poor Anthea, to be saddled with such fiends, thought Green Jean who, as a curate's wife, had never forgiven Galena for pelting her with rotten kumquats.

Anthea, enchanting in Lindka Cierach's harebell-blue suit and David Shilling's cloche, composed of pale pink roses, had never forgiven her Rookhope relations for not supporting her when she gave birth to Charlene, and had therefore not asked them to the silver wedding. This was no hardship because they were all fearfully common. As a result there were no undry eyes in the church, except Raymond's who always blubbed when he recited Tennyson.

'"One praised her ankles, one her eyes, One her blond hair and lovesome mien,"' declaimed Raymond in his beautiful lilting voice, gazing into Anthea's eyes, and briskly editing as he went along:

> 'So sweet a face, such angel grace,
> In all that land had never been:
> Sir Raymond swore a knightly oath:
> This perfect maid shall be my queen!'

'Dad wasn't a knight like when he first met Anthea,' hissed Sienna. 'Silly old tosser.'

'I'm very disappointed by the turnout,' announced a frowning Dora, when she discovered the *Limesbridge Echo* and *Oo-ah!*, clinging tenaciously onto their exclusive, were the only photographers outside the church. 'I expected all Fleet Street to be here.'

'That child's the most frightful applause junky,' muttered Sienna.

'Who d'you think she gets it from?' asked Jonathan as, watched by a tight-lipped Green Jean, who also disapproved of wasting paper, henna-haired Harriet from *Oo-ah!* threw confetti over Raymond and a dimpling Anthea.

And there's Mum in the graveyard, thought Alizarin bleakly, how can she rest in peace with this din going on?

By eight o'clock, guests invited to the church were getting stuck into the Veuve Clicquot, exclaiming that Raymond's irises were even more exquisite than Van Gogh's and admiring the blow-ups of Old Masters, including the Waterlane Titian, in the marquee.

They were soon joined by influential members of the art world, livid at being banished from the house and denied a look at Raymond's pictures, by clients and glamorous celebs who might buy pictures or want their portraits painted and by some dowdy and worthy members of the local gentry: the Bishop and the

Lord-Lieutenant and their wives, whom Anthea felt raised the tone.

A string orchestra booked to play light classics and golden oldies, because Anthea loved ballroom dancing, was already belting out gems from *Oklahoma*. After dinner they would alternate with a heavily vetted pop group.

Raymond, who had swapped his morning coat for a dinner jacket, welcomed new arrivals alone until his wife, having been photographed changing by *Oo-ah!*, put in an appearance. Anthea had looked enchanting in church but really took the breath away as she floated down the stairs in clinging ivory silk shot through with rainbows. Her boyish curls had been swept up into a plaited hairpiece studded with rubies and intertwined with gold leaves – the exact replica of Hope in the Raphael.

Everyone in the crowded hall on their way to the garden clapped and cheered. Raymond couldn't speak for a moment.

'Oh Hopey,' he muttered, 'what a wonderful thing to do.'

Jupiter was less happy, not wanting the world to know that there was a Raphael hidden upstairs.

'Brilliant, Anthea' – he kissed her gold-dusted cheek – 'you've never looked more stunning. All the same' – he dropped his voice – 'on the grounds of security, it's better not to tell *Oo-ah!* who you're supposed to be.'

'Understood.' Anthea smiled up at him. 'This was for your father.'

'Abandon Hopey, all ye who enter here,' murmured Jonathan, catching sight of his stepmother.

Despite the warm night air soft as cashmere on her skin, Anthea shivered as she went into the garden. There was security on the gate, but so many other ways, through the woods or over the river, to crash the party.

Oh please, don't let Charlene roll up unexpectedly.

*   *   *

Many of the guests had retreated from the midges into the marquee and were examining the seating plan. Some were already settled in their allotted places. But not the Belvedon children, who had commandeered their own table in defiance of any placement and, all extremely arrogant, were yakking away, making private jokes.

The waitresses, having read of his laddish pranks, were very taken by Jonathan, who was as naughty and manipulative as he was extraordinarily handsome. Deathly pale with thick ebony curls, a big sulky mouth, a long nose and huge, dark, restlessly roving eyes, he exuded trouble like a thoroughbred colt about to bolt across a motorway. He was now wickedly caricaturing guests on a pile of paper napkins. Each time he finished a drawing, a waitress grabbed it, aware it might keep her in her old age.

Harriet from *Oo-ah!* was equally captivated: 'What artists do you most admire?' she asked earnestly.

'Amanda, my ex-girlfriend, could have told you,' sighed Jonathan, 'but alas we've split up.'

'Oh dear, why was that?'

'I'm dumb-blonding down, and she hated me falling asleep on the job. I need my eight hours a night.'

'Your eight whores,' growled Alizarin disapprovingly.

Tall and thin, despite massive shoulders, Alizarin had short, spiky dark hair, gaunt craggy features, Galena's high cheekbones, her slanting dark eyes framed by big black spectacles and the suppressed outrage of someone who had struggled to the top of Everest to find it wasn't there.

In between reading the latest on Kosovo in the *Guardian*, Alizarin gazed at Hanna Belvedon, Jupiter's big blonde wife. The myth of the eldest son wanting to kill his father, and the second son wanting to kill the eldest, certainly applied to the Belvedons. If Jupiter longed to strangle Raymond for being a whimsical old dodderer, Alizarin wanted to murder Jupiter for stealing and marrying the one woman, apart from Galena, he had ever really loved.

Hanna, sitting a couple of tables away, pretending to listen to the solipsistic ramblings of Casey Andrews, was miserably aware that her diet hadn't worked, that her black dress was too tight and that her long hair needed cutting. She was drawing bluebells on the tablecloth and comfort from Alizarin's dark ferocious passion.

The marriage service earlier had reminded her painfully of the hopes and excitement with which she had, five years ago, made her own vows to Jupiter, who she was convinced was no longer forsaking all others. He wasn't sleeping. He was curt and silent and, having hitherto insisted they spent every night together, had suddenly suggested she remain down in Limesbridge next week because of a forecast heatwave.

'Sprog on the way?' Casey leered at the black silk straining over Hanna's tummy.

Blushing, she shook her head.

'Career minded, are we? Don't want to leave it too long.'

'Somerford is a-coming in,' sang Jonathan, who was drawing the venomous critic as an obscenely fat python. Idly caressing his sister Sienna with his other hand, he asked, 'Why, apart from a crap review, does Casey want to murder Somerford?'

'Somerford's decided to write a monograph on Joan Bideford instead of Casey,' said Sienna. 'More interesting really. Joan's like living on Lesbos with a Swedish bus conductress.'

A swan dressed as a very ugly duckling, Sienna seemed to have studs on every part of her body not covered by her leather catsuit. Only that afternoon she had dyed her lovely long Marmite-coloured hair bright scarlet to match her drooping mouth and bitten nails.

She was now moodily telling a more subtle redhead, Harriet from *Oo-ah!*, about her latest installation on display at the Saatchi gallery, which was called *Aunt Hill* and consisted of piled-up stiff-legged nude models of her Aunt Lily.

'It like illustrates the evils of ageism,' said Sienna with a yawn. 'How like we chuck the old on the scrap heap.'

'Did your auntie mind posing in the nude?'

'Why should she? I gave her a large cheque for Badger Rescue. Lily's like my Auntie Hero.'

'Any plans for the future?'

'Putting her in a glass case with a bottle of whisky. If Damien can pickle sheep and sharks, why can't I like get a hundred grand for a pickled aunt?'

'It's shocking' – Harriet from *Oo-ah!* was not sure how to take Sienna – 'the way we sideline our senior citizens.'

No-one could have looked less sidelined than Aunt Lily, Raymond's older sister, who'd made a killing on the horses that afternoon. Nearly eighty, and still beautiful, with Raymond's luxuriant silver hair and brilliant turquoise eyes, she lived (to Anthea's intense irritation) in Raymond's nicest cottage overlooking the river, and caused coronaries at White's and Boodle's whenever she threatened to write her memoirs. She had a blond streak in her white hair from chain smoking, and was working her way down a bottle of champagne and observing everyone with intense amusement.

'What did you give Anthea and Raymond for a silver wedding present?' she shouted at Jonathan, who was now drawing his brother Jupiter as a lurking wolf.

'A tin of Quality Street. I thought Anthea looked like one of those women in poke bonnets on the lid. But Knightie and I' – Jonathan blew a kiss to Mrs Knight who, in a short and fetching maid's uniform, was directing guests to their seats – 'ate most of them.'

Overhearing this, a hovering Jupiter, who'd scored a hit with his present of Emerald's head, looked smug. Glancing contemptuously at his brothers and sister, unaware that he himself epitomized Envy, Avarice and, since he'd met Emerald, certainly Lust, he thought how they personified the deadly sins. Alizarin, refusing to compromise, was Pride; the constantly raging Sienna was Wrath; Jonathan, who had just nodded off, pen in hand, head on Sienna's leather shoulder, was Sloth; and Visitor, the yellow Labrador sitting in the chair allocated to Jonathan's ex-girlfriend, grinning in his master's Old Rugbeian tie, was certainly Greed.

Visitor, who always appeared to be trying to compensate for Alizarin's hostility, was borrowed by other Belvedons if they wanted to appear more lovable when being photographed by the media.

True to his name, Visitor toured the various Foxes Court houses every day for pieces of cheese from Raymond, rich tea biscuits from Anthea (who was surprisingly fond of him), bridge cake and cat leftovers from Aunt Lily, hash cookies from Jonathan, scrambled egg from Mrs Robens, and even wiggled his plump hips against Hanna's bird table in case there were crumbs left to dislodge.

In the past he had carried the rare cheques received by Alizarin to the bank, where the manager would always give him a piece of shortbread. Alas, Visitor continued to take cheques there, after Alizarin had left the bank in a huff for restricting his overdraft, so Alizarin now posted his even rarer cheques instead.

Visitor's tawny eyes were sparkling. He had already lifted his leg on several guy ropes and made his number with the chef. Visitor loved parties. They meant abandoned food, because there were invariably several Belvedons too uptight to eat, and dancing. Visitor adored dancing, bouncing round the floor with Dora and Dicky, who, drowning his sorrows at the prospect of appearing in *Oo-ah!* in a purple suit, was getting even drunker than Aunt Lily. Xavier Campbell-Black, who was in the same form as Dicky, would piss himself.

31

After an hour and a half of drinking, when the majority of the guests were seated and the waitresses were revving up to bring on the first course, Emerald and Zac arrived. They were late because Emerald kept saying she couldn't go through with it.

Yesterday she had painted a watercolour of herself edging across a high bridge with half its slats missing. Behind her on the bank waved the disconsolate Cartwrights. On the bank ahead stood the hazily drawn Belvedons. Rocks and a raging torrent lay far below.

As she and Zac came off the motorway, a huge red sun was sinking into the downs. This is the last sunset I'll see before meeting my real mother, she thought. Tears welled up in her eyes as she simultaneously experienced intense loneliness and a feeling of coming home.

The moon was hovering on the horizon like a great gold air balloon and the sun had set as they drove under the archway of white blossom. As the big golden house reared up before them, a deafening roar could be heard coming from the marquee.

'I'm about to open Pandora's Box,' moaned Emerald, dabbing at beads of sweat with a powder puff, 'and all the evils of the world are going to fly out and sting me.'

'I've got insect-repellent in the dashboard,' said Zac calmly, 'but your Violetta smells much more exotic.'

'Stop taking the piss,' snarled Emerald.

In her evening bag was the little musical box that played 'One two three four five, once I caught a fish alive', which Anthea had given her as a leaving present when she was three days old and which Patience had hung over her cot. As they walked from the car park through the garden, Emerald only noticed how beautifully the sculptures were floodlit.

'I'm frightened, Zac.'

'No, you're not. I'll be right beside you all evening.' Zac's fingers clamped on her elbow, propelling her through the front door.

'Do I rush forward and hug Anthea or appear cool?'

'Neither – remember our game plan. Don't say a word until she can't escape. Just relax – be yourself.'

'How can I be, when I'm not sure who "myself" is? Oh, what a stunning house!'

Emerald gazed round the hall and through into the drawing room, admiring glittering chandeliers, gilt cherubs frolicking around ancient looking-glasses, incredible pictures on faded terra rosa walls, richly swagged curtains swarming with pink peonies.

At least we've come to the right house, she thought, clocking Emma Sergeant's portrait of Anthea.

'That's kind of kitsch.' A grinning Zac was pointing to a blow-up under a picture light of Anthea and Raymond outside Buckingham Palace.

'Shut up,' hissed Emerald.

Her first glimpse of her real mother was Anthea glancing round in fury because they were so late. Everyone was sitting down. The orchestra were poised to play 'See, the conquering hero comes!' The guests led by Green Jean would clap in time as Anthea and Raymond walked in hand in hand and regally took up their positions at the top table. The whole marquee was already lit by flickering candles.

Anthea's rage however evaporated at the sight of such a good-looking couple. Gushing like a Cotswold stream in February, she seized Zac's hand when he introduced himself and Emerald.

'What a handsome chap. I love the name Zachary, and Sir Raymond and I simply love the States, and of course any friend of Jupiter's.'

Now Anthea was taking Emerald's little sweating hand in her own tiny one.

I'm going to faint, thought Emerald, my heart's going to smash through my ribs. This is my mother, how beautiful she is, a fairy princess, the same height as me, a twin gazing into my eyes, except hers are cobalt violet. But if I collapse into her arms, as I long to, I'll send her flying. She was quite incapable of speech.

Noticing the candle-snuffer hidden by its silver wrapping paper trembling frantically in Emerald's hand, Anthea was touched that some Americans really were unnerved by titles. Accepting the present, she passed it quickly as a relay baton to a hovering Green Jean.

'Thank you ver' ver' much, Emerald. Why, you're a little person like me. What part of the States are you from?' and when Emerald was still incapable of replying: 'Grab yourself a glass of bubbly and rush in, we're about to dine. Your table's on the left, near Jupiter.' Then, seeing Keithie, Somerford Keynes's burglar boyfriend, sidling out of the drawing room, fat handbag bulging, Anthea rushed towards him. 'Catch up with you two later . . . Keithie, I didn't see you arrive. How ver' ver' good of you to come.'

Emerald was appalled to find herself thinking Anthea had a dreadfully put-on voice.

'You're doing great,' murmured Zac.

As they entered the marquee, the room fell silent – then everyone launched into a frenzy of 'Who are they, who are they?'

Amidst the *nouveaux riches* collectors in their white tuxedos and pink carnations, and the upper classes, whose dinner jackets were lichened with age, and the deadpan monochrome art world, Zac dressed entirely in black (his ebony satin dress shirt replacing the traditional white) looked far more a part of the latter group, who far outnumbered the others. But the rest of the art world didn't have Zac's long lean elegant T-shaped body, nor his hard gold features, nor the amiable untroubled smile so completely belied by the unblinking, watchful yellow eyes.

'Wow!' murmured Sienna. '"Tiger, Tiger, burning bright In the forests of the night".'

'More like a Beverly Hills funeral director,' drawled Jonathan, who loathed competition, 'but I would not kick out his girlfriend.'

Jupiter, still pacing, went utterly still, blood flooding his cold marble face, as he fought his way down an aisle of half-in half-out chairs to welcome them.

She's the one, thought Hanna Belvedon in despair. What chance have I got?

The girl looked utterly jolted by Jupiter. She was terribly white, and trembling, and dropped first her scarlet bag, then her crimson pashmina, to reveal a slender fairylike figure. Jupiter was clearly just as fazed, diving to pick up her things, breaking the professional habit of a lifetime by gazing at something beautiful with unqualified enthusiasm.

The girl's handsome boyfriend by contrast looked totally unruffled. With an Adonis like him in tow, maybe she wasn't that interested in Jupiter.

Glancing round, Hanna noticed both Jonathan and Alizarin had stopped bickering about the right home for the Elgin Marbles and were also staring at the girl. Then Alizarin, with utterly uncharacteristic levity, chucked a paper dart at Hanna. Inside he had written: 'You're infinitely more beautiful.'

'Where did that come from?' demanded an icy voice. 'What did it say?' Jupiter held out his hand.

'Nothing,' said Hanna, and as a fleet of waitresses streamed on with the first course, sea trout mousse with a prawn and champagne sauce, to the accompaniment of the 'Trout' Quintet, she defiantly tore the paper dart into tiny pieces.

'Any chink in that marriage and Alizarin will move in,' observed Aunt Lily to Keithie the burglar on her right. 'Jupiter will develop the most frightful squint if he tries to keep one eye on Hanna and the other on the exquisite child who's just walked in. Ugh, here comes Willy of the Valley – even I keep my wrinkly old elbows rammed to my sides when he's about.'

Attention had been temporarily diverted from Emerald and Zac by the even later arrival of David Pulborough, who had only a hundred yards to walk from the Old Rectory, but who kept his watch deliberately slow so he could always make an entrance.

'Of Armani and the man I sing,' mocked Jonathan.

'David, how lovely.' Graciousness met graciousness as Anthea jumped from her chair and ran to greet him.

As David drew her back into the ruched corridor leading into the marquee, Jupiter noticed him bending to kiss Anthea on the mouth, his eyes swivelling to see if Rosemary were watching before groping her bottom. Jupiter hoped David wouldn't poach too many Belvedon artists or clients this evening. But entering the marquee, the little bounder waved at Casey and Kevin Coley.

David was followed by his mistress, Geraldine Paxton from the Arts Council, who wore a navy-blue watered-silk trouser suit, blood-red lipstick and so much powder she looked as though she'd dipped her face in a barrel of flour. A networking nymphomaniac who advised the rich what to put on their walls, Geraldine was gratified to be on the top table on Raymond's right, but irked to be so far from David. Anthea, who was unaware of the extent of David's commitment to Geraldine, greeted her fondly, knowing it would upset Rosemary.

Rosemary, who'd entered the marquee from the garden, had been tormented for nearly twenty-seven years by a tendresse between Anthea and David and had the lack of bloom and quilted jaw of the perennially cuckolded wife. St George's horse had lost its bounce and looked like a riding-school hack, but she was cheered that the Belvedon children were now noisily yelling, 'Come and sit with us, Rosie, you can have Visitor's seat.'

'You're over here, Rosemary,' said Green Jean firmly.

Rosemary knew she couldn't expect a better placing than between gay Somerford and gayish Neville-on-Sundays, who doted on Jonathan and, knowing of his need for sleep, always muffled the church bells when Jonathan was at home. Both men clearly felt they'd drawn the short straw being seated next to Rosemary. Across the table, Joan Bideford, back from Lesbos and roaring away like a sea lion, clearly did not.

'Hello, Rosie,' she yelled, 'still married to that little squit?'

Suppressing a smile, Rosemary jabbed a finger at a far-off table, where Anthea, knowing David's ambition to become High Sheriff, had placed him between the equally dowdy wives of the Bishop and the Lord-Lieutenant.

Rosemary then looked for her son Barney, who worked in the gallery with David, noticing that, perhaps with deliberate irony, Anthea had placed him next to the prettiest girl in the room.

Barney, who preferred his own sex and who looked like a pallid version of his grandfather, Sir Mervyn Newton, did many dodgy deals to feed his cocaine habit. Like most children pushed together with the children of their parents' friends, Barney detested the Belvedons, who used to tease him about being fat.

'The moment I saw you I thought, "She was a phantom of delight",' sighed Barney's father as he gazed into the rheumy eyes of the Bishop's wife.

Glancing round at the great and the good and the deeply iffy, Emerald wondered if any of them would like their heads done. She knew she ought to be doing a number on the rest of her table, but having met Anthea, she couldn't think straight, and, having knocked over her glass of wine, found herself buttering her table napkin.

Any of these men might be my father, she thought. Her panic at being separated from Zac, who was having a lovely time between Hanna Belvedon and Joanna Lumley, was somewhat allayed when she discovered the pasty slob on her left was the son of David Pulborough, who lived next door and who could fill her in with loads of malicious gossip.

'That's Alizarin the tormented conflict-junkie,' Barney was now telling her bitchily, 'waiting to be famous enough to be played by Daniel Day-Lewis.'

'I hear your father's just signed up Jonathan.'

'Much good it'll do him,' snapped Barney, 'Dad's already got him fat commissions from the National Portrait Gallery to paint Rupert Campbell-Black and Dame Hermione Harefield, but Jonathan's done fuck all except squander the advance on booze, drugs and women.'

'He's very attractive,' confessed Emerald, glancing across at Jonathan who was clearly both plastered and coked up to his big bloodshot eyeballs. Seated next to a ferocious beauty with bright red hair, his hands were all over her. Now he was kissing the skylark tattooed on her shoulder, now unzipping her leather catsuit even further, to provide a glimpse of high round breasts and a silver stud gleaming in her belly button. Peering to see if she was wearing a ring, Emerald found she wore them on every finger.

'Who's Jonathan snogging?' she asked Barney. 'She looks familiar.'

'His sister, Sienna, and they're not entirely doing it as a wind-up. With any luck one of them will pass out before they disgrace themselves on the dance floor.'

Fortunately *Oo-ah!* had been diverted from such lewd

behaviour and were busy photographing a beaming Visitor in Anthea's £3,000 wedding hat.

'No-one's really disciplined the Belvedons,' went on Barney, forking up Emerald's untouched sea trout mousse. 'Raymond is used to artists and thinks their behaviour is quite normal. But they've been brought up rather as a cat brings up its food, vomited into the world by Galena's neglect. Yet her charm has somehow extended down the years, enslaving them.'

These are my brothers and sisters, thought Emerald. She had never encountered people so outrageous nor so glamorous. Nor could she take her eyes off Anthea. With the Bishop on one side and the Lord-Lieutenant on the other, their flushed balding heads were bent so far over her, they seemed about to clash like shiny red billiard balls.

'Lady Belvedon is so beautiful,' sighed Emerald.

Loyalty to his mother, Rosemary, was Barney's only decent emotion.

'And an absolute bitch,' he said.

'Surely not.' Emerald longed to defend Anthea, but was scared of giving the game away.

'She's the most ghastly snob,' said Barney flatly. 'Anyone who's not going to advance her socially, or feather Raymond's nest, is ruthlessly rejected.'

Like she rejected me, thought Emerald darkly.

As they were between courses, Anthea had bidden *au revoir* to the doting Bishop and Lord-Lieutenant and was wandering round the tables, air-kissing and charming.

'Watch her doing a number only on the really important,' said Barney savagely. 'Look at her drooling over that guy with the strange eyes. Must say, he's seriously gorgeous.'

'He's my boyfriend,' said Emerald.

Because of the stifling heat, men were taking off their jackets, and a side of the marquee had been opened up to the garden. Beneath the sweet heady scent of clematis and lilac lurked the rank sexy smell of wild garlic, as though some courtesan too lazy to have a bath had drenched herself in expensive scent.

Black fluffy clouds with pearly grey linings were advancing on a primrose-yellow moon. In the distance beyond dark shrubberies gleamed the River Fleet. Emerald longed to race down the hill and swim across the moonlit water to freedom. She shouldn't have come. But, glancing up, she saw Anthea had moved on and Zac, smiling across at her, was making a thumbs-up sign.

After dinner, Jupiter made a smooth speech.

'Practising for when he takes over the Tory Party,' said Barney sourly.

'There are ordinary marriages and delicious marriages,' began Jupiter. 'This is a delicious marriage.'

He then praised Raymond, which he found difficult because he despised his father, then Anthea, which he found easy.

'Anthea's been a wonderful wife to Dad, for whom she planned this entire day, and she's been a wonderful stepmother, compensating so much for the tragic loss of our own mother. I cannot thank her enough.'

'We can,' shouted Jonathan and Sienna.

'Shut up,' snapped Alizarin. 'Let her have her hour of glory.'

For a while they did, even when Anthea, smiling into the *Oo-ah!* camera lens, brimming with tears but not enough to dislodge her blue mascara, rose to her feet. Having prettily thanked her dearest stepson Jupiter, who had always been such 'a tower of strength', she launched into a eulogy to her husband.

'Round the walls are all the Old Masters Sir Raymond has Saved for the Nation.'

'And made a pretty penny for himself,' shouted Somerford Keynes, whose mother-of-pearl binoculars were trained on Zac.

'Unkind, Somerford!' Anthea threw him a reproachful glance. 'Let us all drink to Sir Raymond.'

'She can hardly see over the table,' spat Sienna.

'Thank your lucky stars she isn't genetically modified,' said Jonathan, drawing a giant Anthea on the tablecloth. 'Think of the nightmare if she were six foot two, and no bug could kill her.'

'My one regret,' wound up Anthea in a ringing voice, 'is that Mummy and Daddy are not alaive to witness this wonderful occasion.'

'Bollocks,' thundered Aunt Lily, to the horror of Green Jean, 'Anthea never let them over the threshold.'

'Boo,' yelled Sienna, a lone voice amidst the storm of cheering as Anthea sat down. 'Support me,' she wailed to Jonathan.

But he was gazing at Emerald, who was smiling because everyone seemed so delighted with her mother.

'One praised her ankles, one her eyes,' murmured
    Jonathan:
'One her dark hair and lovesome mien.
So sweet a face, such angel grace,
In all that land had never been.'

'Christ,' he went on dreamily, 'she's incredible.'

'Another demon Barbie,' snarled Sienna. 'What's happened to her Nicolas Cage boyfriend?'

Jupiter, who'd recently flushed Keithie the burglar out of the dining room with an even more bulging handbag, was not amused to discover Zac prowling around upstairs.

'Just looking for the john,' said Zac blandly, 'easy to get lost in these old places.'

'There are portaloos in the garden,' said Jupiter icily. He'd better get Robens to frisk every guest on the way out.

* * *

Raymond, who felt guilty he'd been so foul to Alizarin over the tennis match earlier, had spent much of dinner trying to convince Geraldine Paxton from the Arts Council that his second son was a neglected genius.

'If only he'd use a lighter palette or accept a commission we might have some suitable pictures to hang, but he insists on going his own road.'

'It might help if he and his brother stopped thumping critics,' said Geraldine crisply.

Jupiter was very much looking forward later to showing Geraldine, an expert on being an expert, the head sculpted by his new protégée Emerald Cartwright. Now the official part of the evening was over, he could also ask Emerald to dance.

32

Raymond and Anthea opened the ball to 'This Guy's in Love with You', which they'd discovered was their favourite tune, the year they met. Raymond was a competent but rather straight dancer, and very stiff from too much tennis. Anthea however was dying to show off.

As she and Raymond came off the floor, they bumped into Zac, so tall, lithe and strong. Next moment he and Anthea had exchanged a smouldering glance, and Zac had swept her off to dance. Lighter than an elf in his arms, Anthea was soon telling him she would have taken up ballet, if she hadn't been so tiny.

'Ay made the other principals and the corps seem like hippos. And where do you come from, Zachary? You dance so beautifully.'

'Well, originally I guess from Vienna.'

'So you must love to waltz,' cried Anthea. 'Oh, so do I, whirling around held tightly in your partner's strong arms, so much more romantic than this modern stuff.'

'Where did you get the idea for that fabulous dress?' Zac touched the rainbow-woven silk, letting his fingers linger, pressing the little breast beneath.

'It's a character from a painting,' murmured Anthea, 'but my lips are sealed.'

'Your lips' – Zac glanced down at them – 'are far too soft and pretty to be sealed.'

Jupiter, having fortified himself with a large brandy, ignoring the reproachful blue eyes of his wife, was poised to ask Emerald to dance, when Jonathan pre-empted him.

'I must get your telephone number before I get too hammered. You've got to sit for me.'

Having scribbled Emerald's number on the inside of his wrist, he led her onto the dance floor, opening his arms like the Angel of the North, then enfolding her against his body.

'I can't bear it,' groaned Sienna as Jonathan dropped a kiss on Emerald's dark head, then, tilting up her face, gazed into it with such intensity, fingering it in bewilderment.

'You've got to let him go, lovey,' muttered Alizarin, who was also watching the anguish on Hanna's face as she clocked her seething husband.

Jupiter could hear David Pulborough saying, 'I am appalled Raymond didn't sell out. People prepared to pay twice as much keep asking me if I can find them a Casey Andrews. You're being robbed, Casey.'

There would be time to strangle David later. For the moment, Jupiter decided, it was more important to break up Emerald and Jonathan.

The ever courteous Raymond was back in his seat, beside a restless Geraldine Paxton.

'Did your wife ballroom dance professionally?' she asked him sourly, then she thought: Oh good, David's stopped propositioning that dreadful Casey Andrews and is coming to ask me to dance.

David was just about to twirl his fingers at Geraldine when he suddenly saw little Dora Belvedon in her lilac bridesmaid's dress and asked her instead, letting her ride round on his toes, so that *Oo-ah!* might take their picture, and everyone think what a caring charmer he was.

This also gave him the chance to examine close up the incredibly beautiful girl dancing with Jonathan. Half the men in the room – the rest were gay – seemed to have taken the floor for the same reason. Then David twigged: she was the girl in the leather mini who'd been sculpting Jupiter's head last week. She kept glancing out into the garden, and for once Jonathan looked like the stable boy trying to cling on to the bolting thorough-bred.

As the band crashed to a halt, Jonathan put his hands on either side of her face and, dropping his dark head, buried his lips in hers, kissing her on and on. Everyone whooped, the men somewhat reluctantly. Jupiter's going to kill Jonathan, thought David in delight. But maybe Emerald would perform the task first.

'What a bloody irrelevant stupid thing to do,' she screamed.

Thrusting Jonathan away, she practically knocked him over as she whacked him viciously across the face before running off into the garden.

She's a southpaw, thought Alizarin irrationally. Where the hell had he seen her before?

The heterosexual male half of the party might have followed Emerald out of the marquee if the leader of the orchestra, who'd been taken aside by Zac, hadn't launched into the languorous violin solo which intro-duces Weber's 'Invitation to the Dance'. Then suddenly the whole band launched into the main tune, the most glorious dancing music, conjuring up Vienna, excite-ment, beautiful bejewelled women in ball dresses, glittering chandeliers and handsome men swirling around in tails.

Zac just came up, clicked his heels in front of Anthea, and swept her onto the floor. And the room stopped because they were both such wonderful dancers, circling to this amazingly powerful swooping beat. Everyone clapped and Visitor the Labrador, seeing proper dancing, galumphed onto the floor with Dicky and Dora. As Visitor bounced about, Zac reached down and took Dicky's and then Dora's hands and they joined up with Anthea and all whirled around.

Anthea, iridescent as a dragonfly as the rainbows of her dress caught the light, looked so deliriously happy there was a feeling round the room that Zac might be about to waltz off with a ready-made family.

'I'm amazed he's not teaching her the goose step: vun, two, vun, two,' said Jonathan, ruefully rubbing his reddened cheek. 'Vy don't you elope with Hopey, Herr Ansteig, and leave divine Emerald viz me.'

As the band paused, there were shouts for an encore! The music started up again. This time, leaving Dicky and Dora gambolling with Visitor, Zac whisked Anthea once round the floor, before dancing her out into the perfumed garden. Across the lawn they went, under rose-garlanded arches and pergolas, past floodlit marble nymphs and bronze gods, down shaven lawns between dark yew ramparts, in and out of the apple trees, beneath a ceiling of blossom, their speed pegged by rough grass. But still Zac carried on, driving her with the heat and force of his body, until they reached the boathouse and the silver river.

Laughing, protesting, Anthea tried halfheartedly to escape. 'Ay must go back to my guests, you're so macho, Zachary, what a glorious dance!'

But Zac held on tight, thrusting her into the boathouse. Pressed against his taut hard muscular body, Anthea's knees gave way. He's going to kiss me, she thought in ecstasy.

'We mustn't upset Emma,' she said playfully.

Then her pounding heart jerked to a standstill; her blood froze. Her gasp of horror would have soared to a scream if Zac hadn't clapped his hand over her mouth, as she realized there was someone else in the boathouse. Against the moonlit cobwebbed window, a black silhouette quivered.

'Don't you think you've upset "Emma" enough?' said

a breathless, rasping voice. Then, when Anthea didn't react: 'Hi, Mum, I'm your daughter Charlene, why the hell did you give me up?'

'Ay don't know what you're talking about.' Anthea tried to bolt in panic, but Zac, leaning against the door, black and menacing as Emerald's shadow, barred the way.

Then Emerald flipped.

'How dare you give me away,' she screamed, 'you could have got me back after you married Raymond.'

'You've got the wrong person,' whimpered Anthea.

'Oh no, I haven't. Remember the musical box you gave me?' Emerald swung it in front of Anthea's terrified face. 'One two three four five, once I caught a fish alive. Remember the hippo and your white cardigan to help me sleep because it smelled of you?'

Suddenly Anthea caved in. 'I didn't know where you were, my parents chucked me out. I was at my wit's end, I was only nineteen, I had no money, I tried and tried to find a way to keep you.'

'Not very hard,' hissed Emerald. 'And why did you tell Lynda Lee Potter Dicky and Dora were your first born, and what special joy it gave you to hold them in your arms?'

'Because I could take them home!' Anthea was hysterical. 'It wrecked my life giving you up.'

'Why didn't you search for me like other mothers, why didn't you put your name on the Adoption Contact Register, and wait desperately hoping every day for a knock on the door?'

'I thought it was unfair to disrupt your life.'

Emerald was swaying like a cobra – about to strike.

'*Your* life, you mean. Then why did you blow me out when Zac tried to contact you? You selfish bitch.'

Terrified Emerald was going to claw her face, Anthea backed into Zac and gave a shriek.

'And who's my father?' screamed Emerald.

Next moment, they all jumped at a hammering and banging then Jupiter shoved open the warped door. 'What the fuck's going on?'

'Anthea's my mother,' sobbed Emerald.

In the long pause, she could hear the surflike boom of the band, the croak of frogs, the gentle swishing flow of the river.

Jupiter's face was as pale as a death mask, the moon shining through the cobwebs crackling and speckling it like an Old Master.

'Is this true?' he asked bleakly.

'If she says so.' Anthea sounded almost sulky.

'I'm sorry I tricked you' – Emerald had turned to Jupiter, quailing at the hatred in his eyes – 'but she wouldn't recognize me, so I had to get into your house somehow.'

Anthea took the opportunity of shooting past Jupiter out of the boathouse, racing back up the hill, losing a shoe, twice falling in the stream, covering herself in mud. All the outside entrances had been locked for security reasons, including the side door leading to the marquee. She had to scuttle past the dance floor, packed with couples swaying to Robbie Williams's 'Millennium', their merriment such a contrast to her dark nightmare. As she hurtled through the front door, a worried Green Jean was hovering in the hall.

'Are you OK, Anthea? Raymond's been searching everywhere. *Oo-ah!* want to photograph you with the children and Visitor. Can I get you a drink?' But Anthea had fled upstairs, slap into Raymond, who in horror took in her collapsing hair and mud-stained dress.

'Whatever's the matter, my darling?'

Pushing him out of the way, Anthea threw herself on her new cream linen counterpane and his mercy, sobbing so wildly it was some minutes before Raymond could make any sense.

'Darling, angel, it can't be that bad.' A terrible

277

thought struck him. 'You haven't met someone else?'

'No, no, much worse, there's a girl down in the boathouse who says she's my daughter.'

'Well, is she?'

Having set herself up as the personification of chastity and fidelity for the past twenty-five years and the antithesis of promiscuous Galena, Anthea was not prepared to tarnish this image.

'Yes, but she's yours too,' she cried despairingly.

Raymond was astounded.

'My child? Why on earth didn't you tell me?'

'I only discovered I was pregnant after I'd left the gallery. I knew how much you adored Galena, how desperate you were to mend your marriage. I loved you so much, we'd had our one night – or perhaps two – of love together, then Galena came back and told you she loved you, I couldn't break up your marriage.'

Anthea's hairpiece woven with gold leaves and rubies was all askew like a fallen halo, her face streaked with blue mascara and eyeliner. Although she shivered frantically, sweat was darkening the armpits of her dress.

'Galena would have gone bananas if she'd found out. So I gave my baby, my little Charlene up for adoption. I wanted to keep her so badly.' Anthea clasped her tiny trembling hands to her face. 'The adoption society were so fierce and disapproving, they said I'd be punished by God if I changed my mind. Mummy and Daddy had chucked me out. Oh Raymond . . .' She was sobbing so much she had again become incoherent.

'Oh my precious child.' Raymond was crying too.

Dragging the blue checked duvet off the bed in his dressing room next door, he wrapped it round her shuddering little body.

'Why didn't you tell me when we got together again? We could have gone to court.'

'I couldn't do it to Charlene's replacement parents. They'd sent me such a lovely letter and a beautiful shawl. I've still got it. I couldn't break their hearts. I wanted to tell you so badly. Don't think I haven't cried every day inside.'

'What a terrible secret you've had to keep.' Raymond got out a purple silk handkerchief and wiped both their eyes. 'But she's come home, we've got all our lives to make it up to her. You can tell me the details later, but let's go and meet her, and call the family into the library.'

'But what about the party?' wailed Anthea, quailing too at the prospect of her censorious stepchildren.

'The caterers will keep the drink flowing. That lot have enough to squabble about till dawn anyway, and the band's been paid double. Leave them to it.'

In the distance they could hear strains of 'Hit me, baby, one more time', and wild shrieks as a couple ran off across the lawn.

'Oh Hopey, I can't bear to think what you've been through.'

Anthea caught a glimpse of her red, swollen, grief-devastated face in the mirror. Nor could she.

'I can't cope with people at the moment,' she whimpered, 'I'm still in shock. Will you go and see her?'

'Of course I will, don't worry, wash your pretty face, and I'll get Jean to bring you up a cup of tea.'

If Dr Reynolds had been invited, he was tempted to joke, he could have given Anthea a shot. He felt passionately relieved she was still his.

Buoyed up by champagne, a sense of adventure and the prospect of another daughter to love – what a wonderful seventy-fifth birthday present – Raymond went downstairs. There he found Green Jean, simultaneously avid to find out what was up and having difficulty keeping the team from *Oo-ah!*, who'd heard desperate sobbing, at bay.

'Lady Belvedon is absolutely exhausted,' Raymond told them firmly, 'working her tiny self into the ground, making everything perfect for everyone else, so I've sent her to bed. I'm sure you've got enough material,' he smiled at Harriet, 'but if you need more, we can cobble it together tomorrow. And if you could bear to take her a cup of tea . . . ?' he added to Jean.

On the terrace, he met a stony-faced Jupiter.

'Anthea's told me, Jupe. Where's your new sister?'

'In the library.'

Neither of them noticed Barney, who'd been wondering what had become of Zac, lurking in the shadows.

Raymond almost danced across the hall.

'"A fairy Prince with joyful eyes, And lighter-footed than the Fox,"' he quoted happily as he slid into the library, which was one of the few rooms untouched by Anthea, and locked the door.

First editions, tall art books, leather-bound classics seemed to be falling out of their shelves in excitement. Characters in the paintings, which Anthea had banished from the rest of the house, and which included a Stanley Spencer miracle, and a homosexual threesome by John Minton, seemed about to abandon their activities to witness a more thrilling drama. Alone, on the faded threadbare crimson sofa, tiny as Anthea, huddled Emerald in her pretty dress, like a thrown-aside bunch of flowers. Her face was ashen, her eyes closed.

'My dearest child, welcome home.' Raymond's voice was deep and tear-choked, then, in amazement: 'Why, we've met before! I so hoped we'd meet again, where was it?'

'At Rupert Campbell-Black's,' stammered Emerald. 'You gave me your autograph. I had no idea that Anthea was my mother then. I hope you don't . . .'

'Of course I don't.'

Raymond held out his arms; Emerald collapsed sobbing into them. Raymond's handkerchief smelled faintly of Extract of Lime, his dinner jacket was wet with Anthea's tears and streaked with her make-up. For a moment Emerald luxuriated in the warmth of his body, giddy with relief that he wasn't angry.

280

'You're taking it so well,' she mumbled, 'I didn't mean to upset Lady Belvedon, I hope it hasn't wrecked your party, and it's not too painful for you having her child rolling up.'

'And *my* child too,' said Raymond, proceeding to tell a flabbergasted Emerald that he was her father, and explain the nightmare through which Anthea had been. Emerald couldn't take it in. For so long she'd imagined a father of Rupert Campbell-Black's age, still fit and virile. Raymond must have been fifty when she was born. Now he was seriously old. But he was so kind, sitting beside her, his arm round her shoulders, patting her hand.

'Anthea was only doing what she thought best for you, darling,' he told her gently, 'handing you over to a mother and father who longed for you and would adore you. When she and I finally got together after my first wife died, she felt she couldn't disrupt your life. Anthea always puts other people first. You look so like her,' he added, kissing her forehead.

'May I see her?' begged Emerald.

A minute later, Emerald and Anthea fell into each other's arms.

33

Poor Raymond had the less fun task of breaking the news to the family. The party was thinning out, but a lot of people were still dancing and drinking. Rosemary Pulborough, having endured seeing her husband flirting or caballing all evening, was extremely glad to have an excuse to leave: escorting a very merry Aunt Lily back to her cottage.

'I'd like to have said thank you to my brother and his wife,' protested Lily, 'but they appear to have vanished upstairs to renew their conjugal vows.'

At least Anthea isn't with David, thought Rosemary wearily.

Earlier, Dicky Belvedon, as a result of all that waltzing and a skinful of champagne, had just finished being very sick in the lupins, when he heard raised voices carrying across the hot night air. Stealing down to the boathouse, he had overheard most of the row, including the exchange with Jupiter.

Bolting back to the marquee, he found his twin sister talking to Sienna. Jonathan had nodded off like the dormouse in *Alice in Wonderland*. Visitor was waddling up and down the table finishing up.

'Where's Mummy?' asked Dora. 'Everyone's asking for her.'

'Probably being photographed on the loo in a YSL nightie,' said Sienna.

'She was down at the boathouse,' panted Dicky.

'Whatever for?' demanded Dora. 'Ugh, you've got sick on your shirt.'

'Some girl's saying Mummy's her mother,' gasped Dicky.

'What?' Jonathan was awake in an instant.

'That dark girl you were kissing, Jonathan, she was screaming at Mummy that Mummy was her mother. Then Jupiter barged in and the girl told Jupiter, and he asked Mummy, and she said it was true.'

'Don't tell such wicked lies,' said Dora, going very red. 'Mummy wouldn't do it with anyone else. We're her first born, she said so in the *Daily Mail.*'

Sienna, trying to hide her excitement, dropped a napkin in a jug of water and wiped Dicky's shirt.

'Are you quite sure, Dicko?'

'Quite. Mummy ran up the hill crying, I couldn't keep up with her, she lost a shoe.' He held up a tiny blue high-heeled sandal.

'Wow!' said Jonathan in delight. 'It's like discovering the Virgin Mary's slept with the entire Nazareth rugger team. A new little stepsister and such a pretty one. Alizarin!' he yelled over the din of the band to his brother, who was snatching a few moments of conversation with Hanna. 'Come and hear the latest, Anthea's got a love child.'

Returning to the table, catching sight of Dicky and Dora, both near to tears, Alizarin told Jonathan to shut up.

'Who's going to ring Dempster?' demanded Jonathan unrepentantly, waving to a waitress to bring another bottle. 'You'd better, Al, you need the money more than me and Jupiter.'

Jupiter arrived next, also very pale, outraged at being tricked by Emerald but in control of himself.

'You've obviously heard. Dad wants us all in the library in ten minutes.'

'Then fill up our glasses,' said Jonathan.

'I suggest Hanna puts those two to bed.' Jupiter nodded at Dicky and Dora.

'It's way past our bedtime,' chorused the twins.

'We're coming too – or I'll go and tell Harriet from *Oo-ah!*,' threatened Dora.

'Does that mean I've got two sisters? Oh yuck,' groaned Dicky.

'She's only like a half-sister, like I am,' explained Sienna. 'You share the same father with me and the same mother with what's she called?'

'Emerald. And I know which half of her I want,' said Jonathan evilly. 'Alizarin can have the top half.'

The Belvedons' delight at Anthea's embarrassing lapse after her hogging the moral high ground for so long soon evaporated when Raymond, with tears in his eyes, imparted the joyful news that Emerald was his and Anthea's child.

Alizarin, who'd been gazing at the Stanley Spencer, swung round.

'How old is she?' he demanded.

'Twenty-six in July,' said an unguarded Jupiter, remembering how he and Emerald had discussed both being born in Cancer during dinner.

There was a long pause. Dicky sidled towards the calculator on Raymond's desk.

'So you were shagging Anthea while you were married to Mum,' said Alizarin bleakly. 'Mum always swore you were. I never believed her.'

The others were jolted. Since Galena's death, Alizarin had never spoken her name.

'That means Emerald's like three months older than me,' said Sienna furiously.

Jonathan took a book of Sickert's drawings off the top shelf. 'Dad the stud,' he drawled, 'humping Mum and

Anthea at the same time but still posing as the wronged husband.'

Raymond, appalled at such antagonism, stumbled on.

'Your mother and I were going through a bad patch,' he stammered. 'Anthea came to the gallery and comforted me. I swear I only made love to her about once on the office sofa.'

'You naughty man!' said Dora in horror.

'Galena, or rather your mother found out, not about the sleeping together, but that I was very fond of Anthea, so Anthea unselfishly left the gallery and only afterwards discovered she was expecting a baby and not believing in abortion—'

'Correct-shun,' interrupted an enraged Sienna, 'what about the one she made me have when I was sixteen?'

'My dear,' said Raymond faintly.

'Did you?' Dicky looked up from his calculator in amazement.

'You naughty woman!' thundered Dora.

'Anthea had the baby,' ploughed on Raymond, 'longed to keep little Charlene, but felt she couldn't let the adopting parents down, and kept this terrible secret for twenty-five years.'

Three branches of purple lilac, shrivelled up in the heat, were shedding their petals on the polished table. Hanna sat with her head in her hands. Jonathan got up and poured himself three fingers of sloe gin.

'That's because you're not the dad, Dad,' he drawled. 'It's the tallest story from the shortest person I've ever heard. You may have pulled the assistant, but you've been conned. Emerald and that male model boyfriend, who's a hood if ever I saw one, have cooked up the whole thing to get their thieving hands on some Belvedon cash.'

'Jonathan, please.' Raymond was nearly in tears again. 'I promise you it's all true.'

'You're covering for Anthea. How did Emerald get in here anyway? Who invited her?'

'Jupiter did,' said Sienna.

Alizarin, who'd moved on to Rossetti's drawing of Tennyson, glanced quickly round at Hanna.

'I liked the head Emerald did of me,' snapped Jupiter, 'I wanted Dad to meet her. She's got great talent, and I asked her boyfriend as well. Where is he, by the way?'

'Thought he was probably *de trop*,' mumbled Raymond. 'He's retreated to the Mitre in Searston. Going to ring in the morning. Nice chap.'

'And she brought my brother's head in on a platter like John the Baptist,' said Jonathan. 'I do not believe that girl or her boyfriend are legit.'

'She's the image of Anthea,' pleaded Raymond.

'Nothing like you,' said Sienna beadily.

'She's got Granny Belvedon's wonderful green eyes. It's miraculous we've found her again. I do so want you to love and accept your new sister.'

'Not until she's had a DNA test,' persisted Jonathan.

Dicky, who'd been laboriously pressing buttons, finally looked up from his calculator.

'If it's your twenty-fifth wedding anniversary, Dad,' he said in a shocked voice, 'you must have put it into Mummy before you were married. Why didn't you use a condom?'

Jonathan's shout of laughter was interrupted by a bang on the door, which Alizarin unlocked to find David Pulborough, unable any longer to contain his curiosity.

'Family confab? Terrific party. Everything all right?'

'Fine,' snapped Alizarin, who detested David, 'now bugger off.'

'I thought you'd like to know,' said David, pretending to be concerned, 'that Casey Andrews, feeling rather neglected by our host and hostess, is threatening to batter Somerford to death with a cricket bat. And there's an urgent call for you, Raymond.'

Jonathan grabbed the handset. After thirty seconds, he began to laugh.

'It's the *Daily Mail*, Dad. They want to know all about Anthea's love child. Can they have an exclusive?'

Just for a second, the colour drained from David's flushed face.

'Of course they can,' cried Raymond. Anything to get away from the collective disapproval of his children. 'I want the world to know our beautiful daughter has come home.'

'Someone must have tipped off the *Mail*,' said Jupiter, keen to regain the ascendancy, glaring accusingly round the room.

Dora, however, had folded her arms in fury.

'She's *my* mother, I should have been allowed to tip off the press. They might have paid me enough to buy Loofah a new saddle.'

Suddenly everyone seemed to be hissing Raymond the pantomime villain. Then a whipcrack of lightning followed by a cannonade of thunder sent Grenville diving under the sofa, with fat Visitor practically concussing himself trying to follow. Opening the royal-blue velvet curtains a fraction, Jonathan saw couples racing in from the garden. The heavens had finally opened.

Upstairs Anthea and Emerald were opening their hearts with equal lack of restraint. Chattering, weeping, embracing, they couldn't stop looking at each other as, like picture restorers, they filled in the gaps of the last twenty-five years. Warmed by endless cups of Earl Grey, buoyed up by more glasses of champagne, they kept laughing and finding their laughs identical, discovering they were both left handed, suffered from migraines, loathed clutter and wearing trousers, and that violets were their favourite flower.

Curled up amid the dolls in the cream-linen four-poster, admiring the porcelain, the pastels of Dicky and Dora, the needlepoint cushions (blurting out she did embroidery too), Emerald thought she had never been in a prettier room.

Anthea had banished Raymond's blue checked duvet to the dressing room and taken off her rainbow-woven dress and her hairpiece. Now in a white smocked dressing gown, with her blond curls brushed off her tear-stained face, she looked about fourteen. Giddy with relief that the skeleton had finally emerged from the closet and turned out so pretty, talented and nicely spoken, she was now busily re-editing events to show what humiliation and dreadful deprivation she had suffered to ensure Emerald a better life.

'Ay was only nineteen and a virgin when Sir Raymond seduced me. After one night of love-making to comfort him, I fell pregnant. My parents threw me out, I had no home, no money, all I wanted was you to have a better chance in life than me. Single mothers were treated like scum in those days. Nurses in the maternity ward, social workers, the nuns at the adoption society were all the same.'

Anthea's voice was rising, her fingers drumming on the bedside table in time to the deluge outside.

'You poor thing,' wailed Emerald. 'But tell me about the rest of the family. You're so pretty, I must have loads of glamorous cousins, uncles and aunts.'

'Not very exciting,' said Anthea firmly. 'My grand-mother was dying of cancer at the time, everyone was terrified she'd find out. Ay had to visit her in hospital in baggy jumpers.'

'Where was I born? How much did I weigh?' Emerald was desperate for information.

'Four and a half pounds. The birth was dreadfully long and difficult. I was utterly exhausted. I remember catching a last glimpse of your tiny hands through the window but I don't recall signing the papers or driving away. I blocked out the whole heart-rending experience.'

'You poor thing,' moaned Emerald, patting her new mother's shoulders. But a faint voice of disquiet kept saying, I suffered too, I've had a terrible time.

Anthea seemed more interested in learning about Patience.

'Well, they certainly didn't match us physically,' admitted Emerald disloyally, 'she's large, red-faced and horsey. There was usually a bridle hanging from the bed, and dogs in it.'

'Ugh!' said Anthea, who only allowed Nina Campbell's toile de Jouy monkeys and parrots into *her* bedroom. 'What did she tell you about me?'

'Your name, and that the adoption society said that you were beautiful, young, very brave and er – working in a gallery.'

'I was brave,' agreed Anthea, topping up Emerald's glass. 'I sustained myself through the dark days in a ghastly bed-sitter, dreaming of you growing up in a lovely airy home with the sun pouring through the windows, probably designed by your father.'

'Daddy was in the army,' said Emerald, perplexed.

'They lied to me!' Anthea pleated the counterpane in fury. 'The adoption society swore you were going to a charming architect and his wife, who'd never need to work, but did a lot for charity. I'd never have signed the papers if I'd known you were going to be shunted from one army billet to another.'

She'll flip if she finds out Daddy's driving a minicab and Mummy's working in a pub, thought Emerald. Then, desperate to change the subject: 'I always found it difficult to talk to them about adoption.'

'My parents would never let me mention you,' countered Anthea. 'I couldn't even discuss you with Raymond. Having Dicky and Dora made me realize the extent of my loss. I had to pretend they were my first babies; everyone gave me advice. I wanted to scream, "I've been down that road", but I had to bite my tongue.

'It's so unfair. When I was nineteen, it was regarded as criminally selfish to keep your baby and deny it the security of a mother and father; now society regards you

289

as having been criminally selfish if you gave a baby up. I can't win.'

Like a rescued castaway, Anthea couldn't stop gabbling.

'They said I'd get over it, but I never did. I looked into every pram, thought of you every day, particularly on your birthday.'

'When is it?' asked Emerald idly.

'July the ninth. No, the tenth. No, the eighth. You're trying to trick me,' flared up Anthea.

So Emerald flared up too.

'It's the seventh – actually,' then, changing tack, 'Raymond's so approachable, even if he was married. I'm sure he would have supported you. There must have been oodles of money splashing around. If you'd really loved me.'

'Of course Ay loved you, I carried you for nine months.'

Anthea's tummy was so flat, it was hard to imagine a baby in there.

'I'm sorry, I guess I'm testing you.' Emerald stifled a yawn and shivered.

The thunder had rumbled away. Over the clatter of rain could be heard the distant boom of 'American Pie'. Anthea looked at her watch.

'We must get you to bed.'

Although Anthea lent her the prettiest white broderie anglaise nightgown trimmed with pale pink ribbon, Emerald detected a distinct *froideur*.

'Oh wow,' she cried, trying to make amends as Anthea showed her her room.

Painted on the walls was a riotous jumble of trees, Gods, nymphs, satyrs and woodland creatures peering through the greenery.

'You do have the most wonderful taste.'

'Sir Raymond's first wife did this,' said Anthea icily. 'So self-indulgent. I long to paint over it, but Raymond thinks it's a work of art, and her children are determined to hang on to it.'

Remember never to praise the first Mrs Belvedon, thought Emerald as Anthea whisked about, turning down the bed, switching on lights.

'You are kind.'

'I like to pamper my guests.'

Emerald glanced at their reflections in the big mirror, stunned by how alike they were, except for different-coloured hair and eyes.

'You look like my younger sister.'

Instantly Anthea dropped her guard, putting an arm round Emerald's shoulders.

'I'll find you some lovely clothes to wear tomorrow. Promise not to run away.'

'No, no, I'd love to stay. There's only one thing bugging me, do I call you Lady Belvedon, or Anthea?'

'I hope you're going to call me Mummy.'

The moment she'd gone, Emerald rang Zac, who to her fury had switched off his mobile. How bloody selfish could you get? She was so desperate for reassurance that she was still adored and special, she was tempted to ring Patience and Ian, then caught sight of the bedside clock. Even her doting parents wouldn't want to be roused at five in the morning.

34

Emerald woke whimpering and sweating with terror. On the wall to her right, Galena had painted a lusty Apollo lunging at Daphne, who was slowly turning into a laurel tree: her legs merging with the branches, long eyes and wild hair losing themselves in the leaves. Was this Emerald Cartwright turning into Charlene Belvedon?

She felt defenceless, post natal, utterly exhausted and strangely cheated, as though, having seen the film of a favourite book, the characters were not as she'd imagined. She could no longer fantasize about Rupert Campbell-Black rescuing her in a helicopter if things got rough. She had arrived at Foxes Court believing herself to be the injured party. But Anthea had stolen her role.

She was also freezing and in a hot, jasmine-scented bath felt she was washing away all her Cartwright past. The mirror had misted over; she couldn't see who she was any more.

As she finished drying herself, the bedroom door opened. Not Jonathan on the pull, nor an outraged Jupiter demanding explanations, but a rotund yellow Labrador waddled in. Knowing he was banned from coming upstairs, Visitor pressed his face against the side of the bed. If he couldn't see Emerald, she couldn't see him. Hoping to draw her attention to the tin of sugar biscuits on the bedside table, Visitor wagged his tail.

Hearing whistling, Emerald ran to the window. Below, the forecourt was strewn with petals and shiny with puddles. Through dripping acid-green limes, she caught a tawny glimpse of the Old Rectory. A ginger cat idled along the dividing wall.

This is a glorious place, thought Emerald, running her hand over the little Degas horse on the window sill, this is definitely where I belong.

The whistling grew louder. Alizarin Belvedon, standing by the water trough, was reading the *Observer*. Having conned Jupiter and slapped Jonathan's face, Emerald felt she'd better get Alizarin on her side.

To hell with clothes and make-up, she was now a bohemian Belvedon. Wriggling back into Anthea's ravishing white nightgown, flinging her crimson pashmina round her shoulders, Emerald ran downstairs with Visitor galumphing behind her.

Having left the party straight after the showdown in the library, and been painting ever since, Alizarin had needed to clear his aching head.

Symbolizing the stripping away of the Belvedons' illusions about Anthea's professed virtue, last night's rain and wind had ripped off the blossom and shredded the dandelion clocks and the white starry flowers of the wild garlic. The silver-and-black-striped water thundering into the mossy water trough always reminded Alizarin of Galena's fringe. The whole wedding business yesterday had crucified him. Anthea's spiteful remarks about his mother to Lynda Lee Potter had further banged in the nails.

And now Anthea's daughter, barefoot, pale as her nightgown, black plait falling over one breast, wrapped in her crimson shawl like King Cophetua's beggar maid, stood in the doorway. In the serpentine curve of her body and her wanton confidence that men would find her irresistible, Alizarin, like Zac, was reminded of Munch's Madonna.

Was this the reason Galena had sunk into such despair? he wondered. Had she discovered Raymond had made another woman pregnant?

'It's not my fault,' protested Emerald as Alizarin glared at her. 'My mother was a virgin when your father seduced her.'

Blood all over the office sofa, thought Alizarin with a shudder, blood all over the hall and the Blue Tower when Galena died.

'I didn't ask to be born,' said Emerald sulkily.

The tallest of the brothers, Alizarin towered over her. His dark hair, black sweatshirt, torn jeans and huge hands were spattered with brown and khaki paint like camouflage. His stubbly jaw was set; his eyes hidden by dark glasses, emphasizing his big broken nose. His mouth was tough and uncompromising. The sun had gone in but a purple-black cloud provided an appropriate backdrop. To Emerald, he seemed both savage and mysterious.

'Can I come for a walk with you?'

Receeing her new domain, thought Alizarin bleakly.

'I suppose so. Gumboots are on the right of the front door.'

The pale blue child's pair marked 'Anthea' fitted her perfectly.

'Why does Anthea mark her gumboots?' Emerald raced to keep up with him. 'No-one else could get into them.'

'She's very possessive.' Alizarin glanced down at Emerald's pearly white parting. 'She won't want to share you. Rightly or wrongly, you're going to alter the balance of power here. Anthea totally ignored Jonathan and Sienna once Dicky and Dora arrived. They're all going to be very jealous.'

As they walked down the garden, past weary caterers retrieving glasses from the bushes, Alizarin pointed out Jonathan and Sienna's studio, not mentioning that it had once been Galena's, and Hanna and Jupiter's cottage with all the curtains drawn. Visitor, who was feeling sick after last night's excesses, ate grass and drank noisily out of puddles. Before they reached Aunt Lily's cottage overlooking the river, Alizarin turned right into the trees, where the downpour had lowered the green ceiling.

'I'm chancing my arm going into the woods with you,' Emerald said coyly. 'You're the only brother who hasn't made a pass at me.'

'Jupiter jumped on you?'

'We had dinner after I did his head. He said his wife didn't like sex, but they all say that.'

'And?'

'He asked me back to his house, but instead I leapt into a taxi.'

Detesting himself for having pried, Alizarin turned his disapproval on Zac and Emerald.

'Pretty bloody, conning Jupiter and wrecking a family party.'

'What else was I to do? Anthea rejected me three times, then she threatened me with an injunction.'

'Did she?' asked Alizarin in surprise. 'I suppose there was lots at stake. You probably reminded her of all those feelings of loss and shame when she gave you up.'

'You're very fair,' grumbled Emerald.

'Not always,' said Alizarin.

And terribly attractive, thought Emerald wistfully.

Suddenly, as though they were being pelted with ice cubes, hailstones clattered down. Opening his jacket, Alizarin pulled her inside, smelling of turps and sweat, as he protected her from the bombardment with his huge shoulders. Snuggling up to him, Emerald felt fleetingly safe as she had when Raymond hugged her last night.

It was like holding a child, reflected Alizarin, reminded suddenly and agonizingly of the baby Hanna had been carrying, whose birth had been terminated at Jupiter's insistence. My child, who would be six now, thought Alizarin, churning with loathing for his brother.

The hailstorm only lasted a minute, but the whole steaming wood now reeked of pestled wild garlic. Visitor's back looked as though it was covered in rhinestones. Alizarin let Emerald go.

'Nice to have a big brother,' she murmured.

'Have you told your parents?'

'Not yet.'

'The *Daily Mail* will tomorrow.'

As they emerged from the wood, Emerald gasped: beyond the glittering river, a grey horse had taken shelter under one white hawthorn. Sheep were scattered like daisy petals under another. The pale green domes of the trees were fluffed up against a thundery grey sky. Then the sun came out turning the cow parsley an unearthly white. Everything sparkled as though a shoal of diamonds had been chucked down.

'Borochova's Silver Valley,' sighed Emerald in ecstasy.

'Been at the cuttings?' snapped Alizarin.

'No, I love her work,' protested Emerald, 'I bought a little drawing of a cat with my twenty-first birthday money. I'll bring it down to show you, next time . . .' Her voice trailed off uncertainly.

Alizarin thawed a fraction. As they reached the Lodge, he said, 'That head you did of Jupiter.'

Emerald steeled herself.

'It's very good.'

'It is?' Colour flooded her face, her witchy green eyes widening in amazement.

She's pretty now, thought Alizarin. How lovely she'd be if she were happy.

'Thank you,' mumbled Emerald. 'It matters, because you know Jupiter well.'

'So do you, better than most people. You caught the political animal – or rather the beast – beneath the skin.'

'I'd rather sculpt you.'

'No, thank you.'

And the door slammed behind him.

Back in her room, Emerald found a tight-lipped Anthea.

'I've dreamed of bringing you breakfast in bed for twenty-five years. I thought you'd run away.'

Emerald gazed down at the opaque butter on the toast soldiers, the brown egg probably hard boiled by now.

'I'm so sorry, how gorgeous, I'll get back into bed.'

'You're all wet.' Beadily Anthea noticed the flushed cheeks, the clinging broderie anglaise. 'You haven't been out in your nightie?'

'Alizarin showed me round.'

'Alizarin!' squawked Anthea. 'You don't want to waste time on that pinko. Always whizzing off to places like Bosnia to avoid paying his debts, then having nervous breakdowns when he comes back – so rude and arrogant.'

'He was lovely about you.'

'In what way?' demanded Anthea suspiciously. 'The only woman Alizarin cares about is Hanna.'

'Jupiter's Hanna?' asked Emerald faintly.

'She was Alizarin's Hanna, for several years, then very sensibly she decided Jupiter was the better bet. Alizarin would do anything to get her back.'

Oh my God, thought Emerald in horror. To get Alizarin on her side, she'd lied about Jupiter making a pass at her. Jupiter hadn't mentioned anything about the lack of sex in his marriage either. Oh please, don't let Alizarin say anything to Jupiter, who'd really been so kind.

'Eat up your breakfast,' chided Anthea.

Emerald looked at the skin floating on the top of her cup of coffee and nearly threw up.

'The *Daily Mail* want a telephone interview with you around eleven,' Anthea continued. 'You'd better not mention this to *Oo-ah!*, who want to photograph us all at a family lunch. You must choose something pretty to wear from my wardrobe. And this evening, there's a party for the locals. I can't wait to show off my new daughter.'

Exhaustion overwhelmed Emerald; she suddenly felt quite unable to cope with such a marathon. And where the hell was Zac?

'Where did you meet Zachary?' asked Anthea, reading her thoughts.

'At Rupert Campbell-Black's.'

'Really?' Anthea brightened. 'Rupert's an awfully old friend.'

But when Anthea questioned her further about Zac, Emerald was ashamed how little information she could provide. She must learn to listen more – although she was getting plenty of practice with Anthea.

Nor had she noticed Zac secreting a suitcase into the boot last night. When he banged on her bedroom door half an hour later he was back in his combats and polo shirt, announcing inevitably he was off to Moscow via Heathrow, which threw Emerald into a complete panic.

'I can't cope with this lot on my own.'

'You stick around,' ordered Zac. 'After all the trouble we took to get you in here . . .' Then, pretending to put the little Degas horse in his pocket: 'The pickings are awesome.'

On the way out Zac had a brief encounter with Anthea, who blushed remembering their waltz into the garden.

'I ought to be very cross. You tricked me.'

'Only because I knew how desperate Emerald was to meet with you.' Staring deep into her eyes, Zac murmured deliberately huskily, 'Didn't stop me enjoying that dance. Emerald's my type, I guess, and you are *so* like Emerald.'

All very formal and Austrian, he briefly kissed her hand and was gone. Anthea was aglow. Raymond was already dotty about Emerald because he claimed she was so like Anthea. In turn it was nice to be fancied by Zac.

Lunch for eleven under the walnut tree was a disappointment, both for *Oo-ah!* and Anthea. Zac had already left, Alizarin had gone back to work, Hanna and Jupiter, still burning with resentment, didn't show up, Jonathan was asleep. Dicky and Dora showed off impossibly and Sienna sat with her trainers on the table, ostentatiously reading Joanna Trollope's *Other People's Children.* Emerald, being small, had earlier clocked love bites under Sienna's chin and wondered if they'd been given her by Jonathan.

Raymond had been sweet to Emerald, taking her on a tour of the marvellous pictures and sculptures. But he looked terribly old, particularly outside, where Emerald noticed the grey chest hair, the wrinkly face, and the liver spots freckling his hands.

'Can you move your legs, Sienna?' demanded Anthea, coming out through the french windows with a handful of silver. 'I want to lay.' Then, not wanting a row in front of Harriet from *Oo-ah!*, she added, 'And thank you for the pretty scarf you gave me.'

Sienna's face, that of a captured terrorist, looked marginally less sullen.

'But d'you mind awfully if I change it?' went on Anthea, running a J-cloth over the table. 'The colour is a little too hard.'

'You mean like you're too hard for the colour.'

'Sienna,' chided Raymond.

'I believe in telling the truth,' said Anthea shirtily.

'Not where baby Charlene was concerned,' replied Sienna bitchily.

'Get out,' roared Raymond. 'I will not have you cheeking your stepmother.'

'I know when I'm not wanted,' said Sienna in a relieved voice. 'I'm off to London.'

'Lucky you. Can I go and ride Loofah?' asked Dora.

'No, you can't. You can damn well help me lay,' exploded Anthea, then, remembering *Oo-ah!*: 'If you're good you can stay up and hand nibbles round at the party.'

Lights were flickering in front of Emerald's eyes. She could hardly see out of the right one.

'I'm terribly sorry, I've got a migraine coming on, I'm afraid I can't make tonight's party.'

'Mummy's the one who has migraines,' said Dora beadily.

After that *Oo-ah!* gave up and returned to London.

'Give me your card,' whispered Dora, accompanying Harriet to her car, 'I'll keep you posted.'

Alizarin couldn't concentrate on work, he too had a frightful headache, and he couldn't stop thinking about Hanna. She'd never implied her marriage was in trouble, he was ashamed how cheered up he'd been by Emerald's report, and jumped in hope at a knock on the front door. Looking out of the window he instead found Dora.

'Can I come up?'

Alizarin sighed and put down his brushes.

'Daddy and Mummy's new daughter is something I can do without,' grumbled Dora. 'She really takes the biscuit.'

Hearing the magic word, Visitor opened an eye and wagged his tail.

'Will you give me a pound if I take Visitor for a walk?' said Dora.

During the afternoon a photographer rolled up from the *Mail*, and was very disappointed to find Emerald was too ill to be photographed. A reporter, who'd tagged along to get reactions from Sienna and Jonathan, was equally frustrated. Both men struck gold, however, with Dora, who in return for the money to buy a new saddle, posed with Visitor.

'No-one has asked me how I feel about Mummy and Daddy's love child,' she told them soulfully. 'My brother Dicky was sick four times last night, Visitor was sick three times.' Visitor thumped his tail approvingly. 'My new sister's being sick upstairs at the moment. Sienna says my mother's a slapper, but she only slapped me once when I bit her because she wouldn't let me watch *Brookside*.'

Gazing down from an upstairs Old Rectory window, David was so furious the Belvedons were receiving so much media attention that he rushed down and suffused the area in a disgusting smell by throwing his wife's left gumboot on the bonfire.

Sienna cried most of the way back to her studio in the East End. One of Thatcher's children, she had been taught at college to know her true worth and market herself. To control the art world, you had to be a nuisance because you would only be appreciated for your ability to shock and behave badly.

More seriously she was now working on a huge canvas of animals in hell: bears in China, monkeys in laboratories, veal calves in crates. She could only do a little at a time because it made her cry so much.

Beneath her aggression, Sienna was a little girl lost, who blamed herself for her mother's death. She drank too much and slept with too many men to blot out the fact that she was hopelessly in love with her brother Jonathan. It had always been them against the world. Now she was truly terrified. She had seen Jonathan's reaction to Emerald, and knew life would never be the same again.

35

Oo-ah! magazine were incensed the following morning to find themselves pre-empted by the *Daily Mail*, which contained a double page exclusive headed: 'Lady Belvedon's Love Child'.

Having reported Raymond's gushings at length, they also included a telephone interview with Emerald:

'I've found the end of the rainbow at last. My adopted parents tried, but I always felt an outsider. If they wanted me so much why did they pack me off to boarding school? My real mum and I are so alike. We love clothes and making houses beautiful. We're both size eight, arty, obsessively tidy, terrified of horses and suffer from migraine. My mother was six years younger than I am now when she courageously gave me up for adoption and went on to become a wonderful stepmother to four children. I am very proud of her. I feel I have come home.'

By eight o'clock, the queue of press and television outside Foxes Court's firmly locked gates stretched as far as the High Street.

'This is a much better turnout,' announced Dora, waving happily at cameramen as Robens the gardener drove her to school. With any luck further revelations might buy her a new bridle or even a second pony.

An enraged David Pulborough, on his way to the station and the London train, was tempted to return home and put his wife's right gumboot on the bonfire.

Alizarin, who'd been trying to paint since first light, was equally incensed by the hooting din. As the gates were shut, the reporters rang the bell of the Lodge instead, so Alizarin tipped buckets of water over them. Visitor, who loved publicity even more than Dora – camera crews meant biscuits – was whining to be let out. Any moment he'd be handing out cups of tea, thought Alizarin sourly.

His mother's child, Alizarin, who was as dedicated to righting wrongs as his sister Sienna, was now painting a scene of appalling torture in a Serbian police HQ. One young Albanian was being electrocuted in a revolving chair so he could be flogged at the same time, another was having his fingers broken in a metal vice. On the torturers' faces was sexual excitement; on that of the cleaner scrubbing down the walls, mild curiosity. You could hear the screams and smell the blood.

Every brushstroke was anguish, but Alizarin felt someone had to tell the world. On other canvasses stacked against the walls were further atrocities: human shields; starving Albanians in concentration camps; civilians riddled with bullets, frozen to the hillside. Alizarin had only returned from Macedonia last week, he must get it on canvas before the horror faded.

The room reeked of turps and damp dog. Like a surgeon, Alizarin worked under powerful hospital lights. On the wall, resting like a butterfly with wings of glowing crimson, bright blue, rich green and stinging yellow, hung Galena's palette. Beside it was a beautiful charcoal drawing of Galena herself.

Bloody hell, someone else was hammering on the door. Alizarin was about to empty another bucket out of the window when he recognized the dishevelled black curls of his brother Jonathan. The press were going crazy. As Alizarin let him in, Jonathan announced that he'd just heard the cuckoo.

'Must be Emerald settling into her new nest.'

In fine form after a very long sleep, Jonathan was off to London to prove that Emerald wasn't Raymond's. Accompanying him was Diggory, his extremely self-regarding Jack Russell, who was now yapping round Visitor, grumbling because he'd been shut away during the silver wedding party in case he bit people.

'These are knockout.' Sighing and shuddering, Jonathan examined Alizarin's canvasses. 'But gruesome – I'd squeal in a second if anyone did that to me.'

Alizarin was now holding up a big magnifying glass as he scraped paint off a torturer's face.

'What d'you want?' he asked ungraciously.

'To talk about our new sister.'

'I'm working.'

Jonathan then made the mistake of showing his brother his latest nudes of Sienna.

'Content's bound to raise a few eyebrows.'

'Content's fine,' snapped Alizarin, who couldn't praise where he didn't admire. 'It's the execution that's so bloody vulgar. Frankly, you're too self-obsessed to be any good as a portrait painter.'

'I've always thought of you as Pride,' snapped back a wounded Jonathan, 'but you're getting more and more like Envy, and you should stop painting the working classes, they never pay.'

Gathering up Diggory and his canvasses, he stalked out.

Alizarin put his throbbing head in his hands. He *was* jealous of Jonathan's effortless success, and was ashamed of himself for being so belligerent, but he couldn't throw off his black mood.

Pulling a baseball cap over his nose, Jonathan stormed his Ferrari towards the motorway. Along the verges, cow parsley like some white-faced religious group was being whipped into a frenzy by a vicious east wind. Rain lashed the windows.

Fucking Alizarin doesn't even realize, thought Jonathan furiously, that I only went over to the Pulborough because Jupiter was refusing to show Al's pictures any more.

'It's because you don't want Alizarin making money and taking Hanna back off you,' Jonathan had shouted at Jupiter.

'Bollocks,' had howled back Jupiter, 'it's because I can't sell the bloody things.'

'Then you're not selling me either,' Jonathan had yelled. 'Al's a genius, it's only a matter of time.'

Raymond, who had not been told the reason for Jonathan's defection, had been devastated.

Jonathan Belvedon had always been adored slightly too much. Spoilt by nannies, teachers of both sexes and later by women, he tended to take the easy option. Smoking dope one afternoon on his bed at boarding school, he had decided the best way to pull the most glamorous women in the world was to become a portrait painter.

Now, at twenty-eight, he had socialites, models and actresses queuing up to be painted. Poor Alizarin slogged away for days on a picture. Jonathan dashed things off in half an hour, often from a photograph or a video taken by an assistant. Like Nijinsky, he was a superb and instinctive artist, 'to whom technique is only a servant'.

Jonathan lived in a loft in Hoxton, where droves of young artists, mostly pretty girls in various states of undress, completed all kinds of work – landscapes, installations, as well as portraits that he had started. Recently he'd been too busy modelling Armani suits for *GQ*, punching critics and getting his dick out on television to do much work.

Jonathan never had any money because he was constantly snorting, drinking or buying dinner for his friends. He and Alizarin had once been inseparable, painting or hell-raising all night, then lying on the studio floor listening to the Alpine Symphony as the sun rose. Now they were separated by Jonathan's runaway success and Alizarin's utter failure. But this didn't stop Alizarin castigating Jonathan for selling out and producing rubbish.

Ringing Sienna when he got held up in traffic at the Chiswick flyover, Jonathan was depressed to find her also working.

'I was so pissed off by bloody Emerald in the *Mail*,' raged Sienna, 'I had to get stuck into something.'

She was now channelling her rage against the Filipinos who tied dogs' broken legs behind their backs and rammed their snouts into tins before flogging them as meat in the market place.

'It's like so fucking cruel!' Sienna was sobbing with anger. 'Where are you off to?'

'To take the piss out of David. D'you think Willy of the Valley's Emerald's father?'

'I wouldn't wish that fate even on her.'

Diggory meanwhile, who got wildly jealous when Jonathan spent too long on the telephone, had started yapping furiously.

'I'll call you later,' yelled Jonathan over the din. 'Let's have supper.'

David Pulborough had always been ahead of the game – still driving the bus with 'Further' on the front. As the supply of Old Masters dried up, he increasingly concentrated on young artists. These he kept on their toes by never letting them feel quite sure he was retaining them, by not allowing them sufficient advance to get smug, and by putting on group exhibitions to foster a competitive spirit. He had also copied the Belvedon's habit of producing a much admired Pulborough calendar, which each month featured a painting and a small photo of its artist. Anyone who underperformed or was playing up was left out. David also went berserk if any of his artists sold their work privately.

Jonathan, a free spirit, had no desire to be owned, advised or shaped by David. He just wanted maximum money for minimum work. Having captured Jonathan, David expected all his starry entourage to follow him. He'd have such fun bringing that stroppy little bitch Sienna to heel and Trafford, Jonathan's loftmate, was unlikely to stay at the Belvedon after being banished from the silver wedding party.

The nice thing about young artists was that even the unsalubrious ones like Trafford were always surrounded by pretty girls. Over the years, David had been a serial humper, a ladies' man for all seasons. Thank God the sofa in the back office couldn't talk. He was still Lust in the Seven Deadly Sins, but gradually snobbery was taking over from lechery. The Pulborough had been so successful that he was no longer largely dependent on Rosemary, but he needed her to add gravitas if he were going to have a room in the Tate named after him and to achieve his ambition in 2000 of becoming High Sheriff of Larkshire. And if he left Rosemary, what excuse would he have not to marry all his other girlfriends, including Geraldine Paxton, who had proved so invaluable at securing grants and commissions for his protégés?

This had been his game plan, but suddenly Emerald had rolled up and spoiled everything.

Jonathan reached the Pulborough at midday. Zoe, David's assistant, slim and understated so as not to upset Geraldine, was typing catalogue blurbs. She had a terrific crush on Jonathan and was mortified that her light brown bob had been whipped into a bird's nest after a weekend sailing.

David believed in giving buyers little choice. On the far wall of the ground-floor gallery hung a lone Pissarro of a couple by a river. Peach-pink lupins in a copper vase on a nearby table – a trick he'd learnt from Raymond – picked up the coral of the woman's dress.

In a back room, a restorer was bent over a large oil, painting out the vixen being torn apart by two hunt terriers, and replacing her with a tartan scarf.

'People won't buy anything to do with blood sports these days,' sighed David. 'But I've got a terrier-mad actress who might give me two grand for that. She'd buy that dog of yours.' David glared at Diggory, who glared back.

'I wish you wouldn't bring him in here,' went on David fussily, as Diggory briskly rearranged the purple silk cushions and curled up on the white sofa in David's office.

On David's splendid oak desk was a photograph not of Rosemary nor gay Barney, but of his daughter Melanie, who, like David, had married up and for money. On Melanie's right on the pale green Lutyens bench sat a smug David, bouncing a plump grandson on his knee and looking twice as young as his son-in-law on Melanie's left, who owned the large, ravishing Elizabethan house in the background.

Jonathan meanwhile had picked up the latest Pulborough catalogue and, after reading a paragraph or two, chucked it down.

'The copy's far too lucid. You must obscure it up a bit, throw in a few "pivotals" and "seminals". Can I have a drink?'

David looked at his watch. 'I suppose so.'

As Zoe went off to get a bottle, Jonathan moved on to the subject of Emerald.

'I cannot imagine Dad shagging Anthea out of wedlock. You were around in October 1972, and much more of a stud than Dad. Are you sure you didn't give Anthea one?'

'I was barely back from honeymoon, for Christ's sake.' David, turning purpler than his cushions, moved around the gallery fussily straightening straight pictures, lining up folders. 'Your father was certainly besotted, but so were the clients and the artists, particularly Casey and Joan.'

'Doesn't stack up. Dad's not the sort of person you don't tell you're pregnant. Even if he was terrified of Mum finding out, he'd have supported Anthea financially, and he adores children so much, he'd have accepted Emerald if she'd had two heads. I'm pushing for a DNA test. Thanks, angel.' Jonathan accepted a glass of Sancerre from a blushing Zoe. 'Any crisps for Diggory?'

'We don't keep them,' snapped David, frowning at Zoe for wasting wine kept for important clients on mere artists.

Gone too were the days when he could scoop up crisps like a starved schoolboy. It irritated the hell out of him that despite being twenty-five years older, Raymond had retained his spare, elegant figure and his mane of silver hair.

Jonathan would have returned to the subject of Emerald, if he hadn't wanted a further advance from David, who refused to give him one.

'Gallery owners,' grumbled Jonathan, 'always think of artists lying under trees getting drunk on their advances.'

'Artists,' replied David crisply, 'always think of gallery owners riding round in Rolls-Royces, living off their fifty per cent commission. You've no idea of the overheads of this place.'

Jonathan then produced the two nudes of Sienna.

Cultivating idiosyncrasies to attract the cartoonists, David had recently taken to wearing a monocle, with which he now examined Sienna's body.

'Why does she ruin her beauty with all those studs?'

'I'm thinking of calling these two *Stud Farm I* and *II*.'

'Those legs go on for ever,' sighed David.

Jonathan smiled enigmatically. 'And they start at an interesting place too. How much can you sell them for?'

'I can't,' said David firmly. 'She's your sister, they're far too controversial. When are you going to get started on Rupert Campbell-Black and Dame Hermione?'

'Rupert's always busy,' complained Jonathan, 'and I'm terrified of Diggory disappearing down Dame Hermione's snatch, never to return. That's the trouble with Jack Russells. I'll get someone to video her.'

'She wants you in person,' said David crossly. 'And the National Portrait Gallery wants more from you too.'

'Brian Organ often uses photographs as an aide-memoire.'

'Photographs are only a point of reference. The extent of live sittings *always* enhances the quality. I've also had complaints from clients,' went on David sternly, 'and particularly from the Arts Council and the Tate, that you're not providing enough input, that they'll get a face or perhaps a nose painted by you if they're lucky.'

'I don't understand the fuss,' said Jonathan sulkily. 'With the great portrait painters, Raphael, Van Dyck, Reynolds, it was a huge studio operation, someone did the hands, someone else the clothes and the curtains, horses were done by the horse specialist. The lead painter often only did the face, but he got the biggest fee, because he had to do all the smooth talking to get the commissions and take the flak afterwards – like I do.'

'I'll be taking all the flak from now on,' said David firmly. 'You've just got to get that pretty nose to the grindstone.'

The meeting broke up firstly because an incredibly rich and evil member of the Russian Mafia called Minsky Kraskov (who wanted to launder a pile of drug money and whose visit David wanted to keep secret) was due any minute, and secondly because Diggory suddenly decided to mount David's pinstriped leg.

'Bugger off,' yelled David, 'and the little bastard's lifted his leg on that Sisley.'

A trickle could be seen running down a canvas of a poplar wood, which was leaning against the wall.

'Shows how realistic the trees are,' said Jonathan unrepentantly.

'Get out,' shouted David.

36

Glancing across Cork Street, Jonathan saw the paparazzi gathered outside the Belvedon watching his brother Jupiter grimly hanging the new Joan Bideford exhibition. With olives from the island of Lesbos as nibbles at the private view, thought Jonathan. Pulling Emerald's address, which he had transferred from his wrist onto a bit of paper, out of his jeans pocket, he set out for Shepherd's Bush.

He found Patience, her eyes red and puffy, her crimson-veined face covered in blotches, devastated by Emerald's piece in the *Mail*. After several large whiskys, Ian had gone off minicabbing. She prayed he wouldn't lose his licence.

Patience knew adopted children often sought out their real mothers and one mustn't be clinging, but she'd never dreamt it would hurt so much. It was probably to do with losing the house, working in the bar, and having to boost Ian, who hated having to be endlessly charming to his passengers. It had been rather a grim year and she couldn't stop crying. Plump Sophy had taken the day off, pleading food poisoning, to comfort her mother.

'I told Emo not to do it,' she told Jonathan furiously.

Jonathan was perfect. Used to endless crises at Foxes

Court, he put his arms round Patience and hugged her until she stopped crying.

'It's only a honeymoon,' he soothed her, 'Anthea is such a bitch, Emerald'll suss her out soon. It's just rather a glamorous set-up.'

He'd pinched two bottles of champagne from the party, which he proceeded to open. Diggory got a much better reception than he had at the Pulborough and was soon curled up on Patience's knee, eating crisps and looking interested. Unlike Zac, Jonathan was quite unfazed by the overcrowded sitting room; it reminded him of his own studio. Everywhere he noticed pictures of and by Emerald.

'I feel so awful Emo didn't confide in us,' said Patience dolefully. 'They told us at the adoption society that if we were good parents the children would never feel the need to seek out their real parents. If you can't have babies, you're haunted by guilt that you've done something wicked to warrant it, that you're not worthy and certainly not capable of looking after a child or loving it enough.'

She picked up a Mothering Sunday card, gathering dust on the bookshelf.

'I was so scared of taking on anything as exquisite as Emerald. I nearly dropped her when they handed her over. But by the end of the weekend, I'd fallen in love totally. She was so beautiful, and she had such blue eyes when she was born. We called her Emerald, because it was my mother's second name.'

'Much better than Charlene,' said Jonathan, filling up her glass. 'Diggory was called Spot when I got him from Battersea.'

'Such a dear little dog.' Patience dropped a kiss on Diggory's orange and white head. 'I know we spoiled Emerald, to make up for her losing her real parents, smothering her with love, letting her do what she wanted.

'But it's always been such a privilege to have her. I'm so proud of her. I don't expect she said half the things in that horrible article. She's so talented – you can see where she gets it from now. I always knew we were too dull for her.'

Sophy, sick of her mother making allowances, raised her eyes to heaven and, worried that Patience was getting drunk, went off to make lunch. Being Monday, no-one had been shopping and she could only find a cauliflower, a chunk of ancient mousetrap decorated with her own toothmarks, and a tin of rhubarb. She could make cauliflower cheese. She borrowed a pint of milk from the gay actors upstairs who, having read the *Mail*, were deeply sympathetic.

'Tell Patience there's a large Scotch waiting whenever she wants.'

'Emerald's always had such high expectations,' Patience was telling Jonathan. 'She was so excited when Sophy arrived from Belfast. Mind you, Sophy's typically Irish, so sweet and easy going, always putting camomile on everyone's nettle stings. Anyway, when she arrived, one of Emerald's friends announced: "My baby sister came out of my mother's tummy." "My baby sister," said Emerald proudly, "came out of an aeroplane."'

Jonathan laughed and refilled Patience's glass and let her run on because he was interested, learning that they'd got Emerald from an adoption society in Harrogate, and her mother was definitely Anthea Rookhope, who'd worked in a gallery, but the father had withheld his name.

'We never dreamt it would be someone as distinguished and clever as your father,' said Patience humbly. 'I love his programmes. Ian, Emerald's father, is very unarty.'

'Nice-looking man' – Jonathan picked up a photograph – 'and lovely horse you're riding.'

'I always prayed every night that Tony Blair wouldn't stop hunting, but sadly I stopped instead.'

'Lunch,' announced Sophy. 'I hope you don't mind eating in the kitchen.'

Jonathan, who hadn't eaten since the Quality Street he'd wolfed with Knightie on Saturday afternoon, had two helpings of cauliflower cheese and three of rhubarb crumble, and took a huge shine to Sophy. He liked her merriness, her sweet round face, her beautiful skin, and her soft voice with its faint Yorkshire accent.

Sophy couldn't believe Jonathan. He was the most glamorous man she'd ever met, and so cosy and unfrightening, unlike Zac who was coolly contemptuous and who reined in his emotions like a dressage horse. She could hardly eat any lunch, and kept leaping up to examine Jonathan at a different angle: such eyelashes, such cheekbones, such an amused sleepy smile.

'Goodness, it's five o'clock.' Patience tottered off to get ready for work.

'D'you think I ought to do her shift for her?' asked Sophy.

Jonathan shook his head.

'Some of your pupils are bound to pop in for a drink after work and sneak. I'll drop her off.'

Having delivered Patience, he returned with more bottles and they carried on drinking with Sophy raging against Emerald.

'My parents are absolutely skint, but bloody Emerald still gets a socking great allowance and the use of a studio. And she lied in that horrible piece. Mum and Dad gave her everything, spoilt her rotten to compensate for her losing her first parents. And it was Emo who insisted on being sent to a boarding school, and got the shock of her life when it wasn't as jolly as Malory Towers.'

Jonathan proceeded to give a blow by blow of how Jupiter had been conned, and how Zac had waltzed Anthea out to her doom.

'Not the Blue Danube, but the boathouse by the River Fleet.'

'God, I wish I'd been there.' Sophy's eyes – the innocent azure of the sky after a big storm – were absolutely popping.

'What persuaded her to seek out Anthea?'

'I'm sure it was Zac. He met her when we were rich. It was only after he came back from America and discovered Daddy'd gone belly up that she started searching for her natural mother.'

'Nothing natural about Anthea, ask her hairdresser.' Sophy giggled.

'Zac's been pushing her all the way.'

'Must think Dad's richer than he is. How come you're so much nicer than Emerald?'

'I'm more of a drip. I went to the local grammar school rather than Emo's posh boarding school, because I didn't want to leave Mummy and Daddy and the animals, and I'm a second child,' said Sophy, 'and so as parents they were much more relaxed. The only reason I'd like to meet my birth mother is to see what she looked like and find out my medical history. She must have been fat.'

'Wide birth mother,' grinned Jonathan. 'Have you got a boyfriend?'

'I've got one who takes me to the opera.'

'I bet he bikes to work.'

'How did you know? He tried to make me cycle to school, but I couldn't get up in time, so he paid for me to go to a gym. Last night, I snogged the instructor,' confessed Sophy, 'so I can't go back.'

After that, things became hazy. Fading cow parsley and buttercups slapped against their legs as they took Diggory and another bottle for a walk on Barnes Common.

'If only we could have a dog,' sighed Sophy. 'I thought

of becoming a vet, but I wasn't sure about shoving my hand up cows.'

'I do all the time anyway,' said Jonathan and they collapsed with laughter.

Later they all three dropped into a casino in Mayfair. Under glittering chandeliers, people with obsessive faces gathered round gaming tables. Only the women dragged their eyes away from rattling ball or ace-laced card hand to gaze at Jonathan, whose black curls were flopping over cheekbones increasingly stained with colour.

Jonathan in turn was increasingly taken by Sophy. He liked the way her unpainted cherubic face looked as pretty at midnight as at midday. Nor was there anything to embellish it in her pink beaded handbag – only three packets of Silk Cut.

'I hate to run out.'

'A fag bag,' said Jonathan, helping himself, 'and, talking of fags, that fat slug at the bar in a dinner jacket is called Barney Pulborough. He lives next door to us in the country and sat next to your tricky sister on Saturday night. Probably fed her a lot of vitriol about me.'

'Probably jealous.' Sophy took another slug of champagne. 'You're an icon.'

'I con the public, according to Barney's father, who owns the Pulborough who represent me.' Jonathan lowered his voice: 'Barney has shares in this place, and it's where the Pulborough launder their ill-gotten gains from dodgy deals.'

'Blimey,' said Sophy in excitement.

Barney in fact was very happy. Having overheard Raymond talking to Jupiter on Saturday night, he had made a killing selling the story of Lady Belvedon's Love Child to the *Daily Mail*. For once therefore he was quite amiable to Jonathan.

'That big Saudi at the roulette table,' he told him softly, 'is a client of Dad's called Abdul Karamagi. He collects nudes and is about to launder half a million pounds – just watch him.'

The Saudi, whose huge hands were spilling over with chips, proceeded to put half on red, half on black. Round clattered the wheel, down dropped the silver ball, up came black, which paid double, so exactly the same amount of chips were returned to him.

'If he cashes them in in a couple of hours, they'll be as clean as Anthea's knickers,' said Barney.

'What happens if zero comes up?' asked Jonathan.

'You just pray it doesn't. I'll introduce you,' said Barney.

Abdul's chocolate-brown eyes melted when he saw Sophy's splendid proportions. He had also heard of Jonathan, and over another bottle and a large plate of smoked salmon for Sophy, commissioned him to paint her.

Sophy was staggered by the skill with which Jonathan brokered the deal. £80,000 might seem a lot, he explained, but pubes took for ever to draw, though as he was so taken by Abdul, he would do him a nude of Sophy for £60,000.

'Shut up, you'll get a cut,' he hissed when Sophy protested, then to Abdul, 'And I'd like an advance of twenty thousand.'

A minute later Abdul was meekly cashing in some chips. Sadly he couldn't buy Sophy as well, commiserated Jonathan, but the portrait would be delivered in the middle of June. Once Abdul returned to the tables, Jonathan slipped Barney £4,000.

'We needn't tell your father?'

'Certainly not,' said Barney, and while standing them another drink, told them about his new boyfriend, who was a sister at Guy's.

'What do the patients call him?' asked Sophy.

'"Charge Nurse",' smirked Barney, 'but he loves being called "Sister".'

'I think Barney's sweet,' protested Sophy as she and

Jonathan reeled out into Berkeley Square. All round her the big dark houses seemed to be dancing a quadrille, whilst the floodlit-patterned trunks and branches of the plane trees swayed like giraffes amidst their ceiling of leaves.

Jonathan shoved £500 inside Sophy's bra.

'I can't take it.'

'It'll pay a few bills at home. You could do with a dish-washer.'

'I can't pose nude.'

'Sure you can, won't take many sittings.'

At least it'll be a chance to see him again, thought Sophy.

Jonathan then hailed a taxi, shoving an outraged Diggory on the floor because there wasn't room on the seat for him and Sophy, and kissed her all the way home to his studio in a condemned warehouse off Hoxton Square. Here they found his louche flatmate, Trafford, laboriously making a picture called *Sick Joke* by sticking pieces of sweetcorn and red and green pepper onto a canvas then glazing them.

Trafford had a shaved head, 'You won't regret it' tattooed across his chest and leered worse than Abdul. He reminded Sophy of a knowing old Scottie dog, just back from the butcher's with a large bone and sawdust hanging from his fur tummy.

'The press have been on all day about your new sister,' he told Jonathan. 'So has Sienna, not best pleased.'

'Oh Christ, I forgot to ring her,' groaned Jonathan, who was opening a tin of Butcher's Tripe for Diggory.

'The bitch,' screamed Sophy, who had picked up the *Evening Standard*, where Anthea in an interview had emerged as Mother Courage.

'"I knew Raymond loved Galena,"' read out Sophy through gritted teeth, '"and only turned to me out of unbearable loneliness. The result was my Charlene. Naturally I'm grateful to Patience and Ian Cartwright for holding the fort, but I can only thank God my baby's back where she belongs." What a cow.'

'Another session in the re-edit suite,' said Jonathan, putting down Diggory's bowl. 'Don't let it get to you, darling. Anthea's just in orgasm because she's at last found a smart relation.'

'She's good looking, your new sister.' Trafford peered over Sophy's shoulder at a blurred picture of Emerald. 'When are you going to bring her round?'

The fumes from the glues and resins were making Sophy's eyes water. Diggory was managing to wolf his food and simultaneously growl at a large Newfoundland puppy called Choirboy, who lay on the chaise longue chewing a Gucci slip-on and adding to the general chaos. The cork board groaned with Polaroids of women. Sophy groaned too because they all seemed so beautiful.

Drawing Trafford aside, Jonathan told him to push off.

'I want to take Sophy to bed.'

'Can I watch?' asked Trafford, who'd spent much of the evening looking at porn on the internet, but who preferred the real thing.

'Only if you waive that three hundred I owe you.'

Jonathan's triple bed shared a room off the studio with a hundred canvasses, a large wardrobe and a stuffed polar bear hung with Jonathan's jackets. There were scant curtains. Several windows in the houses opposite, which mostly belonged to artists, were still lit up. Jonathan shoved Trafford, armed with a torch, in the wardrobe.

'How do I escape?' whispered Trafford.

'Women usually belt off to the bog afterwards,' whispered back Jonathan, 'you can nip out then.'

'You on the pill?' he asked Sophy as, in between kisses, he unbuttoned her shirt. 'Good, I am now going to shag the arse off you.'

'If only you could,' sighed Sophy. 'It's much too big, and I'm far too fat. My last boyfriend, the one before the opera buff, nicknamed me "Sofa".'

'You're my three-piece-sweetheart,' giggled Jonathan, pushing Sophy back onto the bed. 'I haven't been so excited since I went on the bouncy castle at Limesbridge fête.'

Sophy was seriously big. Unable to see what was going on over her backside, Trafford started to emerge from the creaking wardrobe.

'What's that?' gasped Sophy, hearing heavy breathing.

'Probably a dog,' mumbled Jonathan, who was blissfully losing himself in mountains of soft flesh. 'Shut up, Diggory, shut up, Choirboy.' He hurled a shoe across the room.

As they carried on, Trafford, frantic to distinguish some of the magnificent heaving flesh, switched on his torch.

'Who's that?' cried Sophy, jumping out of her luscious dimpled skin in panic.

'Light from the knocking shop opposite,' whispered Jonathan soothingly. '"Gestapo bully" is one of their specialities, shining lights into clients' faces and threatening to beat them up. Oh, you gorgeous thing.'

The ensuing romp so excited Trafford he nearly fell out of the wardrobe, knocking over a canvas. Furiously Jonathan kicked the door shut. But by this time Sophy was far too excited to notice. Later, as she ecstatically cradled a snoring Jonathan to her breasts, she wondered if she'd dreamt it, or had a man really slithered out across the floorboards?

Two streets away, Sienna lay on her bed smoking. Work had been interrupted all day by the telephone which she'd answered, hoping it might be Jonathan, but it was always about him – journalists wanting to know where he was and why his ravishing new sister had slapped his face. The last call had been from Dicky, who'd crept out of bed at Bagley Hall.

'All the boys have been teasing me,' he had sobbed. 'Mummy won't give me away like she did Emerald, will she?'

Switching off the telephone, Sienna had sobbed too. On the polished floor, where she had set fire to it, lay the blackened fragments of Anthea's interview with the *Standard*. On the wall was a framed letter from Sir Nicholas Serota, congratulating her on being short-listed for the Turner prize.

In the past, when she was sad, she had drawn comfort from visualizing sweet Hope in the Raphael, but since the silver wedding, she could only see Anthea's smug little face. And nothing could alter the fact that Jonathan was far too preoccupied with his new sister to telephone his old one.

'I feel shocking,' moaned Sophy next morning as she pinched Jonathan's most voluminous shirt to wear to school.

'At least you look as though you're bravely staggering in after food poisoning,' mumbled Jonathan sleepily.

'Thank you both for a heavenly day.' Sophy kissed him and then Diggory.

'We enjoyed it too. You can't remember where I left my car, can you?'

In the middle of Geography, Sophy was called out to take an urgent call from her sister.

'Why haven't Mummy and Daddy rung me and begged me to come home?' demanded Emerald.

'Just bugger off,' shouted Sophy and hung up.

On the Saturday after the silver wedding, Anthea was intoxicated to receive an affectionate airmail from Zac, posted in St Petersburg, apologizing for his cavalier behaviour and thanking her for a memorable party. She didn't show the contents to Emerald, who was bitterly disappointed only to get a neutral postcard of the Hermitage. Scented by lavender bags, Zac's letter took up residence at the back of Anthea's underwear drawer.

It intoxicated her that her face was now in the papers as much as the other Belvedons, that she could manipulate her new daughter into setting those arrogant, defiant brothers at each other's throats, and in addition make Sienna wild with jealousy. She also enjoyed seeing David Pulborough in a jitter. The next few weeks were going to be fun.

37

Jupiter Belvedon was in turmoil. A control freak, particularly where he himself was concerned, he had prided himself on his perfect marriage and, determined to safeguard it, had refused to let Hanna be parted from him for a single night. Now he was devoured with lust for a sister who had pretended to be attracted to him to gain access to Anthea.

Although he had protested to Hanna that he had merely thought of Emerald as a marketable property, Hanna couldn't stop crying. Her tears fell on the huge watercolour she was painstakingly assembling of all the wild flowers in Galena's meadow, creating a ravishing wet on wet effect. Jupiter, never very good at communication, couldn't comfort her. Leaving her in the country, unable to sleep, he worked himself into the ground in London. God knew what Pandora's Box Emerald had opened. He didn't believe she was Raymond's daughter any more than Jonathan did. How could they make their besotted father have a DNA test?

As the days passed, Jupiter grew increasingly fed up with journalists ringing the gallery, wanting to interview his father about the art world and the vain old bugger not realizing they were fishing about Emerald. Raymond was also getting sloppy. Revving up for a BBC programme on the High Renaissance, which meant a lot of research, he had not checked the provenance of a Turner and, having sold it to a private collector, discovered it had been stolen from a museum in Houston, who very much wanted it back. Even worse, far more punters were going into the Pulborough, which had gone above the Belvedon in the dealers' profit parade for the first time.

Raymond had succeeded in the past by selling paintings on brilliantly or hanging on to them until they went up in value. But in recent years he had borrowed huge sums to buy pictures which had slumped instead. Many of the paintings at Foxes Court were held as collateral for the loan.

Jupiter kept trying to persuade his father to have the Raphael revalued so they could borrow against it. Another alternative would be to sell it, or lend it to a big touring exhibition, which could treble its value. Best of all, to avoid capital transfer tax, would be for Raymond to make it over to Jupiter as the eldest son. After his father's death, Jupiter promised he would split whatever the picture was worth between the others. But Raymond, who didn't trust Jupiter, almost hysterically refused. He was only seventy-five, and his ambition, which he hadn't revealed to Jupiter, was to give the Raphael to the National Gallery.

Jupiter was also unnerved by the increasing publicity being given to art looted from the Jews by the Nazis during the last war. More and more of the original Jewish owners or their descendants were trying to reclaim their pictures. What if Pandora had been stolen? Raymond had always been slightly hazy about how he acquired the Raphael, some story about a dying Kraut handing him the picture in return for a glass of water in a burning château.

Finally, was the picture 'right'? Alarming rumours were coming out of the Vatican that one of the most famous Raphaels hadn't been painted by the master at all. No wonder, apart from his obsession with Emerald, Jupiter wasn't sleeping.

Help, however, was at hand. Si Greenbridge, the vastly
rich arms-dealer who had cancelled lunch with Jupiter
the day Emerald had wheedled her way into the
Belvedon, was back in London for Royal Ascot and
the big antiques and art fairs.

Accompanying Si, as well as his four guards, was his
third wife Ginny, a former Miss New Jersey who travelled
with Pascal, her interior designer, and endless colour
swatches. Ginny Greenbridge, who was only interested
in pictures that enhanced the décor, was in her late
twenties. Si was in his middle fifties. A brusque
belligerent hunk who looked as if he could crack safes
with the lift of an ebony eyebrow, Si was a serious
collector with many millions of dollars to launder.

In early June therefore, both the Belvedons and the
Pulboroughs vied to take Si's money off him and entertain him in the most exciting way. Raymond kicked off
with a very smart drinks party at the gallery, with pictures
by his leading artists on the faded burgundy-red walls,
and some enticing Old Masters in the vaults as a cabaret
after dinner.

Despite a damp and dismal evening, the gallery was
packed out. Amid the chattering royalty, the rock stars
and the shadow cabinet ministers Jupiter wished to
impress, Si looked like a huge grizzly who'd gatecrashed
a teddy bears' picnic. Among the sprinkling of ravishing
girls, Emerald, in a little kingfisher-blue number from
Amanda Wakeley which turned her eyes an even
witchier green, shone the brightest.

On her first official outing as a Belvedon, however,
Emerald was desperately nervous. She was also mortified that Alizarin, Jonathan and Sienna had all blacked
the party, whilst Jupiter, who clearly hadn't forgiven
her, was looking more adamantine than his head, which
Raymond had subtly lit and proudly displayed in an
alcove and at which everyone giggled and said 'Good
evening, Jupiter' to as they swanned in.

Seeing Emerald quailing as the paparazzi swooped down on her, Si moved in with the fleetness of a heavyweight boxing champion, whisking her into a corner and shielding her with his massive frame, so no-one could get at either of them.

'Oh thank you,' gasped Emerald, 'I always panic in crowds. I'm so small, I'm terrified of getting trampled underfoot. This is an incredibly smart party, I've just seen Liz Hurley and King Constantine walk in.'

'So smart,' replied Si in a very strong gravelly Bronx accent, 'I can't figure how in hell I got invited.'

Emerald laughed.

'Because you're the most important person in the world.'

Si in fact was incredibly shy and had been so busy dealing in arms and making fortunes in hotel chains, gambling dens, newspapers and television stations, he hadn't had much time to acquire social graces on the way up. He also had a horror of being trapped, because people always wanted things from him.

Examining his pugnacious cave-giant face, Emerald decided he was definitely attractive. She'd always liked rich, powerful, older men; father figures or – in Si's case – godfather figures. In his dark suit, dark shirt, and tie as white as his beautifully capped teeth, he could have walked straight out of a Thirties gangster movie. He was also very brown and fit, his gold-ringed hands were beautifully manicured and nothing could dim his passion for art. Only stopping to see her glass was refilled, he fired questions at her about her sculptures, her taste in pictures and had soon learnt of her elusive New York boyfriend and her tricky new family.

Si's guards, whose chunkiness added to the crush, never took their eyes off their boss. Nor did the rest of the guests, from the shadow cabinet ministers, who wanted vast pledges for the Tory Party, to the princes and princesses who wanted freebies in the Greenbridge jets, to the celebs who wanted their picture taken beside

Si, to the photographers and reporters who were climbing into sofas and chairs to see Emerald over his shoulders, and who all wanted jobs on Si's highly successful newspapers.

Even Anthea, bashing herself like a pale moth against his dark wall of back, had no success.

'Mr Greenbridge?'

'In a minute,' snapped Si.

'We've got to get him away from Emerald,' hissed a white-faced Jupiter. 'People like Michael Portillo are only hanging on to meet him. There are endless pictures he's got to see.'

'Plenty of time for that after dinner,' said an over-joyed Raymond. 'If Si commissions work from the darling child, she's made for life. Look, she's pointing out your head to him.'

Si was so impressed by Jupiter's head that he beckoned over Ginny, his wife, and suggested Emerald did her head while they were in London.

Ginny, who disliked competition, pouted, and said she'd rather be done by Joan Bideford, whose flesh tones matched the poolroom in Long Island. Lesbianism anyway was so hip in the States.

Anthea, outraged that Emerald had been spurned, took Ginny Greenbridge aside.

'My dear, I too married a much older man. Do remember that men of that generation are used to calling the shots, and should be pandered to in every way. If Si prefers Emerald's work . . .'

But Ginny Greenbridge had belted off to try and melt icy Jupiter.

Anthea, used to being the sex kitten centre of every Belvedon party, was not enjoying herself. She had been shoved aside by Si in his haste to rescue Emerald, and how dare Raymond reproach her for spending £2,000 on a Meissen parrot at the ceramics fair, when he was force-feeding everyone Krug? Even Si's guards could be seen discreetly knocking it back, and Ginny

328

Greenbridge was so glittering with diamonds, she must have emptied the jewellery fair at Grosvenor House.

Anthea also regarded it as a personal insult to herself that not only Alizarin, Jonathan and Sienna but also her stepdaughter-in-law had boycotted the party. A sharp-eyed reporter from the *Evening Standard* had picked this up.

'Surely Hanna Belvedon's a gallery artist?'

Another gallery artist, Casey Andrews, noisier and more bombastic than ever, a bottle of Krug protruding from the pocket of his hairy ginger jacket, had decided his destiny was Raymond's new daughter. Not realizing how rich Si was, he in turn shoved Si out of the way, and leered down at Emerald. Noting Casey muscling in, aware of Si's perennially itchy feet, Raymond glided over, murmuring that very shortly they should move on to the Garrick where he'd booked a table. Whereupon, to his horror, Si glanced at his Rolex.

'Ginny and I oughta go, we're meeting with David Pulboro' at eight-thirty.'

'But you're dining with us. I've got some ravishing things to show you later,' protested Raymond, needing all his sang-froid not to betray his fury, particularly when a drooling Casey announced he wasn't doing anything and would be only too happy to take Si's place at the Garrick.

'And I'll take Ginny's place,' boomed Joan Bideford, sliding an arm round Emerald's waist.

'I'm afraid I can't make it either, Dad,' said Jupiter, who was quite unable to face the heaven and hell of dining opposite Emerald.

Game, set and macho to David. In delight, he clocked Raymond's frozen smile as, watched by a scribbling press, and protected by guards with umbrellas, Si and Ginny swept through driving rain twenty-five yards across the road to the Pulborough.

As his contacts were not as starry as Raymond's, David had arranged an intimate little dinner at Le Caprice.

Rosemary had not been invited because among the guests was David's mistress, Geraldine Paxton, whose rich husband Maurice didn't get much of a look-in either. As someone who advised the affluent on what to put on their walls, the sexually voracious Geraldine enjoyed inspiring gratitude in handsome young groovers by introducing them to generous patrons.

David had therefore ordered his newest grooviest gallery artist to be present to chat up Geraldine. Jonathan, who had just returned from Yorkshire, digging into Emerald's past, and who would much rather have done a number on the delectable Ginny Greenbridge, grumbled that he didn't like the Arts Council.

'They're a monument to tokenism and political correctness who spend their time squandering tax-payers' money on works of art by their friends.'

'That's why I want you to become a friend of Mrs Paxton,' said David smoothly.

He had also dragged fat Barney away from the gaming tables to persuade Pascal, Ginny's gay interior designer, how much the work of Pulborough artists would enhance the Greenbridge properties. Both Jonathan and Barney struggled not to laugh when Ginny Greenbridge, on entering the gallery, whipped out a blue and gold side plate and rejected a ravishing Burne-Jones because the blues in Guinevere's dress wouldn't quite match the dinner service on the yacht.

'She's a former Miss New Jersey,' murmured Barney.

'A Miss New Dress and a Miss New Jewellery, judging by that Tiffany cross disappearing down her cleavage,' murmured back Jonathan. 'How's Charge Nurse Bisley?'

'Doing nights,' smirked Barney. 'How's Abdul's nude of Sophy coming along?'

'Nearly finished,' lied Jonathan.

'I like paintings I feel I could fly over or walk through,' confessed Si, admiring a tiger-ridden Rousseau jungle.

'How did you enjoy my father's party?' asked Jonathan. 'Did you meet my new sister Emerald?'

'An absolute knockout,' Si admitted, 'and goddam talented. Sir Raymond is giving her a show in October.'

Dad's given her the slot I would have had if I hadn't defected to the Pulborough, thought Jonathan, trying to suppress an explosion of jealousy.

'She was being monopolized by Colin Casey Andrews as we left,' added Si.

'At least she's met someone with a bigger ego than her own,' sighed Jonathan. 'What was she moaning about this time?'

'Her boyfriend being away, and the antagonism of her siblings,' said Si reprovingly.

'Ah,' said Jonathan lightly. 'We may not be her brothers and sisters much longer. In Yorkshire yesterday I unearthed an old biddy who'd once cleaned for the hospital where Emerald was born. She clearly remembers Anthea being visited by' – Jonathan's big dark eyes rolled innocently in David's direction – 'a very pretty blond man, young, but not very tall, which doesn't sound like my father.'

David choked on his drink.

'Probably her brother,' he spluttered. 'Drink up, everyone, taxi's waiting.'

38

Barney, who'd been looking forward to a delicious three-course blow-out at Le Caprice, was bitterly disappointed. The Greenbridges, like many rich couples who constantly dine out, ate little and drank less except for quantities of bottled water. Si ordered smoked trout and a filet mignon; Ginny, asparagus, then strawberries.

Si, who had no small talk, was only interested in picking David's brains, frequently recording information on a dictaphone. Geraldine Paxton, skeletal thin in a pinstripe suit, and yellow paisley tie, toyed with a plate of vegetables. Jonathan on her left, buoyed up by another line of coke, flirted with her outrageously as he drew first Ginny, then Si, on the backs of two menus. Si had a good face, strong and square. Although the low forehead and underhung jaw added a Neanderthal ferocity, the mournful dark eyes were those of an Alsatian long abandoned in a dogs' home.

Realizing while he'd been quizzing David everyone else had practically finished, Si picked up a steak knife and fork to attack his smoked trout.

'Fish knife, Si,' murmured David.

Feeling he'd done his stuff chatting up Geraldine, Jonathan turned thankfully to Ginny on his left, who was toying with strawberries, enhanced by neither cream nor sugar.

'How long have you been married?' he asked.

'Six months.'

'Happy?'

'Kinda – Si's last wife passed away, but he won't verbalize about her. My analyst told Si he was being very selfish not helping me to work it through and bury her ghost.'

Hence the sad Alsatian eyes, thought Jonathan.

'It would be worse if he talked about her all the time,' he said, drawing the thick black hair on the top of Si's head as a jagged palisade. Next moment his pen shot downwards giving Si a thin gigolo sideboard as Geraldine, on his right, slid a bony hand under his table napkin.

'My clients call me their "hired eyes",' she was simultaneously boasting to Si. 'I help people put art on their walls, not unlike an interior designer' – she flashed big teeth at gay Pascal – 'but art is more intellectually stimulating, and does have an asset value.'

'She helps lame dogs over lifestyles,' giggled Jonathan to Ginny.

'Si keeps buying new properties to accommodate our art,' murmured back Ginny, who was longing to run her hand through Jonathan's hair – he was so cute.

Geraldine turned to Ginny warmly. 'I am sure I can advise you and Si. I'd love to introduce you to . . .'

But Ginny had shot off to the Ladies.

'Every time a marriage breaks up, I make a fucking fortune,' gay Pascal was whispering to Barney. 'The new wife moves in and changes all the décor and needs fifty million dollars of new art to go with it.'

'Can't be bad.' Barney let Pascal do the talking, enabling himself to shovel quantities of Scandinavian ice berries smothered with white chocolate sauce into his face.

As Si was still being clobbered by Geraldine, David pinched Ginny's chair.

'I've just had a call from Dame Hermione,' he told Jonathan furiously. 'I learn instead of videoing her yourself, you sent round that scrofulous beast Trafford with a Box Brownie. Dame Hermione is most displeased and threatening to pull out. And Enid Coley is even more disappointed with her portrait, she doesn't think you even painted her face.'

'I thought she did that herself with a trowel,' said Jonathan sulkily.

'Stop being flip. This cannot go on.'

'It can't,' agreed Jonathan. 'I at least did these all myself,' he added, handing two menus to a returning Ginny Greenbridge, who went into ecstasies.

'Oh my Gard. This is to die for, so like me. May I keep it? You have real talent, and look, Si, Jonathan has made you look like a real gentleman.'

Si was so touched by this miracle – and also because Jonathan hadn't made a pass at Ginny (most men did) – that he promptly commissioned him to paint her portrait.

'Can you do it straight away?' begged Ginny. 'We're off to Berlin on Sunday. Si and I are global citizens.'

Jonathan tried not to laugh.

'Certainly he can,' said David firmly, 'I'll sort out a price.'

I expected David to be fun and easy to work with, thought Jonathan darkly. He's just a bloody Hitler.

'I wouldn't tell everyone,' Geraldine was now confiding to Si, 'but Maurice, my husband, and I have given half a million to Tate Modern.'

'Si gave forty-four million dollars to cultural projects last year,' interrupted Ginny crushingly, 'and Si and I not only give money, we give of ourselves.'

Si was still looking at Jonathan's drawing.

'I'm told the Norwich School is a good buy, I kinda like an artist called John Sell Cotman.'

'Marvellous,' agreed Jonathan.

'Too parochial,' said David dismissively. 'I wouldn't bother.'

'I would,' said Jonathan sweetly. 'My father has a beautiful Cotman of Duncombe Park with the trees turning at home. He might be prepared to sell it.'

David was so cross he overtipped by mistake, and as the rain had stopped, suggested walking back to the Pulborough.

As they strolled along a dripping Jermyn Street, David, remembering how he had benefited from Raymond's example in the Seventies, warmly recommended Raymond's tailors – whom he now regarded as his own – to Si. 'They're excellent and very reasonable. Just mention my name,' he added loftily. 'What are your plans for tomorrow?'

'Going to the art fair. I'm after a Degas drawing of a jockey.'

As they entered Cork Street, David was amused to see Jupiter and Tamzin his assistant still wearily clearing up glasses and chucking out drunks. Across the road, David's assistant, subtle Zoe, had the coffee on and the liqueurs out.

Brandishing colour swatches, Ginny pored over half a dozen of Jonathan's canvasses.

'The rest are sold,' said Zoe apologetically. 'Jonathan's work is rocketing in value, you'd have a real investment here.'

'I just adore the little kid with the pink beach ball.' Ginny turned to Pascal: 'Perfect for the playroom.'

'I didn't know you had children.' Jonathan took a swig of kümmel.

'We're thinking about it. Babies are so hip at the moment.'

'Boom, why does my art go boom,' sang Jonathan, quickstepping Zoe down the gallery. 'Mrs Greenbridge doesn't realize that the pink beach ball is the end of the little kid's cock.'

'For God's sake don't tell her,' giggled Zoe.

*   *   *

Meanwhile, in a white-washed back room lit like a chapel hung a reclining nude by Modigliani priced at £10 million.

'Everyone's after it,' murmured David, 'the Tate, MOMA, the Getty, but I wanted to give you first look.' Then, handing Si a glass of Napoleon brandy, which cost more than dinner, he added smoothly, 'I'd be happy to accompany you to Grosvenor House tomorrow. Dealers at fairs can be iffy if you don't know the ropes. Although you couldn't do better than the Modigliani.'

Si looked at David meditatively. He might be in thrall to the daydreams of his wife's designer, but he was not going to be patronized.

'You can steer me into your smart tailor, David, you can tell me what knife to use, or even how to hold my dick, but not what art to buy.'

David went magenta. 'Only making a suggestion,' he spluttered.

'Well, don't,' snapped Si, 'the Modigliani doesn't grab me and it's way overpriced.'

Jonathan felt increasingly drawn to Si and wanted to stay and talk to him. But not wishing to bug David too much, and having been urged to suck up to Geraldine, he offered her a lift home.

Only when Barney had swept Pascal off to his gambling club, dropping off a weary Ginny at the Ritz on the way, did Si despatch Zoe to make him another cup of coffee, and say to David, 'I have two Leonardo drawings at home, and one by Michelangelo, but my dream is to own a Raphael.'

David's heart leapt. 'My dream is to find you one. I'll put out feelers.'

'Keep it low key. If people figure I'm nosing around, the price will shoot up.'

Getting out his spectacles, Si got up to have another look at the Modigliani. Turning, he caught David with his hand up Zoe's skirt as she put the coffee cup down on the table.

'Mrs Pulboro' doesn't like London?' he asked pointedly.

'No, she's a country gal,' replied David heartily. 'I can only tempt her up to town for the Chelsea Flower Show. Her father was Sir Mervyn Newton, you know.'

'I look forward to meeting her in July.'

'You do?'

'Sir Raymond has asked us to visit Foxes Court.'

David was enraged but not so furious as Geraldine was later.

Although Jonathan thought her a pretentious cow, he made a detour to Hoxton to show her his pictures. All the way, Geraldine boasted about her contacts.

'The art industry is built on relationships, Jonathan. If you play ball your oeuvre could end up on the most influential walls in Europe.'

Reaching the loft, they found a furiously growling Diggory and Choirboy having a tug of war over a Hermès scarf. Trafford, stripped to the waist, was arched over a microscope, drawing his own sperm. Geraldine was enraptured.

'In an increasingly godless age, one's own body is the only site of identity,' she cried.

Trafford had been having an annual tidy-out of his bedroom, which meant using the communal studio as a waste-paper basket. In the middle rose a pile of beer cans, curry trays, Pedigree Chum tins, fag ends, twelve months of unopened bills and bank statements and torn-up photographs of models Trafford had failed to pull. On top was a dressing of pages torn out of porn mags.

Mess created by artists seems to electrify the outsider.

'This is very fine,' exclaimed Geraldine, walking round the pile. 'Does it have a title?'

'Cunterpane,' grunted Trafford, intent on his drawing.

'How apt! Perhaps *Cunterpane One*. I hate to be hard nosed, but is it for sale? Nothing ventured . . . how much?'

'Hundred thousand,' said Trafford, adding another tadpole.

'A very fair price, I know half a dozen homes for which it could form a vital centre piece.'

Jonathan, getting bored, wandered off to his bedroom to find some suitable canvasses to show Geraldine. Geraldine, however, was more interested in sex. Following him, she shoved him back on the bed, attacking him like a Dyson. A minute or two later, she said tartly, 'It isn't a legal offence to move your tongue, Jonathan.'

She was undressing him briskly and Jonathan was wondering whether he was capable of performing at all without more Charlie, when the doorbell rang.

'Jonathan, are you there?' yelled a voice through the letterbox. 'I can see your light's on.'

It was Sophy Cartwright, monstrous crush on Jonathan unabated.

As he tugged on his trousers, Jonathan apologized to Geraldine.

'My sister's rolled up' – well, it was nearly true – 'you stay here while I get rid of her.'

Sophy had arrived with cheesecake, raspberries and a bottle of Tesco's champagne, all of which Jonathan, who had the serious munchies, got stuck into.

'It's so lovely to see you,' said Sophy wistfully.

Only when she asked him twenty minutes later what he was working on at the moment, did Jonathan remember Geraldine.

'Kerist, you've just reminded me. Sorry, darling, there's something I've got to finish off next door. Here's twenty quid for a taxi.' It was pouring with rain again. Jonathan felt a sod as he despatched a desolate Sophy into the cold, wet night.

Trafford was enraged.

'Bloody dog in the manger. Why didn't you pass Sophy on to me?'

'Shut up,' hissed Jonathan.

'How can you prefer that stick insect?'

'She's a stuck insect now.'

Alas, flipping through Jonathan's canvasses, a marooned Geraldine had been enraged to discover portraits of many of her friends in various states of undress. She hadn't dared come out in case 'Jonathan's sister' knew her or Maurice, her husband. But hearing the front door bang, she rushed out in a fury, beating Jonathan round the head with a squash racket. Collapsing on the floor, lying as still as a reclining nude, Jonathan pretended to have passed out. Luckily Diggory, who was frantically licking his master's face to revive him, decided instead to bite one of Geraldine's incredibly thin ankles, sending her shrieking into the night. Outside she immediately rang David on his mobile.

'I'm stuck in Hoxton.'

'Si's still here,' lied David, spitting out one of Zoe's pubic hairs, 'I'll call you in the morning.'

'Tell Si I've discovered an important artist.'

Having applied two more squirts of Right Guard to ten other layers stiffening under his armpits, Trafford caught up with Geraldine in the middle of Hoxton Square. Drenched, limping, waving her thin arms, she had all the pathos of a Lowry grandmother.

'Would you like a lift home?' asked Trafford.

Returning much earlier, Si had found his wife awake.

'Gotta call coming through from LA,' he told her. 'Go get yourself ready, baby.'

Wandering into the bedroom five minutes later, he found Ginny, her long blond hair in pigtails, naked except for a gym slip and white socks, skipping in front of a long mirror.

'One, two, three, four,' she counted in a shrill, childish voice, breasts bouncing, pleated skirt flying, skipping rope hissing through the air, 'five, six, seven, eight.' Her blond bush was darkening. She never got to twenty.

39

As a wet chill June grew even wetter and chiller, Alizarin Belvedon, who travelled his own road and never complained, realized with increasing horror that his sight was going. The streaked black and silver water tumbling into the trough opposite the front door at Foxes Court, which had always reminded him of Galena's fringe, was now only a blur. Used to roaming the valley at dusk, he kept tripping over stones and missing steps. Yesterday he had smashed a treasured possession, a mug Hanna had given him. The hospital lights used by surgeons, in which he'd invested to enable him to paint through the night, were now needed all day.

At first he thought he was imagining things, but he kept having blinding headaches and the vision in his left eye was definitely narrowing, and he had so much left to paint. He was too terrified of being told to give up to go to the doctor. Instead he worked until he collapsed. Nor had he been able to sell any pictures and earned barely enough from his day a week teaching at Searston College to feed Visitor and buy paint.

The news from Kosovo and Chechnya was terrible; he should be there. But he couldn't afford it, he loathed leaving Visitor and a still small voice queried whether he would only be going to escape from the bills, the bailiffs and his hopeless longing for Hanna. As a final injury,

Raymond was giving that spoilt brat Emerald an exhibition. Alizarin groaned so loudly that Visitor woke and waddled across the room to lay a fat paw on his master's knee.

Alizarin had grown up too fast. As a child he had known too many secrets, which he usually blocked out, but which recently had returned to him in hideous nightmares. If Galena set him free perhaps he could paint less tortured, more accessible pictures?

After the silver wedding, there had been much sly media innuendo as to who had really fathered Galena's sons. Jupiter and Jonathan were perceived to be Raymond's, but rumour persisted that Alizarin's father was the late Etienne de Montigny, now regarded as France's greatest painter, who'd been tall and thin, with a beaky nose and massive shoulders like Alizarin. A week before she died, Galena had given Alizarin one of Etienne's ravishing drawings of herself, which hung in the Lodge beside Galena's palette and which Alizarin wouldn't have sold for the world. Alizarin had been nine when Galena died, the same age as Dicky and Dora today. He had spent a lot of time, since Emerald arrived, comforting them both.

'Ouch,' shouted Alizarin, as Visitor clawed his thigh with his paw. 'OK, let's go to London.'

Visitor, who adored jaunts, thumped his tail.

The jaunt started humiliatingly. None of the galleries Alizarin dropped into were remotely interested in his pictures.

'You'll have to become a guide dog sooner than you think,' he told Visitor.

Heavy rain had slowed down the traffic, and it was late afternoon before Alizarin braved the Belvedon. Raymond had gone to the BBC. Jupiter was in the back office sorting out another of his father's cock-ups. A man called Baxter, who'd arrived with a Rolls-Royce and a chauffeur, and who claimed to be staying at the Savoy, had been allowed by Raymond to borrow a charming

Millais for a few hours to show his wife. It now transpired there was no Baxter staying at the Savoy and no sign of the Millais.

Tamzin, Raymond's assistant, yet another comely well-bred halfwit, whom Jupiter referred to as the 'Dimbo', had been ordered not to disturb him. She also didn't recognize Alizarin.

'Mr Belvedon hasn't time to look at unsolicited work,' she told him disdainfully. 'Why don't you send in some transparencies with a stamped addressed Jiffy bag?'

Alizarin's roar of rage flushed even Jupiter out of the inner sanctum, but he only allowed his younger brother five minutes, not even offering him a drink.

'We've got too much of your stuff taking up space already.'

Then, flipping and wincing his way through half a dozen of Alizarin's recent canvasses, he added, 'You must make your work more collector friendly. I'll take that little watercolour of Visitor, if you're really strapped.'

'Fuck off,' howled Alizarin.

He was so angry he drove all the way down a one-way street, ignoring frantic hooting and waving of fists. For a second he rested his aching head on the steering wheel. It would take him three or four hours to get back to Limesbridge in the rush hour.

Thoroughly depressed, he drove east to Hoxton where Diggory and Visitor greeted each other joyfully and where he found Jonathan in high spirits if under siege.

'David keeps hassling me to finish things, and has just buggered off to Geneva to top up his tan and shove more millions into his Swiss bank. Trafford's been arrested for punching a photographer; I offered to bail him, but he said he needed the rest and that having a record will increase his street cred. He had a tidy-up last week, although you wouldn't know it.'

At least the pile of rubbish topped with porn magazines had disappeared to a more elevated location.

'What brings you to London?' asked Jonathan as he rootled under a chaos of love letters and sketches for a corkscrew.

'Not selling pictures, particularly to the Belvedon.' Cussedly Alizarin chucked the watercolour of Visitor that his elder brother had liked into the waste-paper basket. 'Jupiter's a shit, isn't he?'

'Foul,' agreed Jonathan. 'I'm painting a group of people I most dislike including Casey Andrews and Somerford Keynes and calling it *Millennium Buggers*. I'm thinking of adding Jupiter. He'll never forgive you for pushing the frontiers forward and because he knows Hanna admires you more than him.'

Then, as Alizarin blushed and muttered something self-deprecating, Jonathan continued, 'He does too. And he'll never forgive Emerald for conning him into asking her to the silver wedding. I think he even convinced himself she fancied him. How is she?' he asked casually.

'Disrupting the household.'

'Has that Yank boyfriend turned up again?'

Alizarin shook his head. 'Probably what's making her so tetchy.'

Unable to find a corkscrew, Jonathan rinsed a mug and a teacup and filled them both with whisky.

Both brothers, particularly in the face of current family ructions, felt absurdly happy to be friends again. As Jonathan put on the Alpine Symphony, in which Richard Strauss depicts a day on a mountain, starting with basses growling around before sunrise, Alizarin noticed that his brother was looking particularly smart, in a new very white shirt with the creases still in and a dark blue Sixties rock-star suit with a faint cerulean check.

As he topped up Alizarin's glass, Jonathan became very thoughtful.

'Look, I've got myself into a jam.'

'I haven't got any money,' said Alizarin flatly.

'No, for once it isn't that. I've got a sitting in an hour with Hermione Harefield. I daren't cancel. Later I've arranged to see Geraldine Paxton, I daren't cancel her either, or I'll never get anything in the Tate. I've also got a commission to deliver first thing tomorrow morning – a nude. I've already had twenty thousand pounds up front, but there's still forty thousand to come, which I'll split with you if you paint it for me.'

'Don't be ridiculous,' exploded Alizarin, thinking what he could do with £20,000. See a decent eye specialist, stock up on canvasses and paint, mend the hole in the roof, buy a new collar for Visitor or even dinner for Hanna when Jupiter was in London.

The Alpine Symphony was growing louder and louder: the sun was about to burst forth on the snowy peaks.

'Oh please, Al, I'm desperate. You could always copy anyone's style. I'll be reduced to paying a forger.'

'Don't be fucking stupid.'

'I'll give you twenty-five grand.'

'Who is she?'

The doorbell rang.

'That'll be her now.'

Richard Strauss's sun appeared in majestic descending octaves as Sophy's beaming face came round the door. She was wearing her mother's tweed coat over a bright yellow strapless dress, and was weighed down by three bottles of white, smoked salmon, a quiche and a packet of chocolate biscuits for Diggory, who greeted her delightedly, all four feet off the ground.

'Sophy, darling!' Jonathan's manner was unnaturally hearty; he couldn't meet her eyes.

Sophy had a despairing feeling he'd only summoned her because he needed the rest of Abdul's money, but she put on a cheery front as Jonathan launched into the rigmarole of his predicament, leaving out this time, Alizarin noticed, any mention of Geraldine.

'All you've got to do is to sit for my unbelievably talented brother instead,' Jonathan said soothingly, 'I've drawn the short straw. I've got to paint Dame Hermione in the buff. It's going to be called *Expectant Madonna*. She's eight months gone so I've really got to motor. Hope it doesn't pop out, I was never a good slip catch, and that I've got enough paint. She's absolutely vast.'

Sophy, who was feeling vast herself, after misery eating too many chocolates, was not only desperately disappointed, but appalled and embarrassed at having to strip off instead in front of this gaunt angry giant. Seeing her distress, Alizarin wanted to back out. But Jonathan was so charming and persuasive.

'You've got to dogsit anyway, both of you, Diggory chews up canvasses if he's left on his own.' Then, whispering to Sophy: 'I'll be back later, keep the bed warm,' and murmuring to Alizarin: 'Off to ride my trustee steed,' he sidled out.

Alizarin was absolutely livid.

Sophy found taking her clothes off the worst part. At least she was super-glammed up for Jonathan, with pink-painted toenails, shining hair, body lotion rubbed into every acre of her body and no shoulder strap or knicker elastic marks, because Jonathan had ordered her not to wear any underwear.

Alizarin kicked Visitor and Diggory off the big sofa and, spreading a blue sheet over it, arranged Sophy on top. For a second, she fought back the tears, when she saw the plaster on her leg, where in her excitement she'd cut herself shaving. But once Alizarin got going, he was so kind and so quiet. She noticed he kept polishing his spectacles, his tummy kept rumbling, and twice he apologized to her shoes thinking he'd stumbled over Diggory.

Worried she might be cold on such a dank, cold

evening, he whacked up Jonathan's central heating, but she noticed how this made him pour with sweat, obviously not used himself to such warmth. When he whipped off his checked shirt, which had lost most of its buttons, and then his dark green T-shirt, she noticed how little flesh there was on his huge frame.

I wish I could feed him up, she thought, admiring at the same time the endless legs in the ripped jeans. She was dying to ask him what he thought of Emerald, but she didn't want to distract him. Alizarin didn't talk much except to ask if she were all right and occasionally tell her she had a lovely body.

'Too much of it,' sighed Sophy. 'I expect in Saudi Arabia, where Abdul lives, there's lots of sand to stretch out on.'

'How long have you known Jonathan?'

'Four weeks and three days.' She blushed. 'I ought to have seen the writing on the wall. The last time he made love to me, the foreplay was so fantastic, I didn't realize till afterwards he'd been watching *The Bill* with the sound turned down.'

That bloody charm, thought Alizarin furiously, which gets away with things again and again.

'One good thing,' admitted Sophy, 'I wanted to have something interesting to talk to him about this evening, so I went to an exhibition of Raphael's drawings at Buckingham Palace. They were so wonderful' – Sophy stretched joyfully – 'and I had no idea that so many Raphaels were painted by so many different people.'

'Like Jonathan's pictures,' said Alizarin drily.

'But the ones Raphael did himself are so much greater. He seems to paint people as they really are, the pupils' stuff looks chocolate boxy by comparison, as if they were trying too hard to flatter. Sorry, you know all this.'

As the windows darkened, she told him about the children she taught, and Alizarin told her about his students.

'They're so trusting. Once you win their confidence, you could tell them to jump through fire. They've been so short changed,' he went on roughly. 'A whole generation of students has never been taught how to draw or paint because it's unfashionable. Video and the installation are all, and, even more important, marketing. My old college is run by bank managers.'

'I wish my bank manager would go off and run an art college,' sighed Sophy.

Increasingly, she marvelled at Alizarin's obsessive concentration, the tension in his body, and the fire in those long screwed-up eyes.

Four times they were interrupted by a wrong number. Not wanting Sophy to alter her position, Alizarin answered it, on each occasion getting less polite.

'It's some man asking for a Mrs Greenbridge,' he told Sophy.

The telephone rang again. Throwing down his brushes and palette for the fifth time, Alizarin stalked across the room and picked up the telephone.

'No, I'm very sorry, Mrs Greenbridge is upstairs being fucked by the window cleaner,' he snapped and hung up.

Sophy giggled.

'Goodness knows what I've started,' grunted Alizarin. And then he smiled for the first time, which lifted his harsh features, showed off beautiful teeth, and softened the suspicious, angry eyes. He's not ugly at all, thought Sophy in amazement.

At least no-one rang again to break his concentration.

Occasionally, as if in a trance, he wandered over, running his hands over her to memorize a length of nose or curve of her belly.

'My eyes aren't very good,' he apologized, 'I have to use touch.'

Sophy felt increasing quivers of excitement. When he put a hand over her breast, a nipple shot out to meet it. Really, Alizarin wasn't her type.

By two o'clock she had stopped wondering what had happened to Jonathan. At four, Alizarin realized the time, apologized profusely to her and the dogs whom he took out for a pee.

Thinking how lovely he was, Sophy rushed off to find the food she'd bought. In the stifling studio, the white wine was nearly boiling, the quiche had melted and the smoked salmon was practically swimming round the carrier bag, but she laid out a picnic.

As they tucked in, a mood of euphoria took over.

Sophy, Alizarin decided, was like a handful of coloured balloons tied to a garden gate, indicating a party within.

'It's been great having someone to talk to,' he confessed. 'One goes crazy painting away on one's own all day.'

Sophy hadn't looked at the portrait yet. Outside it was getting light. Alizarin didn't want to pull the curtains and let even the fading stars look in in case they broke the spell. Between them they finished the runny quiche and the smoked salmon and gave the chocolate biscuits to a yawning Visitor. Diggory couldn't be bothered to wake up.

By the time the painting was finished, at seven, Sophy was half asleep, only conscious of delicious warmth and rightness, as Alizarin collapsed beside her.

Alizarin in turn felt incredible peace, not just the happiness of producing something he knew was good, but also because Sophy was like summer rain. She would drift through the leaves, reaching plants never watered before, making everything blossom, even sad, uptight, bad-tempered Alizarin.

They were woken around nine by Jonathan, curls wet from the shower, hot from his night on several tiles. Slightly defensive, he had brought croissants and Sancerre, nicked from Geraldine's fridge, as a peace offering. He was amazed not to be chewed out for being so late. He was then decidedly jolted by the extraordinary beauty and rare tenderness of Alizarin's portrait.

'It's awesome,' he said slowly, 'flooded with inner light, like one of Mum's crossed with Renoir. Visitor is the only thing you've painted with as much affection. Fucking marvellous. He's got you, Sophy.' He ruffled Sophy's hair.

Sophy wept when she finally looked at it. She had expected eyes in the middle of her tummy, cubes and triangles, rampant ginger pubes, but Alizarin had made her look absolutely gorgeous, a radiant contemporary Venus with a pink plastic grip comb just containing her gold waterfall of hair and a plaster on her plump leg, celebrating her size rather than hiding it.

'It's the loveliest compliment I'll ever be paid, thank you so much.' And she stood on tiptoe to kiss Alizarin's stubbly jaw.

Jonathan yawned. He looked so beautiful, even first thing in the morning, thought Sophy, with just the right shadows under his eyes. But suddenly she felt he'd only been painted by the pupils, whereas Alizarin's strength and ruggedness was the real Raphael.

Surreptitiously she retrieved the watercolour of Visitor from the waste-paper basket and put it in her bag.

'How was Dame Hermione?' asked Alizarin.

'Ghastly. I stopped her yakking by telling her her face looked most beautiful in repose, when she left her lips together like two lovers asleep on top of each other.'

Sophy caught Alizarin's eye and blushed. She felt sick as Jonathan signed the canvas. Then he said airily, 'Abdul's flying out at midday, I'd better take it round at once. It's so effing marvellous, I ought to charge him ten times as much. How the hell did you get her left boob to fall like that?'

'Paint's still wet,' snapped Alizarin disapprovingly.

'So's Sophy.' Jonathan slid a sly hand between her legs. 'Christ, you are too,' then, as Sophy leapt away and

Alizarin winced, he added, not even bothering to lower his voice, 'Keep yourself warm, darling, I won't be long.'

'I've got to go,' said Alizarin bleakly.

Sophy was appalled how desolate she felt that both her intimacy with Alizarin and the beautiful painting should disappear so fast.

'Sweet, isn't she?' said Jonathan as he and Alizarin walked towards the dirty Ferrari and the ancient van.

'Far too sweet for you,' growled Alizarin.

'At least she's not sexually out of bounds.'

'Whadya mean?'

'Didn't she tell you? She's the Green-Eyed Monster's sister.'

As Alizarin drove off with a succession of bangs, a smoking exhaust and Visitor grinning in the passenger seat, Jonathan reflected it was time his brother bought a new car. He must hand Alizarin's cut from Sophy's portrait over to him at once. Then he started wondering how he could make his portrait of Dame Hermione even more radiant without throttling her, and forgot all about the money.

Jonathan, who was basically good-hearted, returned later to the loft to find Sophy, tidying up as best she could, had unearthed the corkscrew.

'You are an angel. Let's have a drink. What d'you think of my brother?'

'Gorgeous – and a genius.'

'That too. Alas, he won't compromise. No-one works harder to less effect. Mind you, if he made any money he'd give it away.'

'He loves his students.'

'And they absolutely revere him. Although even they find him a bit left wing. Big Al's very politically erect, he could never get it up for a Tory.'

Sophy laughed and accepted a glass of red.

'Er – has he ever been married?'

Jonathan explained about Jupiter stealing Hanna from Alizarin.

'The worst part was that Hanna was pregnant with Alizarin's child, who would be about six now. Jupiter, who's a shit, made her have an abortion. Al's still hopelessly in love with her. I doubt if there'll ever be anyone else.'

Jonathan had picked up the *Evening Standard,* turning to the arts pages. Looking up a moment later he saw Sophy was crying. Embarrassed to say she was miserable she'd probably never see Alizarin again – how fatuous to fall in love in twelve hours – Sophy confessed things were hell at home.

'Bloody Emo appears to have dumped us. Daddy's drinking and cab-driving, Mummy cries whenever Daddy's out, and she's lost her job in the pub, because she kept giving the punters whisky and tonic.'

Sophy also didn't add that she should be handing over her wages to pay bills rather than blueing it on smoked salmon and white wine for Jonathan. Jonathan, who'd just been paid in cash by an ecstatic Abdul, forced another £500 on Sophy as a modelling fee and said he'd see what he could do.

After she'd gone, he rang Raymond and explained the Cartwrights were devastated at losing Emerald. Raymond, even more good hearted than Jonathan, had a brain wave. He and Anthea were planning a twenty-sixth birthday party for Emerald on 7 July, to make up for all the birthdays she'd missed with them. Why didn't they ask the Cartwrights: Ian, Patience and Sophy – he'd just have to square it with Anthea.

Anthea, to his amazement, was wild about the idea. What a wonderful chance to show off and upstage.

'But just in case the Cartwrights are, well, rather humble – after all he drives minicabs and she works in a pub,' she suggested, 'why don't we have an intimate little dinner, instead of a big do, which might faze them.

Just ask the Pulboroughs and us, so all the families can get to know each other.'

Emerald had already dismissively let slip that at parties in Yorkshire Patience had always done the cooking: 'Just plonking baked potatoes and saucepans of bubbling rabbit stew on the kitchen table, and telling everyone to get pissed and on with it.'

In a frenzy of competitiveness, Anthea announced she would cook for Emerald's birthday party.

'We must make a note to have a large high tea beforehand,' Jonathan told Sienna, 'I gather it's black tie.'

'Black eye more likely. Someone's bound to punch someone.'

'I wonder if her sinister boyfriend will make it.'

'He promised to be back for her birthday.'

40

Emerald, meanwhile, had been getting her size three feet under the table at Foxes Court. She had returned to the flat in Shepherd's Bush only to shudder at its squalor and seediness and to pillage photographs of herself at all ages to show Anthea and Raymond. Out of embarrassment and defiance, she had picked a time when the family were all out working.

Raymond, far more interested in the photographs than Anthea, found a lovely art deco tortoiseshell frame for the most beautiful and placed it proudly among the family snaps on the big table in the drawing room. The Belvedon children were furious and kept shoving it to the back.

Raymond had already made a list of rich and famous people for Emerald to sculpt for her exhibition next year. He had also started converting one of the barns into a studio for her and had bought her a new car.

Emerald had in addition become a mini-celebrity, asked to open the village fête, to take part in a photo shoot for *Tatler* and appear on Richard and Judy. The press rang constantly for interviews. Smart locals, out of spite because they disliked Anthea intensely, kept asking her to dinner. Emerald consequently grew more and more uppity.

Raymond was enchanted and kept quoting

Tennyson: 'A rosebud set with little wilful thorns, As sweet as English air could make her.'

Anthea was not pleased. Twenty-six years ago, she'd given up a cuddly little bundle, who'd grown into a critical and opinionated young woman.

Everyone in the household was affected. Dicky, having said: 'Yuk, another sister,' was now swooning with first love. Dora, accustomed to being the rosy-cheeked apple of her parents' eye, bitterly resented them not having time for her any more. Anthea in particular had not forgiven Dora for calling her a 'slapper' in the *Mail*.

'Daddy's going to give Emerald a one-man show,' Dora told Aunt Lily furiously. 'Don't think one man would be enough for her.'

Poor Hanna in particular was utterly miserable. As well as painting flowers, she had before she was married been a successful illustrator of children's books. This, Jupiter had felt, was the ideal career for a politician's wife: something lucrative and creative which could be done from home.

In the past, because he had refused to leave her in the country near Alizarin, Hanna had had to pile everything into the Volvo on Sunday nights and exhaust herself looking after Jupiter, accompanying him to meetings, endlessly entertaining clients and politicians and never having enough time to paint.

How often had she in those days thought longingly of her life before she was married, when she had her own lovely flat, a job she adored, an excellent income (Jupiter, needing vast funds to take over the Tory Party, kept her very short) and half London including Alizarin in love with her?

Now all Hanna could think about was of a time, before Emerald rolled up, when she'd been convinced, even if he treated her harshly, that her husband loved her.

Shopping listlessly in Searston, she passed a second-hand bookshop with a poster in the window:

> 'Marry a wife and you'll be happy for a week.
> Kill a pig and you'll be happy for a month.
> Plan a garden and you'll be happy for ever.'

And she burst into tears.

Alizarin, angry that Hanna was unhappy, watched Emerald with increasing disapproval. Sienna smouldered with resentment. Raymond had never offered to convert a barn for her. But when she raged against Emerald to Aunt Lily, Lily had fairly pointed out that Emerald was clearly still confused about her identity. When Raymond had rung from the gallery to say he'd sold one of her heads, Emerald had burst into tears like Hanna and, saying: 'I must ring Mummy,' had promptly called Patience.

Anthea had been furious about this and got subtle revenge by repeatedly asking Emerald if she had heard from Zac, suggesting they had better think of some other man to ask on 7 July, in case Zac didn't show up.

Next door at the Old Rectory, Rosemary Pulborough, who had not expected to be invited to her husband's little dinner for Si Greenbridge, was still harbouring dark suspicions that Emerald could be David's child.

Rosemary had been half relieved when Galena had died, because she'd had such a hold over David, but she'd infinitely preferred Galena's reign to Anthea's. Galena had been great fun. She, Lily and Rosemary had had merry suppers together, and Galena had never humiliated nor sidelined her.

Rosemary remembered David going ashen that October morning nearly twenty-six years ago, when a tear-stained Raymond had stumbled round to the Old Rectory announcing that everything was going to be all right because Anthea was on her way.

And from that day, Anthea had never stopped tormenting Rosemary, subtly putting her down, letting her know that David had confided some secret, praising everything he did, but quite unable to acknowledge any of Rosemary's achievements: whether it was the brilliant marriage made by her daughter Melanie, or the snow-drop she had propagated in Galena's memory which had won first prize at the Chelsea Flower Show.

Rosemary, however, was planning her revenge. She had recently been appointed Chairman of the Limesbridge Improvement Society and held her first meeting at the Old Rectory on the afternoon of the third Thursday in June. This was packed out because everyone was not only dying to see Rosemary's newly decorated kitchen but also how Lady Belvedon was looking after her skeleton-outing in the press. Radiantly complacent was the answer.

Anthea arrived early and found the new kitchen something else to disapprove of. How could Rosemary have made it so messy so quickly? Look at all that garlic, onions, herbs and lavender hanging from the beams, those ragged recipe and gardening books all jumbled together, those piles of papers and photos of cats and children and all those vases of wild flowers on the table.

And you'd have thought Rosemary had chosen the colour of the walls – the rich reddy brown of newly ploughed Larkshire fields – specially to flatter her three marmalade cats: Shadrach, Meshach and Abednego, who sauntered up and down the long scrubbed table as if they were modelling their opulent ginger fur.

And what was Joanna Trollope's latest doing with the spine up by the Aga? Rosemary should have been making a cake instead of reading. Now she was handing out bought chocolate cake and not even bothering with cake forks and serviettes. Fancy giving kitchen roll to the Lord-Lieutenant, General Aldridge, with whom Rosemary was on ludicrously chummy terms because he was some cousin of Melanie's boring husband. Finally, what kind of bag lady did Rosemary think she looked like, still in her old gardening trousers and one of David's cast-off shirts?

Hanna looked a wreck too, decided Anthea. She deserved to lose Jupiter if she didn't smarten herself up. Hanna and Lily, who was puffing away on some disgusting cheroot, flanked Rosemary like neighbourhood witches, all discussing the wild flowers still needed for Hanna's painting. They made Anthea feel twitchy.

'Cup of tea, Anthea?' asked Rosemary, brandishing a big brown pot.

'Have you got camomile? No? Well, I'll have water.'

'Isn't Rosemary's kitchen super?' shouted Lily, who liked stirring things, to a chorus of assent.

There was a pause while Anthea's judgement was awaited.

'Well, it certainly makes the room look bigger,' she said coolly, then, turning to the Lord-Lieutenant: 'Which Sunday are you opening, General? We had over a thousand through last year. Folk came, of course, to gaze at Sir Raymond as much as the garden.'

'This year they'll gaze at Emerald,' snorted Lily. 'Why don't you plant her in the herbaceous border?'

Anthea's lips tightened.

'Shoo,' she cried as Shadrach padded purposefully towards her.

On the wall by the window hung Galena's *Wild-Flower Meadow*, which Sir Mervyn had given David and Rosemary and which was being admired by two shopkeepers. Anthea was sure Rosemary had held the meeting in the kitchen so everyone would see it. If Galena had been alive she'd have been a bloated old wino, fat as Falstaff, but because she was dead, everyone hero-worshipped her. Anthea wanted to scream. Shadrach settled purring on Lily's lap.

'Shall we begin?' asked Rosemary.

After touching on the village fête which Emerald was going to open on 3 July, and Limesbridge's certainty of being the Best Kept Village in Larkshire (if someone could persuade Alizarin to cut his nettles), and the excessive use of pesticides threatening to wipe out the skylarks for which Larkshire was famous, discussion moved on to a proposed clay shoot in aid of the Distressed Gentlefolk.

'Shoot the lot of them and save a lot of bother,' said the landlord of the Goat in Boots, to sexist guffaws.

Rosemary then brought up the old chestnut of the Borochova Memorial. Galena, she persisted, had immortalized Limesbridge by making it her home for nearly fifteen years and painting glorious pictures of the Silver Valley. These now hung in the greatest galleries of the world and had saved the valley from developers.

'Here, here,' shouted Lily.

Shadrach purred in agreement. Abednego took up perilous residence on the bony thighs of General Aldridge.

'People come from all over the world to honour her,' went on Rosemary. 'Surely there should be a statue in her memory in the High Street, and why can't we apply for lottery money, and turn one of the outbuildings at Foxes Court into a museum about her work?'

'Good idea,' said the landlord of the Goat in Boots.

Nice woman, Mrs Pulborough, he reflected. No side to her. Pity she was married to that shit. One of the joys of coming to these meetings had been to gaze at Jupiter's bonny wife Hanna, but today she looked wretched. Her eyes, once like pale blue lakes on a map, were red and piggy with crying.

Anthea was furious inside, but putting on her martyred virgin face, said she couldn't possibly upset Sir Raymond by evoking memories of Galena's tragic death.

'And as we are already providing accommodation for Sir Raymond's sister' – she nodded coldly at Lily – 'and Jupiter and his wife' – she nodded coldly at Hanna – 'and Alizarin, and Jonathan and Sienna when they deign to roll up, there is no room for a museum.'

General Aldridge, who was known as 'General Anaesthetic' because he was so boring he sent everyone to sleep, had just taken out a subscription to the *Erotic Review* because his wife was going through the menopause. He also had a thumping crush on Anthea.

'No-one does more for the village than Lady Belvedon,' he brayed.

Why didn't they put up a statue to Anthea instead? suggested Green Jean, the vicar's wife, who also had a crush on Anthea, and who had been so pleased she, and not the doctor's wife, had been asked to the silver wedding party.

'We ought to do something in Galena's memory,' said Rosemary stubbornly.

All the local shopkeepers and the landlords of the Mitre and the Goat in Boots, who wanted to attract tourists to the area, agreed noisily.

'We don't want Searston to get the memorial instead of us,' called out Lily.

As the scent of lime blossom drifted in from the churchyard, Rosemary had a brainwave.

'If Lady Belvedon has no room for a Borochova Museum, and as our children have flown the nest' – Rosemary smiled as she imagined fat Barney taking off like a Christmas turkey – 'why don't we convert our empty barn into one instead?'

Resounding cheers all round.

'Ouch,' shrieked General Anaesthetic as Abednego plunged his long claws into his thighs before flouncing off.

Anthea was seething. There was no way she was going to allow the despised wife of her darling David to gang up with Galena's supporters.

'That would be totally unacceptable, Galena is after all a Belvedon.'

No-one could see this mattered a scrap and before Anthea could say 'knayfe' Rosemary was promising to approach her husband and Geraldine Paxton about lottery funds and the best way of launching an appeal.

'Why don't we ask local artists to submit ideas for a statue?' said the doctor's wife, who'd been forced to go away for the weekend so people wouldn't know she and her husband hadn't been invited to Raymond and Anthea's party. 'And then we can ask the best three or four to produce maquettes. We gather your new daughter is an accomplished sculptor, Lady Belvedon, perhaps she could enter.'

'I'm still happy to offer you the barn for a museum,' said Rosemary.

We'll see what your husband has to say about this, thought Anthea.

'My daughter-in-law' – she nodded at Hanna – 'is doing a lovely watercolour of all the wild flowers contained in Galena's *Wild-Flower Meadow*.' Anthea waved a pretty white hand at the painting on the wall. 'Surely Hanna's canvas hanging in the village hall would be a more fitting memorial?'

'It can grace the museum instead,' said Lily firmly.

The meeting broke up because the General was pushing off to award prizes to the Guides in Searston.

'Garden's looking great,' he told Rosemary as he followed her into the sunshine. 'And Isobel wanted you to know she's ordered a thousand of your Borochova snowdrops for the Long Walk.'

Then, as Rosemary went pink with pleasure, he turned to Anthea, who was just behind them: 'You'd better get your order in early.'

'I may be old fashioned,' simpered Anthea, 'but I prefer my snowdrops to look like snowdrops. Lovely news about Melanie, Rosemary.'

'What?' demanded Rosemary.

'About the new baby. She hasn't told you? Oh, stupid me. I expect she wanted to be quite sure. Mind you, she's always been Daddy's girl. David is *delighted*.'

Hanna, who had followed them out through the front

door, looked at Anthea in horror, and put a comforting hand on Rosemary's arm.

'Did you hear that, Hanna? Melanie's expecting,' repeated Anthea. 'High time you and Jupiter got your skates on.'

Still seething, despite delivering such body blows, Anthea paused in the churchyard on the way home. On the lichened headstone were carved the words: 'Galena Borochova Belvedon 1932–1973. Heaven lies around us.'

Someone had left a bunch of meadowsweet and wild roses in a jam jar. In a fit of rage, Anthea kicked it over, then kicked the headstone. Hearing a step, she looked round and gave a gasp of terror. Alizarin was towering over her, blotting out the sun.

'Get away from her,' he roared.

Because Visitor had just bounced into Rosemary's kitchen in search of chocolate cake, Hanna, realizing Alizarin must be in the vicinity, crept into the churchyard hoping for a brief bittersweet word. Then she froze to see him talking to Anthea. No-one would be quicker on the telephone to Jupiter, sneaking about secret trysts.

41

Emerald raged with paranoia at the prospect of her birthday party. She was convinced all the Belvedons, except Raymond, Anthea and Dicky, detested her. Patience, Ian and Sophy must loathe her after the way she'd slagged them off in the press and ignored them since the silver wedding. What would happen if the two families hit it off and united in righteous indignation against her? More likely the Belvedons would sneer at the dowdy, plain and two-thirds overweight Cartwrights. And why had Zac ratted on her, when he'd set the whole thing up? She felt as if both her shrink and her body-guard had gone on permanent leave.

And now four days before her birthday, she had the added nightmare of opening the bloody fête.

'I'd like to thank everyone in Limesbridge for being so welcoming,' Emerald was practising her speech in her bedroom before leaving, 'particularly my new parents, Anthea and Raymond Belvedon.' Emerald smiled at Raymond who was perched on her bed, nodding approval. 'And all their wonderful children.'

The little fuckers, thought Emerald savagely, particularly Dora, who was acting up because Emerald had refused to be run away with in the family trap pulled by a delinquent Loofah through bunting-decked Limesbridge. She had opted instead to arrive at the fête by river in Raymond's boat.

'How could the bitch deny Loofah such a photo opportunity?' raged Dora.

Anthea had already gone down to the wild-flower meadow, where the fête was being held, to rally the troops, but kept ringing up: 'Where on earth are you? The nation's press is waiting, we've got to begin.'

'We'll be with you in a minute,' Raymond told her reassuringly as he topped up Emerald's glass with Moët.

He was as reluctant as she was to get down to the fête, having agreed to stage his own Antiques Roadshow at two pounds a go, which meant all the cantankerous old biddies in Larkshire lining up to have their junk valued.

'You look heavenly, darling,' he reassured Emerald, 'a sight to make an old man young.'

Emerald glanced in the mirror. In her rosebud-strewn gypsy dress with the ruched neckline resting on her white shoulders, and the frilled skirt swirling around her slender hips, she agreed with Raymond she looked heavenly. But how could she open a fête with a broken heart?

'Where's Zac?' she wailed.

'He'll turn up,' comforted Raymond, then as his mobile rang and Anthea could be heard screeching: 'We're on our way.'

Down at the wild-flower meadow, stalls were already trading, because Emerald was so late, and the Belvedons variously helping or hindering. Jonathan, still in a dinner jacket and dress shirt covered in lipstick, was leaning against his dirty Ferrari, drinking a gin and tonic and regaling his supporters with details of last night's adventures. Sloping off from some dull awards ceremony to have a kip, he had mistaken a BMW belonging to a rather stern married couple for Geraldine's Mercedes.

'I didn't wake up until they'd got me home, and things rather went on from there,' sighed Jonathan.

An abandoned Geraldine kept on sending him furious text messages.

Under Jonathan's arm was an Ian Rankin thriller which had been set aside for him by Aunt Lily, who was helping out Rosemary on the book stall. Three sheets to the wind, Lily had already given someone back £4.50 change from a 50p coin.

Next door Anthea had paused at the Nearly New stall brandishing a favourite blue dress, which Rosemary had reluctantly sacrificed, crying: 'Who'd honestly be seen dead in this?'

Alizarin and Sienna, who'd both worked all night, felt like pit ponies emerging into the sunlight. Sienna had wandered barefoot across the footbridge from her studio. Dark glasses covered her reddened eyes. Her huge canvas about sins done to animals was really getting to her.

Last night she had been painting chimps with elec-trodes in their brains, tonight she'd have to move on to the red-hot pokers stuck up the arses of tigers and leopards, so they died with agonizing slowness but without a mark on their pelts. Momentarily comforted to see her brother Jonathan, she had quickly realized he had only driven down to barrack Emerald.

Alizarin was particularly low because he couldn't recognize faces in the crowd any more, and kept being accused of cutting people. Hanna was miserable because she was one of the people Alizarin had cut. Languid Jupiter was manning the loudspeaker and fastidiously pressing the flesh in case he was selected as prospective Tory candidate for the area.

Dicky, back for the weekend from Bagley Hall, had enraged his mother by dying his dark hair blond and parting it down the middle like his idol David Beckham. Ever commercial, he was now doing a roaring trade exhorting people to guess the weight of Visitor. Once Emerald opened the fête and pop music began pouring out of the speakers, Dicky intended branching out and charging people £2 to dance with Visitor. Visitor, loving the attention, was pedalling his back legs like an organist. Every so often he rushed off to drink deeply out of the big bowl in which children were bobbing for apples. This, claimed people who'd already guessed his weight, must make him heavier, and frightful rows ensued.

'That dog weighs at least twenty stone,' called out Jonathan, chucking a fiver into Dicky's tin as he carried large gins and tonic over to Knightie and Mrs Robens, who'd been roped in to do teas, and who were incensed Anthea was refusing to pay them, because the whole thing was for charity. Being referred to as a 'tireless helper' in the parish mag was no compensation.

The minutes ticked by, the press were looking at their watches. Green Jean, not realizing she hadn't been invited to Emerald's birthday party on Wednesday, had already bought one of Emerald's sketches of Anthea. She was livid on the other hand that her husband Neville had bought Sienna's nude drawing of Aunt Lily, of whom he was extremely fond.

'He'll have to hang it in the vestry,' spluttered Green Jean who had already concealed Jonathan's nude of Sienna under a sheet, which everyone lifted to peer underneath and which had just been bought by the landlord of the Goat in Boots.

'I'll 'ang it in the public bar,' he said, handing Jean a fistful of tenners.

There was great excitement because Alizarin's abstract, which Jean had hung upside down, had been bought by a shortsighted General Anaesthetic, who thought he was acquiring a painting of camels in the desert.

'Enjoyed riding them in the Desert Mounted Corps,' he was telling everybody.

The hit of the show, however, was Hanna. Her twelve flower paintings had all been sold, and re-orders were pouring in. David Pulborough, who'd just rolled up having done eff-all, and whose flesh-pressing as prospective High Sheriff consisted of stroking bare arms and patting shapely bottoms, clocked Hanna's great success and suggested he sign her up.

'Your wife's so marketable. You'd better give up running the Belvedon,' David told Jupiter patronizingly, 'and become a kept boy.'

'And use you as a role model,' snarled Jupiter.

'Whoops!' called out a passing Jonathan.

'And you can wipe that grin off your face,' a puce David turned on Jonathan. 'How *dare* you walk out on Geraldine last night, and when in hell are you going to finish Dame Hermione?'

'Do look,' interrupted Jonathan blithely, 'here comes Dad and his alleged daughter – just in time to close the fête.'

What right has the old fool to look so fucking proud, thought David as Raymond in his dark green and black Larkshire Light Infantry blazer, which he could still fit into, drew up and, jumping onto the bank, turned to help Emerald out.

'Where have you been, you're three-quarters of an hour late,' shrieked Anthea, rushing down the path cut through the pink-tipped grasses. 'I have never been so humiliated in my life.'

'It's OK, we're all in one piece,' smiled Raymond as the press went berserk.

Zac the Wanderer – ever unpredictable – rolled up even later, just as Emerald was making her speech. She was so busy thanking everyone and not goofing in front of the Belvedons and making herself heard over a sudden deafening ticking din that she didn't notice the helicopter landing on the edge of the meadow and a suntanned man in the sharpest white suit leaping out.

'"Clothed in white samite, mystic, wonderful,"' breathed an ecstatic Raymond.

'And I now declare this fête . . . Zac, oh Zac!' screamed Emerald.

Dropping her microphone and her notes, ignoring the curtsying little girl with the bunch of salmon-pink gladioli, kicking off her black sandals so her painted toenails flashed like corals in the damp grass, Emerald hurtled across the meadow straight into Zac's arms, whereupon he gathered her up, twirling her round, kissing her on and on, watched with varying degrees of emotion by the Belvedon family.

'Cut,' yelled Jonathan. 'This is a church fête, not the back row of the Odeon.'

And you're one hell of an ugly customer, thought Zac, noticing the hatred on Jonathan's face as everyone laughed and cheered.

Revelling in the muscular strength of Zac's body against hers, Emerald slowly recovered her breath.

'I've missed you so much, please stay the night,' she gabbled. 'Please be here for my birthday party on Wednesday.'

'Sure.' Zac smiled down like the golden sun warming her. 'I said I would, didn't I?'

Joyfully Emerald swung round to the press and the gaping public. 'This is my boyfriend Zac,' she yelled.

Again, everyone laughed, and, having thought Emerald was pale, peaky, stand-offish and much too Sloaney, they all decided that, now her eyes sparkled and her cheeks were flushed, she was very beautiful after all.

Having shaken hands with Raymond and agreed to stay as long as possible, Zac turned to Anthea, clicking his heels, kissing her hand, murmuring, 'Beautiful as ever.'

'This is Charlene's day.'

'Doesn't stop you being beautiful.'

'Oh, Zachary.'

'Zac, you haven't met my sister, Sienna,' said Emerald sharply.

'Sienna!' Zac's eyes, yellow as lime leaves in autumn,

travelled downwards, taking in her paint-stained, clay-matted, hastily piled-up hair, her black glasses, the studs in her ears and her long greyhound nose, the sprinkling of spots on her unhealthily pale complexion, the furious sulky mouth, the tanktop showing off tattooed shoulders, the ripped jeans covering endless legs, and the dirty, ringed bare feet.

'Sienna,' he repeated mockingly, 'are you raw or burnt? A bit of both, I guess.'

Enraged she was looking so awful, Sienna tossed her head, frantic to think up some withering reply. Emerald saved her the bother. Tugging Zac's hand imperiously, she asked him to come and see her studio.

'You have duties, Emerald,' said Anthea coldly. 'You have to draw the raffle at four-thirty.'

Then when Emerald looked bootfaced, Zac said firmly, 'You've got to, babe.'

Anthea, determined not to be sidelined, swept them both round the gaping stall-holders, followed by henna-haired Harriet, ex of *Oo-ah!*, now an eager young reporter on the *Independent*.

'This is my Aunt Lily,' Emerald told Zac proudly, as they paused at the book stall.

'That's why I loathe her,' hissed Sienna to Alizarin. 'My house, my brothers, my father, my studio.'

'She only wants to belong,' said Alizarin reasonably.

'And this is our dog, Visitor. You've got to guess his weight,' went on Emerald. 'He really adores me,' she added as Visitor thumped his tail.

'He's my fucking dog,' exploded Alizarin.

'See what I mean?' murmured Sienna.

'Barney not here?' Anthea was asking Rosemary. 'Sad he doesn't support the village. Gratifying our chaps have turned out in force.'

'Bitch,' snorted Lily, pouring herself another glass of white wine.

'What did you say?' demanded Anthea.

'Bit of a crowd here,' said Lily sweetly.

'And how have your younger children got on with their new sister, Lady Belvedon, any jealousy?' asked Harriet from the *Independent*.

'Certainly not,' said Anthea smugly. 'But Dicky and Dora, probably because they've always been wrapped round with love, are awfully well adjusted. Dora's been giving rides in her pony trap and is about to take Lily home,' *before the old witch gets completely blotto*, thought Anthea furiously. 'And Dicky's been raising money with Visitor all afternoon. We've always tried to instil in them a respect for older people. Visitor's actually won best pet in show for the last five years. Do come and have a look, he's just going into the ring.'

Alas, this year's very large lady judge had other ideas.

'Your Lab is much too fat,' she told Dicky when she reached Visitor. 'He ought to go on a diet.'

'So ought you,' shouted back an outraged Dicky. 'You're much fatter than Visitor, you awful old woman.'

'And Visitor doesn't have droopy boobs,' yelled an equally outraged Dora from the side of the ring.

Jonathan spat out his gin and tonic. Zac met Sienna's eye and burst out laughing.

'Dicky! Dora!' screeched Anthea.

'"Droopy boobs",' wrote Harriet from the *Independent*.

Raymond, not enjoying his Antiques Roadshow, gazed down at a tray on which was printed a picture of an eighteenth-century couple out walking with a fluffy white dog.

'I'm afraid this is not painted by Gainsborough.'

'How d'you know?' demanded the furious old biddy. 'You weren't there when it was painted.'

'Don't forget you're drawing the raffle at four-thirty,' yet again Anthea reminded Emerald.

Fortunately, she was distracted by Dora thundering by in the trap, trying to prevent Loofah from trampling little contestants in the egg-and-spoon race.

'Whoa, you fucking animal,' screamed Dora, 'bloody whoa!'

'"Droopy boobs",' chuckled Lily, who bumped unfazed beside her, by which time Zac and Emerald had escaped across the footbridge.

House martins, flashing their white bellies, were darting in and out of the boathouse, meadow browns waltzed through a blond clump of meadowsweet. All round, the grass was flattened by lovers. Zac put an arm through Emerald's.

'Do you remember last time we were in the boat-house?'

'Anyone who says finding one's birth mother increases one's self-esteem and provides a bridge with the past is talking garbage,' stormed Emerald. 'Come and look at my studio.'

42

Even in a dusty barn, Emerald had created order. Bags of clay were neatly stacked beneath a table on which stood paints, purple and scarlet sweet peas in a glass vase, and an old top hat filled with sharpened pencils and brushes. On the easel was a sensitive and charming drawing of Raymond, in preparation for later tackling his head.

'That is terrific,' said Zac.

'Raymond's been so sweet. He's having a shower put in and a kitchen and a little bedroom on a higher level. At the moment I've only got this.'

Pushed against the bare brick wall was an ancient chaise longue, covered in a white linen sheet, and the bottle-green and white striped quilt from Emerald's bed in Fulham.

'This is perfectly adequate,' said Zac softly. '"Gather ye rosebuds,"' he added, drawing her gypsy dress off one shoulder.

Emerald stiffened.

'I thought I'd never see you again. You never rang, never texted me. The Belvedons have been hell. You weren't here to protect me. Ah . . .' for Zac's big warm caressing fingers had slid under one little breast with the delicacy of a small boy lifting an egg from a blackbird's nest.

'You can't just waltz in here without a word of explanation.'

372

'I had things to do.' Zac's hands were sliding downwards.

'And expect me to roll over.'

'Just belt up.'

Gathering her up, dropping her casually on the chaise longue, Zac unbuckled his own belt, slapping the leather against his palm.

'D'you want me to use this on you?'

Emerald was ashamed to feel herself bubbling with excitement.

'Yes, no, of course not.'

'You ask for it sometimes.'

'Undress me, Zac.'

Pulling her frock upwards and her knickers down he kissed her belly, whiter than any house martin. A moment later he was naked, honed, bronzed, rippling with muscle. I'll never be able to take in all that without some foreplay, was Emerald's last mistaken thought.

The sweat glistened on her pale forehead, her black ringlets flew, the chaise longue creaked, a bluebottle caught in a spider's web buzzed frantically, Emerald closed her eyes mewing in ecstasy.

'Oh Zac, oh Zac.'

Thrusting deeply down inside her, Zac left her on automatic pilot for a moment. Through the grimy window and olive-green treetops, amid the tall chimneys and mossy lichened roof of Foxes Court, he noticed a little turret, topped by a shiny gold weather-vane in the shape of a fox.

'I'm coming,' moaned Emerald, as she stiffened and shuddered.

And I'm getting there, thought Zac, smiling triumphantly down at her.

'Sorry I can't offer you a drink here,' said Emerald. 'Let's shower back at the house and I can show you round while the others are still at the fête. The pictures are fabulous.'

Sliding her hand into Zac's as they walked across the deserted lawn, she pleaded, 'Can we go out tonight?'

'Sure – figured I'd ask Raymond and Anthea to join us.'

Then, when Emerald looked mutinous, he yanked her jaw upwards for a second, stroking her cheek with his thumb.

'It's important that your mom and dad are comfortable with me. Our time'll come later.'

There was no mistaking the seriousness in his eyes. He's ready to make a commitment, thought Emerald joyfully as his beautiful mouth came down to meet hers.

Alas, Jupiter, who'd just been checking the house for burglars and, to be truthful, for Emerald, was looking out of an upstairs window. Ten minutes later, as Emerald flung open Sienna's bedroom crying: 'This is where the Larkshire Ladette sleeps, isn't it a tip?' she found Jupiter sitting on the bed, mending Sienna's reading lamp.

'What the fuck are you doing here?' he yelled, which was all the more frightening because he was normally so controlled. 'You don't own this place – yet – and don't go snooping in other people's rooms. Get out.'

He was quivering with fury.

'Oh dear,' sighed Zac as they reached the safety of Emerald's bedroom, '*he* hasn't forgiven you.'

'None of them has,' wailed Emerald.

'It's quite simple,' said Zac. 'The women hate you because their guys want to fuck you, and the guys hate you because they can't.'

The fête made a record £5,000 but Anthea was far from happy. She was furious with Emerald for bunking off with Zac and failing to draw the raffle. She was livid with Dicky and Dora for behaving badly, and with Raymond, who was exhausted, for suggesting she and he should stay behind with the twins, who were probably only acting up because they hadn't seen much of their parents recently.

'Don't be so selfish,' snapped Anthea, drenching herself in Shalimar. 'I personally am far too tired to go out but we can't let Zac and Emerald down.'

She was determined to maintain her image as the gracious, devoted parent, but Dicky and Dora knew of old their mother's flat voice, her failure to look them in the eye, and her redistributing of favours. That was why, radiant in amethyst chiffon, with a pink rose in her hair, she was all over Zac as they later sat on the terrace watching the ultramarine dusk merge with the blue minarets of Raymond's delphiniums.

Raymond, who'd already had a long chat with Zac, discovering their mutual fondness for bourbon and cricket, had also opened a magnum of Moët to celebrate the success of the fête. Defiantly he gave a glass each to Dicky and Dora.

'You did very well, darlings, with your rides in the trap and Visitor's dancing, and Emerald's speech was excellent, and it's great everyone's paintings sold.'

'Alizarin's didn't,' said Anthea smugly. 'The General soon changed his mind when he saw it the right way up.'

'And guess who tipped him off,' muttered Jonathan, not looking up from Ian Rankin.

'Anyway, an anonymous buyer came in and paid twice as much,' said Sienna happily. Through the trees she could see lights on in the Lodge. Alizarin must be hard at it. She must get on with her poor tortured tigers. Champagne always sapped her resolve.

She was acutely conscious of a lounging Zac, sweating out his bourbon, loafers up on the table, black shirt unbuttoned to show the Star of David glinting on a smooth brown chest. He was so vain, she was surprised he didn't pluck out the grey flecks in his dark hair. Beside his sleek beauty, Jonathan, with his bags under the eyes, his extreme pallor and the suggestion of a gut spilling over his belt, looked thoroughly seedy.

Glancing up, Sienna noticed Zac grinning at her, patronizing bastard, just because she looked so scruffy compared with ponced-up Anthea. He was so like a tiger: strange, predatory, watchful. She wouldn't mind taking that smug smirk off his face with a red-hot poker.

'In what distant deeps or skies Burned the fire of thine eyes?' wondered Sienna.

'What are you thinking about?' asked Jonathan.

'How odd that tigers are both predators and endangered species.'

'Not particularly. I don't imagine antelope and water-buck send many charity cheques to Save the Tiger.'

Zac took a slug of bourbon and turned to Anthea.

'Garden's looking fabulous.'

Lime blossom, philadelphus and jasmine were fighting a losing battle with Shalimar. Roses swarmed up dark trees; love-in-a-mist collapsed over the cooling flag-stones caressing bare legs.

'Raymond and I enjoy gardening, Zac, that's the secret and, of course, keeping one's staff. Robens our gardener, who's been with us for ever, is the salt of the earth.' Anthea rolled off clichés like amazing new truths. 'Robens in fact is one of Nature's Gentlemen.'

'I don't like Robens,' said Dora beadily, 'he waved his willy at me in the shrubbery last week, it was all stiff and purple.'

Sienna and Jonathan exchanged ecstatic glances.

Zac battled not to laugh.

'Why didn't you tell me?' shrieked Anthea. 'Raymond, we must sack Robens at once.'

'Not before Emerald's birthday party,' said Jonathan acidly.

'Don't be cheeky,' squawked Anthea, then, not wanting to get into a dingdong with Jonathan in front of Zac, nor discuss Robens's priapic lapse in front of the twins, she said, 'Time you were in bed, you two. You've had a long day.'

She was distracted by a telephone call from Green Jean. By the expression on her face, and the furiously tapping lilac court shoe, it was pretty serious. Normally Anthea would not have bawled out Dicky, who had turned lime green, in front of an outsider. But such was her dislike of Alizarin: 'Dicky,' she said, switching off the telephone, 'are you the anonymous buyer?'

'Course I'm not.'

'Don't tell porkies. How did you pay for it?'

At first Dicky insisted he'd used his birthday money.

'That wouldn't be enough. Jean says you gave her a hundred pounds.'

'Rotten sneak,' stormed Dora.

'Don't interfere. You're fibbing, Dicky, where did the money come from?'

'It was Visitor's dancing money.' Dicky stood his ground. 'We earned it.'

'That money belongs to the fête.'

'Money going to the fête anyway,' said Raymond reasonably. 'Alizarin donated the picture. I really can't think—'

'Let me handle this, Raymond. Dicky stole that money. You're to give the picture back to Jean.'

'It's mine,' yelled Dicky.

'And where are you going to hang the horrid thing?'

'In my room. Alizarin's the only person round here who cares about me any more,' and, bursting into tears, Dicky ran into the house.

'And about me,' agreed Dora, disappearing into the twilight.

'And about me,' agreed Sienna, draining her glass. Retreating through the french windows, she gave a gasp of horror as she passed Emerald who, not looking her best in orange, had the overpainted look of someone who's tried too hard.

'What on earth's up with Sienna?' she demanded as she came out onto the terrace. But as her sweet, musky scent swept over them like chloroform, Raymond, who had automatically risen to his feet, collapsed grey and shaking on the bench. Why was he terrified, unable to breathe, his lungs filled with poison gas?

'Sorry about that everyone, but one must take a stand,' said an unrepentant Anthea. 'Lovely perfume, Charlene. What is it?'

'Zac gave me it,' said Emerald proudly. 'It's called Mitsouko.'

'Oh bravo, Zac,' drawled Jonathan. 'Didn't anyone tell you? This was the scent in which our mother drenched herself. Even on the day she was found dead.'

Only a further telephone call, this time from Casey Andrews, announcing that he'd be dropping in in half an hour to deliver Emerald's birthday present, persuaded Raymond and the others to escape out to dinner. Before they left, Jonathan drew his still trembling father aside in the hall and hugged him.

'I'm really sorry, Dad. I shouldn't have said that about Mum's death. The smell must have unhinged me, and I don't think Zac's kosher.'

'Seems a nice chap,' said Raymond dolefully. 'I do wish everyone would stop fighting. Poor little Dicky. Anthea insists we don't go up to say goodnight.'

'I'll tuck him in after you've all gone. Do you mind if I go up and look at the Raphael?'

For a second, Raymond glimpsed the deep hurt in the eyes of his favourite son. 'Of course not. Stay as long as you like. Just lock up afterwards. Are you missing Mum?'

'I don't remember her enough to miss her. That's probably why I'm so hard. Thank God for you, Dad.'

43

Zac's return didn't bring Emerald happiness. She had been so excited with the big bottle of Mitsouko, the first thing (except for the clothes and money she had demanded from him) that he'd ever given her, but it had only succeeded in antagonizing the Belvedons even further.

Raymond was sweet. 'Of course it was a mistake, darling.'

His wife, who couldn't understand why Emerald had emptied the bottle down the loo, thought it was a hoot.

'How was Zac to know Galena bathed in the stuff, and chucked a bottle at Raymond the week before she died? It's all such a long time ago, people are much too sensitive.'

Emerald was horrified to find herself sometimes hating Anthea. Every day she discovered other similarities in their character: their love of Chopin and Tchaikovsky; their need for sleep; most scary of all, their liking for Zac. She prayed it was merely Anthea's desire to know a future son-in-law better and kept saying, 'I'm so happy you and Raymond are still so in love. It restores one's faith in marriage.'

Anthea was so frustrated she could scream. Emerald's return had unleashed a torrent of past emotions:

shame, guilt, resentment, heartbreak, and above all deep longings, stirrings of sensuality which she had suppressed during her marriage to Raymond.

Zac didn't help by smiling speculatively into her eyes, asking too many questions, touching her whenever possible.

Anthea had also married a much older man in the hope of never suffering from jealousy again. Now she was eaten up by it, because Raymond, her dear confrère David, her favourite stepson Jupiter, evil Jonathan and even Dicky were all clearly obsessed by Emerald. One should not be wildly jealous of one's own daughter.

She wished Raymond wouldn't keep talking about settling large sums on Emerald for all the years she'd missed out on cultural stimuli.

'Imagine that precious flower growing on waste ground.'

Anthea would have liked to have shown off by making Emerald's dress for the birthday party, but, short of time, she'd whisked herself and Emerald off to Lindka Cierach. On the Tuesday before Wednesday's party, they went up to London for final tweakings and to pick up their dresses. This gave Raymond the opportunity to visit his lawyer in Searston – which made his other children extremely twitchy.

It also left Zac free to prowl round the garden, the boathouse and the woods, studying Foxes Court and all the outbuildings for blocked-up windows and unaccounted-for spaces. Towards dusk he jogged through the village and collected some bottles of red and a steak and kidney pie from the Goat in Boots, where he admired Jonathan's newly hung nude of Sienna. Ending up at the Lodge, he dropped in on Alizarin.

Alizarin in fact had had a very bad day. Hanna, increasingly miserable with Jupiter, was looking to him for love and protection, which he felt he could no longer offer her because he was going blind. For the same reason, he had tried to knock on the head his very real liking for Sophy.

Overwhelmed by guilt that he'd been working flat out for weeks and had done nothing to help Raymond with the forthcoming party, he had risen earlier even than usual and tried with a long fork to fish the algae out of the lily pond, a task he'd always loved doing as a boy, rather like tugging skeins of hair out of the plug hole. Alas, his sight was so bad he pulled up most of the water lilies instead and Anthea had screamed at him like a raped vixen.

Returning home dejected to the Lodge, he had found a beaming Visitor sharing a pork pie with Eddie the packer, who'd just apologetically arrived from London with all Alizarin's pictures from the gallery.

'We can't wait any longer for a discerning buyer,' Jupiter had replied coolly when Alizarin had rung him in a fury. 'Frankly, they're taking up too much space. At least you've got firewood for the winter.'

The Lodge front garden was still an army of nettles – as likely to sting as he himself. Frantically painting to catch the last of the daylight, Alizarin swore as he tripped over canvasses littering stairs and hall, stumbling downstairs to answer the door.

'Whadja want?' he snapped.

'To look at your pictures.' Zac waved a clanking plastic bag: 'And I figured you might like a late lunch.'

Alizarin, who was feeling dizzy with hunger, was won over by the smell of hot steak and kidney.

'Come in.'

Upstairs, having located two plates, knives and forks and a couple of paper cups, he turned back to his easel. He was painting a human shield, a Serb tank with crying babies strapped to its front – each little face was portrayed with such tender anguish. In the background, black smoke and flames poured out of a burning village.

As Zac divided the pie, giving seven-eighths to Alizarin, and poured red wine into paper cups, he noticed cuttings on the Balkans, Sierra Leone, Chechnya and Northern Ireland carpeting the floor, rising in stalactites on every surface, lying along the top of the books. Putting a cup and plate on the table beside Alizarin, out of reach of a drooling Visitor, Zac settled down to look at the pictures, and was absolutely blown away.

He had never seen anything so powerful, nor heart-rending. Poking around, clambering over Galena's furniture which had been chucked out by Anthea, taking canvasses to the fading light so the mysteries and subtleties of colour could be revealed, he was soon unearthing earlier work influenced by the Holocaust, along with the occasional exquisite landscape or portrait.

Having studied them for nearly an hour in silence, he pulled out a last canvas entitled *After the Anschluss,* which was when Hitler brutally annexed Austria in 1938. The painting was of a wood of tall, bare skeletal trees, lashed by rain and gales. Only the occasional beech sapling or little yellow hazel had hung on to their orange and gold leaves.

If you kept below the parapet, you could sometimes hide your treasures from the Nazis, thought Zac.

'These are awesome, absolute masterpieces,' he told Alizarin, with tears in his eyes. 'I'm going to call my old boss, Adrian Campbell-Black, who runs the best contemporary gallery in New York.'

Alizarin, who up to now hadn't been at all sure about Zac, took a lot of persuading; but, gradually succumbing to Zac's enthusiasm and understanding of pictures, he melted, ridiculously touched, almost childlike in his gratitude. Noticing Alizarin had wolfed the pie and drunk most of the red, Zac opened another bottle, and sat down on the corner of the ancient rickety sofa not taken up by cuttings and Visitor.

As they talked, Alizarin abandoned the human shield and idly sketched Zac. As he was losing his sight, his other senses had become more acute: he could hear tones in voices, smell desires.

'Why are you here?' he asked.

'What d'you mean?'

'It's nothing to do with Emerald.'

Zac took the deepest breath. Somehow he trusted Alizarin.

'My great-great-grandfather, Reuben Abelman, built up a furniture business in Vienna,' he said carefully. 'His son Benjamin's even greater success allowed him to indulge his passion for fine art. Shortly after the Anschluss, two Nazis turned up with guns and took Benjamin to party HQ where they threatened to shoot him if he didn't hand over his pictures and sculptures. His collection and the Rothschilds' were to be the first great acquisitions of Hitler's Führer museum. My great-grandfather refused to comply. He was found the next morning clubbed to death. My great-grandmother was sent to the death camps.

'Having stripped Benjamin's house, the Nazis turned their attention to his sons. They stopped my grandfather Tobias practising law, so he committed suicide.' Zac's deep, husky voice was quivering now, as desolate as the rumble of a distant train. 'And they confiscated the pictures from my Great-uncle Jacob's art gallery and sent him to Mauthausen.

'All the Abelmans were wiped out by the Holocaust, except my Great-aunt Leah, Jacob's wife, who escaped early in the war to New York, and my mother, who as a child somehow survived Theresienstadt and joined my great-aunt when she was four.'

Alizarin put down his pencil and, groping for the bottle, filled up Zac's paper cup, missing slightly, so the wine ran like blood down the side.

'My mother never got over the guilt of surviving,' went on Zac. 'At first, my Great-aunt Leah mixed with other artistic Jewish people in New York, as she waited and waited for Jacob. After the war, she heard he'd escaped from Mauthausen, but been murdered by the Gestapo.'

Zac had a beautiful face, thought Alizarin. The scars were all on the inside.

'When I was a kid' – Zac's voice was almost a whisper, a muscle leaping beneath his smooth gold cheek – 'Great-aunt Leah used to show me photographs of our house in Vienna in a smuggled-out family album. The floors were covered with Aubusson and Persian rugs, the rooms filled with eighteenth-century French furniture. On shelf and alcove was beautiful porcelain: Meissen, Sèvres and Dresden. But it was the pictures that excited me. In the hall were a Frans Hals and a Bonnard, in the dining room a Renoir and a Cranach.'

Only Visitor snoring, the tick of the clock, the scratch of Alizarin's pencil, broke the silence. Zac's suntan had taken on a grey tinge.

'Over my great-grandmother's desk in the living room hung the Raphael. My great-grandfather bought it to help out a friend, a profligate count, in whose family the painting had been for two hundred and forty years, who needed to pay his gambling debts. It's small, just twenty-two inches by eighteen. I've only seen it in black and white but I dream of it in colour.' Zac's words were tumbling out in a rush now. 'I've given up on the other pictures, they may or may not surface, but I've searched the world for the Raphael.'

Zac didn't tell Alizarin that he'd picked up clues since he'd been at Foxes Court. On the nursery wall was a framed cast list for a 'Pro-Raphaelite' Christmas play dated 1975. There was Raymond's nickname for Anthea, 'Hopey', and Anthea's rainbow-woven dress, which was hard to identify in a black and white photo.

'Have you tried the Art Loss Register?' asked Alizarin.

Zac shook his head.

'I'm shit-scared of raising the alarm and sending the picture underground. Got to be certain before I make a move.'

Alizarin's eyes were jet black, his face expressionless, as he picked up a magnifying glass to examine his drawing more closely. Zac's jaw needed more strength, the yellow eyes should be closer together, removing any suggestion of innocence. Squinting at Zac he said, 'A lot of looted art's in museums, who won't give it back.'

'Like asking the Mafia to regulate their behaviour,' shrugged Zac. 'I meet stone walls everywhere. Problem is time's running out. Owners of looted art know survivors of the Holocaust are getting thin on the ground and are likely to die off before they can claim. And if you're not a Rothschild,' he went on wearily, 'you're unlikely to get satisfaction through the courts.'

Alizarin began to paint, dipping his brush in a tin which said 'Butchers' Tripe, Lamb and Vegetable Flavour' on the outside. He wondered which ochre to use for Zac's skin, which now had a green tinge. His eyes had retreated into hollows.

'What's the subject of the painting?' asked Alizarin, knowing the answer.

'Pandora's Box,' said Zac.

As the pause went on for ever, Alizarin drenched the paper with water to get a weeping effect.

'It's got a Latin tag along the bottom: "Malum infra latet",' added Zac.

'Which means: "Trouble lies below",' said Alizarin. 'You could be getting warm. That's all I'm going to tell you.'

'Thanks – I sure appreciate this.' Zac was near to tears again. 'I'll talk to Adrian Campbell-Black about you next week.'

'It wasn't a trade-off,' said Alizarin roughly, 'I just believe in justice.'

Trying to keep the quiver of excitement and jubilation out of his voice, Zac asked, 'Why's your sister so screwed up?'

'Like your mother' – Alizarin warmed Zac's cheeks with a touch of rose madder – 'she suffers the guilt of

the survivor. Sienna was two days old when Mum died.'
He went on carefully, 'Mum had decorated rooms for me and my brothers before we were born, but done nothing for Sienna. We pretended Mum was thrilled to have a daughter, but she was really too drunk by then to mind what sex she had. Drink can make a baby undersized, can damage her organs. Sienna looks OK, but I guess it's taken a toll on her heart.'

Alizarin clearly had great difficulty talking about his mother. He suddenly looked, under those punishing hospital lights, as drawn and drained as a surgeon after a nine-hour operation.

'Sienna works so hard,' he went on. 'She feels huge responsibility for the world, particularly for animals.'

Visitor thumped his tail in approval.

'Have you met Emerald's sister?' asked Alizarin casually.

'The roly-poly Rottweiler,' said Zac. 'Not my greatest fan. Mistrusts my motives.'

'With reason,' retorted Alizarin.

The second bottle was empty. A car turned into the drive. Anthea and Emerald were back.

'I must go,' said Zac, 'and I really am crazy about your pictures.'

If Alizarin's eyes had been better, and he'd looked out of the window, he would have seen Zac waltzing up the drive in ecstasy, his face satanic in the moonlight.

44

The morning of Emerald's birthday was infinitely sunnier than the mood of Anthea's servants. Having been paid nothing for the fête, they had been forced to bull up the house for days, and now would have to work until God knew what hour this evening.

'It's worse than getting the place clean enough for the caterers, and it's bleedin' hot,' grumbled Knightie when Jonathan rang in for a progress report. 'Emerald and Zac are still in bed, your dad's supervising the fireworks, and Robens has practically mowed the lawns bald.'

'Where's Anthea?'

'Having her legs waxed in Searston.'

'Hopey de-furred,' said Jonathan joyfully.

'Don't forget your dinner jacket.'

'Alizarin will have to wear a strait-jacket to stop him thumping Somerford. I cannot tell you how much I'm looking forward to this evening.'

Zac answered the next telephone call. A furious, tearful Dicky had broken up, and no-one had remembered to collect him. Scribbling a note for Anthea and Raymond, Zac borrowed Emerald's new Golf and set off for Bagley Hall. Zac, typically American, was charming with children, and on the way home past sun-bleached stubble and bright pink clumps of willow herb, Dicky was soon confessing how fed up he was with life.

He loathed all the publicity about Emerald in the

papers. He was very defensive about Anthea, because people took the piss out of her. Did Zac think she'd forgotten to collect him because she was still cross about him dying his hair blond, or because he'd bought Alizarin's *Upside-Down Camels*?

'That was a good buy,' said Zac, overtaking an Aston Martin. 'Hang on to that painting, it'll be worth a fortune one day.'

Dicky became even more confiding, admitting he was teased at school because he was small, like Anthea.

'There's no such thing as equal rights. Why is it OK for women to be small and not men, and why do I have to go to boarding school and not Dora? I want to be at home like her and not miss things. All Dad and Mummy ever think about is Emerald. I wish she'd go away.' (Or speak to me occasionally, thought Dicky wistfully.)

Stopping for petrol, Zac bought Dicky a family pack of wine gums and a computer game and, driving on, told him about a secret room in his great-grandfather's house in Vienna.

'That's nothing,' scoffed Dicky. 'There's a secret passage in Foxes Court going from the landing down a staircase out of the house into the garden, and' – Dicky looked furtive, he really liked Zac – 'promise not to tell anyone?'

'Sure, sure, Scout's honour.'

'There's a secret room, known as the Blue Tower, above Mum and Dad's bedroom. There's a staircase leads up to it. And I heard Knightie and Mum saying Dad's first wife' – Dicky blushed – 'used to have lots of men there.'

'How d'you get into this Blue Tower?' asked Zac, ultra casually.

'Dunno.' Dicky went vague. 'There's a password, but I don't know what it is. The room's haunted by Dad's first wife, so no-one wants to go up there.'

*   *   *

When Zac returned with Dicky, Raymond and Anthea, back from the beauty parlour, were effusive in their thanks. Dicky promptly dragged his father and Zac off to play tennis. In the kitchen, Anthea was icing Emerald's cake and wrestling with tonight's seating plan. She'd put herself opposite her two admirers, David and Zac, so they could marvel at her beauty in her ravishing new Lindka. The weather was getting very close, but if she got too hot, she could always whip off the little shrug and show off her pretty shoulders. Emerald's replacement father, Ian, she supposed, had better go on her right – perhaps he'd give her a mini-cab discount next time she was in town – then she could have Si, who was the real guest of honour, on her left.

Si's wife Ginny was much too busty and predatory to be put anywhere near Zac: she could go next to Jonathan; and Geraldine, the pretentious bitch, could go on Jonathan's other side. Ghastly Casey Andrews, who had this terrible crush on Emerald, had been angling for an invite all week. Raymond had manfully resisted all his hints, then forgotten and instead invited that vindictive Somerford who was bound to bring Keithie the burglar. Alizarin must therefore be put as far away from Somerford as possible or he might chuck the sarcastic old pansy into the river.

It was such a long time since petfood billionaire, Kevin Coley, Mr Ditherer, had got out his cheque book at Alizarin's first private view to buy a couple of oils, and Somerford had sidled up hissing that they were rubbish. Kevin, as was his wont, put his cheque book away and Alizarin had hit Somerford through Raymond's glass door, as his mother had once hurled the Degas. With Somerford spewing poison, Alizarin's career had ended before it began. Serve Alizarin right really.

And where could she put Rosemary Pulborough? She and Alizarin were very fond of one another – so Anthea wasn't going to give them the pleasure of sitting together. It was stupid to waste heterosexuals on someone as plain as Rosemary. She could go between Keithie and Dicky – although from the way Dicky was gazing at Emerald . . . Anthea supposed it was a relief Dicky wasn't going to turn out gay.

Oh good, here were Zac and the boys back from tennis, not long on the court, it was so stiflingly hot. Having arranged the damp tendrils on her forehead more becomingly, Anthea turned to the more caring pastime of icing Emerald's cake.

'Don't mess up any of the lounges, Dicky,' she called out.

Although the guests probably wouldn't go inside at all. That was the maddening thing about summer, all that time wasted polishing and doing flowers people never saw. Perhaps she could lure Patience inside for a liqueur.

'Dicky,' bellowed Raymond from the study, 'come and fix Sky, and we can watch the cricket.'

That was them sorted for three-quarters of an hour, thought Anthea. Obviously with the same idea, Zac slid into the kitchen. Even though he hadn't removed his black tracksuit top to play tennis, he was hardly sweating.

'Her first birthday at home,' quavered Anthea, as she put a green four-leaf clover on the snow-white icing.

'Beautiful.' Zac was standing much too close behind her. 'You're a great mom.'

'Can I get *you* anything?'

Zac wanted a glass of water. She loved the way he pronounced it: 'Wot-urrr'.

'Evian's in the fridge, help yourself. It's tricky putting in these clover stems.'

Hell, here was Sienna drifting in from working all night, yawning and flexing her aching shoulders. Her hair was in a plait and as usual she had got paint and clay everywhere. One of Jonathan's discarded duck-egg-blue shirts, hardly buttoned up, showed off her long, pale legs. A stud gleamed like mercury in her belly button.

Noticing Zac taking out the Evian bottle, Sienna said, 'Why not try tap water? We're like not on the mains, so it comes straight from a spring up in the woods.'

Peering into the fridge, she was just about to grab a handful of prawns, when Anthea shrieked, '*Don't*, they're for tonight.'

Turning on the cold tap, Zac filled up a mug, then, distracted by the glimpse of a comma of pubic hair between Sienna's thighs, took a huge gulp, and swore as boiling water scalded his tongue and throat.

'Fuck, that's the hot tap.'

'You get like hot water out of both taps here,' said Sienna evilly.

'Very symbolic,' snapped Zac.

'That was wicked, Sienna,' said Anthea in a shocked voice. 'I'm so sorry, Zac, let the tap run for a minute, it'll come out cold as the North Pole.'

'Like someone else round here.' Sienna pulled a face at Zac and, grabbing an orange, sauntered out.

'I'd be grateful if you didn't take any more towels out of the hot cupboard,' Anthea shouted after her. 'Knightie found seven in your bedroom this morning and we do have a lot of house guests. Little bitch,' she stormed to Zac. 'Galena's children are so horrid to me. I tray so hard.'

'The Jews have a legend that the serpent was Adam's first wife,' said Zac.

'Oh, that's priceless,' giggled Anthea. 'You understand everything.'

'And that is such a beautiful cake,' said Zac moving in behind her again.

'I'm off,' said an icily disapproving voice.

It was Emerald, who was driving all the way back to Shepherd's Bush to put her parents and Sophy through a dress rehearsal.

What the hell was Zac doing deserting her to pick up

Dicky and notch up Brownie points with Raymond and Anthea? she wondered furiously. She was their ewe lamb, not Zac.

It's *my* birthday, she told herself. No-one's allowed to be nasty to me all day. Why hadn't Zac offered to drive her the sweltering 240 miles there and back? But she daren't let her family arrive unsupervised. Patience had been known to make a scarecrow look like Beau Brummell.

Zac saw her off, but his goodbye kiss, in full view of the kitchen window, hardly grazed her cheek.

'I'll give you your birthday present when you get back. Safe journey,' and, banging the flat of his hand on the top of her car, he loped back into the house.

Suddenly Emerald hated leaving him with Anthea. No-one warned you in the adoption manuals about your natural mother getting off with your boyfriend.

Returning to the kitchen, hearing bat on ball and clapping from the study, Zac's long fingers met round Anthea's minute waist. Anthea's heart started to thump, and she found difficulty saying, 'Sorry Emerald's being so temperamental. She's very smitten with you, Zac,' and when his fingers climbed her ribs and his thumbs began caressing and lifting her little breasts, the four-leaf clover suddenly acquired a fifth leaf.

'Oh Zac,' sighed Anthea. She tried to move away, but he held tightly on to her. 'I hoped you were going to marry my Charlene.'

'Not when I've got the screaming hots for her mom.' Zac buried his lips in the back of Anthea's very clean neck.

'We can't hurt Charlene,' gasped Anthea.

'I guess not.' Zac's voice was so husky, his breath so warm, his stroking hands creeping inside her shirt. 'If only we could carve out time and find a secret love nest for an hour of heaven.'

Anthea made only half-hearted attempts to finish icing the word 'Happy'.

'I know somewhere,' she whispered. 'I'll tell Raymond and Dicky I've got a migraine coming on. I'll meet you on the top landing in five minutes.'

Hearing the drone of an electric toothbrush, Zac hovered impatiently in the shadows until Anthea beckoned him into her ravishing crimson and white bedroom. She reeked of Shalimar and was still wet from the shower. A white frilly négligé clung to her body.

'Ay can trust you, Zac.'

'Sure you can.'

'You must promise never to tell anyone where you've been or what you've seen.'

'I promise, I won't notice anything but you anyway.'

Anthea wavered. 'I still feel awful about Emerald.'

'Emerald's a kid,' urged Zac, 'you're a woman.' How the clichés tripped off his forked tongue. 'You're what Emerald would have been if you'd reared her.'

How Anthea loved that.

'Kiss me, Zac.'

Zac pressed his lips hard but briefly against hers.

'Hurry please, I want you so badly.' (Come on, you bitch, he thought.)

With a shaking hand Anthea punched out a series of numbers beside a door next to her dressing table. Nothing happened.

'Sugar,' she squeaked, 'I've forgotten the password.'

'What is it?' Just keeping himself from throttling her, Zac put warm, steadying hands on her bare arms.

'*Parsifal* – some stupid opera Raymond likes.' Anthea punched again. 'P-A-S-S—' They could hear someone running down the landing.

'Hurry,' hissed Zac. 'It's spelt 'P-A-R.'

This time she got it right. The door swung open. Softly

closing it behind them, Anthea led Zac upstairs through a door with a mirror set into it. Inside was a bower of bliss, a heavenly little turret room with a blue vaulted ceiling scattered with stars, a faded crimson-curtained four-poster and pictures crowding the walls.

'Ay'm afraid it smells musty.' Anthea wrinkled her nose as she locked the door behind them. 'But Knightie might get the wrong ideas if she cleaned up here.'

The pictures were faint making, all of naked or scantily clad men and women. Zac clocked a Watteau, a breathtaking little Titian, a wonderfully curvaceous white bottom by Boucher, and a Beardsley rake examining a naked nymph through a spy-glass.

'Omigod,' he said slowly.

'Raymond believes some old Italian theory, that if you have paintings of beautiful people on the bedroom wall, you'll produce beautiful kiddies.'

'And you're the loveliest of them all.'

As he buried his lips in Anthea's, she closed her eyes in ecstasy. Zac's, however, remained open, roving round the room, until there on the right of the bed, wham, bang, thanks at least $10 million, ma'am, he saw the Raphael, and felt ecstasy shuddering through his body at such shining beauty. He started to tremble.

How he quivers with excitement, thought Anthea, he truly cares for me.

'Undress me, Zac,' she whispered in Emerald's little girl voice.

He was getting so adept at taking clothes off childlike women, he'd better get a job as a nanny. The white négligé slid to the floor like an avalanche, followed by the gingham toggle holding back her hair. She did indeed have the lovely body of a thirteen-year-old. He could hang a baseball cap on her nipples.

'Oh Zac.' Anthea gasped when she saw the size of his cock. 'Raymond's awfully little. Ay hope ay'll be able to accommodate you.'

It'd be like an elephant getting his trunk down a mousehole.

'Don't worry, babe,' murmured Zac, 'I'll get you so slippery. Just relax.'

Pushing her across the bed, parting her damp blond pubic hair, tongue downwards, he found her tiny clitoris, licking it languorously. Eyes upwards, he joyfully examined the Raphael in glorious technicolour for the first time, revelling in the exquisite folds of Pride's rich purple cloak, in Lust leering at Pandora in her sky-blue dress, and in Gluttony snatching a red and green apple from the table.

'Oh Zac, oh Zac.'

'Oh darling Anthea.'

Shifting his position, coaxing two fingers in and out of her, he studied yawning Sloth on his yellow couch, being kicked in the ribs by a red-faced Wrath. Envy in scarlet glowered at Pandora's wimpish husband and Avarice pocketed a gold candlestick as all the Deadly Sins were evicted from the room.

Anthea was so sticky now, Zac could enter her from any angle. Sitting in an armchair, with her straddled across him, he noticed Mercury in his winged hat peering in through the window.

Laying Anthea on the bed on her tummy, he slowly kissed and licked his way up her pearly white legs, till he reached her dimpled bottom, and slid an oiled finger into her anus.

'Oh Zac.' She gave a squeal of pleasure. 'That is so naughty and lovely, you must stop.'

But Zac was gazing up at Pandora. And as he took Anthea from behind, gently caressing her nipples and tickling her clitoris, he noticed how beautifully drawn was Pandora's arm, despairingly raised to ward off the stinging evils of the world.

Mechanically, almost as if he were grilling a sole, he flipped Anthea over on her back. As she bucked faster and faster beneath him, he noticed she made the same mewing noises as Emerald when she came.

But he had no difficulty in not coming himself, even when later she somewhat cautiously went down on him because it gave him the chance really to examine Hope in her rainbow dress. She was as lovely as the Botticelli Venus or even the Venus of Urbino, haloed in light, her piled-up hair glowing with rubies, and her sweet optimistic face outshining the shining moon behind her.

'My little darling, I'm going to take you home,' murmured Zac.

'Oh Zac,' mumbled Anthea with her mouth full, 'are you truly?'

Pulling out his dick, Zac laid Anthea back on the crumpled sheets, plunged deep, humped joyfully for a moment, then with a shout of triumph exploded inside her. Anthea was in heaven – the nearest she'd been to orgasm in recent years had been when she became Lady Belvedon at Buckingham Palace.

Sated by very different pleasures, they lay back on the bed.

'You're exquisite, like a little Fragonard.' Zac stroked her concave belly.

'Raymond says I'm more like Hope.' Anthea pointed to the Raphael, which gave Zac the excuse to leap to his feet.

'You were wearing her dress when we first met,' he said in pretended amazement, edging closer, frantically working out how the picture came off the wall.

What a back view, thought Anthea dreamily. Raymond was a fine figure in Savile Row pinstripe, but stripped off, he was quite pink and wrinkled. Zac wasn't going to be the only one making arty references.

'You've got a naicer botty than Michelangelo's David,' she cried, stroking it, then sliding her hand between Zac's powerful thighs to cup and caress his testicles.

But as he put his hands on the gold frame to take the

Raphael to the light, Anthea shrieked and her hand tightened convulsively.

'Ouch!' howled Zac. 'Whadja do that for?'

'Don't touch the Raphael, the alarm's wired up to the police station.'

'How does that work?' Zac in his excitement was oblivious of the pain.

'There's a little sensor at the back of the picture, which goes off if it's moved.'

'Like your clit.' Reaching back, Zac put a hand between Anthea's legs. 'Where does it turn off?' he murmured, his fingers becoming more insistent.

Anthea writhed with pleasure.

'In the cellar on the left of the door.'

'And the password?'

'Same as the first four letters to get in here.'

'Why *Parsifal*?' asked Zac, wondering if perhaps he could clamber over the roof and get the painting out through the window.

'It's Raymond's favourite opera.' Anthea ticked the names off with her fingers. 'And although we had to fudge a bit, it's P for Pandora, A for Arrogance instead of Pride, S for Sloth – no, it's spelt with an R, isn't it, so it's R for Rivalry instead of Envy, now S for Sloth, I for Indulgence instead of Gluttony, F for Fury, A for Avarice and L for Lust. It spells Parsifal.'

'That's neat,' said Zac. Getting up, he prowled round the room. He was frantic to grab the Raphael then and there, but out of the window, through a net curtain of cobwebs, he could see men bashing in posts for fireworks, Robens mowing the top lawn yet again, and Aunt Lily's fluffy white cat stalking butterflies in the catmint. Raymond was downstairs, Sienna somewhere; it was too risky.

'You do really love me, don't you, Zac?' begged Anthea, clamouring for affection just like Emerald.

'You have made me the happiest man in the world,' replied Zac truthfully.

'This is a huge thing for me.'

'And an utterly enormous thing for me.' Reaching into his tracksuit pocket, Zac produced a camera. 'Honey, I'm off to the States tomorrow,' then, when Anthea gave a wail of horror: 'I'll be back. May I take a picture to carry against my heart?'

Anthea even posed with her newly waxed legs apart and her hands clasped behind her head to raise her breasts.

'Absolutely sensational,' breathed Zac, as he aimed his lens at the Raphael above her.

45

Sienna often returned to stories from the Greek classics, which Raymond had read her when she was a child. Her favourite had always been about Nausicaa, a maiden who, like Sienna, had three merry bachelor brothers, who were always needing clean shirts for parties. While dutifully washing these shirts one hot afternoon by the river, Nausicaa had surprised naked in the rushes a handsome illegal immigrant called Odysseus, who had hastily slapped an olive leaf over his cock.

Zac must have been rather like Odysseus, wily, wandering, opportunistic, loving them and leaving them, reflected Sienna as she drifted off to sleep that muggy, sweltering afternoon. Waking, she gave a scream to see a dark figure towering over her. Then she realized it was the dark green curtained horizontal bar of her four-poster. Having groped shakily for a ciga-rette, she decided she'd never get back to sleep unless she first had a pee.

Wandering out into the landing, she was stunned to find stealing out of a bathroom a naked Zac. Seeing her, he made no attempt to cover himself with a leaf from one of Anthea's sweetheart plants. He seemed totally unembarrassed, probably because he had such a lean mean marvellous body. For once, he was looking ecstatic.

'I guess I should raise my dick to you,' he murmured as he slid into his bedroom.

Quite unnecessarily for the knowing Dicky and Dora's sake, Anthea had put Zac and Emerald in separate rooms. Sienna therefore assumed he had been returning from shagging Emerald. Bumping into Mrs Robens, who'd been checking the rooms allotted to the Cartwrights, however, she learnt that Emerald had gone to London at lunchtime.

Sienna felt sick. Could Zac have been with Anthea?

Collapsing on her bed she relived the horror of the abortion Anthea had made her have when she was sixteen.

'We mustn't tell Daddy,' Anthea had kept saying.

The father of the baby had been a very attractive married man, and Anthea had had to have several lunches with him to talk about 'the situation', before persuading him never to see Sienna again. He had become quite nasty when Sienna had run away from school and rolled up in floods of tears at his office. Could Anthea be up to her old tricks – but this time nicking Emerald's boyfriend?

An hour later, when Zac disappeared off to Searston in Anthea's car, ostensibly because he'd forgotten to bring a black tie, Sienna crept into his room, breathing in sudden sweetness from the gold honeysuckle clustering round his window and the CK One in which he must have drenched himself before rushing out. Idly Sienna opened a chest of drawers and froze. Under his black evening shirt, she found a gun, a cheque for $10,000, still uncashed, from Si Greenbridge (an arms-dealer no less), a lot of US currency, several £50 notes, some yen and roubles, and Russian, US and Austrian passports. She also found a tattered red-leather collection of Goethe's poems. Sienna's A-level German enabled her to understand that the book had been inscribed in spidery black writing to someone called Jacob from his father Benjamin in 1925, and to translate the quotation:

'At all times, pleasure and grief go together. Have faith in pleasure, meet grief with courage.'

What the hell was going on? How long had Zac known Si Greenbridge?

As Zac stormed back up the drive she could see his mobile glued to his ear, the gleam of his white teeth.

'Tiger Tiger, burning bright In the forests of the night.'

Whatever Zac was hunting, it wasn't Emerald.

A terrific tension was building up in the house. Dark purple clouds bruised the horizon; thunder rumbled threateningly round the valley. It was stiflingly hot. Raymond prayed rain wouldn't douse the fireworks, and turned up the Good Friday Music to blot out Anthea's moaning that his children had put off their allotted tasks until she was forced to do them herself.

'There's no point buttering bread too early, it only curls,' protested Sienna.

Dora was crying. Having returned grubby from horse trials and been ordered to shower at once and not use up too much water, she had mistakenly drowned a woodlouse. Dicky, to distract from the fact that he'd wolfed most of the prawns in the fridge, was winding her up: 'It was a single-parent woodlouse,' he kept saying. 'She's left behind four poor motherless baby woodlice.'

Emerald was on her way down from London with the Cartwrights. Sophy was equally nervous and excited to be seeing Alizarin again. She hadn't dared mention his painting her. Emerald had gone ballistic when she learnt from an unguarded Patience that Jonathan had taken Sophy out.

'Trust you to muscle in on my new family.'

Nor did Emerald approve of Sophy's black dress: far too much of Sophy spilling out. Only because she knew it would trigger off a tantrum and upset her parents had Sophy agreed instead to wear a leaf-patterned shift, a sort of shirt-no-waister which she'd bought for parents' evenings.

Sophy, on the other hand, wasn't nearly so nervous as Ian, who desperately wished he had a job to compete with Raymond's, or Patience, who'd been prevailed upon not to take her cerulean watered silk because Anthea was wearing that colour and 'You'll look like Little and Large.'

Patience's old standby, a brown velvet skirt worn with a pie-frilled collared shirt, had become much too tight. If her mother was so broke, how could she afford to stuff her face? wondered Emerald tetchily. She then dragooned Patience into packing her ancient burgundy taffeta, which smelt of mothballs, but at least had been made for a silver wedding, albeit ten years ago, by Belinda Belville.

'You'd better leave the label sticking out,' giggled Sophy.

It'll clash with my face, thought Patience despairingly.

The drive down was interminable and suffocating because Emerald didn't want open windows wrecking her hair.

Arriving at Foxes Court as the sun was sinking, Patience found the perfection of the whole place utterly depressing. There wasn't a speck of dust or an undeadheaded rose anywhere. Nor had she and Ian ever stayed in a spare room so enchantingly decorated in dove greys and apricots, nor so well stocked. On the beeswaxed William and Mary table beside a vase of pale orange roses lay the latest *Oldies*, *Spectators* and out of date *Tatlers*, which fell open at Anthea's picture. Beside the electric kettle and pretty rose-patterned tea set were sachets of everything herbal and decaffeinated. The bathroom was like a chemist's shop: Floris and Penhaligon's, Alka-Seltzer, Anadin Extra, ibuprofen and Rennie's fought for space. Through the windows, pale roses could be seen cascading down glossy trees. On the way to their room, Anthea had found an excuse to show them her own ravishing toile de Jouy bedroom: 'Just in case you get lost, Ian and Patience. These big old houses are so confusing – you'll find me in here.'

How could Emerald not have originated from such a wonderful place? How could she not have such a beautiful mother? Anthea, still aglow from Zac, fragile in her frilly white négligé, was appallingly gracious.

'Thank you ver, ver, ver much for bringing up Charlene so caringly,' she told Patience the moment they were alone. 'Sir Raymond and I are so grateful. You've really done a great job.'

As if Emerald had been a book she'd returned to them without dropping it in the bath or turning down the pages, thought Patience savagely. Looking down at her feet, still in her driving shoes, she gave a moan.

'Oh bugger, I've left my black high heels behind.'

Anthea, desperate to upstage (she'd never expected Ian and Patience to be – well, so grand), was most sympathetic.

'I'd lend you a pair, Patience, but I'm only size three. I'll phone our daughter-in-law, Hanna, she's got big feet.'

Patience, catching sight of her boiled bacon face in the magnifying mirror, nearly wept. Visitor, a better host than Anthea, heaved himself onto Patience's bed, wagging and eyeing the tin of shortbread on the bedside table.

'Get down, Visitor,' shrieked Anthea.

'Oh, please let him stay,' begged Patience.

Fortunately Anthea was distracted by the fearful news that Casey Andrews was in the area wanting to drop in. Jonathan, who'd just arrived, had grabbed the telephone.

'Casey was on his way back from Cornwall being a Cornish painter,' he informed Anthea. 'I told him to bugger off.'

'That wasn't very wise,' chided Anthea, then suddenly

403

realized if she eloped with Zac she'd never have to suck up to loathsome Casey again.

Emerald was desperately embarrassed to see her mother's big feet spilling over Hanna's sling-backs, but even more so when Patience, on her way out to the terrace, paused to admire the drawing-room pictures, crying out in her ringing, raucous voice, 'I so admire your courage, putting your children's paintings on the walls.'

'Mu-um,' hissed Emerald, 'these artists have paintings in the Tate.'

'Painting's such a lovely hobby' – Patience had turned to Raymond – 'I had a great-aunt who was awfully good at kittens.'

'I may not know much about painting,' muttered Ian Cartwright, firmly averting his eyes from a purple nude with a left breast slung round her shoulder, 'but I know what I don't like.'

'I don't, that's the trouble,' sighed Sophy. 'I'm so easily influenced, I start liking anything anyone tells me is brilliant.'

Oh, please don't let Daddy get onto the subject of elephant dung, prayed Emerald.

'Goodness, that's awfully life-like,' battled on Patience, admiring Anthea's portrait. 'Your eyes really follow one around, don't they?'

'Telling one not to leave drink rings all over the furniture,' said Jonathan, sauntering in looking romantically Byronic in a ruffled white shirt and tight black trousers.

'You haven't had time to shower,' said Anthea accusingly.

'No, but I've used up most of Dad's Extract of Lime from the downstairs bog. Hi, darling.' Jonathan kissed Sophy, then, hugging Patience: 'How's my favourite woman? Will you tie my tie for me? I have mixed the meanest, greenest cocktail just for you.

'I expect you'd prefer whisky.' Jonathan had turned

to Ian. 'We haven't met, but I'm mad about your daughter Sophy, if only she'd taught me at school. You were Armoured, weren't you? My father's got some fantastic Ardizzones in the study, come and see them.'

For a second, as his arm was taken, Ian stiffened in resentment, then he seemed to melt in the warmth of Jonathan's friendliness, particularly when he went on: 'You *must* meet Aunt Lily. Her husband was a diplomat and she knows everyone,' then, waving at a hovering Knightie: 'Can you get Colonel Cartwright an enormous Bell's, darling?'

Why is he all over my family and so bloody to me, thought Emerald. 'I'm going up to change,' she added to Patience.

'I hope into someone considerably nicer,' murmured Jonathan.

46

Jonathan was definitely Lord of Misrule, determined to enjoy himself and stir up trouble. His mean green cocktail soon had most of the guests plastered.

Just inside the french windows, a table buckled under a growing pile of presents. On the top, ticking away like a timebomb, labelled 'To dearest Emerald. All my love, Raymond', was a flat oblong parcel, which looked unnervingly similar in size to the Raphael.

After his trip to the lawyers yesterday, could Raymond be making Pandora over to Emerald? The Belvedons exchanged horrified glances. Anthea was furious. She wanted the Raphael left to her and to be the one to make extravagant gestures.

Sophy was feeling fatter and dowdier by the second. Emerald in her haste to leave London had not allowed her time to dry her hair, so it shot out in all directions. The only answer had been to put it up. I look like the school marm I am, Sophy thought dolefully. She felt even dowdier as a stunning platinum blonde with a drooping scarlet mouth and long, dark, heavily kohled eyes marched out onto the terrace. All in black, she wore a clinging, sleeveless see-through top, a groin level leather skirt, and knee-length high-heeled boots showing off long, slender thighs.

This must be Jupiter's wife, Hanna, decided Sophy,

about whom, Jonathan had said, Alizarin was quite understandably crazy.

'Trust her to copy me and dye her hair blond,' grumbled Dicky, 'and I bet she doesn't get chewed out by Mum.'

'Dar-ling!' Jonathan stopped discussing war artists with Ian, and shot across the terrace. 'You look sensational.'

'Good,' said the blonde, kissing him on the mouth.

'This is my sister, Sienna,' Jonathan, wiping off scarlet lipstick, told an astounded Ian and Patience.

'Hi,' nodded Sienna. 'Excuse us,' then, dragging Jonathan down onto the lawn behind a sapphire rampart of delphiniums: 'We've gotta talk.'

'We sure have,' agreed Jonathan. 'Jupiter's got a buyer for the Raphael, I heard him talking in the study. He'll cop the lot and we'll never see any of the cash. We must get it out of here.'

'We've got to watch Zac even more.' Sienna described the contents of Zac's shirt drawer. 'He and Si Greenbridge must be in cahoots. Si eats Old Masters for breakfast.'

'Hannibal Collector,' sighed Jonathan. 'But that's immaterial if Dad's already handed the Raphael over to Madam for her birthday.'

Si Greenbridge stunned everyone by rolling up without his wife, Ginny. Anthea, envisaging herself as a bluebird of happiness in her new cerulean strapless with the tiny shrug, rushed inside to welcome him.

'Si, Si, so delighted you could make it. Is Ginny freshening up?'

'She's not coming. She's gone back to the States.' Si glanced up the stairs. 'Isn't that a Henri Matisse?'

Ginny, in fact, had been the Mrs Greenbridge that Alizarin, when he was painting Sophy, had told the caller was being fucked by the window cleaner. The caller had been Si, who subsequently discovered his beautiful wife was not having her portrait painted by Jonathan, as she had claimed. Instead she was being boned by Pascal, the interior designer who, not as gay as he pretended, had long had designs on Ginny's interior. Si, who didn't like cheating wives, had put her and Pascal, both protesting bitterly, on the next plane.

'Probably buried her in cement,' whispered Sienna.

'Si will be much easier to sell pictures to without Ginny insisting on everything matching the wallpaper,' whispered back Jonathan.

A spare man, thought Anthea joyfully, and such a rich and macho one. Perhaps Si was a little too old for Emerald, but he'd definitely singled her out at the drinks party at the gallery. He was very sexy in a thuggish way, and if he bought Emerald a few nice things, it would make up for losing Zac.

'Just so thrilled you could come, Si. You and Somerford Keynes, our finest critic, are the only outsiders in a special family gathering.'

More Brownie points for the Belvedons, thought an irritated David, swiftly goosing Anthea as he swept in with Geraldine and Rosemary. David's dark brown tan, essential if one were going bald, was enhanced by a new cream dinner jacket made in the Far East on a recent very successful selling spree. He looked very dashing and Anthea told him so. David smirked. He had a cunning plan for later in the evening.

Emerald, as usual, was last down. Did she inherit her habitual desire to make an entrance from David? wondered Rosemary, as Emerald glided out onto the terrace as if from a different age. Lindka had really excelled herself this time, designing a ravishingly low-cut dress in viridian-and-white-striped taffeta with a ruched hobble skirt to show off Emerald's snaky hips. Only a touch of blusher coloured her milk-white face, her smooth red lips were satin shiny, her dark hair was for once piled up to show off a snow-white neck, around which glittered the Belvedon emeralds, the same lovely green as her eyes.

Sienna and Aunt Lily gasped in horror. The emeralds had been in the family for generations. Jonathan whistled.

'Happy birthday, darling, beautiful dress.'

'Anthea gave it to me,' said Emerald defensively.

'Beautiful necklace. Present from Zac?'

'I haven't opened Zac's present yet.'

Emerald knew she had never looked more seductive, but she felt suicidal because she no longer ignited any spark in Zac. He had made no attempt to lay her since the day of his return. He had not even slid his hands inside her dress when he did up her zip. He was just so detached. Turning away from horrible Jonathan, Emerald went slap into Jupiter, who terrified her even more – as though she'd chucked a cigarette into the bracken a few miles away and found the blaze had suddenly caught up with her. His eyes were so intense, his face twitching with desire and loathing.

'We must talk about your show.'

'Over lunch?' murmured Emerald.

'Depends.' Breathing in sweet Violetta, Jupiter smoothed back a lock of her hair that had escaped from its pins. Christ, she was exquisite.

'You're not to monopolize your sister, Jupiter,' said Anthea playfully. 'I want her to meet Somerford. Charlene, our daughter, is very talented, Somerford. I'll show you some of her heads later.'

Somerford was, for once, looking quite amiable. He was so thrilled he, and not Casey Andrews, had been asked and, having been excited by Zac at the silver wedding party, was glad he'd agreed to leave Keithie behind in the Goat in Boots to watch *Coronation Street* and get up to games of his own.

Leaving Emerald with Somerford, Anthea took Zac over to meet Si.

'You know our daughter Charlene,' she said proudly, 'but not her partner, Zachary Ansteig.'

'Mr Greenbridge.' Zac clicked his heels and, smiling, held out his hand. Taking it, Si smiled back.

'Zachary . . . no, we haven't met.'

'Did you hear that?' hissed Sienna to Jonathan. 'Pretending they don't even know each other.'

'Si's an arms-dealer, probably provided Zac's gun. Lily misheard and thinks he's an art-dealer, therefore even more suspect,' giggled Jonathan as he filled up Sienna's glass. 'Lily's getting terribly pissed.'

'So am I,' said Sienna. 'How could you match your killer cocktail to Emerald's eyes?'

'And her new necklace should be round here.' Jonathan dropped a kiss on the nape of Sienna's neck. 'It soon will be, darling, believe you me.'

It was getting hotter, the garden scents more sweetly seductive, as honeysuckle, philadelphus and rose were joined by night-scented stock and trumpeting lily. There was not a breath of wind; pigeons cooed from the ebony shadows of huge olive-green trees so quiveringly still they seemed about to march on the house. Grenville shuddered at the prospect of an approaching storm. Little Diggory, who'd been licking clean Grenville's eyes and nose like a fussy mother, suddenly barked joyfully.

Here he was at last. Sophy leant against a mossy urn for support as Alizarin, accompanied by a bouncing Visitor, came round the side of the house.

'Here's that big untalented brute,' whispered fat Somerford, hastily employing Emerald as a human shield. 'Can't paint, can't draw – anything except his dole money. I hope Si's brought guards with him.'

Alizarin was wearing a ripped Prussian-blue smoking jacket, and a clean white shirt with the buttons done up all wrong. Taller even than Si and Raymond's delphiniums, he towered over the party like Goya's giant. He looked very pale, exhausted, furious and utterly gorgeous, thought Sophy, wishing some fascinating man was engaging her in sparkling conversation. At least Visitor remembered her and waddled over, rolling on his back, flashing his broken teeth, fat tail threshing like a windscreen wiper. Alizarin, having accepted a large glass of red rushed out to him by Knightie, smiled at Sophy and was about to join her when Zac grabbed him, frogmarching him off to meet Si.

'You've got to see this guy's work. It's awesome.'

Anthea, hardly able to conceal her dislike of Alizarin, was over in a trice.

'Must break up you big lads,' she simpered. 'Si, come and meet our greatest art critic, Somerford Keynes.'

Somerford promptly drew Si aside, urging him on no account to buy Alizarin's pictures.

'You're a serious collector. Don't waste your money.'

Jupiter, overhearing, was ashamed how gratified he felt. He'd been so right to shunt back Alizarin's canvasses.

It was only a fortnight after Midsummer's Eve, but the light was fading and the first stars appearing in the drained blue sky. Ian was having a lovely time swapping friends in common with Aunt Lily. David had drawn Si into a yew glade.

'So sorry about Ginny,' he said. 'Let's do dinner next week. To help you forget her, I'll lay on some amazing young woman.'

'Again,' mocked Jonathan as he sidled up to refill Si's glass. Si laughed. David looked absolutely furious.

Priding herself on being a good hostess, Anthea had introduced dowdy Patience and fat Sophy to skeletal Geraldine – 'You all live in town' – who didn't seem to have anything in common. Desperate to escape, Geraldine's eyes were swivelling like lottery balls.

Awfully gauche, those Cartwrights, thought Anthea, who was floating on happiness. It was priceless the way

Zac was feigning indifference to fool people. She wondered if they dare nip up to the Blue Tower for a quickie during the fireworks. Charlene was looking lovely too. Si, Jupiter and even Somerford had been vying for her attention, which made Anthea feel much less guilty about annexing Zac. She'd better go and organize the first course.

'Run down to the boathouse and light the candles,' she ordered poor rheumaticky Mrs Robens.

She did hope Aunt Lily wouldn't be too tiddly to walk the three hundred yards from the terrace down to the river.

47

Down they trooped, somewhat unsteadily, to the boathouse, breathing in an innocent smell of meadow-sweet and new-mown hay.

On the river bank a string quartet was playing 'Strangers in Paradise'.

David sang along but actually felt more in hell. How could Anthea not have put him on her right or at least left? Now he wouldn't be able to chat up Si across her throughout dinner. When he was High Sheriff things would be different.

'You're here, Mummy,' Emerald called to Patience.

I'm her mother, thought Anthea with an explosion of jealousy, then she realized that utterly bloody Jonathan had been fiddling with the seating plan. For starters he'd swapped over Zac and Somerford, so she'd have the silly old fairy up her end between Sienna and Lily.

Secondly, he'd switched his own place with Alizarin's, which put Alizarin next to Hanna, which would send Jupiter, who was supposed to be familiarizing Geraldine Paxton with the top Belvedon gallery artists, into orbit. Jonathan would now be sitting between Sophy and her sister, which would enable him to indulge in some serious Emerald-baiting.

Sienna clocked Jonathan's move in anguish. He was clearly still obsessed with Emerald. Sophy felt equally miserable. Her father had started to bray with laughter, a sure sign he was drunk. Her mother looked terrified, like a second-class passenger who's strayed into first class, and hopes she won't get caught if she keeps still enough, and Alizarin, after initially smiling at her, was now acting as though he hardly remembered her. She supposed he painted lots of people.

As a final straw, Sophy had taken out a loan this week in order to give Emerald a purple pashmina for her birthday, telling her, 'You can change it, I've kept the bill.'

'Thanks a lot,' Emerald had said casually, 'not entirely sure purple's my colour. It's a bit draining. I'll see what it goes with.'

Sophy wanted to cry with frustration. Why do I always fall for it? Why do I always imagine Emo'll be any different? She must take after her natural mother, Sophy was appalled to find herself thinking. Anthea was absolute hell.

'Move in, Fatso, I can't get past,' ordered Emerald as she edged behind Sophy's chair to sit next to Jonathan, then, hardly lowering her voice: 'Aren't Anthea and Raymond lovely?'

Dinner was decidedly scratchy. The setting was exquisite with the boathouse newly painted duck-egg blue, lit with dark green candles and opened up on one side to the River Fleet, whose flowing water rippled the gold paths cast by flambeaux all along the bank. The table was decorated with jasmine and philadelphus entwined with palest green ivy and enhanced by mauve napkins and the delicate and charming green and purple 'Violets' dinner service.

Anthea made sure everyone knew she'd done the cooking: kicking off with salmon tartlets, untopped admittedly by prawns, and Hollandaise sauce.

'Start at once,' she ordered Patience, 'and tell me what you think.'

Everyone except Alizarin, Jonathan and Sienna dutifully said it was absolutely delicious.

'The tartlet with the heartlet of gold,' murmured Jonathan, who was as high as the glinting weathercock on the church steeple.

Tartlets were followed by very rich lamb and asparagus in cream sauce, which Patience felt uneasily churning round inside her alongside Jonathan's green cocktails. She took a slug of red wine. Raymond, on her left, had been so complimentary about Emerald, Patience wondered rather disloyally if they were talking about the same person. Emerald had been so cruelly unappreciative of Ian and Patience's birthday present of a seed pearl necklace, which had been in the family for generations and which was now the only jewellery unsold. But she supposed they couldn't compete with the Belvedon emeralds.

On Patience's right, in unrelieved black, was Zac, not her favourite person for orchestrating the finding of Anthea. He made no attempt to engage her in conversation, chatting about pictures to Jupiter's wife, Hanna, on his right who, despite a blue satin butterfly fluttering gaily in her piled-up blond hair, looked even unhappier than Patience felt.

I've been such a bad wife compared with Anthea, she thought despairingly. Maybe Ian wouldn't have failed in business if I'd made the house prettier, and ingratiated myself with his customers and colleagues. Look at Anthea dimpling up at the rich and powerful Si Greenbridge. What an asset!

Anthea was so like Emerald in looks and mannerisms, Patience longed to like her. Ian clearly thought her an absolute poppet.

'You and Emerald are just like sisters,' he kept saying. He was looking exactly like Sohrab, their old golden retriever, when he'd met a bitch. Any moment Patience expected a gold plumey waving tail to burst out of his

DJ trousers. Oh please, God, she prayed, let me one day have another dog.

'OK, Mrs Cartwright?' shouted Jonathan, who was busy feeding all his lamb to Diggory and Visitor.

Emerald was delighted that Ian was getting on so well with Anthea and was now nose to nose with Si yakking about the latest lethal weapons. He seemed his own self again, a father she could be proud of.

'Cartwright isn't at all a typical cab driver,' whispered Raymond to Rosemary on his left. 'Got an MC in Korea. Captained the Combined Services at cricket. Likes Matthew Arnold, had a dog called Sohrab, knows about lilies – nice chap.'

'He does seem nice,' whispered back Rosemary, 'I'm sure I've seen her before, it's such a good idea to have them here.'

Beaming up the table, she was amazed to find Si Greenbridge beaming back at her. Buxom Knightie must be hovering behind her offering second helpings of lamb to attract such an approving glance. But when Rosemary glanced round, no Knightie was there and Si was still smiling – perhaps she had asparagus on her teeth.

Hanna, who'd already had far too much to drink, was in a low voice telling Zac, the inspired listener, how desperate she was to have a baby.

'I'm thirty-eight and Jupiter's the eldest son – there's such pressure to produce an heir.'

'Ever thought of adopting?' asked Zac idly.

'Christ, no!' Hanna looked across at Emerald in horror, then, realizing what she'd said, blushed crimson. 'God, that was bitchy. I'm so sorry, she's your girlfriend.'

She was relieved yet unnerved to see Zac was laughing. Didn't he care in the least that Jupiter was devouring Emerald alive with his eyes?

Down the river beyond the wild-flower meadow, people were drifting out of the Goat in Boots, making 'fucking nob' noises as they caught sight of the Belvedon party. Mosquitoes, encouraged by the impossibly hot, humid night, were now biting the guests as voraciously as the evils of the world once fed on Pandora and Epimetheus.

'Such excitement at the West London Gallery,' Somerford was telling Sienna and Lily. 'A ravishing Botticelli loaned by a museum in Venice for their Renaissance Exhibition was withdrawn this very morning because a French-Jewish family are claiming the Nazis stole it from their grandfather in Paris in 1942.'

'Bad luck if you'd forked out millions for a picture only to find it had been looted fifty years before and you'd got to give it back,' grumbled Lily.

'Hits both ways,' agreed Somerford. 'From now on both museums and dealers are going to check the provenance of their stock to see if it's looted.'

'I'd love to own a Botticelli,' sighed Lily.

'I'm a Raphael freak myself,' confessed Si from across the table. 'My ambition is to own a Raphael.'

Suddenly the table went quiet.

He told me not to tell anyone, thought David in fury.

'Dinner tonight is in honour of Raphael as well as Emerald,' announced Raymond, who loved to impart information. 'Agostino Chigi, a well-known Rome businessman who used to bankroll the Popes and actually provided the rubies for Julian II's tiara, was also a great patron of the arts – like one of our guests of honour tonight.' Smiling, Raymond raised his glass to Si. 'Chigi had a villa on the river with a loggia in which he used to hold grand dinner parties. On one occasion, to save washing up, the guests were encouraged to chuck all the gold plate into the river.'

'We're not going to squander our lovely "Violets" plates,' simpered Anthea who, having admitted Zac to the Blue Tower earlier, was unnerved by any reference to Raphael. 'Do fill up Patience's glass, Sir Raymond.'

But utterly bloody Sienna couldn't let the subject rest.

'How does Raphael like come into it, Dad?'

'Chigi had commissioned him to paint a mural on the loggia walls. But Raphael kept moonlighting and not getting down to work. Mind you, he was strutting round Rome like a rock star by this time.'

'Like someone else we know, same birthday.' David tipped back his chair to smile at Jonathan, who ignored him.

'Now the boathouse has been painted, which of you is going to provide our mural?' Raymond glanced happily around at his children.

'I've got too much on,' said Jonathan flatly. 'Perhaps Alizarin?'

But Alizarin, who'd been hitting the red and was spoiling for a fight, was too busy arguing with Jupiter about earlier looting of art.

'Elgin stole those marbles,' he growled.

'Elgin took the marbles because the Greeks weren't remotely interested and considered them worthless,' replied Jupiter coolly. 'Elgin claimed rightly that it was his divine calling to preserve such treasures for posterity.'

'Ought to be returned to the Greeks, they belong to the Greeks.'

'Not if one believes art is of primary importance,' said Jupiter disdainfully. 'The British Museum cherishes the marbles, and this way more people see them.'

Alizarin's huge hands gripped the table. Then he roared, 'So if I make your wife happier, look after her better and allow more people to admire her, I'm entitled to steal her, am I?'

'Touché,' hiccuped a delighted Lily, who was not a fan of Jupiter.

'I said Si should have brought guards,' murmured back an even more delighted Somerford, as both brothers jumped furiously to their feet.

'You keep your hands off my wife,' said Jupiter in a low, furious voice.

'Where did you say your family lived in Vienna?' Hanna turned desperately to Zac.

'My great-uncle had a gallery and an apartment in a beautiful old building on the corner of Singer Strasse and Kärtner Strasse, overlooking St Stephen's Cathedral,' drawled Zac, who was highly amused by the turn of events and who could see Hanna's imploring hand on Alizarin's quivering thigh. 'The Allies bombed it to bits,' he went on. 'There are shops and offices there now. My great-grandfather also had a fabulous house in the fourth district in Schwindgasse overlooking the Schwarzenberg Palace.'

'A gorgeous area,' mumbled Hanna. Oh God, don't let Jupiter and Alizarin kill each other.

As Jonathan surreptitiously scribbled both Zac's addresses on the inside of his wrist, Dora was left to defuse the situation. Wriggling out of her chair between Alizarin and Jupiter, who were still glowering and clenching their fists, she said tartly, 'Chill out, you two yobbos, I do not wish to be used as the Centre Court tennis net.'

Everyone burst out laughing except Jupiter and Alizarin, who, after a lot more scowling, sat down. Dora flounced off down the table to talk to Patience.

'Mrs Cartwright, Emerald said you rode at the Horse of the Year Show.'

'Well, I came second in the Working Hunter, and third in the Foxhunter one year,' admitted Patience.

'Could you come and meet my pony Loofah?' begged Dora. 'He's brilliant at cross-country because I can't stop him, but he always ploughs the dressage, because he won't canter on the right leg and he sits down if I scold him.'

Next moment, Rosemary had cried out, 'Why, it's "Virty" Cameron! I've just twigged.'

Discovering they'd been at school together, Rosemary and Patience, with screams of laughter, started swapping stories about the dorm and the lax pitch. An utterly fascinated Dora sat on an equally entranced Raymond's knee to listen to them.

'Did you really put a drawing pin on the vicar's chair?' she asked in awe.

'I'm afraid we did.' Patience wiped her eyes.

'He was so fat, he didn't feel it!' Rosemary went off into gales of mirth. 'And remember the time we undressed Miss Hinton?'

'Yes, yes,' cried Patience, 'the poor woman's legs wriggled like a bluebottle's, we were awful, and what about putting your rabbit in Miss Murdoch's desk.'

'It was *your* hamster, Virty.'

'Why d'you call Mum "Virty"?' enquired a thrilled Sophy.

'Patience is a Virtue, of course,' said Rosemary.

Everyone laughed.

'What was your nickname?' asked Dora.

'Rosebud or something inappropriate.'

'Mildew more likely. Extraordinary that one school could produce two such ugly women,' Anthea whispered to Si, who didn't react. Too busy gazing at them in horror, thought Anthea.

Smugly she rose to supervise her pièce de résistance. Green chartreuse waterlilies, decorated with Es of angelica, should elicit more admiration and excitement than the fireworks.

'Some enchanted evening', played the string quartet.

Anthea smiled at Zac. Seeing his chance as Raymond also rose to organize the pudding wine, Si abandoned Geraldine on his left, who was bending the ear of an oblivious, still enraged Jupiter, and shot down the table. David, avid to make his number with Si, had already set off round the table to take Anthea's place, only to find Si moved on and himself reduced to squandering vital networking time on his own mistress.

Si meanwhile had pinched Raymond's seat and was producing photographs of horses out of his wallet to show Rosemary, Patience and Dora.

'Much nicer than soppy wives.' Dora pored over them. 'He's great. What's his name?'

'Intensive,' said Si.

'Didn't he win the Arc last year?' gasped Patience.

'That's my boy.'

'I had a monkey on Intensive,' called out Lily, who was still getting on like a house on fire with Ian. 'Thank you, Mr Greenbridge.'

48

'I never see my mother these days,' Dora was soulfully telling Patience, 'she's so besotted with Emerald.'

'I'm sorry,' said Patience humbly. 'They've got a lot of years to catch up.'

Rosemary, taking delight in doing a number on the Cartwrights, knowing it would enrage Anthea, loudly suggested she and Patience should go to an Old Girls' Reunion in London in October.

'Oh do let's,' squeaked Patience in excitement.

'We could have lunch at the Reform first, I've just become a member.'

'I'll be back at school,' said Dora wistfully.

To everyone's astonishment, Si then promised to fly her down to see his horses in one of the Greenbridge jets in the Christmas holidays.

'And if you two ladies would care to join us?'

'We would indeed,' said Rosemary. 'Whatever happened to Biffy Miles?'

Anthea was seething. All these upper-middle-class rituals and talk of people she didn't know. It was as though they were speaking Chinese. Ah, here was her wonderful dessert.

'My God,' said Jonathan, looking down at his plate. 'Are we eating more Belvedon emeralds?'

Drunks being evicted from the Goat in Boots were

having difficulty making their protests heard over rumbling thunder.

'I wish you were our sister, not Emerald,' Dicky was telling Sophy.

'We all do,' murmured Jonathan, Sienna and Dora in unison.

Patience wanted to shout that Emerald wasn't really horrible, that she just got defensive and aggressive when she was insecure and frightened. Emo could be so lovely. Patience took another huge gulp of delicious pudding wine; next moment her glass was filled up.

She had so hoped Emo and Jonathan would get on. Alizarin, the one whose name kept tripping off Sophy's lips, seemed rather an austere chap, watching everyone with those sombre screwed-up eyes, and not addressing a word to poor Sophy. Jonathan's sister looked as though she wanted to knife everyone too. Such a shame when she was so beautiful, despite all those rings and studs.

All through dinner Sienna had been conscious of her beloved Jonathan's preoccupation with Emerald, but images of naked Zac kept flickering before her eyes, upsetting her terribly. From time to time he caught her eye across the table, and his mouth lifted at one corner. Occasionally his eyes travelled lazily downwards. Sienna had never had any inhibitions about stripping off in public but suddenly she felt embarrassed to be wearing such a see-through top, and kept folding her arms aggressively over her breasts like a rugger player in a group photograph. She loathed the idea of Zac in bed with Anthea and even more that he and Si could be after their beloved Raphael.

'Which is the least deadly of the sins?' she asked Jonathan.

'Lust,' replied Jonathan dropping a kiss on the skylark tattooed on her shoulder.

Irked by the ecstasy on Sienna's face, Emerald felt

utterly bewildered. *She* was the birthday girl. Why did so many of the Belvedons seem to prefer fat Sophy and her plain, shiny-faced mother? Dora had just dragged Patience off to meet the appalling Loofah.

'Don't be long,' Anthea called after them. 'Daddah wants to make a speech, and we've got the birthday cake to come, and Charlene, I'm sorry I can't get out of calling her that, has got to open her gifts before the fireworks.'

Anthea grabbed the spotlight again when Emerald's cake arrived and everyone said how pretty it was. But no-one said what a caring mother she had been to have made it. I should have asked Neville and Green Jean as a support group, thought Anthea darkly.

'What are you going to wish for?' asked Jonathan, as Emerald plunged a knife into the white icing.

'That you were at the bottom of the river with Chigi's gold plate,' spat Emerald.

Raymond tried to smooth things over by making an eloquent, charming speech welcoming all the Cartwrights and particularly Emerald.

'Let us all drink to my lovely new daughter.'

'To the green-eyed monster,' said Jonathan draining his glass.

Ignoring him, Emerald rose to her feet: 'I'd like to thank Raymond and Anthea, my marvellous new parents, for being so wonderful to me.'

'Mention Mum and Dad,' hissed Sophy.

'And it's lovely to have Mummy and Daddy and Sofa here and all my family around me,' added Emerald.

Guiltily aware that he had deeply embarrassed Hanna by winding up Jupiter, Alizarin looked across at Sophy in that dreadful green sack dress, whose pattern his eyes were too bad to distinguish, and thought how adorable she was and how anxious about everyone when she should be enjoying herself. He had relived so often that strange peace he had experienced after collapsing

424

beside her in Jonathan's studio. He had longed to ring her, but had nothing to offer but poverty and a guide dog's role. A blind artist was as much use . . .

Another rumble of thunder made them all jump, but it was only Robens trundling Emerald's presents down in a wheelbarrow.

'It looks like rain. You'd better open those after the fireworks,' called out Anthea. 'Robens can wheel them back up again.'

'Just let her open mine,' begged Raymond.

'Seesaw, Margery Daw, Emerald shall have an Old Master,' sang Jonathan.

Everyone held their breath. But Raymond's present turned out to be a beautiful Augustus John pastel of one of his mistresses, which nevertheless caused gasps of admiration.

'Oh how fabulous,' cried Emerald, hugging Raymond in delight. 'You are kind.'

'Ha, ha, ha,' whispered Raymond gleefully to Sienna and Jonathan. 'You avaricious lot thought it was something else.'

'Now I want Emerald to open *my* present.' Jonathan handed her another oblong parcel.

But this time when Emerald had ripped off the red paper wishing her congratulations on her retirement, there were gasps of horror, for inside was an exquisite copy of the Raphael.

'What is it?' demanded Lily, putting on her spectacles.

'*Pandora's Box*,' announced Jonathan happily, 'and most of you are in it. Remember Botticelli painted all the important members of the Medici family into his *Adoration of the Magi*? Well, this is the Unholy Family.'

Taking the picture from a bewildered Emerald, he held it up for everyone to see.

'Look, Emerald is Pandora, opening the box by turning up here. Zac is Epimetheus, I'm Sloth of course, Visitor is Greed, Big Al is Pride, our kid sister natch' – he ran a finger down Sienna's furiously mouthing face

– 'is Wrath, Jupiter is Avarice' – Jonathan started to laugh – 'our dear stepmother is Envy, but she and Jupiter could easily swap sins!'

'Ay am not envious or avaricious,' squawked Anthea.

'How dare you?' thundered Raymond.

'Very easily,' said Jonathan, who hadn't really needed to provide a key, his drawings were so lifelike. 'Here is David with his monocle as Lust, and can you see yourself peering through the window in your tin hat, Dad, Mercury the voyeur?'

'Shut up,' roared Raymond going crimson.

'It's kinda neat,' volunteered Si, raising an eyebrow at Zac, who had gone very still.

'I recognize that picture from somewhere,' mused Somerford.

'What the hell are you playing at?' hissed Jupiter. 'Put the fucking thing away.'

'It's mine.' Emerald grabbed the picture. 'Thank you, Jonathan.'

'I see you left out Hope,' said Sienna bleakly.

I don't understand what's going on, thought Ian Cartwright, but I don't like it one bit. I don't want these pirates stealing my darling Emerald.

Everyone jumped as a mobile rang. Anthea answered it.

'Righty ho, we'll be up in a mo. Will everyone please converge on the terrace for fireworks?'

'Must have a pee,' said Sienna, wheeling off into the darkness. 'You are so drunk,' she loudly chided herself.

As they all trooped up to the house, Anthea surreptitiously slid her hand into Zac's.

'Shall we nip upstairs for a quickie during the fireworks?'

'Sure,' whispered Zac.

'I've left the door to the tower open,' whispered back Anthea.

'Great. For safety you'd better switch the alarm off downstairs.'

'I'll just have to check everything is all right in the kitchen and that my guests are OK.'

'The perfect hostess,' murmured Zac, raising her hand to his lips. 'Don't hurry. I'll wait for you.'

Anthea felt giddy with longing, but as she swayed away from Zac she started like a terrified hare when David grabbed her arm, dragging her into the shadows of an ivied ruin.

'We must talk about Emerald.'

'Not now,' hissed Anthea.

'Well, first thing in the morning then.'

'Righty ho. We'll be up in a mo,' chanted Jonathan, who'd just had another line, as he noticed Anthea and David emerging from the shadows.

'Where's Mummy?' asked Sophy, her heels plunging into the dewy lawn as she panted up the hill after Emerald.

It was very dark in the yew corridors. A thick cloak of indigo clouds had smothered the stars. Hearing shrieks, the two sisters broke into a run.

On the big lawn, illuminated by lights from the house, they found their mother. She was cantering figures of eight, her burgundy taffeta tucked into her knickers, Hanna's sling-backs kicked off, screaming with joy, pissed as a newt, with Dora cheering her on.

'You've got him on the right leg again, Mrs Cartwright, brilliant, one more time,' and Patience cantered a most biddable Loofah into the centre of the lawn again, and executed a perfect flying change, before setting off again towards Anthea's latest splash of colour – a clump of red begonias. Despite her plump mottled thighs, big feet and crimson face, on a pony, Patience looked a goddess. Jonathan, Rosemary, Si, Lily, Dora and Sophy were yelling in approval. Emerald, however, was quivering with rage.

'Mummy,' she screamed, 'for Christ's sake get off.'

Patience immediately stopped. Loofah, who'd been

behaving too well for too long, rolled his eyes and sat down. Slowly Patience slid down his back onto the grass.

'So very sorry, got carried away, so long shince I've been on a horsh.'

'Don't listen to her, you were brilliant,' hissed Dora as she grabbed Loofah. 'You can borrow him to ride out any time.'

As a jumping jack went off, Loofah took off too, towing his young mistress towards the stables. Next moment, Jonathan's mean green cocktail, mixed with three different wines and Anthea's *haute cuisine*, took their toll. Heaving to the right, Patience was sick all over Anthea's begonias.

'Righty ho! We'll throw up in a mo,' cried Jonathan in ecstasy.

49

As the church clock struck midnight, the house went dark, the floodlighting was switched off, the flambeaux and candles doused and the first rocket soared into the ebony night, shaking gold and purple stars into the valley. Both guests and villagers lining the river bank cried out in wonder as this was followed by silver fountains, jade and rose-pink Roman candles and Catherine wheels, jerkily pirouetting like Van Gogh's golden suns.

But between bursts of colour the garden was in darkness, making it impossible to keep track of comings and goings. Jonathan and Sienna had agreed he would trail Si while she followed Zac; but returning from the house, Sienna couldn't find the bastard anywhere. She shouldn't have drunk so bloody much at dinner. Racing in panic round the garden, stumbling down steps, tripping over paving stones, she found nymphs, unicorns, and cherubs, suddenly lit up, but no Zac. Running back to the house, in a blaze of royal blue light from yet another rocket, she found her father on the terrace trying to force a tranquilliser down a shuddering Grenville.

'Come and help me, darling.'

'Can't stop,' panted Sienna, hurtling through the french windows, the drawing room and up the stairs.

Galloping down the dark first-floor landing, she heard stealthy footsteps behind her and quickened her pace; they were getting closer, she stumbled up the next flight of stairs, then gave a scream as she collided with a solid wedge of muscle hurtling in the other direction. Winded for a second, she breathed in Raymond's Extract of Lime, and as her tears were unleashed by alcohol and relief, she collapsed sobbing into the wedge's arms.

'Oh Johno, I'm so frightened, Zac's given me the slip, I can't find him anywhere.'

Drink and drugs had clearly robbed her brother of control. Next moment he was kissing her more passionately than ever before, one warm hand seeking out her bare breasts, the other diving under her leather mini straight between her trembling legs. And she was melting against him, drowning in ecstasy, as he pulled her into a nearby bedroom and slammed the door. They didn't bother to strip off. Desire flickered between them like summer lightning, all the more thrilling because what they were doing was utterly forbidden. Dropping his trousers, tugging off her knickers, he threw her onto the bed, and was on top of her, kissing her face all over, whispering such tender endearments. Then she gave a gasp of joy, he was inside her, the rocket with the joyfully exploding stars invading her. She only wanted to surrender. It was all over in a couple of minutes.

But as the shuddering in her loins subsided, she realized in horror what she'd done. Once you let a deadly sin out of Pandora's Box, you enjoyed it so much, you could never put it back again.

'Oh Christ, Johno, we shouldn't have.'

'Yes, we should.' Lovingly, slowly, he kissed her ringed eyelids, her studded nose and her lips.

'I can't help loving you,' she said helplessly. 'I've fought it so long.'

She'd always known he'd be an infinitely better lover than anyone else. But she hadn't realized he was so lean and fit, nor so wonderfully constructed. Then she felt something metallic against her breast bone, and jumped at a deafening crash outside. As six of the biggest bangers exploded in a drum roll, a flicker of light crept through the curtains falling on a silver Star of David.

As though she'd swallowed a scorpion, Sienna gave a howl of pain.

'You bastard, bastard, bastard, you took advantage of my being drunk.' She was pounding Zac with her fists, slapping his face, then, giving a sob, she leapt to her feet. Falling over a chair and a pair of shoes, she fumbled for the door, and fled.

Jupiter, meanwhile, was on the terrace considering his next move. Fireworks bouncing off the low, dark clouds and the stream made the water and the gardens swim with colour. Deciding to check the house, suspicious like Sienna and Jonathan of Zac's motives, he flicked on the light in Raymond's study and found Emerald on the sofa crying with rage and despair over Patience's appallingly embarrassing behaviour and Zac's defection.

'He doesn't love me any more.'

Jupiter halted, his cold haughty face enigmatic.

'You poor child.'

Closing the door quietly, he dimmed the overhead light and joined her on the sofa. Taking out a grey handkerchief (Hanna was better at flower painting than washing) he wiped away the mascara blackening her blanched cheeks.

'Zac's not worth it, he's a shit.'

'I'm in such a muddle, Jupiter.'

'You don't have to be.'

The comforting arm round her shoulders drew her closer, then tightened like a steel manacle. A moment later Jupiter's lips crashed against hers, his tongue forcing open her mouth, then jabbing deeper and harder until she almost gagged, but was unable to cry out. Now he was ripping her beautiful dress from her

431

shoulders, his free hand clawing at her breasts. Jupiter the beast, beneath the icy façade. Wriggling frantically, Emerald tried to scream and knee him in the groin, but her hobble skirt was too tight.

'Shut up, you bloody tease,' he snarled. 'You've led me on for weeks. Don't pretend you're my sister, we all know you're not.'

Still kissing her speechless, with terrifying madman's strength he forced her back on the sofa. His hand had just burrowed up under her skirt, rigid fingers stabbing viciously between her legs, when the room was flooded with light and a head of piled-up blond hair decked with a merry blue butterfly came round the door. There was a long and dreadful pause, only interrupted by the hiss and mighty crackling of a giant squib.

'Jupiter, oh Christ, oh no,' moaned Hanna in horror and, slamming the door, she stumbled off into the night.

Poor Sophy, meanwhile, was trying to get a plastered Patience to bed: 'I feel so sick,' lurch, 'I feel so sick.'

Dora came along to help.

'I'm quite used to putting my brothers to bed,' she said, taking Patience's other arm. 'Once we get her lying down, I'll get a bowl.'

'Where's Dicky?' asked Sophy.

'He thought Mummy wouldn't notice him watching *Basic Instinct*.'

What a disastrous evening, thought Sophy as Patience finally passed out. Tiptoeing out of the room, she and Dora heard desperate sobbing. Racing along the landing, they discovered Hanna in Alizarin's arms.

'Jupiter's in love with Emerald,' she was howling. 'I've just caught them at it.'

Hanna was so desolate, Alizarin so clearly trying to control his fury. It was as if a raincloud were seeking refuge against a great dark, brooding volcano. Alizarin was stroking Hanna's hair so tenderly.

'You naughty man and woman,' thundered Dora.

Alizarin glanced up. His sight was so bad . . . had he merely imagined the agony and horror on Sophy's face?

I must escape from this evil place, thought Sophy as she stumbled past them down the stairs.

Geraldine and Somerford, who because of their immensely powerful positions in the art world were accustomed to deference, were furious to be abandoned in the garden to the untender mercies of one another. Both, however, had a fondness for rough trade.

'Have you heard of a young Welsh artist called Trafford?' asked Geraldine. 'There's a gritty realism about his oeuvre. One of my clients has not only just acquired his installation, *Cunterpane One*, but also his latest video, *Oh Nan*, which features a masturbating grandmother, as pivotal as it is challenging.'

'I'd like to meet Trafford,' said Somerford.

'I'm not sure he's entirely safe in restaurants or private houses,' mused Geraldine.

'Better meet in a pub then.'

As a swarm of gold tadpoles lit up the sky like anti-aircraft fire, Raymond recognized his son Jonathan emerging from the shrubbery.

'For God's sake go and break up Geraldine and Somerford,' he begged, 'we can't afford to antagonize either of them.'

'I'm taking Lily home,' called out Jonathan virtuously, 'she's even more hammered than Old Mother Cartwright. Break up those silly old tossers yourself, Dad.'

The fireworks were even more thrilling inside than out, thought Anthea as she quivered with anticipation up in the Blue Tower. She had been maddeningly delayed by Si, who'd wanted such a prolonged look at Raymond's Cotman of Duncombe Park in the morning room, that she'd thought he might be about to jump on her. Instead, he finally grabbed a bottle of Krug and shot back into the garden. So now after a quick wash, Anthea awaited her lover. How many times in England was it hot enough to wear just a petticoat after midnight? Not wanting to dirty it, she had left her lovely new dress downstairs in her bedroom.

As David had done a bunk as usual, Si had asked Rosemary to wait for him in a little rose arbour while he collected a bottle of Krug from the house. Then they could watch the fireworks together. Rosemary was not the sort of woman who leapt into men's arms when bats divebombed or bangs got too loud, so they talked about their lives.

Having nipped back to the Old Rectory, ostensibly to get some transparencies to show Si, David on his return lured Raymond into the library. The royal-blue curtains had not been drawn. The leather-bound battalions in the shelves always reminded him of his dreary, repressive youth, growing up in Sorley without a book and hardly a picture. As Raymond handed him a glass of Armagnac, he thought how tired his old boss looked. At seventy-five, it must be wearing to cope with seven kids, plus Anthea who was the most childish of them all.

'I don't want to worry you,' he lied. 'But I'm hearing disturbing rumours that you've got a looted Raphael hidden away. People are onto it.'

The red glow as Raymond pulled slightly faster on his cigar was upstaged by a huge scarlet and silver rocket lighting up the dark room.

'Used to have one – sold it years ago.'

'Well, that's up to you. Know someone who'd take it off you for half a million.'

The green flare of the next Roman candle in no way toned down the carmine flush suffusing Raymond's face.

'Preposterous,' he spluttered. 'It's worth— I mean any Raphael's worth at least twenty times that. Insulting to think I'd harbour anything looted.'

David shrugged and helped himself to one of Raymond's cigars.

'Just warning you as a friend,' he said blandly. 'Once it's on the internet or the Art Loss Register, picture's dead in the water.'

'The Raphael I once had was given to me,' said Raymond huffily.

'That cuts no ice if it was stolen from someone else in the first place. I'd get rid of it at once.'

'What's the subject?' asked Raymond hoarsely.

'Pandora's Box. Hope, appearing out of an oak chest, is allegedly the most beautiful woman ever painted. Rainbow dress, rubies in her hair. Rumour has it that it was originally a panel painting with a motto in Latin, meaning: "Trouble lies below".' David was enjoying himself.

If Raymond hadn't been so flustered, he might have wondered how David knew so much detail.

'I'm not interested,' he snapped.

'I'm just telling you the *on dit*,' said David soothingly. 'If you hear of anyone who's got a Raphael, let me know. I've got a buyer seriously interested. At least you would get some money back.'

Bleating with terror, desperate to find Jupiter, Raymond stumbled through the house. The prospective buyer must be Si or perhaps that dreadful hood Minsky Kraskov, or even Kevin Coley. As the church clock struck half past twelve, the splendour of a blaze of fireworks proclaiming 'Happy Birthday, Emerald' in huge green letters was totally lost on him. Oh, where the hell was Jupiter?

50

Anthea, still awaiting Zac in the Blue Tower, heard Raymond's frantic cries of 'Hopey, Hopey, where are you?' from the bedroom below and dived under the bed. Fortunately he didn't come up the stairs.

When she was sure he'd gone, Anthea, who had lost another kind of hope, crept downstairs. Zac was obviously not going to turn up. Perhaps he couldn't help the delay, but she'd been so sure this afternoon. Wriggling into her cerulean dress, which was so tight-fitting she had trouble with the zip, she was just repairing her face when she realized she'd lost an earring. Grabbing the torch they used for powercuts, she ran back upstairs to the Blue Tower.

She daren't draw attention to her presence by putting on a light. Her eyes went first to the floor, but the torch's beam was wide enough to show up the cruellest gap in the world. Anthea gave a moan of terror, her heart plummeted, then started crashing against her ribs. The Raphael was gone. The beam flashed like a will-'o'-the-wisp into every corner. Nothing.

Could Zac have stolen it before she arrived? She hadn't checked if it was in place when she was hiding up here earlier. Would he shop her, that she had let him into the room? How else would he have known the Raphael was there? Had he left any evidence?

Leaving the door containing the two-way mirror ajar,

racing down the stairs, she collapsed onto her bed, wondering what to do. She felt terribly frightened. Raymond would never forgive her if he found out, and she wouldn't be Lady Belvedon any more. She'd better pretend she'd come upstairs to freshen up, found the door open, gone upstairs and discovered the Raphael was missing.

'Help, help,' cried Anthea, rushing onto the landing, slap into Jupiter.

'Whatever's the matter?'

'The Raphael's gone.'

'What the fuck?' Jupiter barged into their bedroom and bounded up the stairs. 'How the hell did this happen? When did you last see it?'

'About ten days or a fortnight ago. I found the door ajar when I popped upstairs to freshen up just now.'

Being Jupiter, he had time to take in other pictures around the walls. His father had certainly been squirrelling. Outside, the flambeaux had sprung to life again; there was chattering on the terrace.

'Why didn't the alarm go off?' he demanded.

'I've no idea.'

Together they raced downstairs. Inside the cellar door, Jupiter found the alarm switched off and, swearing, switched on his mobile.

'What are you doing?' cried Anthea in horror.

'Calling the police.'

'Oh don't do that, please, Jupiter!' Her voice rose to a shriek. 'It might be a joke, Sienna could have taken it or Jonathan after that stupid drawing, or Alizarin, you know how cross they were about Emerald getting the necklace and the Augustus John earlier.' Anthea was trembling violently.

'Let's ask the family first,' she begged, 'they all know the code to the turret room, we don't want a scandal!'

But Jupiter was already through.

'I want to report the loss of an extremely valuable picture.'

At that moment Jonathan wandered in. He was drenched and there was mud on his trousers and shoes.

'Lily was so pissed she fell in the pond. I'm not mixing that cocktail again.'

Anthea didn't even notice Diggory lifting his leg on her new curtains.

'The Raphael's been stolen,' she whispered.

All the laughter drained out of Jonathan's face.

'I don't believe it, or, Christ, rather I do.'

'Go and round everyone up,' ordered Jupiter. 'The police'll be here in a few minutes.'

Gradually people in states of disarray were shepherded into the library.

'An Old Master has gone missing from an upstairs room,' Jupiter told them. 'I'd like you all to stay in here.'

Raymond appeared utterly demented.

'How could anyone have taken my lovely Raphael?'

Sienna was equally distraught.

'It can't have gone,' she sobbed hysterically, 'the Raphael was the last link with my mother.'

'I was just telling your father earlier, Jupiter,' said David smugly, 'that the word on the street is that you had a looted Raphael here. Perhaps the owner's taken matters into his own hands?'

'*You* could have taken it!' Raymond turned on him furiously. 'You seem to know the picture bloody well. How did you know Hope had rubies in her hair?'

'Dad,' warned Jupiter.

Next moment Zac had erupted through the french windows. Suave and laid back no longer, he had turned into a snarling, maddened tiger, teeth bared, yellow eyes blazing.

'Where's the Raphael? Who's taken it, for fuck's sake?'

'What's it to do with you?' asked Jupiter coldly.

'It's my picture, you asshole.'

'Don't be ridiculous.'

'That picture was on my great-grandfather's wall in 1938. It was confiscated by the Nazis.'

'So?'

'I've got the documentation,' yelled Zac. 'Look, here's a stat of the invoice dated the tenth of May 1931' – he brandished it under Jupiter's nose – 'showing my great-grandfather bought the painting from an Austrian count, and the name of the Viennese gallery who brokered the deal. And here's also the stat of the certificate showing the Nazis confiscated it in 1938.'

'You have been a busy boy,' drawled Jonathan. 'Those could be faked, how do we know it's the same picture?'

'Like this.' Zac slapped a copy of a faded black and white photograph on the table.

'Can't tell from that,' snapped Jupiter.

'How about this then?' Zac brandished the photographs of the Raphael he'd had developed in Searston that afternoon, which were in full colour, and showed the Boucher on the right.

Anthea looked as though she was going to faint.

'How did you get hold of those?' gasped an appalled Raymond.

'I had a tip-off. It's in the room above your bedroom.'

'Why didn't you say anything?' spat Jonathan.

'I didn't want you lot to spirit it away.'

'Who tipped you off?' asked a quivering, white-faced Jupiter.

'A journalist never reveals his sources,' said Zac sarcastically. Then he went berserk, grabbing Jupiter by his lapels, shaking him like a rat. 'What have you done with it, you bastard? My great-grandfather was clubbed to death for that picture.'

'My daughter, o my ducats!' said Jonathan mockingly.

'Shut up,' howled Zac. Throwing Jupiter against the wall, he leapt on Jonathan.

Emerald, who'd been huddled, frozen with horror, on the window seat, the rips in her beautiful dress concealed under Sophy's purple pashmina, suddenly remembering Zac was a black belt, heard herself screaming, 'Don't hurt him!'

439

Zac, who was about to smash Jonathan's face in, lowered his fist.

'One of you's nicked it,' he snarled. 'It'll be an inside job to get the insurance.'

'Rubbish!' screamed Sienna. 'You took it yourself.'

A sulphuric smell of fireworks was drifting in through the windows. Had the devil passed by?

Fortunately, a natural break occurred when Knightie banged on the door and excitedly announced the police were here.

'They've sent that Detective Inspector Gablecross,' she whispered to Anthea, 'the hunky one that cracked Rannaldini's murder in 1996. He catches everyone.' Then, as Anthea turned even greener: 'You'll get your picture back, Lady B.'

The arrival of the police created a diversion, enabling Alizarin to feel his way in through a side door. Sophy noticed grass mowings on his shoes and mud down the back of his trousers; perhaps he had fallen over? He had also taken off his smoking jacket and put on a sweater. A moment later Si and Rosemary came in from the garden, followed by Somerford and Geraldine, who'd all ended up having a jolly party down at the boathouse.

'Have we missed anything?' asked Geraldine in excitement.

As Jupiter explained about the Raphael going missing, Sienna was watching Si. For a second he had looked elated, then, glancing across the library, he had clocked Zac's demented, twitching, ashen face and his own for a second blackened terrifyingly. Then he pulled himself together.

Geraldine and Somerford meanwhile were going into raptures comparing Zac's black and white photograph with his recent colour ones.

'This is definitely the same picture, Inspector,' purred Somerford. 'It's a historic painting: the Raphael Pandora. Been missing for centuries. If I'm not mistaken an American museum, the Abraham Lincoln, has the other half.'

'What *are* you going on about?' asked Jonathan crossly. 'Our picture's complete in itself.'

'Pictures painted on panel in Raphael's day were sometimes constructed in a similar way to pencil boxes,' continued Somerford reprovingly. 'Raphael would have painted the myth of Pandora on the lid, along with the jokey caption: "Malum infra latet", or "Trouble lies below". As indeed it did. Slotted into place this lid would have concealed the painting on the bottom of the box, which was a portrait of a lady who gave Raphael a lot of trouble.'

'If my memory serves me right,' chipped in Geraldine, not to be outdone, 'the young woman in question was called Caterina and nicknamed La Smorfiosa – the Proud One. I've seen it at the Abraham Lincoln – a lovely portrait. La Smorfiosa was rumoured to be a beauty—'

'Like yourself,' chipped in David gallantly.

'—who resisted Raphael's advances.' Geraldine smiled at him warmly.

'At some time,' suggested Somerford, 'Pandora must have become separated from Caterina, her other half. Fascinating.'

'Collectors and museums would give the world to get their hands on this picture, Inspector.' Geraldine waved the colour photographs. 'You must get it back.'

'Well, he won't if you both waste any more of his time rabbiting on about pencil boxes,' exploded Sienna. 'For Christ's sake, let the Inspector do some detecting.'

'Be quiet, Sienna,' rapped out Jupiter, and proceeded to whisk Gablecross off on a tour of the house.

Jonathan meanwhile was counting heads.

Dora and Dicky had disappeared. There was no sign of Patience, Ian or Hanna. Apart from that, everyone else was present. Raymond had aged a thousand years. Anthea was shaking so violently Sophy ran upstairs and found her a cardigan. But as she came back into the library, Anthea was saying, 'The Cartwrights have probably taken it, we know how poor they are. Patience could have pretended to be drunk, to give herself an excuse to be upstairs in bed while the fireworks were going off.'

'We have *not* taken your rotten picture.' Sophy hurled the cardigan in Anthea's direction. 'My mother, I'm afraid, has passed out, and my father's been reading *Wisden* in the loo, he often disappears in there for hours on end. He has now gone to bed. Anyway, he wouldn't know a Raphael from a rhinoceros. My family have never stolen anything in their lives,' she added furiously.

Emerald, remembering the shoplifting of the Joseph dress, went scarlet as her eyes met Zac's.

Jupiter, meanwhile, was showing Inspector Gablecross the alarm in the cellar which had been switched off. They also looked at the secret passage running from the upstairs landing down two flights of steps into the garden on the church side, both doors of which were discovered to be unlocked. The two-way mirror door leading to the Blue Tower was also swinging.

While they were up in the Blue Tower, Jupiter slid his foot over a gingham toggle beside the bed. His stepmother had been wearing it that morning – but he had no wish at this stage to shop her.

'It's a small painting,' he explained, 'cut out of its frame and rolled up, anyone could have slipped it under a dinner jacket.'

Footprints, he went on, had been found under an open dining-room window, making it possibly a burglary.

'Could have come in that way, while the fireworks were going off,' pondered Inspector Gablecross. 'Thief could have turned off the alarm system. Who knows where it turns off?'

'Practically everyone in the household,' said Jupiter.
'Who are?'

'My father and stepmother, all the staff, my brothers Alizarin and Jonathan, my wife Hanna.' Where was Hanna? he wondered. 'My sister, Sienna. Our new sister Emerald Cartwright might not have done.' Jupiter explained about the adoption. 'She came into our lives about six weeks ago, along with her boyfriend, Zachary Ansteig, who I might as well tell you, Inspector, is claiming the Raphael's his, looted from his great-grandfather's house in Vienna in 1938.'

'Ha!' said Gablecross. 'So you think he might have been more interested in tracking down the Raphael than his girlfriend's natural parents?'

'I'm not saying anything,' said Jupiter. 'But he was in the house all day. No, he went to pick up my brother Dicky from school, and he went out this afternoon.'

'Could be an inside job,' said Gablecross. 'How much d'you reckon it's worth?'

'Must be insured for at least four million, but could be worth double or treble that.'

Gablecross whistled.

'Who would have known the password into the secret tower?'

'The immediate family did. Probably my sister Sienna, Jonathan would have forgotten it, Alizarin possibly.'

Alizarin had spent three hours with Zac yesterday, thought Jupiter darkly. Could he have tipped him off?

'Who else might have known of the painting?'

'My mother had lovers up there twenty-five years ago,' sighed Jupiter, 'Rupert Campbell-Black, Colin Casey Andrews, Etienne de Montigny, Joan Bideford.' Then pulling a face, 'My mother had catholic tastes, but I doubt any of them noticed the paintings much.'

'I suppose someone could have come over the roof and dropped in through that skylight' – Gablecross stood on the double bed to look – 'but the cobwebs don't seem to have been broken. We'd better print everyone.'

Going downstairs, they found Jonathan filling up people's drinks.

'The insurance company'll recover it for you,' Si Greenbridge was telling Raymond. 'They know which Mafia's got everything.'

'The police certainly don't.' Jonathan drained the dregs of the brandy bottle himself. 'They are absolutely useless at finding anything. The Yard have cut down their art and antiques squad to two piddling detective constables. The Italians have got thirty.'

'Shut up, Jonathan,' snapped Jupiter, flicking off the overhead light.

And I won't turn a blind eye, young man, next time I catch you speeding through Limesbridge at four o'clock in the morning, thought Gablecross grimly.

'Please find my picture,' beseeched an almost weeping Raymond.

'Someone wanted your painting, sir,' Gablecross told him. 'With such a valuable work, the thief possibly already had a buyer in mind. It could be at the coast by now, and smuggled out of the country by tomorrow, possibly to be sold on the black market, or used as a down payment for drugs or an arms deal.'

'Say no more.' Jonathan bowed in Si Greenbridge's direction.

'Detective Inspector Gablecross believes the thief,' said Jupiter hastily, 'came over the roof or through the house, turned off the alarm and knew the password to get into the Blue Tower.'

'Unless Anthea or Dad left it open,' said Jonathan.

'Ay haven't been there for weeks,' squeaked Anthea.

'Of course not,' said Jupiter. Surreptitiously, so only she could see it, he opened his hand to reveal the gingham toggle.

Anthea gave a gasp of horror. Her world would

444

collapse like a house of cards if anyone knew she and Zac had been making love in the Tower, or worse she had given him access to the Raphael.

The beast, she thought furiously. And on the pretext of snapping me in the nuddy, he photographed our lovely picture.

Jonathan's mind was working in the same direction.

'It's a set-up,' he said to Zac. 'You planned the whole thing from the start, so you could nick the Raphael. There's a gun in his top drawer, Inspector, and loads of illegal currency, not to mention three passports. And I don't believe Emerald's a Belvedon at all.'

'That's garbage,' shouted Zac. 'Why bother to steal my own picture? I was trying to recover it,' he said to Gablecross. 'Search my room if you like.'

While Gablecross's minions belted off to have a look, Anthea, who'd been doing some rapid thinking, asked if she could have a private word.

Facing her across the study table, Gablecross thought how pretty she was. Her slender shoulders begged for a man's jacket to warm them. The violet of her eyes was enhanced by the shadows beneath; he longed to comfort her.

Anthea in turn saw a tough, square, reddish farmer's face, softened by curly brown hair and very green, long-lashed eyes, and wanted to put her trust in Inspector Gablecross utterly.

'Ay could have left the door open some weeks ago,' she confided. 'Sir Raymond and Ay occasionally nip upstairs for a quickie. He's very vigorous for his age.'

'So would I be in his position,' said Gablecross admiringly. 'You can't remember the last occasion? We're just establishing the time of theft.'

Anthea gave a squeak of amazement.

'Now I remember. I did nip upstairs to peak out of the window, just before Emerald's replacement parents arrived. You can't see the front of the house from our bedroom, but the Blue Tower looks straight down onto

445

it. I was very nervous, Inspector, after all they had cared for my Emerald for twenty-six years.'

'Quite understandable,' said Gablecross sympathetically. 'And you used the code to get into the tower?'

'Yes, definitely, but I may not have shut the door, I was so anxious to run downstairs and welcome them.'

'What time was that?'

'Around half past six.'

'That's very valuable evidence.'

David Pulborough was hopping. As someone who regarded paintings as expensive commodities and who fought for his commission as fiercely as any Bond Street crone selling Zandra Rhodes, he had never understood the Belvedons' obsession with the Raphael. But had he overplayed his hand? Had he galvanized Raymond into taking his own painting, knowing it was looted and he could pass it on to Si who would probably pay him the full whack without bothering about provenance? Or could the old fool really not bear to part with it? And what the hell was Anthea rabbiting to Gablecross about?

Raymond wandered distractedly up and down. Jupiter was making lists of people to ring first thing, Jonathan was sketching everyone. Alizarin gazed moodily into space. Geraldine was looking through the *Art Newspaper* for references to herself. Somerford was discussing Raphaels with Si, who'd put his dinner jacket over Rosemary Pulborough, asleep on the window seat beside him. Visitor, impossibly rotund from finishing up other people's dinners, but aware of tension and distress, laid his fat paw on as many knees as possible. Diggory had gone hunting. Grenville the greyhound, tranked up to the eyeballs, lay cross-eyed in the corner. Sophy wished she had a tranquillizer for Emerald, who was shuddering convulsively.

The only person in a worse state was Sienna. How could she have slept with Zac? To wind people up, she and Jonathan had snogged endlessly in public. In private, unwilling to risk her getting pregnant, they had done everything, except go the whole hog. This had only occurred in her darkest dreams and she always woke up dying of shame. But now the citadel had fallen in a couple of minutes to the fiendishly manipulative Zac, who was now aware of her illicit passion. God knew what use he would make of it. Not to mention those moments when she'd believed him to be Jonathan, which had been the most wonderful of her life. She started to cry again.

'It was my last link with my mother.'

'I know, darling.' Jonathan ruffled her hair. 'But just stop going on about it.'

'Art theft is still dismissed as a gentleman's crime by the police,' said David pompously.

'Which means they certainly won't suspect you,' snapped Jonathan.

To his disappointment the police found nothing in Zac's room.

'There was a gun earlier, I swear it,' protested Sienna.

'And what were you doing in my room?' asked Zac bleakly.

Emerald was suddenly jolted out of her torpor. Running across the room, she viciously slapped Zac's face.

'You bastard,' she screamed, 'you bastard! No wonder you found Anthea so quickly. I told you my birth name was Rookhope, you'd probably looked at the cuttings, and knew it was Anthea's maiden name almost from the start. All you were after was your bloody picture. Well, you're too late, I'm glad someone's stolen it from under your nose.'

'I'm sorry.' For a second, a flicker of pity joined the finger marks reddening Zac's ashen face. 'Anyone who has learnt to hate as much as we have, can never love again.'

Emerald gazed at him aghast, gave a sob and fled from the room.

'We'd like a word with you, Mr Ansteig,' said Gablecross.

So it seemed would Anthea, when an hour and a half later she found Zac packing.

'You traitor,' she hissed. 'How dare you lead me on? How d'you think this makes me feel?'

'Well and truly fucked,' said Zac brutally. 'What have you done with my picture?'

'Ay haven't touched it.'

'I went up to the Blue Tower fifteen minutes after the fireworks started, and it was gone.'

51

Raymond's ability as a host was sorely taxed on Thursday morning. He was touched that Anthea had sobbed all night over the loss of the Raphael, but irked she had proved too inconsolable to get up in the morning. Neither Emerald nor Sienna emerged to help him. Mrs Robens, deeply huffy because Anthea had implied she, Robens and Knightie might have stolen the Raphael, had not come in to work. Somerford and Geraldine, who'd been anticipating Finnan haddock and kidneys sizzling in entrée dishes, had to make do with burnt croissants and instant coffee.

But nothing could dim their euphoria that they had been present at the theft of the decade, about which they could regale the art world for years to come. They were also flattered that the notoriously brusque and impatient Si Greenbridge, grateful no doubt to be relieved from that dreary Rosemary, had spent so much time with them – such a powerful contact and with such a murky reputation, probably also grateful they could provide him with an alibi.

Raymond, huddled over a cup of black coffee, was distraught.

'It's ironic how I had planned to give Pandora to the National Gallery.'

'Doubt if they'd have accepted it with such a dubious

provenance,' said Somerford nastily. 'How did you say you'd acquired it?'

Ian Cartwright joined them and, out of habit, forced down a bowl of cornflakes. After the very humiliating press he'd received when he'd been sacked and when Emerald had sought out Anthea, he was appalled to be gathered up into a further maelstrom of publicity. Now he was sober, he'd decided he didn't like the Belvedons one bit. He hated the way they'd sniped at Emerald, and although Raymond seemed a nice chap, one couldn't trust a fellow with so many books.

They had been invited to meet the natural parents of their adopted daughter, he told Gablecross tersely. He had never heard of the picture, and had no idea it was in the house, nor had his wife. He was furious with Patience for being sick and pleased she was being punished by a brain-crushing hangover.

A knock on her bedroom door made Patience moan even louder.

'C-c-ome in.'

It was Dora bearing fizzing Resolve.

'Try and keep it down, Mrs Cartwright.'

'Oh, dear child, thank you. Is it true a valuable picture's been stolen?'

'It's so annoying.' Dora collapsed on Patience's bed. 'I fell asleep in Loofah's shed waiting until the fireworks ended in case he was frightened. I didn't wake up till this morning and my parents never came looking for me. I can't decide whether to ring Children in Need or the press. Can I come and stay with you in London? Sophy and I caught Hanna and my brother Alizarin snogging, which won't please my brother Jupiter.'

Nor can it have pleased poor darling Sophy, thought Patience.

Sophy had spent most of the night trying to comfort a demented Emerald, who had wept that she felt completely isolated.

'Mummy's passed out. Daddy's completely spooked.

Raymond's out to lunch, Anthea's bawling her head off. I'm sure something went on between her and Zac. Four useless parents. Zac was more of a father than any of them. I love him so much, Soph, and before we came to this house, he was mine, and now he's gone.'

I love Alizarin so much, thought Sophy as she wearily patted Emerald's shoulders, and he was never mine and now he's gone too.

Ian was champing to escape from this hell-hole, so Emerald had to get up and drive him and the rest of the family back to London. Raymond, practically in tears, was the only person to wave them off in the pouring rain.

'So sorry it turned out like this. I'm afraid Anthea's too upset to say goodbye. You will come back this evening, won't you, Emerald darling, Anthea's going to need you,' which didn't please Patience and Ian very much.

'Could I possibly say goodbye to Alizarin?' asked a blushing Sophy.

'I'm afraid he's working, so's Sienna. I'll give them your love.'

Sienna, sobbing with rage, was painting horses who'd been imprisoned for forty-eight hours without food or water in airless jolting lorries, portraying them as a tangle of broken limbs. Alizarin was painting a so-called 'Free Zone' in Kosovo: thousands of people, their white faces in stark contrast to their colourful clothes, peering hopelessly through the wire netting of a refugee camp.

Hearing a car storming so furiously through the puddles the spray splashed his window, Alizarin looked out. Catching the briefest blurred glimpse of blond hair and a doleful pink face, he wondered if he was seeing tears or raindrops.

* * *

Inspector Gablecross had murderers, rapists and paedophiles to catch. Realizing regretfully that he would be able to spare little time looking for the Raphael, he dropped in on his wise old friend, Lily Hamilton, with whom he shared a passion for racing.

Approaching River Cottage, Gablecross admired the dark red roses, pale yellow hollyhocks, and first pink phlox fighting for space in her front garden. He also smiled at the teddy bears massed on the back ledge of her ancient Triumph and the large stuffed badger called Douglas secured by a safety belt in the passenger seat.

A hazardous driver – 'Lily never misses a truck,' her nephew Jonathan was fond of saying – she had only retained her licence because of her popularity with the local constabulary. It also drove Anthea crackers that Knightie and the Robenses were always doing extra hours for nothing because Lily gave them cake and sympathy and insisted they sat down and watched racing or exciting bits of *Kilroy* or *Richard and Judy* with her. Lily had inherited from her mother oodles of Irish charm, which the English often dismiss as calculation, but which actually stems from an intensely kind and enquiring heart.

Having been married to a diplomat for nearly thirty years, she had furnished the cottage from all over the world. Watercolours of the Bosporus and the Italian Lakes, African masks and Indian ivory rubbed shoulders with paintings by her nieces and nephews. It was such a relaxed household that all the books had taken off their jackets. On the window ledge were binoculars for birdwatching. A vase of wild flowers, another passion, were dropping their petals on a side table.

Despite getting 'high as a coot' last night and falling in the pond on the way home, Lily had been up since six and didn't feel eleven o'clock was too early to open a half-bottle of champagne which she was sharing with her nephew Dicky, who was averting his eyes from one of Sienna's nudes of Lily, proudly displayed above a red-lacquered upright piano.

'Police are bound to think I took the Raphael,' Dicky was saying gloomily, 'because of my debts. It's going to take me a hundred years to pay the fête committee back for Alizarin's painting. And I got such a lousy report, I'll never get a job when I grow up.' He turned pale when he saw Gablecross. 'I'd better go. Mum might be worried about me.'

'Some hope,' snorted Lily as he scuttled out.

Gablecross refused a glass of champagne but, when she returned from the kitchen, having made him toast with black cherry jam, Lily emptied a miniature brandy into his cup of coffee.

'Ta very much.' Gablecross couldn't get up from the sofa because Lily's vast white cat, Brigadier, was sprawled across his lap, purring thunderously.

'What d'you reckon on last night?' he asked Lily, who poured the remains of the half-bottle into her glass, and lit a cheroot.

'I don't know,' she sighed. 'Rosemary Pulborough rang me first thing. Evidently it was her busybodying little husband who told Raymond all London was saying the Raphael was stolen.

'I cannot understand this fuss about looted art.' She shook her head. 'Raymond rescued the Raphael from a burning château. When I rescued Brigadier' – she smiled fondly at her cat who was covering Gablecross's dark blue trousers with white fur – 'he was as thin as a rake and terrified of everything. There's no way I'd ever give him back. People make such a fuss about the SS too, but it was rather like being in the Guards.

'Oh well, I'm old,' she grumbled as Gablecross raised an eyebrow, 'I'm allowed to be unpolitically correct.'

'Any idea who might have taken it?'

'None,' said Lily firmly. 'Gypsies were camped on the wild-flower meadow last night. Million pounds' worth of art in their possession.'

'This looks like an inside job, made to look like a burglary.' Gablecross bit into a folded piece of toast. 'Footsteps under windows, doors to secret passages left open.'

'Would you still prosecute?' Lily took a thoughtful sip of champagne.

'Probably not, if the thief could be persuaded to return it. On the other hand,' he went on, licking jam off his fingers, 'that American, Zachary Ansteig, who claims it's his, will probably press charges. In America, the fine for that could be half a million dollars, or five years inside. We're not so hot on looted art in the UK, but it could be nasty.'

'Could be an act of defiance,' Lily mused. 'Whole family been upended by Emerald's arrival – such a confused child.'

'Si Greenbridge and Somerford Keynes can provide alibis for each other,' said Gablecross.

'Both could have paid someone else to steal it,' suggested Lily. 'Somerford's boyfriend's a burglar; I should think Mr Greenbridge is dripping with unsavoury friends. Rosemary wouldn't bother to steal it, she's got her own money. David could easily have taken it. As Jonathan walked me home, I remember seeing the little weasel creeping back from the direction of the Old Rectory.' Then, as Gablecross made a note: 'He could be in league with Anthea, very keen on each other over the years. She's also keen on Zachary Ansteig; I saw her slipping her cradle-snatching hand into his as they walked up from the boathouse.'

'Pretty woman,' sighed Gablecross.

'I thought you had better taste,' said Lily tartly. 'Pretty frightful mother, and if anything happened to Raymond, she'd have me out of here in a trice.

'Jupiter could have taken it for the insurance, he's very greedy, and hot on his rights,' she continued. 'Jonathan and Alizarin are chronically short of money. Jonathan spends it as fast as he makes it. It's just the sort of prank he'd enjoy, never dreaming Jupiter'd call the police.'

'What about the punk one? She was hysterical.'

'Sienna's a darling, just mixed up. As the rumour was circulating that the picture was looted, any of the family might have taken it to stop it going back to its original owner, such is their affection.'

'And Jupiter's wife?'

'Terribly unhappy, Jupiter keeps her very short, marriage is very rocky. Jupiter's bats about Emerald. He can't sleep, prowls around his cottage at three in the morning.'

Bird-watching isn't the only thing you use those binoculars for, thought Gablecross, then he said, 'The popular view is that Ansteig and Emerald are in it together.'

'I'm sure not. He was using her. Deeply humiliating for someone that beautiful to be used.'

'What about the Cartwrights?'

'Certainly not. Utterly straight and couldn't have known about the Raphael unless Zac had tipped them off, and there is clearly no love lost between them and Zac. Ian Cartwright detests him. Terrified he's going to marry Emerald.'

'Ansteig's a very tough customer,' said Gablecross. 'Admitted he was poised to nick it himself, then someone pre-empted him. Wouldn't tell me how he took those photographs of the picture.'

'More coffee?' Lily heaved herself out of her chair. 'No, don't get up. House rule: if you've got a cat on your lap, you stay put.'

For someone who was supposed to have been so plastered she fell in the pond, Lily had picked up an awful lot, thought Gablecross. Her eyes and skin were clear. She showed no evidence of a hangover. Perhaps she and Jonathan were in cahoots.

'D'you know how to get into the Blue Tower?' he asked.

'I should do,' Lily laughed, 'I lost my virginity up there.'

'What about the servants?' enquired a rather pink Gablecross. 'Mr Robens was sent to get more wine from the cellar during dinner. Could he have flicked off the alarm?'

'Wouldn't blame him, Anthea pays them such piddling wages. But I think Knightie and the Robenses are far too scared of Galena's ghost, particularly at midnight, to risk going up to the Blue Tower.'

Lily picked up her binoculars. Now the sun had come out, the glare from the river was blinding.

'I saw a kingfisher last week. Oh good, here's Rosemary, I told her to drop in.'

The wind had whipped up the colour in Rosemary's pale cheeks, her eyes sparkled and a beautiful Art Nouveau silver daffodil gleamed on the lapel of her rather dreary brown suit.

'What excitement,' she cried, putting a bottle of Sancerre and a box of cheese straws down on the table. 'I've just seen Green Jean in the village shop, so outraged she missed the fun last night, she couldn't look me in the eye. Green Jean's our vicar's wife, Inspector, always raiding people's dustbins and inveighing against disposable nappies and unrecycled envelopes. She's worse than Visitor. Talk of the devil,' she giggled as Visitor waddled in. 'Hello, darling. Just in time for these cheese straws.' She tore at the cellophane with her teeth.

'Have you been drinking?' asked Lily.

Rosemary shook her head, then, to the amazement of her listeners: 'I think Si Greenbridge is the nicest man I've ever met. He's just sent me an e-mail asking me and Virty Cartwright to Le Manoir.'

'Did he give you that brooch? I'm sure I've seen it before.'

'No, Geraldine did.' Rosemary went off into peals of laughter. 'Before my husband tackled your brother on the subject of looted Raphaels, Lily, he obviously whisked Geraldine home for a quickie and the silly old bat left her lovely brooch on my bedside table as a tip.'

For the rest of Thursday, police interviewed suspects and sifted through the evidence. The theft had been too late for the nationals, but they had moved in in force by Thursday lunchtime, whereupon a devastated Raymond plied them with tea and Mrs Robens's fudge cake, and begged them to help him find his Raphael.

On Friday morning Jupiter had a terrible shock. Convinced the police would take little further action beyond placing the Raphael on the Art Loss Register, he was looking forward to a massive payout from the insurance company. He was therefore insane with rage to discover that Raymond, perhaps nervous of setting off alarm bells, hadn't raised the valuation on the Raphael since the early Sixties when he had insured it for only £80,000. This meant that the insurance company, who only bothered with pictures worth more than £100,000, would now make no attempt to trace it. Jupiter could have throttled Raymond, but for the moment his priority was to find Pandora and prove she wasn't Zac's.

Suspicion was in fact hardening on Zac, when the frame of the Raphael, covered in his fingerprints, was found in the rushes by the pond. Zac, however, had vanished. So had Sienna, Emerald and Jonathan. Ignoring police requests to stay put, they had all dispersed north, south, east and west like Lars Porsena's messengers.

To escape Jupiter's icy rage, Raymond fled to London. Anthea, having lied that she had left the Blue Tower door open at six-thirty on Wednesday night, was panicking that the police might pick up clues that she'd been in bed earlier with Zac. Longing for someone to blame, she turned her fury on Alizarin.

'I'm sure he's involved,' she spluttered to Jupiter. 'He

told the police that during the fireworks he fetched a tranquillizer for Visitor from the Lodge. He could easily have borrowed one of Grenville's tablets and everyone knows Visitor hasn't a nerve in his podgy body.'

Alizarin, in fact, had been with Hanna, whom he'd spent most of the fireworks comforting. Alas, Jupiter had been informed by an indignant Dora that she'd found Hanna and Alizarin in a steamy clinch.

'We'd better tackle him before Dad gets home,' he said grimly. Envy and Avarice, red in tooth and claw, he and Anthea belted down to the Lodge. They found Alizarin working on his Free Zone picture, laboriously painting in each despairing face with the aid of a vast magnifying glass.

'What a mess!' Anthea gazed round the studio in horror. 'And when are you going to cut down those nettles?'

'They provide sanctuary for the peacock butterfly. I'm surprised Emerald isn't seeking refuge there.'

'Don't be cheeky.' Anthea's mood was not improved by a hauntingly beautiful portrait of Zac propped against the wall. A forgotten beef sandwich was gathering flies on the window ledge. Anthea shuddered.

'What d'you want?' demanded Alizarin. 'I haven't got any drink.'

'You spent a long time with Zac on Tuesday night,' snapped Jupiter, 'did he ask you about the Raphael?'

'He said he was looking for it.'

'Why didn't you warn us?' screeched Anthea.

'It was the guy's picture, for God's sake.'

'It bloody isn't,' exploded Jupiter. 'I suppose you tipped him off.'

'I told him he was getting warm. We've got all this.' Alizarin waved his paintbrush in the direction of Foxes Court. 'His family lost everything.'

'How dare you! If he's got nothing, how can he afford all those designer clothes and the jetting around?' exploded Anthea. 'And what right have you to talk about

458

what we've got? Who pays for your Health Service, your dole money, your libraries? Your father does with his taxes. You don't contribute a thing. How dare you take this moralizing tone. I know Raymond slips you a bit. You're thirty-five, for God's sake, not fifteen. Just get out, you disgusting bum.'

At last she could get her hands on the Lodge for holiday lets.

'You lost us the Raphael,' said Jupiter. 'Have you no idea how tough things are at the gallery? Anthea's right. If you had any integrity, you'd pack your bags and get out.'

Alizarin was too proud to protest. But after they'd gone he hugged Visitor in terror. He looked round at his pictures which he'd painted with such love but still the world hadn't liked them. He watched the moon slowly turn from gold to silver, and thought how lovely it would have been to grow old with Sophy and see her blond hair go grey, then found that he was crying.

In the morning he was gone, taking only Galena's palette, the Etienne de Montigny drawing of her, half a dozen canvasses, and Visitor. He left enough money to pay the milkman, Visitor's vet's bills, and for Knightie to put flowers on Galena's grave.

Raymond was horrified to hear when he got back from London that Alizarin had moved out. Why had the Raphael and all his children deserted him? Anthea replied that Alizarin had confessed to tipping off Zac about the picture. She then lied that, after a row, Alizarin had gone of his own accord.

'Just the sort of kick up the backside an artist needs,' she kept saying as she despatched all Alizarin's pictures and Galena's furniture to damp and draughty out-buildings. 'Ridiculous living at home at thirty-five, he'll be grateful one day.'

One of the first tasks of the workmen renovating the Lodge for holiday lets was to paint the walls Alizarin had used as canvasses. Dora and Dicky were devastated by his departure and they particularly missed Visitor. Who would finish up the food they didn't like? Who would there be for Diggory to boss or to comfort poor nervous Grenville?

Dora retaliated by scrawling in lipstick all over the hall wallpaper, and being pronounced as 'thoroughly disturbed' and 'in need of a psychiatrist' by Anthea.

'I'm going to divorce my mother,' raged Dora to Harriet of the *Independent*. 'I'll give you all the dirt if you pay for some new hall wallpaper.'

'We can't afford that.'

'I'll go to the *Sun*.'

'Oh, all right then.'

Jupiter would have felt more guilty about evicting Alizarin if Hanna hadn't flipped when she heard the news. Packing her bags, she had gone off to stay with her mother in Norway.

An enraged Jupiter had visions of Alizarin joining her there. But first things first. Feeling it more important to retrieve the Raphael than his wife, Jupiter flew to Geneva. Here he headed for the Free Port, a VAT-exempt zone, full of safe deposits stuffed with cash, valuables and pictures. He prayed one of the family might have thrust Pandora into the Belvedon vault, but when he arrived, he found nothing but David Pulborough and one of his clients, a Russian Mafia thug called Minsky Kraskov, sniffing around on their way to the Hermitage.

52

Jonathan, convinced that Zac and Si were in league, rang *Mercury*, the New York art magazine for which Zac was allegedly working, and discovered that although he had never written for them, the group was owned by Si.

Determined to find out more about Zac and the fate of the Raphael before 1944 when it fell into Raymond's hands, Jonathan flew to Vienna in early August. At Emerald's birthday dinner, Zac had let slip that his great-grandfather had owned a house in a street called Schwindgasse. Hoping for a slum, Jonathan was irritated to find the street lined with beautiful faded ochre houses with balconies and large gardens in one of the oldest, most charming parts of Vienna. At the end of the street was the Schwarzenberg Palace, a splendid baroque pile in its own park, flanking lovely public gardens.

Jonathan got no joy either from the old house or Zac's family. The present owner, a sleek blonde, initially charmed by Jonathan's helpless smile and melting dark eyes, admitted that a Jewish family had lived there before the war, but clearly didn't wish to enlarge on the speed with which they'd been turfed out. As if weeping for their plight, huge drops of rain suddenly poured out of the dark grey clouds above. As Vienna was in the grip of a punishing heatwave, Jonathan revelled in the impromptu cold shower.

Splashing happily up streets named after Goethe, Mahler and Schubert, past theatres, a sculpture by Henry Moore, and the ice-green dome of the great Charles Cathedral, he paused to listen to the joyful din of the Vienna Philharmonic rehearsing for tonight's concert. On all sides were museums and galleries, many of them showing one of Jonathan's favourite artists, Gustav Klimt, whose ornate gilded portraits of *femmes fatales* had outraged turn-of-the-century Vienna. The whole area, in fact, was the perfect setting for an enlightened bourgeois Jewish family steeped in the arts. Tomorrow, vowed Jonathan, he'd go on a Klimt crawl. Today he had more urgent plans and splashed on until he reached the spot on the corner of Singer Strasse and Kärtner Strasse where Zac's Great-uncle Jacob's gallery had stood in the shadow of Vienna's other great cathedral, St Stephen's. Bombed to rubble by the Allies, the splendid old building had been replaced by shops and a block of flats.

Jonathan was about to seek out the porter, when his heart turned a double somersault. For there, drenched, dressed entirely in black, blown against the front door like a poplar leaf, was his own *femme fatale*.

Fortunately, he had plenty of time to regain his cool. So great was Emerald's self-absorption, she didn't even seem surprised to see him.

'I hoped I'd find Zac here, not you,' she sobbed. 'Maybe he never loved me, but I can't stop loving him. I know I'm going to end up an old maid. Sophy's bound to marry early, she's always had low standards. Anthea married at twenty. Even Mummy, who looks like a horse, got a husband by the time she was twenty-four. I always vowed I'd be married by the time I was twenty-seven – and that's less than a year to go. I know I'm going to be left on the shelf.'

'Can I break into this explosion of shelf-pity?' interrupted Jonathan, who was having difficulty keeping a straight face. 'By telling you the word "Raphael" means

"God heals" in Hebrew, so you're going to be OK. And you don't want to be a bride anyway, white truly isn't your colour.'

'Oh shut up, you've just rolled up to be objectionable.'

She had reddened eyes and a red nose, like a Vick's advertisement; her scraped-back hair had crinkled in the downpour. She looked quite plain, which cheered Jonathan immensely. He felt much more able to carry out his game plan.

'What are you doing here?' she demanded.

'Working – and hoping to find out more about the Raphael.' He held out his hand. 'Let's start again. Brother and sister. Did you know that "yes" and "no" mean the same in Vienna? No wonder Zac was dodgy.'

'Don't take the piss,' grumbled Emerald, but she stopped crying. 'I haven't got anywhere to stay.'

To win her confidence, convinced, like Jupiter, she wasn't his sister, Jonathan booked her into the room next to his at his hotel, which was in a quiet street, and overlooked an ivy-clad courtyard at the back, 'So you can't grumble about traffic keeping you awake. I expect you'd like to unpack and get out of those sopping clothes, then we'll explore the city.'

And what a breathtaking city it was. Each building seemed to celebrate the rampant hedonism of the Viennese. On every ledge pomegranates spilt, leaves sprouted, cherubs gambolled, muscular giants wrestled, horses reared up, heraldic lions raised paws.

'You feel a worship of the Imperial past almost amounting to necrophilia,' said Jonathan as they dined that evening in a stunning restaurant housed in the Schwarzenberg Palace overlooking the park and flood-lit fountains. Emerald for once was starving and was soon tucking into lobster cooked in Chablis sauce to be followed by pigeon cassoulet. Jonathan, who'd seemed awash with cash, had ordered Dom Pérignon, followed by a matchless bottle of red, and was clearly pulling the stops out in preparation for the great pass later, Emerald decided. But his behaviour puzzled her; usually so tactile, he hadn't laid a finger on her, except grabbing her to prevent her being mowed down by a lorry when she forgot that Austrians drove on the right. The Dom Pérignon was also his first drink of the day. There was colour in his normally pale cheeks, his eyes were clear and the bags beneath them as well as his gut had nearly disappeared.

Looking gorgeous on purpose, just to tempt me, she thought crossly.

'Why did you paint me as Pandora?'

'Because Pandora means "all gifted" and because, according to Hesiod, she was the most beautiful woman the Gods could invent.' Then, as Emerald smirked, he added, 'But she was also a silly trivial Nosy Parker, who couldn't resist opening a box she shouldn't and wrecking everyone's lives.'

'Did I really screw things up for your family?' asked Emerald, appalled.

'Totally, but in the end it may shake down for the good.'

'I couldn't help it.' Defiantly she clashed her knife and fork together, telling Jonathan he had ruined her appetite. 'They say it takes a major crisis to force adopted people to seek out their real parents. We lost our wonderful house in Yorkshire, all my stability and roots gone in a trice.' Her green eyes welled with tears.

'Sophy told me you loathed the house in Yorkshire and never went there. Now eat up your lobster and don't be silly.'

'The bitch, how dare Sophy?'

Jonathan put his head on one side.

'Emer*ald*,' he said gently.

For a second she glared at him, then, to his amazement, she laughed. 'Well, perhaps I did loathe it, but I liked it as a status symbol.'

'Good girl.' Delighted at such a concession, Jonathan

patted her shoulders. But when she arched against him, provocative as a cat, he steeled himself to whip his hand away.

By the time he'd settled the massive bill it was approaching midnight, but Jonathan suddenly seemed in a hurry to get home.

'He's going to pounce,' thought Emerald, churning in terror and excitement as she pounded the pavements after him.

Her fears were confirmed when he collected both their hotel keys and bundled her into the creaking Art Deco lift. Feeling his wine-flavoured breath lifting her hair and warming her forehead, she rammed herself against her side of the lift. But having opened her bedroom door for her, Jonathan bid her a swift goodnight.

'I'm off to watch the porn channel. You get five free minutes a night, and if you run them together at midnight, you can get ten minutes on the trot. See you in the morning.' And to Emerald's chagrin, he merely pecked her on the cheek and shot into his room.

As the days passed he continued to behave in the same kind, sober but utterly brotherly fashion. Together they explored the cathedrals, the galleries, bought oysters in the market, ate far too much rich chocolate cake with apricot jam, wandered through the Vienna woods and went to the Vienna Phil in the evenings.

They also sketched each other incessantly. Jonathan disappeared a lot to delve around in dusty archives, not letting on to Emerald he was investigating Zac's past as much as that of the Raphael.

At the end of the second week, Emerald started panicking she hadn't got her period.

'I know I'm pregnant, and Zac's the father,' she stormed. 'I'm not going to be a single parent like Anthea, it'd ruin my life. Where can I get an abortion?

You're bound to know a good doctor,' she added nastily.

Jonathan looked at her meditatively.

'Dear, dear, dear, how can you be so dismissive of Anthea giving you up as a baby, when you're not prepared to give yours even a chance?'

Emerald flushed.

'Look what an awful life I've had. It would have been better if I hadn't been born.'

'It would have saved everyone a lot of earache. See you this evening.'

It irritated the hell out of Emerald that Jonathan's friends were always ringing or texting him. Jonathan, in turn, was ashamed how jealous he felt when he learnt that David Pulborough was giving Trafford a big show next year and Trafford had also been shortlisted for a big prize for his video of a masturbating granny entitled *Oh Nan.* Jonathan vowed to stop squandering his talents, but all he wanted to do was to paint Emerald as they sat for hours in cafés or wine bars trying out bottles of the new vintage.

'According to Giacometti,' he told her, 'who spent weeks painting members of his family, "The adventure, the great adventure, is to see something unknown appear each day in the same face."'

And as the days passed, and yellow leaves began to cover the parks, and cold clear air could be felt again coming off the mountains, Jonathan noticed the little brackets on either side of Emerald's mouth when she smiled, and the red patch in the left hollow of her nose, which she tried to cover with concealer, and the yearning melancholy in her eyes, which softened to sage green when she was caught off guard.

Bored with his curls one day, Jonathan had them cut off.

'Trying to look more like Zac,' Emerald was horrified to hear herself snapping, but only because she was so jolted by the beauty of his forehead and temples and the strength and grace of his newly revealed jaw and neck.

'Sorry, that was bitchy,' she moaned, 'I'm only frantic about not coming on. I need some Prozac.'

'You need some anti-Zac,' drawled Jonathan, 'you're just suffering from PMT.'

Predictably, when her period arrived the next day, Emerald made a fearful fuss about having desperately wanted Zac's child.

'At least I'd have something to remember him by.'

'Don't be fatuous,' snapped Jonathan, 'you've got what you wanted.'

'You've no idea how important it is for adopted children to have their first blood relation. And I'm so late I've run out of Tampax. Jonathan, *Jonathan*,' but he had walked out, slamming the door.

Returning twenty minutes later, he found her in tears and chucked a packet of Tampax on the bed.

'Here you are. A long stop between two short legs.'

'My legs are *not* short and I've got the most terrible cramps.'

Jonathan flicked on the kettle and filled a hot-water bottle, then he got a little bottle of gin out of the mini-bar. Having emptied it into a glass, he added tonic.

'Don't need lemon, you're quite sour enough.'

'Why are you so vile to me?' moaned Emerald as he tucked her up in bed and gently began to rub her rigid tummy. 'Aaah, that's so nice. How d'you know so much about women?'

'I had to try and be a mother to Sienna. Poor darling had her first period at ten. Anthea hadn't bothered to tell her about them. Jupiter, Al and I were all away at school when it happened. Sienna came screaming out of the loo convinced she was bleeding to death. Mrs Robbie had to cope. I know Sienna can be difficult, and it's debatable whether she or Anthea have given each other the harder time,' he added, his hands kneading and caressing away the pain, 'but her life's been pretty good hell.'

The gin was kicking in. Jonathan noticed Emerald's eyelashes, lying on her blanched cheek like ragged rooks' wings.

Oh, please make his hands creep downwards or upwards, Emerald was shocked to find herself praying, as sleep rolled over her. When she woke, Jonathan was gone and it was dark outside. Under her door he'd shoved a drawing of her on her deathbed and underneath had written, *Period Peace*.

When Jonathan returned long after midnight to his room, a page of Emerald's sketchpad had been shoved under his door. On it was an exquisite drawing of Christ with Jonathan's features, complete with halo and Diggory under his arm, instead of a lamb. Underneath, Emerald had written, *Self Portrait by Jonathan Belvedon*.

Jonathan could hear her television on next door, and instead of watching the porn channel, he poured himself a large whisky, and lay on his bed smoking and gazing into space. He wished Diggory were here to cheer him up. Who the hell could have taken the Raphael?

He left the hotel in the morning without making contact, but when he returned he found all his clothes had been beautifully washed and ironed with a note on top: 'Sorry I've been a complete cow. At least I've learnt the Austrian for launderette.'

Emerald felt herself in more and more of a muddle.

'Do you find me attractive?' she demanded.

'Quite,' said Jonathan, then, when she looked boot-faced, he smiled and added: 'Quite exceptionally attractive.'

But he made no pass. It was like living with a vegetarian wolf. And as August moved into September, she found herself increasingly drawn to him, and when he vanished to his archives, she missed him dreadfully.

One warm afternoon, he took her to the Central Cemetery, another splendid park where two and a half million people are buried, and where the Viennese come to walk, chat, and feed the squirrels and sparrows.

'Only when you're dead in Vienna have you really made it,' explained Jonathan, who was watching the exquisite shadows dappling the tawny leaves scattered on the grass as the tree ceiling grew thinner.

In the musicians' graveyard, they found buried many of the great composers: Johann Strauss, father and son, Beethoven and Brahms. Jonathan drew Emerald's attention to a lichened monument, which showed a bespectacled Schubert arriving in heaven, bewildered that a smiling angel was laying a laurel wreath on his dishevelled curls.

'Needs a haircut like yours,' mocked Emerald.

'Schubert never got any recognition during his lifetime,' said Jonathan, 'he had to wait till he got to heaven, like Alizarin probably will.'

Glancing round, he saw tears, for once not of frustration nor self-pity, filling Emerald's eyes.

'That is so sad. Is Alizarin that good?'

'One day he'll be regarded as one of the greats of all time.'

'So could you be,' protested Emerald, suddenly serious.

'Me?' said Jonathan in amazement.

'You just squander your talent and fool around.'

She looked so sweet and fierce, he had to clench his fists not to take her in his arms.

Instead, gazing at the miles of graves, he said, 'Terrifying how many people are alleged to be buried alive. It's rumoured the Viennese used to have a rope inside the coffin attached to a bell, so they could alert the outside world.'

Then, when Emerald shivered, he added, 'Tomorrow we're going to visit the Von Trapps' house.'

'How fabulous,' squealed Emerald, *'The Sound of Music*'s easily my favourite film.'

'I know it is.'

'How?'

'Because it's Anthea's too.'

Sometimes they discussed what had happened to the Raphael.

'What were you doing during the fireworks?'

'Taking Lily home, she fell in the pond.'

'Are you sure it wasn't you that fell in the pond? You were drenched when you got back to the house.'

'I've always been wet.'

'Don't be silly. The frame of the Raphael was found in the rushes. Are you sure you didn't nick it as a practical joke? And how come you're so cash rich now?'

'I had a good win at the casino,' said Jonathan blithely. 'Actually, I've almost run out.' He glanced at her sideways. 'I've got to go back to London to finish Dame Hermione in time for the Commotion Exhibition.'

'When are you leaving?' gasped Emerald.

'Tomorrow. The next day.'

She really minds, he thought in ecstasy as the colour drained from Emerald's face. His backing-off had worked.

'Bloody Jupiter,' she stormed, 'if he'd paid me for that head, we could have stayed another week.'

On the last night, they went to their favourite restaurant in the Schwarzenberg Palace overlooking the park. Watched by everyone, they were oblivious of everything except each other.

'I don't want to go back to London,' moaned Emerald.

'D'you remember the first time we danced, I kissed you and you slapped my face?' asked Jonathan.

'You were so drunk, I nearly knocked you over.'

'What did you think of me?'

'That you were an irrelevance, all I could think about was confronting Anthea.'

Jonathan couldn't prevent his hand reaching out to stroke her face, but just managed to turn it into a summons for the bill.

As they wandered home guided by a huge gold moon floating above the green domes, the rearing horses and the floodlit goddesses, Emerald asked, 'Why were you so gratuitously bloody to me at my birthday party?'

'I thought Dad had given you the Raphael to make up for being adopted and not brought up by him and Anthea. It was the sort of stupid, quixotic thing . . .'

'You were panic stricken about losing your inheritance.'

Jonathan's head was bowed, his face in darkness.

'Well?'

'I was panicking that if you became that rich, Zac the fortune-hunter wouldn't be able to resist marrying you.'

'What a bloody horrible thing to say.'

'I was so terrified of losing you,' muttered Jonathan.

'W-what?'

Emerald was so busy gazing at him in disbelief that she tripped over a paving stone. Jonathan caught her and she melted into his arms, pleading: 'Please, please kiss me,' then, when he didn't, trying to make a joke of it: 'I t-t-thought sisters were your speciality.'

Jonathan shoved her roughly away, throwing back his head, banging his clenched fists against his chest.

'I am not laying a finger on you until you have that DNA test.'

'Why are you so sure I'm not a Belvedon?'

'Because I can't bear you to be,' he said despairingly.

He took her face between his hands, caressing her cheekbones with his thumbs, watching the silvery light playing on her adorably bewildered face.

'I've loved you since the moment you walked into the marquee at Dad and Anthea's silver wedding party,' he whispered, 'but I know too how important it is for adopted children to have their own kids. I've also screwed up one sister by getting too close to her. The moment you've had that test and proved you're not my sister' – his voice broke – 'I'll never let you go again.'

Full of hope, they returned to England.

53

Sienna, meanwhile, had been in Rome and Florence, gazing at Raphaels, wrestling with her demons. In mid-September she returned to the East End to work and in early October flew to New York where the Commotion Exhibition, which had earlier in the year outraged and excited the British public, was about to go on show.

Three huge rooms of the highly prestigious Greychurch Museum off Madison Avenue had been given over to eighty-four exhibits by forty young British artists. Among the most outrageous were not only Sienna's installations, *Tampax Tower* and *Aunt Hill*, but also *Millennium Buggers*, in which, as promised, Jonathan had included Casey Andrews, Somerford Keynes, his brother Jupiter, and a number of Tory grandees whom Jupiter was wooing. A large alcove had been set aside for Jonathan's installation of Dame Hermione Harefield, which was due to be flown in at any minute.

There was great excitement about Trafford's gay rights statement, which showed a gigantic puckered anus surrounded by a halo, entitled *Assholier Than Thou*. At the last moment, Sienna, on her animal rights soapbox, had also contributed *Slaughterhouse*, an incredibly powerful painting of an abattoir, showing fat businessmen hanging upside down from a conveyor belt, having their throats cut and slowly bleeding to death. Sienna would have preferred to tackle the

473

subject as a moving installation, but time had been too short.

Arriving at the Greychurch, she found the usual eve-of-preview scraps going on: artists grumbling that their work was in the wrong place, badly lit or improperly installed and querying whether security was tight enough.

'Who'd want to steal this shit anyway?' grumbled the guards, who were anticipating riots at the preview.

Having supervised the hanging of *Slaughterhouse*, Sienna dropped in on the ultra-cool Manhattan Gallery, owned by Adrian Campbell-Black, Rupert's younger brother, who was also an old friend of Raymond. Adrian's features were gentler than Rupert's, his hair light brown, his eyes pale grey, but he had the same Greek nose and olive skin without a trace of red, and the ability to turn a suit into a poem. Inside the gallery, arctic-white like an igloo, he was easily the prettiest thing, although the competition wasn't great, the only other occupant being a vast dung beetle cast in resin.

'No-one else but museums will buy that,' complained Sienna as she accepted a glass of wine.

'That's where you're wrong, darling.' Adrian had the same light, clipped voice as Rupert. 'I've sold three of those this week. Installations are so hot. In order to accommodate these massive excrescences, the rich are competing to build houses bigger than Buckingham Palace.'

'My brother Jonathan has done a twenty-foot nude sculpture of Dame Hermione with a door in front, so we can all climb inside.'

'That should do brilliantly.' Adrian ran a duster over the dung beetle's shoulder. 'They adore Dame Hermione here, she's singing *Arabella* at the Met tonight, first time back after the birth of her baby. Even though she's ten years too old for the part and about a hundred pounds too heavy, you can't get tickets for love nor money.' He shook with laughter, then confided:

'I'm rather into opera. The love of my life, a tenor called Baby Spinosissimo, is in the same production, he's gorgeous looking. His ex, Isa Lovell, is now working with Rupert and used to be married to Tabitha – our family is so incestuous.'

'Any news of the Raphael?' asked Sienna idly.

'Not a lot, despite massive publicity. I talked to Jupiter on the telephone last week, he says the police are no wiser and the entire family seem to have buggered off abroad.'

As Sienna paced restlessly round the room, Adrian noticed how tired and ill she looked, her face set and sullen, so marred by those rings and studs. She could be ravishing.

'You OK, duckie? You've lost a lot of weight.'

'I'm fine. Oh my goodness!' Flipping through the transparencies and polaroids on the desk, she was amazed to find they were of Alizarin's pictures.

'They're awesome,' admitted Adrian, 'like Galena's in their intense vitality and genius with light, but they're more intensely felt. I'm desperate to contact Alizarin about a show next year. Raymond says he's shoved off somewhere. Any idea where he might be?'

Sienna's joy at such recognition for Alizarin was short lived.

'Who set this up?'

'Zachary Ansteig.'

Zac's name was like a brand on her shoulders.

'He's crazy about them,' went on Adrian. 'Good thing the poor boy's got something to take his mind off the Raphael.'

'I must go.' Sienna leapt to her feet.

'Good luck with Commotion,' said Adrian. 'It's going to be huge. The moral majority are already sharpening their knives.'

'Nothing to Peking,' said Sienna as he opened the glass door for her. 'Some artist there has put a corpse on display.'

'We could always show Geraldine Paxton instead. Look after yourself, darling.'

Returning to the Cameron Hotel on Central Park South, into which all the Commotion artists had been booked, and which remarkably was still standing and had liquor left in the bar, Sienna was bitterly disappointed to find that Jonathan hadn't checked in. Instead, in her pigeon-hole, was a note from Slaney Watts, the Commotion publicity officer. The media were interested in Sienna's work. Could she make herself available for back-to-back interviews and photocalls tomorrow?

Sienna drooped. Having spent the last seven days and nights finishing *Slaughterhouse*, and having flown out early that morning, the last thing she felt up to was a media assault. In the bar she could see Trafford and other YBAs getting hammered. She'd better ring Alizarin before she joined them. But as she took out her mobile, everything was forgotten, for with the relentless prowl of the big cat ever on the hunt, Zac padded into the lobby. He was wearing a dark grey overcoat with the collar turned up and had lost his suntan, but his yellow eyes roved just as speculatively round the foyer.

Sienna had forgotten how fatally glamorous he was. She wanted to bolt into the lift. Then Zac saw her and smiled, and she was quite unable to stop herself stumbling towards him, and thanking him for helping Alizarin.

'No problem, guy's a genius.'

Oh, that deep, husky, caressing voice.

'How's Jonathan?' he added mockingly.

'Haven't a clue,' snapped a blushing Sienna. 'How's Emerald?'

'Haven't a clue.'

For a moment, they gazed at each other, assessing, wondering.

'My office is round the corner, come and have a drink.'

She had expected black leather sofas, pale grey walls and carpets, state-of-the-art computers, purring, ravishing PAs, the light raindrop patter of laptops, Jackson Pollocks on the walls.

She found one small, scruffy office, with internet access and fax machine. Tables, shelves and every surface groaned with books on Old Masters, art magazines and catalogues. On the peeling walls, blown up, were his photographs of *Pandora* and the other looted family paintings Zac was trying to trace. Under the desk, all over the floor were boxes and boxes of bound legal briefs and xeroxed documents from archives all over the world.

It was like a huntsman's tack room, and it smelt of dust and dedication. The only note of tenderness were faded photographs of a beautiful sad-eyed woman and a very dark, vividly handsome man.

'Mom and my Great-uncle Jacob,' said Zac, getting a bottle of red out of a filing cabinet.

Having poured her a drink, he listened to his messages in several languages and flipped through his faxes.

'Have you found the Raphael yet?' Sienna asked.

Zac shook his head.

'Trail's gone cold.'

'Not through want of trying.' She looked round the room.

'I guess not. I gather your brother's digging around in Vienna.'

'With Emerald,' said Sienna flatly.

'They deserve each other. What d'you want to do this evening?'

'I've been up since five, English time.'

'Can't go to bed till bedtime. Only way to get a decent night's sleep. Would you like to go to the Met?'

'You'll never get tickets. Adrian says it's a sell-out.'

'Want to bet?' Not taking his eyes off her face, Zac picked up the telephone.

Having secured two tickets in the stalls, he asked her if she wanted to nip back to the hotel and change, then, looking at his watch: 'You've got forty-five minutes.'

'Why should I?' she asked truculently.

'No reason at all,' grinned Zac. 'All eyes will be upon you.'

They were indeed, as, laughing his handsome head off, Zac led her into the lionhunting den of a diamond-encrusted black-tie audience. Sienna, who'd been temporarily distracted by the huge ravishing Chagalls on either side of the entrance, nearly died of embarrassment. She couldn't believe there could be so many variations on the little black dress. Scents swirled like the garden at Foxes Court in a heatwave.

'Why didn't you tell me it was a first night?' she hissed.

'You didn't ask,' murmured Zac. Because he was so spectacularly handsome, everyone looked to see who he was with, amazed that it should be someone quite so scruffy, with two spots, and rings and studs on her unpainted face, and an inch of dark root to her piled-up straw-blond hair, which had taken on a green tinge since Emerald's birthday party. Jonathan's pink shirt with the collar sawn off and ripped jeans completed the lack of picture.

Sienna tried to bolt, but Zac had her wrist in a vice. The bastard was still grinning as they settled into their seats.

'There's Adrian Campbell-Black waving from that box.' Zac waved back. 'Baby Spinosissimo's got a minor role as Matteo. An amazing Russian piss artist, Mikhail Bulgakov, is singing Mandryka. He and Baby detest Dame Hermione so it should be a riot.'

Then, conscious of Sienna's humiliation, he ran a finger down her gritted cheek.

'New York's obsessed with celebs,' he said gently. 'Once the Commotion opens, this entire audience will be at your feet. I know Strauss is a terrible old Nazi,' he added, almost apologetically, as he handed her a programme, 'but his music is to die for, and the story's set in Vienna.'

How strong his Viennese roots are, thought Sienna.

Thank God the huge chandeliers were dimming and retreating into the ceiling, and people wouldn't be able to see her any more. Emerald would have known how to dress, she thought savagely.

All her life, Sienna had heard opera, mostly Wagner, pouring out of her father's study, and treated it with indifference. She was amazed how much she enjoyed *Arabella*.

Dame Hermione, smug and resplendent, had only to raise an eyebrow to send the audience off into rapturous applause. Her voice was exquisite, her stage manners appalling, masking everyone, and singing so far to the front of the stage that the handsome Russian had practically to climb into the pit to sing back to her. In one duet, Sienna saw Hermione kicking him sharply on the ankle and in the half darkness found herself laughing as her eyes met Zac's.

'That's Adrian's boyfriend,' whispered Zac, pointing out the dashing, slightly decadent-looking Lieutenant, who was keen on Arabella's sister, and who'd just stamped deliberately on Dame Hermione's toes.

Finding too little room for his long thighs, Zac swung them towards Sienna. In panic she swung hers away. Even with jet lag, it was impossible to nod off next to a tiger, but she was soon enraptured by the swooningly beautiful music and the story in which, after a string of misunderstandings, true love triumphs, and Arabella ends up with her solid country squire.

As the bravos rang out, and pink carnations rained down, Zac caught one and handed it to Sienna.

'Hermione's going to be milking the applause for the next half-hour, let's go.'

In the taxi, Sienna asked why at the end Arabella had given Mandryka a glass of water.

'When a woman accepts a marriage proposal in Austria, instead of saying "yes", they traditionally present the guy with a glass of water from the well,' said Zac, adding drily, 'Must remind you of that boiling water you lured me into drinking at Foxes Court.'

'Hot water's your métier,' snapped Sienna. 'Where are we going?'

'To dinner, you've got to eat.' Then, when she protested: 'In the last act, your stomach was rumbling loud enough to drown the timps.'

54

Zac took her to the Four Seasons. Sienna was in despair. She'd always so longed to go there, and now she was rolling up like a tramp. The Four Seasons felt the same and refused to let her in because she was wearing jeans, so Sienna calmly unzipped and stepped out of them. Pulling Jonathan's pink shirt to halfway down her thighs, she handed the jeans to the gaping hat-check girl.

'Is that better?'

'Much,' said Zac approvingly.

The waiters were all over him. Many of the diners, including some very expensive-looking, pretty women, stopped to say 'Hi', no doubt wondering what he was doing with such a dog.

He obviously isn't short of money, decided Sienna as a bottle of spectacular Zinfandel arrived. Maybe she'd misjudged him and he really wanted to recover the Raphael for emotional rather than financial reasons. But she mustn't go soft. After the way he'd behaved, she had no reason to trust him. Unnerved, she took a huge gulp of wine.

'Drink it slowly,' chided Zac, then, as she tossed her head at the reproof: 'I'm Viennese of course, I believe wine, women and song should be enjoyed at a leisurely pace, particularly women.' Mockingly he looked into her eyes and then at her mouth.

That wasn't leisurely, that lightning-bolt coupling on the night of the fireworks, thought Sienna going scarlet. She felt a butterfly of desire flickering between her legs.

Drink on no food soon loosened her tongue, and she found herself telling Zac why she loved the Raphael so passionately.

'I was the only one of Mum's children who didn't lie in her arms and watch the sun rise on it. Somehow I had this fantasy about showing my own child . . .' Her voice trailed off. 'But it's not going to happen.'

She closed up when Zac pressed her on how Raymond had acquired the picture, countering by asking him how his great-grandfather had lost it. All the chattering happy diners around them faded to nothing as the terrible story unfolded.

'Why didn't they get out before Hitler moved in?' asked Sienna in horror.

'If you emigrated they only allowed you to take ten per cent of your belongings, kind of like Zimbabwe today. I guess they hoped things would improve.'

'What d'you think happened to the Raphael after the Nazis grabbed it?'

Zac examined his untouched glass of white.

'I figure it was seized by Goering, the fat fucker had eight huge houses crammed with treasures.'

'Rather like Si Greenbridge,' said Sienna slyly. 'What's your connection with him?'

'Tracking down pictures when he's too busy to do his own hunting,' said Zac, picking up the menu. 'What d'you want to eat? I'm going to have foie gras and Wiener schnitzel, because I'm Viennese,' he added slyly.

Relieved to be able to hate him again, furious with herself for being won over, Sienna weighed in. How could he touch such food? Had he no idea how much the poor geese and calves suffered? Her voice was rising. People were looking round.

'Oh per-lease.' Zac stifled a yawn.

'I bet you approve of experiments on live animals,' stormed Sienna, leaping to her feet.

'Of course I don't.' Once again Zac grabbed her wrist, applying pressure until she winced and sat down again. 'But when Mom was dying of cancer, I'd have OKed any experiment on any living thing in the world to make her pain less terrible.'

Sienna scowled at him, then flushed and apologized. There was a long silence. Zac filled her glass.

'At first Mom didn't mind dying too much. She said life hadn't been much cop.'

'Not very flattering to you.'

'It wasn't that. She felt guilty surviving the death camps. And we were so poor. I didn't care. To keep warm I stayed in bed all day, and read a lot. My Great-aunt Leah took me to museums.'

'What was your father like?'

'A university professor. He survived Auschwitz, so in a way he was a link with my mom's mother, but he was so much older, and in lousy health and couldn't work. He died when I was about two. Mom married a goy second time around – more for someone to support her, me and Aunt Leah, I guess. She paid for it. He was a sadistic son of a bitch.'

Zac was ashen now, his hand shaking as he knocked back a most uncharacteristically huge gulp of wine. 'I guess he couldn't hack Leah living with us. Couldn't beat Mom and me up as he wanted to. After Leah died . . .'

Zac stopped suddenly. He'd told no-one these things.

'What happened?' asked Sienna.

'He finally walked out,' said Zac wearily. 'Then a year before she died, Mom met my second stepfather. He married her knowing she'd got cancer. Willing her to fight it. He loved her so much.'

Sienna longed to put her hand over his.

'I'm so sorry,' she mumbled.

Zac raised his glass.

'To both our moms,' he said softly. 'Yours was such a terrific painter.'

Summoning back the waiter, Zac ordered Sienna tagliatelle with wild mushroom sauce, followed by ratatouille, and then, with a slight smile, chose sword-fish and Caesar salad for himself.

'And don't tell me they stab Caesars in a particularly vicious way,' he drawled.

Sienna burst out laughing. She kind of liked him teasing her and was horrified how increasingly she liked him.

After the second bottle, as they were having coffee, she blurted out, 'Why were you sauntering bollock naked along the landing the afternoon of Emerald's birthday party?'

Zac looked at her meditatively: 'I'd been fucking your stepmom.'

'Oh my God.' Black coffee splashed all over the white tablecloth. 'For Christ's sake, why?'

'The Blue Tower was the only room I hadn't checked out. I guessed the Raphael must be there. I should have grabbed it then.'

'How *could* you have abused my father's hospitality? He really loves Anthea.'

'I know. He's got such impeccable taste in every other direction.'

'Stop being so fucking flip,' exploded Sienna. 'Did you know your prints are on the frame found by the pond?'

'Is that a fact? I tried to take the Raphael to the window when I was up there. Anthea screamed that it was wired up.'

'Hasn't it entered your thick greying head,' snarled Sienna, 'that Anthea could have lured you upstairs to get your prints on the picture? That she might have nicked it herself?'

'Could be in league with David,' mused Zac. 'I saw him belting towards the Old Rectory after the fireworks

484

started, and just after we left the boathouse, he drew Anthea aside. I wonder if he is Emerald's father?'

'Don't change the subject. How could you have shagged Anthea when you were having a relationship with Emerald? Poor Emerald, don't you feel guilty?'

Zac looked totally unrepentant.

'Emerald was suffocating me,' he said. 'Her voice was always filled with longing for something or someone I couldn't give her. She's so fucking needy, just like her mom.' Very gently he tugged the ring in Sienna's eyebrow. 'Neither of them was a millionth as good a lay as you.'

'How dare you?' spat Sienna. 'I want to go back to the Cameron.'

Ramming herself against the side of the taxi, clutching her jeans as a shield, she refused to speak on the drive back. So Zac ignored her, singing Mandryka's part in the love duet.

'If you were a girl from one of my villages,
you would go to the well behind your father's
    house,
and draw a cupful of clear water
and offer it to me at the door, so that I should be
    your betrothed before God
and all men! O beautiful one!'

'Oh fuck off,' sobbed Sienna, falling out of the taxi and rushing into the Cameron.

As she raced across the lobby, she could see Trafford and the rest of the YBAs in the bar still getting legless.

'Sienna,' they yelled, as she dived into the lift.

Once again, like a driven robot, she was appalled when she reached her own floor to find her own bitten finger jabbing the ground-floor button. But as the lift reached its destination, the doors parted like stage curtains on two villains in some dark Jacobean tragedy: Zac and Si Greenbridge standing laughing together, teeth gleaming satanically against their dark stubble. As Sienna cringed against the side of the lift, Si slapped a big gold-ringed hand on Zac's shoulder and shepherded him out through the front door into a hovering limo.

Sienna was terrified. Had Zac lured her out to the opera and to dinner so Si's guards could frisk her room, or leave some terrible booby trap? What secrets had she betrayed about the Raphael? Upstairs she frantically tugged open every drawer, checked every cupboard. Her case lay open on the bed. She couldn't remember opening it; someone must have picked the lock. Thank God there was no balcony outside for someone to climb along, just the trees of Central Park, ghostly in the moonlight.

The only other evidence of invaders was a condom and a chocolate on the pillow of her turned-down bed. Visitor loved chocolate, she thought wistfully. But drawing back the sheet, she half expected to find his severed bloody head. Having chained the door, she rammed every chair against it, but, despite her exhaustion, she was far too scared to sleep.

55

Fortunately the next few days were taken up by endless interviews for the Commotion Exhibition. This caused a world-wide scandal, denounced as so obscene by senators and high churchmen and such a negation of art by incensed critics that the Greychurch Museum's grant was under threat. Hugh Grant on the other hand, along with other celebs and the general public, poured in to see what the fuss was about.

Other critics, including Somerford Keynes, who'd stirred his fat stumps and arrived on Concorde in time for the opening party, in turn praised the show for courageously confronting all our fears. Sienna's work was particularly well received. Feminists admired *Tampax Tower* and thought *Aunt Hill* witty and significant. Alongside Trafford's video *Oh Nan*, it was regarded as a significant step for Grey Power.

But it was *Slaughterhouse* that turned Sienna into an animal rights icon. Critics stood on their heads to examine the terrified faces of the hanging businessmen on their grisly conveyor belt.

Almost as much of a talking point was *Assholier Than Thou.*

'Stonewall are thinking of using it on their writing paper,' boasted Trafford, who hadn't been sober since he arrived.

David Pulborough, tieless and clad in too-tight jeans

487

and trainers to identify with youth, was much in evidence telling everyone he'd be showing Trafford next spring. He had to smile a great deal to hide his outrage that neither Jonathan nor *Expectant Madonna* had made the opening party. Commotion without YBA's superbrat was a bit like *Hamlet* without the Prince. This was because back in England, Jonathan couldn't tear himself away from Emerald, insisting on taking her to Harley Street and staying in the room while she had a DNA test so she couldn't cheat.

'Now all we've got to do is to give Dad a nose bleed.'

'But I love your father,' protested Emerald as she drove him to Heathrow. 'And if he isn't my father, I won't be a Belvedon.'

'He'll make an even nicer father-in-law. The moment we get the results, I'll put a ring on your finger, and turn you back into a Belvedon.'

It was anguish for him to leave her behind but their desire for one another was so white hot, it would be risky to subject it to a media circus. With Trafford in New York, Jonathan also felt safe leaving Emerald in his studio in Hoxton, so she could work on the sculptures she'd been drawing up and, less enthusiastically, look after Diggory.

Thanks to Concorde, Jonathan reached his hotel room by ten a.m. American time. Ignoring a thousand fax messages, he went up to his room, unzipped his suit-case and nearly wept. Emerald had insisted on packing for him, wrapping his newly pressed clothes in tissue paper, stocking up his sponge bag with toothpaste for sensitive teeth, English Fern aftershave and orange razors. Attached to a flat parcel was a postcard of Gustav Klimt's *Judith*. On the back she had written:

Darling Jonathan,
    I so long to be loved, but I lack the inner secur-ity that accepts such a thing. Please bear with me while I learn to trust. Thank you for putting up

with me over the last three months, which contrary to my crap behaviour have been the happiest of my life. Good luck with Commotion. Enclosed is something to make you even handsomer. Please come home soon, I love you,

    Emerald

Blushing with delight, clutching himself in ecstasy, Jonathan danced round the room, reading the card over and over again. Inside the parcel was a Harvie & Hudson silk shirt in Antwerp blue.

'Fuck Commotion.' He was chucking everything back into his case when an apoplectic David Pulborough rang.

'Where the hell have you been? *Expectant Madonna* arrived late last night but her bulge won't go through the front door. It's taken a dozen workmen to winch her through an upstairs window. By some miracle we've kept this from the press. Dame Hermione has graciously agreed to be present at the unveiling this afternoon and Micky Blake, who's curating the exhibition, has even more graciously agreed to lay on refreshments for the media.'

'I'm going back to England.'

'Will you stop pissing about,' David's language became very unbefitting a future High Sheriff, 'and get your ass down here and show us how the fucking thing works.'

To avoid a ravening press and the moral majority brandishing placards saying 'Filth!' and 'Go Home, Blaspheming Brits', Jonathan was smuggled in through a back door. By the time he and a pack of electricians and carpenters had got *Expectant Madonna* up and thrumming behind closed blue curtains and a shield of security guards, it was well into the afternoon.

David, who had designs on Dame Hermione – he'd heard she fucked like a stoat – was still dressed deliberately casually in increasingly tight jeans and no tie. He was very irritated to witness the formal attire of his star artist.

'Where did you get that suit?'

'Armani. *Vogue* gave it me as a modelling fee.'

'I never got my cut on that,' snapped David, 'we'll have to adjust the fee elsewhere.' Then, as Jonathan looked likely to bolt, 'Come on, the media want a good hour before Dame Hermione arrives.'

So much excitement and mystique had been generated by Jonathan's delay that everyone expected him to erupt into the press room plastered and stoned, launch into a stream of expletives, get his dick out, smash a window, punch all the critics who'd slagged him off (who'd all arrived in bullet-proof vests) and then throw up.

To their amazement, Jonathan stalked in sober, clean-shaven, clear-eyed and immaculate. Not only was his beauty astonishing, but he was also cool, focused, extremely detached and not prepared to make outrageous statements on the scandal caused by Commotion, nor about the whereabouts of the Raphael.

The YBAs, who'd been caning it for three days, waiting for Jonathan to lead them into laddish pranks, were bitterly disappointed.

'I've never known anyone come off Concorde sober,' grumbled Trafford. 'The zeitgeist today,' he was now telling a bewildered reporter from CBS, 'is the body and its foundations. As no-one believes in an afterlife' – Trafford reached for his quadruple brandy and Benedictine – 'one's body and everything that emerges from it is the only temple: snot, spit, vomit, tears, pus, sperm, shit, piss, menstrual blood are all sacred.'

'How very true,' chipped in a hovering Geraldine Paxton admiringly.

'Thank you, Mr Trafford,' said the reporter from CBS faintly. 'Can you tell Jonathan Belvedon we're ready for him?'

On his way to a Channel 4 interview, Trafford paused to speak to Jonathan, who'd just finished with *The New York Times*.

'I've sold five editions of *Oh Nan* and six of *Assholier*.'

'That's great, Traff.' Putting down a cup of black coffee, Jonathan got out his mobile.

'See that redhead over there? She's Slaney, the museum PR,' continued Trafford, then, with all the arrogance of the great artist who can pull anyone: 'She's having dinner with me tonight. For five hundred dollars you can hide in my wardrobe.'

'Sweet of you,' murmured Jonathan as he punched out: *Missing you hopelessly*. 'Oh look, there's Sienna.'

Sienna had just endured a grilling from NBC over the theft of *Pandora* and was getting increasingly twitchy over talk of escalating fines for looted art and swarthy, sinister men following her. She nearly wept with relief when she saw Jonathan. His new beauty made her gasp.

But although he ruffled her hair, admitted he'd missed her and asked what she'd been up to, it was soon clear he wasn't hearing a word she said. Nor was he interested that everyone was speculating about the Raphael, not even that Si had been lurking in the lobby. Only when she mentioned Zac did his face harden.

'I'll kill that shit for hurting Emo.'

'How is she?'

'Wonderful, an angel, not at all like we thought.' Then, hearing a double bleep, he whipped out his mobile.

'IM YRS 4 EVR MRALD,' read Sienna over his shoulder.

'Jonathan, stop coffeehousing,' bellowed David, '*Sky News* want to do you now, and after that *Vanity Fair*.'

'See you later, sweetheart.' Pecking Sienna on the cheek, rereading his message, Jonathan rushed off.

'I stood among them, but not of them; in a shroud Of thoughts which were not their thoughts,' quoted Sienna despairingly.

491

Jonathan was so obsessed with Emerald, he'd forgotten today was Sienna's twenty-sixth birthday, as had the rest of the family. She'd been away so long. When Jonathan had loved her, she hadn't needed her friends. Now, working so hard to get over him, she hadn't bothered to get in touch with any of them.

Trying not to howl, drenched by rain, unable to get a taxi, she battled her way back to the hotel, praying someone might have remembered. In her pigeon-hole was one red envelope containing a card of a sleeping Burmese cat.

'Dearest Sienna,' she read, 'Good luck with your exhibition, and have a lovely birthday. See you soon, I hope. Love, Patience (Cartwright).'

The old duck. Sienna bit her lip. How weird that the mother of the girl who was the cause of so much of her unhappiness should be the only one to remember.

'This has just been delivered, Miss Belvedon.'

The receptionist handed her a parcel.

Tearing the gold paper, Sienna felt the softness of cashmere and drew out a black polo neck from Rosemary and Aunt Lily. The card wished her a happy birthday and begged her to come home soon. Rosemary must have tipped off her friend Patience. But who had delivered the parcel? There was no stamp. Perhaps by some miracle Jonathan had remembered and was organizing a surprise party later.

Then a shadow darkened the white card, Sienna breathed in CK One and whipped round with a gasp of horror to find Zac far too close behind her. He had been working out; she could feel the heat of his body, the caress of his dark green tracksuit. His hair was black with sweat.

'Happy birthday,' said Zac, noticing the tears and the terror in her eyes, and the face so pale and vulnerable despite its armour of studs and rings.

Overwhelmed with claustrophobia, Sienna rammed herself against the reception desk.

Zac fingered the cashmere. 'Nice turtle-neck.'

'From Rosemary and Lily. I also got a card from Emerald's mother. No-one else remembered because I've been such a bitch,' sobbed Sienna, and fled for the lift.

Having showered and changed in his office, Zac took a taxi to the Commotion Exhibition to find the building swarming with excited media and public, awaiting Dame Hermione. Zac was greeted warmly by all his friends in the art world, including curators from other museums, who were mostly gay and who'd popped in to catch a glimpse of Jonathan, now being interviewed by CBS.

'Often takes longer to think up a title than make the installation,' Jonathan was telling them airily. '*White Cliffs of Diva, Womb with a View,* were options, but *Expectant Madonna* seemed more appropriate. You'll see in a minute.'

'I gather you employed a team of assistants. Which bits did you do?'

'I did her face and her pubes,' grinned Jonathan, who was still ecstatic about Emerald's text message, 'and the blue veins on her boobs,' then, catching sight of Zac, his face hardened: 'What the fuck are you doing in New York?'

'I live here,' snapped Zac. 'Just wanted to remind you it's Sienna's birthday today.'

'Oh Christ.' Jonathan's cigarette nearly set fire to his hair as he clutched his forehead, then, turning to the CBS crew: 'Sorry, guys, that's it for now.'

'Johnny,' 'Johnny,' 'Johnny,' tape recorders advanced from all sides.

'Beat it,' said Jonathan.

When Sienna, dark glasses covering her swollen eyes, huddled into her new polo neck, fought her way into the Exhibitors' room, everyone cheered and sang: 'Happy birthday, dear S'*enn*-ah.'

493

Jonathan, having unearthed a watch which changed colour that he'd bought for Emerald on the flight over, had charmed Slaney the museum publicist into wrapping it for him. Slaney had also nipped out and bought a huge bunch of white roses delicately tinged with pink, a rainbow cake, which Jonathan had decorated with Smarties, and a big card, which Jonathan had signed.

Greeted by such largesse, Sienna nearly broke down. Strapping on the watch, she fled to the loo to find water for the roses and have a quick blub. She returned to popping corks. Micky Blake, the tall, thin, cadaverous curator of the exhibition, euphoric to have had 300,000 visitors in the past three days, had been only too happy to lay on champagne.

Sienna accepted a glass and hugged Jonathan.

'Such gorgeous presents,' she said shakily. 'I thought you'd forgotten.'

Jonathan blushed slightly as, over her shoulder, his eyes met Zac's.

'Let's get wasted,' said Trafford.

'Again,' said Slaney acidly. 'A guy's just been in wanting to buy *Slaughterhouse*,' she told Sienna, 'only problem is he's going back to Russia in a fortnight, and wants to take it just before the end of the exhibition.'

'I don't know' – Sienna's eyes flickered in sudden panic – 'I wanted to do a copy first.' Glancing up, she noticed Zac's presence for the first time and that he was regarding her speculatively.

'Who invited *you* here?'

'Came to look at the exhibition, love your stuff,' then when she looked mutinous, 'I've brought you a present.'

It was the Decca recording of *Arabella*, with Kiri Te Kanawa singing the title role.

'That's cool,' mumbled Sienna, 'really kind and thank you for dinner the other night.'

'Dinner?' An outraged Jonathan swung round. 'You sleeping with the enemy?'

'Don't be fatuous,' stormed Sienna, blushing furiously.

'I figured you might enjoy *Arabella* sung by a proper actress rather than a lump of lard,' said an amused Zac.

'For God's sake shut up, and put that CD away,' shrieked Slaney as she came off her mobile. 'Dame Hermione has left the Waldorf. I'm off to whip up a spontaneous ovation.'

'Are you going to accompany Dame Hermione through the building, Jonathan, and show her your *oeuvre?*' asked Geraldine Paxton, who'd just walked in and who thought Dame Hermione a self-regarding cow. 'Or will you receive her beside *Expectant Madonna?*'

'When's Jonathan going to do a moony?' chorused the visiting curators. 'We're all dying to see that cute ass.'

56

Nothing turned Dame Hermione Harefield on like a crowd of press. Radiant in her violet Chanel suit, huge amethysts at her ears and neck, soft brown curls framing her round-eyed rosy face, a mauve pashmina carefully concealing her large bottom, she paused in Commotion's entrance a good twenty minutes – thus enabling even the *Christian Science Monitor* and the *Osh Kosh Gazette* to get their pictures.

Then, telling the cheering crowd she had no time for autographs, she swept through the museum, ignoring even the most outrageous exhibits until she reached her own, which was still concealed by its pale blue curtains. Delighted to see her elusive artist for once on parade and looking so tidy and handsome, Hermione kissed Jonathan full on the mouth, smearing him with ruby-red lipstick. Furiously, Jonathan wiped it off with his sleeve. That would be the clip Emerald was bound to see on the ten o'clock news tonight.

'Good people, good people!' Dame Hermione clapped her hands, accepted a glass of champagne, took a hefty slug, then waited until as many people as possible had crowded into the room.

'It is with the greatest pleasure that I unveil this important work.'

Slowly the blue curtains slid back to reveal first a massive pink belly like the globe in the days when everything seemed to belong to England. Then the rest of Hermione appeared, naked except for her gold halo, her hands clasped together in prayer, each arm supporting a massive blue-veined breast. There was a gasp of amazement, a stifling of laughter, then everyone leapt out of their skins as the smiling red lips parted and Hermione's voice launched fortissimo into: 'Once in Royal David's City'.

Finally, as the fibreglass Hermione sang: 'Mary was that Mother mild, Jesus Christ her little Child,' a mighty whirring followed, as if a giant cuckoo clock were about to strike. Then an invisible door in her vast belly shot open and out popped Baby Jesus, complete with halo, and, having smiled and waved, popped in again.

There was a stunned silence. Then Hermione clapped her hands.

'Bravo, Jonathan. Bravo!'

So everyone clapped and cheered too and the press went berserk. Even Jonathan, who'd been looking apprehensive, smiled and posed with Hermione. Baby Jesus popped out over and over again. A beaming David kept getting into shot beside Hermione, which irritated the hell out of Geraldine.

'Why didn't Jonathan do an installation called *Cuckoo Cock?*' grumbled an upstaged Trafford. 'It pops in and out of his trousers enough.'

Having witnessed her brother's triumph, Sienna went in search of more champagne. On the way, she was unnerved to see Zac studying *Slaughterhouse*.

'You lot kill animals just as cruelly,' she snapped.

'Oh, come on, honey, give us a break.' Taking her arm, Zac walked her back to the press room, where the YBAs were getting hammered again.

The indefatigable Slaney was already on her mobile revving up a high churchman.

'You really disapprove, Your Eminence. That's terrific. Could you bear to fax the *New York Times*? . . .

497

Yes, the Virgin Mary in the buff and the Christ child shooting out of Dame Hermione's belly, deplorable, isn't it?'

At that moment, Geraldine rushed into the press room.

'Sienna, where's Sienna, come quickly,' she cried excitedly. 'Some religious maniac's slashing your painting.'

'What!' whispered Sienna in horror.

'Looks like some Arab, clearly upset by your attacking the way they kill animals.'

'What a fantastic story,' yelled Slaney, hanging up on the Cardinal.

But Sienna had gone, Wrath in the Seven Deadly Sins, hurtling into the hall; seeing a man in white robes with a long, curved knife, she leapt on him, screaming, wrestling, trying to knock the weapon out of his hands.

'Pack it in,' yelled Zac, who'd raced after her, attempting both to grab the knife and pull Sienna off the man.

Next moment, Jonathan came running in followed by the world's press and Dame Hermione, screeching with horror at such a loss of limelight. Still grappling on the floor, Sienna felt the sinewy power of the Arab's body, the stench of his breath, the mad loathing in his rolling brown eyes.

'Leave my picture alone, you sadistic fucker,' she howled, 'I'll kill you, kill you.' As she kicked him with her steel-tipped boots, the Arab howled with pain. Only when Zac, Jonathan, Trafford, Slaney and several security guards had dragged them apart and slapped handcuffs on them, and David had crept out from behind *Tampax Tower* and Somerford Keynes from behind *Assholier* and Hermione had stopped screaming, did Micky Blake the curator sidle nervously forward to assess the damage.

'Leave it,' sobbed Sienna, tugging frantically at her handcuffs, 'I can do a copy, I've got drawings. Please leave it.'

Slaughterhouse was in ribbons. Underneath the picture, a grey protective layer had been scraped like the underside of a child's new shoe. To the right at the top it had been sliced open. Sienna gave a moan of despair and collapsed briefly against Zac. Then his hand clenched on her shoulder. For as the protective layer was peeled back, there, out of its frame and in all its shining beauty, lay the Raphael.

'My God!' Startled out of his slug-like languor, Somerford waddled forward. 'It's Pandora. How divine she is.' The press also surged forward, frenziedly photographing both picture and combatants.

'Get back,' yelled Jonathan, then, cool as an Arctic January, he turned to Micky Blake. 'That picture belongs to my father. It was stolen last summer. Some joker, knowing my sister was part of Commotion, obviously decided to smuggle it into America behind one of her pictures.'

Zac seemed to wake up.

'I guess your sister did the smuggling,' he snarled. 'She was so worried about not being able to show Pandora to her children.'

As Sienna winced and leapt away from him, there was a wail of sirens and the police roared in. But as Micky Blake began to explain the situation, Zac, still quivering with rage, took over.

'That is my picture, stolen from my great-grandfather in Vienna in 1938,' he told the police and, from his inside pocket, neatly folded, he produced copies of photographs, stats of the documents and even a neatly folded 'Buyers' Beware' page from the *Art Newspaper*, which showed a photograph of Pandora.

'It's the Raphael,' the policemen told each other in wonder.

Si was so well known in America and looted art such a hot subject here that the theft of the Raphael had been huge news. What a coup it had come to light in New York.

'It's my father's picture,' sobbed Sienna.

The police, however, had been pulling in YBAs for disorderly behaviour all week. Taking one look at Sienna's unhealthily grey face with its rings and studs, her black grunge clothes, and her steel-tipped boots, Sergeant Rubin decided she looked infinitely dodgier than the Arab, and arrested them both.

'And I'll take the painting,' said Zac.

'Oh no you don't.' Jonathan leapt forward.

'Neither of you is taking it,' said Sergeant Rubin firmly. 'It'll go to the District Attorney to be authenticated, and then the asset will be frozen.'

'Cold Master,' sighed Jonathan.

'I had to take it,' muttered a despairing Sienna. 'I was so terrified Zac or Si were going to get there first.'

Her worst moment, as the picture was put in a box, was seeing the reproachful look in Hope's blue eyes as an oilskin was laid over her.

'Don't take her away,' she howled, 'I'll never see her again.'

For a second, a grim, shell-shocked Zac dropped a hand on her shoulder.

'Stay cool, babe, it's OK.'

'It's bloody not,' snarled Jonathan. 'You screwed up Emerald, don't start on my sister. Now fuck off.'

Dame Hermione, meanwhile, had been out of the limelight too long. Seeing the knives had been put away and that Zac was even better looking than Jonathan, she rushed into the fray.

'May I help, officer?'

'Why, Dame Hermione,' Sergeant Rubin blushed, 'we've got everything under control.'

'They're arresting my sister,' protested Jonathan.

'Surely not, officer.' Hermione's deep voice deepened as she beamed round at the frantically snapping media, then, putting her arm round Sienna's heaving shoulders: 'This young woman is the daughter of my old friend Sir Raymond Belvedon, a most distinguished art-dealer and television personality. I am convinced of her innocence.'

'That's for us to find out, Dame Hermione.'

Even though it was midnight in England, David took huge delight in waking Raymond.

'Would you like the good news or the bad news? The Raphael's been found.'

'Oh thank God.' Raymond sounded weak with relief. 'Is it OK? Any serious damage?'

'Not that can't be mended.'

'Where was it found?'

'Hidden behind one of Sienna's canvasses. She's as clever at smuggling as her old dad.'

'Oh my God, poor child, what's become of her?'

'Been arrested. Picture's been impounded. Zac's brandishing his documentation. You'll have a fight on your hands if you want it back.'

The moment a distraught Raymond put down the telephone, the *Sun* rang.

'The Raphael's been found in your daughter's possession, Sir Raymond. Are you going to press charges, or was it an inside job to claim the insurance?'

At first when she reached the police station, Sienna tried to bluff it out. Someone was trying to frame her – not the picture. But she was so tired and shivery from getting soaked at lunchtime, and the cops were too clever for her and she'd kept her secret for so long. It was almost a relief to talk. Conscious of her extreme distress, Sergeant Rubin held one hand, Officer Smithfield the other. Plied with scalding mugs of sweet black coffee and endless cigarettes, Sienna explained about getting drunk at Emerald's birthday party and suddenly feeling brave.

'I pretended I needed a pee, then I raced through the garden, switched off the alarm, belted upstairs to the Blue Tower – I knew the combination on the key-pad but I found the door already ajar, so I took the Raphael off the wall and left the door open behind me. Back in my room, I cut it out of its frame, rolled it up, played the Stars and Stripes on it . . .' Perhaps she was still pissed from her birthday champagne?

'Then I shoved it under the floorboards,' she went on, 'and, racing downstairs, I switched on the alarm, chucked the frame in the rushes, and joined the party. One of the guests was throwing up in the begonias, so fortunately all eyes were on her.'

Sienna gave a ghost of a smile. Hot now, she tugged off her polo neck, and reached for another of Sergeant Rubin's cigarettes.

'Sounds like a wild party,' said Officer Smithfield.

'It was. Later in the evening, my stepmother discovered the picture was missing.' Remembering what Anthea and Zac had been up to earlier in the day, Sienna felt suddenly shot through with misery. 'And my brother called the police. Everyone was under suspicion. Zac whipped out his documentation much too pat. I don't think it's his picture at all. He's after the money. It could be worth ten million.'

Sergeant Rubin whistled.

'So where did you take your ten-million-pound note?'

'Rolled up in a magazine, it went with me to Italy. Then I started painting this picture that the Arab slashed. It was such a gruesome subject I couldn't imagine anyone wanting to steal it, so I slotted the Raphael in behind. Customs didn't bat an eyelid anywhere.'

'You may well go to prison,' said Sergeant Rubin sternly. 'You've wasted a lot of police time.'

'Not that much, they were only with us a day.'

'And a huge amount of paperwork. The Brits were convinced it was an inside job to claim the insurance.'

'Oh God, that'll have to be paid back,' groaned Sienna, then she brightened: 'Thank God it was wildly underinsured. My stepmother would have spent the ten million on clothes by now.'

Under her tank top and combats, both policemen could now see the beauty of Sienna's slumped body. Sexy as hell, yet vulnerable beneath the hard, defiant exterior, they decided.

'Why did you really take the Raphael?' asked Officer Smithfield.

'Because it's ours. You've seen how beautiful it is, I couldn't bear anyone else to have it.'

'Would you like something to eat?' said Sergeant Rubin, switching off the tape recorder.

'Probably. I've always like loathed the police, but you've been so kind.'

'D'you think Dame Hermione's had a boob job?' asked Officer Smithfield.

57

Next morning Dame Hermione the merciful dominated every paper.

Sienna appeared briefly in court and was bailed for a
hefty sum by Jonathan and Adrian Campbell-Black. Her
passport, however, was taken away, and she was ordered
to stay in the States while the American and British
police argued over whether she would be tried in
England (if at all) or America. Later there would
inevitably be a civil case to decide the ownership of the
Raphael.

Back at the hotel, Jonathan poured Sienna a large
vodka and announced he was going back to England.

'You can't leave me.'

'Adrian'll look after you. The museum says you can
stay here as long as you like. You've boosted their
turnover enough. And you're being offered shows all
over the world.'

'I don't care.'

'Yes you do, babe. You and Al are the serious ones.
You'll get your passport back in a week or so. You're so
lucky to have a record. There won't be a party you're not
asked to – like O.J. Simpson.'

'Where's Zac?' asked Sienna dully.

'Opening the champagne, I guess. If he comes anywhere near you, Trafford's promised to bury him. And
try not to talk to the press, darling, the case is *sub judice*.'

Jonathan felt a shit, but he had to get back to Emerald. Before leaving England, he had written to Raymond, apologizing for spending so long in Vienna, but saying it had enabled him to get to know and adore Emerald. He was convinced her insecurity stemmed from not being certain she was a Belvedon.

'I have persuaded her to have a DNA test. Could you bear to have one as well? There's a sweet man called Bredin in Harley Street.'

Jonathan's guilt about abandoning Sienna evaporated as Emerald ran into his arms at Heathrow. Silken violet-scented ringlets snaked over her shoulders, her pale face was flushed with colour like sunset on the snow. New high-heeled black boots meant her luscious scarlet lips were four inches nearer his. Jonathan just managed to stop himself kissing the life out of her.

All the way home she bubbled over with excitement – how she'd spring- or autumn-cleaned his studio, taken Diggory for walks, completed two heads, and made him a monkfish and scallop pie for tonight. As they passed the Lucozade building, with the bottle tipping gold liquid into a glass, she demanded a debriefing. Jonathan was all praise for Sienna's courage in keeping the Raphael secret for so long.

Two further revelations irked Emerald, that that 'bastard Zac' had been taking Sienna out and that 'darling Patience' had sent Sienna a birthday card. Suddenly all her old jealousies reignited. Did Jonathan still lust after Sienna? Did Zac who dumped Emerald lust after her too? Did Patience like Sienna better? Emerald couldn't bear to share.

It was a grey, glaring day. Leaves gathered in the gutters. Flowers in window boxes had been pinched by the first frost. Reaching his studio, not sure why the temperature had plummeted, Jonathan received a delirious welcome from Diggory, praised the heads – one rather wooden of himself – and the unnatural tidiness. Would he ever find anything?

For a minute Emerald pressed a biro in and out then she erupted.

'How could Sienna be so irresponsible, waltzing off with the Raphael, bringing shame on the family? Everyone was under suspicion. You all thought Zac and I were in it together. Zac nearly got arrested. Sienna never thinks of anything but herself and her precious work.'

'D'you blame her?' said Jonathan icily. 'None of us remembered her birthday,' then, as Emerald started to play on an imaginary violin: 'Just stop it.'

Guilt at abandoning Sienna and frustration at not being able to screw all the bitchiness out of Emerald fuelled Jonathan's rage.

'Just remember,' he shouted, 'Sienna never had a mother, just bloody Anthea, who's given you more affection in six months than she's ever given Sienna. And you've got Patience, well named, she needed to be called that, putting up with you. She's one of the nicest women I've ever met, she adores you, so does Ian, and they're proud of everything you do. When did Patience ever miss a carol service, or a lacrosse match, or a school play? Think of all those plusses: boarding and art schools, trips to Florence, lovely clothes, houses in Fulham, fast cars. The whole family's jumped to your whining tune. When your father went broke, all they worried about was how it would affect you.'

'Stop it, stop it.' Collapsing on the sofa, Emerald clamped her hands to her ears.

'Quite frankly,' went on Jonathan brutally, 'you settle once and for all those arguments about nature and nurture. None of Ian and Patience's niceness and attempt at bringing you up to be a decent human being rubbed off. You've remained a bitch just like Anthea. And you were bloody lucky to be adopted too. If Anthea had brought you up in a one-bedroomed flat in Purley, she'd never have coped and you'd have ended up in a children's home, being abused insensible by some bearded goat.'

Emerald was so shattered, she ran out of the studio. Out in the street, two small boys stopped playing football and gazed at her in horror as she began to cry. Jonathan was right. How could she have bitched about Sienna, whose brother she had stolen?

Jonathan wandered round distractedly, noticing the fish pie, the table laid with candles, mint lying on top of the new potatoes, flowers everywhere. There were clean sheets on the bed; Emerald had even cleaned the windows. In the waste-paper basket, he noticed the remains of a green leather belt Diggory must have chewed up, which Emerald hadn't even made a fuss about. Rushing outside, he bumped into her rushing back in again, sobbing her heart out, gibbering apologies.

Taking her in his arms, he calmed her, saying how sorry he was, that he worshipped her, that they were both uptight because any moment they'd get the result of her and Raymond's DNA test.

Raymond, who could never deny his favourite son anything, had dutifully trotted off to Harley Street, but, unable to face hysterics about the lack of trust, he hadn't told Anthea.

And if he wasn't Emerald's father, who was? And what did it matter compared with losing his beloved Pandora? He kept thinking of her imprisoned in some New York warehouse like a shuddering Grenville in kennels.

The Belvedons' attitudes to the discovery of the Raphael were sharply divided. Jupiter was furious with Sienna for stealing his birthright but, ever practical, set about marshalling funds to pay back the insurance and for the civil case next spring. Aunt Lily, Dora and Dicky all felt Sienna had been very brave and resourceful. Anthea was wildly disapproving. How could Sienna have remained silent when everyone was accusing everyone, including her stepmother, of nicking the Raphael? It was also typical that lucky Sienna should be bailed and now housed in New York by a glamorous single chap like Adrian Campbell-Black.

Second wives tend to be snoopers. In search of slights and to discover what was going on, Anthea had always read her stepchildren's diaries. Now they were grown up, she read their letters marked 'private' which had been sent to Raymond. Longing to be outraged, she was disappointed Alizarin had not yet begged for money.

She was also dying to find a recent letter from Jonathan marked 'strictly private'. After days of scrabbling, she tracked it down under the green paisley lining paper in the top drawer of Raymond's desk in the London flat, and nearly died.

On the back Raymond had scribbled 'Mr Bredin, 28 Harley Street, 3.30 October 15'. That was eight days ago.

Whimpering, Anthea snatched up her mobile.

'We've got to talk, I can't discuss it over the phone.'

They met in a dark corner of the Cavendish, St James Hotel, at midday. In the belief that one gained more from people if one looked pretty, Anthea was enchantingly dressed in a little Parma violet suit. She smelled deliciously of Shalimar; her soft crimson nails matched the Kir Royale she was delicately sipping.

'Sugar,' she cried, as her shaking hand spilled a few drops on her skirt.

Whipping out a red silk handkerchief, David's habitually wandering hand caressed her thighs as he mopped her up.

'Well, what is it?' he asked. 'I've got a crucial lunch in half an hour.'

'Jonathan's persuaded Raymond to have a DNA test to discover if he's Emerald's father,' she said.

'So?' David drained his dry Martini and waved to the barman to fix him another.

'They'll find out he isn't,' bleated Anthea.

'Ah, but they won't find out who is.'

'But Raymond will be furious I've lied to him and he will want to know who it is. I'm going to say that you and I had a night of passion, when I was traumatized at being fired over Galena. I'll explain that you comforted me, we got tiddly, and little Emo was the result. I've got to tell him it's you, or he'll start suspecting Eddie the packer.'

She's got it all worked out, thought David bleakly.

'I stood by you twenty-seven years ago,' he snapped, 'I risked my marriage and my job. Raymond will forgive you, he always does.'

'But his vile children won't. Please, David.'

Apply cocktail onion to eye, thought David as the barman placed another dry Martini in front of him. He was now feeling too sick to drink it.

'Raymond must have fucked you enough to believe he was Emerald's father,' he said sulkily.

'We only did it once, he hardly came inside me. I thought it was safe. I never dreamt for a moment Emerald wasn't yours. I only told Raymond he was the father to get you off the hook.' Her voice was rising in hysteria.

The barman looked up and sighed. Mr Pulborough up to no good again. David forced himself to pat Anthea's hand.

'Stay cool, don't confess to anything until Raymond gets the results and you've talked to me. I've got to go. I'll call you later.'

David had booked a private room for another secret assignment, but when he reached Prince Igor's in Bury Street, Casey was already seated at the bar, noisily ordering a bottle of Pouilly-Fumé and a first course of foie gras because he and Galena had always had the same in here. His booming voice was so distinctive that everyone in every nearby gallery must know David was busy poaching the Belvedon's star artist.

'I forgive you for being late, and have ordered double

portions,' announced Casey, shovelling up nuts like a bingeing squirrel.

As befitting the great artist only to be mentioned in the same breath as Bacon and Freud, Casey wore a navy blue smock suit which covered his paunch. A black beret perched on his shaggy pepper-and-salt hair, like a slug on winter grass. The parts of his face not covered by beard and moustache were wrinkled and red from excess, yet he still felt he had a divine right to every woman in the world as he crinkled his eyes at the comely barmaid.

David felt so sick he could only sip still water, but was able to show Casey a photograph of *Millennium Buggers*, in which Jonathan had portrayed Casey as a vast penis.

'The little shit,' roared Casey, rattling every bottle along the bar. 'That's going straight to my lawyer. Think of the fortune I've made for that family.'

'Shall we go through?' urged David, who'd just seen Tim Bathurst and Johnny Van Haeften, two dealers who were friends of Raymond, coming through the front door.

'Raymond's completely out of touch, of course,' went on David as he ushered Casey into the best chair and poured him a third glass of Pouilly-Fumé. 'Only interested in himself and his television programme. A star' – David massaged Casey's musclebound arm – 'should never be handled by another star, only by a back-room boy.'

Casey's demands were endless. He wanted major prizes, exhibitions worldwide including a Tate retrospective, the price of his pictures quadrupled, a slot on television bigger than Raymond's and Emerald Belvedon (maybe Pulborough: David felt sweat trickling down his ribs) on a gold plate.

'How would you like to paint Dame Hermione?' he asked. 'There's no way the NPG are going to accept *Expectant Madonna*, but they'd jump at a portrait by you. Dame Hermione is keen.'

'Lovely breasts.' Casey's mouth doubly watered as a huge helping of foie gras was placed before him. What a good thing Pulborough wasn't drinking. There was a wonderful bottle of Mouton Cadet Rothschild to come with his venison.

'How about a quiet supper next week with Emerald Belvedon?' asked Casey, his voice thickening. 'And with Dame Hermione and perhaps Nick Serota. Or if Dame Hermione can't make it, then just Emerald, you and myself. I am compelled to paint that young woman.'

The thin toast disintegrated beneath the weight of the foie gras Casey was piling on it. David had a vision of frail Emerald similarly crushed beneath Casey's gross body. Casey was now swilling down his vast mouthful with a great gulp of Pouilly-Fumé, smearing butter and pâté all over his beard. Could he really put up with this disgusting satyr for the next twenty years? wondered David.

On the other hand, two Hockneys David had paid £300,000 for last week had turned out to be fakes and Barney, who was supposed to rally the punters, produced nothing but restaurant bills. If Rosemary threw him out, he would need Casey.

'I'm sure Emerald would regard it as a great honour,' he said smoothly.

'I am also anxious to have access to Galena's memoirs,' went on Casey. 'I know they're still in the hands of that stubborn old bitch Lily Hamilton. Your Rowena's a close friend of Lily's, isn't she? Tell her to put in a good word.'

The Belvedon was in trouble. The rumours spread by David had been deadly. Worried about stock valued too high, Raymond's bank was calling in its huge loan, ordering the disposal of everything that had passed its sell-by date. But punters, unnerved by newspaper reports about the Raphael being looted, had lost faith

511

in the gallery and were not coming forward to buy. Had other pictures been stolen?

Raymond had also been preoccupied with a programme on Botticelli, Jupiter distracted by Hanna leaving him. Neither man's eye had been on the ball. They must keep their nerve, Jupiter told his father, and concentrate on Casey's exhibition in February which would bring in a lot of revenue.

At the end of October, however, Casey rocked the art world by announcing he was leaving the Belvedon after nearly fifty years and taking his entire exhibition, lock stock and double barrel, across the road. Summoning a press conference, he praised the marketing skills of the Pulborough. David P. already had a long waiting list for his pictures. The Belvedon had lost its grip and as an act of solidarity to his Jewish friends, he didn't like working with galleries who dealt in looted art.

The catalogue for Casey's show at the Belvedon had already been printed, invitations to the private view were in proof.

'We've got to sue,' fumed Jupiter.

He broke the news of Casey's defection to his father as he was walking Grenville in Kensington Gardens. A distraught Raymond had immediately rung Casey and been subjected to such a long aggressive monologue that a bored Grenville had escaped into the bushes after a rabbit. Poor Raymond had ended up deaf in one ear, and wound up in Grenville's long fishing-rod lead like a maypole.

Dropping in at the Belvedon on the off chance the DNA results might have come through, Jonathan was horrified how much his father had aged and lost weight. The veins stood out on the back of Raymond's beautiful hands as he laboriously tried to answer the fan mail and begging letters which always poured in after a programme.

Dear Ray, [read Jonathan over his father's hunched shoulders]

Can we have a signed drawing for our auction? To be honest I have never watched your programme. *Match of the Day* is more my bag. Can I be a tad cheeky and also ask you to ask other famous friends to donate a signed item, and if you or they would be free to mastermind the auction?

Raymond sighed, and put the letter to one side.

'Dear Sir Raymond, My parents have gone bankrupt and can no longer pay my fees at art school.'

'Dear Sir Raymond, Tick the appropriate box: I would be happy to donate £1,000, £5,000, £20,000.'

The figures swam before Raymond's eyes.

'Dear Sir Raymond, On behalf of Greyhound Rescue . . .'

Raymond got out his cheque book. As an economy, Jupiter had turned down the central heating. The only way to keep warm was to write cheques.

'Those letters are carnivorous,' said Jonathan disapprovingly. 'Why have you both got such long faces?'

'Casey's left us,' moaned Raymond.

'Well, good riddance.'

Jonathan looked so carefree and handsome in his Antwerp-blue shirt, Jupiter lost his temper.

'It's all your bloody fault. Casey was pissed off you told him to fuck off the day of Emerald's party. He was livid we put Joan Bideford on the front of next year's calendar.'

'There was room for her on next year's calendar,' said Jonathan in amazement.

'Don't be fatuous! And as for *Millennium Buggers*—'

'You and Somerford were in that too. I thought Casey would regard it as rather an elitist bunch.'

'Shut up,' roared Jupiter.

'We didn't cherish him enough.' Raymond shook his

head. 'That's the second major artist we've lost this year, who was the other one?'

'Jonathan,' said Jupiter bleakly.

'Emerald's been blitzing my studio,' said Jonathan hastily, 'I thought you'd like this.' He handed Raymond an exquisite watercolour of Grenville stretched out on the study sofa.

'My dear boy!' Raymond took it to the light. 'Worthy of Cecil Aldin, Degas or even Stubbs. I saw a photograph of *Expectant Madonna*, frightfully funny, but I wish you'd do more of this stuff.'

As Jupiter stormed furiously off into the back room, pointedly slamming the door, Raymond added, 'So lovely to have you back,' then, lowering his voice: 'Should have the results of my test any day now. Tell Emerald I'll still adore her, whatever the outcome. Why don't you both come and dine at the flat tomorrow night? Anthea'll be in London, we'll get something nice in from Fortnum's.'

58

A warm west wind was blowing up from Limesbridge to wish them luck. Leaves were falling seriously now, huge pale gold cornflakes, blanketing parks and pavements, as though the trees were determined to strip off before November. It had been raining and their trunks glistened in the street light. People turned to stare as Jonathan and Emerald crossed St James's Square, hand in hand, eyes only for each other. Every so often, Emerald pulled off strands of jade-green feather boa which clung to her scarlet mouth.

Jonathan was so certain of the outcome that in his pocket was a black leather box containing an exquisite ring, four emeralds in the shape of a four leaf clover. He'd checked with Dr Bredin. The results had gone first-class post to Raymond yesterday. Emerald was the one panicking. If Raymond were her father, she'd lose Jonathan for ever.

As they went up in the lift, Jonathan took her tiny cold face in his hands.

'It's been worth every moment of the waiting,' he said softly. 'Tonight I will make love to you until the dawn rises. The stars won't dare to set in case they miss something and the sun will hang back knowing he's been knocked off the number one spot for ever. I love you.' He dropped a kiss on her trembling mouth as the lift doors opened into Raymond's flat.

Normally when she entered a new place, Emerald's first move was to look at the pictures. But having quickly kissed Raymond and Anthea, she ran to the sitting-room window gabbling, to disguise her nerves, about the wonderful view of the Houses of Parliament and the tawny towering trees of St James's Park. Then she swung round, wide-eyed, flushed and about to be all mine, thought Jonathan in ecstasy.

As memorial services were an increasing chore of the much younger wife, Anthea had felt justified in spending a bomb at David Shilling on a ravishing midnight-blue feather hat for such occasions, which she had left on the hall table. Jonathan couldn't resist putting it on and wrapping Emerald's feather boa round his neck to make her laugh. Then he noticed Anthea looking extremely smug, and felt an icy hand clutching his heart.

'Glad you've both had a nice long holiday in Vienna,' she said. 'Lucky for some.'

'And there is some good news in the world,' said Raymond. 'I think we can manage this between us, don't you?' Then, as the cork burst out of a magnum: 'Let Raphaels and Casey Andrewses fall about our ears.'

'What are you talking about?' asked Jonathan numbly.

'I've just got the results of my DNA test' – Raymond brandished a chart of waving black lines which could have been painted by Moholy-Nagy – 'and Emerald is definitely my daughter. So there are no more doubts,' he went on happily as he filled up four glasses.

'I feel a little hurt you doubted my word, Emerald and Jonathan' – Anthea smiled at them graciously – 'but I do understand you wanting to be a thousand per cent sure.'

'This is definitely one to file under "Oh Fuck",' said Jonathan slowly.

There was a thud as Emerald fainted, sending a vase of scarlet and purple anemones flying.

'Overwhelmed by relief and happiness,' said Anthea complacently.

Still wearing Anthea's frivolous feather hat like Picasso's weeping woman, Jonathan gathered up his sister, carried her next door and laid her on the bed. For a second he gazed down at her, running his hand slowly over her death-mask face to memorize it for ever. Then he kissed her briefly on the lips, returned to the drawing room and went berserk.

'All your Seventies crap about love and peace!' he yelled. 'All your bloody permissive society!' Then, turning on Anthea. 'If you hadn't shagged my father when he was married to Mum, none of this would have happened. By your bloody adultery, you've totally destroyed my and Emerald's lives.'

'Get out,' yelled back Raymond, 'don't you *dare* to talk to Anthea like that, you spoiled brat.'

'It was you two who spoiled life for us.'

'Bring back my hat,' screeched Anthea as he stumbled into the lift, groping for the ground-floor button and the descent into hell.

Tears pouring down his face, walking distractedly into the Piccadilly traffic, he lost Anthea's hat and watched it disappearing under the wheels of a 22 bus. With the satisfaction of the serpent after a good afternoon's mischief, Emerald's green boa slithered off into the gutter.

Tempted to give up his life in Savile Row police station, two leaves for happy days nestling in his curls, Jonathan ended up at the Pulborough.

'Vine leaves in his hair,' murmured David, who was reading *Private Eye*'s account of Casey's defection: 'King Rat leaves sinking ship', and waiting for a call from New York before going out to dinner.

Jonathan was so unhinged by unhappiness, he told David everything.

'I love Emerald, and she's my sister.'

517

David, who hadn't yet heard from Anthea, felt like Christian at the wicket gate.

'Never deterred you in the past,' he said bitchily.

'Bloody does now. Sienna and I were just a wind-up, I never believed in a million years Emerald was Dad's daughter.'

Nor had David. Raymond had clearly done a good deal more than fiddle with Anthea. Since Emerald had rolled up in May, David had been in a continual panic he'd be outed as her father. The last three days since his meeting with Anthea had been a nightmare, in which he had bidden farewell to Rosemary's millions and the post of High Sheriff.

Being stingy, he was also incensed at having had to fork out unfairly, twenty-six years ago, for all those hotel bills in Yorkshire, train fares, gynaecologists, supporting Anthea after the birth, giving her a holiday in Spain, not to mention all the people he'd had to buy to keep quiet so Rosemary didn't twig, particularly when he'd been using her money. There had been no need for it; he had been fleeced and conned. Thank God he had always refused to sign the birth certificate. Just wait till he saw Anthea.

Irrationally, a tiny part of him had wanted to be Emerald's father, and now 'Shrimp Villy' would be strutting round like an old buck. And so David vented his rage on Jonathan.

'I can't think why you're making such a fuss,' he said nastily. 'As your well-read father is always quoting: "Never morning wore to evening, but some heart did break." It just hasn't happened to you before. Should give your work more depth. Anyway, you'd be useless for Emerald.' David put Casey's cuttings back in a blue cellophane folder. 'You're too libertine, too lightweight. Emerald needs someone stable, responsible, possibly much older.' David licked his smirking lips.

'Like you,' whispered Jonathan in horror. 'Don't you dare lay a finger on her, you bastard.'

'Don't be ridiculous,' said David smoothly, 'I must call her first thing – although she'll need a body-guard – Casey is determined to immortalize her on canvas.'

'I've already done that,' snarled Jonathan. 'Tell the fucker to stay away from her.'

'I doubt if you have "immortalized her". You've blown your career: fooling around, drinking, shagging, hell raising.' David picked up his purple cummerbund, which he only just managed to tie round his waist. He must take more exercise; he and Emerald could jog in the park to get her in training for running away from Casey.

'No-one's asking for your stuff any more,' he went on, shrugging on his dinner jacket. 'I've had no orders for *Expectant Madonna*, nor *Millennium Buggers*. The world was at your feet, but today's taste is fickle. Everyone's clamouring for the latest thing, but it's not you any more.'

'Thanks a bunch,' said Jonathan, who hadn't regis-tered a word, 'I've just got to leave Emerald alone.'

'She's got Anthea and Raymond now,' said David sourly. Then, seeing Jonathan looked near to death, and not wanting to lose him as an artist, only to shock him into working harder, he added more gently, '*Vogue* are planning to make Kate Moss an artist's muse. The Chapman brothers, Tracey, Gary Hume and Sam Taylor-Wood are all doing her, they want you as well.'

'I'm not interested.'

'Not in Kate Moss? You must be in a bad way.'

'I need to talk to Alizarin,' muttered Jonathan. 'He went through the same thing over Hanna. I'm going abroad.'

'Well, don't forget to leave a forwarding address – look after yourself, dear boy.'

But Jonathan had staggered off into the night.

*   *   *

Back in Duke Street, St James's, Anthea was flabbergasted when a revived but distraught Emerald confessed she was hopelessly in love with Jonathan.

'I thought you loved Zac.'

'Zac's just a feckless opportunist. Jonathan's the warmest, sweetest, most loving man I've ever met.'

'I agree about Zac, but I don't think Jonathan's any more capable of being faithful—'

'Than his father was, humping you when he was supposed to be Galena's besotted husband,' said Emerald hysterically. 'Was I conceived right here? Did Galena ever find out you were shagging her husband in the marital bed?'

'How dare you!' An enraged Anthea slapped her daughter very hard across the face. 'High time someone taught you some manners, young lady.'

'Well, it won't be you.'

As she hadn't brought any money with her, Emerald ran most of the way back to Shepherd's Bush, losing her bag and her shoes on the way.

Hearing the outside doorbell ring just as *Peak Practice* ended, Patience picked up the receiver by the front door.

'Hello,' she called out.

There was no reply. It was spooky round here at night when Ian was out minicabbing. Goodness knows what wickedness was luring her to open the downstairs door. Then Patience heard desperate sobbing, her big heart prevailed and she pressed the intercom button. The pattering up the three flights of stairs could have been made by the paws of a little lurcher. The next moment Emerald had collapsed into her arms.

'Oh Mummy, oh Mummy, I'm sorry I've been such a bitch, please help me.'

The Belvedons did not enjoy the Millennium. No matter how many times Anthea expressed relief at a step-free Christmas, Raymond, still fretting over the Raphael and the gallery's fate, couldn't get used to such a depleted family gathering. Only Lily, Dicky and Dora, who ought to have been in bed, saw the New Year in with them. Grenville, without the support of his friends, Visitor and Diggory, was having a nervous breakdown over the fireworks, which had been banging away for days. Every time Raymond coaxed him into the garden, another rocket would go off and Grenville would bolt back into the house. Dicky and Dora were equally miserable about the dearth of their elder brothers and sisters.

'I even miss Emerald,' said Dora in amazement.

'So do I,' sighed Dicky.

Nor could Anthea and Raymond invite their old friends, the Pulboroughs, over, even for a drink. David was still punishing Anthea for conning him and Raymond had not forgiven David for annexing Casey Andrews.

Jonathan, meanwhile, unhinged by unhappiness, wandered the streets of Vienna mocked by the manic jollity of the singing Glühwein-swigging revellers, as he relived all the happy times he'd spent with Emerald. He was trapped in his Viennese coffin of despair, with no bell to ring ever to free him.

Back in England, on New Year's Eve, a landscape by Cézanne was stolen from the Ashmolean, triggering off much talk of a crackdown on art theft, which didn't bode well for Sienna. Still in New York, she refused to join Adrian Campbell-Black, his boyfriend Baby and their pals in Connecticut for a party. Instead she worked feverishly trying to amass enough pictures for an exhibition to raise money for the court case.

Dora and Dicky were further lowered by the continued absence of Alizarin and Visitor.

'I want to ring them up and wish them a Happy New Year,' wept Dora. 'Visitor always recognized my voice on the telephone.'

Nor were there any lights in Jupiter's cottage. Since word had sped round that there was a glamorous new spare man in London, an eldest son, who would inherit Foxes Court and who had a dazzling political career in front of him, Jupiter had been bombarded with invitations.

On Millennium night, a stunning divorcee had asked him to a party in her flat overlooking the Thames to watch the River of Fire. But gazing down at the leaping blaze of fireworks as her jewelled hand crept into his, Jupiter realized his heart had already turned to ashes. How utterly meaningless life was without Hanna!

Feeling an utter shit – again – he left the party, like Cinderella, and now, alone in the gallery, was drinking himself insensible and trying to hang pictures for a sale starting on 2 January, in the hope of raising some quick cash.

He had already smashed the glass on a watercolour and had insufficient strength to lift a vast Landseer into position. Only Alizarin could have done that. Jupiter took another slug from the Armagnac bottle.

'Unhappy New Year, Jupiter,' he told himself.

If it weren't for his stupid pride, he'd have begged Hanna to come back. But he was convinced she was with Alizarin. He groaned in despair as he imagined them laughing over Visitor's antics, making love, throwing snowballs in a bridal-white Norwegian landscape.

Going into the back room to collect two Dutch still lives of fruit that would look lovely in a group with the Boucher bottom, which he'd hijacked from the Blue Tower, he heard the doorbell ring. Glancing in the monitor, he gasped with joy. For outside the glass door, her sweet face and exuberant gold hair framed by a black velvet hood, stood Hanna. Jupiter rushed out into the main gallery, then groaned with disappointment. Not Hanna – too young, but familiar. Then he realized it was Emerald's plump sister, Sophy, swaying, with a bottle of Chardonnay in each hand.

'I'm really sorry,' she stammered. 'I was just passing and I wondered if you had any news of Alizarin.'

'Come in,' said Jupiter. 'It's a bit of a mess.'

'I was at a party.' Sophy, clearly drunk, hung her head.

'So was I,' said Jupiter.

'It was such an important time, I suddenly couldn't bear not to be with someone important,' mumbled Sophy.

'I've been putting up pictures,' explained Jupiter, 'but I'm not seeing them, or anything, very straight. How's Emerald?' he asked, as he handed her a glass of Armagnac.

'Ghastly. I've never seen such unhappiness.' Sophy explained about Jonathan and the DNA test.

'He was so wonderful for Emo. She's never been properly loved or in love before. It's made her really appreciate Mum and Dad. We'd be such a happy family, if . . .' Sophy's voice trailed off: 'she wasn't so in love with Jonathan and we weren't so poor.'

'Poor Jonathan,' murmured an appalled Jupiter, who'd been so wrapped up in his own misery, he'd not realized what was going on. 'I just heard there'd been a row, not unusual, and that Jonathan had pushed off abroad.' He shook his head. 'I didn't think she was Dad's daughter either, or I'd never have jumped on her.'

'You mustn't feel guilty, everyone falls in love with Emo.'

'I just wish Hanna hadn't caught us.'

Jupiter put a frightful nude up on the wall and took it down again. Who the hell had bought that?

'What's happened to Alizarin?' Sophy's elbow shot off the table. She heaved it back.

'Anthea and I chucked him out,' Jupiter was amazed to find himself admitting it. 'I've always been jealous of him. He inherited all Mum's talents. Only thing she handed on to me was a passion for caviare.'

'You're a terrific organizer,' said Sophy comfortingly, noticing that Jupiter's dinner jacket, which he'd hung over a chair, had an unexpectedly dashing cherry-red lining.

'I'm fed up with running a gallery,' he went on. 'Dad loves saving pictures for the nation; I just want to save the nation.'

'You could save the Tories. My father would certainly vote for you.' Sophy couldn't resist asking: 'How's Hanna?'

Collapsing into a chair, putting his head in his hands, Jupiter said despairingly, 'She must be with Alizarin, no-one's heard a squeak out of either of them.'

Ask a silly question, thought Sophy.

'Alizarin's got more integrity than I have,' said Jupiter bleakly.

'She married you,' said Sophy stoutly. 'You're extremely attractive.' And terribly like Alizarin, she thought wistfully, as Jupiter squinted up at her with narrowed eyes and his hair all ruffled. It must have been very confusing for Hanna.

'Extremely attractive,' she repeated owlishly.

And so are you, decided Jupiter in surprise. Very Dawn French, or rather Dawn English Rose with that exquisite colouring.

'Our assistant, Tamzin, has failed to return from Gstaad, claiming to have fallen in love with a ski instructor,' he told Sophy. 'Would you like a job for the rest of the week? We've got a sale on.'

'Oh please, how gorgeous, thank you.' It would bring her nearer to Alizarin.

'Look!' She leapt to her feet. 'There's a man in the

doorway, slumped like a great black wounded crow. Shall I offer the poor thing a drink?'

'Christ no, he's asleep. Don't encourage him,' snapped Jupiter.

When he was running the country, he'd get all those homeless scroungers off the streets.

59

Little did Jupiter realize, as the bitter winter kicked in, that his own brother was sleeping rough less than a mile away around Centre Point. After he had been evicted from the Lodge, Alizarin had eked out a living painting portraits in Leicester Square. But with his sallow skin, black hair, and slanting dark eyes above high cheek-bones, he looked too like the asylum-seekers flooding in from the Balkans, allegedly up to every con trick. Too many drug-dealers and criminals were also posing as pavement artists, threatening to beat up customers if they didn't pay outlandish prices. Consequently the police kept fining Alizarin and seizing his painting equipment. Just before Christmas, his landlady had chucked him out because he couldn't pay the rent.

He had now been sleeping rough for three weeks. All his dole money went on food for Visitor and in bunging other tramps to pose for him. Too proud to beg, he was stockpiling drawings he hoped he would sell.

Matters were not helped by his last pair of spectacles being smashed in a punch-up and his sight having deteriorated so badly that he could only see faint shapes. He was in addition plagued by murderous headaches. He had suffered terrible humiliations, wandering by mistake into the Ladies near Tottenham Court Road, falling down the escalator with Visitor in his arms. Scared to risk the tube any more he walked everywhere and rationed himself to one shower in the public baths a week.

On the second Wednesday evening in January the temperature dropped to seven degrees below zero. Overhead Alizarin could just distinguish a fuzzy little crescent moon, lounging on an eiderdown of fluffy black cloud. He could have used that eiderdown, his hand was too frozen to hold a pencil. He had wrapped Visitor, whose fur had grown so thick he looked like a yellow husky, in his ancient greatcoat and taken temporary refuge in a doorway at the bottom of Charlotte Street.

Just up the road were the head offices of Saatchi & Saatchi, whose founder had never bought any of his pictures, and Channel 4, who had often employed his father. Tantalizing smells of wine, garlic and herbs kept drifting towards him from the Charlotte Street Hotel and from one of Raymond's favourite haunts, the fish restaurant Pescatori.

It was like looking out of a basement window, as a blurred tangle of black fishnet legs, velvet cloaks, silver sequinned skirts, pinstripe creases, shining brogues, jeans and trainers passed before his eyes. Alizarin breathed in sweet wafts of scent, newly applied to encourage kisses on the way home.

'Tax-aaaaay,' bellowed the Hoorays.

Alizarin had already seen three people he was at school with and two ex-girlfriends of Jupiter. But none of them noticed him as, with a stream of merry chat, they stepped over and round him. Don't ruin our lovely evening with your embarrassing poverty.

It was gone midnight. Coughing racked his body as the rumble of the last tube shook the pavement. Alizarin eased onto his other hip. He was so thin, a bomber jacket and an old sweater were no protection against the vicious cold.

Before the soup vans went home, he had wangled a bowl of turkey broth for Visitor. Later, as they lurked in a McDonald's doorway for warmth, a departing customer had chucked a half-eaten hamburger into the gutter. For a second Visitor held back, wagging his tail in case Alizarin's need was greater, then, at a nod, gobbled it up. Alizarin could never sleep if Visitor hadn't eaten.

When he'd applied for a bed in a hostel, the counsellors had advised him to take his old friend to Battersea.

'You don't stand a chance of accommodation with a dog.'

And Alizarin had shouted that it was the only thing he did stand a chance with. He'd have walked into the Thames if it hadn't been for Visitor.

Taking refuge in a side alley near the Middlesex Hospital, Alizarin crept into his sleeping bag. It was getting colder. He'd pawned his watch but he could read the hours of the night like Braille. People were still coming out of clubs, being sick in the gutter, swearing because taxis very sensibly refused to take them. Alizarin could hear the dull thump of Visitor's tail as other tramps put their sleeping bags beside his, particularly if there were dusty mince pies on offer.

Because Alizarin was large, the rest of the homeless community hadn't messed with him. He also had a dignity, a kindness and an ability to listen which had inspired a similar love in his students. He had made friends since he had been on the streets, not with work-shy scroungers, but quietly desperate people who, like himself, had lost their way in life.

Alizarin adjusted the greatcoat around Visitor, always so cheerful and uncomplaining, and, drawing together the strings of his own sleeping bag, waited to be warmed by his own breath. His thoughts strayed wistfully to Foxes Court and the dry leaves flying out of the hedgerows laying a warm blanket over the tender green shoots of the winter barley. Then he dreamed of Sophy, and falling asleep beside her sweet softness.

He was woken by a din. Tramps were always getting

drunk or stoned, and picking fights. Best not to get involved. But the screaming was getting louder. Alizarin shoved his head out, gasping at the cold. In the street light, he could see shadowy forms in frenzied movement and just make out a woman bent back over a dustbin, her skirt up over her breasts. A man was fucking her. She must have been having a period; blood, black in the moonlight, was streaming down her white legs, awakening some terrible distant memory. Alizarin found himself screaming, yelling, sobbing for them to stop. Visitor staggered onto his arthritic legs, barking. The man swore, pulled out of the woman, lurched over and viciously began kicking Alizarin.

He must have passed out. He woke to even more excruciating pain in his head and Visitor licking his face – sweet Visitor always there for him. A drunk was kicking a tin in the distance; Alizarin could hear the hiss of the dustman's lorry, banging bins, a clatter of bottles like the emptying of a fisherman's net.

Then, gradually, as consciousness reasserted itself, he groped round in panic. Not only had the case containing his dole book, his sketchpad, Etienne's drawing of Galena and her palette been stolen from inside his sleeping bag, but he couldn't see a thing. Perhaps it was still dark, but there was the first tube shaking the pavements. He could hear the whirring bristles of the cleaning machine sucking dirt up from the gutter, the thud of newspapers being sorted: it must be nearly morning.

Every so often as the hours passed, last night's horror returned and he trembled with terror. It must be the kick on the head. Oh dear God, bring back my sight. If he were blind how could he feed Visitor? He could hear cars going in and out of the Middlesex Hospital and footsteps approaching. As an ultimate humiliation because he couldn't find his cap to lay upside down in front of him, he was forced to thrust out shaking hands.

'Please help me, I'm blind,' he stammered.

'Another of those scroungers from Kosovo,' said a voice disapprovingly. 'Why don't you stay in your own country?'

'I'm fucking English,' Alizarin heard himself shouting.

He was drenched in icy sweat which made him even colder.

The next couple, women, judging from the click of their heels, also clicked their tongues, muttering how disgusting it was for work-shy folk to use poor old doggies for begging, then spend the money on themselves.

'It's my dog I'm trying to feed,' yelled Alizarin. Then, as their heels clicked hastily away, remembering other tramps telling him people sometimes came back if you were polite, he added: 'Have a good day.'

Tubes rumbled, the pavement was filling up with footsteps, buses roared, ambulances jangled into the Middlesex. Alizarin breathed in cigarette smoke as the next passer-by quickened his pace, not wanting to be caught. The next approached tentatively, pausing, smelling faintly of eau-de-Cologne like an aunt.

'Please, please, help me feed my dog,' begged Alizarin.

There was a long silence. Then a desperately embarrassed female voice with a soft Scottish accent murmured, 'I think your wee doggie's passed away.'

How could he have forgotten to check Visitor? He had been so distraught about not being able to see. Frantically Alizarin reached out, hugging Visitor's shaggy body, calling his name, waiting for the familiar thud of his tail, realizing how cold and stiff he was.

'Don't be dead, please don't, Visitor.'

Crouched over him, parting his matted hair, Alizarin listened desperately for the faintest heartbeat – nothing. 'Oh, please, God.' His howl of desolation must have wakened the dead in Limesbridge churchyard.

The kind Scottish lady burst into tears and was joined

by the two secretaries, who, feeling guilty at muttering about 'work-shy folk', had returned with a tin of Pedigree Chum. One tried to comfort Alizarin, the other fetched a policeman.

Gordon Pritchard, a heart specialist so revered that God was rumoured to walk six paces behind him when he toured the wards, was on his way to hospital when his Rolls was halted by the traffic. Seeing a crowd gathered round some kind of accident, he lowered the window.

'Can I help?'

For a second, the man slumped over a shaggy yellow dog looked up. Tears streamed down his grey face. Like Munch's *Scream*, his wide-open mouth was a hollow of agonized outrage.

'Alizarin?' called out Gordon Pritchard in horror. 'Alizarin Belvedon?'

Pritchard had often stayed at Foxes Court and bought Old Masters from Raymond, who in turn he'd looked after when Raymond had had a heart murmur, five years ago.

'Alizarin, it's me.' Pritchard jumped out of the Rolls.

Only when Alizarin totally failed to recognize him did Pritchard realize he was blind. When he tried to get him admitted to Casualty, the main stumbling block was that Alizarin wouldn't part with Visitor. Such was his colossal strength, no-one could prise his dog away from him. Racked by coughing and tears, he kept crying out for Sophy.

Getting no answer from the flat in Duke Street, St James's, Pritchard grimly rang the gallery. Sophy, who was opening the post, handed the receiver to Jupiter.

'I see, I see, I'm terribly sorry. We'll be over at once.'

As he put down the receiver, Jupiter was trembling violently.

'Hanna?' whispered Sophy.

'No, Alizarin, he's been sleeping rough' – Jupiter's voice broke – 'and he seems to be blind, and Visitor's just died. Oh my God, how could we have done this to him?'

Then, pulling himself together: 'I must go to him.'

'Can I come too?'

Forgetting to lock up, forgetting the stock sale, they ran up Cork Street, up Regent Street, across Oxford Street.

It was rush hour, the sales were on, but not an orange 'For Hire' sign appeared anywhere. Shoving shoppers and commuters out of the way, they passed All Souls and the BBC on their left and raced along Mortimer Street. Jupiter was ten times fitter. Sophy thought her lungs would burst as she pounded after him.

There was still a crowd around Alizarin. Two policemen, a couple of nurses, an ambulance man and Gordon Pritchard were trying to reason with him. Seeing him sitting like a child clinging to a giant teddy bear, Visitor in his arms, the picture of despair, Sophy fought back the tears. She mustn't add to his misery.

'Alizarin, it's me.' Jupiter patted his brother's shoulder.

Sophy fell to her knees. 'Alizarin, it's Sophy,' she panted. Putting a hand round his agonizingly aching head, she pressed it to her heaving breast. 'I'm so terribly sorry. Thank God we've found you.'

'Sophy?' Alizarin looked round in bewilderment. 'It is really you. Oh, Sophy.'

'Really me. There, darling, it's going to be OK. You must come inside and get something warm inside you.'

'I can't leave Visitor. He took care of me. If they take him away, I'll never see him again.' Helplessly Alizarin ran his hand over Visitor's face, smoothing his fur, stroking his velvet ears.

'He looks really peaceful.' Sophy's voice was choked with tears. 'His eyes are closed, and his tail looks as though it's about to wag as he arrives in heaven.'

'Promise he's dead, it's not just a trick to take him to Battersea?'

'I promise. We'll take care of his body. Feel.' She took a blanket from the ambulance man and rubbed the rough wool against Alizarin's hollowed cheek. 'We've got this to wrap him in.'

'I'll take him straight down to Limesbridge' – Jupiter's voice was choked too – 'and bury him beside Maud.'

Only then did Sophy manage to remove Visitor from Alizarin's clutches.

He was admitted to hospital with pleurisy and pneumonia. There was no flesh on his body to protect him from the cold. Only his colossal strength had saved him. Clutching on to Sophy's hand, he raved on and on about Galena pouring with blood.

'I couldn't save her and I couldn't save Visitor. He froze to death because I couldn't afford to feed him. Oh, Sophy.'

'He was fifteen, he died of old age, darling.'

As the morphine kicked in, Alizarin lost consciousness.

Jupiter was in shock, wondering how on earth to get Visitor home, when his mobile rang.

'What the fuck's going on?' demanded Rupert Campbell-Black. 'I've just rolled up at your gallery after a cheap bargain for Ricky France-Lynch's birthday, place deserted, door open, pictures on the walls. Tempted to help myself.'

When Jupiter told him, Rupert was very sympathetic, and offered his helicopter. Visitor had been, after all, the great-great-grandson of Rupert's revered black Labrador, Badger.

Gordon Pritchard, however, hadn't finished with the Belvedons. Having handed Alizarin over to the top eye specialist, who'd promptly admitted him to Intensive Care, he proceeded to give Jupiter a very nasty five minutes.

'What the fuck happened?'

'There was a row over the Raphael.' Jupiter flushed slightly. 'I thought Al was having an affair with Hanna. Anthea wanted the Lodge for holiday lets. Together we chucked him out.'

'Anthea was always a bitch,' said Pritchard. 'He knew in June he was going blind. Told no-one.'

'Oh my God.'

'We'll run some tests, but it doesn't look good.'

'I'd better ring Dad,' said Jupiter.

Raymond, in bed with flu and a persistent cough, was devastated not least by the death of Visitor, whom he, Grenville and all the family had loved so much.

'Jupiter's bringing his body down later,' Raymond told Anthea. 'Pritchard found Alizarin sleeping rough in Mortimer Street, in seven degrees below. Pritchard claims you and Jupiter slung him out. It can't be true.'

'Course it wasn't. You know how paranoid and shirty Alizarin is. Jupiter and I reproached him mildly for tipping Zac off about Pandora. Al went into a sulk and stormed out.'

Raymond's eyes fell first.

'Poor old boy, poor darling Visitor. I must go to him.'

'You can't, you've got a temperature. I'll go' – Anthea sighed to indicate huge sacrifice – 'and bring him back. We'll get a nurse in, he can sleep in Dicky's room till half-term.'

Anthea caught the next train. Alizarin must be made to come home before such a damaging story reached the press. She and Jupiter must also get their stories straight – but Jupiter wasn't answering his mobile. After all, she kept telling herself as the train rumbled past grey frozen fields, Alizarin had been the one to walk out.

Arriving at the Middlesex, having redone her face and drenched herself in Shalimar in the taxi (she had always thought Gordon Pritchard most attractive), Anthea was horrified to find Emerald's fat sister *in situ*, looking quite awful. Sophy's eyes were swollen, her hair unbrushed, and she was bound to sneak to the Cartwrights.

'Where's Jupiter?' demanded Anthea.

'Taking Visitor's body back to Foxes Court. He should be home by now. Rupert Campbell-Black gave them a lift in his helicopter.'

Anthea was hopping. No opportunity to get her story straight, and to miss a chance of receiving Rupert Campbell-Black! Alizarin seemed to have tubes coming out of everywhere. He had the dreadful pallor and sunken features of Christ just down from the cross, and Sophy that sanctimonious stricken bustle of all those Marys who hung round him.

'How is he?' demanded Anthea.

'Asleep.' Sophy put her finger to her lips. 'He's had a massive dose of morphine.'

'I've come to take him home.'

'Well, you can't.' Sophy lost her temper. 'You chucked him out, and as a result he's got pneumonia, and isn't going anywhere. Why don't you bugger off?'

Anthea would have stood her ground if Gordon Pritchard hadn't rolled up, whisked her into a side room, and subjected her to an even more unpleasant five minutes than he'd given Jupiter.

After all I've done for that family, thought Anthea as she flounced out. And she couldn't even ring David for sympathy.

Jupiter was back at the Middlesex by evening. He looked utterly exhausted, his face drained of colour except for huge purply crimson shadows beneath his eyes, but he was calmer. They had buried Visitor in the orchard beside Maud. Raymond had insisted on staggering out in his dressing gown.

'I didn't tell him Al was blind. He couldn't handle it at the moment. Have you had anything to eat?'

'I'm not hungry.'

'Nor am I, but I could murder a large whisky. Let's go

and have dinner.' Then, when Sophy looked doubtfully at a sleeping Alizarin: 'He won't wake for ages.'

Jupiter took her to his local: Mulligans in Cork Street. They sat side by side on a banquette, which made conversation easier. Sophy chose leek soup because it was the cheapest thing on the menu and she'd heard from Emerald that the Belvedons were broke. Jupiter told her not to be silly, so they both had Irish stew and pickled red cabbage and a lot of red wine.

Sophy kept crying; Jupiter held her hand.

'I know I should ring Sienna and Jonathan, but I just feel it's better if the old boy's kept quiet at the moment,' he said, then, taking a deep breath: 'Look, I've had an idea. Casey Andrews's exhibition was scheduled for the second half of February. But he's walked out, so I'm going to show Alizarin instead.'

'That's wonderful!' squeaked Sophy, flinging her arms round Jupiter, then recoiling in horror. She hadn't washed since six that morning and she'd sweated so much with worry and pounding across London, she must pong worse than a skunk on a fun run.

But as she wriggled away, Jupiter clung to her.

'Tamzin, Dad's dimbo assistant, is showing no signs of coming back from Gstaad.' He begged: 'I can only do Al justice if you help me.'

'Oh God, I'd love that. It's half-term on the sixteenth of Feb so I'll be free.'

Jupiter ordered a couple of large brandies.

'You've got school tomorrow, I ought to take you home.'

'The hospital says I can stay the night.' Sophy's voice trembled: 'It'd be so awful if he woke up and there was no Visitor, and he didn't know where he was.'

'I'm so ashamed,' muttered Jupiter. 'Because he wasn't with Hanna, I feel as though a great poisoned thorn has been tugged out of my side and I can love him again.'

*   *   *

He and Sophy were less euphoric a few days later when tests proved that Alizarin had a dangerous and very rare tumour, known as Norfolk's Disease, which was pressing increasingly on his brain and the optic nerve. Doctors knew very little about the condition.

'His best hope,' Gordon Pritchard admitted privately to Jupiter, 'would be an operation in the States, which would cost a fortune.'

The truth could probably be kept from Raymond, reflected Jupiter, but Alizarin was too intelligent and tuned into people's voices ever to be fobbed off with lies. This made it even more important to make his exhibition a success.

60

With the private view scheduled for 15 February, Jupiter had just over a month to get things organized. Tipped off by Mrs Robens when Anthea and Raymond would be away, he drove Sophy and the gallery van down to Limesbridge. Crossing the bridge, he could see Foxes Court behind its prison bars of leafless trees – a frequent subject of his mother's paintings. Had Hanna felt as trapped? The house would be his once Raymond died, but what would be the point without Hanna to share it?

His desolation increased as they passed the Lodge. In the front garden, the nettles had been replaced by neatly edged beds and a wheelbarrow planted with mauve and yellow pansies. Net curtains twitched behind a Tory poster. Alizarin would have gone ballistic. Jupiter felt even more guilty at chucking him out.

With renewed determination he and Sophy were soon dragging canvasses, often mildewed and escaping from their stretchers, from packing chests, barns, potting sheds, and outside lavatories. Having loaded these, they raided the attic, finding earlier pictures, not just of out-of-work miners and shipbuilders, but of dogs and children, even tennis parties, which had somehow escaped Anthea's skips.

'Thank God she's frightened of spiders and seldom comes up here,' said Jupiter.

'Who's this? She's beautiful,' sighed Sophy, as from

behind a headless rocking horse she dragged a ravishing nude with her blond pubes cut in the shape of a heart. Then she blushed furiously, realizing it was Hanna.

Jupiter's face was expressionless as he examined the picture.

'When did you get married?' stammered Sophy.

'Ninety-four.' Then, after a long pause: 'You can date it by Alizarin's paintings. They get steadily darker, no more industrial landscapes, just an obsessive catalogue of disaster, atrocity piled on atrocity.'

Hearing a step on the stairs, Jupiter glanced at his watch. He didn't want to bump into Anthea. But it was Dora, full of plans for a Labrador puppy, which she could look after until Alizarin needed it as a guide dog.

'What I really came to say,' she went on, 'is that Dicky's seriously broke, so why don't you put *Upside-Down Camels* into the exhibition?'

The next few weeks, when Sophy wasn't teaching, were spent shooting out invitations and press releases, proofreading a makeshift catalogue, framing, hanging, lighting and visiting Alizarin who, because he refused to let the family pay for a private room, was now in a public ward full of eye diseases and the aftermath of dreadful operations. Locked away in darkness, the noise must have been driving him crazy.

Nor did he seem remotely roused out of his despair by the prospect of an exhibition, which would not sell enough pictures to pay for the operation. Aware that he had lowered his guard, clinging to Sophy the morning she and Jupiter found him, he was dauntingly offhand when she rolled up to read him the *Guardian*, bearing quiches rather badly baked by Patience and freesias he could smell if not see. She would have stopped coming if Alizarin's favourite nurse, black Molly Malone, hadn't confided how much he looked forward to her visits.

'"Where is Sophy?" he demand all day.'

*　　*　　*

The story of Alizarin's sleeping rough had reached the papers. His homeless friends around Charlotte Street did extremely well giving interviews about the Tender Toff. Dora also cleaned up. The *Sun*, much beguiled by her stories of Visitor's body being flown home 'just like Princess Diana's' in Rupert Campbell-Black's helicopter, promised to give her a chocolate Labrador puppy the moment Anthea's back was turned.

Although Alizarin's story was rather overshadowed by a by-election and the coming out of a rock star, it had not been good for the Belvedons' image. Not only did they harbour suspect Raphaels, but neglected their own.

Meanwhile, there was an exciting development in Hoxton. Jonathan's seedy friend, Trafford, who was now the protégé of Geraldine Paxton, had just landed himself the £20,000 Whistler Prize for *Shagpile*. This was an eight-foot tower of male nudes engaged in the sex act, plugged into each other like Lego, which those 'in the loop' thought both 'pivotal' and 'challenging'. There was even talk of a board game.

Although Trafford, according to Jonathan, would be willing to service a musk ox, he didn't like Geraldine – old Needy in Toyboy Land – and yearned for the long, ringed and studded white body of Sienna Belvedon. Even more, he missed the high jinks he had enjoyed with her brother Jonathan, who was far too devastated he couldn't marry Emerald to come home from Vienna.

One morning in late November, Trafford had taken a call for Jonathan from Abdul Karamagi. The Saudi was still so enraptured with the nude which he believed Jonathan had painted of Sophy that he wanted to fly Jonathan out to the Middle East on his private jet to paint his favourite stallion for a seven-figure sum.

Having cosily explained that Jonathan had gone permanently abroad, Trafford accepted the commission. He was also convinced that he had earned his fee. Abdul's stallion was even rattier than Jonathan before he left for Vienna. Trafford, nevertheless, felt guilty enough to persuade Abdul, who longed for recognition as a discerning collector, to enter *Sophy of Shepherd's Bush*, as the nude was now known, for the British Portrait Awards.

At the beginning of January, Trafford and a troupe of Jonathan's cronies (none of whom had any idea Alizarin was the artist) collected the nude from Abdul's house and delivered it to the British Portrait Museum in Gower Street. The winner of the £25,000 prize would be announced at a big dinner at the Dorchester on Valentine's Day.

'No-one's to tell Jonathan,' ordered Trafford, 'then he won't be choked if he doesn't win.'

Also among the 700 entries was one of Alizarin's portraits of Visitor, which Dicky and Dora had submitted as a joke.

The Awards themselves were sponsored by Doggie Dins Petfoods, whose chairman, Kevin Coley, had recently become a Labour peer. Having failed to grapple his way up the social scale through show-jumping or polo sponsorship, Lord Coley had turned in the Eighties to art and, with the help of Raymond's eye, had built up a fine collection of pictures.

David Pulborough and Geraldine Paxton, both avid to snatch Lord Coley's custom from Raymond, were on his judges' panel. They spent their time manipulating the other judges, on the premise that they were 'the experts', and enjoying several excellent lunches together on expenses. Naturally they wanted Jonathan to win because he was a Pulborough gallery artist, but after the bollocking he'd received in October, Jonathan was refusing to answer David's calls.

David was also furious when he saw the magnificent nude of Sophy. Jonathan had yet again failed to pass on the commission on the fat fee that Abdul must have paid him. This, however, could be rectified once Jonathan had been lured home to receive the first prize.

The other judges had already spent two days in the museum boardroom, drinking coffee, eating ridged fawn biscuits, getting on each other's nerves, and sulkily being bullied into shortlisting four of David's artists, including Jonathan and Casey, when yet another judge rolled up. This was Casey Andrews's ex-wife, Joan Bideford, who'd been delayed by a freak snowstorm in Peru. Wearing a charcoal-grey suit and a Guards' tie, roaring like a sergeant major that the entire panel was in need of a decent optician to have selected such junk, Joan chucked out three of the Pulborough artists, including her ex's oil of Margaret Jay.

'Gather you've taken on the old bugger,' she bellowed at David. 'You'll regret it.'

The only entries that were worth a toffee, she went on, were Daisy France-Lynch's portrait of Tabitha Rannaldini, Jonathan's nude of Sophy and Alizarin's painting of Visitor.

Kevin Coley was enchanted. Like Joan Bideford, he loved pretty women, and had bought many of Joan's erotic nudes in the past which had rocketed in value. He trusted her opinion and longed for a wonderful dog portrait to win. He could then put Visitor's beaming face on every tin of Doggie Dins. The rest of the judges agreed, except for David and Geraldine – the experts – who said Visitor wouldn't dignify the competition.

'And the dog has just passed away in rather tragic circumstances,' said Geraldine quietly. 'It wouldn't be available for publicity.'

'Nor will his master,' insisted David, 'chap's unlikely to paint again.'

'All the more reason to give it him,' snorted Joan.

'How much more on message would be a beautiful plump young woman, with glorious flesh tones,' urged stick-thin Geraldine. 'Fat is after all a feminist issue. Jonathan's nude has greater artistic merit than his brother's Labrador.'

Joan lit a cigar and took another look at Sophy's sleepy smile and sand dune curves.

'Sorry, Kev, Lab's wonderfully painted but this does have the edge, bursting with energy, staggeringly confident. Never thought Jonathan was capable of such innocent unguarded lyricism.'

Joan mopped her brow. *Sophy of Shepherd's Bush* was declared the winner, Visitor the runner-up, with Daisy France-Lynch, who had won last year, in third place. Joan even allowed Casey to be fourth.

'Then I can watch the vain old tosser's face when he doesn't win.'

David was shocked to find himself agreeing with Joan. Casey was getting far too above himself. Geraldine belted off to ring Jonathan in Vienna. Trafford, as a lover, although vigorous, didn't bathe enough and Jonathan had looked so handsome when he'd rolled up at the Commotion in New York.

In his dingy digs in Vienna, Jonathan had reached rock bottom. The room, which was the size of a whelping kennel, was only furnished with a narrow bed, a wireless, and a hundred canvasses, on which wistful variations of Emerald's wan, white face gazed at him from different landscapes. He had failed to dig up any dirt which might jeopardize Zac's claim on the Raphael. Having not sold a thing since the summer, he was flat broke. He was shocked by his jealousy that Trafford had won the Whistler and become a media star.

Deciding not to buy a litre of whisky and get plastered because his rent was due tomorrow, Jonathan switched on the radio. The Vienna Phil were about to play Tchaikovsky's Sixth Symphony.

'The irony,' the announcer was saying, 'is that before Tchaikovsky wrote perhaps his greatest work, he had lost all confidence in himself as a composer. "What I need", he wrote to his brother Modest, "is to believe in myself again".'

'Tchaikovsky *et moi*,' sighed Jonathan.

The ascending scale of the opening bassoon solo coincided with the telephone ringing.

'Jonathan, it's Geraldine.'

'Oh, go away.'

'Don't be silly. You've just won the British Portrait Award, and twenty-five thousand pounds.'

'What for?'

'Trafford submitted one of your nudes.'

'Which one? I've done so many.'

Outside there was a rosy blur on the linden trees. One day he wanted a shirt like the purple and white striped crocuses being flattened by the rain.

'Doggie Dins will pay for your flight home,' insisted Geraldine.

And I'll be 800 miles nearer Emerald, thought Jonathan.

'OK. I'll come.'

'Don't tell anyone you've won. The press will only know you've been shortlisted.'

Jonathan was fractionally cheered up. Perhaps he wasn't such a meretricious, forgotten artist after all. The BP Award was hugely prestigious. He hoped Emerald would be proud. It would also give him a chance to see Alizarin.

61

The ballroom at the Dorchester was packed. The Doggie Dins logo of a jaunty mongrel adorned every menu, and flashed orange and green, like the Cheshire cat, above the platform. The shortlisted portraits would be later shown on a huge monitor. The future High Sheriff hopped from table to table, massaging dinner-jacketed shoulders, caressing bare backs, charming, networking, David the player.

'I wouldn't be giving away secrets if I told you the Pulborough's got the winner.'

News that Jonathan had been shortlisted had been just the tonic Raymond needed. He hadn't seen his darling boy since October. The Belvedons had there-fore taken a front-row table and sod the cost. Anthea, on the other hand, was feeling paranoid. David was still livid she'd let him think he was Emerald's father. Jupiter, who'd always been so affectionate and supportive, appeared to have gone over to Alizarin's side. Last time she'd seen Jonathan, he'd called her a whore and stolen her David Shilling hat, and now he'd won a prize, God knew what he might get up to.

Anthea was also irked that on a table to the right, David had annexed most of the Belvedon's big clients. The newly ennobled Lord Coley, looking like a thatched pig with his brick-red face and brushed-forward grey hair, who'd always made passes at Anthea in the past, was now chatting animatedly to Si Greenbridge and Rosemary Pulborough, who looked irritatingly better than usual in dove-grey chiffon. On Si's right was frightful Geraldine with even more frightful Trafford next to her. Hopefully Trafford would get drunk and embarrass them all. Anthea had never seen anything so disgusting as *Shagpile*. And next to Trafford, like a fuchsia barrel, was Kevin's ghastly wife Enid, who was ecstatic about becoming Lady Coley. She had been dreadfully patronizing towards Anthea as they'd queued to leave their coats.

'How embarrassing to find your stepson sleepin' rough in the gutter,' she had yelled, 'and what's this about you havin' looted art in your attic?'

Everyone had turned round.

Anthea was also livid with Emerald, who'd flatly refused to show up because it would be too agonizing to see Jonathan. Nor was Emerald very happy about *Sophy of Shepherd's Bush*.

'You never told me you'd posed for Jonathan,' she'd stormed.

'I sort of forgot,' mumbled Sophy.

'Did he sleep with you?'

'Oh no, no, no,' lied Sophy, then, truthfully: 'He was never interested in anyone but you.'

Sophy was worried stiff that Jonathan would be lynched if it leaked out that Alizarin had painted the portrait.

To David, Geraldine and Lord Coley's consternation, Jonathan's flight was delayed, and he only reached the Dorchester as the guests were scraping up the last of their mango and ginger ice cream and drifting off for a pee break.

Jonathan, who was wearing Emerald's blue shirt with his dinner jacket and no cufflinks, was far too nervous to face the family and the agony and the ecstasy if

Emerald were with them, so he hovered in a side room, sketching the judges.

Over at David's table, Lord Coley, talking across dull Rosemary, had been highly gratified by his long chat with Si Greenbridge. You certainly networked when you dined with the Pulboroughs.

Somerford, who didn't feel that Casey Andrews winning the award was much of a story, and who was looking for a better lead for his column, paused beside Si's chair.

'Is it true you're planning to build a Greenbridge Museum in Detroit?' he asked. 'And fill it with works of art for the benefit of the city?'

'What a wonderfully philanthropic gesture,' cried Geraldine, 'I hope I may be allowed to make suggestions.'

'Bloody good career move, Si,' grunted Trafford, 'you'll be able to launder your dirty money and your murky reputation at the same time.'

'Trafford!' thundered a horrified David. Geraldine looked as though she was about to faint, but Si, who seemed in an amazingly good mood, roared with laughter.

'I'll remember that remark next time you want me to buy a picture, young man.'

'Lord Coley and I,' butted in Lady Coley, who was determined to keep her very big end up, 'also feel it is our duty to open our collection to the public next year. As yet we cannot decide what to call it.'

'What about Art Nouveau Riche?' murmured Trafford, scooping up all the table's allocation of petits fours and washing them down with a glass of Barsac.

As a roll of drums sent people racing back to their seats, Casey Andrews could be seen combing his beard in anticipation of accepting the award. As the lights dimmed, Rosemary was amazed to feel Si's huge warm hand closing over hers and the pressure of his iron thigh against her own. Overjoyed but disbelieving (perhaps he was just stretching?), she edged her leg an inch away. Immediately Si's leg followed.

Geraldine, looking thin and graceful in silver – like the twigs Anthea used to paint at Christmas, thought Jonathan – mounted the rostrum to give away the prizes.

'My lords' – big flashing smile at Lord Coley – 'ladies, and gentlemen, welcome to the tenth British Portrait Awards sponsored so generously by Doggie Dins.'

After that Jonathan couldn't take in what she was saying.

'Although we rejected nine-tenths of the send-in, blah, blah, blah, we were struck by the extraordinary skills, blah, blah, blah, keeping figurative painting alive, blah, blah, blah, Lord Coley, whose huge enthusiasm for art brought this competition into being, blah, blah . . .'

Jonathan, who was busy drawing Kevin Coley's fourth chin, didn't look up at the monitor as the winning names were flashed up to loud cheers.

'I have to confess that this was Lord Coley's favourite,' shouted Geraldine over the din, as a beaming yellow face appeared on the screen.

'Visitor!' gasped Raymond in delight and anguish.

'But on balance, we were unanimous about the winner, who has long been regarded as the wild man of the art world,' continued Geraldine to more cheers and catcalls.

Casey smirked and recombed his beard.

'But over the years,' called out Geraldine triumphantly, 'he has matured astonishingly and produced on this occasion a work of towering genius.'

Next moment, *Sophy of Shepherd's Bush* flashed up on the screen. A few seconds of silence was followed by tumultuous whoops and wolf whistles.

'That's Emerald's sister,' cried Anthea in outrage. 'Why doesn't she do something about her bikini line?'

'And the winner of the British Portrait Award 2000,' shouted Geraldine, 'is Jonathan Belvedon.'

Looking up from his sketch, Jonathan caught sight of Alizarin's portrait and felt, like his hero Byron before him, as if 'an elephant had trodden on his heart'. Not for a moment, however, did he betray his disappointment. Only pausing at David's table to down a third of a bottle of champagne, he sauntered, cigarette in hand, up onto the platform. The blaze of flashlights showed up his unhealthy pallor and the stone and a half weight loss, but he smiled amiably.

The Belvedon table, who knew that smile of old, wondered nervously what he was about to do next. Massed polyanthus along the edge of the stage cringed, expecting him to throw up. But Jonathan merely seized the mike. It was half a minute before he could make himself heard over the uproar.

'Abdul Karamagi commissioned me to do this portrait of Sophy in good faith,' he announced calmly. 'I hadn't got the time, so my brother Alizarin got me out of a jam and painted Sophy instead. My only contribution to this picture was to sign it. Hence the work of towering genius.'

Geraldine looked as though she was going to have a coronary.

'Alizarin's always followed his own road,' shouted Jonathan over the din, 'never shirking, never compromising. He works more hours than anyone I know and has continued to work in this intensely personal way, irrespective of fashion. It's great, he's got a big show opening at my father's gallery in Cork Street tomorrow and an even bigger one at the Campbell-Black in New York later in the year.

'I am glad to accept the award on his behalf and to be able to bank the cheque' – Jonathan grabbed them both from a helplessly mouthing Geraldine – 'to stop him giving it away to even poorer artists. Thank you.'

Having glanced at the Belvedons' table, to make sure

Emerald wasn't there, only pausing to nick another bottle of David's champagne, Jonathan looked neither to right nor left as to deafening cheers and a few boos, he sprinted out into Park Lane. Here he shook off the press and, leaping into a taxi, went to see Alizarin.

After the champagne, the beautiful people, the soft lights and the merry bitchy chat about nothing except whose pictures were unjustifiably selling better than others, the contrast was hideous.

Under that glaring fluorescent light in an over-crowded ward surrounded by other desperately suffering people, Alizarin seemed to have become part of that persecuted world he was constantly portraying. How well he would have recorded the scene if he could have seen it.

In his striped pyjamas, his thinness emphasizing his beaky nose, sightless closed eyes, Belvedon eyelashes feathering his wasted cheeks, Alizarin could have been any one of the Holocaust victims Jonathan had been reading about so obsessively in Vienna.

Typically he was not particularly excited by the news he'd won. There was nothing original or visionary about his portrait of Sophy. His imagination hadn't been stretched.

'Everyone was knocked out by it.'

'Shows what lousy taste they've got. And twenty-five thousand won't pay for the operation.'

'You'll make a lot more tomorrow. After tonight they'll flock to the private view.'

'Doesn't bring Visitor back.'

'Oh, Al! Your portrait of him came second, which means another ten grand. Casey Andrews will go apeshit to be beaten by a dog.'

Alizarin smiled faintly.

'That's something. Good of you to come.'

'I wanted to see you.' Oh Christ, why did everything come back to sight?

On the bedside table, Jonathan noticed scribbles intended as a Valentine card in which the arrow kept missing the heart, and nearly wept. Then he remembered he'd never paid Alizarin his share for Sophy's portrait. He must get the money somehow.

'Let's open this,' he said, whipping out David's bottle of champagne from inside his dinner jacket.

'Oh no you don't.' A nurse who'd been redressing the eye of a patient opposite grabbed the bottle. 'Alizarin's on extremely strong medication at the moment. Time you pushed off anyway. We're about to turn out the lights.'

They were already turned out for Alizarin.

62

By nine o'clock on the morning of Alizarin's private view, a large sign saying: 'Winner and runner-up of the British Portrait Award 2000' had been plastered across the front window of the Belvedon. At midday, Raymond's assistant, Tamzin the dimbo, who could sniff out a party all the way from Gstaad, returned from her six-week sabbatical with a Mars-brown tan. Having arranged white daffodils still tightly in bud in large glass vases round the gallery, she proceeded to drive Jupiter crackers ringing her friends and describing the sexual prowess of Heinz her ski instructor.

'It didn't matter one bit that there was hardly any snow.'

Later, as Sophy charged round polishing parquet, buffing frames with black boot polish, touching up the walls with white paint, Tamzin painted her nails.

'I wanted to go to art school, Sophy, but Mummy and Daddy thought I'd get into drugs so they made me take a sekky course.'

'Not so's you'd notice,' muttered Jupiter, who'd just bought six more light bulbs and was busy adjusting their beam onto different pictures. 'For Christ's sake, start ringing round the press, Tamzin.'

'Just nipping out for a sandwich. D'you want anything, Sophy?'

Sophy shook her head, for once too nervous to eat.

An increasingly edgy Jupiter had brought in a ghetto blaster and was playing tapes of battle sounds to create atmosphere. Guns booming and shells exploding seemed to sum up his mood and that of Alizarin's thundery dark pictures, which, properly lit for the first time, looked spectacular. Pride of place on the ground floor had been given to *Upside-Down Camels*, which glowed like amber and citrine. *Heatwave*, loaned by Dicky Belvedon, said the description.

'It all looks wonderful,' Sophy told Jupiter soothingly.

But outside a vicious north wind whipped down Cork Street, and the sky had turned a sickly yellow presaging the snow which Tamzin had been denied in Gstaad. Bad forecasts would certainly deter the country punters, thought Sophy in anguish as she set off in a taxi to collect two crates each of red and white, and a huge chunk of mature Cheddar from which guests would hack pieces.

When she returned, Tamzin was waving the *Standard*.

'You're in the paper.'

'"My brother painted my winning portrait," admits YBA's bad boy', said a large headline.

Oh Christ! Sophy winced at her even larger naked body sprawled across the centre pages, with a caption: 'Sophy's extremely choice'.

If she didn't get sacked for bunking off, the head would boot her out for this. No wonder education was in a parlous state in England.

'At least they've plugged the private view,' said Tamzin, waving a sponge bag. 'It's nearly five-thirty, I'm off to change.'

Outside the icy pavements glittered under the street lamps. Jupiter had just returned from righting a blown-over bay tree when Anthea rang in. She and Raymond had reached the London flat, but Raymond had developed a raging temperature, was clearly going down with flu and wouldn't be able to make it.

'I really can't leave the old boy.' Anthea lowered her voice: 'Ay'm so disappointed.'

'Bloody liar,' said Jupiter as he hung up. 'But it'll be easier without Dad, he gets more uptight than the artists.'

Thank God Alizarin wasn't here either: he was always so rude to the press. Nor would he have been happy, if he weren't blind, to see how much of his earlier, carefree work, before he lost Hanna, was on display. Oh Hanna, sighed Jupiter.

Seeing he was shivering worse than Grenville at the prospect of fireworks, Sophy made him have a hot shower upstairs. Inside she was even more apprehensive than Jupiter. If they didn't sell pictures tonight, Alizarin would be condemned to an eternity of darkness. But she killed her nerves by keeping busy, opening bottles, putting out blue glass ashtrays and polishing Jupiter's shoes. When he came down with his hair slicked back, she gave him a good-luck tie: red silk covered with black cats.

'That is fabulous.' Jupiter put it on. 'God, we're going to need it.'

David Pulborough was absolutely furious. He and Geraldine had been made to look complete idiots at the awards last night. They both detested Alizarin, and now he'd been proved the winning artist, David wouldn't be owed a fat cut any more.

In revenge, he had decided to hold a spoiler party across the road at the Pulborough and give selected press a preview of one or two of Casey Andrews's latest pictures, before his exhibition opened next week. By six-thirty, therefore, David, Geraldine, Casey and Somerford Keynes were peering out like a witches' coven, furious to see despite the falling snow so many people going into the Belvedon.

'Jupiter and Raymond's faces will be alizarin crimson by the end of this evening,' bitched Somerford. 'They will not sell a single picture. Talk about the flop of the Millennium.'

David kept popping out into the street, diverting critics and diary writers he knew.

Bastard, thought Jupiter.

All three floors of the Belvedon were soon packed with clients, artists, other dealers, press and beautiful people, looking at each other rather than the pictures. Abdul Karamagi was among the first arrivals, ecstatic at the publicity. *Sophy's Bush*, he kept telling everyone, would shortly be as famous as the Botticelli Venus.

Sophy herself, now falling out of the black lace dress which Emerald had vetoed for the twenty-sixth birthday party, was to her embarrassment much photographed. Jonathan, who had turned up merely to support Alizarin, received his usual share of hysterical media attention, particularly after last night's misunderstanding.

'When did Alizarin paint that portrait?' 'Where is he?' 'Where's Raymond, and what's happening about *Pandora*?' clamoured the journalists.

'The civil case, which we will win,' said Jonathan firmly, 'is scheduled for late April. Sienna's case – she'll be totally exonerated too – comes up at the beginning of March.'

'I told you not to distract the press,' hissed Jupiter.

'Why does everyone keep murmuring "Interesting"?' Sophy whispered to Jonathan.

'Because,' he whispered back, 'if you slag a picture off, you're bound to be talking to the artist's mother, who'll thump you. If you say it's wonderful, you're bound to be talking to the artist's best friend, who'll be so jealous, he'll thump you even harder. Much easier to be neutral and murmur: "Interesting."'

'Interesting,' murmured Sophy.

'How's Emerald?' asked Jonathan ultra casually.

'Trying to work.'

'Why wasn't she at the awards yesterday?'

'I think she was jealous you'd painted me, not her.'

Jonathan felt the faintest lift of the heart. He could just handle things if Emerald still loved him.

Many of the major players had now arrived: Lord Coley, very pleased with himself: 'We chose the artist last night, Al Belvedon's going places'; Minsky Kraskov, the terrifying Mafia thug alleged to like paintings of tortures. There was a rumble of excitement as Si Greenbridge walked in, watchful as ever, flanked by guards so he needn't make small talk.

Jupiter was in a quandary. He'd learnt from Sienna that she'd seen Si and Zac plotting in New York. He was tempted to show Si the door, but he needed him to buy a picture to egg on the other rich apes, so with gritted smile he moved forward to welcome him.

'I'll ask if I need help,' snapped Si. He seemed tired and distracted.

It was also sadly obvious that both collectors and press had turned up expecting more voluptuous nudes, with or without a bikini line, like *Sophy of Shepherd's Bush*. People were yakking at the top of their voices to be heard over the booming guns and the explosions, but no-one was buying. The gallery's reputation had been more damaged than even Jupiter had thought.

Everyone nudged as Somerford and his claque of queens could be seen mincing through the snow from the Pulborough, careful not to slip, pens poised to annihilate Alizarin. On the way in, Somerford met Judy Collins, head of Twentieth-Century Acquisitions at the Tate.

'You won't find anything in here,' he told her bitchily, 'I'd pop across to the Pulborough and look at a real artist.'

'I like that,' said Judy Collins, walking over to examine *Upside-Down Camels*.

A diversion was created by a group of Alizarin's

students, who had raised £2,000, and wanted to buy a picture for their common room to go towards Alizarin's air fare. They were clearly devastated he wasn't at the party.

'What a photo opportunity missed,' sighed Tamzin.

This show is going to bomb more spectacularly than anything we've ever done, thought Jupiter, but that isn't enough to distract me from the agony of Hanna not being here, to hold my hand, to laugh it off with me over supper later, to soothe my wounds in bed.

Lady Coley, who looked like a Windsor violet barrel this evening, had been admiring the charming water-colour entitled *Dog Stars*, which showed Visitor gazing up at a night sky dominated by Canis Major, and which Sophy had retrieved from Jonathan's waste-paper basket the night she met Alizarin.

'Tracey's thirty next month,' Lady Coley reminded her husband, who promptly asked the price.

'I'm afraid it's sold,' gasped Sophy, hastily sticking a red spot on the description. Although Jupiter would murder her, she couldn't bear the Coleys to have Visitor.

Jupiter, however, had been distracted by the arrival of a tall blonde. Tears spilled down her anguished features, like a waterfall over grey rocks. Snow had whitened her hair; she had lost so much weight around the face, she looked like a Victorian waif seeking refuge from a storm. Jupiter, jaw gritted to stop himself breaking down, fought his way through the crowd, seized the blonde's hand, pulling her into the back office and locking the door.

'I was worried no-one would turn up,' sobbed Hanna.

'For Alizarin?' asked Jupiter bitterly.

'No, for you. It was so brave of you to give him this show.' Then, as he gazed down at the bulge: 'I'm nearly seven months pregnant, and it's yours, you idiot.'

'Oh my darling.' Jupiter's hand went down, his trembling fingers splayed out over her tummy, then travelled slowly up over her left breast, curling itself round the back of her neck, drawing her lips towards his.

'You can't leave people in the middle of a private view.'

'Wanna bet? I have so much apologizing to do,' muttered Jupiter.

Tamzin had disappeared upstairs with Abdul. Jonathan, hackles up, teeth bared like an angry cur, was pursuing Somerford. Sophy was left as chief salesman. To whom?

Si had been poised to buy one of the big oils of Macedonia, and all the other major players, spurred on, were reaching for their cheque books, when he had suddenly glanced across the street and clocked David and Geraldine through the window of the Pulborough. Next moment he had shot out of the gallery, with his guards pelting after him, and disappeared into his limo and the night. All the other major players promptly put back their cheque books and the party began to disperse.

The battalions of red and white had been depleted by the onslaught, the chunk of mature Cheddar looked like a desert ant heap. Beautiful people were on their mobiles checking the whereabouts of the next party and ringing for cabs. The press were packing up their cameras and putting away their notebooks. Nothing had sold, an empty spike waited wistfully for yellow invoices. Somerford was still badmouthing Alizarin, Jonathan was moving in to thump him, when Sophy hissed in excitement: 'Look at that!'

For a tall man in a dinner jacket, oblivious of the cold, was loping down Cork Street, his gold hair silver in the moonlight. The gallery fell silent as Rupert Campbell-Black stalked in. All the things Sophy had ever heard about his utter self-confidence and dazzling, unnerving beauty were true, but she loved him already because he had two children he adored who were adopted like she was.

Ignoring the visitors' book, refusing a drink, Rupert picked up a catalogue. The crowd divided, still in silence, as he circled the rooms, looking quickly and intently at each picture as though he were examining yearlings at a spring sale. Just in time, Sophy managed to peel the red spot off Visitor's portrait.

Pausing in front of it, Rupert smiled slightly.

'How much is that?'

Sophy took a deep breath.

'Five thousand pounds,' she gasped. Jupiter, who'd priced it at £500, would murder her a second time.

'OK.' Rupert moved on.

I've blown it, thought Sophy wretchedly.

As Rupert went round the rooms again, the chat began to soar. This time he put crosses in his catalogue against a few landscapes and the worst torture paintings, but sadly not beside Visitor.

'I said those were the most challenging,' said a man in a beetle cap, who'd been slagging the torture paintings off as grotesque earlier.

Rupert handed the marked catalogue to Sophy.

'Thanks.'

He's going, thought Sophy in despair.

'Oh, please buy something just to encourage the others,' she pleaded.

For a second, Rupert's face betrayed no emotion, then he said: 'I've marked the ones I don't want, I'll take the rest,' and, seeing Sophy's look of joyful incredulity, he smiled.

'Are you s-s-sure?'

'Quite,' said Rupert, who'd had a tip-off from his brother Adrian, who was going to take most of the pictures for his New York gallery.

'D'you think Jupiter'll give me something on them?' he asked.

'I can give you ten per cent,' said Sophy grandly.

'Fifteen,' suggested Rupert.

'Twelve and a half,' said Sophy. Heavens, she'd soon

be haggling away like a carpet salesman.

'Done.' Rupert got out his cheque book. 'I'll give you a deposit and pay for *Dog Star*. I'd like to take that with me now to show my son Xav, who's got a black Lab. I'll get the rest collected at the end of the exhibition.'

Pandemonium followed, red spots going up like an attack of scarlet fever, yellow invoices falling on the spike like Roman soldiers at Philippi. Lord Coley, who'd had a vicious run-in with Rupert years ago, when he'd had an affaire with the wife of Rupert's best friend, still admired him as a businessman, and immediately bought three landscapes. Abdul bought two. Minsky Kraskov snapped up the torture paintings, leaving nothing for the head of Twentieth-Century Acquisitions at the Tate.

Tamzin came belting downstairs.

'I've just been chatted up by the Chapman brothers – where's Rupert Campbell-Black? Oh look, the daffodils have all come out.'

Hanna and Jupiter, who'd just emerged dazed but starry-eyed from the back room to learn the incredible news, were soon pulling Alizarin's other paintings out of the stock room. They all went. Even the mature Cheddar in its sculptured form was sold for £800.

Sophy started giggling and found she couldn't stop. Somerford, who'd harboured an unrequited crush on Rupert since the days of Galena, decided to give Alizarin a rave review.

'Alizarin Belvedon's work appears gloomy and harsh, but the more one looks, the more visual and emotional strength one finds,' he wrote on the back of his cheque book.

Suddenly everyone was talking about the dynamic use of colour, the unique complexity, originality and energy of the paintings.

Judy Collins put a reserve on *Upside-Down Camels*.

'Could you ask Dicky Belvedon if he'd be prepared to sell? The colour is wonderful.'

'Dicky'll be able to pay back the fête committee ten times over and buy an Aston Martin,' said Jonathan gleefully. 'And General Anaesthetic's going to be furious.'

Crossing the room, he thanked Rupert for buying Alizarin's paintings.

'I've got a lot of your mother's stuff at home,' admitted Rupert.

'You're not Alizarin's father, by any chance?' murmured Jonathan.

Rupert shook his sleek golden head.

'Alizarin was born long before I – er – knew your mother. My money would be on Etienne de Montigny.'

'Look,' Jonathan blushed, 'your brother Adrian's been fantastically kind to my sister Sienna. She's the one who nicked the Raphael. Could I ask you a colossal favour?'

'Almost certainly not,' said Rupert, looking wary.

'Sienna never knew our mother,' pleaded Jonathan, 'I was only two when she died. Alizarin is so traumatized, he can't talk about her at all. Jupiter never liked her much. Dad's blocked her out and won't speak about her in case he upsets Anthea. Aunt Lily and Rosemary only knew her socially. Sienna's so desperate for info.'

'Not sure my recollections would be entirely suitable.'

'Perhaps not, but there must have been inter-intercourse bits. With the court case coming up, she's terribly low.'

And you too, my poor boy, thought Rupert, looking at Jonathan's gaunt, shadowed face and big haunted eyes.

'I'll try and take her out to lunch, next time I'm in America,' he conceded. 'But I don't promise anything.'

Everyone was dying to talk to Rupert but he had Zac's ability to freeze people out, thought Sophy as she handed him the wrapped-up *Dog Star*.

'Thank you,' said Rupert gravely. 'You're much

prettier than your gatefold, and those are sensational
tits.'

'There's that bastard Campbell-Black,' stormed Casey
Andrews, buckling his big red bulbous nose against
the Pulborough front window. 'Little shit was always
hanging round Galena in the old days.'

Highly unamused to see such evidence of transaction,
David drew Casey and Geraldine into the back room for
another bottle of Veuve Clicquot. Now that Somerford
had waddled over to the Belvedon, they could discuss
the real purpose of the evening: the erection of a
Borochova Memorial in Limesbridge.

Anthea was still stalling, explained David. She'd
always had such a hang-up about Galena, but public
feeling was so strong, she'd be overruled. Sucking up to
his new gallery artist, he then said that he and Geraldine
felt Casey was the ideal artist to do the memorial.

'You knew Galena intimately. Like Picasso, you're as
mighty a sculptor as a painter.'

Casey stopped smirking over his entry in *Who's Who in
Art*, which was almost as long as his beard.

'Of course I'll do the memorial. Better order in some
Portland stone, there's been a run on it recently. As you
know' – he flashed green teeth at Geraldine – 'I'm at
work on my memoirs, which will be, I may add, sensational.' Then, pursing his lips pompously: 'The world
should know I was the great love of Galena's life.'

'Hardly surprising. You're so dynamic,' murmured
Geraldine.

'Were you the only one?' asked David innocently.

Casey held out his glass for a refill.

'The only serious one – Raymond of course is a
pansy.'

'You're not worried about upsetting the family?'
queried Geraldine.

'Not in the least,' boomed Casey, 'Raymond's lost his
marbles, and I don't owe anything to those malevolent

562

scallywags.' Wandering out into the main gallery, he caught sight of Rupert laughing with the scallywag who had told Casey to bugger off the night of Emerald's birthday party. 'The Belvedons deserve everything coming to them. When are you proposing unveiling this memorial?'

'Early 2002,' said Geraldine, which would give her plenty of time to work on the Arts Council and the Lottery Committee and ensure a huge fee for Casey and a nice cut for David and herself.

'But as a formality,' went on David smoothly, 'to placate the committee and the people of Limesbridge and Larkshire, who will put up half the money, we'd better throw the competition open.'

'People love competitions,' urged Geraldine, seeing Casey's look of disapproval.

'I'm sure the *Western Daily Press* will run a piece,' added David soothingly, 'and Nigel Reynolds might put something in his *Telegraph* diary, so we can say we've given people a chance to enter. Your ex-wife would probably like a crack. Christ, she was a pest at the British Portrait Awards. The best twenty can bring in their portfolios. We'll pick out the three best of those besides you to provide maquettes. Then in July we'll announce the winner, which of course will be you.

'Better if we go through the formalities.' He filled up Casey's glass. 'Show you've despatched the competition, give you splendid publicity as a multi-faceted artist.'

Anything to distract Casey from the pandemonium across the road as the press slid all over the ice to photograph a departing Rupert.

'Mind you, the Belvedons will be dead in the water after the court case in April.' Geraldine picked up her bag. 'Just going to spend a penny, then shall we go and dine?'

As soon as she'd disappeared, David let slip he was going to become High Sheriff in April: 'Total surprise, must have been lobbied by my friends. Just wondering if I could ask you to paint me in my regalia outside the Old Rectory?'

'Only if you arrange for me to do that nude of Emerald Belvedon,' said Casey roguishly.

63

With the return of his beloved wife, a baby on the way, and a colossally successful private view under his belt, Jupiter was ashamed that he still had time to be secretly miffed that Alizarin wasn't more grateful.

'A sodding great cheque will be shortly on its way to pay for his operation in America,' he grumbled to Sophy as they washed up glasses the following morning. 'But Al will hardly acknowledge it. I've run a gallery for fifteen years. I've sold art all over the world, worked from dawn to dusk. The only words I've never heard are "Thank you".'

'Thank you,' said Sophy, kissing him on the cheek. 'It was a gorgeous party, and thank you for giving Alizarin the chance to see again and for my lovely bottle of Joy. It smells like a garden in June.'

Alizarin had, meanwhile, prevailed upon his favourite nurse, Molly Malone, to collect his sickness benefit. Jupiter was therefore staggered the following morning to receive a large jar of his favourite caviare and a startlingly colourful 'thank you' card chosen by Molly.

When Sophy, drenched in Joy, with her hands smothered in hand cream in case Alizarin wanted to hold one of them, went to see him the following week after school, she found him very cantankerous. Perhaps he was sad about Hanna going back to Jupiter.

His post, he grumbled, contained nothing but

requests for money from impoverished artists and charities.

'I've even had a begging letter from Limesbridge Conservatives.'

When Sophy read him his press cuttings, he said nothing, even when Somerford Keynes wrote: 'I once described Alizarin Belvedon as a rotten painter. I was wrong. I retract every word. It was the tenderness of his latest exhibition that moved me, as though even in the most horrific war scenes, he'd dipped his brush in the milk of human kindness.'

Glancing up, Sophy saw tears trickling out from Alizarin's poor blind eyes and seized his hands.

'They're wonderful reviews.'

'I know. A successful exhibition fires you up to start again but I can't . . .' His voice broke. '. . . do that now.'

'You will again, after the operation.'

'There's only a ten per cent chance of success.'

'I'm coming with you.'

'You've got a job. You can't let those children down.'

'I can. They'll understand. You're what matters to me.'

'I'm fine on my own,' snapped Alizarin. 'Adrian Campbell-Black's promised to find me a minder in New York. Sienna's coming to the airport to meet me.'

'I'd still like to come,' pleaded Sophy, but she let go of his hands.

'You can't. Just bugger off,' said Alizarin roughly. 'Thanks for everything, but I'm leaving tomorrow, and I've got masses to organize.'

Sophy managed not to cry until the door to the ward shut behind her. Then she howled. Sweet Molly Malone, however, came racing after her, waving the most hideous bunch of mauve, yellow and red asters.

'They're from Alizarin,' she said. 'He made me take him down to the hospital shop, he was determined to choose them himself.'

Sophy still went home in utter despair.

Next morning, Alizarin gravely thanked the nurses and doctors who'd been so kind to him. Then, the picture of desolation, he was led shuffling out of the hospital and for a moment enjoyed the soft rain on his sweating face and was transported to the wet walks of Limesbridge, feeling the green silken caress of the wild garlic, which would be soon sweeping over the woodland floor.

'Taxi's waiting, Mr Belvedon.'

From then onwards it was all under cover. He was overwhelmed with panic as, trapped in his own tunnel of darkness, he was led by a kind hostess down another tunnel onto the plane. It was like being engulfed for ever in the belly of a whale.

They put him by the window, so he could 'enjoy the view'. The moment the plane was aloft, he was again transported back to Limesbridge on a warm June evening as a heavenly scent of flowers overwhelmed him.

'What would you like to drink, Mr Belvedon?' asked a steward.

'We'd like two glasses of champagne,' said Sophy's sweet, trembling voice from the seat beside him.

64

Despite the beauty of the March morning, Rosemary Pulborough was in low spirits. Not only had Forbes, her gardener, pruned all the buds off the viburnum intended to smell sweetly under the kitchen window, but he had also mowed away the pink and black fritillaries she'd been nurturing on the edge of the lawn.

To add to her misery, David was catting around more than ever, and, even more lowering, the *froideur* between him and Anthea had clearly melted. Anthea was once more imparting advance information to Rosemary about Melanie's second baby, which was due any minute, and more painfully this morning about Si Greenbridge, who was evidently in London and had popped into the Pulborough yesterday.

'The busiest people always find time,' had said Anthea smugly.

David had been so incensed by his public humiliation when Alizarin had won the British Portrait Award last month that he had whisked Rosemary away from the Dorchester before she had had time to say good-bye to Si. As Si hadn't been in touch since then, she became more and more convinced she had imagined the pressure of his leg and the warmth of his huge hand closing over hers. She had clipped out of *Hello* a photograph of David, herself and Si, with his arm proudly round her shoulders, at the awards, and tucked it into her notecase, behind her credit cards and snapshots of the cats and Melanie's first baby. Her sole act of defiance had been to cut David out of the picture.

David was forced to be nice to her at the moment because from April as High Sheriff he would need a wife. The prospect of struggling into coats and skirts and little black dresses for an eternity of engagements depressed her even more.

She must pull herself together. It was past eleven and she was still in her dressing gown. Rubbing in moisturizer in front of the bathroom mirror, she wished the hand running down over her face and neck was Si's instead of her own, stroking her as tenderly as outside the first acid-green criss-cross leaves of the weeping willows were caressing the white sweep of daffodils.

'"Continuous as the stars that shine and twinkle on the milky way",' murmured Rosemary, so lost in sad thought she didn't at first hear the telephone.

'Rose-*mary*?' Only one voice emphasized the second syllable. 'This is Si.' Then, when she couldn't speak for joy: 'Si Greenbridge.'

'How lovely!'

There was an indignant squawk as Rosemary's knees buckled, and she collapsed on Abednego, who'd been stretched out on the window seat enjoying the sunshine.

'Sorry, darling.'

'Is someone with you?'

'Only one of my cats.'

'Are you free for lunch?'

'Golly, yes.'

'I'll pick you up.'

'No,' squeaked Rosemary, catching sight of Lady Belvedon gathering narcissi next door, 'Anthea's home.'

She kicked herself. How presumptuous to think Si was planning anything clandestine. Then her spirits soared as he said, 'Christ, we don't want to give that bitch any ammunition. Where's somewhere safe and quiet for lunch near you?'

Rosemary's mind went as blank as the untroubled blue sky outside. Finally she stammered, 'There's the Grasshopper and Sixpence on the Limesbridge–Rutminster road.'

'See you there, a quarter after one. If I'm a few seconds late, order a bottle of Krug.'

Switching off the telephone, Rosemary threw her head back, breathing deeply, clutching herself in ecstasy.

After that, everything went wrong. She had just showered and washed her hair, and sent Abednego scurrying out of the bathroom by spraying on deodorant, when Green Jean, that enemy of aerosols, arrived lobbying for jumble and gasping for herbal tea.

Green Jean was followed by the doctor's wife collecting for the Lifeboats, accompanied by her fox terrier, who promptly treed Shadrach. By the time Rosemary had coaxed Shadrach down, her un-blow-dried hair was sticking out wildly like a greying sunflower.

A sassy new bra gave her a good shape, but if one rammed one's breasts together over a certain age, one's cleavage wrinkled like an Australian drought area. Her body hadn't seen the sun since last September but gardening in all weathers had left a satsuma net of red veins on her pale cheeks.

You're a very unattractive property, she told herself despairingly, an old wreck coming out of an old rectory.

At least she had a terribly pretty frilly cream silk shirt to wear with her brown velvet suit. But her hands were shaking so much that she pricked her finger while pinning on her cornelian brooch, and bled all over the cream silk, so she had to wear her dreary grey poplin instead. By the time she'd picked a bunch of daffodils and polyanthus for Si, it was twelve-forty-five.

Rushing outside, she found her car battery flat. She was being punished for sinful intent. The only answer was to take David's vast new Range Rover. She felt so plain she couldn't bear to glance in the driving mirror. But as she gingerly manoeuvred the great double-decker tank along the twisted Larkshire lanes, it was impossible not to feel optimistic. The cottages were wearing plumes of yellow forsythia in their hats. Flocks of gulls, like outsize snowflakes, followed the tractors over the rich brown earth. Primroses, anemones and celandines shining like little suns crowded the banks on either side of the road. St George's horse was off to the races.

'Going to see Si, going to see Si, going to see Si,' sang Rosemary to the last movement of Beethoven's Fifth Symphony.

But drawing up outside the Grasshopper and Sixpence, she gave a moan of horror as she realized she'd picked a motel. What would Si think? Inside, presumably because everyone was busy humping away in the surrounding bungalows, the self-service dining room was deserted. A bored-looking waitress, who occasionally lifted a silver lid and gave some sickly yellow chicken marengo a stir, had clearly never heard of Krug.

There was no sign of Si. Catching sight of General Anaesthetic and his wife driving decorously past in their ancient Rover, followed by a furiously hooting convoy of motorists, Rosemary collapsed into a chair in the foyer, taking refuge behind the *Financial Times*.

Then she jumped out of her skin as on page three she found a belligerent Si glaring out at her, looking far too busy to take anyone out to lunch. 'King Midas', said the headline.

'So sorry I'm late.'

Through the swing doors came a grim-faced Si, navy-blue coat collar turned up against a jaw already blackened with stubble.

'I'm so sorry,' began Rosemary, then, lowering her

voice in case she hurt the feelings of the staff, 'that I chose such a sleaze hole.'

She was so nervous as she leapt to her feet, she overturned her bag, which spewed out its contents. Next moment Si was on the floor beside her. As he retrieved a little paperback of Matthew Arnold's poems and her notecase from under the table, the photograph of them both at the British Portrait Awards fluttered out. A smile of such delight softened Si's heavy features.

'I clipped the same picture. I cut out David too,' he said.

As they were both on their hands and knees, and her mouth, open in amazement, was so near his, he kissed it very gently, then, edging nearer, extremely hard.

'Just adore your new hair-do,' he added, ruffling her hair.

'It's a hair-don't, actually. Oh, Si, I've only driven past and never noticed it was a motel . . . I don't want you to think . . .'

'Best idea you ever had.' Si squeezed her hands. 'How hungry are you?'

'Not very.'

'Nor am I. I'll get a room, and we'll have a bottle and some sandwiches.' Then, seeing the terror in her eyes: 'It's OK, we can just talk and smooch. No big deal.'

Si was overjoyed with his bunch of flowers, unwrapping them from their silver foil and putting them in a tooth mug beside the vast bed. This had a headboard like the console of some touring opera, complete with telephone, lights to dim, air conditioner, music controls, levitating television set, electric window blinds and a button to make the bed do the humping if you were feeling tired. An ice bucket holding a chilled bottle of Moët came up through a trap door.

Rosemary got the giggles and wanted to try everything as they talked about Tiger Woods's swing, Si's new horses and his airline company, and, best of all, in between lingering kisses, how they had missed each other. Si was so huge and hunky, he made her feel by comparison as fragile as Anthea.

By the second glass, he had most of her clothes off and in the rose-coloured lighting, her flesh didn't seem nearly so pleated, particularly when they snuggled under the sheets, and he stroked her and told her how pretty her body was until she stopped trembling.

'The first time I saw you, I thought what a *fritefly* attractive man. What did you think?' asked Rosemary.

'That's the woman I'd like to spend the rest of my life with.'

'Oh, Si.' Rosemary buried her blushing face in the pillow. 'I'm so plain.'

'You're beautiful,' snapped Si.

Then, rolling her towards him so he could look into her face: 'I had a pretty rough childhood, my mom drank and knocked me about, there wasn't any money, but my dad promised me a puppy, and after a lot of nagging he took me to the Dogs' Home. There, amid all the din and barking, I saw a brown crossbreed, about nine or ten I guess, whom no-one wanted. She'd been there for months, her despair and loneliness was palpable' – smiling down at Rosemary, Si caressed her cheek with the back of his hand – 'I said, "I'll have that one".

'I called her Sunny, and she lived for another eight years. She was the sweetest, best, most loving dog I ever had, and never stopped wagging her tail. She made my adolescence bearable.' Si couldn't speak for the moment. 'The day she died was the blackest of my life. I've been looking for another Sunny ever since.'

'Woof, woof,' muttered Rosemary, to hide how touched she was, turning her head to kiss his fingers.

'And once she was loved,' added Si softly, 'she became beautiful.'

Rosemary couldn't believe that a man normally in such a hurry seemed to have all the time in the world to kiss her breasts, her tummy button, even her chilblained toes, and all the way up her thighs.

'Sorry it's taking so long,' she muttered, rigid with tension.

'Hush, honey, relax.'

Wearing her dark forest of pubic hair as a moustache, Si looked more like a bandit than ever.

His chunky gold rings grazed her breasts as he caressed her.

I mustn't fake, she kept telling herself. This is the really real thing, I mustn't.

'Oh! Oh! Oooooh! Oh Si!' she cried as suddenly she toppled over the cliff into the lovely warm ocean, shuddering in wonder and amazement.

But soon she was panicking again. It was clearly her turn to give Si pleasure. Feeling dreadfully amateurish and out of practice, she began licking him, as nervously and surreptitiously as a child warned not to accept lollipops from strangers. But soon nerves gave way to joy at his obvious delight.

'That is so good, honey, but I want to come inside you.'

'I don't think you'll be able to get inside,' confessed Rosemary. 'My gynae says, after a certain age, women close up if they aren't used, like rusty old gates, padlocked and entwined with goose grass.'

'That's bullshit. I'm so fired up, I'll probably shoot before I get inside anyway.'

They were both wrong.

Afterwards, Si ordered another bottle.

'What are you doing?' he asked, as Rosemary examined herself in the mirror.

'Seeing if I've turned to gold, Mr Midas. I could use my clitoris as a torch on dark nights.'

'You are not to take the piss.' Pulling her back into bed and into the crook of his arm, Si asked idly, 'What's happening to all those mad Belvedons?'

'Oh, masses. Jonathan's still trying to dig up dirt for the court case in Paris, Berlin and Vienna I think. Jupiter's frightfully excited about his new baby and is treating Hanna like a discovered Leonardo.'

'What about the blind one?'

'Alizarin? He's had his op. Jonathan, Sienna and Sophy were all with him. They've got the tumour out. Now he's got to bite his nails to see if his sight comes back.' Rosemary sighed. 'Such a tragedy. Evidently that snake Zachary Ansteig had the temerity to send Alizarin a basket of fruit. Jonathan chucked it out of the hospital window. Poor little Sophy was rather cross. She's trying to diet and could have lived on it for days. Jonathan said it was probably poisoned like in *Snow White*.'

'What about the deranged daughter?'

'Sienna? She got off with a six-month suspended. The prosecution tried to prove she took the Raphael because she knew it was looted. But she clearly had no idea and stood up to cross-questioning extremely well.'

'Lucky she was tried in the UK.' Si filled up Rosemary's glass. 'They really hammer you in the States for smuggling art. How's the old boy?'

'Desperately missing his picture.'

Leaning on his elbow, Si ran a finger down Rosemary's flat tummy. 'How did he acquire it in the first place?'

'Found it in some burning château during the war. He was in the Larkshire Light Infantry. My cousin Nicky was in the same regiment before they amalgamated with the Rutshire Yeomanry. Leo Cooper published an awfully good regimental history. Anyway, Raymond and his platoon took a village and found the nearby château ablaze from a direct hit.'

'Where was it?'

'Somewhere in Normandy. It was called the Château des Rossignols, because the nightingales sang so sweetly there. After the war it was rebuilt and turned into a hotel called the Coq d'Or, rather like yours.' Rosemary put a fond hand on Si's penis.

'We stayed there as a foursome,' she went on, 'after Anthea married Raymond. The village was called Bonfleuve. Actually, it wasn't very *bon*.' Rosemary shivered. 'I caught David kissing Anthea behind a fig tree, which rather spoilt things. Raymond never found out, thank God. I anaesthetized myself with lots of calvados.'

'Poor baby.' Si's hand was creeping upwards, finger circling a tawny nipple. 'And Raymond told you about discovering the Raphael?'

'Evidently, he burst into the château, discovered some dying Nazi, gave him a glass of water and a last glimpse of the Raphael, and was given it in return as a keepsake. Awfully romantic, Raymond would have carried the Nazi out of the château if he hadn't died. He never dreamed the picture belonged to Zac's family; such a ghastly coincidence. It's all so long ago. If the Nazi gave it to Raymond, surely it's his?'

'I wouldn't know. It's certainly going to cost them a fortune in legal fees. I love you,' said Si jubilantly. 'How about a replay?'

Rosemary adored the way Si refused to let her drive home, following in the Merc which he was also too drunk to drive. Goodness knows what his poor chauffeur, who had to drive Rosemary and the Range Rover up to the gates of the Old Rectory, thought to have this giggling, garrulous granny beside him.

The rush hour had come and gone. The yellow houses of Limesbridge looked appropriately flushed and post-coital in the last red rays of the sun. Thrushes, robins and blackbirds were giving thanks for such a lovely day.

Once home, reality reasserted itself. There were eight messages on Rosemary's machine. Before she had time to listen to any of them, the telephone rang.

'We've been trying to trace you *all* afternoon.' It was a smug, delighted Anthea. 'You forgot the Limesbridge Improvement meeting. I had to take the chair. David and Geraldine turned up. We thrashed out details of the Borochova Competition' – Anthea was clearly so pleased to have David back, she was actually now pro the idea – 'and David's going to be so busy with his extra High Sheriff functions, they want me to take over as Treasurer. "Because you're a treasure," David said, which made General Anaesthetic awfully jealous.'

Which means a lot of lunches for Anthea and David, reflected Rosemary, and for the first time in twenty-six years she didn't mind.

'Gerry's such a poppet,' continued Anthea, 'she wants to throw the competition wide open.'

Like my legs, thought Rosemary and, putting the receiver carefully on the window seat, swayed off to feed the frantically mewing and complaining cats. When she picked up the telephone five minutes later Anthea was still chattering.

'We've scrapped your idea of a Galena Museum. David wants to move his mother into the barn.'

'"To keep herself warm and hide her head under her wing, poor thing,"' sang Rosemary and rang off.

All the same, she was sweating. How could she have gone missing for nearly six hours, pinching David's car when he and Geraldine were in the area? Had he noticed it was missing? She didn't care. She was just knocking back a glass of Sancerre when a spluttering David rang.

'How could you forget a Limesbridge Improvement meeting? Geraldine came down specially. And I've just had a furious call from *Larkshire Life*, they were supposed to be interviewing you about being a High Sheriff's wife at two o'clock and found no-one at home.'

'Sorry, I forgot.'

'How can you be so self-centred? Ring them at once and grovel. And I suppose you've forgotten Casey's coming to stay on Friday to paint my portrait.'

Rosemary was defiantly pouring herself a second glass when the telephone rang yet again. It was Emerald.

'Can I ask you a colossal favour, Mrs Pulborough? David's just told me about the Borochova Memorial Competition. I'd so like to enter and do something to please the Belvedons to make up a little for wrecking their lives, particularly Jonathan's.' Her voice trembled. 'I want to do a sculpture of Galena and try to capture some of her charisma.'

'What a good idea.'

'I'd ask Anthea, but I don't think she'd be too keen, and I know how much Galena liked you. Could I come and pick your brains?'

'Of course,' said a blushing Rosemary. 'I've got loads of photos, so has Lily. I'm coming up to London next week. Just let me look.'

Reaching for her bag, tugging at the crimson satin book mark, she opened her diary and nearly dropped the telephone, for across a whole week, Si had scrawled, 'I adore you, don't ever change.'

'Actually, I could make it this Friday,' she told Emerald. To hell with Casey, he and David could fend for themselves. 'Let's treat ourselves and see if we can get into the Ivy.'

As she drew the landing curtains, Anthea glanced into the Old Rectory garden and saw Rosemary waltzing round the lawn with a large ginger cat in her arms. The silly old thing must be going potty.

'"And then my heart with pleasure fills,"' sang Rosemary, '"And dances with the daffodils."'

General Anaesthetic, still angry that David had hijacked the Borochova Memorial meeting, popped into the Goat in Boots for a glass of beer and to admire the nude of Sienna on the wall. He found the locals chuntering over the fact that David Pulborough's new Range Rover had been parked outside the Grasshopper and Sixpence throughout the lunch hour.

'Talk about shittin' on your own doorstep.'

'Man's a bounder,' agreed the General happily.

65

As neither Zac nor the Belvedons were prepared to settle, the case deciding Pandora's fate was listed for just after Easter on the fourth Tuesday in April with the Mr Justice Caradoc Willoughby Evans presiding. Several judges had regretfully refused the case, feeling they had enjoyed too many evenings carousing in the Garrick with Raymond to provide impartial judgement.

Heartened that Sienna had not been sent to prison, that Alizarin, albeit still blind, had survived his horrific operation and that Hanna in early April had given birth to a beautiful son, Viridian Edmund, with whom the entire family was besotted, the Belvedons perhaps didn't take quite enough trouble amassing evidence for their case.

They were also relying on their smooth-tongued QC Sampson Brunning. The only rival to the revered and renowned George Carman at whipping rabbits out of hats, Sampson had grown famous getting Belvedons off everything from hitting fat critics through glass doors to, more recently, smuggling Raphaels. They were in no doubt Sampson would triumph again. Sampson was in no doubt either – if Sienna didn't shoot them all in the foot.

Goodness knows, he stormed to Jupiter, how he had kept that opinionated, slovenly, ungrateful little tramp out of gaol. In the middle of her trial, Sienna had even given the judge a lecture on the rights of animals, comparing their fate to far worse than the Holocaust. Mr Justice Willoughby Evans was known to have a fondness for pretty, feminine, agreeable women. Sienna must bloody well learn to be polite.

Sienna had already produced a written statement for the civil case giving her version of events and hoped the matter would end there. Sampson wasn't remotely surprised when Zac's side didn't accept this version and expressed a desire to cross-examine her in court.

'What are they doing this for?' demanded Jupiter.

'They clearly don't believe the story Sienna told last time, that she had no idea Pandora was looted. Looking like she does, they probably think she nicked it for drug money.'

'Oh come off it, Sampson. Will Sienna have to show up?'

'Course she will, or it'll look ten times worse. She'll just have to keep a civil if studded tongue in her head.'

Despite her air of truculent indifference, Sienna had been terrified that she might go to prison last time and was panic-stricken at the prospect of being grilled in court again.

On the Tuesday before Easter, she had sulkily agreed to lunch with Rupert Campbell-Black at the Ritz, and rolled up twenty minutes late, looking deliberately awful. Her paint-stained hair hung in rats' tails, a shapeless sleeveless black top showed off her tattooed arms, black baggy combats wrinkled over dusty trainers.

Out of the big dining-room windows could be seen the first pale olive green leaves of the plane trees in the park. Their innocent freshness was an unhappy contrast to Sienna's sickly grey face and the indigo shadows beneath eyes reddened as much by tears as by working all night. A drastic weight loss made her face armour of rings and studs the more obtrusive.

Rupert, equally fed up at having to come up from

Penscombe on such a lovely day, was only there because his brother Adrian as well as Jonathan had begged him.

'She's a really good kid, Rupert, she needs help.'

Needs a bath for a start, thought Rupert sourly.

All round the room, people who'd recognized him were nudging each other, speculating whether this was another illegit come out of the woodwork.

'What d'you want to drink?'

'Water, I can't stay long.'

'Don't be fatuous.' Rupert ordered another whisky for himself and a glass of champagne for Sienna, who shook her shaggy head when the waiter offered her first a menu and then a basket of bread.

'I'm not hungry. What are you staring at?' She scowled at Rupert.

'You. I thought Alizarin was the one sleeping rough.'

Sienna glared up at the ceiling, on which were painted garlands, musical instruments and happy little pink clouds floating across a turquoise sky.

After a long pause, Rupert said, 'The more I look at your brother's pictures, the more I like them. I'm supposed to be selling them on to Adrian, but I'm tempted to hang on to the lot.'

'In case his sight comes back, and his pictures soar in value.'

'You really are a bitch, aren't you? I never dreamt I'd feel sorry for Anthea, having you as a stepdaughter.'

But as he waved for the bill, Rupert heard a sob, and saw a tear was glittering beside the diamond in the hollow of Sienna's nose.

'You shouldn't cry,' he said, not unkindly, 'salt water rusts metal, like wrecks at the bottom of the sea.'

'I'm s-s-s-o-orry. I don't like know what gets into me.'

'It's OK,' then, as the waiter arrived: 'You'd better make that a bottle rather than a glass.'

Waiters, used over the years to Mr Campbell-Black lunching with tearful women, obligingly rearranged the seating so he and Sienna had their backs to the room, which was transfixed with interest.

'D'you think he's got her pregnant?' hissed the editor of the *Tatler* to the Chilean ambassador's wife.

In between sobs, Sienna told Rupert of her terrors at appearing in court again.

'I know Zac will produce some barrister who'll tie me in knots. I acted up so much last time, Sampson's convinced I'm a liability.'

Rupert was being so kind that after the third glass and some delectable Provençal vegetables in a tomato coulis, she was telling him everything.

'How on earth did Zac manage to photograph the Raphael in the Blue Tower?' asked Rupert.

Sienna's eyes darted round the trees of Green Park for lip-reading squirrels.

'He shagged Anthea.'

'Christ! He must have wanted the Raphael back. Tell Zac's lawyer that if he gives you a hard time.'

'I can't, it would crucify Dad. He's awfully frail at the moment.'

Rupert looked at her meditatively.

'Can I give you several words of advice? If you want to win that case for your father, get that hardware off your face. Frankly, you look like a scrap yard.'

'I'm like making a statement,' snarled Sienna. 'You're just out of touch.'

'I'm sure.' Rupert was unmoved. 'But people my age and older, which includes Mr Justice Willoughby Evans, find it absolute hell.'

'Why should I conform to please some old judge?'

'Because you want the Raphael back, and because your father's been hurt enough.'

'That's rich coming from you. You and Mum hurt him enough in the old days.'

There was a pause. He will walk out now, thought Sienna in despair. Longing overcame her.

'Did you really like Mum?'

'I adored her. She was irresistible, uncompromising, outrageous, sensational in bed – because she didn't give a damn. Painting always mattered more. I was making it in showjumping, everything came second to winning and the horses. We were well matched, the eighteen-year age gap didn't seem to matter at all. We enjoyed each other without clinging.'

Lucky Mum, thought Sienna.

As the waiter put two plates of fettucini with sliced truffles in front of them, Rupert wished he could tell her some of the pranks he and Galena had got up to.

Sienna picked up a fork. 'Goodness, I am hungry after all. You gave Mum a Jack Russell called Shrimpy.'

'So I did.' He certainly couldn't tell her who Shrimpy had been named after.

'Why did you and she break up?'

'I married, and tried to behave myself for about a week. In a way we were too alike, both damaged by our childhoods. Hers under the Communists was far worse.'

'Like Zac's,' murmured Sienna, thinking aloud, and then flushing. 'He's too damaged by his past to commit himself.'

'Is he attractive?'

'Kind of, not my type really, but he's sexy and dangerous.' Her sudden smile lifted her sullen face, showing off wonderful teeth. 'A bit like you.'

Rupert smirked and filled up her glass.

'This is so divine,' sighed Sienna, 'I'm sure I shouldn't be eating truffles.'

'It's a fungus.'

'Think of poor pigs having to hunt for it.'

'They enjoy it, like foxhounds,' added Rupert slyly.

'Oh, shut up.' Colour flooded Sienna's face. 'When you made love to my mother, did you notice the Raphael on the wall?'

'Frankly, I didn't notice anything except your

mother. Although she once said I had the same Greek nose as Pride.'

'I wonder if any of her other lovers clocked it and tipped off Zac. Oh God . . .' At the thought of seeing him, Sienna put her face in her hands. Rupert found the paint-stained bitten nails oddly touching.

'If you took that chainmail off your face,' he said gently, 'you'd be much prettier than Galena – and much more likely to bring the Raphael home.'

'D'you think we'll win?'

'Yeah. Everyone loves your father so much, he can do no wrong in a jury's eyes, and Sampson Brunning, however much you dislike him, is ace at springing surprises.'

Rupert's optimism, however, was misplaced. The conduct of civil cases had changed due to reforms brought in recently. The whole procedure had been speeded up. Witnesses had to produce – several weeks before the trial – written statements along with any relevant documents, birth certificates, photographs, invoices, authentications, for the other side to pick over.

After this, if neither claimant nor defendant were prepared to settle, as Zac and the Belvedons were not, the case would go to court in front not of a jury, but a single judge, who would have been given every statement and document to peruse, so he was clued up on all the material on which each side intended to rely.

Once in court, apart from calling the occasional witness to provide background, each side would be allowed only to cross-examine and try and blow huge holes in each other's witness statements. This meant that immediately the case was under way, the producing of dramatic new evidence, Sampson's whisking rabbits out of hats, to unnerve the opposition, was forbidden. It would only be permitted if the side in question could prove that this evidence had only just come to light, for example, a hitherto untraceable witness emerging from the woodwork.

This was supposed to be a fairer system. But for the Belvedons, it meant that Raymond could no longer wow an already well-disposed jury, nor Sampson spring surprises. It also favoured the side with the larger financial resources. Zac together with Si's army of lawyers had spent months producing watertight evidence. In retaliation, a desperately impoverished Jonathan had been single-handedly ferreting round in dusty foreign archives, certain that Zac's evidence didn't stack up, promising but failing to provide a breakthrough.

This had resulted in a terrible row over the telephone on the eve of the trial, with a maddened Jupiter accusing Jonathan, who was now in Paris, of living up to his nickname of Sloth.

'You've just wasted everyone's time getting stoned in the capitals of Europe.'

'Everything's shut for Easter,' yelled back Jonathan, 'I can't get into the public record office until tomorrow.'

'It's too fucking late, the case starts tomorrow. You've failed us yet again.'

Hearing Jupiter crashing down the receiver, Raymond retreated trembling to the church next door, taking refuge in the family pew. Despite his arthritis, he had no truck with perching on the edge of the seat. Kneeling on the pale blue hassock Anthea had embroidered with the Belvedon crest, he prayed for the return of Alizarin's sight, for Baby Viridian to allow Jupiter and Hanna a little sleep, for Dicky and Dora who were spitting to be missing the court case, and for Sienna, Emerald and most of all Jonathan to find people to love rather than each other. Almost worse than the loss of the Raphael had been the absence over the last six months of his favourite son, whose life he knew he had ruined.

Raymond also asked God not very optimistically to curb his wife's spending. Aware she might not be able to afford clothes afterwards, Anthea had bought new outfits from Lindka Cierach for the expected duration of the trial; she was now upstairs trying on hats.

Raymond sighed. He dreaded being cross-examined. He was getting so vague. He loathed leaving his burgeoning garden at its loveliest and particularly Grenville. It had been different in the days when Visitor's reassuring presence had kept Grenville calm. Visitor had so looked forward to Easter – all that chocolate.

Great vases of wild cherry were already scattering their white petals on the church floor. Bluebells picked by Lily were shrivelling and fading. Like me, thought Raymond. Perhaps the case would only last a few days.

'"Oh God of battles!, Steel my soldiers' hearts,"' prayed Raymond. 'Bring my Raphael home and Hope back into my life.'

He smiled slightly as he noticed the word 'Tits', which Jonathan had carved on the pew with a compass during a boring sermon. Creakily rising to his feet, he heard a rhythmic thudding. Grenville, having tracked his master down, was banging his bony tail against the church door. Raymond was less able to identify the sound of clanking from the Old Rectory. Had he peered over the wall, he would have seen David Pulborough marching up and down practising walking with a High Sheriff's sword.

The sun setting behind the wood had left an apricot flush along the horizon: an exquisite backdrop for all the differing greens of the young leaves. Admiring the sky-blue blur of forget-me-nots round the water trough, hearing a robin singing in the poplars, Raymond breathed in a heady smell of balsam. He longed to seek solace in his garden, but wearily remembered the hundreds of letters from fans, wishing him luck for tomorrow, that needed answering.

*　　*　　*

Up in London, having restlessly roamed the streets all day, Zac watched the same sunset as Raymond. Guiltily aware that he only turned to God in times of fear or anguish, he pulled a rumpled black velvet capel out of his suitcase and set out for the synagogue in Great Portland Street. He was exhausted because he and Si's lawyers had been closeted for weeks closing every loophole in his evidence. He was sulking because he'd wanted to spend the weekend skiing high up in the Alps to clear his head and work off his aggression, but his barrister, Naomi Cohen, had put her Gucci-clad foot down.

'A tan'll make you look too rich.'

For the same reason, she'd ordered him to put aside his expensive clothes for his court appearance tomorrow, and buy a tacky off-the-peg suit in polyester pinstripe to wear with a cheap white nylon shirt and sickly yellow tie, like some middle-management geek. He must also leave off his Rolex and arrive in a hired Vauxhall, rather than Si's helicopter, or even Si's Merc. Si, although closely overseeing events, had meekly caved in when Naomi had suggested he stay away from court in the early stages.

'If Si rocks up, you won't appear destitute, for Christ's sake,' she told Zac.

Sienna would laugh her head off, thought Zac furiously. Why did she keep drifting back into his thoughts like bonfire smoke?

Evening prayers were drawing to a close as he entered the synagogue, which was filled with men, heads bowed, murmuring in accompaniment to the strong voice of the rabbi. Women seldom attended evening prayers, and, at all times, had to sit up in the gallery or behind a screen so as not to distract the men. Sienna would never agree to being sidelined like that.

The rabbi had launched into the Kaddish: the beautiful memorial prayer for the dead, intoned at the end of all services. So many dead to remember, Zac felt weighed down by their expectation – Reuben; Benjamin and Ruth; Leah and Jacob; his grandparents, Tobias and Sarah, his father and all his family and above all Rebecca, his hollow-eyed mother, as utterly emaciated as any death-camp victim before she died. Tomorrow, like a ghost army, they'd be willing him on as he rode into battle.

I will avenge you, he promised. Please God, let me bring home the Raphael.

He must harden his heart, knowing it would break Sienna's. Her howl of anguish when they dragged Pandora away in New York had haunted him like his mom's imagined scream when her own mother was dragged off to Auschwitz. In his wallet was a London *Times* clipping of Sienna's trial with a photograph of the defiant defendant in torn jeans, flashing her tattoos. He was so relieved she'd not gone to prison. He couldn't bear to think of that free spirit in chains.

Why did she get under his skin?

Dear God, bring me to my senses, prayed Zac.

The rabbi was nearing the end of the Kaddish. 'God is our hope,' joined in the deep voices of the congregation in Hebrew, 'Let us put our trust in him and strive for the coming of the day, when his sovereignty will be acknowledged and his will obeyed throughout the world.'

They were still chanting as he left. He had promised to take Naomi, his barrister, out to dinner. Her parents had fled from Germany during the war. She had been born and called to the Bar in England, but half her family, like his, had been murdered by the Nazis; her legacy, a burning desire to right hideous wrongs. Although she was an expert on restituted art, and had already clawed back several Old Masters from museums for Jewish clients, she had never before handled anything so huge or so public. Zac appreciated that if barristers were any good they got impossibly strung up

589

before a case.

All that was left of the sunset was a dark red glow in the west anticipating the blood that would be shed when they joined battle there tomorrow. Naomi was very good looking, but he hoped she wouldn't expect him to make love to her tonight to ease her tension.

66

At nine-thirty a.m. on a sunny Easter Tuesday, Raphael's *Pandora* was packed into an air-conditioned silk-lined box, loaded into a police van and with an escort of motorbikes and police cars driven ten miles from a warehouse in Searston through narrow lanes softened with cow parsley and the first green foliage of spring.

Her destiny was the already overflowing crown court in Larkminster. Arriving early, Sienna had hidden herself high up in the public gallery. She had been commissioned to produce daily sketches of the chief participants by the *Telegraph*, who she was sure had only chosen her because Jonathan and Alizarin weren't available. Her hands were trembling so much at the prospect of seeing Zac, she could hardly draw.

The court lay below, an intensely theatrical cross between opera house, chapel and classroom. Dark polished rows descended like an amphitheatre, divided by crimson carpeted aisles. Directly opposite, the bench rose like a huge oak counter. Behind it reared up the judge's imposing red-leather chair, and behind that a carved snarling lion and a sleekly snorting unicorn hoisted up the Royal Coat of Arms, their paws and hooves obscuring the motto: 'Honi soit qui mal y pense.' 'Let shame come to him who thinks evil.'

In front of the bench sat a clerk and ushers in black gowns reading documents, checking the tape machine which would record every bitter word. In front of the barristers' rows was a big table, strewn with more law books, brightly coloured ring binders, and briefs tied up in cyclamen-pink ribbon. Above, like huge ash buds, hung microphones. The press had squeezed themselves into rows to the left. Facing them to the right like a brass play pen – which would be needed to contain Zac, thought Sienna sourly – was the witness box.

Sienna's brooding was interrupted by a great cheer from the huge crowd, who had assembled in the sunshine to welcome Raymond and sadly notice how pulled down the dear soul was looking. Anthea by contrast looked perky and pretty in a fuchsia pink suit and mauve striped beret from David Shilling.

Once inside, they sat down in the row behind their QC, Sampson Brunning, and his team. Sampson, who had sleek fair hair, a high colour and hard roving blue eyes, was wearing a square-collared black silk gown, and a wig tipped over the beetling blond brows of a man who means business.

In the barristers' robing room, he had clocked Naomi Cohen's full scarlet lips and glossy black hair flopping from a side parting over proud pale gold aquiline features. He had also noticed her slender ankles and swelling bosom beneath her white-frilled high-necked shirt and black gown.

She had been distinctively frosty, probably nerves at squaring up to such a QC as himself, thought Sampson smugly. Like himself, she and Zac were staying at the Black Swan in Searston. He would probably bed her on night three, reflected Sampson, when her crush on her moody tormented client had subsided.

Ah, here was Jupiter rushing in at the last moment, the only sensible Belvedon in Sampson's book. Sienna was a mouthy urchin, Jonathan, who'd failed to produce any of the promised evidence, a useless cokehead.

Sliding into the row beside his stepmother, Jupiter, despite his air of cool, was worried stiff about losing the

Raphael, which was now acting as collateral with the bank, who would probably foreclose if Zac won the case. Raymond still hadn't paid back the £85,000 to the insurance company and God knew what the costs would be. Jupiter was late because he'd been viewing a sale in the nearby auction rooms, where, in a dark corner, he'd spied a possible 'sleeper', which in art world jargon meant an undetected masterpiece. He prayed David Pulborough would be too busy High Sheriffing to view as well. Surreptitiously he switched on his mobile to check on Hanna and little Viridian, who was now sleeping peacefully, after keeping them up all night.

Interest rumbled through the court as Zac and Naomi Cohen walked down the aisle and, totally ignoring the hissing Belvedons, turned into the pew on the left. With a shaking hand, Naomi undid the cyclamen-pink ribbon tying up her brief and, spurning the water jug provided by the court, produced a bottle of Evian.

Trust Zac to roll up with a designer lawyer, thought Sienna furiously. Trust ghastly, pompous, sleek, lascivious Sampson Brunning, who so disapproves of me, to gaze at Naomi with all the delight of an otter who's just inherited a fish shop.

Savagely Sienna began to sketch them both, but her chalk seemed to take control of her hand and draw Zac instead. Not even cheap shiny suits or cadmium-yellow ties could dim his prowling beauty.

Everyone in the Belvedon row giggled and edged up as Aunt Lily clattered down the aisle. Ignoring the 'No refreshments in court' sign, she'd brought a flask of brandy and a two-pound jar of glacier mints. They must keep a seat for Rosemary who was bringing a picnic later.

Restlessly, Zac undid the button of his awful shirt and loosened his even more awful tie.

'Do it up,' hissed Naomi.

'Museums quail at that girl's approach,' murmured Somerford Keynes, who was taking up at least two seats in the press box, and who'd been kept very busy, as he was telling David Lee, the editor of *Art Review*, authenticating the Raphael with colleagues from the Frick and the National Gallery.

'Ah, here it is.'

As Pandora was unpacked from her box, releasing God knew what new evils, Raymond quickly suppressed a sob. Aunt Lily put a gnarled hand on his knee. Sienna swore as tears fell on her sketchpad. Even Jupiter had a lump in his throat.

Everyone in court craned their necks to catch a glimpse as two policemen propped the picture on a red leather bench at the back of the court, with more policemen guarding it on every door. Even at a distance the clear glowing colours had a radiance. Like King Cophetua's beggar maid, thought Jupiter, you could suddenly see what the fuss was about.

The big hand of the clock edged towards ten o'clock.

'All rise,' cried a pretty blonde usher. Like books crammed too tightly into their shelves, the court found it hard to struggle to their feet as Mr Justice Caradoc Willoughby Evans, a long name for a small, rotund but impressive man in red robes, came through crimson velvet curtains and was helped into his splendid red chair. Having breakfasted on bacon and eggs, black pudding, mushrooms, toast and Oxford marmalade served by a butler in the judges' lodgings overlooking the park, Willoughby Evans was delighted by the turnout. A fine profile could always do with raising.

His wig looks as though a lot of grass has frozen on his head, thought Sienna drawing frantically. And with his plump square face and twinkling eyes, he looked like Ratty in *Wind in the Willows* after thirty years of picnics with Mole. Then she couldn't suppress a scream of laughter as through the crimson velvet curtains, with his sword clanking, resplendent in white ruffled shirt, dark blue tail coat, knee breeches, black hose and with an expression of great self-importance on his face, came David Pulborough. It was the High Sheriff's duty to look after visiting High Court judges and sit in on cases, particularly when they were as fascinating as this one.

Down below, Lily gave a snort of laughter.

Raymond's shoulders heaved.

'Shut up, both of you,' hissed a grinning Jupiter as David, smoothing his hair, settled himself into the chair next to Willoughby Evans, solicitously lowering the judge's microphone and pouring him a glass of water.

'I'm sure he'll put in a good word for us,' whispered Raymond, wiping his eyes.

'Like hell he will.' Jupiter tapped Sampson on the shoulder. 'Can't we object? David's bound to drip poison into the judicial ear, and he'll try and flog him pictures. Willoughby Evans bought a van de Velde at Christie's six months ago.'

Oblivious of the mirth and bitching around her, Anthea's heart swelled. Never had David looked so manly. Imagine him whipping out his sword and challenging Zac to a duel in her defence.

Willoughby Evans immediately asked for the Raphael to be brought over, then shook his head. No wonder men were prepared to fight over such beauty. He'd never seen 'so exquisitely fair a face' as Hope's.

'That must be Sloth and that one Avarice.'

'I've lived next to that picture for thirty years and never known of its existence,' lied David, leaning forward to have a look. 'Like the princess in the tower.'

The proceedings kicked off with Naomi opening her case by giving a short history of the Raphael's journey from Vienna to New York. The first witness was Detective Inspector Gablecross, who described briefly how he'd been called to Foxes Court in July, when the Raphael had been reported stolen, how it had been recovered at the Commotion Exhibition and was now in possession of Searston police who under the Police

Property Act would like guidance on where to dispose of it.

Gablecross was followed by Somerford Keynes. Oozing self-importance, only just fitting into the witness box, lecherous little eyes roving in Zac's direction, the great critic dated the picture at around 1512.

'Painted on panel, the fable of Pandora formed the lid of a box, on the bottom of which was painted a portrait of Caterina, a proud beauty whom Raphael was rumoured to have admired unrequitedly. Hence the lid's caption: "Malum infra latet" or "Trouble lies below".' Somerford leered down at Zac.

'In the seventeenth century,' he went on, 'this box consisting of both pictures belonged to the Roman Cardinal Aldobrandini, who, during a diplomatic mission to Vienna, presented it to an Austrian grandee, Count Heinrich von Berthold' – Somerford's slack lips watered at the thought of such august personages – 'in whose inventory of 1695 both pictures are listed.'

'Silly Old Master-bator,' grumbled Sienna, who was furiously sketching Somerford in the witness box as a great pot-bound man-eating plant.

'The lid,' continued Somerford, 'was probably separated from its companion picture in the late eighteenth century when both were transferred from panel to canvas to avoid cracks, woodworm and susceptibility to temperature changes. Caterina now hangs in the Abraham Lincoln Museum outside Washington, Pandora remained in the Berthold family's castle in Hungary for some two hundred and forty years before being sold to Benjamin Abelman of Vienna for approximately ten thousand pounds.'

'How much would you now estimate the value of the picture?' asked Willoughby Evans.

'At auction, it could possibly fetch between eight and ten million pounds.'

Everyone gasped and craned their necks. The police flanking Pandora edged closer. Naomi Cohen adjusted her wig and, having asked permission of Sampson Brunning, gave further background to events.

'Austria,' she explained, 'was the recipient of Hitler's worst hatred, because Linz Academy of Fine Arts had refused him admission as a student. In 1938, his secret police had therefore moved into Vienna, humiliating and arresting Jews and stealing their treasures. The collection of Benjamin Abelman was one of the first to go.'

Mr Justice Willoughby Evans, meanwhile, was making notes on his laptop, proving judges could be computer literate too. What a case! he thought happily. A beautiful picture and some beautiful women to admire if the proceedings got boring. Lady Belvedon was a cracker. Being small, Willoughby Evans liked little women, and he liked Naomi Cohen's flashing dark eyes. Once she got into her stride, her voice had lost that harsh, high, nervous edge. He must ask her and Sampson Brunning to dine at the judges' lodgings later in the week.

Peregrine, Sampson Brunning's junior, also on his laptop and supposed to be keeping track of the evidence, was playing Solitaire.

Now it was Zac's turn. Naomi smiled up at him reassuringly as he tugged at his hideous yellow tie before being sworn in on the Old Testament.

I hate her, thought Sienna, drawing Naomi as a crow in her black robes.

Zac was so pale that his white knuckles didn't show up as he gripped the rails of the witness box, but he performed sensationally. Only rarely, like a bonfire under wet leaves flaring up and dying down, did he show his aggression and desire for vengeance. His love for the Raphael, and his desperate need to repossess it, were obvious to everyone.

With a set face, his deep husky voice quivering with emotion, he made the court weep as he described how Benjamin was cudgelled to death because he tried to hide the Raphael, how Benjamin's seventy-five-year-old wife had been forced to clean pavements with a tooth-brush before her frail body was chucked into a gas oven, and how heroic Uncle Jacob had sworn he would avenge them by recovering the Raphael but instead had been murdered by the Gestapo for smuggling out Jews before he could join his beloved Leah in the States.

I've heard all this before in the Four Seasons, thought Sienna, I'm not going to feel sorry for him. Zac, she decided, was not so much a tiger burning bright, as a narrow-eyed, flaring-nostrilled unicorn, quite capable of stabbing his horn into anyone's front or back.

'What d'you think happened to the Raphael after it left your great-grandfather?' asked Naomi.

'Hitler ordered everything confiscated in Austria to stay in the same country to stock his new FührerMuseum in Linz,' answered Zac, 'but I figure the Raphael ended up with Goering, an obsessively avaricious collector, who managed to siphon off many looted paintings for his own private collection. In the records that came back from Karinhall, Goering's mansion, after the war, the Raphael was listed as having been taken there. After that, there is a question mark by its name.

'Goering knew little about painting,' went on Zac disdainfully, 'and often handed the most exquisite pictures, not realizing their true worth, on to his trusted advisors. He had already rejected one Raphael, *A Portrait of a Young Man*, looted from Cracow, in favour of a Watteau. Perhaps Hope and Pandora' – Zac pointed across the rapt court at the picture – 'were not nude or fat enough for the crude taste of the Reichsmarschall.'

'Have you been back to Vienna?' asked Naomi gently.

'I went back to the family apartment in Singer Strasse and to Jacob's gallery. They had both been bombed flat and replaced by modern buildings.' For a moment Zac, white and cavernous-eyed as an El Greco, couldn't speak. 'All my life, I have had a sense of loss,' he whispered finally. 'The Raphael is the only part of my past left.'

A very good morning for Zac.

'Poor boy looks awfully upset,' sighed Raymond.

'Ought to be given a scholarship to RADA,' snorted Aunt Lily.

The judge called an adjournment and bore a clanking David off to lunch, which made the Belvedons very twitchy.

Outside the court, the photographers and reporters swooped on Zac.

'Over thirty billion dollars of looted art is still missing,' he was telling them. 'We are determined to score a moral victory, so our case will give real support to other Jewish families for their own claims. Ouch,' he howled as someone kicked him sharply on the ankle.

'I hope you're going to donate between eight and ten million pounds to helping their causes,' mocked a voice.

Swinging round in fury, Zac found a ravishingly pretty girl, with a smooth brown face and Marmite-coloured hair drawn back in a neat French pleat. She was wearing a beautifully cut holly-green suit. Only the long legs were recognizable. It was Sienna, studless, ringless, tattoos concealed, Belvedon diamond hanging from her neck, pallor despatched by three days on the sunbed, posing as a cool young Portia for the court.

'Aren't you sorry your side opted to cross-question me?' she said, laughing in Zac's face, before scampering off after Raymond for vegetable lasagne and a large vodka and tonic in the pub.

Zac was totally thrown. For the rest of the afternoon he couldn't get his head together at all.

'What on earth's happened to Sienna?' hissed an equally fazed Anthea.

'Rupert Campbell-Black took her to the Ritz and told

her to take the heavy metal off her face,' said Jupiter in amusement.

'Ay bet it wasn't the only thing he asked her to take off,' said Anthea furiously.

She had also noticed David engagingly crinkling his eyes at that uppity Naomi Cohen all morning. Life was very hard.

During a long hot afternoon, Sampson Brunning's cross-examination took Zac apart. Why had he changed his name to Ansteig? Wasn't it a shame his mother was dead and beyond a DNA test or Zac could have proved he was really Benjamin's great-grandson rather than a wide boy on the make.

Naomi leapt to her feet. 'That's not a proper question,' she cried reproachfully, then, peeping at Willoughby Evans under her lashes, 'as my learned friend well knows.'

'I agree. Mr Brunning,' reproved Willoughby Evans, 'you know how to behave; please do so.'

'Sorry, m'lord,' said an unrepentant Sampson.

Why, he asked, had Zac abused Emerald's trust, using her to worm his way into the Belvedon household, accepting its generous hospitality as he snooped around spying?

'I wanted my picture back, for Christ's sake.'

How had he managed to photograph the Raphael?

Zac looked meditatively across at a terrified, tight-lipped Anthea. He would have been quite happy to drop her in it, but both Si and Naomi had persuaded him it would make him appear too much of a cad.

'It was the day of Emerald's birthday,' he drawled. 'Lady Belvedon must have been fazed because she was meeting Emerald's mom and dad for the first time, and left the door up to the Blue Tower open.'

'So you invaded her bedroom.' Sampson must have put his upper lip in rollers during the lunch hour. You would have thought Zac had raped a Mother Superior.

'A member of the family had told me I was getting warm. I had to check everywhere.'

'Of course, ten million would come in very useful.'

'The money was irrelevant.'

'Are you acquainted,' sighed Sampson, 'with the English expression "pull the other leg . . . "? Why didn't you take the painting at once?'

Everyone jumped as Lily's mobile rang.

'Hell-o?' Lily held it like an unexploded bomb.

'Lily,' hissed Anthea in horror.

An usher tapped Lily on the shoulder, waving a finger.

'That was Rosemary,' announced Lily, switching off. 'She can't make it. She's awfully elusive at the moment.'

Everyone except David suppressed smiles.

Peregrine went back to playing Solitaire on his laptop.

'That night of the theft,' persisted Sampson, 'you admitted, did you not, you had never loved Miss Cartwright and had used both her and her two families.'

'I said,' Zac answered bleakly, 'that anyone who had reason to hate as much as I had, was incapable of love.'

'And you admit you pressured her into the finding of her birth parents.'

'I guess so.'

'Shady, and cold as the grave,' observed Lily, taking a swig from her brandy flask.

By the end of the afternoon, if Sampson had tarred and dropped him in soot, he couldn't have blackened Zac's character more effectively.

67

Keeping his laptop free for Solitaire, Peregrine, Sampson's junior, wrote 'Day two' at the top of a lined foolscap pad. The temperature had plummeted. The day was grey and overcast, lamps were being turned on all round the court. Sienna was due first into the witness box.

'Don't let her near the media,' Sampson had begged Jupiter, 'or she'll cook all our geese.'

Sienna, however, rolled up at court wearing a little crocheted suit in the burnt orange of a robin's breast. She was greeted by a chorus of wolf whistles from the press and a large bunch of flowers sent by Rupert.

'Saw you on television looking sensational,' he had written on the card. 'Go and annihilate them.'

'I'll put them in water for you, Sienna,' said Peregrine, adoringly.

She's got some guy, Zac thought furiously as he passed them on his way into the courtroom.

Rupert's flowers apart, Sienna was bubbling over. Charles Moore, the editor of the *Daily Telegraph*, had just faxed her saying how much they all liked her drawing which had appeared on page five next to the report of the case. Judge Willoughby Evans's clerk had also called her asking if the judge could buy the original. This showed him, Sampson and the new High Sheriff ogling Naomi as she quizzed Zac, or rather an arrogant head-tossing unicorn, in the witness box.

'I don't have a double chin,' complained Sampson.

'I don't have eyes so close together,' fumed Naomi.

'I think it's an excellent likeness,' said Willoughby Evans, who'd been absurdly flattered.

David, who had not, queried whether Sienna should be allowed to do any more sketches, 'Bearing in mind what side she's on,' he added pointedly.

'Oh, I don't think I could be influenced in any way by a cartoon,' said Willoughby Evans, smiling warmly at Sienna as she entered the witness box.

After she had been sworn in and told Sampson she had nothing to add to her witness statement, Naomi took over. Clocking Zac's and everyone else's partiality, she prepared for battle.

'Miss Belvedon, why did you steal the Raphael on the night of the seventh of July?'

'Pandora's been in our family for nearly sixty years,' began Sienna gently. 'The court has heard about Emerald being pushed into finding her natural parents. But taking Pandora away from us would be like wrenching a child away from adopted parents, who'd loved and brought her up.

'People in museums walk past pictures. We looked at the Raphael and lived it every day. It may be part of Zac's past, but it is also a part of a mother we all lost. It inspired four artists: my two brothers, myself and my mother. Her paintings were so full of light, you can see how she was influenced by the Raphael.'

Sampson Brunning was looking up at her in ecstasy. What a transformation. Perhaps he should bed her rather than Naomi on night three.

'My brothers lay in my mother's arms as it grew light,' went on Sienna. 'First they could see the moon, then Hope in her ivory dress, then Pandora in pale blue, a colour which emerges first from the darkness.'

With her back to the picture, Sienna described every detail.

'My mother died when I was two days old, so I had to teach myself to love the Raphael.' Her hands clenched on the brass rail to stop herself breaking down.

The windows had gone dark. Outside a deluge was assaulting the first soft leaves of the horse chestnuts. Willoughby Evans's hands paused on his laptop.

'Would you like five minutes to compose yourself?' he asked Sienna fondly.

Sienna shook her head. 'I'm fine.'

Good witness, thought Naomi, we're not out of the woods yet.

Then she felt a tug on her gown and Zac was hissing in her ear, 'She's a hellcat, go bury her.'

'Miss Belvedon,' asked Naomi, 'why did you really steal the Raphael?'

'Because I was terrified someone else would. Zachary Ansteig had been prowling round the house for days. I kept finding him in upstairs bedrooms, so I searched his drawers, and found . . .' Sienna ticked off the items on her fingers.

'Do you usually snoop in the rooms of your guests?'

'Not often, but I don't often find them sauntering naked down the landing in the middle of the after-noon.' She pulled a face at Zac, who scowled back.

'You were worried about losing a ten-million-pound picture?'

'No, a picture I loved.'

And so the sniping went on until finally Naomi said, 'I suggest you stole the Raphael because you realized it was looted.'

'In my father's house,' replied Sienna mockingly, 'are many pictures. I have no idea how ninety per cent of them were acquired. I felt Pandora was in danger so I took her.'

At that moment a bright shaft of sunlight came through the window, falling on her face.

Raymond, who'd nodded off, woke up with a start.

'Galena!' he gasped.

'Mum!' muttered an unnerved Jupiter.

Is there no escape? thought Anthea despairingly.

'Well done, Sienna darling.' Sampson, who decided to forget about the double chin, hugged her afterwards.

Naomi didn't fare any better that afternoon when she had to cross-examine Emerald who, also terrified of appearing, had been sustained only by the hope that Jonathan might be in court.

Emerald had been amazed how much she'd missed Sophy since she'd been in America. Today – solid, merry, reassuring – Sophy would have been the ideal companion. Patience, hanging precariously on to another barmaid's job, hadn't dared take the day off, so Emerald arrived alone.

Both press and public, having drooled over her photographs, had expected a raving beauty, and were appalled to see this stricken little ghost in last year's flowered Joseph dress, now two sizes too big. The rose-red blusher and lipstick she'd slapped on to brighten her blanched face looked as incongruous as make-up on a corpse. The news that Jonathan hadn't even showed up was the final straw.

In faltering tones she told the court how she had met Zac.

'Only when he discovered Lady Belvedon was my natural mother did he start pushing me to find her.'

'Can you speak up?' demanded Naomi, as rain rattling on the roof and windows made Emerald almost inaudible.

'Perhaps you could adjust Miss Cartwright's microphone,' reproved the judge, smiling at Emerald.

'Sir Raymond and Lady Belvedon immediately admitted they were my parents and took me and Zac to their hearts,' mumbled Emerald. 'After that Zac became increasingly distant. The night the Raphael went missing, he went berserk, admitted he'd never loved me, and had only used me as a way to get into the household.'

'Boo!' shouted Sienna from the gallery.

'Rotter,' agreed Lily, crunching a glacier mint.

Zac examined his fingernails, a muscle leaping in his cheek.

Was Emerald denying, queried Naomi, that Zac had given her huge emotional and financial support in finding her affluent family?

Emerald said she could not.

'Didn't he buy you a beautiful dress for the silver wedding party?'

'Yes.'

'And other beautiful clothes?'

'Yes,' whispered Emerald.

'Wasn't he in fact putting a silver spoon in your mouth? In your new life, didn't Sir Raymond and Lady Belvedon smother you with gifts, a studio of your own, your own bedroom, an Augustus John, a flash car, clothes from Lindka Cierach, the Belvedon emeralds on the night of your birthday? There was even fear in the family of Sir Raymond making over the Raphael to you. I suggest you found yourself in clover and enjoyed it very much indeed.'

'I didn't enjoy it at all, because I knew Zac didn't love me and, like Pandora, I'd opened up a can of worms, and brought misfortune on my new family who loved their Raphael so much.'

Suddenly the realization that she wasn't going to see Jonathan after all, overwhelmed Emerald and she burst into tears, which echoed heart-rendingly over the microphone and round the room.

Poor little duck. There was not a man in court who, like Willoughby Evans, didn't want to draw David's sword, leap over the bench and challenge Zac the bounder to a duel.

'I had no idea she was so keen on that promiscuous shit,' boomed Lily, handing Anthea her hip flask.

'Nor had I,' snapped Anthea thrusting it back in horror. I'm the one who deserves sympathy, she thought fretfully. Zac wronged me far more than he did Emerald.

Willoughby Evans called a short adjournment. The press rushed out to telephone. Sienna raced down from the gallery to get into the Ladies before a queue built up. She was just having a pee when she heard a sharp distinctive carrying voice. That cow Naomi Cohen must have walked in.

'So presumptuous of Emerald Belvedon to think Zac would have ever married her,' continued the sharp, carrying voice. 'Zac would never marry out. As my father's always grumbling, we lost more Jews to marrying out than in the entire Holocaust.'

Why should that information make me want to slit my wrists? wondered Sienna.

After the adjournment, it was Anthea's turn to go into the witness box.

She looks even prettier today, thought Willoughby Evans, as Anthea, in David Shilling's little straw Breton trimmed with daisies, played the disappointed prospective mother-in-law for all it was worth.

'My long-lost daughter was in a fragile state adjusting to her new family. She was so in love with Zachary. We all gave him such a welcome as our son. But her hopes were built on sand. Why did he have to break my Emerald's heart?'

A murmur of disapproval drifted round the court. A faint waft of Shalimar floated towards Willoughby Evans as Anthea drew out a little lace handkerchief and carefully mopped her eyes.

What a poppet, thought Willoughby Evans.

A *Daily Mail* reporter forced through lack of space to sit in the gallery was enchanted to find himself rammed next to the ravishing Sienna. He was also amused that she was drawing a sobbing crocodile, but was having difficulty balancing a daisy-trimmed straw Breton on its head. Catching his eye, Sienna giggled and drew a line through the sketch.

'The whole country and the press are firmly on your side,' he told her. 'Ladbroke's are offering three to one on a Belvedon victory. I myself had a hundred-pound bet this morning. Whatever Zac's right to the Raphael, he's coming across as a crook and a bastard. We're all looking forward to your dad going into the box tomorrow. That should nail it for your side.'

Having shaken off the press, Zac drove the hired Vauxhall through the pouring rain into the Larkshire countryside. On the car radio, tolling hauntingly, was Mahler's Ninth Symphony, the last piece the Vienna Philharmonic had played before the Anschluss. Simon Rattle had conducted the same symphony at a concert last week in memory of the dead at Mauthausen, the terrible death camp from which Great-uncle Jacob had somehow escaped.

Zac knew he had let down Jacob, his mother and the entire ghost army. He knew he'd behaved appallingly to Emerald and Anthea and that Naomi was feeling rejected because he hadn't made a move on her. He was clearly going to lose the Raphael, and never see Sienna again. Even Si had deserted him, buggering off to Munich on some deal.

Zac pulled up on the edge of a dripping green wood to watch a watery sunset. Both billowing clouds and the sheep in the field ahead appeared to be ringed with fire. He hadn't even heard the fucking cuckoo this year. But as the Mahler drew to its quiet, unbearably poignant close, deep in the wood a cuckoo, clearly inspired, began singing, like a flute practising a perfect third: 'cuckoo, cuckoo,' floating on and on, echoing through the drenched greenness, as if to apologize for his earlier absence.

Moved to tears, Zac flung back his aching head. He

must pull himself together for the sake of the ghost army. Maybe Raymond would screw up tomorrow. He was roused by a bleep on his mobile. Checking the screen, he gave a whoop of delight.

Stop fretting, Boychic, Si had texted, *I've found Trebich in Munich, who's agreed to testify. Don't tell anyone until I get there tomorrow.*

68

Day three brought back the fine weather and twice as many people to welcome Raymond as he arrived at the court, with Viridian's copy of Tennyson in his breast pocket to ward off any metaphorical arrows. After another sleepless night he looked frailer than ever. You could get two fingers inside the collar of his pale blue striped shirt and his right hand was painfully swollen from still trying to keep the increasing flood of fan mail at bay. Anthea had been very snappy, poor child, because he kept calling Sienna 'Galena'.

All the morning press had insisted that the case was going the Belvedons' way, but Jupiter, Sampson and Sienna were edgy as they conferred in the corridor outside the courtroom, a dingy place of peeling radiators, dejected plants, and a sap-green carpet, speckled with coffee spilt by trembling witnesses.

'You don't think Dad's too gaga to testify?' asked Jupiter, who was pulling on a rare cigarette.

'I hope not,' sighed Sienna. 'Naomi Cohen just whisked past looking as smug as hell.'

'That may be because I caught Zac coming out of her bedroom at two o'clock this morning,' said Sampson.

Sienna turned to look out of the window. In the block of offices opposite, she could see people typing, chatting, xeroxing, having meetings, and envied their peaceful lives, free from the dreadful pain she was enduring. Zac and Naomi. With his track record, it was to be expected. Why did it hurt so much? 'I love, I hate, I know not why, but it is excruciating', she quoted despairingly to herself. Out loud she said: 'Ah, a Merc has just drawn up disgorging Si Greenbridge and several guards.'

Shit, thought Jupiter. I hope he isn't after my sleeper.

'I've just got to nip down the road to an auction,' he told Sampson.

'Raymond won't notice you've gone,' said Sampson reassuringly, 'he'll be in the box most of the morning.'

Willoughby Evans wished he hadn't drunk so much port last night, and also that he hadn't overheard one of the High Sheriff's remarks. He'd been commenting idly on Raymond's great charm.

'Used to great effect on customs officers in the old days,' David had interjected jealously. 'Before political correctness kicked in, Raymond was the most effective smuggler of pictures in Europe.'

'I didn't hear that,' Willoughby Evans had snapped, 'and you didn't say it.'

He didn't like David, he decided, and any man who wore lifts on his buckled shoes was distinctly suspect.

David was equally unamused to see his wife in court for the first time, sitting on the Belvedon side to cheer on Raymond, an unwarranted amount of blusher on her pale cheeks, giggling and taking nips from Lily's hip flask, and wearing much too snazzy a peacock-blue suit. He was the one who bought clothes, Rosemary only spent money on plants.

Rosemary was very happy. Si had been abroad for a few days, but had promised to be in Larkshire today. David's Range Rover had become almost a fixture outside the Grasshopper and Sixpence. In the post, Si had very indiscreetly sent her a bracelet made up of ten gold squares, on each of which was engraved one of the Ten Commandments. Except on the seventh: 'Thou shalt not commit adultery', he'd had printed on the underside: 'with anyone but Si Greenbridge.' Rosemary couldn't believe such happiness.

It was ten o'clock. 'All rise,' shouted the usher.

'"Cannon to right of them, Cannon to left of them . . . Into the jaws of Death . . .",' murmured Raymond. But as he entered the court, he veered away from the witness box. Everyone held their breath as he wandered over to the Raphael. The policemen guarding it edged closer, but Raymond ignored them, gazing at his picture.

Had his father finally lost it? wondered Jupiter in horror.

'Sir Raymond,' hissed Anthea, 'his Lordship is waitin'.'

'So sorry.' Raymond returned meekly to the witness box to be sworn in. 'I just got used to looking at it every day.'

'Sir Raymond,' said Sampson warmly, 'tell the court how you acquired the Raphael.'

The Belvedons and Sampson held their breath, but Raymond put on a command performance, rich Irish charm and telly megastar to the fore. By the time he'd raced down wartorn France, cleared the Falaise Gap of poor dead men and horses, 'the stench was unbearable, my dear,' stumbled on a Nazi in a burning château, 'whose life-blood was ebbing away,' given him a glass of water, and lifted down the Raphael for him to have a last look, there wasn't a dry eye in court.

'In the midst of this dreadful war, two enemies were united as brothers.' Raymond's beautiful silvery voice vibrated like an oboe. 'He spoke a little English. With his last words, he thanked me, gave me his blessing and the Raphael.'

'I wish he'd kept the chit,' Jupiter muttered to Aunt Lily. His father was always too busy gossiping to taxi drivers to get receipts.

Giving a sigh of relief, feeling it was OK to slip out between overs, Jupiter disappeared off to the auction rooms in Lower Fresh Street.

Naomi began her cross-examination and Raymond was soon happily relating how he'd cut the Raphael out of its frame and rolled it up in a shell case.

'I recognized it as a Raphael because my father took me to a loan exhibition in aid of the Red Cross in 1941. Lady Hampshire had lent Raphael's working drawing for Pandora.'

'I thought Dad bought it in a flea market,' muttered Sienna to Archie from the *Mail*, as she drew her father as a cormorant. 'He is sweet, isn't he?'

'In your witness statement, Sir Raymond, you have said you didn't know the Raphael was looted,' confirmed Naomi.

'I had absolutely no idea.'

Hearing a rumble of interest, Rosemary glanced round and her heart leapt for Si Greenbridge, huge, tanned and looking uncharacteristically straight and un-Mafiaesque in a blue button-down shirt, brick-red trousers, a blazer with big gold buttons and a dark blue pashmina scarf she had given him, had walked in and was grinning in her direction.

'There's Si,' bristled Anthea, 'with the gall to smile at us.'

Si was followed by one of his sharp legal boys, who sidled into the row behind Naomi, tugged her gown as she was about to launch into her next question, and handed her some papers.

Glancing down at them impatiently, she started dramatically.

'M'lord!'

Willoughby stopped scrabbling away at his laptop and peered over his bifocals.

'Yes, Miss Cohen.'

'I am very sorry,' lied a triumphant Naomi, 'to interrupt my cross-examination of this witness, but I have just had a message that a potentially vital new witness, with evidence that goes to the heart of this case, has made himself known.

'I have been handed this statement by my solicitor,' she shouted over the rumble of excitement as she passed copies first to Willoughby Evans, then to a stunned, stony-faced Sampson. 'May I please ask for an adjournment?'

Having devoured the document with bloodhound-furrowed brow, Willoughby Evans turned to Raymond.

'I'm extremely sorry. The claimants have unearthed new evidence. I need to confer with both sides. As you're under oath and in the middle of your testimony, Sir Raymond, perhaps you could have a cup of coffee in one of the witness rooms, and please do not discuss the case with anyone, while I call a brief adjournment.'

'Of course.' Raymond smiled happily. He could finish 'Ulysses': 'Some work of noble note, may yet be done,' and the *Times* crossword.

The moment he left the court, both sides pitched in.

'M'lord,' spluttered an outraged Sampson, conveniently forgetting he had whipped more rabbits out of hats in his time than Paul Daniels, 'it's highly irregular to produce new evidence at this late stage in the proceedings.'

'I appreciate my learned friend's misgivings,' said Naomi patronizingly, 'but we would like to call Major von Trebich, m'lord, a friend of Colonel Feldstrasse, who was the senior German officer at Le Château des Rossignols in 1944. He has crucial evidence about the Raphael. We didn't know his whereabouts until last night when he returned from six weeks in Tunisia. He was anxious to fly straight here this morning.'

'The timing seems singularly inappropriate, m'lord,' snapped Sampson, 'just when my client, who's an old man, easily confused, is in the box and I cannot confer with him.'

'I'm afraid you can't, Mr Brunning. As an even older man . . .' said Willoughby Evans drily.

'Sorry, m'lord.'

'My job is to find out the truth,' continued Willoughby Evans. 'If this witness has something important to say, let us hear it.'

'I'd like to call Major von Trebich, immediately after I've finished cross-examining Sir Raymond,' said Naomi.

Belting out the moment the arguments had started, Rosemary rushed to the Ladies to have a cigarette to calm her nerves and powder her shiny face. It was so hot in court.

As she applied a very becoming new pinky-brown lipstick appropriately entitled Lust instead of her usual dash of scarlet, she saw a disapproving Anthea's reflection beside her own.

'You're not meant to smoke in here, Rosemary, that's what gives you all those little lines round your mouth, although I read of a wonderful new lipstick that doesn't creep down wrinkles, called "No Wander".'

'Pity I can't use it on David,' giggled Rosemary, who'd had too many nips of Lily's flask on an empty stomach.

Anthea's lips tightened.

'You missed another Borochova Memorial meeting last Friday.'

'Oh hell, did I? Geraldine and David seem to have hijacked the whole thing.'

'It was your idea to involve them and Lottery money in the first place.'

'But none of the Belvedons has been consulted.' Rosemary drenched herself in Trésor given her by Si last week.

'Excuse me, Rosemary, Ay'm a Belvedon. I also saw you wavin' at Si, I'd watch him if I were you.'

'I find him absolutely charming,' snapped Rosemary.

'Well, he's no friend of ours.'

'Why ever not? He buys enough pictures.'

'Because he's bankrolling Zac with all the dirty money he gets arms-dealing. You don't think that little Ess Haitch One Tee could have afforded to bring a case like this on his own? Si's just turned up with some Nazi to rattle Sir Raymond.'

Oh my God. Rosemary felt an icicle being dropped down her spine. She'd been too overjoyed to make the connection. Si had never told her he knew Zac. What terrible incriminating details had she let slip in bed with him? Ve have vays of making you pillow talk.

Back in court, Naomi straightened her black gown and flicked her shiny dark hair behind her ears before replacing her wig.

'Sir Raymond,' she asked gently, 'according to your statement, your platoon took the village of Bonfleuve on the twenty-fourth of August and you found an unknown Nazi dying in the burning Château des Rossignols nearby and he gave you the Raphael.'

'That's right.'

'How old was this man?'

'Early forties, hard to tell, war ages people.'

'Is this him?' Naomi produced a grainy cracked photograph.

Raymond put on his spectacles.

'Again, hard to tell, his face was blackened with smoke.'

Naomi took a deep breath: with her beaky nose and fierce eyes, a sparrowhawk poised to swoop.

'Sir Raymond, ten days before your platoon captured Bonfleuve, the senior Nazi living in the château and in charge of the area, a Colonel Feldstrasse, had in fact moved on to a safe house, fleeing the closing in of the Allies.'

Raymond looked at her in bewilderment.

'No, no, my dear, you've got it wrong. If it wasn't a

Colonel – Feldstrasse, did you say? who gave it me, it must have been some other Nazi billeted there.'

'All the other Germans billeted at the château had already fled,' said Naomi triumphantly, 'and were all captured. Colonel Feldstrasse, the only one who spoke English, had been sent to a POW camp for high-ranking officers by the time you reached the château. Far from dying, as you gave him a last glimpse of Pandora, he was released in 1946 and was killed in a car crash in 1970.'

Peace ages men too. Raymond had gone grey; he seemed to shrivel. 'This can't be true,' he stammered. 'Another German must have sought refuge there.'

The witness box had become the loneliest place in the world. Raymond had told his version so often, he'd almost come to believe it. Glancing round, Si Greenbridge noted the collective horror on the faces of press and public.

'Dear God, poor Raymond,' muttered Lily.

'Dear, dear,' sighed Anthea, not totally displeased that chinks had been found in Raymond's breastplate of righteousness.

Glancing up, Rosemary saw David with his head on one side, attempting to look shocked and concerned, but having difficulty hiding his delight.

I loathe him, she thought numbly, and through my shameful indiscretions I have felled a dearest friend.

Trapped in the gallery, Sienna was reminded of occasions when Grenville and Diggory had torn a rabbit apart before she could drag them off. Naomi was now ripping her father to pieces. The court was in uproar. Press, switching on their mobiles and stampeding the fire doors, met Jupiter running the other way.

'What the fuck's going on?'

'I'm afraid your dad's been blown out of the water.'

*   *   *

After the adjournment, Naomi called her star witness. Major von Trebich was tall and willowy with smoothed-back silver hair, a Tunisian tan, and teal-blue eyes emphasized by a blue silk shirt, worn with a carefully arranged lilac silk scarf secured by a big pearl pin. His pale grey suit was exquisitely cut. As languid as Grenville, he moved with natural grace, wafting expensive lemony scent.

'Germans do have style. What an attractive old boy,' sighed Anthea.

'Heil Hitler,' snorted an outraged Lily.

You could have heard a spider tiptoe across the court.

'Major von Trebich, how long did you know Colonel Heinrich Feldstrasse?' asked Naomi.

'Nearly thirty years.'

'What was your relationship?'

'Heinrich was my lover.'

The court gasped with collective amazement. Willoughby Evans hit several wrong keys including the delete button.

They had met, went on Trebich, during the fall of Paris, when Germans were in a state of euphoria.

'We kept our love secret. The Führer disapproved of homosexuals almost more than Jews. Perhaps some rumours spread. Heinrich's career advanced less dramatically than expected, and he was posted to le Château des Rossignols to oversee the area of France round Bonfleuve, an increasingly dangerous place after the Normandy landings. I begged him to leave.'

Naomi then read extracts from Major von Trebich's battered red leather diary:

'"August 10, Heinrich telephones tonight, he is forced to leave Les Rossignols. He can hear enemy fire, they are sweeping across France. Will I ever see him again?"' Naomi's red talons flipped over several pages: '"August 18, Heinrich has been taken prisoner, and got word to me today, deliriously happy he is safe."'

Naomi put down the diary.

'So he was captured at least six days before Sir Raymond's platoon took the village?' she asked Trebich.

'Long, long before.'

'What did he feel when he left the château?'

'Heartbroken that he'd left in such a hurry he couldn't take the Raphael. "Oh my Pandora," he wrote in a later letter – you have it there, Fräulein Cohen – "how could I have left her to burn in the fire?"'

Incredulity rippled round the court. Raymond was turned to stone. Zac couldn't look at the Belvedons. He felt utterly sick relying on the evidence of a Nazi.

'When did Colonel Feldstrasse acquire the picture in the first place?' smiled Naomi.

Trebich seemed to grow inches taller with pride.

'In early 1941. It was a gift from the Reichsmarschall, Hermann Goering, at that time a hugely popular and admired figure, as a mark of his affection – and admiration,' said Trebich warmly. 'Heinrich knew a great deal about art and had great charm. He was so proud to be singled out by the Reichsmarschall.'

'He never thought to search for the picture after the war?'

Trebich shrugged. 'What for? He know the château burn to the ground.'

'Would he have given it to an English soldier?'

'Nevair.' Trebich's shudder was like Grenville's after a bath.

'Did Colonel Feldstrasse know it was looted from the Abelman family?'

'Certainly not. He was merely overjoyed to own such an exquisite picture.'

'Who was his heir?'

'I was. He had a charming wife, who died before he did, but no children. He left me everything.'

Oh Christ, thought Jupiter.

'How, as a German,' asked Naomi idly, 'do you feel as the owner of a looted picture?'

619

'I feel ashamed,' said Trebich quietly, bowing his silver head. 'Even if I have title, there is a moral obligation to return such a picture to its rightful owner. I couldn't hang a stolen picture on my wall,' he added sanctimoniously. 'And I know if Colonel Feldstrasse were alive today and he knew the history of the painting's confiscation, he would want it returned to Zachary Ansteig.'

Major von Trebich smiled at Zac, who was gazing at the floor.

'It's only because Zac's so bloody good looking,' hissed Sienna to Archie from the *Mail*. 'Si Greenbridge probably bribed that Nazi woofter and faked all the documents.'

'Thank you, Major von Trebich,' said an overjoyed Naomi.

Sampson did his best. If it were such a treasured possession, why didn't Feldstrasse take it with him?

'Not being a dealer,' replied Trebich haughtily, 'Heinrich didn't know you could cut a painting out of its frame and conceal it rolled up in a shell case.'

'Honi soit qui mal y ponce', wrote Sienna furiously. Where the hell did this put her poor father?

Raymond was recalled briefly to the witness box, and, capitulating faster than the French in 1941, broke down and wept, admitting he had stolen the painting from the deserted château.

'We detested the Nazis. They'd just killed my brother Viridian. I was twenty. It was the most beautiful painting I'd ever seen. How could I leave it to burn? I'm sorry I lied,' he added despairingly. 'I'm just a foolish, fond old man who loved his picture.'

'You're just a very greedy old man,' said Willoughby Evans sternly, 'who wanted to hang on to something that wasn't his.'

'No, he's not,' screamed Sienna, suddenly galvanized

in the gallery. 'Anyone who loved pictures would have done the same thing.'

A couple of officials frogmarched her outside, and Willoughby Evans agreed to an adjournment until the following day, so that everyone could get their breath back.

69

Leaving the court, Zac bumped into Sienna.

'How dare you humiliate my father?' she screamed and, before Si's guards could stop her, slapped him viciously back and forth across the face. 'I see you manage to conquer your loathing for Nazis when you need their help, you fucking hypocrite.'

Back at Foxes Court, the Belvedons spent a dreadful night. Raymond gazed into space, shuddering with horror.

'How could I have let you all down? I'm so sorry.'

'No good being sorry,' snapped Anthea. 'You've brought shame on all of us telling porkies at your age. I've just had poor little Dicky on the phone in floods.'

Guilt that he'd sloped off to the auction made Jupiter crueller than usual.

'Why the fuck didn't you tell the truth in the first place, Dad? We might have stood a chance.'

And where the hell was Jonathan? All Jupiter's jealousy spilt over. The only thing Jonathan was any good at was cheering up Raymond, and he wasn't even here to do that.

Thank God for Hanna and Baby Viridian, thought Jupiter. Thank God he had at least bullied Raymond into making Foxes Court over to him seven years ago, so the bank couldn't take that.

Remembering the sleeper in the back of the car, which might after all be a Constable, Jupiter decided to escape from the wailing and teeth-gnashing and drive up to London, so the restorer could get to work.

No-one slept at Foxes Court that night.

Sienna tried to comfort a sobbing Dora.

'Daddy'll never survive prison, particularly if he can't take Grenville with him.'

Naomi Cohen, dining at the judges' lodgings with Willoughby Evans and Sampson Brunning, was having a wonderful time. Rather like nurses able to switch off at a party after tending dying cancer patients all day, they managed not to discuss the case.

There was only the final speeches by the two counsels to come in the morning, after which Willoughby Evans would probably postpone his judgement till Monday. Sampson was an old enough hand to congratulate Naomi warmly on the way home.

'We'll make our speeches. Willoughby Evans will give the picture back to Zac. End of story.'

'I wish Zac was more kind of grateful,' sighed Naomi, 'he's still furious we had to rely on Trebich's evidence.'

Over at the Old Rectory, Rosemary couldn't stop crying. Thank God, David was out at some dinner giving prizes to achieving policemen. Si had utterly betrayed her. But she in turn had betrayed the Belvedons. Without her account of holidaying in Bonfleuve at Le Coq d'Or the first time she and Si had slept together, Si would never have been able to track down Major von Trebich.

She jumped as the telephone rang. It was Si going against every rule and calling her on the house telephone.

'You bastard,' yelled Rosemary, 'you've made me break the ninth commandment and bear false witness against my neighbour. I never want to see you again.'

* * *

Haunted by Sienna's anguished face, Zac paced up and down his room at the Black Swan. Naomi was fast asleep. She had come home drunk, euphoric at having smashed the Belvedons and watched herself walking prettily from court on *Sky News*. What a pity one wasn't allowed to talk about ongoing cases to the press.

She did however talk to Zac. Like a champion baseball player after a game, she took him through every triumphant sentence, every move. Now she was deservedly luxuriating in the sleep of achievement.

Zac was in despair. He hadn't really minded upsetting Anthea, nor Emerald. From what Si had said (who had got it from Rosemary who was helping Emerald with her maquette) Emerald was over him and now crazy about Jonathan. But he felt dreadful about Sienna. As she had led a tottering Raymond towards the car park, yelling expletives at the press, he'd been reminded of Cordelia and Lear: 'So young, my lord, and true.'

He could still feel her fingers on his cheek and he had to his surprise detested seeing Raymond so humiliated. The old guy had been really sweet to him, ordering in bourbon when he came to stay.

He felt even worse on Friday morning when the papers crucified Raymond.

'Mr Greedy,' shouted the *Sun*.

Mac of the *Mail* had drawn the Raphael on the wall of Raymond's study, with all the seven Belvedon children asking: 'What did you do in the war, Daddy?'

The telephone rang at Foxes Court as the family were failing to force down any breakfast. It was Dicky's headmaster.

'Poor Dicky's so terrified of being recognized by the press,' Anthea reported back to Raymond indignantly, 'that he's shaved off all his lovely hair.'

'Rubbish,' stormed Dora, 'Dicky just wanted any excuse to look like David Beckham. Why are they being so horrible to Daddy? He'd have been a hero in *London's Burning*.'

As he shuffled down the steps to the Bentley on Robens's arm, Raymond crumpled and collapsed. Dr Reynolds, despite not being asked to Anthea and Raymond's silver wedding, arrived in ten minutes. At the least, Raymond was suffering from shock and exhaustion, he said. There was no way he could go to court.

'I must,' whispered Raymond, 'people'll think I'm such a sissy.'

'No, they won't,' said Sienna. 'If Willoughby Evans gives his judgement this afternoon, I'll come and get you.'

'I'll stay home and look after you,' announced Dora, who was avid to miss maths and scripture, having been far too upset last night to do any homework, 'then I can walk Grenville.'

'Viridian, Dora and I will look after you,' said Hanna, who'd come over to the house to wish everyone good luck. 'You must all go,' she added, kissing Jupiter, who had just arrived back from London and the restorer.

A worried Sienna knew she should stay behind but couldn't bear the thought of not seeing Zac one more time.

In a day promising rain and sunshine, the pale acid-green spring leaves lay trustingly against a brooding purple-lake sky. The Belvedons found the court in an uproar. Peregrine, Sampson's junior, had abandoned his Solitaire and was grinning from ear to ear:

'Jonathan'll be here in half an hour, with a sensational new witness.'

'Who is it?' demanded Sienna. Then, when Peregrine whispered in her ear: 'Oh my God.'

'As we speak,' went on Peregrine, 'Sampson is arguing in court that Jonathan didn't get the breakthrough till late last night. Willoughby Evans can't refuse, having given the fair Naomi free range yesterday.

Thank goodness Sampson hadn't begun his speech.'

Next moment, Si Greenbridge, who'd been trying to get through to Rosemary all night and didn't dare storm the Old Rectory because of David, shoved past them, ran out to the car park and roared off alone in his Mercedes. Feeling suddenly isolated, Naomi had just managed to keep down two Alka-Seltzers when Rupert Campbell-Black's dark blue helicopter landed on the greensward.

The pretty archivist at the Public Record Office in Paris the previous evening had felt so sorry for the handsome young Englishman. Every morning for the past month he had rolled up first thing to scour newly declassified documents on the Resistance and on the Nazis' corrupt dealings in art, rootling frantically through yellowing documents written on ancient typewriters. Since Easter he had developed a dry cough not helped by the dust and grew hourly paler and more desperate. He was always the last to leave. It was now nearly six. Time to chuck him out. She longed to invite him for a glass of wine and a walk in the Bois where she would kiss away all his sadness.

She jumped at the sound of a low whistle. The Englishman was excitedly smoothing out scrumpled-up papers which had been stuffed to the back of a buff folder. His dark eyes darted back and forth. Dropping the folder, he rushed to the counter.

'What's the French for "Bingo"?' demanded Jonathan, then, over the striking clock, he begged, 'Will you please make six copies of this letter for me?'

'There are forms to complete.'

'I'll fill them in while you copy. Please.'

As she switched on the copying machine, the pretty archivist glanced down at the letter stamped with the Nazi eagle and read: 'Our valuable agent "Le Tigre" has been murdered in Paris. The Gestapo is blamed, but suspicion falls on the degenerate artist Le Brun.'

'It's my last hope. I'll buy you a drink next time,' promised Jonathan as he vanished into the warm spring evening.

Even though Raymond had shown Jean-Jacques Le Brun's watercolours at the Belvedon in the Fifties and Sixties before the Frenchman became famous, Jonathan couldn't get in to see him. The first call had been answered in a strained, cracked, shaky voice by Le Brun himself. After that the housekeeper answered both the telephone and the door, explaining in increasing disapproval that M. Le Brun was ill and couldn't see anyone.

Le Brun's house in Montparnasse, lofty, semi-detached and with a pale green roof had one more floor, probably a studio, than the other houses in his street. In the gap between it and the house next door, Jonathan could see a garden, and then a garden beyond that belonging to a house in the next street. He might have given up, if at that moment Sienna hadn't texted him.

Dad's been totally trashed. We've lost the Raphael. If you can't come up with any evidence, at least come home and comfort him.

Racing up Le Brun's street, Jonathan turned left then left again into the next street, running down it until, over the roof of Number 20, he could see Le Brun's pale green roof.

The door, thank God, was answered by a couple of students, who thought it a great lark. M. Le Brun did indeed live in the house behind and on warm evenings sat in the garden. They hoisted Jonathan over the wall, which was covered in spikes more treacherous than any unicorn's horn.

'Fucking hell,' he muttered as he tore first his combats, and then Emerald's blue shirt, and nearly lost his manhood before landing on some white irises.

He was just unhooking Emerald's shirt when he felt hard cold metal rammed into his bare back.

'*Es-tu un cambrioleur?*' demanded the voice that had cracked and quavered on the telephone.

'No, I'm an artist but I don't want to show you my pictures.'

'Thank God for that.' The pressure of the gun eased.

Jonathan edged round and found himself looking down on the black beret and beneath that the watchful, wizened face of France's greatest painter since Etienne de Montigny. There was no time to waste.

'I need to ask you about "Le Tigre", or rather Jacob Abelman.'

To Jonathan, Le Brun's long, sad sigh was like the first murmur of cool breeze after an interminable heatwave.

'I knew one day you would come.'

'My father, Raymond Belvedon, has been crucified,' pleaded Jonathan. 'Pandora is about to be taken away.'

'I have watched the news and followed the case in *Le Monde*. Your father doesn't deserve this. He had faith in my work before anyone else and so did Jacob Abelman.'

Le Brun led Jonathan through a painter's garden – intensely scented, ghostly white with lupins, lilac and tulips, to a veranda smothered in white montana, where he had been drinking very black coffee and peeling an apricot. Next moment, the housekeeper rushed out brandishing a saucepan.

'It's OK.' Le Brun handed her his gun. 'Please bring us more coffee and a bottle of cognac.'

'You're not allowed to drink, *monsieur*.'

'Tonight I need the Dutch courage.'

On a record player Karita Mattila was singing Strauss's 'Four Last Songs'. Inside, the walls glowed with stupendous pictures, but there was no time to look. Le Brun pointed to a chair:

'Sit down and tell me what you want.'

After ten minutes, he agreed that if Jonathan could dredge up a lawyer, he would be prepared to sign a statement.

'It would be better if I flew you to Larkminster. I know

it's a hideous imposition, but you'll adore the countryside, it inspired my mother.'

'I am ninety and beyond inspiration.'

'Now that the day has tired me' sang Karita Mattila,
'my spirits long for
starry night kindly to enfold them.'

Le Brun let Jonathan sweat, gazing on his ghostly
garden, unwilling to invoke the spectres of the past.
Then he drained his little glass and refilled it.

'I will come.'

Out in the street, Jonathan rang Rupert Campbell-
Black.

'Can I borrow your helicopter tomorrow?'

'No, you can't. I've got six horses racing in different
parts of the country.'

'Dad's been annihilated.'

'I know. I'm extremely sorry. Oh, all right, have it
then.'

70

Rupert's helicopter landed outside Searston County Court at half past ten. Leaping out, Jonathan lifted down Jean-Jacques Le Brun, settling him on the daisied lawn, straightening his beret, then waving an expansive hand towards the pale gold town, with its river sauntering round the castle walls and its cathedral spire piercing the lowering navy blue cloud as if to unleash a shower of rain.

'I told you it was beautiful.'

'Good God!' Willoughby Evans nearly fell out of the window of the judges' chamber. 'He really has brought Jean-Jacques Le Brun. I've got two of his watercolours at home. I wonder if he'd sign them.'

Sienna raced across the grass into Jonathan's arms.

'Thank God you're here. Sorry I was such a bitch.'

'But you've grown so beautiful,' said Jonathan in amazement, and, aware of scowling Zac taking a breather on the tarmac outside the court, he kissed Sienna lingeringly on the mouth before introducing Jean-Jacques.

'This is my fabulous new best friend, M. Le Brun, you've got to look after him while I go into the witness box.'

Knowing he could be relied on to stir things up, the press and public gave Jonathan a great cheer as he was sworn in. He was still wearing Emerald's now torn blue

630

shirt and ripped combats. His big laughing mouth was set in a hard line, his dark eyes glittered dangerously. Two spots of colour glowed on his blanched cheeks like red sold stickers.

Sold to the devil, thought Zac savagely. Jonathan his Nemesis, the one Sienna loved.

Up in the gallery, having portrayed Zac as the sleek long-eyed unicorn, Sienna was now drawing Jonathan with his wild mane and furious eyes as the snarling lion. No two men could think more evilly of one another.

Helped along occasionally by Sampson, Jonathan gave evidence rather like a one-man show, his conversation confiding, almost chatty.

'With the high profile of this case,' he explained, 'people have emerged from the woodwork. Zachary Ansteig's charismatic Great-uncle Jacob was certainly deported to Mauthausen but recalled after a few months. This was because the Nazis had embarked on the biggest looting spree in history and they needed his expertise in identifying and valuing the pictures they'd bagged.'

Then, over the rumble of amazement, smiling round at the flabbergasted faces, Jonathan continued: 'Jacob had *such* impeccable contacts in Europe, he was able to lead the Nazis to the best collections. And when this happened' – Jonathan shook his head ruefully – 'their Jewish owners were packed off to the death camps.'

'That's a lie!' Zac had leapt up, yelling abuse until two policemen shoved him back in his seat.

'You'll have to leave the court if you can't restrain yourself, Mr Ansteig,' reproved Willoughby Evans. 'Let Mr Belvedon have his say.'

'Later,' went on Jonathan, 'Jacob settled in Paris where the Nazis allowed him to trade as long as he produced the pictures they wanted. War in fact was a godsend in France for those dealers who collaborated.

'Jacob also vowed, as the court has been told, to avenge his murdered father by hunting down the

631

Raphael. How convenient that whilst he was working for Hermann Goering, he stumbled on his beloved Pandora. There are, as you've also been informed, records of the picture going to Goering's palace, Karinhall, but a question mark over its whereabouts after that. Great-uncle Jacob was the question mark. As Pandora belonged to his family, he naturally felt justified in repossessing it.'

Zac was unable to contain himself.

'Bullshit,' he shouted.

'What was less understandable,' said Jonathan in mock sorrow, 'was that two years later Jacob sold the Raphael on to another Nazi, Colonel Feldstrasse, who hung it proudly in his distant château, fantasizing it had been given him by the Reichsmarschall.'

'M'lord, this witness has been misinformed,' cried Naomi, terrified Zac was going to leap across the court and strangle Jonathan. Why the hell had Si shoved off instead of staying here to control Zac? 'This is groundless speculation unbacked by any evidence,' she added furiously.

'Except this.' Smiling gently, Jonathan brandished some torn faded sepia papers. 'Here's a letter dated the eighteenth of April, 1942, from Jacob to Feldstrasse arranging for them to meet in Paris. Here's Jacob's invoice and copy of the receipt for the looted Pandora: a picture Colonel Feldstrasse bought in good faith, not perhaps for a mess of pottage, but for five hundred thousand Swiss francs, which was about thirty thousand pounds in those days. So,' Jonathan added coolly, 'it is no longer Abelman property.'

The stunned silence was only broken by a car backfiring, which made everyone jump. The press were poised to bolt for the doors.

Somehow Zac had regained control of himself, but his face had shrivelled as if struck by lightning. Sienna couldn't bear to look at him.

As Jonathan leant over, took a pile of photographs

from Sampson and started flipping through them, it was as if SS guards were systematically kicking Zac to death with their jackboots.

'Here,' Jonathan told the court amiably, 'are pictures of Great-uncle Jacob showing Pandora to Colonel Feldstrasse, who clearly liked his own sex, particularly when they were as handsome as Jacob. And here's Jacob with Goering – make a nice couple, don't they?' Jonathan waved the photograph. 'Jacob was so charming, so amusing, no wonder he was one of Goering's pets, and he was as good at exploiting women as his great-nephew Zachary.'

'My lord, that is totally inappropriate,' interrupted a furious Naomi.

'I agree,' said Willoughby Evans firmly. 'Please stop making wild accusations, Mr Belvedon. There is no jury for you to impress.'

'All that guff about Jacob wanting to join his wife Leah in America was crap too,' went on Jonathan unrepentantly.

'Your language, Mr Belvedon,' snapped Willoughby Evans, who nevertheless like everyone else was transfixed with interest.

'Sorry, my lord,' drawled Jonathan. 'Here is a last photograph of Goering, Jacob and Jacob's French mistress, Georgette Le Brun . . .' With raised eyebrows, Jonathan repeated the name: '*Le Brun*, at a Nazi party in 1943.'

'You've been working very hard,' admitted Willoughby Evans, as he and David examined with ill-disguised approval the photograph of ravishing Georgette, 'but I hope you have other evidence substantiating these claims.'

With so much evidence piled against her, Naomi had an uphill struggle, particularly when Jean-Jacques Le Brun went into the box.

He had taken off his beret; his bald head freckled with

liver spots looked like a robin's egg. He wore a red-and-black silk bow tie and had combed his neat triangle of moustache and goatee beard. On the lapel of his frock coat was a red Légion d'honneur. He refused to sit down.

'Just like darling M. Poirot. Don't these old Froggies keep themselves nicely?' murmured Anthea.

'I remember Le Brun staying at Foxes Court in the Sixties,' Lily whispered to Jupiter, 'such a sweet, sad man, who used to compare notes with Raymond about being cuckolded.'

What on earth had happened to Rosemary? she wondered. They were supposed to be lunching at the George. Lily was looking forward to beef and ale pie.

In excellent English, Le Brun proceeded to inform the court that Jacob Abelman had been a highly respected dealer.

'When the Nazis confiscate and burn my pictures, regarding them as degenerate and obscene, he had the great courage to show them in his gallery in Vienna.'

'There.' Naomi smiled round as tears of gratitude filled Zac's eyes.

'In 1942,' went on Le Brun, 'my wife Georgette and I were living in Paris, and met Jacob again. He was staying at the Ritz, a favourite haunt of the Nazis, and from his beautiful coat with a fur collar and the open car he was driving around on black-market petrol, he was doing well. My pictures were banned. I was not prepared to collaborate. Georgette and I were very poor. Jacob suggested we took him as a lodger, and was very generous. Georgette was beautiful. She loved silk stockings, pretty clothes, delicious food. I was out a lot, painting in an underground studio, working for the Resistance . . .' Le Brun's voice dropped. 'I didn't realize she was falling in love with Jacob.'

Poor old boy. Everyone was shaking their heads.

'What a darling,' murmured Anthea.

'How long did Jacob Abelman stay with you?' asked Sampson.

Le Brun took a sip of water and his time.

'Until he was killed by the Resistance.'

A gasp went round the court. Naomi jumped to her feet.

'With respect, m'lord, this witness has also been misinformed. Jacob Abelman was murdered by the Gestapo.'

'*Non*, the Resistance,' persisted Le Brun.

'How d'you know this?' asked Sampson gently, praying the old boy hadn't lost it.

'Because I killed him,' said Le Brun.

Zac jumped to his feet, then slumped back. Lily dropped her handbag. Hip flask and glacier mints crashed to the ground.

'He was having an affaire with my wife,' went on Le Brun. 'You can see them with Hermann Goering in the picture Jonathan show you.'

'Was that why you killed him?' asked Sampson.

'No, no.' Le Brun smiled wryly. 'I am Frenchman, we accept these things.'

The killing, he went on, had occurred on 8 March 1943. Love had made Jacob and Georgette careless.

'She tell me she was going to spend the night with her mother in Illiers.'

'Proust holidayed there as a child,' murmured Willoughby Evans, peering over his glasses, 'very built up now.'

'It is, my lord. While she was away, Georgette's mother rang joyfully to tell Georgette her sister had had a six-pound baby boy. I summoned three colleagues in the Resistance, one a safe-breaker. They all suspected Jacob was the notorious "Le Tigre". We raided his room and found a chest hidden. We broke it open like Pandora's Box.'

'Bloody hell!' Jupiter accepted a slug from Lily's flask.

'We found letters of authority,' went on Le Brun sadly, 'from Goering, from Field Marshal Walther von Brauchitsch, one of the first military commanders of occupied France, allowing Jacob to travel as a purchasing agent throughout Europe. There was even one from the East Tyrol Resistance. Jacob was clearly playing a triple game. We suddenly heard the roar of his car . . .' Le Brun had gone yellow. He clutched the brass rail.

'Would you like a break?' asked Willoughby Evans in concern.

'*Non!*' like a rifle shot. 'I must finish. We heard the exhaust of Jacob's car, one of the few running in Paris. We shoved everything back and met him in the hall in his beautiful fur coat, smelling of Chanel No. 5, my wife's perfume.

'We took him to the forest of Fontainebleau,' said Le Brun bleakly, 'where we held brief kangaroo trial. He deny everything, only as we raised our guns, he ask: "Who betray me?"' Le Brun put a shaking hand to his forehead. 'To my eternal shame, I lied that it was Georgette. "Then I am ready to die," said Jacob, so we killed him.'

Glancing across the aisle, Jonathan noticed tears like snails' trails glittering on Zac's face and was enraged that he suddenly felt sorry for him.

'For the rest,' sighed Le Brun, 'Jacob's collaboration was total. I have records of all his dealings with the Nazis, lists of paintings he looted and their owners who he betrayed. Being Austrian, he kept impeccable records: including love notes from Georgette. Already they were making plans to escape to South America if the Nazis lost the war.'

Sampson Brunning was so fascinated by the story, he had turned into Michael Parkinson, asking the questions that everyone wanted answering.

'Why was Jacob nicknamed "Le Tigre"?'

'Because he was a killer and prowled when he walked and was *beau comme un dieu*,' added Le Brun almost wistfully, 'like his great-nephew over there.'

Zac gazed stonily into space.

'How did your wife react when you told her?'

'She shout that she love Jacob and didn't care how many Jews he kill. They would meet in another life and she would tell him I'd lied. Then she leave me.' Le Brun closed his eyes in sudden anguish. 'Today for the first time I tell the truth.'

Naomi couldn't dent Le Brun, even when she tried to prove he had killed Jacob in a fit of jealousy, because the Austrian was handsomer, richer, more successful and had stolen Georgette.

'According to official reports,' she went on accusingly, 'Resistance papers were found on Jacob, so he couldn't have been working for the Gestapo.'

'We put them there,' said Le Brun wearily. 'The Gestapo had already killed forty-one thousand people in reprisal. "Le Tigre" was so valuable to the Nazis, they would have butchered scores of us in retaliation. So we put the letter of authorization from the East Tyrol Resistance in his inside pocket. Maybe he had worked for them at some time, but not when we knew him. He was a turncoat of many colours.'

Then Le Brun squared his little shoulders and with a great effort, raised his voice.

'I am here today because Raymond Belvedon is a good and honourable man, whom I have known for fifty years, who, having saved Pandora from the flames, acted as any art lover would have done. I am deeply sorry, however' – he turned to Zac – 'to have destroyed a young man's hero.'

Zac seemed to wake out of a trance, stumbling to his feet, stunned with horror, beads of sweat mingling with tears on his face, his eyes cavernous. 'It can't be true,' he mumbled over and over again as he lurched out into the aisle, staring round in bewilderment.

Next moment a fire-exit door burst open and Sienna hurtled down the red carpeted steps. Ignoring Willoughby Evans and the hissing disapproval of both camps, she flung her arms round Zac, frantically patting his shoulder, holding him close, trying to warm and revive him with her body, gibbering how sorry she was.

'What the fuck are you playing at?' hissed Jupiter and Jonathan in unison as two policemen prised her off.

'That's enough, Miss Belvedon,' said Willoughby Evans, who was privately very taken with Sienna. 'I think this is a good time to adjourn for lunch.'

What a difference from yesterday. Everyone, even Jupiter, was thumping Jonathan on the back.

'What a shame Rosemary missed it all,' grumbled Lily, linking arms with M. Le Brun as the Belvedon contingent swarmed off to the George to celebrate.

After lunch both sides addressed the court. Zac didn't even stay to hear Sampson, after two large gins and tonic, triumphantly tying up the loose ends. The Abelmans had sold the picture, forfeiting any claim, he told the judge. Trebich on oath had also waived any right to it.

'Bet he's sorry,' chuckled Lily, who'd also been at the gin, 'eight million would have kept him in boyfriends for the rest of his life.'

'Thank you, Miss Cohen,' said Willoughby Evans as an utterly deflated Naomi ended her muted peroration, then he beamed benignly at the contestants: 'I will give my judgement on Monday morning.'

Archie from the *Mail* lent Sienna his telephone to wire her sketch of a snarling shaggy Jonathan and a sleek snorting Zac, fighting over an oval-shaped Raphael, which she'd substituted for the Royal Coat of Arms, through to the *Telegraph*.

'Bloody good drawing,' he told her approvingly. 'You deserve to get your picture back.'

71

By Monday, Ladbroke's were offering two to one on a victory for the Belvedons, who consequently set off to court with their tails up. Jupiter, vastly relieved that the gallery and Foxes Court appeared to be saved, insisted Hanna accompany them. Baby Viridian, who'd had a busy weekend trying to cheer up his grandfather, could be left to sleep in the care of Mrs Robens.

Raymond was desperately ashamed of lying and breaking down in court. All seemed to have been saved, except honour. But despite looking close to death, he put his favourite yellow rose, the early Canary Bird, in his buttonhole and insisted on tottering into court on Jonathan's arm. Predictably he felt very sorry for Zac.

'Poor fellow, learning those dreadful things about Jacob.'

Anthea was dressed especially delectably in lemon-yellow with a big Antwerp-blue picture hat. Winners, she felt, were entitled to obscure the views of those behind them.

Jonathan had put six bottles of Veuve Clicquot in the fridge for a celebration later. Aunt Lily clattered down the aisle with two hip flasks and a switch to lemon sherbets. Glacier mints, like toothpaste, she had decided, made drink taste disgusting.

Lily had promised to call Dora the moment the result was through, hopefully during break, when the *Independent*, the *Guardian* and the *Mail* would be ringing in for Dora's reactions. Having discovered a massive hat bill from David Shilling in her mother's knicker drawer, Dora was planning to auction it to the highest bidder. A second pony was definitely on the cards.

Jean-Jacques Le Brun had stayed over, boosting Raymond's spirits, reacquainting himself with several of his pictures, delighted, on balance, he had saved the bacon of the Belvedons, particularly that of Jonathan, such a dear boy, who'd made him realize how much he'd missed not having a son.

Only Sienna was in turmoil. Even though the *Telegraph* had devoted nearly half a page to her Lion and Unicorn drawing, which included Willoughby Evans chucking a bucket of water over the contestants, it was too facile an interpretation of Friday's tragedies.

The weekend papers had also had an embarrassing field day, speculating on Sienna's transformed appearance and her public embracing of Zac. Had Zac notched up another Belvedon scalp? they wondered. Was that why Emerald had wept in court? 'Ladette to Lady', and 'The Sloane-ing of Sienna' were among the headlines. Zac, Emerald and Sienna had all been 'unavailable for comment'.

I'd have been only too available if Zac had picked up a telephone, thought Sienna desolately. Holding him fleetingly in her arms had brought back all the divine madness of the fireworks evening.

On her right, as she approached the court, had gathered a large Jewish contingent waving placards demanding the return of all looted art.

'Give Zac back his Raphael,' shouted a fearsome brunette.

'Oh, fuck off,' snapped Sienna. 'And you can fuck off too,' she added as a torrent of press surged round her. She was flaming well going to sit with her family today.

David Pulborough was spitting. On Saturday, Rosemary's cat Shadrach had died of old age, and David thought he'd been especially caring, digging a grave beyond the tennis court. It was only a cat. But Rosemary couldn't stop crying, refusing to accompany him to a regimental dinner in the evening. Even worse, it looked as though his next-door neighbours were poised for a famous victory.

Five minutes to blast off. April storms had been forecast. The lights of the court kept flickering on and off. A mean east wind was thrashing horse-chestnut leaves against the window pane.

A restless Jonathan wandered off to look at the Raphael. Hope and Pandora must be getting gate fever at the prospect of coming home. Sloth on his yellow sofa had probably slept through the whole ordeal. Would Emerald be pleased, wondered Jonathan, that he had been less slothful recently? Or had she wept in court, nagged a nasty little doubt, because she was still carrying a torch for Zac?

'This judgement will be frightfully boring,' Sampson was telling the rest of the Belvedons. 'Endless citings of cases and procedure and we won't get the result till the very end. Oh, here comes the Royal House of Darkness.'

At least Zac, in Ray-Bans, dark grey polo neck, softest black leather jacket and black cords was sartorially back to normal. He was followed by several guards and a stony-faced Si. The Jewish contingent, who'd moved to the gallery, gave them a round of applause.

'To the victor, the trophy,' spat Jonathan, as Zac slipped into the row on the left.

Naomi Cohen looked tired and in low spirits. Cases were like boat races, there was no kudos in coming second.

Serve her right for turning me down on Friday night, thought Sampson smugly.

'Be upstanding in court,' called out an usher, as

Willoughby Evans appeared smiling broadly through the crimson velvet curtains.

'Hi, Sheriff!' Taking a slug from Lily's hip flask, Jonathan waved happily at a clanking bootfaced David, who did not wave back.

Willoughby Evans was exhausted but elated. Never had a case engendered such publicity. With any luck he'd notch up enough brownie points to be promoted to the Court of Appeal. He liked the idea of the black and gold robes of a Lord Justice. He had worked very hard on his judgement, which would take around forty-five minutes to deliver, and had treated himself to a glass of champagne with his morning kipper.

'The Raphael *Pandora*,' he began in his sonorous Welsh baritone, 'passed to Benjamin Abelman on the eighth of August 1931, and was stolen from him in Vienna on the twelfth of April 1938. The subject is the opening of Pandora's Box. I doubt when Raphael painted his exquisite picture, captioning it "Trouble lies below", he had any idea how prophetic these words would be. In the last few days, all the deadly sins, Pride, Avarice, Lust, Wrath, Envy, Sloth and' – as Lily crunched a lemon sherbet – 'even Gluttony, have stalked this court.

'Zachary Ansteig's family,' he went on, 'must have suffered unimaginable horrors and, in seeking what he believed was his birthright, he opened a Pandora's Box releasing all varieties of evil, not only shredding the reputation of Sir Raymond Belvedon' – Sienna slid her hand over her father's – 'but also of his idol, his Great-uncle Jacob.

'But before you judge these men too harshly, remember the words of L.P. Hartley, "The past is a foreign country: they do things differently there."

'Jacob Abelman' – Willoughby Evans looked at Zac – 'has been described as a turncoat of many colours. But he was once a highly respected dealer, courageous enough to show art forbidden by the Nazis. He also belonged to the Resistance in Austria. Later he was seduced by the potentially vast profits gained by throwing in one's lot – as many others did – with the Nazis.

'But remember it was only when the war looked likely to be lost by the Germans that suddenly every man and his dog in the occupied countries claimed to have belonged to the Resistance. Caught between the cross-fires of Nazi and Communist rule throughout Europe, people changed sides as often as their shirts. It was a very grey area.'

Willoughby Evans beamed at Anthea, far from grey in her lemon-yellow. He'd love to put her in his button-hole. Straightening his wig, gathering his thoughts, he turned to the stricken grey ghost, shrivelled with shame, gazing into space on her left.

'Raymond Belvedon was one of the most admired and beloved figures in the art world until last Friday. But you must remember that, after the war, everyone was souvenir crazy. When my father, among others, liber-ated Belsen, he remembers soldiers seizing watches off the guards and even taking home lampshades made of human skin.' Willoughby Evans shuddered.

'Sir Raymond,' he added kindly, 'found the Raphael in a blazing collapsing building. If he hadn't rescued it, none of us would be in court today. He knew he had looted a painting, but had he admitted this, it would have been taken away from him. And when you see the beauty of Pandora, like Helen of Troy amid the burning towers of Ilium, you understand exactly why men have joined battle and suspended moral judgement for her sake. So I repeat, judge neither man too harshly.'

'There, Daddy.' Patting her father's cheek, Sienna's hand felt the wetness of tears.

'I don't know which way this judgement's going,' muttered Jupiter, as Willoughby Evans launched into a prolonged flurry of citings, subjections, proprietorial claims, pursuyvants, and X versus Ys.

Raymond passed the time by reading 'Ulysses': 'It may be we shall touch the Happy Isles.' Jonathan read *Viz*. Hanna played battleships with Aunt Lily. Jupiter hoped Willoughby Evans would wrap it up quickly, he'd just received a text message to ring his restorer.

Sienna was drawing Willoughby Evans as a sweet little field mouse. Zac, she thought, looked like a bombed-out town. Then she realized Willoughby Evans was talking about his beloved uncle.

'Jacob Abelman appropriated the picture in 1941 from Hermann Goering. *His* painting, you might say. He was the younger son, whose older brother Tobias had killed himself. But Tobias had a daughter, Rebecca, who survived the horrors of Theresienstadt and had a son, Zachary Ansteig. You may think Zachary Ansteig abused both the hospitality and the daughter of the Belvedons' – Willoughby Evans shot a reproachful look at Zac – 'but it was his past and his inheritance for which he was searching.'

Noticing Sampson shaking his head, so the little tassels at the back of his wig shook like lambs' tails, Sienna redrew her field mouse as a vicious-looking rat. She thawed a little as Willoughby Evans praised the tenacity and enterprise of Jonathan Belvedon.

'Nor can anyone, having heard his evidence and that of Miss Sienna Belvedon' – glancing up, a surprised Sienna encountered a smile of such approval that she promptly softened the vicious rat's eyes and thickened his whiskers – 'doubt that the Raphael is as much a part of their past and a link with their dead mother as it is of Zachary Ansteig.'

'Two sets all,' muttered Sampson.

'I realize how deeply they would feel its loss,' went on Willoughby Evans.

'Eight million smackers,' muttered Jonathan. 'You bet we would.'

'Hush,' reproved Anthea, who'd been planning a holiday in St Lucia. Raymond would be too frail to make the journey, but she could perhaps take Green Jean as a bag-carrier, whose plainness would be the perfect foil for her own beauty.

More cases, more statements, more incomprehensible jargon.

'The law is a foreign country,' Jonathan whispered to Hanna, 'they say things differently there.'

The clock had moved round to ten-forty.

It was getting darker. Outside the rain was hissing on the little green parasols of the horse chestnuts, spattering reporters' notebooks. Photographers were putting their coats over their cameras. Willoughby Evans was now paying tribute to the skill and industry of all counsel involved, ably supported by their respective teams.

'Oh, get on,' groaned Jupiter. 'It was much more exciting on the other days,' he whispered apologetically to Hanna. 'I really love you,' he added.

Like audiences at boring concerts, everyone was craning to see how many pages Willoughby Evans had left to read. Only two now. Sienna took Raymond's hand. Please God make it OK.

'For these reasons I have given, I conclude . . .'

'Here we go,' muttered Sampson, who was playing with his pink brief ribbon. Peregrine parked his chewing gum and stopped playing Solitaire.

'The painting was taken from Benjamin Abelman in 1938,' intoned Willoughby Evans, 'but the Nazis who stole it did not become full owners. None of the subsequent transfers established title. Who knows to which son Benjamin would have left his picture, but in the law of this country, the elder son inherits.'

The pink ribbon snapped in Sampson's hand. Feeling the blood drumming in his head, Jupiter closed his eyes. They'd lost it. Involuntarily rising out of her seat, Sienna could see a jubilant Naomi's hand on Zac's arm. Her pencil broke as she turned Willoughby Evans back into a vicious rat.

'Although Benjamin's younger son, Jacob Abelman, recovered the Raphael and sold it to Colonel Feldstrasse,' he was saying sternly, 'it was not in fact his to sell. Benjamin's elder son already had a daughter, whose son Zachary Ansteig is the direct heir.'

As the ecstasy on the faces of the Jewish supporters was illuminated by a biblical flash of lightning, Willoughby Evans's voice rang out like a chapel bell.

'I will therefore recognize Zachary Ansteig's title to the painting, as derived from the law of the twelfth of April 1931.' Then, as a cannonade of thunder rocked the building: 'Sir Raymond never obtained good title to this painting.'

Utter pandemonium followed. Everyone was yelling their heads off, except the Belvedons.

'Oh no, no, no, no,' whispered Raymond.

We're going to need that Veuve Clicquot for a wake, thought Jonathan numbly.

'Never – hic – trust a Welshman,' muttered Lily.

How dare conniving beastly little Willoughby Evans crinkle his eyes at me all week, thought Anthea furiously, then take away our lovely Raphael?

'We must appeal,' she cried.

'There isn't any fucking money,' snarled Jupiter. 'We'll have to pay costs now. With all Si's dirt-gathering trips in his jets, they'll be massive.'

There was no time for tears. Naomi and Sampson were already up at the bench, arguing terms. Naomi haughtily demanded costs and Sampson, wondering if the Belvedons would ever be able to pay him, complained this was far too high and he'd like a more detailed assessment.

'It seems reasonable to me, Mr Brunning. Costs follow the event, do they not?' said Willoughby Evans, trying and failing to make himself heard over the uproar.

Sienna sat utterly stunned. Her longing for Zac had

fooled her into thinking she didn't mind so much about the Raphael. Now its loss hit her like an overhanging branch.

Equally stony-faced, having secured a Pyrrhic victory, idol in smithereens, proud heritage a mockery, Zac stalked out into the downpour. Such was his suppressed fury, he had no need of guards to fend off the press, who split open like the ground in an earthquake as he disappeared through them into Si's Mercedes.

Deprived of their interviews with Zac, the maddened media stampeded the Belvedons, knocking Raymond's Canary Bird out of his buttonhole, trampling it in the mud.

'I'm so sorry,' Raymond mumbled in bewilderment as the storm flashed and crashed overhead, 'I must get back to Grenville, he's terrified of thunder.'

Desperate to get a shot of Pandora before she was packed away, photographers raced back into the court.

How could Hope still be smiling? wondered Sienna.

'You lying bitch,' she said slowly.

72

Jonathan was relieved not to go back to Foxes Court. He couldn't face Anthea's martyrdom, Raymond's anguish, Jupiter's cold rage, Sienna's despair. Le Brun had been coming home for a celebration, but felt now he should return to Paris. Jonathan insisted on accompanying him. As Rupert had repossessed his helicopter, they caught a late afternoon flight and dined at Chez André where Jonathan sunk into deeper and deeper gloom. At least hunting for evidence had distracted him a little from Emerald. Now, alive in his dark coffin without any bell, the bleakness of a future without her terrified him.

'Don't try to eat,' said Le Brun, who'd been watching the poor boy pushing exquisite langoustine round his plate. 'You're exhausted, which is ninety per cent of depression.'

'I wish,' sighed Jonathan. If only a decent night's sleep could get him over Emerald. Then, pulling himself together, he apologized for dragging Le Brun over to England and forcing him to admit such painful things.

'And thank you for trying to salvage Dad's reputation.'

'You're not just sad because of the Raphael,' observed Le Brun.

'I'm pissed off that shit Zac has finally got it.' Then Jonathan told Le Brun about Emerald.

'Everyone bangs on about the benefits of finding one's birth mother,' he said finally. 'No-one warns you of the hell of falling in love with your real brother.'

Despite a very long day, Le Brun insisted on coming back to Jonathan's dusty little room to look at his pictures, which were all of Emerald. Le Brun refused a drink and said nothing because the suffering they conjured up was so excruciating, it reminded him of losing Georgette.

Oh well, thought Jonathan.

'I'm sorry I've been such a bore,' he muttered. 'Do you think the pain ever goes away?'

'*Non*,' said Le Brun tersely.

'Right.' Jonathan took it on the chin. 'I'll get you a taxi.'

'It will never go away, because you have immortalized this girl and your unhappiness.' Le Brun put a consoling hand on Jonathan's arm. 'People's hearts break all the time, but only a handful have the genius to portray this suffering: Catullus, Sappho, Housman, Yeats, Mahler, Munch, now these . . .' Le Brun waved the other hand round at the pictures. 'They are also extraordinarily beautiful.'

'Thank you.' Jonathan fought back the tears. 'That does help – a lot. But I'd still trade Emerald for any immortality.'

'That's because you are young. I am old and tired.' Le Brun sat very suddenly down on the bed. 'We will talk more tomorrow. Now get me that taxi.'

Switching on his mobile, Jonathan found a text message from Jupiter.

'Dad's had a massive stroke,' he told Le Brun shakily, 'he's unlikely to last the night. Can I drop you off on the way to the airport?'

The first British Airways flight left Charles de Gaulle at a quarter to seven in the morning. Trafford, who met Jonathan at Heathrow, was somewhat the worse for wear after an all-night preview party celebrating the opening of Tate Modern.

Some prudes, he announced proudly, had dismantled *Shagpile* and knocked off all the cocks.

'Bloody good publicity. Thinking of replacing the cocks with Brillo pads and renaming it *Hagpile*,' then, just sober enough to take in Jonathan's reddened eyes and corpse-like pallor, he added, 'Sorry about your dad.'

'Thanks. Sorry to drag you out here, but I wanted to repossess my dog.'

Perhaps it was desire to escape from a petrol-stinking car park, but any worries that Diggory might have forgotten him were dispelled when an orange-and-white bullet exploded out of Trafford's filthy jeep, screaming, wriggling, covering his master's salty face with kisses.

'Don't be too nice to me,' mumbled Jonathan.

Diggory reeked of hash, cigarette smoke and various scents. He had clearly been partying as full-bloodedly as Trafford, who, reflecting that both Sienna and Emerald would probably be *in situ* and in need of comfort, suggested he accompany Jonathan to Foxes Court.

Jonathan shook his head.

'I'll drive myself. Need time to adjust to being an orphan.'

'Nice bloke, your dad. Let's have a drink.'

'Have one on me.' Jonathan shoved a bottle of Bell's into Trafford's shaking hand.

'Sure you're OK?'

'Fine.'

All the same it took Jonathan three-quarters of an hour to remember on what floor he'd parked his car.

What would Van Gogh have made of rape fields? wondered Jonathan, putting on dark glasses to fend off glaring lakes of yellow beneath a white hot sky. As he stormed into Limesbridge, scattering the pink and white petals in the gutter, crossing the fingers of both hands on the steering wheel, he prayed that his father would stay alive long enough for him to say goodbye.

It was therefore an anti-climax to be greeted by a grey-faced, exasperated Sienna: Raymond hadn't had a stroke at all.

'It's something much milder called a T.I.A.'

'Sounds like one of those things one should buy before the fourth of April to avoid tax.'

'It stands for Transient Ischaemic Attack and evidently simulates the symptoms of a stroke.'

'Is he OK?'

'He's got to keep quiet for a few days, then they'll do some tests. D'you want some breakfast?'

'I'd like a drink.' Wandering into the kitchen, Jonathan poured them both duty-free brandies. 'Where is everyone?'

'Jupiter's belted back to London to sweeten the bank manager. Anthea's sobbing on her bed, rehearsing her role as unmerry widow. In reality she's hopping because she overheard Robbie and Lily discussing how pleased Dad would be to see Mum in heaven.'

'I'll go and see him.'

'He might not recognize you. He keeps calling me Galena and Grenville Maud. Such an insult, no wonder poor Grenville's refusing to eat. Dad thought Limesbridge had been taken over by the Russians last night and that Neville-on-Sunday was Boris Yeltsin and offered him a huge vodka.'

Jonathan grinned. Out of the window he could see little Diggory hurtling round the garden in search of Grenville and Visitor.

'Where's Alizarin?'

'He rang, he's in the middle of another op, and can't fly back at best till later in the month.'

'Poor darling.' Jonathan put an arm round Sienna's shoulders. 'It's all fallen on you.'

Sienna battled not to cry. It was so shaming that even when she was convinced her father was dying, she could only long for Zac's arms round her.

* * *

Raymond had retreated to his dressing room. On his way up there, Jonathan bumped into Anthea, who expressed horror at his brandy bottle and the two hundred Gauloises.

'You mustn't drink and blow smoke all over your father. He's been dreadfully ill. He won't recognize you. He asked Lily to bowl to him this morning.'

Being nice, Jonathan decided, was the easiest way to get rid of her.

'Poor Anthea, you look whacked.'

'I haven't slept for weeks, months actually, what with the trial.'

'I'm sure. Go and lie down, I'll sit with him.'

One of Anthea's eyelids was turquoise, the other violet, he noticed; perhaps in her way she did love his father.

Raymond, elegant as always in Turnbull & Asser blue-and-white-striped pyjamas, was lying diagonally across the bed to accommodate the long legs of Grenville, who languidly waved his tail, before jumping down to greet Diggory.

Raymond's face lit up.

'"This is my son,"' he quoted in wonder, '"mine own Telemachus."'

'I told you he wouldn't recognize you,' said Anthea smugly.

'Hi, Dad,' said Jonathan, shutting the door firmly in her face.

As he stooped to kiss his father, he was shocked to be grazed by stubble. Raymond had never not shaved.

'I expect the Grim Reaper will soon be doing it with his scythe,' murmured Raymond wryly.

'Don't be morbid, Dad, you're not dying at all. Do you want a drink?' Then, when Raymond didn't, Jonathan refilled his own glass and, pulling up a chair, took Raymond's hand.

'I've always loved this room.'

Every inch of the wall was covered with favourite

pictures: portraits of the family, past sporting achievements, dogs on the lawn, sketches of Raymond by
friends: Lucian Freud, Francis Bacon, William
Nicholson. In the wardrobes were countless beautiful
suits, a rainbow of coloured shirts, dashing hats. In
the bookcases, poetry. On the dressing table, silver-
backed brushes nestled with a pottery Cheshire cat
Jonathan had modelled at prep school.

A faint smell of Extract of Lime hung over the room.
The Good Friday Music was on the CD player. Viridian's
dilapidated lichen-green leather volume of Tennyson
lay on the bedside table beside a saxe-blue vase of
cowslips and kingcups, picked by Lily.

Although putty grey and shrunken in the face,
Raymond's smile was as sweet as ever. 'Good, Larkshire
bowled out Rutshire.'

'Do you want the commentary?' Jonathan glanced at
his watch. 'It'll be on in a minute.'

'No, I want to talk. Jupiter and Alizarin are good
fellows but not brilliant at cherishing. I worry about Lily.
I've left her her house, but she may not have enough to
live on. Jupiter's awfully tight with money, and I don't
think he'll allow darling Anthea to buy many clothes. Do
encourage her to marry again. So pretty, needs a nice
young chap to take care of her, someone who'll be kind
to Dicky and Dora.'

'Dad, stop it,' said Jonathan gently.

'And I worry about Sienna, so loving and sweet lately,
and dear little Emerald, I wish I'd got to know her
better, I'm so sorry about her and you, all my fault.' A
tear trickled down the crow's-feet; Raymond was having
difficulty breathing. 'And don't let poor Grenville
starve, Anthea's not his greatest fan.'

'Dad, you're not dying.'

'So they tell me, but I don't feel very well.'

'I'll look after everyone. I'll become the Van Dyck of
the twenty-first century and make a fortune.' Jonathan
felt wiped out by tiredness.

'No, no, you have too much talent. You must paint what you want to. If Jupiter sells one or two pictures, that should be enough.'

The smell of crab-apple blossom and clematis was drifting through the window, honey sweet yet sharp, taking Jonathan back to Le Brun's garden. Perhaps he wasn't so lousy an artist – Le Brun had liked his stuff.

'See that my post's answered,' begged Raymond. 'Jupiter likes to bin everything, but if people are kind enough to write, tell them I'm so dreadfully sorry I let them down.'

'You didn't. Listen, there's the cuckoo.'

'How good of him to turn up.' Raymond lay back in ecstasy. 'That pastel of my father's awfully good, he was such fun. I let him down too. Oh dear, I worry about you all, particularly little Viridian. The ozone layer, and now the Arctic Circle melting. I don't want Germans running Europe, or even worse the Chinese over-running the world. You will look after Robens and Esther? I don't know if Jupiter will keep them on.'

Raymond was gasping for breath.

'Don't talk, I'll read to you.' Jonathan pressed the repeat button on the Good Friday Music, and picked up Tennyson. The gold-tipped pages fell open at 'The Passing of Arthur', who, like Raymond, was looking back on a world that was coming to an end.

'I found Him in the shining of the stars,' read
  Jonathan,
'I marked Him in the flowering of His fields,
But in His ways with men I find Him not.'

You could say that again, he thought, or He wouldn't have made me and Emerald brother and sister.

All day Diggory slept off his excesses on Jonathan's knee, while Raymond, watched by a yawning Grenville, drifted in and out of sleep. Waking, he was delighted Larkshire were 270 for 2.

'Zac liked cricket, you know, can't be entirely bad, all his relations wiped out, have to feel sorry for the poor boy.'

'I don't,' snapped Jonathan.

'Difficult to underestimate the importance of roots,' sighed Raymond. 'Look at that lot on the wall. Take them for granted, but you know where you are. Poor little Emerald's torn between us and the Cartwrights. I've left her a little money. You will look after her?'

Jonathan smiled crookedly, lit a cigarette and got up to blow the smoke out of the window. At this time of the evening and the year, the slanting sun behind the trees revealed ebony branches beneath the pale mist of green, reminding one of death. Robins and blackbirds sang to distract him.

'St John Evangelista,' muttered Raymond as his son turned back from the window. Jonathan had such a lovely face, hollowed cheeks, sweet, sensitive mouth, curly hair, even curlier eyelashes, around sloe-dark soulful eyes – so like a Raphael.

'When you're dying—' he whispered.

'You ain't.'

'"Truth sits upon the lips of dying men." You were always my favourite – by miles. Alizarin, Jupiter, Sienna – all awfully tricky and critical. I dote on Dicky and Dora, but you were such a dear little boy.'

'I wasn't a very good little boy.'

'Maud was my favourite too,' whispered Raymond, spreading his stroking fingers to block Grenville's ears. 'I shouldn't say it in front of him, but Maud was so sweet guarding your playpen. Her only crime was sticking her long nose through the bars and selecting the occasional toy like a cocktail snack.' Racked by a fit of coughing, Raymond continued, 'That Gauloise reminds me of your mother. Not sure I feel up to meeting her yet.'

Jonathan stubbed out his cigarette and, sitting on the bed, took his father's hand.

'Maud and Visitor are up there, they'll guard you. I can just see you riding through heaven in the Bentley, with Maud and Visitor beside you, reading your own obituary in *The Times*.'

Raymond smiled faintly.

'The Bentley's failed its MOT,' he mumbled. 'Time for us both to go.'

Suddenly he gave a stifled cry, shuddered, went rigid and stopped breathing.

'Dad,' yelled Jonathan in panic. 'Dad!'

Leaping up, Grenville nudged his master frantically, whimpered, then threw back his brindled head and howled. As Diggory joined in Anthea burst into the room.

'What's going on?'

'I think he's gone.' A stricken Jonathan was cradling Raymond in his arms.

'You should have called us, shutting us all out not giving us a chance to say cheerio . . .' Anthea started to scream.

73

Jonathan was utterly devastated, sobbing his heart out, deranged with grief.

'Far too distraught,' observed Aunt Lily, 'just for the death of a father . . .'

Anthea was also shattered. She'd always got more attention than any of the children, and had tantrums if she didn't get her own way. Who would indulge her now? There were, however, compensations. She looked lovely in black. Everyone was fussing over her and for once her stepchildren, even Sienna, were being nice to her. Letters also flooded in. Anthea skipped the guff about Raymond, reading out the bits about herself.

'You were such a wonderful wife to Sir Raymond, Lady Belvedon, you kept him young.'

'How am I not going to throttle her?' muttered Sienna to Knightie.

What really upset Anthea, however, was the conspicuous absence of David. He had been so charming and attentive earlier in the year, when he'd wanted to muscle in on the Borochova Memorial Award. Now he and Geraldine had control, he had no time for her.

'You always said if anything happened to Raymond you and Ay would end up together,' she sobbed.

If you'd managed to hang on to the Raphael, we might have, thought David.

A great sadness for the Belvedons was that Margaret

Cassidy, MP for Searston, a jolly backslapping Tory predictably known as 'Butch', had died the same day as Raymond and bagged the more flattering obituaries. Even Raymond's adored *Times* criticized his shameful lying and breaking down in court and implied an intemperate scattering of seed, as they pointed out he had left behind a second wife and seven children.

The good news was that Margaret Cassidy had vacated a possible safe seat for Jupiter. During his trip to London, he had missed his father's death, but as ample compensation, his sleeper had turned out to be a lovely little Constable, which, after a clean, should fetch the odd million, which would help him and Hanna with death duties.

Margaret Cassidy's funeral in Searston Cathedral was on the same afternoon as Raymond's, but far less well attended. Not an inch of St James, Limesbridge, was unoccupied. The press, having poured down from London in anticipation of high drama, found the Belvedons in tears of hysterical laughter. The local flower shop, overwhelmed with orders, had muddled the two funerals. Raymond as a result had received several wreaths for 'Darling Butch, ever in our thoughts', and even a bunch of lilies for 'A Dear Godmum'.

The Belvedons needed a laugh. They were all so sad.

'Darling Butch,' sighed Aunt Lily, 'would have loathed the weather,' which was bitterly cold with a vicious east wind once again stripping off his beloved blossom.

'Why can't families all die on the same day?' sobbed Dora. 'And why can't Loofah come into church if Diggory and Grenville are allowed?'

'Because Grenville hasn't eaten since Dad died,' said Sienna.

David Pulborough was furious – not just at even more media than ever concentrating on Foxes Court, but because an equally heartbroken Robens and Eddie the packer, rather than he, had been asked to join Jupiter, Jonathan and Dicky in carrying Raymond's coffin. Anthea had made Dicky hide his shaven head under his school cap.

'Everyone'll think he's got ringworm,' hissed Dora.

So many of her media contacts were in church, she couldn't decide who to sell the latest titbits too.

The organ played Raymond's favourite hymns and the Good Friday Music. People read poems and made careful speeches. Jonathan was only aware of a ravening press who had crucified his father a week ago, who were now scribbling away or muttering into their tape machines. There was a bleep on his mobile. His heart lightened briefly as he read: *Darling Jonathan, I'm so sorry. Say goodbye to Raymond for me. Still all my love, Emerald.*

Dropping Diggory on Sienna's knee, startling the vicar who was poised to launch into the final prayers, black hair curling over his navy blue overcoat, eyes blazing in a deathly pale face, Jonathan stalked up the steps of the pulpit.

Oh God, what's he going to do next? wondered the Belvedons, as he adjusted the mike and waited until the rumble of excitement had faded.

'Tennyson was my father's favourite poet,' he began quietly, 'but today an earlier poet, Shelley, seems more appropriate.

'"He has outsoared the shadow of our night . . ."' Jonathan spoke very slowly, emphasizing every word.

> 'Envy and calumny and hate and pain,
> And that unrest which men miscall delight,
> Can touch him not and torture not again;
> From the contagion of the world's slow stain
> He is secure.'

Glaring round, Jonathan gripped the sides of the pulpit.

'Here we go,' muttered Jupiter.

'I'd like to know what you're all doing here,' asked Jonathan softly. 'Last week you carved up my father in your newspapers and on your programmes. The rest of you from the art world' – he scowled particularly at Somerford – 'have been gloating over his downfall in restaurants, pubs and galleries. In a minute you'll all pour into his house to guzzle his champagne.'

There was total silence, as Jonathan plucked a yellow rose from the branch of Canary Bird decorating the pulpit.

'My father worked harder than anyone I know,' he said defiantly. 'Charisma is an impossibly overworked word, used to describe rock stars and YBAs who turn heads when they roll up drunk at parties. In fact it comes from the word "Charites" – or rather "the Graces". It means goodness and whatever bestows the gift of grace. Predictably my father was born, nearly seventy-six years ago, on a Tuesday; Tuesday's children are proverbially always full of grace.'

Looking round, Jonathan was amazed to see how many people were crying openly, and nearly lost it.

'There is no-one in this church' – his voice shook only for a second – 'who at some time hasn't been touched by my father's grace and, to quote another poet, by "that best portion of a good man's life, His little, nameless, unremembered, acts Of kindness and of love." So in future bloody well say nice things about him.'

No-one made a sound as Jonathan bounded down the steps. But as he stopped beside the Belvedon pew to present Anthea with the yellow rose and gather up Diggory, Dicky stumbled to his feet, shouting that Jonathan was right and clapping wildly. Next moment everyone had followed suit. An impassive Jonathan walked out into the sunlight with the cheers ringing in his ears.

Everyone came back to Foxes Court, as Raymond would have expected, except Jonathan, who, having seen

Raymond's coffin safely into his grave next to Galena, shoved off to London. Sienna, fed up with behaving well, decided to get drunk and later to have a swim in the pool, which was still full of algae and leaves. On the way, she bumped into David. Why did he always undress her with those horrible hot eyes? You didn't need a bathing hut with him around.

'Heard about the Raphael,' he sneered.

'What?'

'Zac never took it home. Sent it straight to Sotheby's.'

'What!' Sienna clung on to a stone dolphin. 'I don't understand.'

'He's flogging it – in an Old Masters' sale in July. Sienna . . . *Sienna.*'

But she had plunged fully dressed into the icy water, vanishing beneath the leaves. For a moment David thought she wasn't coming up. Perhaps he'd better leap in and hoick her out – good excuse for a grope. But Sienna had emerged, paler than Ophelia, algae greening her hair, murder in her eyes.

'Bastard! Traitor! So much for recapturing his past. From the start, he and Si were in it for the money.'

74

Rosemary stayed away from the funeral, pretending she'd got flu, still devastated by the misfortune she'd brought on the Belvedons. Emerald didn't go, for the same reason. If it hadn't been for her, they'd never have lost the Raphael, nor been faced by this vast bill for costs, and an utterly stressed-out Raymond would be alive today.

She felt even guiltier when she learnt about the will. Having already made over Foxes Court and its contents to Jupiter, Raymond had also left him the gallery as well on condition that he provided for Anthea, Dicky and Dora. Raymond had also given Lily her house, £100,000 each to Sienna and Jonathan, £200,000 to Alizarin because of his blindness, £50,000 apiece to Dicky, Dora and Emerald and £5,000 each to the Robenses, Knightie and Eddie the packer. Far too much, in Jupiter's mind. How the hell would he keep Anthea in hats and Dora in ponies?

Emerald meanwhile was having no success in getting over Jonathan. How could she when his doings were constantly in the papers, particularly his glorious outburst at Raymond's funeral?

As Raymond had left her so much, she was even more determined to give something back to the Belvedons. She was therefore delighted and relieved when, having shown her portfolio and ideas to the Borochova

Memorial judges, out of hundreds of entries, she had been shortlisted. Along with three others, she now had to produce a suitable maquette – or little model – by late June. The winner, to be announced on 6 July, would then complete the sculpture.

Seeing Emerald working night and day, Patience was equally amazed by the change in her daughter. Compared with Sienna, who was now so chic and glamorous, Emerald would go for days without bothering with make-up, hardly running a comb through her hair. Apart from the occasional flare of temper, she was also so quiet and sad.

Both Rosemary and Lily had been marvellous, helping her with photographs and tales about Galena. If the submission day had been a few months later, observed Lily, Emerald would have been able to read Galena's diaries, which, locked in a drawer at River Cottage, were ticking away like a timebomb, only to be opened in October 2000.

In early June, Emerald had a particularly bad day. It was muggy and baking hot in London. On a rickety table in her bedroom, she was trying to sculpt Shrimpy, Galena's little Jack Russell, which made her cry because it reminded her of Diggory and Jonathan. Next door her mother and father were glued to the European Cup. Portugal was playing and the gorgeous Portuguese players, with their dishevelled curls, big rolling eyes, mobile features and mock-serious ways of crossing themselves before they bounded onto the pitch, were so like Jonathan, it made her cry even more.

'Telephone for you, darling,' called her mother.

It was David Pulborough, his voice smooth as white chocolate pouring out of a vat.

'My dear, sorry we didn't have time to chat the other day. The Memorial Committee simply adored your portfolio. Thought I could give you a few pointers. How about a bite of supper tomorrow?'

663

And a chance to hear news of Jonathan, thought Emerald.

'Oh yes, please.'

'Prince Igor's at eight o'clock then.'

The following night was even hotter and stickier. Even though the waiters at Prince Igor's had been allowed to take off their satin embroidered waistcoats, their white muslin shirts already clung to their bodies. David had reserved a table in an alcove partly concealed by a large bamboo plant.

At first Emerald was touched by his kindness as he filled her up with white wine, ordered her a tiny helping of gulls' eggs and shredded pigeon salad, to be followed by poached salmon. But he sat much too close to her on the red velvet banquette, which scratched the bare undersides of her thighs, and talked so grandiosely about himself, how he was advising Derry, Cherie and Tony and how last Friday he'd dined next to the Princess Royal: 'a tireless worker for good causes like myself.'

He would be happy to represent Emerald, he went on, and was definitely going to put in a good word for her in the competition, but she needed proper advice if she were going to fly. To punctuate this monologue David kept putting hot hands on her bare arms and thighs, or brushing her breasts with his arm.

'You've broken one heart besides mine,' he teased. 'Casey Andrews longs to paint you. He's been captivated by your beauty since he met you at Raymond's party. Will you sit for him?'

'He's a terrible lech,' protested Emerald. 'Jonathan says he puts girls on a revolving podium and crawls round gazing up their skirts.'

'But think of the kudos,' urged David. 'It would be a terrific career move. I've just firmed up a big exhibition for him at the Tate next year. Imagine if your portrait were included. We could simultaneously put on a little show of your heads at the gallery. I'll come to every sitting and chaperone you, how about that?'

David crinkled his eyes engagingly, and was just giving her bottom an encouraging squeeze, when Emerald said, 'Oh, look, there's another of the judges. Will she think it unethical we're having dinner together?'

Geraldine clearly did and shot across the restaurant.

'Hello, David, hello, "Rosemary",' she said sourly, 'I hope he's not giving away secrets,' then flounced off to join her party at a nearby table. If I mixed purple lake with alizarin crimson I could just about capture the colour of David's face, thought Emerald.

'What was that about?' she asked.

'Must have got the wrong end of the stick,' stuttered David, 'and thought I was dining with Rosemary.'

Emerald took a deep breath which pushed out her enticingly high round breasts.

'How's Jonathan?'

'Fine, I think.'

'What's he working on?'

'New ideas.'

No need to tell Emerald that the little snake had sent an e-mail that very morning, saying he no longer wanted to be represented by a pompous crook. David had been tempted to pass the e-mail on to his solicitor.

'Like to come back to the gallery and see them?' he asked.

'Oh, please.'

Shoving a £50 note into the hands of the waiter who had just arrived with two plates of poached salmon, muttering he'd settle up tomorrow, David whisked Emerald out of the restaurant. Anything to get away from Geraldine, peering slit-eyed through the bamboo like approaching Vietcong.

Emerald was jolted to be in Cork Street. Across the road in darkness, except for one of Joan Bideford's outrageous lit-up nude sculptures in the window, was the Belvedon. She was so upset, she didn't notice David slapping on Paco Rabanne and smoothing his hair in the underside of an Ella Fitzgerald CD, before slipping it into the CD player.

Pop went a cork, flying out of a very cheap bottle of sparkling wine.

'"I have dreamt that your arms are lovely,"' sang Ella.

'I've got something to show you,' called David from the back office.

Wandering in, Emerald found a splendid white sofa piled with mauve and dark purple cushions. On the desk, beside a very flattering silver-framed photograph of David in his High Sheriff's uniform, and a pile of faxes and transparencies, was the most charming unframed little watercolour of Shepherd's Bush meadows.

'Vintage bubbly for a fair lady.' David handed her a glass. 'And an early Turner for your delectation.'

'It's beautiful.' Emerald bent over the picture.

'Changed a bit, hasn't it? Can you work out where your parents' flat might have been?'

Feeling his hot breath on her neck, and his body pressed against hers, Emerald asked hastily if she could see Jonathan's stuff, hoping it would include some of the portraits of herself in Vienna.

'I'll get it out,' promised David prophetically as he disappeared through a second door into the stock room.

'Sorry,' he cried unrepentantly a minute later, 'must have left Jonathan's canvasses down at Limesbridge. Got something much more exciting to show you.'

Swinging round, Emerald shrieked, for David was wearing nothing but a rainbow-striped condom.

Remembering Jonathan's professed loathing of condoms: 'It's like washing your feet with your socks on,' she burst out laughing.

Interpreting this as approval, David was on top of her – oh that scent of violets, oh that soft white skin. One hand expertly unhooked her bra, the other scuttled like a tarantula up her thighs.

'I love Jonathan,' screamed Emerald, as David's warm wet lips came down on hers. Falling backwards, she sent trannies, Polaroids, faxes, watercolours flying.

'You're too good for him.' David whipped off her scarlet knickers. She's as tiny as her mother, he thought excitedly as he explored further. 'You need an older man to guide and cherish you.'

Emerald lost her temper.

'Get off, you disgusting creep,' she yelled, shoving him violently away.

For a moment David's portly body barred her exit, but as she took a run and hurled herself against him, he gave way like a warped door and she fled out into Cork Street.

Unable to face another night alone at Foxes Court, Anthea had been to the theatre and supper with a sympathetic girlfriend, before returning to the flat in Duke Street, St James's. As she always seemed to be cold these days, she'd just had a hot bath. This part of town always reminded her of first meeting David and the half-hours they always managed to snatch together. Now he was continually busy. Sadly she looked across at St James's Park. The blossom had gone, giving way to the uniform green of summer. Jupiter'll be selling this place next, she thought fretfully.

Some drunk was leaning on the doorbell. On and on, now in fits and starts, growing more frantic. Anthea would have been spooked if it weren't for Gubbins the porter.

When she finally picked up the telephone, it was several minutes before she could identify a name from the hysterical sobbing. When Emerald finally fell into the flat, her lipstick was smeared, her floral dress ripped. David, she wept, had made the most ferocious pass. But she seemed far more upset over the loss of her purple pashmina, given her by Sophy, who could ill afford it, and a little black sequinned bag, which had been a present from Jonathan.

'If David starts using my cheques they'll bounce.'

At first Emerald was touched by her mother's fury.

'The beast, the brute, in fact the bastard,' raged Anthea.

Having found desperately shivering Emerald a thick jersey, she made her a cup of cocoa. Emerald hadn't the heart to ask for a stiff drink.

'Did he – er – did he – put his thingy inside you?'

'No, no.'

The last time she was here, Emerald remembered, was when the DNA tests proved she was Raymond's daughter and could never marry Jonathan. A revelation so terrible, nothing afterwards, not even a pouncing David, could really dent her for long.

Anthea was pacing up and down, her suddenly aged face an ugly contrast to the spring flowers on her cotton dressing gown. Outside large cranes hung over St James's Park like malignant birds. In the distance, Big Ben reared up like a floodlit sugar-sifter.

'Now Sir Raymond has passed away,' muttered Anthea, who was shaking worse than her daughter, 'there's something I must tell you. Try not to hate me.'

Oh God, what new evils are going to fly out of Pandora's Box? wondered Emerald. That was such a sweet photograph of Jonathan going off to prep school in a cap and short trousers, she might try and nick it before she left.

'When I first went to work at the Belvedon,' a still pacing Anthea was saying, 'I worshipped Raymond, he was so caring and such a gentleman. Then David came back from his honeymoon, all tanned and handsome in his lovely sports car. I fell for him laike a log. I simply couldn't help myself. After Galena made Raymond sack me, I discovered I was pregnant with you . . .' Automatically Anthea ran a finger over a Dresden shepherdess checking for dust. 'I was convinced you were David's baby. David accepted this and paid for everything, hospital bills, accommodation, on condition no-one found out and I gave you up. I thought he'd relent once you were born, but he was so petrified of Rosemary and Raymond finding out, and losing his new wealth and his nice job.

'When I gave you up the pain was so terrible, I thought it would blot out the agony of David not marryin' me, but it didn't.' Anthea hung her head. 'I married Raymond because he was so safe.'

'And you went on having an affaire with David?'

'Yes, yes,' whispered Anthea.

'Poor Raymond, poor Rosemary,' said Emerald in bewilderment.

'Rosemary should have made more of herself,' snapped Anthea. As the green flame of jealousy hissed out of the damp log, Emerald couldn't help smiling.

'Raymond wasn't very exciting in bed,' confided Anthea, 'but David was such a wonderful, imaginative lover . . .' Then, seeing Emerald shudder: 'Well Ay thought so. He always knew the right buttons.'

Like an ace casting director for *Cinderella*, thought Emerald, fighting hysterical laughter. She was getting as silly as Jonathan.

'When you rolled up with Zac' – Anthea was frantically straightening coloured paperweights – 'I couldn't bear to be reminded of the terrible unhappiness of giving you up, and I was petrified . . .'

'David would flip.'

'Yes. I feel so ashamed. At our silver wedding party I thought only of myself, panicking and fibbing to Raymond that he was your father then biting my nails through the summer. The biggest shock was the DNA result.'

To her amazement, Emerald was smiling.

'David must have had kittens.'

'He did. He'll never forgive me, and you know' – Anthea looked up in amazement – 'I suddenly don't care.'

'Hurrah!' cried Emerald. 'I'd have behaved exactly

the same. I only dined with David tonight,' she confessed, 'hoping for news of Jonathan. What I could never understand was why you hadn't told Raymond I was his, but if you were convinced I was David's, it all falls into place.

'Poor Anthea.' She put an arm round her mother's heaving little shoulders. 'What a nightmare it's been for you.'

'I hated living a lie,' sniffed Anthea.

'Can we have a huge proper drink to celebrate?'

'Do let's, there's some brandy and an untouched bottle of crème de menthe Raymond gave me for Christmas.'

Since it was true confession time, Emerald took a deep breath and told Anthea about sculpting the maquette of Galena.

'I really need your help, now I've got into the last four.'

Anthea, to her amazement, was thrilled.

'There are some of her clothes in the dressing-up box at Foxes Court, so we can get her measurements right, and lots of photos. There might even be some here. She was quite fat, you know.'

After that there was so much to talk about that a pink dawn gatecrashed the party just as the crème de menthe ran out.

'Let's have some breakfast.' Anthea cannoned off a William and Mary winged chair as she tottered towards the kitchen. 'The moment the Pulborough opens, Ay'm going round to sort out that rotter.'

Anthea found the Pulborough in uproar. Arriving earlier, David had been unable to find his Turner of Shepherd's Bush and was furiously accusing his son Barney, his assistant Zoe, his cleaner Marlene and the office cat of stealing it.

Most of Cork Street, in order to listen, were rubbing non-existent smears off the insides of their front windows. Jupiter, Tamzin and Eddie the packer were all busily dusting Joan Bideford's nude.

'You always complain if the bins aren't emptied first thing, Mr P.,' Marlene the cleaner was now protesting.

'Here comes the US Cavalry,' murmured Jupiter as Anthea came storming up Cork Street.

'How dare you try and rape my daughter, you rotten swayne,' she screamed, rushing into the Pulborough.

Whereupon most of Cork Street decided their outside windows needed cleaning.

'Ay've come to collect her pashmina.' Anthea snatched it back from a disappointed Zoe. 'And her new handbag' – Anthea grabbed that from an even more disappointed Barney – 'and her scarlet panties, which you tore off her, you scoundrel. How could you abuse a young woman's trust?'

'Is this what you're looking for, Mr P.? Must have fallen into the waste-paper basket,' interrupted Marlene. From one finger and thumb were suspended Emerald's red knickers; from the other, marinaded in pot noodles and bilberry yoghurt, hung the Turner of Shepherd's Bush.

75

Soon after Raymond's funeral, a big piece had appeared in the *Evening Standard* saying how delighted Sotheby's were to be including the Raphael *Pandora* in their Old Masters sale on 6 July. This was not entirely true. Having seen glamorous photographs of Zac all over the papers during the court case, Sotheby's staff were understandably excited when he asked them to sell his picture.

Alas, they soon discovered Zac was not as other Jewish heirs who sought their help in selling restituted art. These tended to be fragile, a little bewildered and touchingly grateful for any advice, free valuations and help with research. They were only parting with this infinitely precious part of their past because there was no other way they could pay the massive legal bills or because a Monet or a Sisley cannot physically be divided between five grandchildren. These heirs also spoke of their picture with such pride and longing, praying, like a single mother giving up a beautiful baby for adoption, that it would go to a loving, appreciative home.

Zac, by contrast, seemed only interested in making as much money as quickly as possible and showed no affection for the Raphael at all. From the start, he insisted on a terrifyingly high reserve of £15 million and that the picture must go into the sale on 6 July.

Sotheby's begged him to wait until their next big Old

Masters sale in December. This would enable them to put the Raphael on the catalogue cover, produce a CD-Rom and a hardback for promotional purposes and send the picture on a triumphal tour of the art capitals of the world, so all the major players would be in town to view it.

To which Zac had replied that if they didn't do all these things in the eight weeks before 6 July, he would take Pandora straight round to Christie's. The contract hammered out between Sotheby's and Si Greenbridge's sharp-suited lawyers was an absolute brute. Nor did the Old Master experts, who'd been working on catalogue footnotes eulogizing the Raphael until four o'clock in the morning, enjoy having their exquisite prose torn to shreds by Zac.

The press, meanwhile, egged on by David, who intended to bid for the picture and who wanted to bring the price down, were spreading rumours that *Pandora* might only be a school painting and wasn't anyway in the best condition.

To refute any rumours, Chris Proudlove, Sotheby's kind and genial press officer, suggested they call a press conference.

'Get along the broadsheets, the big art magazines and of course television. Our experts Richard Charlton Jones and Lucian Simmons,' he went on, 'will then talk about the picture, its history and its excellent condition. And for you, Mr Ansteig' – Chris Proudlove smiled at Zac – 'it will be a unique opportunity to put the record straight. You had a lot of adverse publicity during the court case and since – quite unfairly,' he added hastily. 'Now's your chance on an open stage to give your side of the story.'

'I have absolutely no desire to justify anything,' snarled Zac.

'What a beast,' sighed a secretary longingly as he stalked out of the building.

*   *   *

673

Jupiter no longer minded about losing the Raphael. The Constable had sold extremely well. A valuation of the paintings in the Blue Tower had convinced him that flogging a few would sort out death duties and the gallery's money problems. The General Trading Company, thrilled with Hanna's flower paintings, had placed a big order. Searston Conservatives, having been assured Jupiter could control his wild family, were poised to adopt him as candidate and little Viridian was making eyes bluer than a Tory rosette at everyone.

Jupiter was also preparing to move into Foxes Court. Empathizing with his father's beloved Tennyson: 'That man's a true Conservative Who lops the mouldered branch away,' he had coolly informed the family he'd like them out by Christmas. Anthea was already looking for a cottage in the area for herself and the twins with a paddock for Loofah.

All the Belvedons found it horrible at Foxes Court without Raymond to welcome and fuss over them – none more so than Alizarin who finally came home at the end of June. There was no reason why he was still blind, but the American doctors felt they had done all they could.

The moment he arrived, Alizarin asked Sophy to take him to Raymond's grave, which was still covered in flowers. The limes were in bloom in the churchyard – the scent of his childhood. Seeing tears once more escaping from under his dark glasses, Sophy tried to comfort him, but as usual he shrugged her off.

Wretched pride again. Alizarin couldn't tell her of his despair that he'd never paint again, nor see the pale yellow lime blossom, nor, saddest of all, her sweet trusting face. She was only twenty-three. What use was a painter without eyes? If only Visitor were still alive to be hugged and confided in. If only he could have retreated to the Lodge to bawl his sightless eyes out, but Jupiter had decided against chucking out the retired bank manager and his wife. They brought in too good a rent.

It was still impossibly hot. As soon as supper was over, Alizarin, lying that he was drooping with jetlag, retired to bed, leaving Sophy and Jonathan, who happened to be the only other member of the family at home, to watch television.

Missing Raymond desperately, Jonathan was huddled in one of his father's old jerseys and trying not to pump Sophy too much about Emerald. Grenville shuddered at their feet panting and dribbling, knowing a storm was near and there would be no Raymond to comfort him. Diggory sat in his basket under the television set convinced his master and Sophy were looking admiringly at him rather than watching the late-night Wimbledon round-up. John McEnroe, discussing the day's matches, was being charming, intelligent, reasonable and not slagging off a single player.

He used to be an obnoxious, mouthy brat like me, thought Jonathan. Perhaps I could improve?

'What the hell are we going to do about Alizarin?' he asked.

'I think he's about to crack,' sighed Sophy. 'He's like one of those stone walls that fills up with rain – or tears – and suddenly collapses.'

They were roused by terrifying screams.

'Jesus!' said Jonathan as Diggory leapt out of his basket, barking furiously.

'It's Alizarin.' Sophy had gone very white. 'He keeps having these nightmares.'

Racing upstairs they found Alizarin sitting up in bed drenched in sweat, his huge frame racked by frenzied sobs, screaming for Galena and shouting, 'He said I mustn't tell anyone.'

Gradually, Sophy calmed him. Jonathan paced up and down. Alizarin had been put in the spare room on whose walls Galena had painted the myth of Daphne turning into a laurel tree. Leering satyrs and wild beasts peered out from every tree – none of which Alizarin could see. Perhaps Galena's ghost had returned to derange him.

Jonathan took his brother's hand.

'What happened the afternoon Mum died?' he asked gently.

At first Alizarin would only mumble about some tramp fucking some woman who'd bled all over the pavement the night Visitor died.

'She was crying out, I couldn't help her.' Alizarin was wildly agitated again. 'I suddenly couldn't see where she was.'

'Go on.' Sophy stroked his sodden hair.

'I couldn't help Mum either.' Alizarin's normally deep voice had become a little boy's. 'I wanted to but he locked me in. Mum was pouring blood like the woman in the street.'

They all jumped as lightning lit up the room, followed by a deafening crack of thunder. Diggory shot into Jonathan's arms; a panic-stricken Grenville disappeared under the bed. But there was no time to find him tranquillizers. Alizarin's need was greater.

Gradually, a few stumbling words at a time, the story spilt out. Alizarin had been alone in the house with Galena and baby Sienna.

'Mum told me to watch television. She'd been drinking all day, yelling on the telephone. I heard a car crunch on the gravel . . . Someone ran up the stairs, Mum shouted at me to stay in my room. Then I heard more arguing . . . I can't tell you any more.'

Jonathan, who'd been cuddling Diggory and watching sheets of water falling out of the sky, swung round, frantic to know the truth.

'For Christ's sake, go on.'

'It'll help,' urged Sophy, trying to still his shuddering. Despite her desperate concern, it was such heaven to hold him in her arms.

'Mum's screams grew so loud,' he whispered, 'I took my wooden sword and crept up the stairs to the Blue

676

Tower. She was yelling at him for shagging Anthea' – for a second Jonathan's eyes met Sophy's in amazement – 'then I heard him say: "You never stop grumbling you're not getting it any more, well now you're fucking well going to."

'I pushed open the door . . . Oh Christ . . .' Alizarin's huge hands obscured his stricken, disintegrating face. Sophy clung on to him, terrified he was going to bolt.

'It's all right, Jonathan and I are with you.'

'I thought he was killing her,' said Alizarin, childishly again, 'he was on top of her, fucking her, blood was gushing all over the floor. I rushed at him with my sword. "Get out, you nosy little bugger," he bellowed. Mum screamed: "Go away," over and over again. I ran back downstairs and along the landing; next thing I knew he'd locked me in my room, shouting: "Don't you ever dare tell anyone what you've seen." I tried to call for help . . .' Alizarin went on hopelessly. 'Then I heard the front door bang, Mum screaming again, then this terrible crash. Chasing after him, she must have toppled over the banisters, falling down the stairwell onto the flagstones.'

'Jesus,' said Jonathan, 'the bastard left her to bleed to death.'

As if recognizing a greater need, Grenville emerged shivering from under the bed, jumped up and pressed his long length against Alizarin.

'I climbed onto the roof,' said Alizarin, exhausted but back in his normal voice. 'It was dusk, no-one heard me calling. Poor little Sienna was bawling her head off, Shrimpy was whimpering. Finally the Old Rectory gardener came over and let me out. They thought Mum had locked me in. Everyone asked me questions. I couldn't answer, the words wouldn't come out, even when they arrested Dad.'

Alizarin gazed at them like a skull, his face bone-white, his eyes huge black caverns.

'It was the same with the tramp and the woman.' He

shook his head in despair. 'I couldn't save her either. Christ, that must have been the moment my sight went. I can't tell you anything else.'

As Jonathan opened his mouth to protest, Sophy raised a warning finger.

'You've done brilliantly,' she told Alizarin, 'Jonathan'll get you some more blankets and a large drink. There, darling, you've been such a brave little boy.'

Reluctantly, Jonathan collected a double brandy and a couple of Anthea's sleeping pills, but by the time he returned, Alizarin seemed curiously calm, his eyelids drooping. After that one deafening clap, the thunder had also retreated. Alizarin's hand was smoothing Grenville's striped head, reminding Jonathan agonizingly of the dying Raymond.

'Who was the man?' he demanded roughly. 'Rupert, Casey, Etienne?'

'No, no, no,' protested Alizarin sleepily, 'it was Willy of the Valley.'

'Kerist.' Jonathan collapsed on the end of the bed as Alizarin drifted off. 'I never knew David was Mum's lover. The dirty sod. Ugh!' Then, becoming thoughtful: 'I wonder when that started. He was miles younger than Mum. I always thought Dad was the one who was keen on him, that's why he forgave the ghastly creep so much.'

'Your dad forgave everyone,' sighed Sophy.

After sleeping most of the next day, Alizarin woke at dusk and, after a bath and a shave, insisted Sophy took him for a walk. The sun had just set. Fluffy vermilion aeroplane trails were drawing kisses all over a drained blue sky. Pigeons were crooning their young to sleep. Last night's downpour had intensified the scent of the flowers. But Alizarin could only breathe in their sweetness, occasionally feeling the rough scratch of a yew hedge, hearing the babble of Raymond's brook. Regret overwhelmed him that he had never opened up to his father, always pushing him away, and now it was too late.

Leading him across the big lawn, Sophy turned right and then left.

'Where are we?' grumbled Alizarin.

'Visitor's grave. It's next to Maud's and Shrimpy's,' explained Sophy, reading the inscriptions. 'He's got a lovely headstone, feel.' She placed Alizarin's hand on it. 'Oh, and such *beautiful* words.'

'No-one consulted me,' growled Alizarin. 'What do they say?'

'"Visitor Belvedon 1985–2000."' Sophy's voice was suddenly choked with tears. '"Be comforted, little dog, thou too at the Resurrection shall have a little golden tail."'

Alizarin couldn't speak, battling not to break down. Sophy in turn was terrified. Now they were back in Larkshire, she knew Alizarin, too honourable to chain her to his side any longer, was about to give her her marching orders.

He had no idea he had pulled out of the drawer an inappropriately festive scarlet shirt, which she had given him and which now emphasized his desperate pallor. All the buttons were done up wrong. He had only managed to slot his belt through two loops. He wore a loafer on one foot and a black slip-on with the sole hanging off on the other. Glancing round at the ravishing garden, remembering the joyful pictures he had once painted of it, the family and the animals, Sophy thought how viciously cruel was his punishment. Beethoven at least could compose when he went deaf, Milton still wrote when he was blind, but Alizarin could see nothing, least of all where to put his paintbrush. Overwhelmed by the pathos of his situation, she could bear it no longer.

'I love you,' she yelled at the top of her voice. 'I want you to know, I really love you.'

'No need to shout,' snapped Alizarin, 'I'm blind, not deaf.'

'I wanted Visitor to hear me say it,' sobbed Sophy. 'Now that he's no longer alive to look after you, I want to instead – f-f-for always – please let me.'

Reaching out trembling hands until he found her lovely plump shoulders, Alizarin drew her towards him. He could feel her soft clean hair tickling his clenched jaw. He couldn't imprison her for the rest of her life. Then, looking up for divine guidance, he started violently, blinking then rubbing his eyes, then frantically gazing – it must be a dream. No, it wasn't. Above the trees, slightly hazy, he could make out a tiny gold crescent moon. Hanging below a dark cloud, it looked exactly like Visitor's tail, sticking out from underneath the drawing-room sofa.

'"The little golden tail." I can see! It's come back!' Alizarin's voice was hoarse with excitement. 'I can see the trees, the clouds, a star and the new moon exactly like Visitor's tail. And, oh Sophy,' his voice cracked as he pressed his lips against her forehead, 'I swear I saw it wag. Visitor's giving us his blessing, oh my darling, darling Sophy.'

76

'My knees completely gave way when he kissed me,' Sophy giggled to Jonathan afterwards. 'Only Alizarin would have been strong enough to hold me up.'

Jonathan was terribly pleased for them. He'd never seen two people so deliriously happy, but it made his own deprivation even harder to bear. Loving Emerald was like a cancer, a gnawing pain that never went away. Vienna and Paris had been hell, London and Limesbridge were even worse, all fogged with her ghost, which vanished as he reached out to hold her.

The morning after Alizarin's sight returned, after yet another sleepless night, Jonathan took a bottle of champagne from Raymond's cellar, which he supposed now belonged to Jupiter, and went to see Lily, who was looking very diminished. She missed Raymond dreadfully and being the so-called head of the family made her feel frightfully old.

She had, however, been vastly cheered by the barracking of Tony Blair by the Women's Institute and was now inveighing against the banning of blood sports.

'And what are they going to do about twenty thousand foxhounds? I can't see Cherie and Tony keeping a couple at Number Ten. Oh, lovely!' Lily accepted a glass of champagne. 'I so like drinking at nine in the morning.'

As he slumped down on the red rose-patterned sofa

beside Douglas, the stuffed badger, Lily noticed Jonathan was trembling violently. He looked terrible, grey and shadowed, with new deep lines etched round his mouth. All his larkiness had gone.

'You look like a painting by Francis Bacon.'

'I'm sure. Can we talk about Mum?'

'I thought you might want to.'

'Who's my father?'

Lily gave a long sigh, and took a huge gulp of champagne.

'I'm awfully afraid it may be that little shit, David Pulborough.'

To Lily's amazement, Jonathan gave a Tarzan howl and, gathering up Douglas, waltzed round the room knocking over a little table and the piano stool.

'You don't seem very upset,' chided Lily.

'If it's true, I am the happiest man alive.' Collapsing back onto the sofa, Jonathan told her about not being able to marry Emerald.

'Yes, I can see that would pose problems,' agreed Lily. 'I suspected something was up. I couldn't tell you before, Raymond loved you so much better than any of the others, it would have broken his heart. And he loved David too, which would have left his poor heart in smithereens.'

As Jonathan reached for his glass of champagne, Brigadier, Lily's vast white Persian, eyed by an outraged Diggory, landed like a little elephant on Jonathan's knee.

'What happened?' he asked, not daring to hope.

'David arrived for the summer holidays,' began Lily, 'to coach your brothers. Your mother wasn't sleeping with your father, they'd had some row, which gave her the excuse not to. Raymond was in London a lot. He knew Rupert, Etienne, Casey and Uncle Tom Cobbleigh were all giving her one, as you so euphemistically call it, but somehow he trusted David, because David seemed to prefer him, and Raymond felt singled out and special.

'It would have destroyed him if he'd known your mother and David were at it all the time. They had some close shaves. But David has always had the ability to lurk undetected like a dishcloth in a washing machine.

'After David married Rosemary, it was all downhill. He didn't like Galena's exhibition being a flop. Failure terrified him. Raymond got a silly crush on Anthea. David was after her too, thought he was the one that had got her pregnant. Claimed he paid for everything – in fact he borrowed vast sums from Rosemary and Galena. Then told Galena about Anthea's baby to hurt her, taunting her that he was fed up with her demands. To hurt her even more, he told her Raymond was nuts about Anthea too.'

'Jesus, what a bastard.' Jonathan, weighed down by a thunderously purring Brigadier, reached out to fill their glasses.

'This sent Galena roaring back to your father,' went on Lily, 'but the truce was fleeting. Galena was too hooked on David; she confided in me a lot. She was also tormented with doubts about her painting, experimenting with a less figurative approach. Marvellous stuff, but she was frantic for reassurance. David told her she'd gone soft.'

Heaving herself to her feet, Lily weaved through the crowded room to a desk and, creaking to her knees, unlocked the bottom drawer, which was crammed with blue leather-bound diaries. Picking one out, flipping through the pages, she handed it to Jonathan.

'You'd better read this. I'm breaking the embargo, but your mother would understand.'

What bold, flamboyant writing, thought Jonathan, balancing the diary on Brigadier.

'September 8th, 1970,' he read, 'Raymond and I have had no sex for four months. Thank God for David. At first he was a little lapdog, yapping round my feet, now his warmth, energy and passion have enslaved me. He burrows into my body and my heart.'

'You were born prematurely at the beginning of April 1971,' observed Lily drily. 'Don't need to be very good at arithmetic to work that one out. They didn't have calculators in those days. Raymond, like Dicky, could never add up.'

'Mum and David, wow!' Jonathan shook his head. 'When I drew him as Lust, I was spot on.'

'He had a sort of hedonistic life force that gets away with things again and again, rather like you.'

'Am I like him?' asked Jonathan, suddenly appalled.

'You're what David should have been. He was clever and charming, but he came from a very rigid, repressed, lower-middle-class background. Stumbling on all the music, books, pictures and beauty at Foxes Court, plus Galena's arms and Raymond's uncensorious understanding, he must have felt he'd found Paradise, and was determined never to lose it again.'

'Dad didn't love me best because I was so like David?'

'No, no, because you were lovable.'

'And you will go on being my aunt?'

'If you go on bringing round champagne like this.' Lily patted her nephew's cheek fondly, then sighed. 'I don't want to blacken David's character, but he has been appallingly treacherous. It was he who tipped Si Greenbridge off about the Raphael.'

'He didn't,' said Jonathan in horror.

'He'd seen it enough times when he was poking Galena and then Anthea up in the Blue Tower. He described it exactly to Si and said it was in the house. Si told Zac. Zac didn't trust David and double-checked with Alizarin.'

'My God, how d'you know all this?'

Lily looked smug.

'Si's distraught Rosemary won't speak to him any more, so he asked me to mediate. Rosemary was desperately worried because she told Si that Raymond had found the Raphael in a château in Bonfleuve. She thinks that lost you all the picture. She didn't realize that Dirty Dave had already told Si everything.'

'I don't believe all this.' Jonathan clutched his head. 'Are you trying to tell me Si and Rosemary . . . ?'

'They were' – Lily emptied the bottle into their glasses – 'but she's blown him up, because she thought he was merely sleeping with her to get information.'

'Dear, dear, everyone seems to have been shagging their brains out except me,' grumbled Jonathan.

'Makes a change.'

But Jonathan wasn't really interested in Si and Rosemary.

'I need to be sure,' he said slowly. 'I daren't hope. They've presumably still got Dad's DNA profile in Harley Street from when they tested him and Emerald. I'll just have to trot along there and bung them to speed up the process. Christ, how could David have done that to Dad?'

'The Judas factor,' observed Lily. 'There's more frisson in betraying best friends – and they are always the ones we want to beat.'

'I don't go along with that,' mused Jonathan, 'although I'm seriously pissed off Trafford's got a room in Tate Modern.'

'A sickroom?' suggested Lily.

Jonathan laughed; then, after a pause: 'Was Dad gay?'

'Slightly,' admitted Lily. 'Didn't do much about it. Like Tennyson's dog, he hunted in dreams. He was much more hooked on beauty. That's why he couldn't bear to part with Pandora and was so mad about David, who was extraordinarily good looking when he first arrived at Foxes Court . . .'

'And probably why he immediately fell for Emerald,' said Jonathan.

Over in Shepherd's Bush, Emerald was finding her maquette the hardest thing she had ever sculpted.

Trying to capture Galena's blazing vitality, which never came across in photographs, she chucked out one attempt after another. Leaving herself too little time, she had to stay up all night before submission day, hardening the clay with a blow-drier.

She'd also had terrible trouble getting Shrimpy right, taking every book on Jack Russells out of the library, but Shrimpy still looked like a pig. She even dogsat for a sculptor friend's Jack Russell puppy over the weekend, but the little terror ran about, chewing her brushes and her shoes and only stayed still when he fell asleep. So in the maquette, Shrimpy flopped down exhausted across Galena's feet.

In return, the fellow sculptor lent Emerald his estate car for the day and with the maquette laid on foam rubber and cocooned in bubble wrap in the back, she set out to deliver it. The trip down was anguish. She was so tired, she was terrified she might drop off at the wheel – and every deepening green leaf reminded her of Jonathan and darling Raymond, her loving, welcoming father.

There was the church ringed by trees so tall and proud they seemed convinced they were entirely responsible for holding up the sky. She hadn't visited Limesbridge for nearly a year, and would have delivered the maquette to the village hall and fled, if Anthea hadn't begged her to give them a preview at Foxes Court.

Having thrust some red roses into Anthea's hands and nearly dropped the maquette in her nervousness, Emerald unveiled it on the dining-room table.

Oh help, she thought, as Anthea burst into tears, I've made Galena too glamorous.

'I didn't mean it to hurt you.'

'You haven't, it's so beautiful. Everything: the bluebells, her water jar, the little sleeping dog, the cheesecloth dress, her haughty Slav face held up to the sun . . .' Anthea skipped excitedly round the table.

'The straw hat cast aside – she was so untidy. She could be standing there. Raymond would have been so proud.'

'I couldn't have done it if you hadn't dug out all that stuff.'

Mrs Robens bustled in then crossed herself like the Portuguese football players.

'Heavens, it's brought her back from the grave.'

Then Emerald froze as Sienna, her traditional enemy, her rival for Jonathan and possibly Zac, wandered in, as usual covered in paint. How would she react to such a subjective interpretation?

To her amazement, Sienna fingered the thick, straight hair and the tilted face in wonder.

'Christ, it's miraculous, I feel like I've met Mum at last. It's got to win. It'll look fantastic in the High Street. Shrimpy's adorable. You are like so bloody talented.'

Emerald, unbelievably touched and gratified, couldn't speak. She had never known Sienna enthusiastic.

'Galena was so strong and beautiful,' Anthea was now saying wistfully. 'You can see why Raymond worshipped her.'

Sienna, however, had been wised up by Jonathan about the perfidy of Galena and David. To everyone's amazement, she suddenly blurted out: 'Mum was like an absolute cow to Dad. You made him a million times happier.'

'Why, Sienna.' Anthea blushed a deeper red than Emerald's roses. 'You can't mean that.'

'I do seriously. He loved you infinitely more than Mum.'

'Oh, thank you.' Anthea, near to tears again, held out a shaking hand. After what seemed an eternity, Sienna reached out and took it.

'Let's have a huge drink to wish Emerald good luck,' she said gruffly.

'I daren't drink,' sighed Emerald, 'it's not my car.'

*   *   *

Aware that Anthea and Sienna were embarrassed yet dying to talk, Emerald left immediately, only pausing to put six pale pink lilies on Raymond's very new grave. Then, on impulse, she divided them, propping three against Galena's mossy headstone. Having spent so much time agonizing over her rebirth, she had grown very attached to Raymond's first wife.

Limesbridge was full of tourists taking photographs. After dropping off the maquette, Emerald drove past the site earmarked for the memorial, praying she would win, not least because she was absolutely skint. Probate wouldn't be through for weeks because of the wrangling. She'd spent so much time on Galena, she must get down to the other commissions Raymond had found her. At least her tears would keep the clay wet. I've just got to get over Jonathan, she told herself hopelessly.

If only she didn't have to return to Larkshire next week for the announcement of the winner by ghastly David Pulborough. She hoped their last scuffle wouldn't totally prejudice him against her. The ceremony was taking place on 6 July, ironically on the eve of her twenty-seventh birthday. How anxious she'd been to be married by then.

The sun was gilding the willows along the river bank as she drove over the bridge. What a bitch she'd been at her last birthday – making sure her parents and Sophy were dressed as she wanted, taking family heirlooms, beautiful dresses and Augustus Johns for granted. She'd also still been besotted by Zac, public enemy number one in the Belvedon household, particularly as the Raphael was coming up at auction on the evening of the 6th.

As Sophy was now blissfully living off Putney Common with Alizarin, both besotted with their new Labrador puppy, the Cartwrights had turned Sophy's bedroom into a tiny studio for Emerald. Here, as midnight

688

approached on 5 July, she was still up, desperately trying to finish the head of a Cuban heiress in time for the girl's father's fiftieth birthday next week. Her back ached, and so did her little hands, which were engrimed with clay as if she'd been scrabbling down a rabbit hole. It was stiflingly hot. Moths crashing against the window made more noise than Patience's timid knock as she brought her daughter a cup of chocolate.

'Please go to bed, darling. We must leave by eight-thirty, we've got this detour to make on the way. Daddy mustn't be late.'

Patience was trying not to get too excited that tomorrow Ian had an interview for a bursarship at Bagley Hall, a school in the next county to Larkshire. Perhaps by some miracle she might be able to have a dog and a horse again. But all Patience could really think about was the despair and exhaustion to the point of collapse of her elder daughter.

77

The 6th of July dawned very hot and beautiful, with not a breath of wind nor a cloud in the sky. After such a rainy summer, the woods seemed to be boiling over more Prussian blue than olive green and the farmers were still haymaking. Patience listened to the clunk of the baling machines as they spewed out vast fawn cotton reels of hay and gazed longingly at glossy horses grazing in every other field.

As they crossed over into Rutshire, and Ian swung the ancient Volvo up a little road called Bagley Hall Lane, Patience smiled at a huge notice in the barley saying: 'The Countryside is for Life not just for Ramblers'.

How had she existed in London so long? she wondered. Please God, let Ian get this job.

Searston Town Hall slept gold and proud as a lioness in the midday sun. The press, revved up by David and Geraldine, were out in force. Inside the great hall, a splendid room with goddesses gilding the walls and a stage flanked by dark-red velvet curtains, was already packed in anticipation of an exciting result and drinks and canapés afterwards.

As Patience changed into black high heels in the car park, an utterly untogether Emerald noticed for the first time that her mother was looking unusually smart.

'Lovely dress, Mummy. That blue really suits you.'

'Can't let you down on your big day.' Patience blushed slightly. 'I thought we might have tea in Bath later and buy you something nice for your birthday. Have a think what you'd like.'

Only Jonathan, thought Emerald.

Inside, she was amazed to find the Belvedons packing the front rows. Alizarin, still in dark glasses although his sight was improving all the time, was actually wearing a tie and Sophy looked adorable in a sort of flowered nightdress. And there in a suit flaunting a large blue rosette and rather self-consciously pressing the flesh, was Jupiter. With him was Hanna, suntanned and stunning in cream silk with her figure back at phenomenal speed, and little Viridian, adorable in a sailor hat, whom Jupiter liked kissing much more than other people's babies.

Anthea, finally out of black, and equally stunning in Schiaparelli pink with a new crimson-and-white-striped halo hat, was actually giggling with Rosemary Pulborough, whose hair had become softer, blonder and longer, and who looked almost glam in a citrus suit and a terracotta straw boater. Aunt Lily wore her standby, a dashing vermilion Stetson. Even Sienna had washed her hair and put on a skirt.

How embarrassing they were all tarted up and she was only wearing jeans and a purple T-shirt. At least it matched the shadows under her eyes.

'You're supposed to look arty,' said Patience reassuringly.

Then Emerald realized why they were all so smart, as David clanked in in his High Sheriff's dark-blue velvet and frills.

'He's only supposed to wear that fancy dress on ceremonial occasions,' fumed Lily.

'Good luck, Emerald,' called out Mr and Mrs Robens

and Knightie, who were sitting in an excited row with the landlord of the Goat in Boots, and who all agreed the poor lamb was looking dreadfully peaky.

'We're rooting for a Belvedon victory,' boomed General Anaesthetic. Green Jean perched at the end of the row, waiting to disapprove.

Biting her lip to hide her disappointment that Jonathan hadn't shown up, Emerald looked so small and vulnerable as she took her seat between huge leering Casey and massive Joan Bideford, who both knew they'd won. Beyond Casey, the fourth finalist, a sleek Indian called Ranjit Chitajan, sat with his eyes closed, praying that he might.

Casey, who'd dyed his beard a startling orange, promptly suggested that Emerald and he had lunch afterwards.

'I wouldn't,' hissed Joan Bideford from her other side, 'he'll make you pay for the honour. Come and have a bottle of fizz and a sarnie under the haycock with me.'

On a table on the stage, the four entries of the finalists had been covered in green plastic, which two minions had been practising whipping off all morning. Geraldine had organized a big screen and monitors all round the hall, so everyone could see what was going on.

Rather muted clapping greeted her and David's appearance on the platform. David was not quite so popular in the county as he imagined. Smiles weren't even suppressed when he nearly tripped over his sword. Suavely he introduced Geraldine, with much play on how privileged Larkshire was to be graced by her presence.

Geraldine, the sort of woman who made even linen too frightened to crease, was immaculate in a pale grey trouser suit. She told the audience how happy she and the High Sheriff were to bring glory to Larkshire by commemorating their greatest painter, Galena

Borochova, thanks to the co-operation of Lady Belvedon – Geraldine smiled coolly in Anthea's direction – who had urged them to go ahead.

'We had four outstanding entries,' she went on. 'Galena was a powerful but very subtle artist, and we wanted something subtle to illustrate her special qualities. The first is a marvellous contribution from arguably our greatest painter and sculptor, Colin Casey Andrews.'

Casey Andrews leapt to his feet, raising clasped hands in the air. But the storm of clapping died almost instantly as a ghastly upended palette with huge breasts and pubic hair round the thumb hole was unveiled and appeared on the big screen.

'What's that supposed to mean?' shouted the landlord of the Goat in Boots.

'You're not supposed to ask,' hissed Green Jean.

'Great art of course defies explanation,' said David smoothly, 'but in principle, Mr Casey Andrews's palette symbolizes Galena the artist, the breasts Galena the woman, and the thumbhole the fecundity of her womb producing so many talented children.' He nodded sourly at the Belvedons.

'Load of crap,' shouted Robens.

'Be kwy-et,' said David furiously.

Little Viridian started to cry. Sophy and Sienna got the giggles.

'A work of towering genius. Imagine the impact when it is enlarged to eight or nine feet high,' exhorted Geraldine.

'Jonathan can train Diggory to jump through the hole,' whispered Hanna.

'It will fit very comfortably into the space,' said David.

Remembering how David had tried to fit his rainbow-condomed cock into her space, Emerald jumped out of her skin as she felt Casey Andrews's nicotined fingers stroking her left breast. He didn't even remove his hand to clap when his wife's entry was unveiled. A large nude,

693

with no head, feet or hands and riding a bicycle, it was greeted with even more boos and yells of derision.

'On yer bike,' yelled Robens.

'How does she change gear?' shouted Knightie.

Joan Bideford turned purpler than Emerald's T-shirt.

'Philistines,' she thundered.

Little Viridian bawled even louder.

'He's a discerning critic already,' said Jupiter proudly.

Sienna nudged Emerald from behind.

'You'll walk it,' she hissed.

'Anything's better than biking it.' Sophy wiped her eyes.

Ranjit's entry, a monkey who was simultaneously eating a banana and defecating, evidently to symbolize the artistic process, got given even shorter and noisier shrift.

Here we go, thought Emerald, dear God make the Belvedons like it.

Back slid the green plastic, catching in Galena's paintbrush, making the maquette sway alarmingly for a second, before a minion leapt forward and steadied it. There was a long pause, as Galena was shown from all angles on the big screen, then an explosion of cheering.

'That's the one,' yelled the audience.

'We don't want any junk in Limesbridge,' piped up Knightie.

'And Emerald's a Belvedon,' shouted Sienna.

'Other lot are a waste of taxpayers' money,' roared the General and was shushed again.

Geraldine was unable to make herself heard, so David took over.

'Emerald Belvedon's entry is quite excellent, particularly for a young woman of only twenty-six,' he said coolly when the din had died down. 'All the judges feel she has a promising future.'

Emerald put her burning face in her hands.

'A-a-a-ah,' cooed the audience, as the camera panned

in on a sleeping Shrimpy. Little Viridian was gurgling with joy.

'Brilliant,' hissed Jupiter, 'it's exactly like Mum.'

Alizarin, who'd taken off his dark glasses, stretched a long arm down the row and patted Emerald on the back.

'It's extraordinarily beautiful and incredibly like her,' he whispered, which pleased Emerald most of all.

'Please let us have silence.' David glared at the Belvedons. 'This is excellent work, but the judges felt it was too representational, too predictable, utterly charming admittedly, but lacking the imagination and vision of the other three entries.'

'Bollocks,' thundered General Anaesthetic to the horror of Green Jean and his wife.

'I worked for Mrs Belvedon,' shouted Mrs Robens, going very red, 'it's the spitting image of her.'

'Anyway, the judges' decision is final,' cried Geraldine, feeling her input had so far been insufficient to make the headlines. 'The winner of the Galena Borochova Memorial Prize is Colin Casey Andrews and here to present him with a commission to complete the work, and a cheque for twenty thousand pounds, is your High Sheriff, David Pulborough.'

'Bloody rigged,' roared Alizarin.

The press were going berserk as Casey Andrews stalked up to collect his cheque to a chorus of boos and slow hand claps. Not for nothing had Searston WI been in the forefront of the Women's Institute's roasting of Tony Blair. Emerald, meanwhile, had bolted out of a side door. Racing after her, Sienna found her sobbing piteously inside the green curtains of a weeping ash.

'I'm so sorry, I'm not being a lousy loser, I don't mind about not winning. It's coming here again, and you all being so lovely, which I don't deserve, and not seeing Jonathan. Everything reminds me of him and I love him so much.'

Emerald accepted Sienna's proffered piece of loo

paper to blow her nose, then confessed: 'I loved Zac more than anything else in the world this time last year; I now realize what a bastard he is.'

'He is,' agreed Sienna, thinking darkly of the Raphael on sale in New Bond Street that very evening. 'What we need is a large drink.'

78

A terrific din was still coming from the town hall as Sienna frogmarched Emerald out of the municipal gardens down the sunlit High Street into the gloom of the Bear and Honeypot. Slumped on a bar stool, Emerald gazed up at a row of teddy bears and tried not to start crying again.

My life is over, she thought helplessly, I'll never get over Jonathan.

'Thanks,' she muttered as Sienna gave her a large glass of champagne. 'What the hell's this?' she demanded ungraciously as the landlord handed her an appallingly wrapped parcel. 'It's not my birthday till tomorrow.'

There was so much sellotape cocooning the red tissue paper that it took her ages to unwrap. Inside was an exquisite silver loving cup with handles in the shape of lions' heads. Inside that was a tiny envelope addressed to Emerald. As she recognized Jonathan's black script, she started to tremble. Her eyes were so awash with tears, it took some time to decipher the note inside.

'Darling Emerald, you wanted to get married before your twenty-seventh birthday. If this is still true, get your-self over to St James', Limesbridge, by two o'clock, your utterly adoring, no longer brother, Jonathan.'

'I don't understand,' whispered Emerald, swaying and clutching the bar.

Sienna put out a hand to steady her.

'Dad wasn't Jonathan's father.'

'Oh my God, how did he find out?'

'He got the DNA results on Monday.'

'Poor Jonathan,' whispered an appalled Emerald, 'he loved Raymond so much.'

'Doesn't matter, he always had Dad as a father, knew he was more bats about him than anyone else.'

'Who is his father then?'

'Almost certainly David Pulborough.'

'Oh yuck, that disgusting lech!'

'Jonathan wanted it to be Rupert Campbell-Black, but anything rather than Casey Andrews – or Joan Bideford for that matter.'

Emerald gave a shaky laugh.

'Is he gutted?'

'No, ecstatic, it means he can marry you, *that's* the only thing he cares about.'

Emerald gazed at Sienna, tears spilling down her face.

'But this must hurt you so much,' she stammered, 'I know you love him too.'

'Not that way any more, and I know how happy you'll make him.' Then, when Emerald couldn't speak: 'Don't you want to marry him?'

'Oh, more than anything else in the world.'

'Well then?'

'Poor Sienna, you'll have to put up with me as a sister-in-law.'

'I've been such a bitch,' they cried simultaneously, collapsing laughing helplessly into each other's arms.

Then over Sienna's shoulders Emerald saw the pub clock, which said five past one, and gave a wail.

'I can't get married in jeans.'

'Of course not.' Grabbing her hand, Sienna led her past a large stuffed bear and several grinning utterly riveted punters upstairs to a bedroom with a long mirror, a basin, and an open window looking out over the High Street.

698

On the bed – so like doll's clothes that Emerald half expected them to have cardboard tags attached – lay pale stockings, the palest pink bra and knickers, little pink shoes and the prettiest dress in palest pink silk dupion. Just above knee length, it was edged at the hem and neckline with slightly darker pink feathers. In a little hat box were matching feathers attached to a comb for her hair. In the basin, keeping cool, was a bunch of pink freesias. On the dressing table, a big bottle of Violetta.

'Jonathan did this?' gasped Emerald.

'With a little help over sizes from Anthea and Patience. He really loves you, no, don't cry any more, and the mums have really like bonded in an unimaginable way putting this together. And Rosemary P. and Lily were roped in to do the flowers in church, which are stupendous. Jonathan chose pink because he thought you might be too pale for white, although' – Sienna opened her make-up case – 'I've bought buckets of blusher.'

'Thank God I washed my hair this morning,' gabbled Emerald. 'I nearly had an extra hour's lie-in instead. Oh darling, darling, Jonathan, I do not believe this.'

'Have another drink then.' Sienna filled up her glass.

'I must have a shower.'

'How's David taking it?' yelled Emerald over the sound of running water.

'Doesn't know yet. Rosemary does. She's getting out her rolling pin.'

Emerald's hands were shaking so much, Sienna had to paint out her dark circles and put on her eye-liner. The pink dress hung so beautifully, no-one would notice it was now much too big.

'You look absurdly gorgeous,' sighed Sienna as she slotted the comb, with the pink feathers attached, into Emerald's piled-up hair, 'like a little squaw.'

'It's twenty-five to two, we must hurry,' begged Emerald.

'I think Jonathan will wait.' Sienna peered out of the window. 'Transport's outside.'

Charging downstairs, hanging on to her feathers, clutching her flowers, Emerald went slap into Ian, who was putting a white rose into his buttonhole.

'Oh Daddy, so you were in on it too. How on earth did you get your morning coat here?'

'Jonathan brought it down last night, felt it might have given the game away if you'd seen it in the boot. You look absolutely lovely, darling.' Ian kissed her on the cheek.

'Don't make her cry again,' pleaded Sienna, wriggling into a tight scarlet dress as she ran down the stairs, then turning for Ian to do up her zip.

'You're not going to like the next bit,' she added to Emerald, 'but Dora insisted. Better have another slurp first.' She handed Emerald her glass.

Outside, surrounded by punters and photographers, stood Loofah, chestnut patches gleaming, malevolent eyes rolling, mane and tail plaited with pink bows, harnessed to a shiny dark-blue trap. Dicky was hanging on to him for grim death.

'Oh no!' Emerald retreated into the pub in terror.

'He'll be as good as gold,' said a grinning Dora who, brandishing a long-tailed whip, was already ensconced in the trap.

'Theirs but to do or die,' cried Sienna, helping Emerald into the nearside seat, as Ian clambered on the far side into the other.

'Dicky and I are going in my car,' Sienna added maliciously, 'let go of the reins, Dicko.'

'What happens if he sits down?' wailed Emerald.

'He won't, he has a great sense of occasion,' said Dora confidently, 'and he loves crowds.'

As Loofah broke into a brisk trot, the word, it seemed, had got around. All down Searston High Street, people stopped to wave and cheer.

Dora was in an excellent mood. She was in the process

of selling the story to the *Telegraph* and the *Standard* and was due to rendezvous with them in the churchyard.

As they hurtled towards open country, past cottages decked out in pink and yellow rambler roses, narrowly missing cars and dog-walkers, a dazed Emerald got out Jonathan's letter, reading it over and over again.

'Oh Daddy, is it really true, how long have you known?'

'Just over a week. Jonathan was determined it should be a surprise. Had a bit of good news myself while you were changing upstairs, got a call on my mobile telephone from Bagley Hall, offering me this job. Evidently the other bursar's been fiddling the books. They want me to start as soon as possible. Seems a good school, Rupert Campbell-Black's children go there.'

'So does my brother Dicky, which lowers the tone,' said Dora, steering stylishly round a lorry buckling under a load of hay bales. 'Giddy-up, Loofah. The deputy head is a bitch.'

'That's wonderful, Daddy, congratulations,' murmured Emerald, clutching on to her feathers as dark strands of hair kept escaping, but all she could think was: If I don't get killed first, I'm going to marry Jonathan. So there is a God and an end to the rainbow after all.

At last there was Limesbridge, with its idling river and the tall chimneys of Foxes Court peering through the billowing trees. Realizing he was nearly home, Loofah thundered down the High Street, ignoring posters showing Jupiter's thin, haughty face in nearly every window, exhorting people to vote Tory in the forthcoming by-election.

'At least this job means I can make a contribution to the wedding— Jesus Christ!' Ian clapped his hands over his eyes as Loofah swung off the High Street into Church Road, nearly mowing down Rosemary and Aunt Lily. No wonder everyone had dressed so smartly this morning. It was the first bit of happiness, except for

Sophy and Alizarin in a lower-key way, that the family could celebrate since Raymond's death. They were determined to enjoy it.

'That hat cost Rosemary five hundred pounds,' confided Dora. 'David will go apeshit.'

There were the dark yews and soaring scented limes. There was the church with its gold weathercock and its bells ringing out joyously. Flanked by crowds hanging over the iron gate, as deathly white as the rose in the buttonhole of his morning coat, his dark curls for once brushed, was the handsomest bridegroom in the world. And wearing a red bow and yapping round his master's (for once) polished shoes, was Diggory. Charging down the slope, Jonathan lifted Emerald out of the trap.

'Thank Christ, you're alive.'

'Charming,' said Dora.

'You look so beautiful.' Jonathan dragged Emerald behind a nearby yew tree, covering her face with kisses, taking off all Sienna's make-up. 'I haven't press-ganged you, I know it was presumptuous,' he muttered as they paused for breath, 'but I love you so much. This is going to be the shortest engagement ever. Will you marry me?'

'Definitely,' gasped Emerald, then she gasped in even more delight as he slid the emerald four-leaf clover set in tiny seed pearls onto her finger.

'Oh how lovely, it's beautiful.'

'I bought it to give you the day we got Dad's DNA test.'

'Thank you, I love you so, so much.' Emerald flung her arms round Jonathan's neck. 'I cannot believe you organized this.'

'Who normally cannot organize a piss-up in a brewery, as Jupiter keeps telling me,' grinned Jonathan as once more he buried his lips in hers.

'I must be seeing things,' Sophy muttered to her mother as Emerald's shiny hair collapsed round her shoulders. 'Emo is actually allowing her face to be totally mussed up before her own wedding.'

The extraordinarily happy couple only let go of each

other when Ian, getting bossy with the confidence of a new job, tapped his future son-in-law on the shoulder.

'Can't keep the parson waiting. You push off up to the front pew, Jonathan.'

'Can't I walk up the aisle with you two?' protested Jonathan.

'No, you can't,' said Neville-on-Sunday, getting his hairbrush out and smoothing Jonathan's curls. 'Off you go, Emerald will join you in a minute.'

Grumbling, blowing kisses to Emerald, Jonathan gathered up Diggory and disappeared into the church, where Green Jean was remonstrating with an unusually tidy Trafford for drinking brandy out of a bottle.

'It's OK, it's organic,' said Trafford, passing it to Jonathan.

Outside, Anthea descended on a dazed Emerald, tidying her hair, readjusting the feathers, straightening her dress, reapplying lipstick and blusher, taking the shine off her nose.

'I chose the dress with Jonathan,' she couldn't resist whispering.

'It's lovely, everything's lovely, I'm in a dream.'

Emerald only had time for a brief word with Patience, who had lipstick on her teeth, but who was redeemed by a dashing green hat lent her by Rosemary.

'You look terrific, Mummy.'

'So d'you, divine. I'm so excited, darling. I couldn't tell you before. Jonathan swore everyone to secrecy, I've always loved him so much, Daddy and I couldn't have a nicer son-in-law. Not that Alizarin isn't awfully nice,' Patience added quickly. She was rather in awe of Alizarin. 'Anthea's been absolutely super too, she made me up. Such a dear person. Neither of us has any mascara on our lower lashes in case we cry.'

'It's all fabulous,' said Sophy, pausing to allow Emerald to arrange her pink beret at a more becoming angle, 'so like Jane Austen, sisters ending up with brothers. And Jupiter's lovely wife's been up all night making and icing the cake,' she added as Hanna paused to peck Emerald on the cheek before scuttling into church.

Up in the front pew, Trafford was saying smugly, '*Shagpile*'s been nominated for the Etienne de Montigny Erotic Prize.'

'Well done,' said Jonathan.

I don't mind, he thought truthfully, I've got Emerald, she's the only prize that matters.

Miss Prattle, the village gossip, resplendent, uninvited, but taking up most of the fourth pew, sat like a recording angel, fulminating over misdemeanours.

'The groom and the best man are both smoking,' she hissed, 'and that dog shouldn't be in church.'

'At least the dog's not smoking,' replied Jupiter gravely.

'And I'm sure Alizarin's young lady's expecting.'

'Hard to tell really,' observed Jupiter as plump Sophy bounced up the aisle.

'And who is Jonathan marrying in such a hurry?'

'His sister,' said Sienna with a sweet smile as she plonked herself down beside Jupiter. 'Oh, look who's arrived from Paris.'

Everyone swung round as a beaming Jean-Jacques Le Brun, blowing kisses in toutes directions, settled happily into the seat up the front that Lily had kept for him.

Ian Cartwright admired the banked blue delphiniums and the coronets of pale pink roses on the end of every pew. He was unable to believe such happiness and change of fortune as he took his elder daughter's arm.

'I'm so proud of you, darling, Raymond Belvedon was such an awfully nice chap, I feel he ought to be taking your other arm.'

'I'm sure his ghost is,' whispered Emerald, 'I'm so lucky having two families.'

The organ launched into Bach's Toccata. With a

smile as radiant as the new moon, the bride floated up the aisle.

'She can't marry her brother,' hissed Miss Prattle as Jonathan sprinted down the aisle to collect her.

'I've missed you so much,' he whispered.

The congregation giggled, particularly when Jonathan during the vows announced, 'With my body, I cannot wait to worship you.'

But when they knelt down later, both Emerald and Jonathan shut their eyes, and begged God to help them make each other truly happy.

'Why are weddings so soppy?' muttered Dicky in disgust as Anthea and Patience mopped each other up yet again.

After the marriage service, Jonathan kissed his bride throughout all four verses of 'Dear Lord and Father of Mankind' until Neville tapped him on the shoulder, then cried, 'Ouch!' because Diggory had bitten him sharply on the ankle.

'Diggory's very up himself because Jonathan's got him a dog passport to go on the honeymoon,' whispered Sophy.

'I hope Emerald can cope with his breath,' whispered back Alizarin.

Then he stroked Sophy's cheek.

'You look so pretty. We could get married, if you wanted to.'

Sophy beamed up at him.

'You and I don't need rings on our fingers.'

'Tum, tum, ta, tum, tum, tum, tum, tum, ta, ta tum, ta, ta, tum, tum,' went the Wedding March.

Never had two such pale people looked so glowingly happy, decided Sienna as, chattering nineteen to the dozen, bride and groom came down the aisle.

I cannot bear it, she thought. I can't behave beautifully any longer. She put a hand on poor Grenville who stood shivering in the side aisle, hoping eternally for his dear master's return.

Outside, Jonathan broke away for a second to kiss Anthea and Patience.

'Now you're my mothers-in-law, I can refer to you both as the Old Witches.'

'I thought you already had,' said Anthea drily.

After the photographs, Emerald took Jonathan's hand, leading him over to Raymond's grave, on which she laid her bunch of pink freesias.

'I just want him to know that he didn't ruin our lives after all.'

'I do like Jonathan,' insisted Ian, as he opened the iron gate back into the garden of Foxes Court, 'so much more congenial than that absolute bounder Zachary Ansteig.'

'I agree.' Anthea smiled up at him. 'Congrats on your new job, by the way, terrific news. I'm very excited too. I'm having a rose named after me, very pale gold streaked with salmon pink. They're calling it Lady Belvedon.'

'If it's as pretty as you, I'll buy lots,' said Ian happily, realizing that now he was moving to the country, and had a job again, he could.

Dora was due to join Dicky at Bagley Hall next year, reflected Anthea. She was sure Ian would be understanding if she were late with the fees. Although there might be someone to pick up the bills quite soon. Caradoc Willoughby Evans was phoning every day, and the rose-grower was a charmer, quiet, but with lovely hands and piercing blue eyes.

The terrific party under way at Foxes Court was soon deserted by Sienna. She couldn't bear to hear anyone else slagging off Zac, and the thought that he might be at Sotheby's this evening was too much for her.

Jonathan, leaving Emerald's side only for a minute, tried to dissuade her.

'Are you sure it's a good idea seeing the Raphael sold? It's going to hurt like hell. Stay here and get hammered.'

'Dad insisted we always waved people off until they were out of sight,' said Sienna. 'Pandora deserves that. Dad would expect it.'

'I'd come and hold your hand,' Jonathan assured her, 'but I'm off on my honeymoon later. I never dreamt I'd be so excited about getting my dick out in private.' Then, misreading the desolation in her eyes: 'You OK, darling, not jealous of me and Emerald?'

Sienna shook her head violently, unable to speak.

'As Jupiter's bidding for Rupert Campbell-Black, who's sending his helicopter to fetch him in an hour or two, why not get a lift with him?' suggested Jonathan.

'I need to take my car back to London,' said Sienna. 'Go on back' – she kissed him on the cheek – 'be wildly happy. Don't tell people I've gone, I don't want to break up the party.'

As she ran out to her car, she passed Dora in the shrubbery talking confidingly into her mobile.

'I just wanted to tell you, Harriet, that my brother and my sister Emerald have definitely not committed insects.'

Only Grenville, who'd been chewed and nagged by Sophy and Alizarin's puppy all afternoon, followed Sienna, begging her with sad onyx eyes to take him with her.

'I'll fetch you the moment I'm sorted,' she promised. 'You're in no state to be abandoned for hours in my studio.'

79

Only in the car did Sienna break down, sobbing all the way back to her studio in the East End, to the sforzando accompaniment of *Arabella* – the only present Zac had ever given her. The love duet, disc two, band five had been played into the ground. Sienna hadn't eaten properly for days and in the driving mirror noticed a large spot on her chin, which made her cry even louder.

Her studio was a disgusting tip: dirty mugs and plates everywhere. She deserved rats – other than Zac. Desperate to pay off the costs of the court case, too busy to tidy up, she'd been working twenty-four hours a day.

On her big easel, virtually finished, was the huge canvas of *Sienna's List*. Unable to contemplate the many dreadful ways the animals were being tortured, she had pinned a sheet over the lower black and grey half of the picture. In the top half, in brilliant colour, dolphins, tuna, whales and other fish, all restored to health, swam joyfully up a bright blue river. On the grassy bank gambolled every kind of animal. Overhead flew the birds – even battery hens and poor foie gras geese – all sweeping along in a joyful rainbow riot towards God, waiting with arms outstretched to welcome them to heaven.

Only God's face was missing. Sienna had tried every variation: black, white, old, young, men, women, even children, wearing out palette knives scraping off the pigment, but none of them seemed right. God had let such terrible things happen to animals and he hadn't given her Zac. Once the Raphael was sold, she would buckle down and find a solution. Idly she picked up her sketchbook of the court case, dominated by drawings of Zac, which had sold all over the world.

The love affaire that had never existed was over. Yet why did her fingers keep walking the lonely road of 1471? Why did she check her mobile every minute and sleep under the fax machine in case, by some miracle, he'd got in touch? Tonight would be the last she would see of him or Pandora, who would vanish into a bank vault or onto some rich man's wall, to be flaunted like the wife of a captured general.

Wearily she put on disc two again. Feeling she owed it to the Raphael to look beautiful, she turned on the shower. It was so hot her hair dried in a trice, and because Zac hadn't seen her in it, she wriggled back into the clinging red sleeveless dress she'd worn for the wedding.

Bugger! Her spot was bigger than ever, shining through each added layer of base. At least it matches my dress, she thought sulkily.

'If you were a girl from one of my villages,' sang Arabella's suitor, Mandryka, 'you would go to the well behind your father's house and draw a cupful of clear water and offer it to me at the door, so that I should be your betrothed before God and all men! O beautiful one!'

And I offered Zac boiling water out of a tap at Foxes Court, thought Sienna dully.

Henry Wyndham, the Chairman of Sotheby's, slipped home on the afternoon of 6 July. As well as the Raphael, he had to sell eighty-eight other pictures, many of great rarity and beauty, that evening and he needed to clear his head and get focused.

Later, in a deep, English Fern-scented bath, he

practised the increments: 'Ten million, ten million five hundred, eleven million, eleven million five hundred . . . Fifteen million [God willing], sixteen million, seventeen million . . . twenty million [God even more willing].'

He hadn't been so excited since June 1998, when he'd sold the Monet of Giverny for £19.8 million – which had been a record for a Monet. If only he could steady his nerves with a large whisky, but you couldn't drink before a sale. You had to keep your wits about you, to smile and be charming when your brain was going round like a hamster on a wheel. If no-one was bidding, it was easy to drop one's shoulders and lose the plot – and he didn't want Zachary Ansteig coming after him with a baseball bat.

Thank God any worries about no-one bidding on the Raphael had been dispelled. The National Gallery weren't bidding because they already had enough beautiful Raphaels. But at least they hadn't made a pre-emptive strike, which gave the other museums a chance. He knew the Abraham Lincoln Museum who owned the companion picture to *Pandora*, although not hugely rich, were desperate to buy it.

Arriving at Sotheby's, Sienna was mobbed by the press.

'Looking fantastic, Sienna!' 'What yer going ter shock us with next?' 'To me, a bit happier, Sienna.' 'How much is *Pandora* going to go for?' 'Very sad day for the Belvedons.'

'Very,' snapped Sienna, pummelling them out of the way.

Inside the foyer, towering spires of sapphire and purple delphiniums in blue Chinese vases reminded her agonizingly of Raymond, as did the excited glamorous crowd, gabbling away in every language, which included so many of his friends.

There were the great American curators, whose heads

seldom left the Middle Ages, lean-faced and ascetic-looking in their pale linen suits. There were strutting charming Italians, heartbroken their homeland wasn't rich enough to retrieve the Raphael, but who nevertheless cheerfully embraced cool, bearded, pale-eyed Danes and genial Germans, whose curls spilled over their ox-like necks.

A great many Jews, their big hands seldom leaving their wives' glittery shoulders, were there, less to bid than to see the financial outcome of one of the first looted art cases. Jaunty British dealers, sporting fob watches and ties pretty enough to frame, arrived gossiping in pairs, with invariably a long-limbed, golden-haired beauty sandwiched between them.

The women tended to be even more spectacular than the men. Not just the celebs: Jerry Hall, Joan Collins and Joanna Lumley, but the wives and girlfriends with their clean shining hair, their pashminas sliding down suntanned arms and their faces as zit-free and glowingly polished as the furniture, already labelled in the next room for tomorrow's sale.

More formally attired, but just as glamorous, Sotheby's staff in neat little dresses or pinstriped trouser suits hovered solicitously, both reassuring and revving up their clients. No wonder Raymond had nicknamed them 'Sootherby's'.

Prospective bidders were already registering for paddles, flipping through the catalogue, adding coloured stickers to lots they coveted, examining *Pandora* on the cover.

Stop drooling over our painting, Sienna wanted to scream. Not in the mood for chat, she was accosted as she sidled up the stairs by Barney Pulborough, his bland sallow face sweating like Cheddar cheese in a heatwave.

'My father,' he informed her happily, 'has been in secret talks with Zac about flogging the picture to some pharmaceutical billionaire.'

'Well, that's at least ten million the bastard won't spend experimenting on live animals.'

'Dad's going to have competition.' Barney peered over the banister at the ever-increasing crowd. 'Lots of the major players are here or bidding over the telephone. Sotheby's are hoping for twenty million. The *on dit*' – Barney lowered his voice – 'is that Zac is the most bloody-minded client they've ever had to deal with, although' – Barney licked his fat lips – 'I wouldn't mind taming him.'

Seeing Barney most unusually waylaying a gorgeous girl, realizing in amazement it was Raymond's daughter, people moved in to commiserate.

'Won't be the same without the old boy.' 'Helped me so much when I was younger.' 'Most influential figure in the art world since the war.'

'Why didn't you bloody tell him when he was alive?' snarled Sienna.

Turning, so no-one could see how close she was to tears, she went slap into Kevin Coley, Lord Ditherer, who'd given Raymond so many headaches, changing his mind constantly, ratting on deals.

Kevin and Enid Coley had spent 4 July in America, and Kevin should have stayed over for a big board meeting of Doggie Dins (US). How macho to have been called out in the middle to bid. Imagine the publicity in the States, where there was huge interest in Pandora, if he were outed as the buyer. Kevin, on the other hand, had lost a lovely Stubbs last year when his mobile had cut out on his jet at the penultimate bid. There would also be kudos if he were in the sale room, with David Pulborough bidding for him, and was later photographed accepting the Raphael from Sotheby's chairman – so he had flown home.

Now, like a bull in a very upmarket picture shop, he was trying to claim noisy acquaintance with half the room. Why the hell wasn't David here to smooth his path?

'Hi, Sienna,' he said, recognizing a familiar, much improved face. 'Looking very tasty. When's the memorial service?'

'You won't be fucking invited.'

'I see that girl's lost none of her charm,' exploded Lady Coley as Sienna pushed past them.

Fortunately everyone was distracted by the arrival of Rupert Campbell-Black, bronzed from racing at Catterick and Chepstow, and his wife Taggie, stunning as always in sleeveless fuchsia pink and an orange cashmere shawl.

Rupert was sulking, he'd wanted to go to Wimbledon, but his brother Adrian had persuaded him the Raphael was an excellent investment. The bloodstock market was showing alarming fluctuations, Wall Street was poised to dive, property was too high, but the top end of the Old Master market was holding up well.

'If I put a foot inside Sotheby's, New Bond Street,' sighed Adrian, 'it'll just push up the price.'

'Whereas a philistine like me—' snapped Rupert.

'I'll sell it on very quickly,' Adrian reassured him. 'Several museums are hanging fire to see how much it goes for.'

Taggie and Rupert were shortly joined by Jupiter who'd been registering for a paddle and who had taken off his tie and exchanged his morning coat for a blazer. As they all looked around for Sienna, she leapt behind a bust of Julius Caesar. Rupert and Taggie'd been so sweet at the funeral, but at the moment she couldn't handle people being nice to her. Although if the Raphael went to Rupert, she'd mind less – at least she could go and see it.

There was an explosion of flashbulbs, and shouts of excitement. Sienna, who'd just emerged from behind Julius Caesar, shot back again, as Zac walked in alone. Creeping forward, she could see he was wearing a white shirt and black trousers. His face was darkened by sunglasses and stubble. He seemed taller, thinner, angrier.

Perhaps the truth about Jacob really had destroyed him. But edging her non-spot side out further, Sienna's compassion turned to fury. Zac was being mobbed by beautiful, eager women. If the Raphael only makes its reserve, she thought savagely, he'll be one hell of a catch.

714

80

Over in his flat in Bury Street, David Pulborough was concealing his receding hairline with engraved silver-backed brushes, given him by Geraldine, and brooding on his day. The Borochova Memorial Award ceremony had not gone well. Casey had probably banked the cheque by now, but David wasn't sure that he could rail-road the people of Larkshire into accepting Casey's finished sculpture. And he was not sure he wanted to. At lunch after the awards, bloody Casey had presented him with his portrait in High Sheriff's uniform. Not only had Casey given his subject puffed-out cheeks and paunch, he had also drastically slimmed down the Old Rectory and not included a single blade of grass nor flowers nor splendid trees. David could have been posing in front of any suburban semi.

When reproved, Casey had announced sententiously that he could only paint as he saw with his inner eye. David was so livid he was tempted to see if the prize, due to public pressure, could be awarded instead to Emerald. She'd be so grateful, he still might get his leg over.

He and Geraldine had made wonderful love in a field on the way back to London, but he wished she wasn't pushing quite so hard for marriage. Rosemary's rich aunt was about to croak and leave Rosemary a very great deal of money, which David was dying to spend.

A dream had been forming in his head for the past

few days. He was bidding up to £27 million for Kevin Coley, which would mean a flat fee of £100,000 in his pocket. But if the fat ape had stayed in the States, David, who two-timed his clients as blithely as his women, had been planning to arrange for Barney to bid for Minsky Kraskov, who was on a yacht in the Med, and to see which man packed it in first.

When Kevin dropped out this evening, however, David was tempted to carry on and buy the Raphael himself. Even if he 'flipped it', art jargon for selling on very quickly, he could make a nice little killing of two or three million – particularly as he had a new hugely rich South American client who might easily bite. The gallery was doing brilliantly, and with Rosemary's aunt's money and the Old Rectory recently valued at £1.5 million, there was plenty of dosh floating around.

All this rather left marriage to Geraldine out of the equation. Even so David was irked that Rosemary, who'd claimed she was going to some local wedding, had just rolled up. He hoped she hadn't overheard the telephone conversation in which Geraldine had been asking him why on earth he'd asked Rosemary to become his wife in the first place.

'If you marry a rich old dog,' he had quipped, 'you can sleep with the pretty ones in the afternoon.'

'That's obnoxious,' Geraldine, who still had grass seed in her linen turn-ups, had been saying furiously. Hearing Rosemary's step in the hall, David had rung off.

But Rosemary seemed calm enough, smiling as she examined his ticket for tonight.

'I'd like to come to this. They've just predicted on the wireless that *Pandora* could make twenty million pounds. Poor Belvedons.'

Slapping Eau Sauvage on his sunburnt cheeks, David said he hadn't been able to get her a ticket, and he had to dine with Kevin Coley later.

'Going to be a hell of a scrum.'

'What time are they selling her?'

David glanced at his watch.

'About eight-twenty. You can watch it later on the news.'

He and Geraldine must remember not to stand together in front of the television cameras.

Five minutes later, he walked up Old Bond Street, past the beautiful clothes shops, the galleries and the flags swooning in the heat above the great jewellers.

England at its most elegant, thought David, his heart swelling. And there, most elegant of all, emerging as her driver admiringly opened the car door, smiling at the battalion of cameras, was Geraldine. She would be a wonderful adornment to his life. He must try and work something out.

He was gratified when the press surged forward to talk to him.

'About Jonathan Belvedon . . .' asked Adam Helliker.

'One of our most exciting gallery artists,' said David smoothly. 'Along with Colin Casey Andrews, who of course today won the Borochova Memorial Award. Now, if you'll forgive me.'

He and Geraldine had hardly crossed Sotheby's threshold before an enraged Kevin Coley bore down on him.

'Where the fuck have you been? Thing's nearly over.'

Old Masters other than the Raphael were already selling briskly. A portrait of a court siren by Cranach the Elder and a little Grimmer winter scene of people skating, dogs barking and falling snowflakes mingling with the stars had already gone for vast sums.

Never had so many folding chairs been crammed into the main gallery. People, particularly the old, were arguing and grumbling, trying not to be moved out of seats they had wrongfully appropriated, hoping chivalry would prevail – chivalry did not. Others were crowded four deep in a great horseshoe round three of the cranberry-red walls and spilling out of the room's two entrances.

Facing them on the rostrum, Sotheby's charming, outwardly languid chairman, Henry Wyndham, a shaggier much taller Hugh Grant, a giraffe crossed with Michelangelo's *David*, was flipping through his ring-binder. This gave him the number, name, reserve of each lot and the commission bids from people who couldn't make the sale. The Raphael, the star lot at eighty-nine, would be the last to be sold, but there was an El Greco, a speculative Rembrandt and two stunning Canalettos along the way to keep people interested.

Against the right wall, a mass of photographers and television cameramen were lined up. Forbidden to film the actual punters, who might prefer to remain anonymous, they concentrated on Sotheby's team of telephone bidders. Confined like Rupert's thoroughbreds to a big mahogany pen with only their shoulders and tossing heads of newly washed hair on show, these beauties of both sexes were busy laughing and speaking in every language as they alerted clients in jet, boardroom, Lamborghini or in Abdul Karamagi's case on top of his finance director's daughter, that the picture they wanted would be coming up for sale in a few lots' time.

David eyed them with pleasure, hailing the prettiest by name, and sat down in his favourite place, halfway up the room, on the edge of the central aisle, next to bloody Kevin, who kept nudging and plucking his sleeve and asking to be introduced to everyone. Beyond Kevin, Enid Coley, massive as a hippo in grey satin, had spread over three-quarters of snake-hipped Geraldine's chair.

'Did you fly back from the States in the Lear?' asked Geraldine, who liked to show off her familiarity with jets.

'No, no,' said Enid crushingly. 'The Lear is for the servants.'

At the back of the hall, Rupert Campbell-Black, in an

increasingly bad mood, was watching Wimbledon on a pocket television, and wondering why the hell he'd allowed himself to be hemmed in by these popinjays.

'That shit' – he scowled at the back of Kevin Coley's thatched grey head – 'nearly broke up my best friend's marriage. I've always wanted to bury him.'

'You'll have the perfect opportunity when he bids against us for the Raphael,' murmured Jupiter, who believed in firing up his clients.

The El Greco went for £8 million, followed by a somewhat sugary Fragonard of a girl with a puppy which sold for £1.5 million.

'Puppies always add ten per cent in England,' observed Jupiter.

David was now boasting to Kevin that he was intending to bid for lot sixty-one, an exquisite van de Velde of sailing ships on a choppy grey sea.

'A new good friend, Mr Justice Caradoc Willoughby Evans actually' – David gave a light laugh – 'asked me to keep an eye out.'

Bidding was brisk, hitting the van de Velde's lower estimate right away and soaring up to £1,200,000 offered by a museum. Was David going any higher? asked Henry Wyndham.

David shook his head.

Everyone swung round, trying to read the thoughts of the dispassionate thin-faced man beside Rupert. After a long pause, Jupiter nodded.

'One million, four hundred thousand at the back.' Henry Wyndham looked round with polite incredulity. Was no-one going to bid further?

As the hammer crashed down, Jupiter switched on his mobile.

'Hi, Caradoc,' he murmured. 'I got it. One point four million. Once it's been cleaned, it'll blow your mind. Talk to you later.'

Smirking slightly, ever machiavellian, Jupiter went back to firing up Rupert.

'Did you realize that David Pulborough used to be Mum's lover?' he said softly. 'And almost certainly fathered my brother Jonathan?'

'What?' roared Rupert, then, lowering his voice, 'When, for Christ's sake?'

'Summer of 1970.'

'Jesus,' exploded Rupert, 'I was in there—' Then, remembering Taggie on his right: 'And Casey Andrews and Etienne as well. That little toerag screwed Galena? She must have been four-timing the lot of us.'

Standing up to glare at David, Rupert nearly bid by mistake for *Five Wise Virgins* by Rubens, who were showing no sign of making their £300,000 reserve.

'Galena and that self-regarding little tosser. I do not believe it.'

A still life of strawberries went for £50,000, making everyone realize how hungry they were. It had gone eight o'clock, only a handful of lots before the Raphael.

'Trust that little shit Pulborough to get into cahoots with that bastard Kevin Coley,' muttered Rupert furiously. 'Kev probably got into Galena's knickers as well. Jesus!'

'Where's Sienna?' whispered Taggie, unsure of the cause of her husband's wrath.

Jupiter glanced round. 'Can't see her anywhere.'

'Got a boyfriend yet?' asked Rupert.

Jupiter shook his head. 'Difficult day for her. Jonathan getting married, she was always a bit too crazy about him.'

'Thank Christ, I never had a sister,' said Rupert. 'If she'd been as pretty as my brother Adrian, I'm sure I'd have shagged her.' Then, as a frightful picture of a courtier having his head cut off sold for £20,000: 'That should have happened to bloody Pulborough.'

Sienna had taken refuge against the wall between a bulky NBC cameraman and an even bulkier Somerford Keynes.

To the back of the hall, on the right-hand side, half hidden from her by NBC's camera and tripod, stood Zac. He was flanked by two of the sharp-suited lawyers who had hammered out the contract, and who now told everyone who tried to approach him to piss off. Zac quivered with the same tension – the tiger poised for the kill – that she remembered from Foxes Court.

Oh, why wasn't she the white shirt clinging to his divine, hard body, or the cranberry-red wall against which his head had fallen back with such deceptive languor? Surreptitiously, he seemed to be searching for someone. Then, like two tiny total eclipses, his dark glasses focused on her. Perhaps she was imagining things? Perhaps he knew the NBC cameraman? But he started violently, then instantly jerked his head away, his face totally expressionless.

'What are you working on?' asked Somerford, bringing her back to earth.

'A big animal rights project. It's nearly finished, but I can't like work out how to portray God.'

'Like Rupert Campbell-Black?' suggested Somerford.

Sienna laughed then moaned in despair as to loud cheers a young porter wearing a blue apron and white gloves, aware that this was his finest hour, carried in the Raphael and placed it reverently on the easel by the rostrum.

'A lot to be desired,' wrote Somerford in his note-book. 'Far more ravishing in the flesh – like yourself,' he murmured. Then seeing how dishcloth-grey she had gone, he added with rare kindness, 'This must be hell for you.'

'Pandora looks so small and defenceless,' mumbled Sienna. 'Like a gorgeous little filly that's been dragged away from her mother at Tattersalls. I just want to take her home.'

81

'Lot eighty-nine, Raphael's *Pandora*.' The Chairman of Sotheby's smiled down at his excited audience, a conductor on the brink of a symphony. 'I am starting the bidding at ten million pounds.'

Hope beamed out of the little painting.

'You could all buy me if you tried.'

There was a long pause when all you could hear was a woodland cheeping of mobiles, and the atmosphere crackling with electricity. Then two anonymous punters started pushing the bidding up. These were actually Minsky Kraskov in a yacht off Cannes and Abdul the Amorous, who'd just rolled off his finance director's daughter in Dubai.

Both men were barking instructions in broken English over the telephone: Minsky to russet-haired Natacha, Abdul to Patti with the ebony bob – two Sotheby's beauties in the mahogany pen.

'Ten million. Ten million five hundred thousand, eleven million, eleven million five hundred thousand,' called out Henry Wyndham, his sleepy come-to-bid eyes scanning the room in case he missed anyone.

'Eleven million, five hundred thousand on the telephone,' he repeated. Then, noticing that the man from the Getty had removed his spectacles, indicating a bid, he turned back to beautiful Natacha in the mahogany pen, who was still gabbling away to Minsky on his yacht, saying: 'Twelve million against you now, Natacha. At twelve million.'

Minsky took even longer to make up his mind than Lord Ditherer. So Rupert, as a sign to Jupiter, pointedly examined his fingernails. Catching Henry Wyndham's eye, Jupiter nodded.

'Twelve million, five hundred thousand at the back,' called out Henry.

Everyone swung round, or stood up unashamedly to find out who had bid.

'Jupiter Belvedon's just bid for Rupert Campbell-Black,' whispered David.

I hate that bastard, thought Kevin, plucking at David's sleeve.

'Go on,' he hissed.

'Thirteen million on the aisle,' said Henry, as David raised his eyebrows, then, turning to the telephone bidders, 'Thirteen million against you now, Natacha.'

Minsky Kraskov was watching the lights of Cannes rippling orange across the dark-blue waters of the Mediterranean.

'Who is damned opponent beeding against me?' he growled.

'I can't tell you,' said Natacha, 'but it's thirteen million against you. Do you want to bid?'

'I'd rather haf you against me. It is a dealer or a museum?'

'Perhaps. You can't keep them waiting.'

'Ees it the Getty?'

'D'you want to bid?'

'Oh, OK.'

A gold pen glittered in Natacha's waving white hand.

'Thirteen million, five hundred thousand on the telephone and against you, sir, I'm sure there's another bid in you.' Henry Wyndham smiled at Kevin, who again plucked David's sleeve.

There were audible groans from the Americans, the French and the Danes when, like favourites falling in the National, the big museums gradually dropped out.

Henry was stepping up the drama now, whipping the bidders to a frenzy of competition. He knew Kevin and Rupert detested each other and there was no love lost between David and the Belvedons. If he could get a dog fight going between the two sides, bidding could soar beyond the reach of astronauts.

David went up to £17 million, Jupiter to eighteen, Minsky to nineteen, and on it went.

A pale intense woman from the Abraham Lincoln Museum, who owned *La Smorfiosa*, *Pandora*'s companion picture, had been waiting to jump in at £20 million, but to her horror the bidding soared past her limit.

Gazing up at the window in the roof, Sienna was amazed it was still light. She longed to escape from this venal hell into one of those untroubled eighteenth-century landscapes and sleep for ever on a village green or wade into a reed-strewn river until the waters closed over her head. She was brought back to earth by a fracas.

Minsky's yacht appeared to have gone under a bridge.

'I'm afraid my client's telephone has cut out . . . please wait a second,' begged Natacha.

'It's twenty-four million against you, Natacha.' There was a slight edge to the Chairman's voice as the seconds ticked past.

'Who's running this sale?' snapped David.

Seeing the tension was getting to him, Jupiter glanced at Rupert, who again examined his fingernails. Another million was only after all a two-bedroomed flat in Chelsea. Jupiter nodded.

'Twenty-five million at the back.'

Behind the Chairman's head, a flickering blackboard

turned Rupert's bid into dollars, euros, marks, lire and Swiss and French francs. It looked huge in whatever currency.

There goes the new roof, the children's school fees, half the horses and probably Penscombe as well, thought Taggie in terror.

'It's an awful lot of money,' she whispered.

'Money isn't everything,' snapped Rupert.

David was poised to bid £26 million – nearly the top whack for Kevin, who was already looking green. Then suddenly David saw Rosemary fighting her way through the crowded doorway on his left. She was wearing a new, very becoming, slate-blue suit, her face lit by stunning diamond earrings. What in hell was she doing squandering the housekeeping at a time like this? Thank God, he and Geraldine were respectably divided by a Berlin Wall of Coleys.

David was so jolted he forgot to flicker his eyebrows at Henry Wyndham, and the Raphael nearly went to a reconnected Minsky, who'd actually been ringing his astrologer, who'd advised him it was a good day for shopping. Thus encouraged, Minsky had bid £26 million.

The hammer waits for no man. David nodded hastily.

'Twenty-seven million on the aisle,' said Henry jubilantly.

He was delighted to see an even more major player had just appeared at Rosemary Pulborough's side. Such was the force of Si's personality, as though a big bear had entered the forest, that all the jam-packed lesser animals breathed in, allowing him and Rosemary through to join Zac and his lawyers at the back.

'Bloody monster,' hissed Sienna to Somerford. 'D'you remember him telling us how he longed to own a Raphael, the night of Emerald's birthday party? And what's Rosemary doing fratting with such a fiend?'

Jupiter went to £28 million.

I wouldn't mind living in a council flat, thought Taggie in despair, but Rupert would hate it, and he couldn't have any dogs.

David glanced round at Rupert, and thirty years fell away. He was back barring the way to Galena's studio and this glittering blond bastard, as arrogant and glamorous as he was today, was loping up the stairs towards him, picking him up like a bollard.

'Get out of my way, you little twerp.'

David felt equal rage against Jupiter, who had never made any secret of his contempt.

I was the one Galena loved, thought David.

A God-like feeling assailed him. Chucking reason aside like an overcoat in a storm, he lifted his head and gazing straight at Henry, raised his eyebrows.

'Twenty-nine million on the aisle.'

As a ripple of excitement went through the room, Kevin plucked at David's sleeve in horror.

'What the fuck,' he hissed, 'you've passed my limit . . .'

'I'm not bidding for you any more,' hissed back David.

All the world would realize he was buying for stock and appreciate how dazzlingly the Pulborough was doing. He felt as if he'd scored a try at Twickenham.

This galvanized Abdul the Amorous, who, bored with pleasuring the finance director's daughter, was chatting again to Patti with the ebony bob. Suddenly her face lit up as though a restorer had covered it in white spirit, her scarlet fingernails flashing as she waved a hand. Abdul would just have to sell a few oil wells.

'Thirty million on the telephone,' said Henry, having difficulty, like Patti, hiding his elation.

The room was boiling over, chat subsiding to total silence between bids.

David bid thirty-one and a half, Jupiter thirty-two. David thirty-three. It was no longer a question of money. Avarice had been overtaken by Pride, Envy and Wrath, as mutual loathing spurred on the two sides. They were greyhounds flat out after a hare. David could no longer hear the figures he was bidding.

'Thirty-three million on the aisle.'

Jupiter glanced enquiringly at Rupert, who glanced across at Taggie. A drop of blood trickled down her chin, where she'd bitten her beautiful lip through in terror. Reality kicked in. Rupert shook his head. Thirty-four was his unlucky number, he'd have to win a lot of Derbies and put Taggie on the game to recoup it.

'Are you sure, are you absolutely sure?' drawled Henry, as if he was pressing another dry martini on Rupert rather than a £34-million bid.

Jupiter smiled and shook his head, just managing to hide his bitter disappointment. Bang went the generous cut Rupert would have given him. If only Raymond had let him sell the Raphael, in May '99, long before Emerald's birthday.

Taggie, dizzy with relief, reached across for Rupert's hand. For a second he glared furiously into space, then he smiled wryly and lifted her fingers to his lips.

Abdul went to £35 million. Campbell-Blacks and Belvedons should stay out of the kitchen, thought David scornfully, then clutched himself in ecstasy: the Raphael was going to be his. He'd sell it on at once, but for a few days, it would hang in the drawing room at the Old Rectory and he and Rosemary would throw a grand party to show it off to the county.

As he once more raised his eyebrows at Henry, a great cheer went up. The entire room was caught up in the drama. David was very near the record.

'I suppose he won't have to fork out for Barney's wedding,' bitched Somerford to Sienna, who was reeling with horror that it was going to David. Patti, after more consultation, had ruefully shaken her gleaming ebony bob, Natacha her russet mane, which meant both Abdul and Minsky were out.

David has taken everything, both my father's wives, he left my mother to die and now he's going to get the

Raphael . . . Sienna wanted to scream, to snatch up the NBC camera and hurl it at him. Glancing up the room, Zac caught sight of her anguished despairing face, and turned to Si, talking urgently.

'Any advance on thirty-six million? Fair warning.' As Henry lifted the hammer, his eyes swivelled intently over the crowd, as if searching for four-leaf clovers. It was so easy to miss a bid. To the right at one o'clock, Si Greenbridge lifted a gold-ringed hand.

'Thirty-seven million in a new place,' cried Henry in delighted surprise.

Another explosion of applause and a collective gasp of anticipation, as everyone cricked their necks jerking round to look.

That's it, thought Sienna numbly, Si's been hovering. Now he's got her.

But the latent Guggenheim had been unleashed in David. All reason suspended, he bid again.

'Thirty-eight million on the aisle.'

'Have you gone raving mad?' hissed Geraldine across the bows of the Coleys.

The press were going crazy, scribbling frantically, the cameramen all fretting to break the rule about not photographing punters. The Chairman looked down at his rostrum. On the right, where so many right-handed auctioneers had brought down the hammer, rings ran into each other like a rain shower on a pond. There were only a few rings on the left; he glanced up smiling at Si.

'Thirty-eight million against you, Mr Greenbridge.'

Si went to thirty-nine, David to forty.

'Si's running the little shit up,' muttered Jupiter, 'going to leave him with ego on his face.'

The longest pause of all followed; not a mobile cheeped.

'I'm selling now for forty million,' said Henry Wyndham softly, 'going for forty million on the aisle.'

I've thrashed the Belvedons and Rupert, thought

David in ecstasy. Oh please, please God, prayed Sienna. Si Greenbridge glanced at Rosemary, who smiled and nodded.

There's something going on between those two, thought a momentarily distracted Sienna.

There was another flash of big gold rings as Si lifted his hand.

'Forty-one million at the back.'

A yell of ecstasy went up from the press office, the record had been smashed. Cheering, clapping and stamping rocked the room. The din brought David to his senses. With the buyer's premium, that would be over £45 million. Reality asserted itself. Like Portly the baby otter at the Gates of Dawn, the moment of his glory faded and he felt alone, bewildered and rather cold.

As the hammer came down, Sienna gave such a howl of despair that, even amid the tumultuous applause, the pandemonium and euphoria, people turned uneasily in her direction and a Spanish dealer crossed himself. Zac by contrast was smiling, hugging Si and kissing Rosemary, then pumping the hands of his lawyers. Sienna had never seen him look so happy, as well the bastard might. The Raphael had more than quadrupled its reserve.

The press had erupted, surging through the hall towards Si and towards the rostrum.

'Must get a shot of the Chairman handing over the picture to Mr Greenbridge.'

'Give us five minutes,' said Chris Proudlove, the press officer, totally failing to hide his euphoria. 'We're going to hang *Pandora* in a side gallery. There'll be champagne and canapés on offer. You can get your pictures of the Chairman and Mr Greenbridge then.'

'Should have told me you were going on bidding,' said Kevin bullyingly, 'nearly gave me a coronary. Who the fuck were you bidding for?'

'For stock,' said David.

'Made me look a right tit.'

'Again,' snapped David. He was fed up with brown-nosing Kevin. He was the major player now.

But infuriatingly people were surging forward from all sides to commiserate with Kevin: dealers, buyers, Sotheby's staff, looking at him with new respect. He must be loaded to underbid a lot like that.

Jupiter felt wiped out by anti-climax, as though he'd turned up at his own wedding and found Hanna married to someone else, and not even a bridesmaid on offer. It was always worse when you came down after champagne. All the same, seeing Taggie and Rupert together made him gladder than ever that he and Hanna had patched it up.

'Shall we go and have dinner at Green's?' said Taggie. 'To cheer ourselves up? It's only eight-thirty. It seems like midnight.'

'I've had a brilliant idea,' said Rupert, putting a hand on Jupiter's shoulder as they fought their way towards a side door. 'You're going to be the next Tory leader, and take the party out of the wilderness.'

As David and Kevin struggled through the scrum, more and more people were commiserating with Kevin.

'Back luck, Lord Coley, you nearly made it,' called out Johnny Van Haeften. 'How about lunch next week?'

'I'm sorry you didn't get it, Lord Coley, come and have a drink next door,' said Henry Wyndham.

Bloody Kev, thought David furiously.

Ahead he could see Si and Rosemary ringed by press.

'Better not leave together,' he muttered to Geraldine. 'See you in Green's in half an hour.'

Battling on alone, he decided he'd better say 'Well done' to Si, after all he'd want to sell him more pictures. Si's unusually frivolous tie covered in bright pink roses looked familiar. Hadn't he seen it in Searston High Street that morning?

'Congratulations, Si.'

'Sorry about Pandora.' Si grinned down at him, then, putting his father-bear arm proudly around Rosemary: 'And I'm afraid I'm taking another little lady off you.'

Rupert and Jupiter, following behind, exchanged incredulous glances.

'What d'you mean?' spluttered David.

'It means there's life in the rich ugly old dog yet,' giggled Rosemary. 'I'm afraid you're a high and dry sheriff now, David.'

A stunned silence was broken by the sound of clapping.

'Good on you, Mummy,' cried a delighted Barney, 'as long as you and Si have care and custody of *moi*.'

When an apoplectic David tried to frogmarch Rosemary back to Bury Street, two of Si's guards grabbed him. Next moment he was bearded by Adam Helliker of the *Sunday Telegraph*.

'Evening, David, what's this rumour about you being Jonathan Belvedon's father?'

'Don't be fucking stupid, Jonathan's Raymond son.'

'I hope not or he married his sister this afternoon,' said John McEntee from the *Express*, brandishing a copy of the *Evening Standard*. 'Just have a look at this.'

'Daddy's first wife mated with David Pulborough', announced the large caption beneath the charming picture of Dora and Loofah.

'No comment,' shrieked Larkshire's High Sheriff, as he was engulfed by a tidal wave of press.

In a side gallery, Sienna discovered another rugger scrum as photographers fought to take Si and Rosemary's picture as they gossiped with Henry Wyndham. Around them, celebs and luminaries of the art world embraced and fell on smoked salmon, angels on horseback and glasses of champagne, praying that some Midas gold would rub off on them if they managed to rub shoulders with Pandora's new owner.

Everyone was so busy chatting forty-one million to the

dozen that, like a bride neglected at her own wedding reception, because the guests feel she's too special to waste time on them, the Raphael hung on the wall temporarily unattended.

What a beautiful picture, thought the curator from the Abraham Lincoln Museum tearfully, I should have ignored the board and gone higher.

The next moment, a strange, staring-eyed, pitifully thin young woman had slunk across the room and lifted the picture off the wall.

'Don't touch it,' cried the curator in horror.

'I only came to say goodbye,' sobbed Sienna, and before anyone could stop her, put her blanched lips to the pale cheek of Pandora, and then to the glowing forehead of Hope.

Two kindly Sotheby's porters, who'd been devoted to Raymond, pulled her away, and smuggled her weeping out of the St George Street entrance.

Not even the sight of David yelling, 'I've already told you, "no comment",' as a pack of baying reporters chased him down Clifford Street, could bring a smile to her face.

82

By the time she came off the motorway, Sienna was beyond tears, beyond the bitter-sweet comfort of *Arabella*: disc two, band five. Moonlight was seeping through the tree tunnels, dappling the long silver road. Pale ghosts of willow herb brushed her car. Combines, like dinosaurs, lurked overnight in shorn fields. The stars were brilliant as though an overjoyed Jonathan had chucked a handful of confetti against the face of the night, but the moon was hemmed in by furry sable clouds – like the Raphael guarded by an escort of Zacs.

As Sienna dropped into the Silver Valley, however, the moon shook off her dark entourage and, dimming the stars with a switch, sailed radiant and solitary into a pearly-grey sky. The church clock was striking midnight as Sienna crossed the bridge. She had no interest in the helicopter landing on the cricket pitch like a swarm of fireflies. Perhaps it was Rupert dropping off a disappointed Jupiter.

Sienna had rung and asked Mrs Robens to leave the front door unlocked. As she went inside, Grenville pattered lightly down the stairs in eternal search of Raymond. Hoping for a miracle like me, thought Sienna, gathering his desperately thin, snaking body into her arms.

The wedding party had been cleared up except for the odd glass and plate. On the hall was a note in

733

drunken writing: 'Masses of food in larder. Great party had by all. Hope you wasn't too sad. Have a nice hot toddy, see you in the morning, love Knightie.'

In the fridge, she found a half-empty bottle of Moët with a silver spoon in its mouth. Pouring herself a glass, kicking off her high heels, she took Grenville out for a pee. The garden had been neglected since her father died. The parched unsprinkled lawn scratched her bare feet. Flowers wilted, their leaves cast down, heads hanging.

The moon was now hidden by the house, which cast its long ebony shadow across the lawn, its chimneys like pointing fingers saying: 'Go from this place.'

It would be Jupiter's house soon – a West Country Chequers with politicians landing in helicopters and intrigue going on all night. Rupert had been a very successful Tory Minister for Sport. Jupiter had clearly begun networking.

Despite the heat she shivered. There was no room for her here. Why had she driven down? She'd forgotten even to bring a toothbrush. In the hall she noticed another gap on the wall: Jupiter flogging another family picture.

Tiptoeing upstairs so as not to wake Anthea, she found her stepmother's bedroom door most unusually ajar. Then she remembered: Anthea, not wanting to sleep in her lonely marriage bed after a wedding, had gone to stay with Green Jean.

Peering inside to double check, Sienna noticed the door up to the Blue Tower was open. Climbing the steps, remembering how she had made the same journey the night she stole the Raphael, she found the second door also unlocked.

Then as she pushed it open, her heart failed. For there in the moonlight to the right of the bed, where it had always hung, was the Raphael. It had to be a fake. Someone was playing a hideous joke.

Putting down her glass, she rushed across the room,

climbing onto the bed, throwing aside a pile of old Belvedon catalogues to get closer. It *was* the Raphael. There was the little nick in the moon's chin, which the madman's slashing knife had made in New York.

In bewilderment, she fingered the winged evils of the world, touching the normally choleric face of Wrath, now drained of colour in the moonlight, touching terrified Pandora and Epimetheus, arms raised to ward off the dazzle of Hope in her gauzy dress.

As a shadow fell across the bed, Sienna gave a scream and swung round. A man stood in the doorway, a white shirt emphasizing the breadth of his shoulders, the black trousers the leanness of hip and length of leg. His grey-flecked hair gleamed silver; his eyes were black hollows; his face ghostly and deeply shadowed as though he'd wandered without sleep for a hundred years.

'I've brought Pandora home,' he said slowly.

'Stop taking the piss,' snarled Sienna. 'Have you bought our house as well? You've taken everything else that matters, my father, our good name, the Raphael. How the hell did you get down here so quickly anyway?'

'Si lent me his helicopter.'

'After the crooked bastard bought the picture,' spat Sienna. 'Way back at Emerald's birthday party, he was saying he wanted a Raphael.'

'He was bidding for me. I was so uptight, I figured I'd screw up if I bid myself.'

Sienna shook her head.

'I don't understand. Why've you bought back your own picture? What sort of dodgy deal have you and Si been involved in all this time?'

'Hunting for the Raphael. While I was digging, Si made noises above ground, to flush it out.'

Zac spoke matter-of-factly, hardly a tremor in his deep husky voice.

'So you weren't an art correspondent at all.'

'Not for a year or two. I was too busy searching.'

Little by little he was edging into the room. Huddled

on the four-poster Sienna was in a complete panic, heart thumping, brain zigzagging like a hunted rabbit.

'So why's the Raphael hanging here like a sodding trophy?'

'It's for you.' Zac's voice broke. 'I saw you across the sale room, you looked so hurt, I couldn't sell it.'

'But for Christ's sake, you'll be clobbered for the buyer's *and* the seller's premium *and* huge costs for the tour *and* the CD *and* the hardback.'

Zac shrugged. 'It's only money.'

'Still doesn't answer my question.'

'You were the only person who loved Pandora for herself. And I love you for yourself,' Zac went on despairingly, 'I've loved you from the moment you caught me coming out of the bathroom after screwing Anthea. It was the worst moment of my life. I felt the hangman's noose tightening round my neck. To track down the Raphael, I'd fucked Anthea and Emerald without a shred of contrition, only to discover I did have a heart after all, big as an ox's, thawing slowly and painfully inside.'

'I still don't get it,' whispered Sienna, rearing up on the bed, clutching the nearest bedpost for support.

'I had to win the court case,' stammered Zac, who was now shaking so much, he had to grab the same bedpost, his hand above hers. 'If your side had won, the others would have flogged the Raphael, and split the money between them: Jupiter on the fucking Tories, Jonathan on living it up, Alizarin on struggling artists, Anthea on hats, Raymond on a Poussin or a house in Tuscany.'

Seeing his desolation and totally uncharacteristic uncertainty, Sienna longed to slide her hand up to meet his, but she was still numb with disbelief.

'I had no hope at all,' muttered Zac, 'until you crossed the court and put your arms around me. Even in that bleakest moment when I realized the extent of Jacob's treachery, I felt safe, as though you were Mom back from the grave telling me some frightful nightmare wasn't true. I nearly made a move then, but I had so much to work through. I accept now I can't change what Jacob did. I don't want to unravel the past any more, just make a future.'

He was so close, she could smell traces of CK One and the faint peppermint of his breath. As a lamb bleated down the valley, a ewe gave a reassuring rumble.

'I might have won the case' – they both jumped violently as, almost with a mind of its own, Zac's shaking hand closed over hers – 'but what was the point of having the second most beautiful woman in the world hanging on my wall, when I wanted easily the most beautiful one?' With a tentative quivering finger, Zac traced the contours of Sienna's cheek. 'In my bed all night, sitting by the fire with me in the evening, raising kids and growing old together. Don't cry, baby, I can't bear it.

'It's your picture now.' For a moment his voice was too choked to carry on. 'If by a millionth chance, you'd like to share your life with me, we can love it together. If not, it's still yours. Without you, everything's pointless: pictures, money, existence.' His other hand crept shyly up her arm, then retreated. 'Say the word and I'll quit.'

Then, as Sienna said nothing, unable to speak, Zac turned towards the door. Seeing utter desolation on his moon-blanched face, Sienna gave a cry.

'Don't go,' she sobbed. 'Never like go away again.'

Gazing at him for a second, seeing the tears sparkling on his black lashes, she let go of the bedpost, held out her arms and fell into his.

'Oh Zac,' she whispered, pulling his trembling mouth to meet hers, 'it's not just the Raphael that's come home.'

Too tired and happy to go to sleep, Zac and Sienna found another bottle and, welcoming a delighted Grenville onto the bed, watched the sky slowly lighten, as they waited for the sun to rise on the Raphael.

'I've suddenly realized,' murmured Zac, running a finger along her high cheekbones and long heavy eyelids, 'why I fell in love so instantly with Alizarin's Balkan paintings – because they were filled with people who looked just like you.'

'And I've got to kiss you again,' sighed Sienna happily, 'because you are so beautiful and because that was the most brilliant fabulous sex I've ever had.'

'Better than last time,' murmured Zac when they finally paused for breath.

'I thought you were Jonathan,' cried Sienna in sudden outrage, 'I'd just stolen the Raphael. I was pissed. I was so off the wall, I'd have let Somerford shag me.' She pummelled his chest furiously. 'That was such a shit's trick.'

'I know. It was diabolical.'

The tiger eyes, still a little bloodshot, were full of laughter. She was so unused to Zac being happy.

'God I enjoyed it.' Zac ran a hand over her hipbone, dipping down into her waist. 'You have such a great body, and it locks into mine so perfectly. What did you do with the Raphael that night?'

'Shoved it under the floorboards where I used to hide booze and dope from Anthea. Where were you going when you bumped into me anyway?'

'On my way to nick the Raphael. Weird if we'd met up in the Blue Tower. I'd arranged for Anthea to leave everything, including herself' – Zac grinned ruefully, his fingers playing idle tunes on Sienna's ribs – 'open for me. Then I met you, and here is an indication' – he buried his lips in her shoulder – 'of how passionately, even then, I wanted you, that I could forget the Raphael – and you know how passionately I wanted that – for a few minutes.'

Twisting her head to kiss his hard cheekbone, feeling the soft flutter of his lashes, Sienna asked, 'What did you do after you left me?'

'Found the Raphael gone – and went apeshit. Si nearly buried me for screwing up.'

Sienna was still puzzled.

'I don't understand why Si's involved.'

'He was bankrolling me.'

'Whatever for? Is he your boss?'

'No,' said Zac, sending ripples of delight through her body as he gently caressed the underside of her breast. 'You have the cutest boobs.'

'Don't change the subject,' pleaded Sienna. 'Tell me – how does Si come into it?'

'He's my father,' said Zac simply. Then, at Sienna's look of incredulity, 'Well, my stepfather actually. Si really loved Mom, married her four years ago knowing she'd got cancer. He and I fought like pitbulls at first, but whilst she was dying and afterwards, he carried me. I just love the guy. I was so bent out of shape, he suggested as therapy we search for the Raphael.'

As Sienna's mouth was still so wide open, Zac had to kiss it, then he said, 'Si didn't want me to flog the Raphael. He and Rosemary warned me I'd bitterly regret it, that the hurt over Jacob would fade. What they didn't realize was the only thing I cared about was you. I was convinced I hadn't a hope in hell. It made me really mean.' Zac whistled, and shook his head. 'I've got to send Sotheby's several crates of Krug to apologize.'

'Not when they're going to sting you for the buyer's premium and all those expenses,' said Sienna in outrage.

'I don't give a fuck.' Zac pulled her on top of him, so she gasped and arched with pleasure. 'I'll pay Si back somehow. Anyway, I'm the richest guy on the planet now I've got you.'

Unnerved at the prospect of more erotic enterprise, Grenville shot off the bed. For Sienna, things were still going too fast.

'Am I imagining things or is Rosemary about to become the fourth Mrs Si Greenbridge?'

'I guess so – but there's only going to be one Mrs Zachary Ansteig.' Looking up, Zac took her face between his hands. 'You are so beautiful.'

'Except for this zit,' said Sienna ungraciously, because her mind was suddenly careering off again. Had Zac really said what he'd just said?

'It's a cute zit.' Zac squinted up at it. 'Makes you more human if you've got one imperfection.'

As he kissed her, his tongue roving caressingly around her mouth, she could feel his glorious cock leap upwards. But instead of joyfully impaling herself on it, Sienna had to battle not to burst into tears. Utterly confused she rolled off him. Outwardly unmoved, Zac filled up their glasses and started singing the love duet from *Arabella*.

'If you were a girl from one of my villages,
you could go to the well behind your father's house,
and draw a cupful of clear water . . .'

'I've played that song into the ground,' mumbled Sienna. 'You have no idea how revoltingly miserable I've been, or how hopelessly I'm in love with you.'

'Only if you prove it by marrying me.'

'That cow, Naomi, said you'd never marry out.'

'Ah changed ma mind. I guess I need rescuing just as much as Grenville. Well?'

Sienna turned towards him, her pale face suddenly radiant. Then Zac realized it wasn't just happiness making her blush. The sun had risen, casting a soft pink glow on her face and on the Raphael.

'Look, look,' he said, pointing towards the picture as the characters sprang to life.

But Sienna had sprung to her feet too. Wrapping herself in a big orange towel, chucking the remains of her champagne out of the window, she ran clutching the glass from the room. A minute later Zac heard the front door bang. Suddenly terrified – perhaps he was going to lose her after all – he ran to the north window, and then smiled. For far below, with Grenville frisking round her, was Sienna, parting the ferns and filling up her glass with ice-cold water from the spring. Glancing up, she waved and smiled at him, her orange towel slipping as, very carefully, she carried the glass back into the house.

EPILOGUE

The ancient warder in charge of the Old Masters Gallery at the Abraham Lincoln Museum was taking the weight off his legs during a hot crowded Sunday afternoon. As the sun poured in through the half-open window, a young girl student joined him on the bench and introduced herself.

'My name's Zelda. You are just so lucky to work here and see these pictures every day.'

The ancient warder agreed that he never got tired of them, adding that the gallery had never been so busy before the Raphael *Pandora* arrived.

'It's that little picture over there, Zelda, glows like a jewel even on the darkest day, always got folk round it. There was a big court case over it years ago.'

'Isn't that portrait next to it by Raphael too?' asked Zelda.

'Sure is. That's *Pandora*'s companion picture,' explained the old man enthusiastically. 'Sitter was a feisty young beauty called Caterina, who evidently gave Raphael the run-around. He nicknamed her "The Proud One", but at the big ceremony here when the two pictures were reunited after more than three hundred years, folk swear there were tears in The Proud One's eyes. Probably just a trick of the light.'

'That's really cool,' sighed Zelda.

As she climbed onto the bench to have a better look, a family walked in through a side door and the room fell silent. From the back, the tall guy, who had thick grey hair, looked oldish. He must have brought along his daughter, Zelda decided, and her two teenage kids, a boy and a girl.

But as he glanced round, waving and smiling at the warder, Zelda said 'Wow!' because he had such an extra-ordinarily alive, young face and was probably only in his late forties. The family all looked so excited and because of their beauty – like visiting angels – the crowd round the Raphael dispersed to let them through. The grey-haired guy had his arm round the woman as they both pointed out aspects of the picture to the kids.

'They come here two or three times a year,' said the old warder, offering Zelda a toffee. 'Seem such a happy family, and they're always so pleased to see the picture.'

'She looks kinda familiar,' said Zelda.

'Sure – she's Sienna Belvedon.'

'Oh wow! Isn't she British? I've heard of her.'

'Should have done,' reproved the old warder. 'Stirred up enough controversy around the Millennium. Churchmen and public figures in an uproar over some picture she painted, all threatening to withdraw public money in the UK.'

'I've heard of that picture.' Zelda wrinkled her freckled forehead. 'Wasn't it called *Visitor's List*?'

'That's the one. Made a helluva difference,' conceded the old warder. 'Drew attention to terrible things we once did to animals. What upset folk most was to have all the poor critters arriving in heaven and being welcomed by God portrayed as a big yellow dog. But the fuss died down. Now it's regarded as one of the finest pictures of the twenty-first century. Always thought Visitor was a funny name for a dog.'

A furry tail ending.

THE END

ACKNOWLEDGEMENTS

Life may be brief, but art, and consequently *Pandora*, my novel about the art world, is long. Which means a huge number of people to thank.

Nobody, for a start, could have been more helpful than Sotheby's and I'm particularly grateful to Diana Keith-Neal, a senior director, for introducing me not only to the Chairman, Henry Wyndham, but also to Richard Charlton-Jones, Lucian Simmons, Natacha Chiaramonte, Patti Wong, Chris Proudlove and Tatiana von Waldersee. All experts in their fields, they were unstinting with both their time and their advice.

I had fantastic help from many art dealers, who allowed me to infiltrate their private views, took me to auctions, showed me marvellous pictures and beguiled me with outrageous anecdotes. They include Johnny and Sarah Van Haeften and their assistant Camilla Clayton, Tim Bathurst, Christopher Burness, Francis Kyle, Jay Jopling, William Darby, Peyton Skipwith, Edward Horswell, James Colman and Maurice Howard.

Excellent technical advice or more outrageous tales were supplied by ace picture framer Mark Wallington; by Rungwe Kingdon and Claude Koenig, whose Pangolin Gallery and Foundry is one of the splendours of Gloucestershire; and on the insurance front by Aaron

Shapiro, Michael St Aubyn, William Marler and Andrew Colvin.

There are many sculptors and painters in *Pandora*, so I am deeply indebted to my dear neighbour Anthony Abrahams, and other fine artists including David Backhouse, Daniel Chadwick, Paul Day, Paul Grellier, Christopher Dean, Hamish Mackay, Caroline Wallace, Tory Lawrence, Charlotte Bathurst, Anna Gibbs-Kennet, Michael and Sybil Edwards and the mighty Maggie Hambling for either allowing me to invade their studios or sharing their secrets with me.

During my research, my portrait was painted for Yorkshire Television by Alan Hydes and my head sculpted by Frances Segelman. Both artists gave me invaluable insight into the creative process as well as an end product of great beauty.

In earlier books I have been accused of making my young heroines too attractive, but anyone meeting Emma Sergeant, Tanya Brett or Georgie Taylor, all three of whom helped me hugely, will vouch that where the art world is concerned I have not exaggerated.

Most of all I must thank artist extraordinaire, Sargi Mann, who heroically continues to paint despite failing sight. His extraordinarily beautiful oil of a pale blue canal idling through golden autumn fields, which hangs in our bedroom, constantly revealing fresh enchantments when viewed from different angles and at different times of the day, was the initial inspiration for *Pandora*.

I never fail to be touched and astonished by the magnanimity of intellectuals prepared to enter into the fun and adventure of producing popular fiction. The Pandora of the title is an invented picture by Raphael of the opening of Pandora's Box. In her creation and historical background I was enormously privileged to be given advice by Dr Nicholas Penny, Keeper of the National Gallery and one of the greatest experts on Raphael in the world. David Jenkins, a

745

brilliant classics master at Monmouth, threw light on the myths of Pandora and the Seven Deadly Sins. Peter Clarkson, Associate Lecturer in Art History at the Open University, specializing in the Renaissance, lent me endless arcane art books and allowed me to pester him with questions. Denis Napier corrected my Latin. Caterina Krucker, Lecturer in Modern Languages, brushed up my French and Italian.

On the art establishment side, I am grateful to Robert and Kate Gavron, John Cooper, ex-Head of Education at the National Portrait Gallery, Maggie Guillebaud, formerly of the Arts Council, Christopher and Angela Dowling of the Imperial War Museum, and Francis Corner of Cheltenham and Gloucester College of Higher Education.

As *Pandora* is also a novel about art that belonged to the Jews being looted by the Nazis, I was unbelievably lucky just before I started writing to lunch with the mercurial, perennially innovative Tom Rosenthal, who was not only illuminating on the contemporary art scene but also dreamed up the way in which my picture could be looted. For further illumination I must thank Karen Pollock and Rosie Barton of the Holocaust Trust; Constance Lowenthal, Commission for Art Recovery, New York, and Eva Kurz, a solicitor specializing in looted art.

I am especially indebted to Ruth Redmond Cooper, Director of the Institute of Art and Law, and her team. On my way to their conference on Art, Law and the Holocaust at the Courtauld Institute in October 1999, I was involved in the Paddington train crash. Arriving at the conference, I couldn't have been treated with more kindness and sympathy; and as the speakers in turn described how the Nazis had tried to eradicate not only a people but their art and culture as well, they put any horrors I had experienced earlier in the day into perspective.

I am extremely grateful too to British Transport

Police for later retrieving early chapters of *Pandora* from the wreckage of the train.

The law surrounding the restitution of looted art is extremely complex, often involving the legal systems of several countries. I would never have been able to tackle a big court case had it not been for the advice of my dear friends, the Right Hon. Dame Elizabeth Butler-Sloss, President of the Family Division, and the Right Hon. the Lord Hoffman, Lord of Appeal in Ordinary, who also lent me a brilliant and famous judgement on a looted art case by the Hon. Mr Justice Moses, presiding judge at the Royal Courts of Justice. Lawyers John Davies, Elizabeth Jupp, Hetty Cleave, Martyn Daldorph, Graham Ogilvy, Gillian Geddes and Michael Flint also helped me.

In my travels, I was incredibly lucky to meet Jamie Tabor, QC, who, while wrestling with a long and gruelling case in Norwich, nobly spent his evenings reading my court case chapters for howlers. But as in every aspect of *Pandora*, I took his, or anyone else's, specialist advice only in so far as it suited my plot. Any mistakes are mine and in no way reflect on their expertise.

I am also indebted to Stephen Burrows, Chief Security Officer at the Royal Courts of Justice, to Emma Macdonald, Bob Parry and the staff at the County and Crown Courts at Gloucester, and to Gil Martin, ex-Gloucestershire CID, for his encyclopedic knowledge of matters criminal.

Writers need geographical locations on which to anchor their stories. Since moving to Gloucestershire, I have been haunted and captivated by two beautiful, historic and adjoining houses flanking our local church. On them I have based Foxes Court and the Old Rectory in *Pandora*. I should therefore like to thank Simon and Mindy Reading and John and Elizabeth Cowan for allowing me to range freely round their glorious gardens, but would emphasize that they and their sweet families bear absolutely no resemblance to the Belvedons and the Pulboroughs in my story.

I must equally thank our former High Sheriff of Gloucestershire, Major John Eyre, for explaining the duties of and historical background to the appointment, but would again stress that as a man of great charm and integrity he bears no resemblance to my frightful High Sheriff in *Pandora*.

Everyone, in fact, in *Pandora*, unless they are so eminent, like Joanna Lumley or Sotheby's Chairman Henry Wyndham, as to appear as themselves, is made up and in no way based on any living person.

My characters sometimes fall ill and make miraculous recoveries. It was invaluable to be able to seek medical information from Joe Cobbe, Sarah Morris, Pat Pearson, Graham Hall, Tim Crouch and Martin Joyce.

On a Ritzy front, interior designer Nina Campbell dreamed up a beautiful bedroom for my heroine's glamorous mother, while Lindka Cierach, Mariska Kay and David Shilling were a constant inspiration for lovely clothes and hats. Aspreys, Tiffany's, Alfred Dunhill and Robert Young the florists in Stroud were also a great help, and I must especially thank Denise Dean and David Risley of Zwemmers and Stephen Simpson of Hatchards for so tenaciously tracking down books I needed.

Writers do not always expect kindness from their own profession. Few, however, could have been more welcoming and helpful than Lesley Garner, Nigel Reynolds, Will Bennett, David Lee, Bevis Hillier, Lucinda Bredin, Peter Harclerode, Matthew Collings, the sublime Brian Sewell, Esther Oxford, John Hawkins of Gloucestershire News Service, Robert Pearson of UK Law News, Peter Davies, Philip Jones and Maria Prendergast. I am also grateful that the *Art Newspaper*, *Art Review* and the *Jackdaw* kept me up to date with events.

I should like to thank Chris Wood of Decca Records for permission to quote five lines from his translation of

Richard Strauss's *Arabella*, and also William Mann for permission to quote four lines of Hermann Hesse's poem 'Going to Sleep', which form part of the lyrics for Richard Strauss's *Four Last Songs*.

The press offices at Middlesex County Cricket Club, the British Show Jumping Association, the All-England Tennis Club, Wimbledon, Conservative Central Office, the Lord Chancellor's Office, and the staff at the Public Records Office at the Angel, Islington, were wonderful, always stopping whatever they were doing to provide crucial helpful information.

Another theme in *Pandora* is an adopted child's quest for her natural parents. I am eternally grateful to Marjorie Dent, who formerly ran the Phyllis Holman Richards Adoption Society, for her wisdom and constant support; to social workers Clodagh Howe, Sue Jacobs and June Sellars, and to Felicity Collier, Chief Executive of the British Agencies for Adoption and Fostering, for their advice and ideas and for providing helpful literature on the subject.

I am also much beholden to the authors of the following books, which provided illumination or factual background on looted art, the art world and adoption. They include *The Lost Masters* by Peter Harclerode and Brendan Pittaway, *The Faustian Bargain* by Jonathan Petropoulis, *Portrait of Doctor Gachet* by Cynthia Saltzman, *Raphael* by Roger Jones and Nicholas Penny, *Blimey* by Matthew Collings, *Boogey Woogey* by Danny Moynihan, *Duchess of Cork Street* by Lillian Browse, *Sotheby's* by Robert Lacey, *Groovey Bob* by Harriet Vyner, *The Sorcerer's Apprentice* by John Richardson, *Birth Records Counselling* by Pam Hodgkins, *Adopters on Adoption* by David Howe and *Ithaka* by Sarah Saffian.

My friends as usual came up with endless ideas. They include Dominique Bagley, Pussy Baird-Murray, Francis Burne, Ailsa Chapman, Sarah Collett, Mike Coppen-Gardner, Fran Cook, my stepdaughter Laura Cooper, Michael Cordy, Susan Daniel, Pam Dhenin, John

Ferguson, Dorry Friesen, Glyn and Vanessa Hendy, Bill Holland, Ute Howard, Tidl Jefferies, James Johnstone, David Laurie, Bruce and Janetta Lee, Ava Myers, John Parry, Patrick Scrivenor and Heather Ross.

On my way home from the courts a couple of years ago I met a delightful and elated woman who told me about her daughter's boyfriend who had longed to be married before he was forty and how the relevant families effected this. Leaping out at Stroud, I asked her if I could use the story in *Pandora* but failed to catch her name. Wherever she is now, I would like to thank her, and anyone else I may have forgotten.

Transworld, my publishers, have all been marvellous in every way, but I would particularly like to thank Mark Barty-King, their Chairman, to whom *Pandora* is dedicated, and my editor Linda Evans, who is simply a darling, who has constantly supplied me with comfort, joy, support and good advice. Richenda Todd has also been a terrific copy editor. Henry Steadman designed the wonderful hardback jacket, on the front of which is a beautiful painting of the myth of Pandora by Chris Brown. Henry has also designed the equally wonderful new cover for this edition. Neil Gower also drew a beautiful map.

I am extremely grateful to Steve Rubin, president and publisher of Doubleday, Broadway Publishing Group, and Jane Gelfman my agent in New York, for so kindly reading the chapters set in America.

I cannot thank my agent in London Vivienne Schuster enough for her kindness, enthusiasm and sympathetic encouragement in the many dark days when I thought *Pandora* would never be finished. Her colleagues at Curtis Brown, Paul Scherer and Jonathan Lloyd, and Euan Thorneycroft, her trusty lieutenant, were also always there when I needed them.

On the home front I am singularly blessed. My PA Pippa Birch is owed a huge debt of gratitude for typing the lion's share of the synopsis and the penultimate draft, and for checking and seeking out endless facts and figures. Pippa came up with many ideas, as did Annette Xuereb-Brennan, Mandy Williams and Caterina Krucker, who heroically typed the rest of the manuscript and refused to go crackers over the endless corrections. To them all I am truly obligated – and also to dear Ann Mills, our housekeeper, for her sweetness and patience in keeping us all sane and comparatively tidy. Phil Bradley, of Cornerstones, drove me to endless places while I was writing the book and always got me there on time.

Most of all I want to thank my darling family, for putting up with shameless neglect for months on end. My husband Leo, who was encyclopedic on military matters, our son Felix and his wife Edwina, our daughter Emily, Bessie the Labrador, Hero the lurcher and our four cats, all provided their essential mix of good copy and endless cheer.

A LIST OF OTHER JILLY COOPER TITLES AVAILABLE FROM CORGI BOOKS AND BANTAM PRESS

THE PRICES SHOWN BELOW WERE CORRECT AT THE TIME OF GOING TO PRESS. HOWEVER TRANSWORLD PUBLISHERS RESERVE THE RIGHT TO SHOW NEW RETAIL PRICES ON COVERS WHICH MAY DIFFER FROM THOSE PREVIOUSLY ADVERTISED IN THE TEXT OR ELSEWHERE.

12041 3	LISA & CO	£5.99
14696 X	HARRIET & OCTAVIA	£6.99
14697 8	IMOGEN & PRUDENCE	£5.99
14695 1	EMILY & BELLA	£6.99
14103 8	RIDERS	£6.99
13264 0	RIVALS	£6.99
13552 6	POLO	£6.99
13895 9	THE MAN WHO MADE HUSBANDS JEALOUS	£6.99
14323 5	APPASSIONATA	£6.99
14579 3	SCORE!	£6.99
14662 5	CLASS	£6.99
14663 3	THE COMMON YEARS	£5.99
99091 4	ANIMALS IN WAR	£6.99
04404 5	HOW TO SURVIVE CHRISTMAS (Hardback)	£9.99
14367 7	THE MAN WHO MADE HUSBANDS JEALOUS (Audio)	£12.99*

* including VAT

Transworld titles are available by post from:

Bookpost, PO Box 29, Douglas, Isle of Man, IM99 1BQ

Credit cards accepted. Please telephone 01624 836000
fax 01624 837033, Internet http://www.bookpost.co.uk
or e-mail: bookshop@enterprise.net for details

Free postage and packing in the UK. Overseas customers:
allow £1 per book (paperbacks) and £3 per book (hardbacks).